STONEHAVEN

A Romance for the
Divine Feminine

By
CURTIS MITCHELL

Please direct all correspondence
and book orders to:
Flying Key Ventures
PO Box 505
Hampstead MD 21074
flyingkey@earthlink.net

Library of Congress Control Number 2018912941
ISBN 978-0-9907067-2-4
eISBN 978-0-9907067-3-1

Editing and production assistance by
Otter Bay Books, LLC
Baltimore, MD 21218-2513
www.otter-bay-books.com

Printed in the United States of America

For She who makes the cool head flame and smoke,
Then cools the fever with the water of delight:
The Antecedent One with a dark star cloak,
The refuge for my soul's long night.

*"Look, don't take my word for it.
Work it out for your own Self."*

—The Prophet of Conscience

TABLE OF CONTENTS

1) ANGELICA 1

2) BRONZE AGE, THE HIGHLANDS 7

3) STONEHAVEN 17

4) PROPHET OF GAWD 27

5) STONEHAVEN BOUND 33

6) WATCHING ALAM 39

7) FOUNDATION 47

8) CHESTER AND MISSY 56

9) JUST IN TIME ARRIVAL 64

10) DINNER 76

11) NEW YEAR 1953 85

12) CHESTER AND MICKEY 95

13) FIRST DAY OF CLASS

       PART 1 MORNING 108

       PART 2 AFTERNOON 133

       PART 3 EVENING 152

14) ALAM ARRIVES 180

15) CURRICULUM

       PART 1 PREPARING SACRED GROUND 204

       PART 2 BOUNDARY RIDING 224

       PART 3 VISITING THE TEMPLE 251

16) CHESTER AND THE TATTOO 276

17) BLOWOUT 296

18) THE BLISS OF HOUSE DOMESTIC 325

19) CURRICULUM TWO..335

20) RETURN OF THE PRODIGAL.................................346

21) RECOVERY..360

22) CHILDREN 375

23) CURRICULUM THREE..384

24) PATROL...400

25) WALKING...434

26) REGINA AND THE LAMA'S GHOST.........................456

27) CURRICULUM FOUR..470

28) QUINN AT THE MEN'S CIRCLE...............................482

29) MAITHUNA, STORMS, AND THE MOON 517

30) CALLEY'S RELEASE...548

31) LUCKY MAN 562

32) QUINN AND THE PRIEST..568

33) CIRCLES OF WEN AND MEN 581

34) THE HIDDEN LANDS..594

35) INITIATION...605

36) RUNNING AWAY 628

37) ANGELICA'S DREAM..636

38) THE MOVING OF THE HIDDEN LANDS 656

39) RACHEL'S RIDE 661

40) ON THE HUNT...666

41) BLOOD ON THE GROUND......................................676

42) ASSIGNMENTS..689

43) A PRIME NUMBER...698

EXCERPT FROM BOOK 3 OF THE SIDDHI WARS SERIES, **WALLID ISLAND** 699

ACKNOWLEDGMENTS 703

1

ANGELICA

She was a free woman, ready to take on the world.

Angelica paused at the top of the ramp to the dais, and looked around. As she gazed out over the crowd, she vowed to remember this moment. She looked inward at her feelings. She felt good—strong and powerful and accomplished. In combination, it was exhilarating.

She stood straighter and smiled, waving to her family and friends. Confidently stepping forward, she strode to the Chancellor handing out diplomas.

Later, saying goodbye to friends, she realized that she was not going to look back at college with nostalgia. She felt a strong sense that whatever happened next, whatever she chose to do next, would work out well.

She knew she still had much to learn. Her studies in ethnology had taught her that. But she had a good mind for seeing patterns across cultures and understanding the roots of those patterns in nature. She had developed this capacity into a kind of expertise on human cultures. She had no doubt that, with her contacts, she would land easily in a government, law firm, or think tank position.

She had decided the first thing she wanted to do, however, was go on a retreat. She loved yoga and wanted to ground herself in her body again. After much research and a recommendation, she had chosen a two week Kundalini Yoga residential course at a retreat center on the western side of the Appalachian Mountains. After talking with her parents, they agreed to pay for the course as a graduation present.

Among her circle of friends she had no real boyfriend, preferring to be free to interact, or not, with one boy or another. Her strategy had paid off well: she'd had a number of lovers, some for a few months, but no serious relationship in the present moment requiring her to work out details of where she went and for how long.

She had the support of her family, and she liked them. They were good to her and had given her something that she believed was probably close to an ideal American life. There was no abuse and no substance issues, though she figured it would probably be years before she swapped stories with her parents about smoking weed.

At dinner after the ceremony, the family shared memories about her childhood and her accomplishments. Her brother teased her about having no serious beau, and hence no grandchildren on the horizon. She teased him back about having three before he was thirty. But her brother and his family were happy; they were intelligent people and were already looking forward to an early retirement. He was a skilled electro-mechanical engineer and was a partner in a firm doing development work for the government.

Angelica's father, on the other hand, was a little worried for her. He wondered aloud whether or not she was ready to just step out into the world. It was, he asserted, a much more dangerous place than she had experienced. Rather than dismiss his concerns, as she often did, she decided to take him seriously this time and listened to him.

When he was finished she told him, "Look, Dad, I know what you're saying is true. I know I'm naïve. But the only way to correct that is to go out and gain experience. And I promise, I'll be cautious and careful. I'm not going to retreat from the world, either, Dad. I'm just going off to stand on the mountain and get my bearings."

He looked at his daughter with pride in that moment, confident that wisdom would bring her beauty, and secure in the certainty that wisdom was what his daughter sought.

On the second night back at their home—Angelica's childhood home—while packing up some of her things for storage, she was overcome by a feeling of gratitude for the life that she had been given. She had to sit down on her bed and cry for it. Tears of joy at her good luck, tears of sorrow for all the millions who weren't born so lucky, tears of gratitude for her family that had worked hard and been so good to her. All these poured through her in quiet waves, washing out any sense of taking her life for granted. Finally, there were tears of relief that she'd actually realized her great good fortune and privilege. She cried for a long time.

She called down from her room to her parents that she wasn't feeling very well—that she was tired, and going to bed early. Her mother called up the stairs, "You OK, honey?" Angelica called back, "Yeah, I'm OK. I think I just need to rest."

And as she lay down under the blankets, she curled up around an old stuffed elephant and the tears returned. She cried a long time for the suffering of all the people who would never have a chance like the chances she'd had; no chance to make a life like the one she was going to get to make. She cried herself to sleep.

The next day she was to help her mother paint different walls in the house different colors as an experiment. As the day went on she began to develop a feeling that gradually rose up in her and got more intense as the day continued. She thought first it was a feeling she was missing something, As she paid attention to it, it seemed to spread everywhere inside her, becoming almost a sensation in her limbs and on her skin. It became a kind of felt-sense that she had forgotten something. As she thought about it, she realized there was something she didn't understand.

The feeling started to move around from one place to another. Sometimes the felt-sense was one of urgency and the need to do something. At other times it felt like a burden on her back and shoulders. It moved around to other places in her body, giving rise to different feelings and mental images wherever it dwelled for a moment. The felt-sense settled down then. It oscillated between the need to do something and a sense of burden.

She was in the kitchen painting one wall a deep warm red. She thought suddenly about her student loans—her parents insisted that she help pay for her education—and they felt like a burden. But this was only a slightly similar sensation to what she felt. What she felt was a different, more intense, deeper sense of burden: a felt-sense of owing, a sense of… then she said it out loud, "I have a debt. I have a debt for my existence."

And then, standing there with her roller dripping on the drop cloth, she said, "How can I pay for that?"

Later that evening she sat with her parents after supper and tried to explain the felt-sense to them. They assured her that she didn't owe them anything. They'd done what they had done for her because they loved her and because it was their duty as parents.

She replied, "Yes. I know. But you didn't have to be so good about it. You guys have been really good parents, creative and patient. And I know I don't owe you for all that. But I do owe you acknowledgment and respect. That I will always do.

"I'm talking about something else. Because all this was given to me, in effect by the world, I feel I owe something back to the world. It has given me life through you, and by modelling generosity like that, I have come to feel that I, too, have to be generous and give back something to the world.

"This feels like something I can't forget. It's a debt, yes, but not a burden, unless I start to forget about it. So I have to pay attention to it and figure out how to pay it back. I have to figure out what to do. And I don't know what that is, yet. I intend to use my time at Stonehaven to start figuring that out."

Her father and her mother said they understood, that they were proud of her for figuring it out, and for being such a good person. Since it was late and they both had to work the next day, her parents went to bed. Before they went, there were hugs all around, and they told her they loved her. They were sure they'd be gone before she got up.

It wasn't so, in the end. Angelica didn't sleep well. The feelings of being indebted, not just to her parents, but to something larger, wouldn't leave her alone. It was not that it was painful. It was just intense. Breathing was sometimes difficult. She would focus on her breath, and reassert, almost like a mantra that she would think over and over as she was drifting down, "I will pay the debt of my existence." Eventually, she knew, she would sleep.

Sleep brought her dreams that, while not exactly bad, were disturbing and intense. Beautiful images would cause feelings and sensations in her that seemed more intense than the images would usually have inspired.

She dreamed of her parents, surrounded in clouds of white light. As she pulled away, presuming she was leaving, she thought it meant she was leaving them to go start her life. They, too, seemed to be pulling away, drifting, eventually vanishing in the white light background field. She also dreamed of her brother, appearing just like he always did, good-natured, industrious and happy with his young family.

Then she dreamed of Stonehaven, starting with the picture of the Mansion on the internet. She felt-sensed herself arriving there, as if she were flying standing up, and arrived on the yard below the veranda. She flew-stepped up onto its floor. There were four ten-foot high sets of French doors open with a breeze from somewhere inside blowing diaphanous curtains outside toward her.

As she stepped up to the doors, the breeze died and the curtains hung still. It was like looking at a split veil, ready to part and reveal the interior. Then a new breeze blew up behind her back. It passed her, blowing the curtains inward. She felt welcomed, Putting one hand on the door frame, she leaned in and looked around the furnished parlor. There were bookcases with rolling ladders going to the twelve foot ceiling, ceiling fans, stuffed chairs of all kinds, not a set of furniture, but a collection of furniture, each beautiful in its own right.

Then she saw the grand piano in the corner, and the top of someone's head on the other side leaning toward the keys in the dim light of the music lamp. She couldn't tell, quite, whether it was a man or a woman. She stepped through the doors and suddenly woke up in her room, almost panting with the anticipation of happiness. She smiled, rolled over and went back to sleep.

In the next dream, her last of the night as it turned out, she was up late at night, lying in her bed reading. It was a fiction book, a romance adventure, and the main characters were moving toward each other.

They were panting with passion and longing for each other, having just arrived safe from some harrowing escape. As she read, her hand dropped between her legs, touching herself, and she felt the thrill run through her.

Then she lost the image of the book in her mind's eye. It was replaced by her looking out her window, over a distance. In that distance a man's form appeared; small at first, then looming larger. She thought she should be afraid, but she wasn't. The form was clearly a man by the silhouette of his build. He stopped, full-size and hovering in the air, waiting outside her second story bedroom window.

She sat up. Her left hand still between her legs, she dropped her right leg over the side of the bed, and gestured to the form with her free hand, inviting it to come in. Slowly the dark shadow grayed, then whitened, then came into the room, pushing her backward onto the bed. She resisted, and turned completely to the side, getting both feet on the floor. The shadow came around and fell to its knees between her legs. She never could remember whether she hesitated or not before she opened her legs, and shortly felt the shadow's hot breath filling the room with the scent of passion. Then his lips were upon her.

When she woke it was first light. The white shadow was gone. She was on her back and turned completely sideways to the bed, legs over the side, her toes just touching the floor. The silk slip in which she slept was pulled up, over her hips and buttocks, and the straps of the slip were halfway down her arms, her breasts exposed. One arm was splayed across the bed and the other rested on her belly.

She laughed out loud at herself, that she could have an imagination like she did, and then she breathed a deep sigh of satisfaction.

2

BRONZE AGE, THE HIGHLANDS

Thirty-five hundred years ago, Calley pushed aside the hide covering the door, jumped into the house with both feet and shook like a dog, throwing water everywhere. Her sister squealed, and the dogs got up and moved away from her. Laughing, she pushed back her hood and took off her cloak. Throwing it to the side, it promptly slid off a stool onto the floor. She shook herself again, driving the dogs further away, cringing as if they expected another shower. They glowered at her. Then they rolled their eyes at her when they realized they'd been had—no more water.

Calley called to them. They came to her hand, still suspicious but happy to see her. "I'm happy to see you, too," she said. "What about you, sister?"

"Always happy to see you, dear. Welcome home," she said, bending back to the fire, uncovering a rising loaf of bread on the elevated section next to the fireplace and poking it with her finger to check for readiness. "Not my day for bathing, though," she said, recovering the loaf and standing up.

Turning, Bree saw her sister had dropped her skirts and was pulling her underdress up over her head. "Come on then," Calley said. "Turns out today is the day!" Naked, Calley reached for Bree's hand, and pulled her toward the door.

"No! No! I am not going out in this weather with you." Bree resisted, trying to pull her arm from the older and stronger sister's grasp. "I'll not do it!"

"Aye, you will!" Calley said. "Sky clad or no, you're going out with me! You smell of old smoke and sour meat. Your hair needs washing with heather and storm water. Come on, I'll do it for you!"

Calley pulled her sister toward her and gave the waistline of Bree's skirts a yank. They fell open, dropping to the floor. Bending her over, Calley started pulling the underdress up over Bree's head when she said, "Enough, enough already! I'll do it myself before you rip it!" She grabbed the bar of soap from the washstand and ran out under Calley's arm that held up the door hide for her.

Emerging into the yard, Bree stepped into a ray of light from the afternoon sun. The air was warm, and so was the rain that poured on her. She gasped with pleasure. "Hair first," her sister said.

Calley picked up one of the buckets she'd brought up with her from the cold stream that ran through the compound and poured it over Bree, making her gasp, but with shock this time. "Oh! Oh! You nasty girl," Bree sputtered. "You shameless, sneaky girl!" But she stood for it.

Calley took the soap and grinned. "So you say! But you'll be needing it sooner rather than later."

"Why? Bree asked, suddenly stiff with curiosity.

"Company's coming," Calley said simply.

"Company?" Bree repeated. "Company?"

Calley grinned and nodded. "Here. Close your eyes. Your mouth, too," and started soaping her sister's hair.

Bree was lost in her own thoughts already, thinking, wondering who it could be. Was the house clean enough? Company was so rare here, this far up in the Highlands. And how should she act? She got out so seldom this time of year, sometimes going months without seeing anyone but her sister.

"Whoozh coming?" she burbled through her sister's still cold rinse. Then, making a "Whooshing" sound while she caught her breath as Calley's other bucket of cold rinse water poured over her, she raised her face to the sky as she waited for the warm rain to cut through to her skin.

"Alam," Calley said, smiling. "I found him in a shelter last week. The rain had driven him in. He'd stacked rocks snugly around the cut at the base of the outcropping on Wolf's Head Mountain. He'd snared a rabbit and was roasting it over a small fire. The light through the rock wall drew me in close." She paused. "The wind pushed the skin of the door back and I stuck my head in to see. And he saw me! Here now," she said. "Ready for the heather rinse?"

"Really?" Bree gasped. The heather rinse was kept in a bucket under the thatched eaves, the infusion still rich with the scents of summer. Calley poured it slowly over her head, letting her sister work it in.

"Yes, yes really. He saw me! Can you believe it? Never, I mean never..." Calley exclaimed.

"I know, I know: How? What happened next?" Bree asked, raising her eyes to the sun shining from the west through the rain.

"He saw me, that's how. I don't know!" Calley replied. "I just brought my face to the edge of the light, and his eyes looked up and he saw me! And then he spoke to me!"

"What did he say?" Moving into the mental space of inner vision, Bree stilled her mind so she could see every picture.

"He said, can you believe this, 'Hail and well met, stranger'. I, of course, flashed back out of the entrance, but it was too late. His dog was outside keeping the sheep rounded up under the overhang, and he growled at me. Growled at me! Come on, Bree, let's go inside and get you dried off.

"Anyway, he said, 'Come eat. I have more than I can eat alone.' So I, I don't know why, decided to give him the Generosity Test. So, I stepped up to the entrance, got down on one knee and pushed the hide aside, and, still crouching, I duck-walked in.

"And now, you know me, you know how I am. You know how I look when I'm working. So, there I was, nothing on but the great cloak and the hood, all gray and shadowy. My hair hung down over half my face, all gray, and stranded and dripping. One tooth, hah-hah! So I squatted there." Calley paused for breath.

Bree, reaching for another towel, said, "What? What did he say?"

"Well, he was just finishing a hare; he had the thigh in his hand. And on the spit he had a rabbit going. He nodded his head toward it and said, 'Well, and that's yours if you want it.' Then he reached forward and lifted the spit off the forks entire and held it out to me. 'Here,' he said. 'Take it,' he said.

"So I leaned out and flashed him some of that old dug, the hanging boob, you know? And you know what? He didn't react! Well, he react-ed a little. His lip twitched a little at the corner, you know? Like he was going to smile, but he was so serious. So he was safe, you know? So I took it! I took the whole thing and put it in a pocket under the cloak. And he just smiled at that and made the give-away gesture with his palm."

Calley paused. Then she said, "I know this, you know. I know it when the magic is afoot. And you know what he said? You know what he said then?"

"No, Calley. Tell me." Bree looked at her sister from the corner of her eye, beginning to brush out her hair.

"He said, 'I know who you are, Guardian of Storms.'"

"No," Bree said.

"Yes!" Calley said emphatically. "Can you believe it?"

"No!" Bree said, with emphasis.

"Yes," Calley said. "Yes! Oh, my Mother. I swear, that's what he said. 'Guardian of Storms' he called me. I couldn't help it. I smiled. It was like 'Food, and Flattery, too'. You know? I couldn't help it. I snaggle-tooth smiled at him! Then I turned and used the Wind to pull open the door and slipped out along the edge of the hide and into the night."

"No, you didn't!" Bree exclaimed again.

"Yes, I did!" Calley asserted.

Then they both fell into a momentary silence, contemplating the potential impact of Alam passing the test.

"I went to see him again the next day," Calley resumed.

"You did, did you?" Bree asked, her eyes narrowing. "In what form?"

"Still under the cloak," Calley replied. "But younger; softer and more solid. I stood above him as he moved off down the mountain the next morning. He turned and looked back up at the shelter. When he saw me, I stood there, still, for a moment. Then, again, I do not know why, I went Mist and sailed down to him and then reformed there, just out of arm's length. And he went to one knee and bowed his head."

"Oooo," Bree said, getting dressed now. "Food, flattery, and good manners! So what did you do?"

"I reached out," Calley said. "I reached out and touched his head with the fingertips of both hands. And then I went Wind on him, and dis-appeared again. Oh, I almost forgot. I laughed when I touched him."

"Why?" Bree asked. "Why'd you laugh?"

"Because it felt good, and I didn't expect that." Calley didn't know whether to laugh again at the memory or scowl at her surprise. So she scowled, and feeling the scowl on her face, she laughed.

Once again, she had that bad memory, of a time when touching a mortal had gone very wrong. She knew her sister remembered this time also, when they'd had to team up to put down someone hungry for power. But this time felt different. Calley said, "This one is different.

He already has power, and he's offered it to me."

"What power?" Bree wanted to know.

"He's already met the Hunter. He knows how to go Stag. I've watched him practicing when he doesn't know I'm looking. But he's not interested in that so much. He's working on going Ram, and I think I've seen him thinking about Bull and Stallion, too. He seems much more interested in evoking the domestic archetypes, rather than the wild ones."

"Right," Bree said. "It seems less likely that he'd be going for an Old Power. More likely to be trustworthy. You sure?"

"No," Calley replied. "But I've invited him to supper so you can see for yourself. If you think it's too risky, we'll wrap his mind in the Mist, and he'll even forget about ever seeing me. Let alone finding his way back here."

Calley paused, again, then both she and Bree sat in memory and contemplation.

Putting down her brush, beginning to braid her hair along one side, Bree sat back, smiled slyly, and asked, "So how did you come to give him an invitation?"

Calley stepped up and said, "Here, let me do that." She stood behind her sister, her back to the light coming through the window and slightly to the side, allowing the light to illuminate the rich red browns of her sister's hair, its length sifting through her hands.

"Hmm," Calley said. "I kept following him, of course. The rain stayed right on him, herding the strays down from the top of the mountain. I'd let the sun shaft down right where he'd been, or shaft it in front of him twenty feet down below him, so he'd want to head to it, but it was off the path and over through the gorse. I was teasing him with the sunlight. Eventually he caught on, and he stopped and turned and looked all around, looking for me. So I laughed out loud! I couldn't help it!"

Bree laughed at her sister's surprise, seeing everything her sister saw. Calley began to braid the hair on one side into a loose weave, thick bundles of strands crossing each other to make a loose French-braid, keeping the hair back just enough but still comfortable.

"So he said," Calley began, "he said, 'Where are you, Storm Driver? I know you're there, for I am Storm Driven.' And he began looking for me, turning slowly first one way then the other. When I laughed again, I decided to stop teasing him, and stood still on the path behind him, the cloak covering me completely. When he turned and saw me, he dropped to one knee again and bowed his head. I felt the earth pull at my feet. I reached out to touch the top of his head again, and as soon as I did I slipped on the wet path, my feet went out from under me, my cloak caught on the gorse and I slid bare-arsed down the path. He stood up and I slipped under him. I came to a stop when he grabbed for me, catching my shoulders and pinning me down and then there I was, lying there under him, naked up to my teats, hood still over my face."

"Oh no. Oh, my goodness. What did you do?" Bree asked.

"Oh, I went Mist on him, of course. There he was, bent over holding a handful of fog, and I sparked a bolt right behind his arse, that's what I did. I was so startled and angry. The effrontery, you know? To lay hands on me like that."

Bree nodded, pulling back when Calley pulled too hard on her hair. "Ouch, you're squeezing it. Give it some slack."

"Sorry," Calley said, and let her hands grow slack as she remembered how she was startled, and then thrilled, and then angry at herself for the thrill.

"Ha!" she said. "After I sparked him I just let it pour down on him. The sheep had scattered. And you know what he did? He sat down. He just sat down, right on the path, knees up, arms on his knees and lowered his head. And he just sat there. After a while he laughed. I could hear him laughing with his face toward the ground. And then, still laughing, I heard him say, 'I am defeated, Storm Guardian. I am surrendered to you. Have Mercy!' but when he raised his face up I could tell he'd said it smiling. He was still smiling, having fun!"

Calley paused. "And, oh, you know what? It made me angry that he was having such fun. So I sparked another one. Cracked it down right next to him. It was his turn to startle. Then he said, 'Storm Guardian, I am sincere in my request for Mercy.'"

"So I said, 'Not yet you aren't' and then I let him have it. I sparked down bolts all around him. I drove him to turn over in the path, belly down, face in the mud and hands over his head. Until he moaned for Mercy, I hammered the ground all around him. I don't know why I didn't kill him on the spot!"

Bree grinned as she asked, "Food, Flattery, and Manners?"

Calley responded, "Yes! No! I don't know!" shaking her arms and gripping Bree's hair in frustration.

"Ouch!" Bree said. "Put my hair down!"

Calley dropped Bree's hair and said, "Yes. No. I don't know," in mock despair.

"So, what then?" Bree asked.

"So then he started calling out, 'What did I do wrong?' and for some reason I decided to answer him. I said, 'You touched me! You should have moved to the side!' and he said, 'I understand. I'm sorry! Have Mercy, Storm Guardian, please!' And I couldn't do it anymore."

"Couldn't scorch him? Really?" Bree asked incredulously.

"Yes," Calley sighed. "I couldn't scorch him. I couldn't kill him. Mercy came up in me."

"So what then?" Bree said. "You must tell me!"

Calley said, "I went up to him. I took this form, my hair spilling forward around my face in the wind, and I walked up to him and said, 'Look at me. Roll over and look at me.' And he did. And, would you believe it? He was erect under his kilt. Erect! Hard as that pestle over there!"

"Oh no," Bree said and started laughing. She stood up, turned around and looked at her sister. She laughed so hard she had to bend over and put her hands on her knees. Calley was laughing, too, leaning against the stone wall of the house and pressing her hands to the cool hardness.

"Oh! Oh!" Calley recaptured her breath. "And guess at what he did then! Guess!"

"Oh...I...can't," Bree replied, taking a whole breath between each word, trying to get the laughter under control.

"He sat up, and looked down at it. Then he looked up at me and smiled. He said, 'Sex and Death, Goddess. Sex and Death.'"

"Oh, my. So what did you do?"

"I pointed at him. I pointed at him like I was going to blast him into little black charred bits. And I said, 'Yes, I am. That I am, too.' And then I floated up to him, and when I got there I slowly moved my pointing hand and pointed at that pestle."

She paused.

"Then I reached up under his kilt and took hold of it, and sat down on it."

"Just like that?"

"Just like that. I put him in me. I lifted his kilt and took hold of it. I bent it toward me and slid it in. Just like that."

Bree's hands went to her face to cover her blush. "Ooooh, ooooh," she breathed, seeing it all in her mind's eye, and feeling in herself what her mind's eye saw. "What, what happened then?"

"I had a vision of him becoming a mountain and me covering him like a cloud, wisps of faint caress and then a covering in close. I felt him, I felt the mountain rise up under me, and in no long time I was ready. And so was he."

Again Calley paused.

"And then I took hold of him and stood up and pointed it down away between our legs and, exploding through my grasp, he spread his seed upon the ground, and then I rained upon it. My thighs were shaking."

Calley became silent and Bree looked at her sister, her eyes filled with excitement.

"I let go and raised his face in my hands. I kissed him in the middle of his forehead. He fainted dead away," Calley said after the pause.

Bree whispered, "And then?"

"And then I became Rain."

"Yes, oh yes," Bree said, quietly. "So Beautiful. So much Beauty."

Calley sighed. "I wonder what will grow there."

Bree said, "I have to get out more often." And then, "Wait, what did you mean by 'Yes, I am. That I am, too?'"

Calley replied, "I meant, that—I meant that I am a Goddess of Sex and Death. And I am also a Goddess of Sex and Death, among other things. As are you, sister."

Bree said, "Seriously. I've got to get out more often. But we need to wait, Sister. We can't bring him here yet. We have work to do so that he will see this as we wish him to see it."

3

STONEHAVEN

There are fields in the mind.

There are fields in the mind's eye that stretch and roll away forever. Other fields are held in a deep embrace. Enclosed. Enfolded in a mother's arms; they are held in the arms of love. There are fields filled with wild flowers, in the mind's eye. And fields of blood.

And mountains. It is in these fields and mountains that Stonehaven exists.

There is a mountain to the west, a long high hump of a mountain crest, sitting along the top of a ridge running north by south. The mountain slopes down in shoulders to the main ridge on either side and become saddles leading to lower peaks in either direction. From these saddles lower ridges extend down, opening to the northeast and the southeast, as if they were arms or hands opening to embrace the rising sun.

From these arms extend smaller ridges, out into the central valley, fingers creating coves and steep vales, each ending in headlands of parallel limestone walls, sometimes several, ranging in thickness from a foot to a few feet thick, standing fifteen to twenty feet apart, with an old dark red clay sandwiched between the walls. In the fog and mists the rock walls looked like concentric rings, ruins of some old and buried citadel.

In the winter the mountain casts a long shadow, bringing early darkness to the valley and the vales in the east below.

The Mountain had long been called Pine Eye Mountain, now shortened on the maps to Piney Mountain. Directly below the peak a few hundred feet and below the level of the saddles is a small forest of great White Pine. It is an old, old stand, drawn to particular soil or water, with fallen trees so thick in every direction the woods seems to be an impenetrable tangled nest: a mare's nest. Looking from the valley and the ridges, the stand of trees was shaped like an eye, a single eye of green, surrounded by deciduous forest or bare rock. In winter the eye stared stark in contrast; in summer hidden almost. In moonlight it seemed to move.

Below the Eye the mountain is steep, in places a vertical face of exposed rock, in other places a steep curtain of trees providing a patchwork blouse or tunic, the browns and grays of buckskin lichens alongside a mossy green, descending to a skirt of elderberry forest at the bottom.

Small streams emerge from springs near the head of each cove, in some places leaping, in others winding, down to a central stream: Stonehaven Creek. The creek runs almost two miles, folding back on itself, from the base of the Pine Eye to a notch between two headlands, rushing away to the southeast.

About 600 acres of this valley are cleared. The bottom-most lands are farmed and gardened. Farther out are hayfields, some small fields of corn and wheat. Beyond that, up to the edge of the woods, are cleared pastures.

It is an oasis of the temperate rain forest, and life grows abundantly and quietly there. Along the boundaries of the 3,000 acre farm are vacation properties and some timber holdings, all owned by shell corporations, which in turn are owned by Stonehaven, acquired over a long period of time. Together with a few parcels of land leased from the government, there are about 6,000 contiguous acres under Stonehaven's control.

The main route to the farm is from the northwest, climbing into the mountains, and crossing the Stonehaven ridge three saddles to the north of Pine Eye Mountain. The Ridge is broad there, almost a plateau, and a gravel road called the North County road runs along the plateau and through the vacation rental houses. It intersects with another road, the South County Road, less travelled. The entrance to Stonehaven is near this intersection on the southern road.

The driveway descends from the flat slowly, then around a curve by a Gate House with a remote controlled gate, invisible from the county road. After the turn past the Gate House the driveway is improved to the extent that it is in better condition than the county road. This drive emerges from the woods, continues to wind down along through pasture, over cattle gates, and then it forks; one fork leading into a parking lot near one of the smaller barns. The other fork leads down to the lot behind the Mansion, standing east of the barns and farther south.

Both the main house—the Mansion—and the wings were constructed of brick, built on rock masonry foundations beginning in the late 1870's and finished in the early 1920's. It stands four stories high on a knee of ridge between two coves. The main length of it faces south, with a long three story columned veranda along the south side. Both ends of the main house end in large circular rooms called the Ballrooms. The wings at each end attached to the main house and the Ballrooms at a forty-five degree angle, on the west heading northwest, on the east heading southeast for an over-all length of almost three hundred feet, although the wings are only three stories high. From above the house, the metal roof looks like a dark red lightning bolt laid out along the highlands.

There is a full basement under all of it, the land graded so that there were windows opening into the basement all along the southern faces. The first floor is twelve feet high. There are many fireplaces, leading to chimneys along the ridgeline and at both ends of the main house, at the middle and both ends of each wing, and at the furthest extent of each circular ball room. These chimneys were all lined at great expense, and even the fireplaces in some of the upper floor bedrooms and in the basement are fully working, although some have inserts and are fueled by natural gas. A re-fit in the 1950's had installed a hot water heating system fed by a boiler installed in a specially built shed near the Mansion. The boiler, originally fed by coal, had been upgraded to run on heating oil or natural gas. There are no air-conditioners at the Mansion, only lots of ceiling fans.

The land has been occupied by humans for a long time. Any rock shelter, especially one facing south or southeast, holds signs of habitation if one digs down, sometimes thousands of years old. During the surge of interest in archeology in the 1920's, the owners had requested a survey from a university. Only small occupancy sites were discovered. These were small camps, perhaps a family group or a few hunters, in what had been a deep forest at the time, so the ownership of Stonehaven declined any more surveys, and decided instead to add their own layers of habitation.

The bottom land was first cleared for farming in 1783, and the first stone house completed in 1795. The labor was done by a mixture of poor whites and about 20 slaves. The living sites of these people were found just up from the bottom. Nearby, up a ravine to the southwest, a graveyard was discovered. When it was discovered during the survey, the ownership built a stone chapel there, above the graves, with double doors facing the north east, looking over the cemetery yard. Markers were placed over each grave. No words were written on these stones, but at different times of the year flowers were placed on them and feasts were held in the chapel.

There was another cemetery, called the family cemetery, up behind the Mansion in the woods to the north. It lay on a short promontory from a ridge. A chapel was built here, also, with doors opening to both the south and the west, atop the rocks, the view unobscured trees. Many of the headstones had names and dates, and the yard was kept up and flowers planted and feasts held.

The amount of work that had gone into clearing the land and preparing it for farming was visible and substantial. The entire farmed bottom was fenced off by stacked stone fences—the stones washed down from above or limestone quarried from the wall outcroppings. The stone from the walls of the original house was torn down and repurposed in building the Mansion. The foundation of the stone house had been incorporated into a new barn first built in 1872.

The original property had been purchased by a man named Adams from Massachusetts who owned several small mills. He began building his fortune before the Civil War and prospered supplying clothing and ammunition for the Union military.

He bought the property, about a thousand acres, when it was very inexpensive and out of tax compliance, right after the War. The original family's men had gone off to war, and none had returned. The widow and her sister were both glad to sell the place, take the money—a fortune to them—and move away with their children, starting over again out west.

Stonehaven came to be organized in its current form by the last surviving member of the mill owner's family. Rachel Adams had been one of those daughters of the aristocracy for whom not much was planned, and from whom not much was expected, except that she would marry a member of her class. Her brother David was intended to inherit the estate, about which he had mixed feelings, at best.

It was she who had named the place Stonehaven as a precocious child of ten. Once, standing on the veranda steps, she'd looked out over the land, up to the Piney Mountain, and sighed. She'd turned to her parents, dining outdoors on a fine summer's evening, and said, "Everything is safe here. It is a haven for everything. Even the stones are safe."

"Yes," her father had said, "It is a haven. Even for the stones."

And her mother had nodded, "Yes, it is. It is a stone haven."

"Then that should be its name," Rachel said. "Stonehaven." And it came to be so.

Rachel showed signs of wildness at an early age. Having been taken to a circus at age six she was astounded at the young woman performer standing and galloping around the ring on the back of a horse. Upon returning home she promptly began training one of the farm horses to the task and soon was galloping around the pasture doing stunts on horseback, working up to even doing a handstand.

This was known and marveled at by the farm hands, but remained unknown to her parents until they received a call from the boarding school where they'd sent Rachel. Her behavior, standing up while galloping around on one of the school's riding horses, represented an unacceptable danger to herself and others, especially since she was training others to do the same. Apparently she'd had the idea to create a school circus act, intending it to be an ironic comment on the school itself.

Throughout her entire educational history she proved to be both brilliant and untamable. Released, finally, from college with a degree in
anthropology, she decided to travel for a short period that, inevitably,
turned into several years abroad. She left New York having obtained
passage on a steamer leaving for Africa. They docked first in Morocco,
then traded down the coast and around the Cape.

She travelled to Windia and Tribhat, studying with Masters of different disciplines from Shamanism to Magic. She stayed a while in Flora, where she encountered the cult of the Trants, who believe in the
achievement of the enlightenment through sex, and where she heard
about the secrets of the Seven Sisters. She travelled to Windonesia and
Wallid in the late 1920's, where she bought a house in Buduna. One
morning she saw a column of light rising from Tanah Headland at
sunrise, and realized she was at a psychic outpost on the edge of the
wilderness. She vowed to return.

She arrived in Europe sometime in the early 1930's, some said, with
sufficient skill to have been considered 'Dakinisiddah', having studied
Tantra and several forms of yoga. It seemed to those around her that
she had become very intuitive, even to the point of being able to occasionally 'read the minds' of people around her.

Rumored, again, she took initiation in the Old Grove Coven in southern
England, and was trained as a Priestess. In the summer of 1932, she visited Paris and took in a performance called "Conflict of the Siddhus".
The performance was a dance production that used the principles of
Temple Dancing. She had been trained to dance like all the daughters
of the aristocracy. And during her travels she'd studied temple dancing
when she could. She was fascinated by the performance and made the
acquaintance of the author, a Mr. Dzordza. Mr. Dzordza was considered to be a Tribhatan Lama, and a renegade from his order. In truth, he
had been blessed to bring his teaching to the West.

She was so taken with what she saw there, weeping silently for some
reason that she couldn't explain, that she vowed that she would study
and learn these movements and dances.

During her time studying, she became pregnant. The father was never
known to many, but of course the rumors spread that the aforemen-
tioned author and teacher was due the paternal nod. However, Rachel,

being a person of means herself, never felt compelled to confirm or deny any of this, considering it no one else's business.

In early 1939, sensing the impending start of World War II, she returned to Stonehaven, with her young son David in tow. Her father had suffered a stroke and her mother asked her to return home for comfort and support. He died in April, 1940, when the dogwoods were coming into bloom.

Her brother David enlisted in the Army in 1942 after Pearl Harbor and died on the beach at Salerno in 1943, leaving Rachel as sole heir to the estate. Her mother also passed away in late 1943.

The estate was now firmly in Rachel's hands. The family businesses of arms and ammunition manufacturing, and uniform clothing mills, was bringing in a large steady income from wartime government spending. Rachel soon found herself with millions of dollars of discretionary income and a controlling interest in revenue sources that would bring in tens of millions in the next decades.

She decided first to upgrade the buildings and grounds, restoring the mansion and putting in a formal garden. The garden was replete with standing stones, dolmens, sacred symbols, groves, niches, a fountain, and a sunken garden with a small spring feeding a pool next to an intrusion of vertical rock. She started a program of managed care for some of the forest, leaving other parts to wilderness. She raised the farm hand's salaries and upgraded their houses.

She took up riding again, teaching her son and the farm hands' children. They worked most on training to be hunters, riding through the woods.

Since the farm was far from any town, she brought in a certified teacher and got the blessing of the County Board of Education to set up a private school. The farm hands' children attended free of charge. David, her son, grew up there with these boys and girls as his friends. Eventually the school began accepting children from off the farm, including children of friends of hers. Rachel, due to her wealth and travels, knew many people.

It is unknown, exactly, of what the curriculum of this school consisted, but one could see that, as a younger generation took over from their parents, the people stopped going to church. Rachel had a few different chapels built, but they were used only for special occasions.

It is certain that Rachel and the Teacher became lovers, and possibly had been before he moved to Stonehaven. An unpublished memoir of a life-long friend recounts Rachel's telling of a tale of one of their love-makings, first told in New York, April 1950.

"Oh, Beverley, I have to tell you. He came into the room yesterday, drying his hair on a towel, naked, and he saw me looking at him and he smiled. I smiled back and he started to grow, you know? No touching, he was across the room. He just watched me looking at him, and the way I was looking at him pulled his erection up. I was directing him, pulling him with my eyes. I raised my hand and his erection raised up. Side to side? It went side to side. He just stood there grinning like a fool, and I laughed out loud.

"I feel your hand, you know." That's what he said. So I swatted it, just hard enough to make him say "Ow!"

"So I said, "Come here, pretty thing" and made a movement in the air like I had closed my hand over it, and pulled, and, I swear, Beverly, we both saw the skin move. He came over to the bed, following his erection, me pulling him with just the gesture of my hand.

"When he got close I held up a hand and stopped him. I imagined him in my mouth, opening it, extending my tongue, and he gasped.

"I feel you, beloved. I feel that."

"Then come," I said. "Come here."

"Then I did to him what he'd just felt, taking him in, extending my tongue, just holding him there, and he started to shiver all over. He went into ecstasy, standing right there, but staying on his feet. He didn't collapse!

"And then he said, voice all quiet, "I feel two of you. One just inside the other." And suddenly I became aware of two of me, two skins, as it were, two surfaces. Then my awareness went inside and it was as if my mind exploded in light. I was in the Palace of a Thousand Lights. When I brought my sensation back to the room and went to open my eyes, I found they were already open! And that I was looking up at him through another set of eyes. Someone else's eyes!

"He spoke. He said, "I see you." My head pulled back, and I took his erection in my hand. And then a voice in me, a soft voice, deeper than mine but using my throat and my lips said, "Whom do you see?"

"And he, so softly and seriously, said, "I see She by whom I was made." Then he went to his knees so that we were at eye level.

"I realized it was Her! It was She in me. Then he said, "And I see you, too, beloved."

"I rolled over on my back so I could take him in embrace. He stood up and entered me, no hands, I just received him. Well, I should say 'We' just received him. He slid all the way in, simply, smoothly. Then I felt Her start to shudder inside me! We wrapped our arms around him and pulled him down for a kiss. We wrapped our legs around his back and held him in, held him still.

"Then, as Her shuddering built, my shuddering built. I heard Her voice in my head, saying, "Beloved, thank you" to me. I felt Her gratitude, gratitude toward me! Then I felt Her love! Her Love of me! I swear it, oh! And then aloud She said, "Beloveds, thank you."

"Then we made love. He became everything I wanted in each and every second. Any movement I could want, he anticipated it. And I just dissolved into his arms, into the bed, into Her love for me, and for him. I went out. I went out of mind. When I came back all was still. He wasn't moving, and he was out of me, pressed against me, still hard, just holding me, looking at my face, waiting for me to come back.

"Later, he told me that for part of the time I was gone he could only see Her. And that She talked to him, that She told him things that She wanted of him. How She wanted him to spend his life.

"Oh my, oh my dear. She came, Beverly. She came to us! She came within me! I felt this new kind of fullness, the deepest satisfaction I'd ever felt, deep, deep into my womb it went, and settled there. And ever since I have only to think of it, and the satisfaction arises and feeds my soul.

"He, too, was satisfied. Even with the erection, he just held me. And let me sleep.

"All those years of training, all those years of practicing, and practicing with men I didn't want, but had to do. And it led to this power to extend my reach. And the power to call Her into me. And just imagine, Beverly, if I can be trained to do these things, if any woman can be trained to do these things, just imagine what it would be like if men learned to do the things he did.

"Beverly, stop writing now, and listen. I have an idea."

4

PROPHET OF GAWD

Chester Tillings considered himself to be a man of Gawd. He was an ordained minister in the Great Smokey Resurrection Church of Gawd's Son Laud. The church had folded, but the ordination didn't. He would travel from one small town to another, looking for a pulpit, sometimes sharing the pulpit with a local pastor, and getting a cut of the collected offering.

He considered that the ordination made him an upright man in the eyes of his Gawd. He had moved in with a woman, living in sin in the eyes of the state, perhaps, but married in the eyes of the Laud. Chester had presided over their own ceremony one evening in a church devoid of worshipers. It was a ceremony he had performed many times in different towns, having by now, to his own reckoning, almost a dozen wives. In his mind he was simply claiming the harem he deserved, as if he were some kind of re-incarnated Old Testerment prophet.

He was thinking about all his wives, sitting there at the table in the double-wide, holding a coffee cup in one hand and looking at his current wife's butt slide under her housedress as she bent to get the bacon from the refrigerator on this one particular morning. Melinda didn't speak a lot in the morning, which suited him just fine, as he was not much inclined to listening to women speak at all.

Suddenly Melinda said, without turning around, "Do you remember how we met?"

Taking a moment to recover from his shattered fantasy of having wives number Two and Seven in bed at the same time, Chester replied, "Sure. I met you at the Stop and Hop. I came in and bought some gas and a pop and asked for directions to the church. You sure were pretty, Missy."

"Not that, Chester. About how I came to you for help."

"Oh! You mean Fat Bobby!" Chester said.

"Yeah, Chester, Fat Bobby," Melinda replied.

She didn't like the nickname. She thought it was gross, even though he had been fat. Maybe it had caused his stroke, or maybe it was suicide that made him drive through the abutment on the bridge and into the creek. She thought the nickname was disrespectful to the dead. He'd been her boss at the store, and he never stopped pressuring her to perform oral sex on him. At least that's what Chester thought. She'd never told him the whole truth, the truth that she'd been doing it for a long time, almost a year. Most days it was once a day at the beginning of her shift. Sometimes again at the end of the day. She was afraid for her job and she had a child who stayed with her grandma all day, and her job supported the three of them.

Instead she'd gone down to the church after work the day Chester had come in. Bobby was getting more demanding and she was so grossed out and so sickened by it now that she went to the Preacher and asked for help. She'd told Chester only that he'd been pressuring her and that she didn't have a man to protect her. She asked that he go talk to Fat Bobby and tell him how wrong it was.

Chester promised he would speak to Bobby when and in a way that the Laud told him to. Three days later Bobby showed up for work with a black eye and went directly to his little manager's office and closed the door without even looking at Melinda.

Later, after a couple more days, and on a Monday after giving a sermon about sin and damnation at the church the day before, Chester stopped by the store and asked Melinda to come by the church that night. Melinda was happy to, although she suspected what she might be getting into. She brushed her hair and her teeth, and put on a nice dress, pale blue with bare shoulders and a white collar, and heels; she even put on a little pale lip gloss and body scent.

Chester was overcome with unexpected lust when Melinda walked down the aisle and emerged in the small spot light over the lectern he was leaning on. She stood there, on the edge of the light, and Chester said, "You must repent of your sins. The fat boy told me all about it, all about what he had you doing. So you must repent of your sins. And the only way I can bring down the spirit of the Laud that you may be washed in the blood of forgiveness is for me to know exactly what it was that you did to him. You must show me, daughter of Laud, in order that you can be cleansed and that righteousness be yours."

Chester hadn't planned, exactly, on doing this, but now that the words had come out of his mouth he knew he better follow up. He stepped from behind the lectern, not bothering to hide the erection straining against his khakis, and stepped down from the stage into the center of the circle of light. Melinda went to her knees in front of him, being careful not to scuff the toes of her shoes.

She reached up and pulled his zipper down and reached in. Finding the opening in his boxers, she pulled out his erection. She contemplated it for a moment; its length, its girth, the veins, the way the head emerged from his foreskin. Then she smelled it, comparing it to all the other men she'd ever gone down on. He certainly smelled better than Bobby. She knew some techniques for making this go more quickly. She went to work on it.

As Chester neared completion he put both hands on her head, and said, "Oh, missy, missy, you truly are a good girl. Such a good girl." Then Melinda was flung way far into surprise when his hands lit up blue-white and so did his erection on the roof of her mouth. The three lit up and formed an electric channel between them which gathered energy and shot a blue-white bolt straight through her and out her clitoris. Chester said, "Praise the Laud!" as Melinda fell away from him onto her side, twitching with the spasms of the orgasm. "Praise the Laud!" Chester said again, but quietly this time. "The Holy Spirit has entered you and you are being cleansed, and when it stops, you will be forgiven."

Melinda didn't particularly want it to stop so she faked it a little near the end. Chester still had his erection. Standing there, flush with conquest, cock waving, he raised his hands to the sky and said, "Thank you Laud!"

Melinda sat up, leaning on one hand. Chester stepped down to her and grabbed her by the hair. "Daughter of Lilly," he said, gesturing at himself, "Look what you've done to me."

"We are sinners born into sin. Like the animals of the field, we are. Your evil ways have brought me to sin, you have brought me low, woman, friend of serpents. I am helpless, Laud help me!" Chester said as he guided Melinda by the hair to kneel down on the steps of the dais, facing the symbol in the back of the church. He stood behind her, still holding on to her hair with one hand and with the other he reached under her dress and pulled down her underwear, glowing faintly white in the dusky light of the church. He positioned himself behind her, lowering himself until his erection was approximately in the right place. He thrust against her indiscriminately, sometimes slipping between her legs, sometimes up her back, sometimes against her anus, banging around, pushing blindly, looking for entry, all the while muttering, "We are animals, Laud help me."

Melinda, not wanting to take it in the asshole, reached back between her legs and guided him in. She kept her hand there, not just in case he slipped out, but to also work her own little hardness, knowing she had to be responsible for her own pleasure. Since the rape was inevitable she would relax and enjoy it. She turned her head sideways and rested her cheek on her other hand on the floor. She simply repeated to herself, "It's just a dick" over and over.

After almost a minute of thrusting Chester was near finishing. Melinda could feel it building and she squeezed from deep inside, pushing him out at the final moment. He came, stepping up over her, drizzling and splatting along her back, the floor, and the side of her face.

Melinda thought to herself, "And this is the knowledge of Good and Evil. Which is which? And where's the Good?"

Chester stepped back, looking at the image spread out before him and then raised his eyes to the symbol. Suddenly he was outside himself, seeing a white glow surrounding the symbol, and a glow the same color enveloping Melinda. He saw himself standing there, erection sagging, dripping once on the floor. He wasn't glowing at all. Then he saw the shadow behind him, dark, some nebulous dark hand-shaped shadow reaching out for his shoulder. Quickly he jumped to the side, stuffing himself back in his trousers.

"It is not safe," he said. "We have sinned and opened ourselves to Evil."

"I did not sin," Melinda said, pulling her panties up. "I simply submitted. I obeyed. Was that wrong?"

"You tempted me and I fell. We are both sinners. There is only one way to protect ourselves. We must be married in the eyes of the Laud. I am holy in His Name. I can perform the ceremony. We must get married and do it right now. Stand up."

Melinda stood up, wiping the mess from her cheek, keeping it out of her hair, and pulled down her dress. Taking her hand, Chester led them up the dais and knelt down before the symbol, pulling her down with him.

He said, "Dear Laud, hear our prayer, two sinners come before you seeking mercy and, and protection. We come here seeking your blessing on us sinners, bless us as man and wife. Do you Melinda, take me as your husband in the eyes of the Laud?"

She thought to herself, "He's a crazy man. What if I say 'No'? What will he do? Oh, man, I'm fucked here. I'm scared. I might as well say 'Yes'. It don't mean much anyway. At least it gets me out of here alive." So she said, "Yes."

"Praise the Laud!" Chester said. "By the powers vested in me I now pronounce us man and wife." Then he pulled her toward him, put his other hand behind her head and held it still so he could kiss her quickly. He said, "To seal the deal."

Then he got up and stepped back and said, "We have to go. I don't have a car. We're going to your house," and then he pulled her by the hand out the door.

He paused at the threshold and looked back. The shadow was gone, but he failed to see the set of eyes looking at him from above the podium, a woman's eyes in a rectangular section of face.

When they got to the car he got in the driver's seat, fished around in her purse and took the keys.

Melinda was standing there, wondering "How did this happen?"

Chester said impatiently, "Come on! Get in the car! I don't know where you live."

The next morning the church caretaker was driving by when he saw one of the double doors was open. He pulled into the lot, and went up the steps of the church to see if everything was all right, and if anyone was there. He walked to the front of the church and saw the mess on the dais. He looked up to the rafters and thought, "Bats must of got in. Look at this, a gawddamn mess." And then he thought, "Naw, bats just doin' what they do. Damn the man who left the door open." Then he went to get a rag and some water.

That had been a little more than 15 years before. Chester, his mind returning to his present moment, said, "Yeah, Missy, I do. I do remember. What about it?"

5

STONEHAVEN BOUND

Angelica sat up. Crossing her arms to finish lowering the straps and shaking her hips to drop the slip over her backside, she laughed again, grabbed a robe, and slipped lightly down the hall to the bathroom to take a shower. She knew her parents would be up soon and wanted one more chance to hang out with them.

The shower felt more alive somehow, which must have meant that it was her that felt more alive. She sensed each drop as it pounded onto her. Turning in the water was a luxury, and soon became an ecstasy. She shivered with pleasure in the steaming heat. Washing her hair became a dance under the water, slow and sinuous, as she put all her attention into sensation. Slowly the tingling drops became like little pinpricks on her skin, then little slashes, passing down and rolling like tiny thorns. Her entire body flushed a bright pink, then a deep red and it became hard to breathe.

All of her was engulfed in a flash of fiery pain and she thought she would burst into flames there in the water. She became dizzy and tunnel-visioned and she slowly dropped to her knees, sliding down the shower wall. She reached up and turned the water completely cold. She knelt there until she cooled down and could breathe again. She adjusted the water back to warm, finished rinsing her hair and turned off the water. She stood slowly, thinking, wow, now that was a hot flash, and wondered if this was going to become a problem. She opened the glass shower door and stepped out onto the rug. She looked at herself, standing naked in the mirror mysteriously free of steam, and saw her eyes spiraling in her reflection. She closed her eyes to clear her vision and suddenly sensed the spiral images she'd seen moving lightly on her face. Slowly the sensation faded. Dizziness from the hot flash, she thought.

She turned from the mirror, grabbed a towel off the rack, and let her mind move forward into contemplating the day. She thought about the clothes she'd wear—one set for the morning and then a change for travelling. She looked at what was left to pack. She checked over her car in her mind. She saw herself leaving for Stonehaven, her parents gone to work, closing the door behind her, standing at the car and looking back at the house. These things she could foresee. But beyond that, nothing. Even the road to Stonehaven was unfamiliar to her, and it would be at least a seven hour drive.

She had been told about Stonehaven by the yoga instructor in an evening class she had taken at college. The poses were mostly from a line of Kundalini yoga. She had begun having shifts in her emotions and thoughts and she couldn't figure out how they related to her sensations. She had decided to ask the instructor, Jonathon, about it one night after class.

He was cute and seemed approachable. Usually cute meant vain and she wasn't interested in more vain boys. But, at around 30 years old, he seemed more solid and more at ease than men her age. He smiled easily. When he talked to people, he looked them directly in the face, without his eyes wandering. When somebody needed some assistance with something, his eyes and hands went directly to that place on the student's body, with no wandering and no inappropriate lingering.

There was something in his presence; something calming and assuring. But he accomplished this not with the gravitas of the role of the teacher. It seemed he accomplished this with something less heavy, like some kind of calming oil laid over troubled skin. It smoothed out the emotions of everyone else in the room. And it made the rest of the men less creepy to be around.

In one of the early classes he'd said something that had really caught her attention. Her reaction had been to turn quickly and focus on him in an effort to discern if he were telling the truth. He was working on simply getting everybody to stand up straight. He said something like, "The Goddess who created you designed you to occupy a certain space. And it is disrespectful of you to refuse the invitation."

She was about to dismiss him as some kind of Neo-Pagan type, but again, there was something in the way he said it that felt more present than it usually would have felt. Perhaps it was the atmosphere, or the container of the room, or something else, but it certainly seemed that he was sincere about himself believing what he said. And underneath that belief she discerned a confidence and relaxation about his assertion that left her feeling a little intrigued. In fact, when she watched him, he seemed unusually confident and relaxed. Sincere, confident, relaxed, "What's not to like?" she'd said aloud to herself.

But coming into the end of her time at college, she thought that she didn't really have time to start an affair. Even a one-nighter would complicate things; she wanted to keep coming back to the class until the end of the semester. So after class one night she went up to him and said she had a question about something that was happening when she went through the routine. He said, "Go ahead, Angelica. Tell me what's going on."

She said, "As I'm going through the routine I feel something start to happen in my belly, lower down below my navel. And this feeling is exciting, maybe even sensual, and it rises up and changes as it rises. When it gets here," she said, pointing at her solar plexus, "it changes. The feeling becomes something emotional but I don't know what the emotion is. It keeps rising up to my heart where it changes again into something intense but emotionally beyond that other feeling. When it gets to my throat I want to moan, but of course I can't, not in class. Most of the time it stops there, but I discovered that when I put my tongue on the roof of my mouth this weird kind of felt-sense rises to my forehead and it seems like there's a sense that out there in the world I could hear and see something else if I could just pause long enough, but then it keeps going and my mind flashes with light, and then it's gone. Is this normal?"

Jonathon said, "It's unusual. It's kind of rare actually. But it is normal in terms of the kind of yoga we're doing. What's happening is that your chakras are activating. Do you know what they are?"

She nodded affirmatively, "Yes, I do. I've read about them in some of my classes on Windu culture."

Jonathon smiled, "Windu culture, eh? Really?"

"Yes," she said, nodding her head, her hair, now down, rolling with the nod.

"Well," Jonathon went on, "the chakras are being activated by what we're doing. The energy you're feeling is accumulated by the effort and the breathing. It builds up in certain places and then gets released into this kind of channel. That's what you're feeling. It can be refined a lot, and you'll sense a lot of different things. It can get pretty intense."

"Where can I learn more about this?" she asked. "I want to know more about what this is and how to work with it. Can you teach me?"

He said "Well," slowly. "I could probably teach you some. But I know a better place for you to learn more about it. There's a place, a retreat center, where I took a lot of yoga classes over the years. It's called Stonehaven. And there are a lot of really experienced people there with a lot understanding about this stuff. They run courses there, sometimes for a month or more. I think there's a class starting for two weeks in early June. Could you get there?"

"Yes," she said. "I graduate in early May. After commencement I'm free for the summer."

Jonathon said, "OK then." He pulled a little paper pad and a pen out of his nearby pack. He wrote something on the top sheet. "Here's the website, and you can fill out the application. This place is pretty selective and you'll need a reference. You can use my name. I wrote down my number, too, so they can contact me. But you should do it soon. The classes do fill up."

He handed the paper to her. "There you go," he said. "Did that answer your question well enough?"

She nodded and smiled at him, suddenly realizing that his attention was very focused on her. It felt a little odd, a little too direct, and she glanced away.

"I'm just looking to make sure you're alright," he said. "I kind of have a responsibility here to make sure you're alright, that you'll be OK when you leave. We'll see each other again next week. I'll make sure that if the energy comes up like that again you're able to just be with it, and be OK. You understand?"

She nodded, starting to turn away for the door.

"It'll be OK," he said, watching her back, smiling at how beautiful she was. "Blessings upon her," he thought as he walked to the closet to get the dry mop and sweep the floor before he left. When he was done he took the mop outside to shake it off, and looking to the west saw the crescent moon. He held an image of her in his mind and said aloud, "Blessings upon her."

She remembered these events standing beside her car in the driveway. Then it was as if she suddenly woke up. She remembered getting dressed, making coffee, having a light breakfast with her parents before they went to work. They hugged and said "Be in touch," as they went off. Finishing packing and brushing her teeth. Finishing the dishes. Loading her car with two small suitcases and a backpack.

And suddenly she was standing there, her hand on the car door turning and looking back and the sensation was as if she had just awakened. And now she was remembering the things she had done as if she hadn't been aware of them while she was doing them.

She realized that she had crossed under her third arch. The first was the door to the building where her apartment had been. The second was the Campus Gate. And the third was the door to her parents' house, the third arch that it was said in certain African rituals wakes up the Spirit. At the first arch the Senses wake up. At the second the Soul wakes up. And then the third wakes the Spirit. So now, paying attention, she was ready for anything.

She stood there, hand poised on the door handle of her car, and sighed--one of those ambivalent, ambiguous sighs. She sighed for all her past, her parents, her education, her friends, knowing somehow that crossing that last threshold was the end of all that she had known. And she sighed for all the future that lay ahead of her, knowing deep in her mind, with a certainty that she couldn't explain, that her life would never be the same.

A tear rolled down one cheek as she looked around her old neighborhood. She looked at her parent's house and another tear came down. She tried to sigh again, and it almost became a sob. She had no idea why she would sob. It was a new beginning, and she should be crying for joy. As soon as she thought it, it was so. Wiping her cheek with one hand, opening the door with the other, she smiled broadly.

She started her car, set the sights of her mind's eye on Stonehaven, and drove away.

6

WATCHING ALAM

Alam woke up chilled and still soaked when the sun went behind the shoulder of the mountain. He lay still and listened, extending his awareness seeking to hear any signs of his sheep, not yet remembering why he was lying in the open on the path. Then he remembered.

He sat up quickly, clutching the grass with both hands, hanging on in case he had to. He looked around, even twisting behind himself. He looked to see if She was there again, waiting for him to figure it out. But there was nothing he could detect. There was only the circle of scorched grass all round him. His detumescence, laying on his thigh, twitched at the memory. He looked down, and he felt some surprise at seeing himself, lying there, fully exposed to the sky. Quickly he flipped the hem of his kilt back in place.

Then he noticed a hemisphere of red light glowing on the ground by his feet. He quickly pulled his legs back under him. He leaned forward to look more closely and he could see it softly pulsing. He backed away from it up the hill on his hands and knees, only standing up when he was across the circle of the black scorch marks. He turned and looked back up the mountain, and he saw the flash of a rack of antlers silhouetted against the sky, which immediately disappeared.

"Hmm," he said to himself. "So He knows." He looked off down the slope, looking for the scattered sheep, seeing only a few. "So that's it then," he said aloud, then promptly shifted shape into a stallion. He trotted off down the hill, and began rounding up his sheep.

Calley watched him, wrapped in gray, sitting in the shadows of the crag, with Her back against the rock, unseen. She saw the Stag look at Alam, could feel the Stag's impatience and flash of anger at the loss of a student. Now She knew for certain the source of Alam's skill at shape shifting. She mused that Alam must have been caught out one day: the great Stag, the one who is both Hunter and Hunted, appearing behind him, ready to kill. She wondered why the Stag, the Hunter, had taken mercy on him.

Opening her mind, a scene unfolded before her. The first image was of Alam crouching in the branches of an oak just up a steep slope from the river. The imagery bounced back in time from that moment. She saw flashes of him walking along the bank, days before, looking for the places where his stock came down to drink, where they crossed it sometimes and would escape up into the hills. She saw him get down to examine the tracks on one path, saw him seeing that there were deer tracks mixed in with the tracks of sheep and the occasional cow or horse, as if the deer were using them for camouflage on their way to water. He guessed there were seven or so, with three yearlings, several days of fresh tracks coming and going. He got down on one knee in the grass alongside the path worn to dirt, careful, and noticed the tracks of a big deer, slid under the older tracks of a cow. She watched him puzzle it out, frowning, probing the dirt with a small stick, checking for how the soil crumbled. She watched as comprehension dawned on his face—this deer, this buck, hiding his tracks under the tracks of a cow. The buck's tracks were almost as big.

She watched as he looked up the path to where it disappeared, spreading out in a meadow; watched him scan toward the uplands, trying to discern where the small herd might be bedding down. He studied the tracks again closely, remembering the weather of the past few days, and figured out that the herd came this way only every third day, and that it had been a day since their last venture down this path. That meant in two days they would come again. She watched him stand up, and back away from the path, having resolved to be there when they came.

When he'd gotten far enough away, he'd stopped and said a prayer to Her, calling out her name, and asking for rain to come and wash away his scent, promising to feed Her with his success. She remembered then that She'd heard that prayer, and answered him. She'd answered him with a light rain and a wind that raised the grass as if he'd never been there.

That had not been her first notice of Alam—he'd sent voice to Her several times in the past. But She knew now which stag it was, and lost no love on this one. This stag had tried in long past times to bring Her under his control, weaving a web of deceit with love, trying to trap both Her and Bree into being in his thrall—the Hunter tried to hunt down Thunder, and free passage into gardens and fields. It hadn't worked, but it had been painful, and She was completely disinclined to have Mercy on him.

Then She had been called to Sea, asked to summon a storm to stop those who would invade the land from ships, and had forgotten about Alam's prayer. She shook Her head to clear that memory, the memory of ferocity, breaking timbers, and the cries of dying men, and looked back again to see what had happened with the deer.

She saw Alam in the late afternoon two days later, making his way silently through the woods on the other side of the river, stepping then pausing. She watched him test the wind, making sure it was steady towards him, blowing his scent away from the drinking spot. She watched him pick a tree, an old knobby-side oak, climb it to a branch that hung out over the river, unsling his bow, and settle down to wait.

The sun set on him, holding still, bow in hand and arrow nocked, resting, waiting. In the final pale light of gloaming the deer appeared. First a hind and her yearling fawn, then another pair, then the third. Then the Stag emerged, suddenly, yet somehow also slowly, appearing like a shift in the long grass of the meadow. Alam leaned forward, breathing so silently and slowly he seemed almost not to breathe at all.

The Stag was massive with a heavy mane. Its huge antlers stretched back as far as the rump, with seven tines on each side radiating from the cup past the fifth tine, spreading so broad as to make the rack almost three times as wide as its heavy shoulders. The Stag stopped, just visible at the top of the path, tines seeming to wave like the tall grass, waiting, scanning for any signs of trouble. It was almost at eye level with Alam. When it stepped onto the path and began to come down toward the water Alam shivered with excitement. Never had he seen or heard of a Stag like this, except in stories.

It came down the path, the others moving out of its way, and dropped its heavy head to drink. Alam leaned forward and aimed down, drawing slowly, sighting in just in front of the left shoulder, and then he held it. Some thought stopped him at full draw, some memory of some story of old, and, overcome with a sense of the presence of the Mysterious, and the Grand, he eased the draw. In the easing the bowstring sighed, almost a groan of disappointment.

The Stag had lifted its head from the water and, free of the river's sounds, heard this groan and froze, water dripping from its lips. They all froze. Then, in a remarkable display of courage the Stag reared, straight up on its legs, and looked right at Alam, eyes to eyes, while the others turned and ran.

She watched Alam's jaw drop and then his face turned to a huge grin. The Stag landed, and snorted at Alam. "Go on then!" he shouted at the Stag. "Go on then with your proud self!" The Stag turned and slowly trotted up the path, turning once when it reached the meadow. Looking over its shoulder at Alam, it snorted again, huffing at him, fixing the slightest of scents in the now still evening, and then disappeared into the gathering dark.

Calley shivered and returned to the present, remembering the power of the Stag, surprised to find her hand between her legs. She shook her head at herself, withdrew her hand, and settled back in to return to journeying to the past. She saw Alam at his forge, some time a few days later.

He had been working at it all afternoon, making rings and spikes for tying down hide tents, and it was evening. He was standing in the doorway, having just banked the fire for the night. He turned and the Stag was standing there, head low, looking at him with eyes so red Alam knew it wasn't just the light reflected from the forge; the eyes glowed with their own red light. The Stag huffed at him once. Alam backed into the forge house slowly, knowing the huge rack wouldn't fit through the door. He tripped just as the Stag leaped. He landed hard and when he opened his eyes, expecting the crash of bone on stone, there was only a man. But what a man, tall and broad and covered with reddish hair, breathing hard through his nose, nostrils flaring

The man stepped through the door, standing over Alam. In the shadows above his head Alam could make out seven dark spikes on each side. The man reached down and grabbed the front of Alam's tunic, pulling him up toward his face, looking at him closely, eyes to eyes. The Horned Man looked Alam in the middle of his forehead and huffed again. He turned and threw Alam out the door.

Alam landed in a heap, raising a cloud of dust, and rolled over on his back to see the Horned Man advancing on him. The Horned Man reached down and gathered up a handful of dirt from the yard and spit on it. Hefting it in his hand, mumbling words, he then threw it on Alam. Alam felt a change happening, felt his bones moving, felt his skin shifting to become hide, hair covered hide. Suddenly he felt his skull split open and he screamed in pain. Putting his hands to the top of his skull he felt the horns, the antlers emerging like trees growing quickly, fast, too fast to be true. And then his hands were gone, his fingers coalesced into hooves. Dirt from the yard swirled up around him, adding bulk and features like modelling clay attached to a frame. When it was done, he was on his back, legs up in the air, head twisted around by the antlers digging into the ground.

"Up, then," the Horned Man said. "Get up!" Alam scrambled to his legs, all four of them. "Go on then with your proud self." The Horned Man waved his hand away and Alam ran.

Calley returned to her present moment. "So that's how He does it. He uses the dirt, he uses the ground. Hmm."

The Horned One watched Alam leap over the stone wall that surrounded his house, tail flashing, and disappear. Snorting, faster and faster, he gave a mighty shout, a shout that echoed off the mountains, and took off after Alam, hurdling the wall like his form was still powered by the pumping heart of the Stag, leaping into space.

Alam ran, changing course in a zigzag, heading for the thickets at an angle, racing through the brush. He came to a log sitting on the edge of a steep hill bottoming out at the river and, turning around, kicked it over the edge. In the noise of it crashing down the hillside he stooped and then crawled deep into the thickets, slipping among the tight weave of branches, almost doubling back, going back the way he had come. He froze when the Horned One passed him heading for the hill where log went over the side.

The Horned One went to the top of the hill and stood there, snuffing, relaxing his eyes to let the star light in. He thought the imbecile could have lost his footing and fallen, but his nose was telling him different. The scent trail went another way. And then suddenly it rained. The Horned One looked at the sky and huffed and shook his fist at it, because the rain would damp down the scents. He got down on his hands and knees, nose to the earth like a dog, and started snuffling around looking for the trail.

Calley remembered that night. She had been elsewhere, paying attention to someone else, when that rain came. She didn't send it deliberately, it was just the natural spread of Her.

In the meantime, Alam had crawled further through the thickets, faster now as the noise of the rain covered the sounds he made brushing through the chaotically woven branches, and was emerging again in the meadow. As he emerged, he sent a silent prayer of thanks to the Storm Goddess.

Calley thought, "So that's what opened the door by which he found me. True gratitude for his life." She returned to Her journey.

As Alam stood up, the Horned One caught scent of the trail down low through the thicket. He shouldered his way in, using all the half man/ half Stag skills he possessed. He plowed through the thicket at speed, nose to the ground, and emerged just in time to see Alam disappear, bounding over a rise that ran through the meadow. The Horned One bounded after him.

Hooves slipping in the rain, Alam fell just as the Horned One was reaching for him. The Horned One overshot Alam and landed on one knee, sliding in the grass. As Alam was regaining his feet the Horned One leapt backwards, turned in the air and landed on him, flattening him to the ground, knocking the wind out of him. The Horned One reached for his throat, trying to pin him down, holding the antlers with the other hand. Alam went still.

In that stillness he caught his breath, and rolled, kicking into the body of the Horned One, slicing with his hooves. The Horned One bellowed in pain, and stepped around to Alam's head, holding him down, now with two hands, pinning his head to the ground. Enormously strong, and despite all Alam's struggles to lash with his antlers, slowly, slowly he felt his head being driven down into the earth; slowly, slowly, he could draw less and less breath, drowning in the soft earth. As Alam lost consciousness, falling into a sea of blackness, his heartbeat in his ears slowing to the slowest drum, he heard the Horned One say, "You'll not threaten us again."

Alam awoke in the soft gray light of dawn, naked in the meadow, surrounded by a small rise of dirt all round him, holding the impression of his body. Slowly, without moving, he extended his senses of smell and hearing, and could detect no presence. He opened an eye and looked around, seeing nothing. The Horned One was gone. He lay there, remembering everything before he moved. When he did move, everything ached. He tried to stand, and couldn't, so he crawled home, scraping his belly and his knees when he crawled over the rock wall. He crawled into his house and lashed down the hides so no one could enter, climbed into his pallet, and crashed into sleep.

Calley stood up and stretched. She had seen enough to know the beginnings of Alam's powers. She decided that She'd seen enough. Then something in Her intuition told her to look more. She needed to know what happened when the Horned One found out Alam was still alive. She looked forward and saw into Winter. There had been snow. She saw Alam pouring out little piles of barley near the edges of the muddy cleared space on the trail down to the river. In that evening She saw the small herd of deer come down the trail, find the barley and pause, frozen, looking through the human scent still lingering there to see if they could catch the faintest scent of something fresh. There was nothing, but the scent from Alam's fire. Then, they heard him singing in his house. The Great Stag, paused at the top of the trail, huffed.

She saw three days farther forward, and, in the night, the Horned One changing into human form at Alam's door. He paused, listening to Alam singing within, an old lullaby for a baby, to put it to sleep in the presence of a frightening storm. Alam had left the hide unlashed, and the Horned One stooped and went in. Alam was waiting for him.

"Understand, Great One. I was no threat to you. I spared you. Hence, no threat," he said. "I will help you if I can."

Calley drew back from the scene, and rested with Her eyes closed. "Signs and portents," She said aloud. "Signs and portents he'd come looking for me. Maybe that's what he'd been thinking all along, deep down." Tired now, She ventured back once more into the past.

The Horned One, still towering over Alam sitting by the fire, humphed and asked, "At what price, mortal?"

"That you teach me," Alam had replied.

The Horned One sat down. She saw Alam's eyes grow large, drawn to the erection rising between the Horned One's legs.

"I do what I am," the Horned One said. He reached forward for Alam and put him on his hands and knees before Him and pulled his face in between His legs by the hair.

She knew the contours of the Horned One's member, long and thin and pointed. Knew it well, indeed. This one had tried to ride her to another level of power, thought himself cunning enough and dominant enough to manipulate her. Although the deer were Hers to herd, this one, the Horned One, was as much Hunter as Hunted, and She had no control over it but Death. He did not know this in Himself, thinking that by embodying the whole cycle of Life and Death within Himself in the way He had, He was virtually immortal. It had cost Calley dearly simply to convince Him that He had no control over her.

She knew Alam would be taken; that he would pay a price for what he wanted to know. She knew he would survive.

This was all Calley needed to see. She stood up, went mist and spread out over the hills, resting in the dispersal. She closed all her eyes, closing the single eye of her visioning, and let the drops of her blow around in a cloud of sleep.

7

FOUNDATION

The first Teacher employed by Rachel, a biologist whose name was John Craft, became a kind of model for the young men and boys on the farm. They did what he did, learned to carry themselves like he did, sometimes even talking like him. He would take them out on patrols in the woods, camping, showing them survival skills. He taught them judo.

It is clear now that they had imprinted on him, becoming men like him, and that they came to believe in and understand the world the way he did. And what he believed, being the romantic that he was, was that the Masculine should be in Service to the Feminine, not in service to itself. He believed that the Sacred Masculine should be in Service to the Sacred Feminine, as a Consort is to a Priestess.

In the classes for the girls this relationship came to be taught also, usually by Rachel, and eventually by other teachers. There came to be a system of knowledge reflecting the nature of the world, recognizing the Antecedence of the Feminine.

From these archetypal relationships, taught and lived out, came the curriculum of Stonehaven.

This idea, the idea of Service to the Feminine, was not taught directly, at least to the younger students. But it was incorporated into everything so that the students learned it indirectly while they were learning something else. The parents of the farmhand children didn't object because the quality of their lives was so much better than they'd thought it would be. They were occupied and happy.

The parents of the other children sent them to Stonehaven because they already knew the kind of education that would be received. It was an education that they wished they'd had. There was physical education: yoga, martial arts, and outdoor skills. There was emotional education: the psychology of Jung and the history of religion, art and music. There was mental education: algebra and geometry, even the fundamentals of calculus. The basic sciences were taught, too. This necessitated a small laboratory being built. Anatomy was taught, as were higher anatomies.

Rachel's idea was to turn it all into a different kind of school. The farm children were growing up and moving away. Her son David was going off to college soon; the children of her friends would be also. Yet she knew that she and Craft had the core of a great idea, and she didn't want to let it go. She knew it was time to let go of educating young people and teenagers. She wanted to start a different kind of school, kind of like an ashram or a temple school, but not quite like those. She wanted to start some kind of retreat center, offering classes to the adult public. Actually, she wanted to start a college, but a very special kind of college. She wanted to teach everything about all that she knew, all the training that had earned her the designation Dakinisiddah. She wanted to start a college to train Priestesses of the Sacred Feminine.

This was not an entirely new idea for Rachel. She had been wanting to formalize what she had learned, and had wanted to teach it to others, both men and women, for a long time. She knew there were people who would want to learn what she knew, but they mostly lived in cities, and she did not want to live anywhere other than Stonehaven now.

Rachel recalled a dialogue between herself and Craft in January 1948. In the winter the bedrooms in the southeast wing were used almost exclusively, as they were easier to heat, whereas the northwest wing was used more in the summer since it was more naturally cool. It was morning and the sunlight streamed in the windows from the east. Craft and Rachel were sitting at the table in the sunshine. Craft had dressed for the morning; Rachel was still in a gown and robe. She had slipped them off her left shoulder, shining in the light. Coffee was in a pot in the center of the table. Both were writing.

Rachel was working on a letter to her friend Beverly in the New York City house. She stopped writing and sighed. Sitting back, she started to tap the pen, then remembered it was a fountain pen, and the ink would spill. She sighed again and put her elbow up on the table and rested her chin in her hand, looking out the window.

Craft, writing text for a lecture when classes resumed in the spring, watched her out of the side of his eye, finishing the sentence he was working. When he saw her start to work her jaw he put down his pencil. She reached across the table and grabbed it, and started tapping it on the table. "Need your drum?" he asked, smiling.

"Maybe," she said. "It's just damn frustrating. There's no word for it. So if I make a word for it I have to think it's right, and it just isn't. "

"What word, hon?"

"Women." The word slid out of her mouth like an ooze, and she clicked her teeth at the final 'n'.

"It's too long. It sounds funny. What's it for? What's the word trying to say?"

"Men with wombs; womb-men," Craft replied.

"I know. I know that. But it's too much. We know we have wombs. You know we have wombs. We both know you don't. We don't have to be reminded of it all the time, do we? Do you need to be reminded of it all the time? No. Of course you don't. So why do we have to talk about it all the time?"

"Maybe men do need to be reminded of it all the time," Craft said.

"That's your problem, Craft," she said. "You have to remember on your own, you're not so stupid that you need to be reminded by the word every time you refer to us. It's not the only job of the language to remind you all the time. But do you understand why it bothers me?"

"Tell me," he said.

"It gets awkward. It gets tiring. There is more to us than just our wombs. What can we say when we are talking about how we're more than that? How do we refer to that?"

"You can't just use the word 'man' of course," Craft offered.

"No, we can't. That's you. That's your word. That subsumes us into you, and leaves you dominant, and us less than equal. It means, at best, that we generalize into you. And that's not what I'm talking about. There are still differences to recognize, like the other ways we can't compete with you, and those ways in which we can, and in those ways in which we, actually, are your superiors."

"And in what ways would those be?" Craft asked, wiggling an eyebrow at her.

"Watch it, buster. I'm onto something here."

He shrugged but kept wiggling discretely.

"We need one word," she said. "We need one syllable. Something to refer to us when we're talking about the rest of us, beyond the womb." She looked over at him, and noticed he was now waggling one eyebrow then the other. "Watch it, asshole." She scowled.

He kept at it, although more subdued, just the slightest waggle, watching her think.

She glanced over at him, and said, "Do get my drum, will you?"

"Sure," he said, as he stood up and walked to the cedar chest under the western window. He opened it, got the drum bag and removed the drum and the beater. He brought them over to her and sat back down.

She picked up the beater and banged it on the table. "Damn it. We need a word." She stood up and leaned on her free hand. Leaning across the table, she gestured toward Craft, as if to use the beater on him, since as soon as he had sat down he had resumed waggling his eyebrows. "And you. Watch it. Or I'm really going to give it to you."

"When?" he wanted to know.

"That's it!" she said. "That's the word! Wen! Men and women? Men and wen! That's it!"

"Really? That's it?" he asked, somewhat incredulously.

"Yes!" beating the table once. "Yes, damn it!" beating it again. "And stop waggling your eyebrows at me!" She came around the table at him, raising her arm as if to whack him with the beater. When he raised his arm to counter the blow she slipped inside it with the beater. She shot her left hand forward and grabbed a handful of his hair. Then, stepping inside his counter move, pulled his head down toward her thighs, and said, "There. Put those eyebrows to work down there."

Later, carrying her to the bed, when they were in each other's arms after he had picked her up off the table, where she'd reclined while he was on his knees, he said, smirking into her hair, "Maybe we should call you tits-men."

"Oh no you don't."

"How about Boobs-men? Moon-men?" laughing while she pummeled him, laughing between expressions of mock outrage.

Laughing they fell on the bed. His hand slipped between her legs. She relaxed, and arched against his hand. "And what of this?" he growled. "What words for this should we put before man?"

She wrapped her hand around the bulge in his pants, "What about a name for this? Cocksman?"

"Yes, that will work" he grinned. But growling again, he pressed down on her clitoris with his hand and said, "But what about this? What shall we call it?"

She whispered huskily in his ear, "Because now we mean it: Woman will do…"

Later, interposed between her legs, he said, "Wench?" She laughed, and bit his ear, and squeezed her sex around him, sounding it, making the sound of "wench" from there.

"Wench" came the sound from their coupling, sending them both into such laughter he had to roll off her, so they could catch their breath.

Craft, when they finished making love, returned to his writing as Rachel dressed and went down to the kitchen to prepare lunch. What Craft had been working on was a short piece, intended to serve as part a lecture or perhaps an article for a magazine. In it, he was trying to organize his thoughts about the nature of the relationship between men and wen. He was following his intuition that the wen were more important in some ways than men. He wanted it clearly spelled out. In his mind he had come to think of this as the Antecedence of the Feminine.

The care and keeping of this lecture was passed on from one successor of Craft to the next in a holarchy of archetypes under which the College came to be organized. His role, as Consort to the High Priestess, was preserved. It was felt poetic that this archetype should bear his name.

The lecture became the responsibility of Craft, the Maker. It was updated and edited as new knowledge became available; science, specifically the science of Craft's original training in Biology, being the area of inquiry where the lecture began.

This is the lecture in its contemporary form:

THE ANTECEDENCE OF THE FEMININE

I awoke this morning under the influence of a dream I could not recall. I knew only that it was bright. I awoke to the dark, warm and comfortable, listening to the sounds of my own heart pulsing and my beloved's breath gentle and steady. I awoke feeling at ease, but also feeling that I did not know where I was. I could not remember where I was. The question, "Where am I?" soon led to "Why am I here?" This one led to "How did I get here?" Finally, circling around, stalking questions, I asked myself "Where did I come from?" and my answer to this last question was:

"I came from something greater than myself."

In the darkness, I sat up. I realized that I was a part of all that lived, animate and inanimate, yes, but I had a sense of something else, the origin of myself. I felt the part of myself that came from my mother. All the stuff, all the substance of me, came from my mother when she bore me in her womb.

It was she that created me, fashioning the parts of me, sustaining me within her until I was complete enough to come into the world. All that I am, as I appear before you, was first created by her. And so it is for all of you. Your blood, your sinews, your bones; all created by her. We know this to be true. It is she that first sustains us.

We are born from her.

We are not born from our fathers.

Our fathers supply instruction. Our fathers contribute to our form by altering the instructions on how the substance of ourselves is made. The contribution of our fathers is small, invisible to the naked eye. But the substance of ourselves comes from our mothers.

And this substance is antecedent to any contribution of our fathers. The substance that is us was born with our mothers when they were born. This was the egg, the ovum, the massive. We now know that a wen is born with all the ova she will ever have, and that these ova are made, not by her, but by her mother. The mass that became us was made by our grandmothers.

The feminine is antecedent in time.

The feminine is antecedent in evolution as well. We have learned that sexual dimorphism is an evolutionary development. For eons the cells of life replicated themselves through division, each cell a mother cell that would split off a daughter cell from herself. In this way it can be seen that Life itself began in the Feminine, and the Masculine evolved out of it.

In this way it can be seen that the Feminine is antecedent and the Masculine is consequent.

Today we know that, embryologically, the feminine sex organs develop first, with the masculine sex organs only developing later; that is, in the womb, we all start out as feminine.

The Feminine is antecedent and the Masculine derivative.

And, finally, in species as evolved as sharks and snakes the feminine can give birth to genetically identical daughters, without the help of the masculine in any way. Nothing male could accomplish the same phenomena.

The masculine may contribute to the making of life, but it is the feminine that creates life.

The Feminine creates, the Masculine makes.

I had risen from the bed, the floor was cold under my feet, and I went to the table to make notes of my revelations. A new question came to me. What does this, what do these facts have to say about the relations between the sexes? About the meaning of my relationship to wen? What does it mean to say the Feminine is Antecedent?

Sitting there, a blanket thrown over me, chin on my hand, and looking out the window at the autumn colors, I fell into a waking dream. In this dream I was pursuing something, something bright in the darkness, running through the woods. So bright it was that it illumined the path beneath my feet, stopping when I paused for rest. At those times it seemed to come closer, teasing me, drawing me further on.

Then I realized that, if I let it, it would come to me.

And what came to me was this: an understanding of the Proper Accord, what my relationship to wen should be.

The Feminine creates, the Masculine makes.

And what is the relationship of a Maker to a Creator?

I was created by the Feminine and in my life I am a Maker.

The Feminine sustains, the Masculine maintains.

Without the sustainer there would be nothing to maintain.

Therefore everything the Maintainer does is in Service to the Sustainer, for without it there would be nothing to maintain.

The Feminine is the Sustainer, the Masculine is the Maintainer.

And therefore the Masculine is in service to the Feminine.

And this is what I was told by the voice in the light that came to me as I stood in the Forest of my Dreams. As I stood still, still and waiting, the light came to me and these are the words the light spoke to me, the words I heard within me when the light touched me.

The Feminine is Antecedent. Serve Her upon whom you depend.

Finally, the voice gave me a prayer to use that would invoke this understanding in me whenever I might need to remember:

The Prayer of Invocation

Oh, Great Sustainer,
Keep me Well 'til the end of my days.
Sustain me Well, that I might be Good.

Oh Great Maintainer,
Work me Well 'til the end of my days.
Work me Well, so my Would is the Should.

8

CHESTER AND MISSY

"It's not Missy, Chester," Melinda said. "It's Melinda. Missy comes from Melissa. And don't you dare call me Milly, either." This was an irritation to Melinda, his insistence that he call her 'Missy'. She wondered how many women he called 'Missy'.

"Call you what I want, little sister. Come here," Chester said, gesturing, mind filled with the image of wife number Four on her knees in front of him, thinking that he'd have to go visit her soon.

"Can't, Chester," she said, turning back to the stove. "Bacon's on."

"Well, I'll just come to you, then," Chester said, using his arms to push his rangy body up and away from the table.

He got up and came around the island counter and there was Marylou, Lulu, Melinda's seventeen year-old daughter coming down the hallway of the doublewide. Her long light brown hair was stringy and dirty and unbrushed. She was wearing a t-shirt cut off at the mid-riff with no bra and tie-on pajama bottoms cut-off at mid-thigh. She was weaving side to side a little, still seeming to be half-asleep.

Chester's eyes went immediately to her breasts, staring at her nipples, just a little too long. Lulu felt him, felt his attention, and came wide awake. She looked up just in time to catch him looking away.

She turned and walked back up the hall. Chester stopped so he could look a little longer at her back-side, seeing no panty-lines, enjoying the image of her naked ass in his mind's eye, muscles bunching on one side then the other. She turned into her room, looking down, hair hiding her cheeks flushed with embarrassment, and closed the door.

Chester came up behind Melinda then, hugging her, pulling her bottom into his groin with one arm, reaching around to grab her breast and squeeze it with his other hand. Melinda submitted with only a little resistance. She knew that if she resisted him, he would make it bad for her later, waiting until he could find a time to prove to her that he could take her how he wanted her. She knew she would have to pay with sex for the favor she was about to ask him.

He held her still while he let go with one hand to unbuckle his belt and drop his pants and shorts. He lifted the back of her house dress and fingered her roughly. He pulled her breast out of her dress and leaned her forward toward the stove. She still had the long fork for turning the bacon in one hand and she thought briefly of stabbing him with it.

The bacon spattered, shooting a small blob of hot grease on her exposed breast. "Ow, Chester, Gawd damn it! Stop!" she said, backing up hard into him to push him away and slamming the fork on the counter. "You burned me!"

Chester, his pecker bent by the push, hurt, narrowed his eyes. "Hell's gonna burn you, not me. I'm takin' what I want. It's my right as your husband." He pushed her back.

She was just able to grab a potholder and move the frying pan to the back of the stove, and turn the burner off when she felt him forcing his way between her legs and then up inside her.

"Lulu's awake, Chester, for Gawd's sake," she whispered.

He leaned forward over her back, thrusting. "Then you better not make no noise."

Lulu sat on her bed, listening to the grunting sounds Chester made with each thrust, feeling the thump travel through the floor into her feet, realizing that the hissing sound she heard was no longer the bacon but her mother breathing through clenched teeth. "Great," she thought. "Another fucking Saturday."

Chester knew Lulu was listening and it made him harder. Lulu felt him think it, and thought "Creeper. Jesus, what a Creeper." Chester felt her thought and grinned, not quite aware that he was doing so. Lulu grabbed her towel and went to the bathroom to shower and wash her hair. The sex didn't last long, and by that time the noise from the shower was drowning out any other sound.

"There," Chester said, stepping back and pulling his pants up. "Good way to start the day. Maybe tomorrow it will be breakfast of champions, eh? A little sugar on top?"

"Maybe," said Melinda sullenly, thinking she didn't know if she should eat first or not. Sometimes just the smell of Chester's crotch made her gag. She turned on the stove and pulled the pan back over the burner.

"I need your help, Chester."

Melinda had been able, over the years, to make enough friends to get a job in the County Clerk's office. It was a steady government job as an Assistant Clerk. The boss might change with an election, but her job remained secure. It had enabled her to take care of her mother in her last days, raise her daughter, and buy this doublewide. She almost had enough saved for a real house.

But her new boss, David Harris, elected County Clerk only a few months before, had started to notice her, pay attention to her in ways she didn't like. They were the same age, and she didn't think he'd notice her, but the others in the office were either younger or older. She'd worked hard to appear invisible, dressing conservatively, never asking a question, and never drawing attention to herself. But he'd noticed her anyway. And when she'd caught him looking she turned away, but she couldn't keep the smile completely off her face.

And then, when he'd approached her, coming closer than he'd needed to one time when they were in the break room, she'd turned her head away again, but with a little fear and embarrassment. He'd moved in, touched her arm, and brought his face around trying to see hers. She'd withdrawn, but something in her withdrawal showed her vulnerability, some sag of powerlessness sent him a message that she was vulnerable, so he had been persisting in his attentions whenever he could; the little touch, the surreptitious glance, the smile that edged into a leer.

She knew the attentions wouldn't stop. She knew also that if she complained, or even threatened to, she would lose her job. Her boss was a popular man, "happily married" with children. She knew also that if she submitted to him there would come a time when he tired of her, and would stop it, and then she'd lose her job anyway.

Chester had helped her before with a similar problem, only it had gone much farther with her boss the first time. She didn't want it to get that far again, and she had to preserve her job. So she told him about the situation and asked him to have a little talk with Mr. Harris.

Chester said, "In the Laud's time, I'll do that. I think, maybe, I'll just take Mickey along with me this time."

Mickey was Mickey Dyson, Chester's best friend, driver, and sidekick. Over the years, as Chester had gotten older, he felt he needed help in fighting the evil in this world. He'd come to feel that the Evil One, the source of moral darkness, was expanding his powers, threatening the good gawd-fearing people with irresistible temptation, and that he needed help in this war assisting the holy spirit in emerging victorious. Mickey was just the perfect man for the job; strong yet easily swayed, not well-educated but very cunning, and filled with pride that he was able to help Chester with his holy work.

Mickey knew about Chester's wives, but it was a secret he could keep once Chester explained it to him; explained how Gawd had prepared his path and made sure he had all his mortal needs met so that he would commit no sins. Besides, Chester always made sure he was taken care of, manipulating some woman from whatever congregation they were visiting into having sex with him. Sometimes Chester would persuade whichever 'wife' they were visiting to have sex with him when Chester was finished, telling the woman that Mickey was a guest in his house, and the obligations of a host were to provide for the needs of the guest.

Chester had never offered Melinda to Mickey, however. Melinda's house was his main homestead, and he didn't want him that close in. He never discouraged Mickey from paying attention to Lulu, though. Once he even stated that it would be a good thing if Lulu would get married off, and he implied that he thought of Mickey as a son, and as family. This was because Chester had a thing for Lulu, and he knew he'd get in trouble if it wasn't diverted.

For Mickey, this was all the encouragement he needed. He'd hang around the trailer waiting on Chester, but in truth he was waiting for any opportunity to get next to Lulu alone. He'd even begun to stalk her, sometimes at a distance, sometimes up close. Sometimes he would show up near her bus stop after school, pretending to be on his way to see Chester, and offer her a ride home in his truck.

Lulu, out of the shower and dressing, heard Chester mention Mickey's name and shuddered. Mickey was even creepier than Chester. Mickey would try to corner her whenever he could, and draw close to her, pestering her with questions about boyfriends. She tried to avoid getting within arm's reach because he would touch her, holding an elbow or a shoulder, and then holding them a little too long or running his hand down her back.

Lulu had halfway listened to her mother telling Chester about the situation at her job. She didn't know about what had happened to this man 'Fat Bobby' and wondered what Chester could do about Melinda's situation. "Maybe he'll pray about it," she thought sarcastically, shaking her head while brushing out her hair.

Lulu shook her head again, turning her thoughts to her plans for the day. She was done with Chester's religionism and its rules. If she could, she'd be done with going to church at all, but she was afraid it would mean more pressure on her mother. She thought of Mickey, sitting in the back row during worship, staring at the back of her head, and was afraid that Chester would send him after her. Safer to keep up the illusion by going along, she'd reasoned.

But she had to rebel. She had to disobey; she felt like her sanity depended on it. But she had to do it in secret, do it in a way that nobody would know, nobody would see. She'd decided to get a tattoo. She'd have to use her fake ID, the one that said she was 21, the one she'd bought through a kid at school. It had taken most of her savings, but she'd already gotten good at using it. She would take more adult clothing with her to school, changing in the restroom at the Stop and Hop, and get rides with her girlfriends to shows on Friday night when she'd told her mother she was just hanging out at the girlfriends' houses, usually overnight.

There was a small tattoo parlor two towns over, close to the interstate. She'd designed the tattoo herself, working on sketches she could take with her. It was a tattoo of a tornado, like the one in the cartoons, the little devil-whirlwind speeding along the ground. On top of it, partially concealed by the coils of the tornado, was a heart symbol. The way she'd drawn it you couldn't tell if the heart was being sucked in or pushed out the top, or maybe even just riding along. She was thinking of adding one last element to the drawing, a small smile in the middle of the heart. She hadn't made up her mind yet. She might even make it a wicked grin.

It would have to be small, and hidden. She'd chosen a spot low on her belly, the tornado to be inked on her mons, right on the pubic bone, and the heart to be riding right above it at her hairline. She'd shaven that morning to make it all clear for the artist. The whole thing would be less than two inches high. She'd been told it would be painful but she didn't care. She was already in pain; she thought that maybe it would take her mind off her life. She hoped it would bring her into focus, concentrating the energy that would build in her low belly every day and that she relieved every night with her hands, laying on her belly with her face in the pillow, muffling the small sounds she would make so no one would hear. Sliding her panties up, she squeezed her knees together.

That was how she felt the desire within her, building during the day, becoming a whirlwind at night, waiting to be dissipated by the dancing of her hands. At the same time she knew that she was keeping her heart safe, carried along on her desire. Giving her heart to no one, moving too fast for any to keep up with her, she knew it was dangerous. It could never be seen by any, unless she chose to let someone get that close to her. She didn't know anyone in her circle of friends that she could trust her heart to. She wasn't a virgin; she'd picked up a guy at a bar in the next town the year before, done him fumbling in the dark in the back seat of her girlfriend's car, but she'd never gone with him again. She was determined to get out and use the power of her secret sign to keep her moving, and take her heart with her.

Sliding her jeans up, high riders that went almost to her navel, she thought about how Chester would call Mickey soon, and about how she'd have to dissemble, telling her mother that she was just going to do a little shopping with her girlfriend, and how much she wished she had her own car. But that would come, that would come in time. She'd take a change of clothes and shoes in her bag, along with her make-up. She'd paint today, no doubt.

Buttoning up her button down shirt she wasn't sure what she'd say to Chester, if he asked. Probably that she was going to do her nails and her laundry, and then maybe go see a movie with her girlfriends later in the afternoon.

Chester would lecture her about the virtues of cleanliness and self-care, and the vanity that painting her nails represented. Calling it a sin, he would then pretend to resign himself to its inevitability and the trial to his soul it was to live with such temptresses as she and her mother. But her mother had long ago laid down the law about it. It was her house and she'd damn well do anything she pleased, and if she wanted to dress up her toes and wear a little eye-liner to fit in then by Gawd or Pall she'd do it.

Breakfast was prepared and Lulu went out to the kitchen. She kissed her Momma on the cheek and said good morning then sat silently at the stool, looking down, deliberately not looking at Chester.

Chester said, "What, girl, not good enough for a good morning?"

"Good morning," she mumbled, rubbing her eyes and yawning, feigning sleepiness. Her mother, turning to put a plate in front of her, was surprised when she saw her daughter looking at her, near eye wide open, and the eye closest to Chester covered with a rubbing fist, showing her mother that she was faking it.

Her mother scowled. "Be nice," she said. Lulu made a pouty face. She mouthed the words, "I am." And said aloud, "Thanks, Mom."

Chester picked up his cell phone and made a call while he was waiting for Melinda, who prepared and brought him a plate. "Mickey, yah, Mickey. We got work to do today. I got a 'calling'. Yeah, yeah, come on over now. Maybe we got food for yah." Chester grunted when Melinda set his plate down.

Lulu groaned inwardly.

9

JUST IN TIME ARRIVAL

Angelica arrived at Stonehaven after an overnight stay in a motel off the interstate. Her dreams had been disturbed but she was unable to remember them, probably due to the highway noise, she thought. While during her first day of driving her mind had been focused on leaving, the second day it had been focused on where she was going, marveling at the scenery while winding her way up into the mountains.

She thought about the program at Stonehaven and the application process. She'd been asked a lot of questions about her practice—not just her yoga practice as it pertained to class, but what she did in her daily life connected to her spirituality. She'd answered honestly, which, basically, was that she hadn't done much spiritually in a daily way. The course information was clear that this was an immersion experience into a multi-dimensional practice which would occupy her entire day. It included teaching the spiritual practices in which Kundalini yoga was embedded. She was so looking forward to it. It was something that would not only help her with the odd sensations and feelings she'd been having at Jonathon's studio and at home recently, but would also take her completely out of the life she'd lived up to this point. And if two weeks of it weren't enough, there was a Phase 2 of the class running immediately after the first Phase. She could sign up for it if she wanted. And she'd told her parents that she might just be wanting to do that.

She arrived at Stonehaven without incident. The directions were precise, and on the last stage down the dirt roads in the mountains there were exact mileage amounts for turns that she could follow. It was a slow beautiful drive in the woods and, in places, past charming little vacation cabins and houses set back off the road, set apart from each other with plenty of woods for privacy. The last stretch, a descent toward the entrance was lovely, the road dappled in gorgeous gold light filtered through the green.

Turning into the driveway, she slowed and, rounding a bend, stopped at a gate with a security cabin. A young woman and young man were there waiting for new arrivals. Angelica observed a flush to the woman's cheeks when she came over to the car, trying to tuck an escaped strand of hair behind her ear. Angelica smiled, thinking that the girl had been messing around with the man, and when she looked over at him she saw him busying himself, looking away from her. Angelica asked if it was OK if she got out, and the woman was surprised and pleased. Her name tag said Emmalia. Angelica said it out loud and reached out to shake her hand, naming herself, "Hi, I'm Angelica."

Emmalia nodded toward the booth and the uncomfortable man and said, "He's Jackson."

"You work here?" Angelica asked.

"Yes, sometimes. It's a kind of internship."

"Cool," Angelica said, looking around. "It's so beautiful here."

"Yeah," Emmalia said. "We feel pretty lucky to be here." And, turning toward Jackson she raised her voice and said, "You feel lucky, don't you? Jackson?"

"Yeah!" Jackson looked up from what he'd been doing, which was waiting for his pecker to become soft enough that he could get it back inside his pants. Apparently, he'd just been zipping up trying not to get any skin caught. "Ouch," he said, zipping in a little pinch of skin, startled by Emmalia calling to him. "Very lucky."

Angelica looked away smiling. Emmalia raised a small clipboard Angelica hadn't noticed before and said, "OK, you're on the list. It's a small class, with a lot of us interns in it, so you'll be staying in the Mansion. It's beautiful. You have a single room on the fourth floor with a nice window facing south. There's a fan in the room in case it gets too warm. You've missed supper for today but stop by the kitchen in the basement and introduce yourself. Tell them I said to warm you up some leftovers. Breakfast tomorrow is served from 6:30 to 7:00, and you have to be finished by 7:30. Class starts at eight, in your yoga clothes, in the large studio near the west end of the Barn. I think that's it. Any questions?"

"Yeah. You in the class?"

"Yes," Emmalia said, touching a finger to the corner of her mouth. "We both are."

Grinning, Angelica said, "Then I'm sure it will be a fun class."

Emmalia grinned back, knowing that Angelica was referring to the kind of 'fun' she'd been having with Jackson. "Yeah, it will be. See you tomorrow."

Angelica got back in her car and waved, still grinning. Emmalia turned back toward the Gate House and picked up the two-way radio from its solar powered charging station. "Gate House to Base, come in, over." When there was no immediate reply she did it again. The reply, "Base here, over." The Base station was in one of the "vacation houses" Angelica had just driven past. Emmalia said, "Last one's in." Base replied, "Alright, shut her up and lock her down. Come on home." When Angelica has disappeared around a curve in the road she walked toward Jackson unbuttoning her shirt, asking, "Do you think you can find that thing again?"

After a couple more curves Angelica came out into the open and caught her first glimpse of Stonehaven lit by the setting sun. Everything was bathed in a red-gold light. She stopped briefly to look at it. The graveled road levelled out and bore to the right with a side road coming down behind the Mansion. Further on were side roads coming down into two large structures that could be barns and a few smaller buildings, now quickly falling into shadow.

She arrived at a parking area behind the Mansion and pulled off, stopping her car and just sitting still for a minute. She got out, grabbed the duffel bag out of the back seat and a backpack that she slung over a shoulder. She looked up at the Mansion with its wings and plethora of chimneys. She crossed the parking lot and stopped to pet an old tan dog with hound ears and a gray muzzle lying in the shade against the cool of the marble steps. The dog sat up, thumping its tail as she approached and then made a very strange sound. 'Ehhh ohhh'. To Angelica it sounded like an extended 'hello', but without the 'L's'. She looked at it quizzically, tilting her head toward her shoulder. The hound tilted its head, too. So she said, "Hello to you, too," and patted its head.

She walked up the steps to the great door. She knocked but no one came, so she pushed the door open and stepped in. Immediately in front of her was an easel with a sign saying 'Welcome!' She looked around. A handsome, no, beautiful woman with dark brown hair streaked with gray, pulled back in a bun, broke away from a small group of women and men gathered by the window on the first landing of the stairway and came toward her, hand out in greeting.

"Hi, I'm Madeleine," she said. "You must be Angelica. We've been waiting for you. Would you like to get something to eat or go up to your room first?"

Mindful that others might be waiting for her to eat, Angelica said, "Eating first, I think, would be the right thing."

Madeleine smiled, nodded her head, and said, "Great! You can put your stuff down right there on the bottom steps and follow me."

Angelica looked around for the first time then. She was standing in what looked like a great hall with a fire place on one end and a door leading to a dining room on the other. There were rooms set off by built-in sliding doors and an amazing staircase with three landings that turned back on itself and ended on a balcony that ran in opposite directions along the second floor wall. Her jaw dropped a little as she looked up and scanned the immensity of the space. The staircase continued up to other floors.

She looked over at Madeleine, who was smiling at her. "Hard to heat," Madeleine said and smiled more broadly. "Ready?" she asked, turning.

"Yes, sure," Angelica smiled back and followed her to a door that led to an extension of the steps that wound down into the basement. On the way down Madeleine said, "I see that you met Homer."

Angelica realized that the group had been watching her as she came up to the door. "Yes," she said. "He's a sweet old thing."

"Not to everybody," Madeleine said. "But he said 'Hello' to you, so we know he likes you."

At the bottom of the steps, which had three shorter turns, Angelica followed down a short hall with mops standing in floor sinks and stacked 5-gallon bottles of water, through a swinging door, and into the kitchen.

There were four people there: one, a woman of about thirty, standing at a table working on some kind of list, another, a man also about thirty, at a workbench putting bread back in its wrappers. Over at the row of large sinks an older woman was working with a younger man, apparently showing him how to scrub the outside of the large pots.

Madeleine said, "Hannah! Here's our last guest for the class. This is Angelica. Do you have any leftovers we can feed her?"

The tall, strong, woman at the sink turned toward them, smiling. "Yes, indeed!" she said. "Indeed we do. Come on in, honey. It'll take just a minute to heat up some food. How does soup, bread, and salad sound?"

"It sounds wonderful. OK if I eat in here?" Angelica asked.

"Certainly," Hannah replied. "You can sit over there on that stool by the counter where the bread is. Pick out what kind you like."

"Hi, I'm Max," the man at the counter putting away the bread introduced himself.

"I'm Angelica," she nodded, sitting down.

"What kind of bread would you like?" Max asked. "We have our own recipe of fresh whole wheat, and these white breads were made here this morning."

"That," she said, pointing to the latter, "And do you have any butter?"

As Max walked around her to go to the walk-in refrigerator, he passed close to her. They both felt a pushing, like the fields of two bar magnets, on each other. They both sighed a little at the same time, the synchronicity of which made them look at each other, eyebrows raised.

"Excuse me," Max said.

"It's OK," Angelica said. "I don't know what that was, but you didn't bump into me or anything."

Max said, "It's our fields. They're both strong. I don't know what it means."

"It means you're both at about the same level," the woman who'd been working on the list at the other bench said. She was not as tall as Hannah, brown hair pulled back in a ponytail. "My name's Delores. Call me Del. I'm running this shift." Del came over and held a hand over Angelica's shoulder. She slowly lowered her palm and stopped when she encountered resistance, about eight inches away. "Do you feel that?" she asked.

Angelica felt the pushing on her shoulder. "Yes, yes I do. What is it?"

"It's your magnetic field. Has a lot of strange stuff been happening to you lately? Strange sensations? Powerful dreams?" Del asked.

"Yes. It's one of the reasons I'm here. Strange things started happening in me in my Kundalini Yoga class, and my teacher Jonathon referred me here. He said the people here know a lot more about what was happening to me than he did, and that you all could explain some things to me. Can you?" Angelica asked, looking from Del to Max and back.

Del looked at Hannah, who was leaning against the sink with her arms crossed, and the young man washing dishes had set down his large pot in the sink and turned around to watch the conversation also. Hannah nodded her head for Del to continue.

Del took a breath and started in. "Yes, we can help you understand. Begin with trying to understand this. Everything that is, we are. There is some way in which every process that is happening, every substance that is, either actually is, or can be, is what we are. So. You generate a magnetic field that can be detected across a room. As I get closer to you the field gets stronger, more dense, and at this level I can sense it with my hand. I can sense it with all of me."

Del stepped closer and Angelica swayed a little on the stool. Angelica nodded she understood.

"Here," Del said. "Use your hand. See if you can feel it on Max. Raise your hand up, palm flat, like this, and slowly move it forward until you encounter resistance."

Del showed Angelica how, using her own hand and together they moved their hands slowly forward. Angelica's hand stopped before Del's did. "You feel that?" she asked Max.

"Yes," he replied.

"Describe what you feel." Del said.

"I feel pressure. If I pay attention I can feel a contour around your hand. I can feel the difference between your hands. And if I pay closer attention I become aware that what I'm sensing is actually a mixture of our fields—the field around your hands blending with me, and resisting at the same time."

"Yes," Del said. "It is a boundary and there are boundary conditions. We can communicate this way. OK, Angelica. Slowly move your hand along the surface of his field. Tell me if you can feel any variations in strength or density, or any patterns in it." Del withdrew her hand.

Angelica moved her hand toward the midline. There was a ripple there as she moved over it, like there was a cord embedded within. She paused and traced the cord vertically, moving upward to the top of Max's head. She encountered spots on the cord that had motion to them, especially at the top. She moved her hand down crossing it over his belly and turning her palm so her fingers pointed down. She saw him wince a little and she pulled her hand out of the field.

"It's OK," he said. He stepped back a little so it would be easier for her to move her hand.

"Follow the rest of the field down," Del said.

Angelica held out her hand, palm forward, fingers pointing down. She closed her eyes, moved her hand forward until she felt the boundary, pushing back at her. She ran her hand along the edge down his belly, pausing at the field variations around his genitals, and moved her hand around between his legs until her palm was flat. She could feel the variations as the field divided down into his legs. A cylindrical flash of red light appeared then disappeared over her head. Everyone in the room saw it.

"Yes. I understand," she said. Her face composed itself into a thoughtful expression and then she made a noise like "Hmp." She looked up at Max. "Could you get the butter, please?" She turned on her seat and took a spoonful of soup, brought over by Hannah while they were playing with energy fields. It was good broth, the base for what must have been French Onion soup.

"Whoa," Max said. "Whoa. Whew. Wow," and he walked around Angelica and Del to the walk-in.

Del looked at Hannah. Hannah nodded, approvingly, and smiled. Del looked back at Angelica. "How did that feel?"

Angelica replied, "Like playing with bar magnets. Except instead of just sensation there was also feeling and imagery. But a lot of it was confusing. Some seemed to be mine, some seemed to be his, some seemed to come from somewhere else altogether."

Del stayed with her while she ate. When she finished everyone else had gone so they washed her dishes and Del took her upstairs to her room on the fourth floor of the Mansion.

Del opened a door to a small room on the south side. Angelica stepped in and set her belongings on the bed. Del said, "You OK?" Angelica nodded.

"Some of us do a sitting meditation sit at 6:00 in the Ballroom at the east end. The door is on the far side of the dining hall. You're welcome to join us. Bring a shawl to wear. It can be chilly in there in the morning."

Angelica nodded again and said, "Thank you."

They exchanged 'Good nights' and Del closed the door. Angelica looked around. There was an open window in an extended dormer, with a small stool below it, and a circular oscillating fan set on the seat. She went over to the window and looked out on the lawn to the edge of rocks into the river valley below. She watched the fireflies leaving the grass and heading for the tree tops.

She turned around and looked at the room. There was a single bed on her left. It had a nice mattress set on a black steel frame with a short wrought iron foot board up under the eave of the roof, and a larger ornamental headboard toward the north. It looked old. It was made up already with a light quilt and two pillows. There were two towels and a wash cloth on it. There was a reading light on a small table at the head of the bed; the switch could be reached through the ironwork. Then there was a small free-standing wardrobe alongside the door.

To her right stood a narrow wooden desk and chair, with another lamp, and three small drawers. Then came the stool with the fan on it. She turned on the fan and watched it blow air around the room. She put the bag she was still carrying on the bed and unpacked, putting her clothing in the wardrobe, her notebooks on the desk along with her phone. She checked it; there was no coverage this far out in the mountains, but the alarm function would work. She set it for 5:30.

She took her necessities bag and went down to the east end of the hall to the bathroom to clean up. She noticed there were no gender signs on the door, so it was co-gender. There were six shower stalls, four sinks, and four commodes. She put her hair up and took a quick shower—the water never got really hot—put on her pajamas, brushed her teeth, then her hair, and put her hair back up for sleeping.

On the way back to her room she encountered a woman coming down the hall toward her. For a moment Angelica thought it was a ghost. The woman was wearing a long dark blue robe belted loosely and open to the waist, with a flowered shawl over her shoulders and her dark hair was down.

Angelica shook her head when the ghost spoke. "Hi, I'm Janice. You in the class?"

"Yes, tomorrow. I'm Angelica. I thought you were a ghost."

"Nah, I don't look that old, do I?" Janice teased.

"No! No, it's not that. You just look, I don't know, kind of classic, rather than modern. I mean, look at me. P.J.'s and all," Angelica responded.

"Oh, that. Well, thank you Angelica. It just seems to fit around here. You'll see. Everybody wears casual stuff when they're not in work clothes, but they all look elegant in it, even the guys. A lot of them wear sarongs," Janice said.

Angelica didn't know what to make of that, so she asked "Are you in the class? Are you one of those, what did she call it, interns?"

"Yes, I'm in the class, but I'm not an intern. I work at a yoga studio and my boss sends me out here for continuing ed. It's where he learned."

"Really? Cool boss. Well, it's late for me, a long day on the road. I'll see you in the morning then," Angelica said.

Janice said, "Good night, then." She turned to watch Angelica go down the hall to her room. Turning at the door, Angelica looked back at Janice and they waved at each other briefly.

Angelica turned off the lights and looked out the window, turning off the fan as she passed it. She felt out into the night, which felt immense to her here. Hot, filled with sounds and yet, no sound. The wind in far off tree tops, the sawing of the locusts, the river just out of sight below, but no traffic hum, no wheezing of air conditioners. And the sky filled with stars above and tens of thousands of little lights below, blinking on and off. She felt herself pulled into the trees, watching the little insects up close, then she saw herself turning from that lofty place and staring west into a dark eye-shaped shadow up on the side of a great mountain. She recalled that her mind had registered an image of it on the way down the drive; the dark eye seeming to be just an island of a different kind of trees.

Now it seemed more shadowed than it should, deeper, as if it led to a great cave, deeper into some giant mind. Then she saw it as a whole, saw it as an eye of the Great Mother, the Earth; an eye of the great planet's awareness looking out on this valley. Then she was overwhelmed with a sense of great beauty and caring. A wave of caring seemed to come out of the eye and wrapped around her and she felt welcomed and safe and blessed.

She turned from the window and lay down, and slept on that wave of Love.

About two hours later she felt another presence near. She opened her eyes and listened and heard the door knob turning. She sat up in the dark. The door opened and she heard a rustle of fabric brush against the frame. She breathed the air, scenting a woman, and recognizing it as Janice in the faint light.

"You awake?" Janice whispered.

"Yes, am now," Angelica replied. "What do you want, Janice?"

"I just thought, you know, the way we waved at each other at the end. I thought it may be a sign, an indicator, you know? Maybe an invitation. And I've just been laying there, unable to sleep, thinking about it, because if it was, you know, I wouldn't want to miss the opportunity. Too hot, you know? And you're so beautiful. I just, I just wanted to know. You know?" Janice said, all the while sliding across the floor until she was alongside the bed and kneeling down.

Angelica, reaching through the ironwork to turn on the reading lamp, said, "Janice, it was just a wave. A wave good night. Really."

Janice was wearing just the robe now, open and loose, slightly down off one shoulder, leaning forward. "Well, do you think, well, would you let me make love to you? I can't get you out of mind, watching you, smelling you, all I could do was lie there and imagine it."

"Maybe," Angelica said. "Maybe some time, but not tonight. OK? I just want to sleep." Angelica had never been with a girl, and, although she'd fantasized about it, she'd never met a girl she was attracted to in that way.

Janice sighed. "OK. You don't think bad of me do you? I'd hate to think I'd upset you."

"No," Angelica said. "I'm not upset. I just want to sleep. It was sweet of you to think of me, though. Kind of flattering." Angelica held still, waiting.

Janice sighed again and stood up, the smell of her desire wafting over Angelica. As she stood up the hem of the robe caught under her foot and Janice was suddenly standing there naked and smooth in the soft light. She laughed, and Angelica giggled. Janice bent to pick up the robe and leave, and said, "Good night Angelica."

"Good night," Angelica said, and turned off the light as the door closed.

10

DINNER

"So," Bree said, her back to her sister, bending toward the fire and smiling to herself. "You still haven't told me how it is that a mortal has been invited to dinner."

Calley, sitting at the table, waking from her reverie, the reverie of being Rain, 'tsk'ed' at herself, shook her head, and said, "Well, darlin', I'm not yet quite sure 'how'. I can tell you 'what', I'm pretty sure, but it got a little fuzzy, and tangled up like a hank of shed wool hung up in the heather.

"I stayed Rain a long time, moving back and forth along the high tops, steadyish down and drifting around, dreaming. And when I'd wake, thinking and thinking and feeling. Oh, by Mother, my mind kept returning to how it felt. How it felt, you know, to have him in me, only some part of me didn't want to think about it, dwell on it, but some part of me did. Once I even dropped out of rain and found myself squatting down in a saddle, hand on my chin, looking down the valley toward his farm, remembering when I'd squatted over him. So solid, too solid, for one who needs to be Mist.

"After dwelling in this way, back and forth, light then hard, steady on for a long time and then not, feeling into it, I'd move from feelings for him, and into feelings against him. And then I'd remember the feeling of him rising under me, feeling the good of it, and then I'd get angry at myself for ever showing myself to him again that morning.

"You remember when he came to the valley, right? Banished by his father for fighting with his elder brother. Well, it was more than that. He hurt his brother badly. I listened to the waggoneers, his father's men, talking about it on their way back down from the farm. They were of the opinion that his brother deserved what happened to him. He was always cruel, always a bully, and Alam grew to be larger than him, and one day he couldn't take it anymore. Alam clubbed him unconscious with a rod he'd taken from a bundle of wood. His brother lost a couple teeth. Not good.

"So here he was sent, to the small cottage with its yard and sheds. He was given a few sheep and a sow with piglets and two goats. He was given some weapons to keep the wolves away and some tools to work the bronze and leather. His cloak, some salt, and some sacks of barley-corn, and that was it. And he was lucky to have it, and indeed, to have gotten away with his life.

"Slowly, his life came together and he had more time on his hands. In fact, with his life being set up, he often had more than time on his hands, if you know what I mean."

"Ah, that? His pestle?" Bree asked, grinning and gesturing.

"Yes, yes I do mean that. I paid pretty close attention then, I tell you," Calley continued with a grin. "It was amazing. I mean, not so much his tool—amazing as that was—but how often he had it in his hands! Once always in a day, often two and three times. Occasionally, four!'

"Four?" Bree asked, fingers over her mouth.

"Yes, four!" Calley replied. He'd walk around outside with it in his hand, too! Swinging it around, pulling on it, standing on the wall around his yard and bringing himself off, spreading it everywhere in great white gouts and streamers, festooning the weeds."

Bree started laughing.

Calley continued, "He'd leave little wads of himself everywhere, here and there, through the woods, or alongside the river. Splats on the rocks.

"Then, after a time, he started to walk about to learn the country. He loved taking it out in the sunlight. He'd get up among the outcroppings and sit on a shelf, exposing it to the sun, regarding it as if it were his pride and glory, wanking off into the open sky.

"So I had plenty of chance to regard him, too. You know, sometimes I'd catch it, catch his stuff, and carry it off, gathering the little droplets with the breeze, cupping them together in my hand out of sight around the crag. I would taste it." And, leaning forward conspiratorially toward Bree and lowering her voice, Calley said. "Sometimes I would tongue it off my palm and eat it!

"No!" Bree said in a whisper, also conspiratorially. "And it tasted how?"

"Like food, a little sweet, a little salt," Calley said with a mock dismissiveness, grinning sideways at Bree while she pretended to study her nails. "Like a pudding of uneven texture, I suppose.

"I had not much to occupy myself in the summers while you went down to the lowlands, so I would watch him. Always I avoided getting seen and caught. But he would nap in the sunshine and it would start to grow all by itself. Sometimes he would even wake up hard and groaning with desire, and finish it right then, and then go back to sleep.

"I took to breezing up to him, and working it up with the air."

"You didn't."

"I did," Calley continued. "I would wake it up on him, stroking it gently. Oh, I tortured him and I loved it. The thing had a mind of its own, I'd swear an oath upon it.

"Really? You'd do that? You'd swear an oath upon the thing?" Bree asked, eyebrows raised.

"No, no. That's not what I mean," Calley shook her head. 'But then again, I might," she mused thoughtfully. "If it was the right oath. But I will show you, so you know."

Calley slipped into reverie, Bree tracking her mind to mind.

Up in the mountains to the south of Alam's farm there was a saddle, hills on either side folding away like open thighs, with a large stone, standing like the lone sentry overlooking the valley running east and west below. After a short meadow the land fell away steeply and a fall of water emerged from the rock face.

It was foggy in the saddle that morning. A breeze rose up the mountain as the rising sun warmed the peak and made the fog waver and wobble, shredding a little bit along the edges, and then it coalesced into the shape of a woman, wearing a cloak the color of the rocks, hood pushed back to reveal a head of oat straw colored hair, perched squatting on the top of the stone, regarding a man in the yard far below.

Across her face the shadows crossed, dark and angry, like the shadows of the thunder clouds turning the light below them dark. She was angry, and stewing with it, not quite sure why. She had an image of a great salmon on a hook pass through her mind and she couldn't tell if it was Alam or herself struggling against the line. When she narrowed her eyes just the right amount she could see it; she could see the line, long and thin, white and sparkling in the light. It made her angry, like some force had been arrogant enough to try to bind the wind. Narrowing her eyes even further, she leapt down off the rock and rematerialized in his yard.

"I know you love me," Calley said from right behind him.

Alam froze, not turning around, and then relaxed. "Aye, that I do."

"All my other mortal lovers went crazy." Calley said, as she stepped back.

He straightened up and said, "Aye, so I've been told."

"They died, they all died," Calley said.

Alam turned his head slightly toward her. "We all do, my lady. We all do," emphasizing the word 'all' the second time.

"It was not a pretty death."

"But was it a good one?"

"In their eyes, perhaps. Some of them anyway."

"I want mine to be Good. I want mine to be Beautiful."

"There is no starting over. Live or die. Do you wish to remember me or not?"

He turned then, going to one knee, bowing his head. "Every bit, Goddess. Every bit."

"Then I will give you something else to remember." She went off thirty yards, flying backward through the air, and became a standing bolt of lightning—a standing bolt of lightning, flickering only slightly, not flashing on and off. It grew high, and then touched down, but, instead of the bolt flashing, it travelled through the ground, making a luminous path straight to Alam.

Alam watched it come and when it got close, he stood up. When it reached him, it stopped under his feet. His feet started to tingle. The tingling sensation passed up his legs and spread throughout his groin and his pelvis, caused him to grow erect, tickled by the sensation. He raised his kilt and looked at it, then straightened up and showed it to the lightning, grinning.

"Do not play with fire," a voice said, sounding like the hiss coming from a flaming twig.

The stream of lightning colored light travelling through the ground became more intense, the tickle becoming a warmth that filled him, caressing his cock with pulsing waves of pressure, pulling more blood within it. Alam groaned.

The hissing voice went soft. "Did you trick me?" Calley asked. "Did you try to trap me, Alam?"

"No, Storm Former, I did not." But then Alam paused. "I thought only that there was a chance to be with you. So often I have dreamed of you in the high places. Dreamed you were there with me, and that I was under your caress. It was through my dreams I came to love you. And in that love I have dreamed about you all the more. I thought—I only thought—that somehow, sometime, you might really join me. So I went about prepared. I had food for you. I made beds in which you might lie down with me."

"You made beds?" Calley asked.

Alam nodded.

"You presume to make beds? Calley asked, again, feeling anger rise within her. "How dare you presume to make beds? How dare you presume that I would sleep with you?"

"No presumption, Goddess. Only hope," Alam's voice rising in alarm.

"You dare to hope?" Calley's query now imperious. She boomed into anger, the sound seeming to spread in a wave from the lightning bolt that knocked stones off the fence and would have thrown Alam to the wall behind him had not Calley held onto him by his cock. But She held onto him up in the air. She powered up the energy in the bolt and he began to burn. The wave of pulsing desire turned into a heat that soon felt like scalding water.

Just before he passed out from pain, Alam's mind closed in on a memory of Calley—the image, the desire, and the way he felt—the love he felt that blossomed up out of the desire, and he whispered "Only hope."

Then Calley realized what had happened: that She had been playing with him while he slept, and She had entered his dreams in that way. He had been dreaming of Her, dreaming of the Goddess. "It is Me he loves," She thought. "If he loves Me, then it is by My hand it has happened."

She eased back on the power She had placed in the bolt, lowering Alam to the ground. She flew in toward him, hovering in the air just above him. "I made you love Me," She said, in an ambivalent and uncertain voice, as if it was unclear whether it was a query or a conclusion.

Lying on his back now, one hand covering his balls and the other shielding his eyes. "Yes," he said, almost breathlessly.

"Do not play with fire," She said. Then She disappeared.

Later that night Alam was lying in his bed, sore, bruised, and feeling the despair of failed love when Calley appeared, assembling Herself out of a mist that had formed along the floor. She pulled back the sleeping skins, and climbed up on Alam, covering them both with her cloak. She took him with gentleness and warmth and sweetness, all beyond anything Alam could have imagined. She took him, healing him, cultivating him, taking him to the edge and then along it, but not over, for a long time.

With each cycle of arousal and rest She became more solid to him, more real. Finally, at the peak moment of intensity, Calley became liquid. She simply changed the material state of Her manifestation. The slight surface tension burst, soaking Alam and the bed.

Alam was stunned. Looking around he saw no sign of Her form. Then he heard Her speak, seemingly from all sides, saying, "Do not betray the fire."

Calley and Bree returned to their present.

"I felt bad, Bree. Really, I'm not sure why. I saw his pain, and knew it came from the Love I induced in him, without intending to do that," Calley said, wondering at what She had done and how it made Her feel.

"I don't know. I don't know why, and I don't know what I'm going to do for sure, in the long run. I kept going back to him, you know, to see if he really loved me—me, you know? And not just that he'd fallen under my spell. In the end I just decided that I couldn't tell, and neither could he. But we agreed that if we make a conscious decision about it every time we engage, or do something together, then it really doesn't matter if it's true Love, or just a spell. By making a conscious choice in the moment we're doing the best we can do."

"But don't you ever doubt?" Bree asked.

"Yes, all the time. I would anyway, but I make him do it, too. Those mortals are funny," Calley answered.

"Why? Funny how?" Bree wanted to know.

"Well, you know, we talk about it. We talk about the doubt stuff. We talk about being bespelled. We talk about the future impact of his death. Cheerful stuff, you know? But he always returns to this thought: 'That I'm the best thing that's ever going to happen to him.' No matter what, anything that happens will not be as beautiful as this, and that's true despite doubt, magic, and death. So it doesn't matter. Those things don't matter, and he'll take all the time he can get with me." Calley paused, her eyes searching side to side for what next to say.

Bree asked, "Yes, but is that good enough for you?"

"I look in his eyes and I see devotion. How can devotion not be good enough?" Calley responded

"Right. Well, we are Goddesses after all," Bree responded.

"No, that's not what I mean. We are Feminine. Manifestations of an even Greater Feminine. And as Feminine, is it not in our nature to respond to devotion?" Calley inquired.

"It is in our nature to respond," Bree said. "But what is our response to be? Do we accept it as our due? Or do we reward it?"

"It ought to be rewarded, ought it not?" Calley asked.

"Yes, but, then, rewarded how?" Bree asked back.

"The boon," Calley answered. "The boon—the fulfillment of a desire. Devotion is a food for us, we respond by feeding the devoted in some way. That is the way of the boon."

"So, he is devoted; then, what is his desire?" Bree continued.

"His desire is all for me." Calley paused, looking inwardly. "Then, that means…I am his boon."

Bree said, "Yes, you are. You are his boon." Very slowly she said it, letting the words sink in. "Will you grant it to him? Will you grant him the boon of yourself?"

"I do not know. I have told you how I came to it. That question is why

I invited him to dinner with us. His devotion draws me closer now. I can feel it, and I do not want to surrender to the pull, even should The Mother ask it of me. Closer in, I can see less; farther out, I lose the sense of the devotion. And the future, though far-seen, is less certain for the loss of sense."

"A paradox, clearly." Bree responded, "How are you to solve it?"

"I can only embody it," Calley answered, distracted by trying to look both closely, and far, simultaneously.

"Mark your words, Sister!" Bree said sharply. "Mark your words!"

Her reverie broken, Calley looked up. "Oh. I see. Yes, I see. I can embody the paradox by embodying the boon. I must become the fulfillment of his desire in order to see where devotion leads on down into the future."

They were both silent.

"This choice, Sister," Calley said, "is a choice I cannot make alone. This is a choice I must ask your advice and consent about."

"When is he coming?" Bree queried.

"He arrives on the next full moon, near sundown," Calley answered.

"Well, then, we have work to do. And you need to change. And you still haven't told me exactly how you invited him."

11

NEW YEAR 1953

"Well, alright Beverly. I'll see you soon. Much love." Rachel concluded her letter and lay down her pen. Cold, bright sunlight filtered through the bare tree branches outside the east wing. The trees, old oaks, hickories, and beeches, surpassed in height by the younger poplars, left shadows across the writing table and the floor in different densities of darkness. Rachel went over to the small fireplace and stirred the grate.

The Mansion had been closed down to just one part of the east wing for winter. There had been a new heating system and electricity installed in the east wing over the summer, replacing the older system installed before the War, along with the phone line and the indoor plumbing.

The new system was powered by the small steam plant that ran on coal, with a diesel backup for the electricity. It was in sheds and garages that had been built along the north side of the formal gardens, at the end of the garden wall. She had made the decision to keep the chimneys cleaned and repaired, knowing that modern things could break down often. This morning had been one of those times. She kept chamber pots in the rooms for the same reason.

John Craft was out in the sheds with Morton, the hired help who lived in the Hand's House further up the valley. He and his wife were the only couple left at Stonehaven with Rachel and John. The rest of the help, recruited by the Help Service Beverley ran for her in New York, was seasonal, and they had all been given leave to go home for the Holidays. Morton's wife Maggie cooked and, with Rachel and the men's help, did the cleaning also.

There had been a problem with the water feed for the boiler during the night. The power from the main line had gone out and the diesel generator had failed to kick in. The men had gotten the generator running but were taking the time to check the underground pipes for leaks. They were looking for melt patches in the frost, and hopefully even some steam escaping from the ground between the steam plant and the house. Then they were going to walk the feed line up to the pond.

The well had an electric pump and a windmill backup system. That water was stored in a pond, and gravity had been used to feed downhill to the cisterns under the mansion, where it had been hand pumped into the kitchen and washrooms. Now those pipes were closed off and the water was diverted to the steam boiler in one of the sheds. Sometimes this water fill line either got clogged, or the water level in the pond got too low, and the system safety valve would shut it all down. Now it was up again and the radiators were banging, and were probably going to have to be bled to get the air out.

Rachel sighed as she bent to put more wood on the fireplace in her bedroom. Sometimes the new systems took as much work as the old way of doing things, if not more.

She went over to her altars for her morning sit before she got on with the plans for opening more of the mansion for the holidays. She unrolled a small carpet and placed a low stool on it. Spreading her robes in a curtain around her, she knelt down facing the altars set below an east facing window and closed her eyes. Feeling the rising sun on her forehead, she smiled. From a bowl on the floor she took a pinch of mixed Artemisia leaves and placed them in a small shell brazier on the floor between her knees. She struck a match to the leaves and blew out the match. She fanned the leaves with her hand, and when the smoke rose she picked up the shell and offered it to the cardinal directions. Then she washed herself in the smoke with her free hand, pulling it in between her knees, toward her midsection, and then over her head.

Placing the shell down on a flat stone to the side, she lit another match and set it to a low votive candle on the side of the altar. Smoke rose in a thin line from the shell, forming a flat cloud over her head. She sat back on the stool, and, resting lightly on her knees, with her hands on her thighs, she breathed into the Meditation phase of the sit.

An image formed in her mind almost immediately, an image of the Divine Feminine, the Goddess, looking at her, smiling at her. After some moments of contemplation, she raised her hands chest high, palms up toward the image, and began the Devotion phase of the sit. She summoned the feelings of Love and Devotion within her and then released it toward the image. The image raised its arms—the Goddess raised Her arms—from Her sides slightly, palms up, and received the energy of Rachel's gift.

The image of the Goddess before Rachel was one she called 'Diosa'. She was an older, more mature version of her image of the daughter Salakta. Behind Diosa was the image of an old wen, the first projection from the true Source. All three of whom, as one being, were the true creators of the Universe; the first three projections of the awareness of that which would become all of Creation. Diosa was more reserved in some ways than Salakta, whose tantric energetics were manifest through Rachel during ritual and sacred sex. Salakta laughed a lot.

Diosa's hair was dark and she wore robes, usually a dark robe over a white or pale tan underdress. She was tall and appeared to be a mature woman, perhaps the equivalent of the human age of forty. Her skin would change shades, in some way Rachel neither understood nor could predict; sometimes the color of ivory at dusk, other times brown or red or black. Rachel understood Her to be the same entity-awareness energetic archetype that was known in ancient times as Ishtar, Inanna, and Isis, but with a major difference. This deity was definitely an Earth deity, not a deity representing the planet Venus. Perhaps She was closer to the pre-classical Hera, before the poets, patriarchalists all, started to reduce Her to a ridiculous figure. At the same time it was clear to her that the imagery and presences she worked with were an archetypal microcosm of a much larger macrocosm, the true universe, and its true creators.

Their relationship, the relationship between the Divine Feminine and Rachel, was one of long standing. The Goddess had appeared to Rachel early in her tantric training in Windia and Flora, at first watching and then aligning in union. Much of the time Rachel would converse with

Her, asking simple questions, getting yes or no answers in the nod of Her head. As the amount of time spent in union with Her increased Rachel became able to hear Her voice, first because they were aligned. Then, when the Goddess was external and facing her, Rachel could hear the words She spoke.

Rachel began to work through her Illuminations; a series of visualizations combined with inner energetic manipulation. She activated the pulse of the Higher Heart and dropped it down to her root, the spot in the middle of her perineum. After a moment of resonance there she divided it and slowly brought it up the back and the front simultaneously in a feat of divided attention. She allowed it to activate the minor chakras as it passed through them, pausing at her clitoris and allowing the energy to activate and pulse at the 'good spot' just inside and opposite her 'little man', as she thought of it. She allowed it to activate the gland buried just inside her there. When it rose to the level of her low belly and low back she paused it again, feeling the chakra pulse open and closed, leaving a residue of resonance pumping each center.

She brought it up then to each chakra, or center, or wheel, pulsing each open and closed, matching these with the corresponding points on her spine. When she got to the top, to the sixth wheel in her forehead she differentially activated the visual and audio portions of it separately, creating three wheels of vibration there. Then, allowing the light to stream into her mind, she illuminated herself as far back and as far down into her head as she could go.

Then she felt the crown arise upon her head, golden light streaming up with a red flame in the middle. Rachel allowed her head to drop back and shivered in ecstasy.

In her mind's eye Rachel saw Diosa smile at her and gesture, pointing first to Herself and then to Rachel. Rachel smiled back and raised her arms over her head, making a 'V' shape. A wisp of whirlwind stirred the motes of reflected light in the morning sun directly over her head. And then the Goddess was within her.

The feeling in Rachel, the sensing of the Goddess, felt large and light, expansive. Rachel went into trance tracking the feelings and sensations. The two, feelings and sensations, combined into one thing, one felt-sense. Rachel heard Her voice say, "Go. Write. Beloved."

Dropping her arms, Rachel stood and bowed to the altars. She went to the writing table, sat down, and took up a pencil. Holding it over the paper she paused to listen.

She heard the voice say, "This is a script for the ninth movement. It is a movement to feed the moon, feeding the Dark Light when it is in shadow. This is the choreography of coupling. From the sit she stands, he bows. She touches him on the shoulder…"

Two hours later, exhausted from holding the energies necessary to pay attention in the tension of being dual, Rachel stopped. The scripts for the Sacred Dances were difficult to transcribe, as each position required descriptors for the hands, head, legs and bodies of both participants. She would see the image completely and simply formed in her head, but describing these images took many words.

The Sacred Dances, sexual dances based on the principles of Temple Dancing, were expected to raise a power that would feed some aspect of Life itself. The food was to be physical, emotional, and mental; using the three bodies Soma, Soul, and Spirit. The motions and actions of the Dancers, moving through the energetic fields, were to act as transformers, not just of the electricity and magnetism of human beings—they were also to act as generators of power for each of the three bodies and as generators of increasing or decreasing frequencies of vibrations.

These three types of generators would create a magnetic field around the participants, and a magnetic bubble or toroid around the Dancers, then around the Observers and Musicians, feeding them.

At some time during the Dance, the High Priestess would direct this accumulated energy toward the object of the Prayer, the aspect of Life that the Dance was designed to feed. Learning to sense and then direct these energies was one of the requirements of a High Priestess. It was a skill that took learning, much like the Siddhi power of moving objects at a distance. This was an energetic phenomenon. It required the ability to sense and feel, as well as both attention-mindfulness and appropriate exact intention. It required Will to accomplish the energetic task.

Rachel, with her eyes closed, replayed in her mind the Dance she had just transcribed. She realized that she heard music along with the visual imagery.

"Music!" she thought. "There must be music. We will have to teach them how to play the music." In her mind's eye she turned to the Goddess, looked through Salakta (veiled and naked and sweating, having served as the Exemplar of the Dance) to Diosa, and asked "Is the music to be transcribed, too?"

The Goddess nodded, with a serious expression of inquiry on her face. Rachel read that as concern for herself. She sighed, thinking of the work it would take. She knew how to write music, and play the piano. It had been expected that she learn these as a child. In a drawer under her writing table she had blank music paper. She removed a sheet, and began recording the opening bars of the piece, including chants. Beginning with simple melodies and leading to complex chords in point and counterpoint. She wrote for piano, knowing that the instrumentation—string, percussion, and woodwind—would come later.

Two hours later, her hand trembling, Rachel put the pencil down. Her back and neck ached, so she stood up and stretched. She was in this position, bent backwards, legs and arms spread, eyes toward the skies when she heard a knock she recognized as Craft's.

"Come," she said, holding the position. He opened the door and stepped in, closing the door behind him.

Craft looked at Rachel, hair hanging free, still not dressed for the day. Then he saw the pile of papers on the table, the empty water pitcher, and knew why Rachel had not come down for breakfast, and why she was still not dressed, with lunch only a short time away.

She said, "Come. Hold me."

So he did. He came to her side, braced himself with one leg almost behind her, and reached under her back with his left arm, in a classically romantic pose, as if Rachel was going to swoon.

"Take me," she said.

So he did. He dropped to his right knee, still holding her up with his left hand in the small of her back. With his right hand he reached down and slowly lifted the hem of her floor length night gown, sliding it slowly up her legs and thighs. As he slowly stood up he shifted his left arm so that it encircled her waist and he brought his right arm up between her legs and reached it through so that he could grasp his left forearm. He hugged her to him and picked her up that way, carrying her to the bed.

He laid her down on a corner of the bed, her legs hanging down on either side. He was careful not to lay her on her hair by swinging her once out and away so that her hair swayed above her head then lowered her, hair on the bed as he swung her back towards himself. It created the effect of her hair spread above her head like a halo.

She lay on the bed, arms and legs still spread, eyes closed, breathing softly. Craft withdrew his arms, the hem of the robe still high on her lower belly, leaving her displayed before him. The scent of her rose up to him. She took a deep breath, rocking her hips with it at its furthest extent, and exhaled slowly.

"Have me," she said with her next breath.

Craft slipped out of his vest and stepped out of his house moccasins. He slipped his suspenders off his shoulders and unhooked his belt, dropping it to the floor. His pants slid to the floor and he stepped out of them. He breathed her in again as he dropped to his knees, erection rising. He leaned in and kissed her at the top of the line of her lips, gently at first, then slowly going deeper, pushing the folds of her apart with his lips and tongue.

Rachel's breath came faster and shallower. Craft found the spot, the concealed button he was seeking. He used his tongue to push back the concealment and, pursing his lips, he held it up and back, and tongued the button, making her gasp. He sucked it gently, pulsing it and releasing it so that her breath became an "Oh" sounding with each pulse.

Standing then, still not having touched her with his hands, he put the head of himself against her. Slowly opening her, he entered, stretching against the wetness, stopping half way to allow her to catch up. He withdrew almost to the end, then slowly forwarded himself through the place he had stopped before, and, with her gasping, sank in all the way to the end. He pressed his pubic bone against the button and she began to shudder.

The shudder began at the point he pressed against, spreading up her torso through her belly then out her arms and legs, vibrating out into the room, changing the color of the light toward a white like the moon.

Then, from the edges of the extended pool of herself, the pool suddenly collapsed. The bubble of the field reversed its flow, entering her hands and feet, collapsing through her arms and legs, vibrating, pulsing, collapsing concentrically until they gathered in her womb, building, pounding, then collapsing once more, draining through her into his still, embedded member, exploding into him and through him. He collapsed to his knees again, head bowed. Then, tremors centered in her hips, she rained for him, rained all over him, blessing him, straining herself toward him, then bucking her hips, her body collapsing into spasms of ecstasy.

Slowly the bucking eased to twitching, a small spasm of ecstasy. Craft worked hard to slow his breathing, marveling at the sparking energy within him, little electric shocks sparking at little barriers, buffers to his full sensing. He became a heat, cooled only by the pool of rain in which he knelt, evaporating her blessing until he steamed in the now cool room.

He waited, watching until the tremors stopped, and she sighed. "We should eat, you know. We cannot live on rain alone," he said and he grinned, touching the pool on the floor and bringing the taste of it to his lips. He looked down at his still full erection and had an idea of what food she had been really talking about.

"Feed me," she said.

He rose, walked around the bed and mounted it, climbing for her head. He gathered her hair and rolled it into a gentle twist and laid it alongside her ear and over onto her heart. He knelt on either side of her head from the top, leaned forward with his hands alongside her hips and slowly lowered himself to her face, spreading his knees across the sheets. He lowered himself until he could feel her breath on him, and waited.

She opened her eyes, gazing on his form and all it symbolized. The Goddess was in her now, and She gazed, too.

"Lower," she said in a husky voice, a voice of two voices.

He lowered himself, focusing the tip of himself on her breath, panting upward at him. He came to rest at the tip of her nose. She reached up with the tip of her tongue, and wrapped it around the tip of the head of him, tilting her head back into the bed, and sucked him in, in one elegant move. He held still, letting her bring her face up to him, taking in as much as she could. She felt him come to rest against the roof and back of her mouth. She held him there within her, connecting an internal circuit that filled her mind with light.

Panting through her nose, head back, she tongued the topside of him, working the rim of the head, coaxing it into release. It was not long coming, this coming. He filled her mouth with food. She continued to tongue him, coaxing him for all of it. When she had it she released him, holding his offering in her mouth, mixing it with saliva, beginning the process of separation of the elements.

She had a fleeting thought, "We shall have to teach Alchemy as well." And she heard the Goddess answer, slowly and softly and drawn out, "Yes."

She swallowed, and swallowed again, putting her tongue against the roof of her mouth, fitting into his imprint, connecting that circuit herself. The energy rose up from her belly, feeding into her head, filling it with light again. It gathered into a cloud as it rose that rained down again within her, filling her with the same spark she had ignited in Craft.

He moved off her and sat cross legged at her head, within the 'V' of her arms. He fell into meditation, tracking the flow of the internal energies, until she stirred.

She asked him, "How did you know?"

"How did I know what?" he asked.

"How did you know that some, so many, of the movements you made were movements from the Dance I was working on?"

"I didn't," he replied. "I just felt the field in the room. It felt like a kind of tracking, tracking the imagery of your mind."

"Her mind. Diosa's mind. That was the track you were following."

"Hmm," he said. "Are you hungry yet?"

She laughed, "Not as hungry as you."

They rose, and she dressed for an afternoon at the barn caring for the horses, and went down to the kitchen.

"Languages," she said, closing the door.

"What?" he said.

"There will be languages," she said, speaking in a quieter voice. "There will be languages."

"And Dancing," she whispered, sliding down the hall on socking'd feet.

12

CHESTER AND MICKEY

Lulu ate quickly, hopeful that she could be dressed, have a load of laundry in the washer and be out the door before Mickey arrived. She needed 20 minutes and maybe Melinda would loan her the car real quick.

"Mom, can I borrow the car and run to the store?" she asked. 'Run to the store' was code between them for getting hygiene products; that way they never had to talk about it in front of Chester. The subject nauseated him.

Melinda turned around and looked at her daughter, knowing it wasn't the right time but also knowing things could change quickly. Lulu still had her back turned, so she couldn't see her daughter's face. "Sure, honey," she said.

Lulu was almost out the door when she heard Mickey's truck pull up. Her stomach tightened with fear. She would have to run a gauntlet now to get past him. She opened the door and looked out. "You're blocking the car," she shouted, but Mickey was already out of his truck and walking toward the house.

"Stop yelling, the neighbors will hear you!" Chester yelled at her, grinning at his own joke. Had there been any neighbors they would have heard him yelling just as loudly.

Lulu, jacket and purse in hand, went down the steps toward Mickey and hissed at him, "You have to move the truck, you're blocking the car."

Mickey held one hand up to his ear, pretending clownishly that he still hadn't heard her. She got up to the car door and told him, "You have to move the truck."

"What, no please?" he asked.

"No, no please," she said opening the door and turning her back to him, bending to throw her purse across to the other seat. He reached out and grabbed the back of her pants and pulled her toward him, grinding her backside against his crotch. Then he reached around with his other hand, pinning one of her arms, and grabbed a breast, squeezing it hard enough for her to give a small cry out.

She tried to hit him with her free hand. He laughed and hugged her to him, trapping that arm as well. "Gotcher please right here," he growled into her ear, grinding his hips against hers. Then, holding her head pinned to a shoulder he leaned around and licked her cheek. Lulu struggled against his grip and broke free enough to make a lunge for the open car door.

Mickey shoved her in. "See you later," he smirked.

"Not if I can help it. Fuck you, Mickey!" she said, closing the door and locking it.

Mickey shrugged and laughed. He turned and backed up the truck. Lulu sped past him in reverse, giving him the finger as she drove off. Mickey laughed again and grabbed his erection, squeezing it. "That's right, Chubbs," he said, speaking to it. "You and me are gonna party with that one someday, that's for sure." He pulled the truck into the driveway and went into the house without knocking. "Hey, y'all. What's cookin'?"

"Missy, get the boy a plate," Chester said. Melinda got up with her plate and Mickey sat down in her seat. Melinda brought a plate of scrambled eggs and bacon back to the table and disappeared down the hall to her bedroom to get dressed for the day.

"What's up, old man?" Mickey asked teasingly.

Chester was studying a map. "Now, looky here, boy. That's enough of your disrespect." Then, showing the map to Mickey, he said, "You know anything about this territory?"

Mickey spilled the eggs off his fork when he leaned over to look at the map. He brushed them onto the floor.

Chester was pointing at a spot on the map northeast of Atlanta. "I had a sign last night in my dreams. There were big sheets of stone with writing on them set up by those damn Masons or something. I saw some kids spray painting them, one of the girls was painting something about some "Goddess of Love" on a stone. Can you imagine? Goddess of Love."

"Nope," Mickey said. "That where we're heading?"

"No. At least not yet. I been there once. Maybe I'll take you someday. I got some other signs closer in, things that need straightening out."

"That's a long way off, Chester. Be gone at least a week for that one, and I gotta work."

"Like I said, not yet."

Mickey grunted and shoveled another forkful of scrambled eggs into his mouth, dropping some as he did. The eggs rolled off his chest, bounced on the edge of the table and fell to the floor. He looked down and stepped on it like it was a bug.

"Say the word, boss. I'm there," Mickey said, turning his attention back to his plate, this time leaning over because he didn't want to lose out on any more food.

"Nah, well, I had this other dream. Somethin' bad happened there but nobody knows it. We gotta go see if we can figure it out, over Harpersville way," Chester said. Chester didn't believe in paying insurance, so most of the time he was not driving himself around. Insurance was for people who didn't believe in the Laud and the Providence ordained by the divine for the faithful. Insurance represented an imperfection of faith, and sometimes that was the theme of his sermon. Mostly, though, his sermons were about the sins of sexuality. He stood up, reached into his back pocket and removed $40.00, tossing it on the table.

Mickey grabbed it with his free hand, tilting his fork to the side to stuff it in a front pocket, spilling more eggs on the table. "Good enough, man."

Chester walked down the hallway to take one last piss before they got on the road. Melinda was sitting on her bed, head in her hands. She had gone very still, listening to his footsteps. She listened as he dribbled at the end, hoping he wasn't shaking himself off while he dribbled and spreading drops of pee everywhere. Chester didn't clean up after himself.

He finished and stepped out in the hall, zipping up. Melinda exhaled when she heard him walking away up the hall toward the front door. She hadn't realized she'd been holding her breath. When she heard the door slam, then the truck doors slam, she started to breathe hard, gulping air like she'd been drowning. She fell back on the bed, slowing her breathing and finally relaxing her pelvic floor, allowing her bladder to relax, soaking her housecoat beneath her. She realized she'd been holding that in, too, all this time. She trembled with some sense of horror she didn't understand and sat up, putting her face in her hands again.

She felt like she wanted to cry for a second, sensing the pain from the bacon splatter burn on her breast. And then a stronger urge rose up in her, an urge to not cry. She said aloud, "I have to get out of here. I have to get that house." She rose, shrugging off her clothes, and made for the shower.

Lulu had left the car on a side street where it couldn't be seen, watching from behind a neighbor's garage, waiting for the truck to leave. When she saw it go she walked back to the car and drove home. Melinda heard the door slam when Lulu returned.

"Momma?" Lulu called out.

"Yeah, baby, I'll be right out. Just washing my hair," Melinda called back.

Lulu looked at the kitchen table, the mess on the floor and around where Mickey's plate sat. "Ugh," she said and started to clean up.

She had carried the plates to the sink and was wetting a paper towel to wipe up the floor when Melinda hollered again. "You leave that mess to me!"

"It's OK, Momma," Lulu said. "Take your time."

Lulu got down on her hands and knees to wipe up the eggs on the floor. It reminded her of the assault she had just endured from Mickey. She felt a wave of revulsion and the spasm of it made her gag.

Melinda emerged from the bathroom with her hair in a towel and saw this: saw her daughter gagging on her hands and knees on the floor. She rushed over to her and got down on one knee. "Baby, baby, are you OK?" she asked.

Lulu sat back on her heels. "Yeah, Momma. I'm OK."

"What's wrong, honey?" Melinda pursued the inquest. "You're not pregnant are you?"

Lulu shook her head. "No, Momma. Mickey grabbed me."

"When, just now?"

"Yeah, when I went outside."

"Grabbed you how?"

"Just grabbed me from behind. Pulled me to him and rubbed himself on me. He wouldn't let me go."

"Are you OK? Did he hurt you?"

"No, he didn't hurt me. Except when he grabbed my boob. I'm OK. I'm just afraid. I'm afraid of him."

"Why's he doing it? You leading him on? You teasing him?"

"No, Momma. He thinks it's cute. Or funny. He thinks it makes me want him. I'm afraid, Momma. One of these days he's gonna really do something."

"Well, then, you just gotta stay away from him as best you can."

"Momma, I can't stay away from him. There's no place to go around here. Everywhere I go he can find me."

"Just do the best you can, honey," Melinda said, using the table to stand back up. "You've got to do the best you can. Now help me clean up a little and tell me what you're going to do today."

Mickey drove through town and took the road to Harpersville. It would be about a 4 hour drive. As soon as they were out of town Chester reached into the glove box and pulled out a pack of cigarettes, lit one, and exhaled out into the summer morning.

"We'll go out this way awhile and then take Barber's Mill down to the one lane bridge and look around. That's what I saw in my dream, that bridge and the 'One Vehicle at a Time' sign. We're supposed to go down that way and stop at the bridge and get out and do a little walk around."

They stopped once for gas and drinks, rolling steadily to their destination. They arrived in the early afternoon. There was a pull-off area to the right, where a car could wait for an oncoming vehicle already on the bridge. The bridge was an old steel bridge, built during the Great Depression, with a wooden plank deck, the planks loose and banging when a car passed over.

They turned down the access road to the riverside and parked. The site was popular with the locals as a party spot on weekends, and a lover's zone late at night during the week. Fishermen would sometimes park there and walk upstream to get away from the trash. "Stop here," Chester said, and they sat a moment looking at the river going by. "Let's look around a bit," Chester spoke, breaking from the reverie. He opened the door and off the dashboard he grabbed a length of stiff copper wire stripped from heavy gauge electric insulation. It had a T-shaped handle bent into one end with one arm of the T set into a rotating handle. It was a dousing rod; Chester called it his "probe".

They got out and looked around. Mickey scuffed through the trash while Chester scanned the trees. Chester always scanned the trees, looking for imps and demons, which he knew would often hide there when they were around. He knew, as they did, that people never looked up anymore.

Then he stopped. Looking down, scanning the ground around him systematically, he laid out his plan to quarter the grounds. In his hand the probe started to twitch, slowly, and then bend in a direction off to the right. Chester turned to follow the direction of the bend and the probe twitched more quickly. The closer Chester got to whatever the probe was pointing toward the faster it twitched. The probe stopped bending when Chester stood over a drifted plastic bag, hung up in the low plants and ground clutter. The probe was vibrating so quickly it couldn't be seen, almost burning Chester's hand with its heat.

Chester squatted down and gingerly lifted the bag by an edge, revealing a used condom, twisted and folded and glistening. He touched it with the probe and fell into vision, seeing what had transpired in its use.

He saw a girl, a teenager, naked below the waist on her hands and knees in the back seat of a car, tube top pushed up around her shoulders, exposing her breasts. The hem was tucked into her mouth to muffle her cries, her back lit white by the waxing moon coming through the rear windshield.

She was being taken from behind by an older man, pants down to his knees and shirt unbuttoned at the bottom exposing his belly. He was not being kind. He was alternating between the girl's vulnerabilities, and she was crying, not so much from physical pain as from humiliation and grief. Her grief was genuine. The sobs that wracked her body caused her flex against him. He was amused, thinking it was from enjoyment. Chester sensed him thinking that women always cried when they enjoyed it.

Chester sent a pulse of inquiry down his arm through the rod and immediately the vision changed to a new scene. He saw an older woman, lying in bed passed out, empty whisky bottle and an overflowing ashtray on a nightstand. She was tangled in the sheet, sweating in the bed. Chester looked closely and saw she was weeping in her sleep. He felt a presence behind him and turned to see a silhouette of the girl from the car in the doorway, just staring at the woman in the bed. Chester knew it was the girl's mother. He heard a man calling from another room and in vision Chester could see it was the man from the car, standing at the front door, calling the girl to come.

A shadow fell over Chester in the afternoon sun of his present time. He shuddered and looked up to see Mickey standing over him. "You alright?" he asked. "Whatchoo see?"

Chester went down on one knee and leaned on the other. "Get me to the truck," he said, standing up shakily. Mickey stood by him, and then walked beside him, not really watching for a stagger or a fall. Chester thought, "I'm getting old," and leaned on the hood. After a minute he turned around and looked up into the sunshine. "Get me a smoke," he said.

Mickey reached through the open window and took the pack off the dashboard, shaking one out for Chester, then one for himself. Lighting them, Mickey looked at Chester from under his eyebrows. "Whatchoo see?" he asked again.

Chester took a breath and held it, choosing his words. "A daddy taking his step-daughter. Momma's a drunk." Then he looked down.

Mickey made a grunting sound. "Whatchoo gone do next then?"

Chester closed his eyes and went back to the vision of the scene of the taking in the car. He watched it finish. The man, stepping backwards out of the car, pulling up his pants with one hand, holding the condom on with other, turning to the moon, removing it and throwing it out into the weeds. Chester heard the man tell her, "Get dressed and go sit in front," as he wiped himself on his shirt tail and finished dressing. Chester heard one door open and close, then another. The man turned and got in and started the car. Chester heard the girl say something and then watched the man punch her in the side of the head. The car backed up, turned and drove up to the road. Chester could see the girl, her bare feet pulled up under her knee-length pleated skirt, huddled against the door.

"This didn't end good," he said, looking hard at Mickey to see if he understood. Mickey nodded. They got in the truck and took off, rattling over the bridge and up the road toward Barber's Ridge. About six miles on, the road started making switchbacks and hairpin turns along the coves. Coming around the first one there were tire tracks that went straight on, leaving parallel prints across the dusty shoulder, and disappearing over the edge. Mickey stopped the truck to let Chester out, then backed up across the lane to park on the shoulder as Chester went to the edge and looked down. Mickey got out and joined him.

They could see where the car had bounced down the hill, smashed through young trees, and come to rest, nose crushed against a large rock. They went down to the car side-footed, careful in in their descent. They got to the car, about a hundred feet down. Mickey, on the driver's side, looked in. The man was sitting back in his seat, his neck obviously broken from hitting the roof. The girl was lying across the seat, her knees on the passenger seat floor with her head in the man's lap. Her skull was crushed and stuck on the bottom of steering wheel.

Mickey let out a low whistle. Chester reached in through the broken window with his probe and touched it to the girl's leg. The vision hit him with a visible shock. As the step-father had been coming around the rising bend he accelerated. The girl's expression was an almost impossible mix of despair and rage. Knowing where they were, the expression changed to resolve as she clicked out of her seatbelt, and launched herself across to the steering wheel, holding it so the car continued on straight off the side. He saw the girl looking calmly at the moon, the man screaming and fighting to take back the wheel.

The girl screamed back at him, raging in his face, while her left hand went down and unclasped his seat belt.

At the first impact the force shook the girl from the wheel into the man's lap as the following bounce lifted him out of his seat, smashing his head against the roof, and breaking his neck. The second impact pinned her head under the bottom edge of the steering wheel, breaking her skull when the final impact bent the car almost in half, driving the wheel column down.

"Not good," Chester said to Mickey. "Murder and suicide. She did it." Chester turned away from the car and raised his arms overhead. "Laud, Laud, have mercy on these sinners, both these sinners. I com-mend them into your hands."

And, as Mickey watched, a glow began around the bodies, rising above the bodies and through the roof of the car. The glows coalesced into two forms, the man's dark and the girl's white. The dark one shot off to the north and the white one to the east. Chester's mind's eye saw the vision of what the girl had seen looking at the moon—her momma's smiling face, nodding her head yes—and he shook his head.

Mickey watched them go. "Whadja think that means?" he asked.

"I don't ask questions I don't wanna know the answer to," Chester replied, looking up the hill to the truck. "Gotta get to Harpersville. Got one more stop to make."

"Whatchoo think people gonna think? Mickey asked.

"Don't matter what people think. They dead. Don't matter, and that's why I don't ask. Sinners all. People gonna think what they want," Chester replied.

"But people gonna think she was..." and Mickey reached in to move her bloody hair and brain smeared head.

"Stop!" Chester commanded. "It don't matter what people think. It don't matter what sinners think. Think about it."

Mickey thought about it, as if he could think. He stayed his hand then, and withdrew it from the broken window.

As they approached Harpersville, Mickey became happy when Chester directed him to turn down a single dirt lane that ended with a trailer in a small yard at the edge of the woods. He knew this place, knew it as the home of one of Chester's wives. He'd seen her in church, and he was hoping that Chester, who sometimes hinted that it would be "biblical", could persuade Doris to allow herself to be shared with Mickey. Chester indicated that maybe this would be the time.

They pulled up to the trailer and parked. Mickey had asked Chester if they were going to report the accident to the police. Chester had said, "Nope. We done our business there. Now it ain't no longer none of our business. They're dead now, and they're gonna stay dead until somebody else finds 'em."

Mickey sat in the truck and mused on this, not really thinking, just projecting the image that the girl had been going down on her father when they went over the edge. He shifted in the seat, starting to imagine what Chester was doing in the trailer, starting to massage his growing erection. He was just beginning to consider taking it out of his jeans and masturbating when, twenty minutes later, Chester came out on the top step tucking in his shirt tail. Chester scanned the yard, then looked at Mickey, smiled, and nodded. Mickey grinned, got out of the truck and went in the house.

Chester, who had stepped back into the living room gestured down the hall. Mickey turned and could see 'Dory' standing in the doorway to the master bedroom at the end, leaning up against the doorframe, in a long slip with a strap down over one shoulder.

Dory tossed her red-brown hennaed hair over that shoulder, indicating Mickey was to come on down behind her, and smiled. Dory liked Chester, liked his sex, but she knew him for what he was. And, seeing Chester only once in a while wasn't enough. She'd been playing shy when Chester brought up having sex with Mickey, not wanting Chester to think that she was too eager, because, in truth, Chester wasn't really enough for her when she was with him. Getting Mickey thrown in the deal was a boon for her. "Two for the price of one," she thought, smiling as Mickey brushed past her.

She turned and closed the door. In the dim light of closed curtains she dropped to her knees in front of Mickey, unbuckling his belt, opening his jeans, and pulling those and his shorts down to his knees. He was nearly hard when she took him in her mouth. By the time he was fully hard she had adapted to the smell and shape of him, and took her mouth off, holding him in one hand, regarding her handiwork.

She smiled and was about to go down on him again, thinking that she would finish him off that way, letting him ejaculate on her breasts, exposed by both straps having slipped over her shoulders. He grabbed her by the hair, holding her face away from him. Using her hair he turned her around. Keeping her on her knees, he dragged her over to the edge of the bed, then up on it, belly down.

He pressed her down into the bed, pulling up her slip, exposing her back side, and kicked her legs apart. Chester's seed ran down the front of her as Mickey stooped and pressed against her anus, forcing it open with the head of his erection.

"Slower, slower," Dory pleaded in a voice muffled by the bedspread, knowing what was about to happen was inevitable. She winced, and struggled, trying to rise, but Mickey held her pinned down. She cried out, but Mickey forced her face down into the bed again. In the end, all she could do was submit, reaching back and holding herself open for him with both hands. It was all she could do to ease the sensations and the pain. "Open, open, open," she thought, willing herself not to fight, not to struggle against the invader.

Chester, in the living room, drinking a pop and watching professional wrestling on the TV, heard her cry out and smirked, thinking that she was enjoying it.

Mickey never took 'sloppy seconds' as a point of pride, but it didn't occur to him what he was splashing his balls in.

It was over soon.

Mickey got up and wiped himself on his shirttail before he pulled up his pants and tucked it in. He was making growling noises and grunts of satisfaction but he said nothing to Dory.

Dory relaxed completely into the bed, saying nothing, wishing for them to leave. Before they left Chester came back to the bedroom, saw her dimly lying there on her belly, bed clothes in a twisted heap around her.

Chester said, into the darkness, "Thanks, Missy." It was what he called all his 'wives'. "Y'all come down to Meeting tonight, praise the Laud. I'll see you there." He turned and left.

When she heard the truck drive off Dory got up and went to the shower. When she washed between her legs the cloth came away with something that made her smile, thinking of Mickey's surprise.

Down the road Chester suddenly started to sniff the air. "Laud almighty, what's that smell?" He identified it as coming from Mickey. "Laud shitting son of Gawd, boy, that's you! You smell like shit, boy. What did you get into? Oh, my Gawd, boy! Take me to the gawdamn tent and go find a stream somewhere and wash off. Don't come in unless your clothes are dry. Laud almighty boy. Laud Gawd almighty." Then he understood what his sermon would be about tonight: plenty of steaming lurid forbidden sex. Get the crowd all heated up and they'd be rolling around in a frenzy of tongues and the money would just pour in.

That night Chester gave one of the best sermons of his life. Passing the hat brought in tens and twenties instead of spare change.

13

FIRST DAY OF CLASS

PART 1 MORNING

Angelica woke before the alarm, her eyes suddenly opening in the early light. She felt both tired and rested; tired from dreaming—dreams she couldn't remember, chaotic flashes of what seemed to be other people's lives—yet rested, she assumed, because she had slept more deeply in the darkness and quiet of the deep countryside. Even though the night had been filled with the sound of insects—cicadas mostly—and tree frogs and the calls of mocking birds, there was no hum from traffic or electric motors.

She rose, putting on panties and a midriff sports bra, and sat down to brush her hair. While she was brushing, she paused. A wave of energy—a spike almost—of exquisite, intense pleasure passed through her. Beginning at her perineum, and passing through her clitoris, it rose up her belly, making her breath catch and her heart jump. She panted quickly as it passed her throat. As it shot through her face she saw an image of a gorgeous green phallus, rendered in exquisite detail. As her head rolled back on her shoulders, she saw it twitch. Then, as her face turned skyward she saw an image of a vagina. "Mine," she thought. It was over in less than a second.

She looked down, letting her free hand fall into her lap, lightly touching her clitoris. With her middle finger she could feel it buzzing. She shuddered. She slowly drew her hand away, curious about the sensation but reluctant to be late for the sit.

She wrapped an opaque sarong around her hips and slipped on a light cotton shirt. She settled a shawl over her shoulders, slipped on sandals, and quietly opened the door, looking either way down the hallway. Seeing no one else, she went to the bathroom and brushed her teeth, leaving her kit hanging from a hook.

She moved quietly down the stairs and into the dining room, past a tea service on a side board. She could hear sounds from the kitchen through the servery. She was tempted momentarily with the thought of a cup of tea, but decided she wanted to be in the room early. She went in through one side of a large double door that was slightly ajar, adding her sandals to the small pile of shoes to the right of the door. The door made no sound from its hinges.

The room was high, large and circular, with a semicircular dais raised three levels on her left. There were large fireplaces on opposite sides of the room, and a door on the far side leading, she assumed, to the East Wing of the Mansion. There were tall windows where possible, with an inside balcony running the entire circumference. There was an assortment of pillows, meditation stools, and benches to her left. She took a pillow and a stool and looked around the room.

The tall, strong woman she had met in the kitchen the night before was seated on the dais. There were about a dozen people already seated in the room. The arrangement was peculiar. Men and women were seated opposite each other about three feet apart, but in a pattern, she realized, that would become a spiral if enough people joined them.

She looked at Hannah, who opened her eyes and stared at her, smiling. The question on Angelica's face must have been clear, for Hannah inclined her head toward the end of the line of women and nodded. Angelica smiled and nodded back, moving to take her seat. As she went, she noticed the others and was immediately curious about the first woman, the woman at the center facing east. She was an older woman, black hair streaked with gray, sitting on the bare floor on her heels, a thick robe tucked under her legs.

Sitting opposite the first woman was a man of middle age, tall and athletic looking. Then she looked closely at everyone, and saw that all the people sitting in the spiral were in good shape. They were strong without being over developed, straight without being rigid, fluid rather than stiff in all their movements.

She sat in the line of women, curving around to where she sat facing south with the woman on the dais to her right. She used her peripheral vision to get a better look at the first woman in the line, obviously some kind of Elder, a Caucasian woman but with a slight cast to the old eyes, a face that had seen much sun and would, she could tell by the skin, darken easily. Her hair, mostly black with some white—rather than gray—streaking, was full, and fell down her back in waves like an extra shawl in the cool morning.

She emulated the sitting style of the women, her heels under the stool, sitting up tall with her head slightly inclined, eyes half open gazing at the spot on the floor where a complimentary person would sit.

More people entered, taking up the pattern, eventually creating a spiral of thirty people in pairs. A man sat down opposite Angelica, settling himself on a small mat. He appeared to be just a few years older than her, with his hair in dreadlocks pulled back in a bundle. He was dressed the same, she realized, as all the men: in a dark, navy blue cotton, floor length, full skirted robe with full sleeves over a white shirt with a low collar. The women, however, showed all kinds of variation in their sarongs and shawls. Then she noticed that every man wore a different belt, most of them woven, in bright colors and patterns.

"I am The Hearthkeeper. Let your eyes rest," Hannah began. "Fall into the gaze before you, let your eyes rest there." Angelica's gaze stopped just at her partner's knees. She felt him glance at her before his eyes settled just off her on the floor.

"Hold your gaze there," Hannah continued. "Breathe." And as one, they inhaled slowly and exhaled together. The breathing continued in unison. Suddenly Angelica felt a wave of energy, like a breeze, pass along the lines, beginning with the Elder. The air grew brighter. She saw the pathways of gazing light up with a white light, and where the gazes crossed in the middle the white light turned to a sphere of golden light, scintillating.

"Oh, Beauty," Angelica sighed, sending a ripple of energy along the line. Then she felt a calming wave emanate from the Elder at the Center.

"Yes, Beauty," Hannah spoke. "Feel into it." Angelica felt into the Beauty and her mind collapsed into a field of golden light. She stayed there.

About 20 minutes later she heard Hannah say "Turn. Return. Breathe. Remember. Be grateful." And with that everyone lifted their gaze and raised their arms aloft palms up. Angelica's gaze crossed the face of her partner as his crossed hers. She felt his rising gaze flow over her, lighting her up within. When their eyes crossed each other's face they smiled brightly at each other. As her eyes looked up she saw the line of golden balls in a spiral string above the group, little spherical flames that went out in a sequence from the center to the end, buoyed on a cloud of pale green. As she watched the whole vision faded. She thought she heard a little 'pop' sound at the end.

"Stand," Hannah commanded. Angelica watched and did as the others did, coming first to her knees, then up on one such that the Feminine and Masculine were in mirror image, then coming to their feet together into a bow to each other that was held for a breath.

Then the sit was over. Angelica couldn't meet the eyes of the beautiful man who had been her partner. As she turned she saw Hannah beckon to her and she went over, realizing that the Elder was coming over, too.

Hannah asked, "What did you see, child?" As the Elder listened, Angelica described her visions and feelings during the sit.

The Elder said, "Turn to me, child." The Elder held her hand up over Angelica's forehead for a moment. Angelica felt both held and as if she was being read. The Elder said to Hannah, "She is verging."

Hannah nodded and said, "Understood." Turning to Angelica she said, "Angelica, this is the Moon Halter." Angelica looked at her, not comprehending, and when she turned back to the Elder, the Elder had already turned and was walking out the door into the dining room. When Angelica looked back at Hannah again, Hannah said, "You did well. Go eat."

Angelica went into the dining room, and stood a moment, getting her bearings. She realized that she was feeling lightheaded, wobbling a little in a circle, and that she should probably get her food and go sit down. She watched Moon Halter go through the line and then go take a seat at one of the straight tables in a solarium on the south side of the room.

Breakfast was laid out on a sideboard against a wall: oatmeal or dry cereal including granola, hard-boiled eggs, fresh fruit, yogurt, sliced bread and butter. Coffee, tea and juice. Angelica got a tray, a small bowl of oatmeal and put yogurt on it, an egg, a banana and a cup of tea. She looked around. She saw Moon Halter still sitting alone at the far end of the long table. There were two women, women who had been in the small group in the foyer when she'd arrived, sitting at the near end. She saw no one sitting yet with Moon Halter so Angelica went and sat opposite her.

Moon Halter looked up with surprise as Angelica sat down. Angelica smiled and Moon Halter smiled back. "Is there some sort of seating protocol here? I mean, is this OK?" Moon Halter smiled and said nothing, returning to her food. Angelica took this as assent. "What happened in there?" Angelica asked. "Never seen anything like it, except maybe in dreams. Did you do that? I mean, did you make that happen? Why? What was the purpose?" As Angelica spoke, almost in a torrent, Moon Halter stopped eating and began to stare at Angelica—the wide eyed stare of someone who may be a little deaf, staring at someone to read their lips when they spoke. When Angelica looked up she thought this might be the case.

Moon Halter spoke, "I am not deaf," as if Angelica had spoken her thought aloud. "You, however, require attention. We nourish the world here, and the world, in turn, nourishes us. This is what you saw. Eat now. You have only a little time to get changed for class."

Angelica felt the sound of Moon Halter's voice wash over her like a caress, brushing her hair back, sliding down the side of her face, the touch of a mother for a beloved child. They ate in silence for a moment, Moon Halter spooning the rest of her oatmeal out of the bowl. Then she stood up. She leaned forward toward Angelica and said, "Attention is a form of nourishment." For some reason she couldn't understand, this made Angelica want to cry.

When she looked up Moon Halter could see the lack of comprehension on her face. She said, "Attention is a kind of food. You are what you pay attention to. You are what pays attention to you."

Angelica, overwhelmed by the compassion in Moon Halter's eyes, suddenly found herself with tears running down her cheeks. She lowered her face and looked within, trying to understand why she wept. She felt a quick flash of fear when she realized that one of the meanings of what Moon Halter had said was that when Moon Halter was paying attention to her, she could be, in some way, what Moon Halter was: a woman of power who could read minds, make lights appear, and extend the sense of her touch well beyond her hands. This was a woman of age and power.

And there was something else, as well: a sense of light within and behind Moon Halter, a golden light that, when Angelica looked at it, made the normal sense of herself dissolve into a point of light, cradled in a sea of light. Angelica's head dropped back, her face toward the ceiling, her tears ran down her cheeks over her throat in twin rivulets.

"It is the Divine Feminine in me you are sensing. This is what Her attention can feel like," Moon Halter said into the pool of Angelica's melting. The sound of Moon Halter's voice, grown deep, brought Angelica's awareness back into the room. Her face came forward, and she felt the tears stop. She inhaled raggedly and exhaled solidly. When she looked up, Moon Halter had gone.

Angelica looked over at the two women sitting at the other end of the long table. They were looking at Angelica, watching the exchange with Moon Halter, watching Angelica. When they caught Angelica's eye, they smiled at her, and nodded. Angelica smiled at them. Angelica looked down and realized she'd been eating the whole time she'd been talking to Moon Halter. She also realized that these two women had been listening and observing the entire conversation. She blushed and looked away, still smiling to herself. She rose, took her dishes to the servery, and went upstairs to change for class.

The two women at the other end of the table watched her go. These women were Eva Gardner and Madeleine Morgan. If Angelica had known, she might have stopped to speak to them, also. They were, respectively, the High Priestess of Stonehaven and the Seeress. They were part of the

Council of Seven wen, who, along with their Consorts, ran the Stonehaven enterprise. The High Priestess also served on the High Council of the Order of the Fleur de Vie. This High Council was composed of seven wen, also: initiated High Priestesses all, and their Consorts.

The High Council ran all the various enterprises the Stonehaven group had started over the years that supported all the works and endeavors of the Order globally. These businesses consisted of interlocking shell corporations that ran yoga and martial arts studios, book stores that stubbornly refused to close, security firms, accounting firms, law firms, retirement facilities, real estate development and rental companies, and many others. The vacation rental houses that ringed the core Stonehaven property were owned by these companies. These houses were used for various purposes: housing for staff and guests, and communications with the larger world. There were no televisions and no computer access from Stonehaven proper. Not even cell phones worked, which was what the Council wanted.

Initiated members of the Order were guaranteed employment and an income that secured their future, even in firms where not all the employees were members. These people worked as yoga teachers, security and body guards, private detectives, book sellers, occupational therapists, and workers on organic farms. What bound the members together was their common belief in the Antecedence of the Feminine, and the vow of secrecy they took at their initiation.

These vows were so strongly embedded in the members by the magic of the ritual that there was almost no possibility of them speaking about it to anyone who was not a member, until they had completed their training as either Consort or Priestess. This training granted them the power of discernment about whether or not to speak to someone. It was only by invitation from someone who knew, and had discernment, that new people were invited to begin the process of becoming members. Once someone had passed the tests of the Consort or the Priestess it was the power of the knowledge of the Truth, and the need to protect it, that kept them from speaking inappropriately.

It was by the apperception of the Seeress that Angelica was accepted into the program. Angelica was the first candidate for a class accepted directly to Stonehaven in four years. It was what Madeleine had seen about Angelica's condition that enabled her to be admitted. Madeleine's training as a Seeress had included the ability to use intuition to determine which people or events should be looked into and which to exclude. Angelica had shown up in her vision on the morning the application had arrived, including the audio impression of her name. Madeleine saw her as a column of white stone surrounded by fire; the stone impervious to the flames which rotated through all six colors of the spectrum. This was an extraordinary sign, a sign that the candidate was—or could shortly become—a liberated and completed human being. This vision of Madeleine's was enough to vouchsafe Angelica.

After watching Angelica leave the dining room the wen looked at each other. Eva raised one eyebrow and Madeleine smiled. Madeleine said, "I'll be watching her closely. When the buffer burns through it will be tricky for her."

Eva nodded. "It will be a full blown thing with this one. She'll need help, but her lack of attachment to any specific world view will leave her susceptible to the Truth."

"And her ability to sense the energies somatically will keep it real for her. But what's unknown is how much sensation she can tolerate and still return with her awareness intact," Madeleine replied.

Eva agreed. "That's always an unknown, Sister. People work years to overcome what she is likely to overcome in a matter of hours. It will be our job to make sure she can keep it together. Do you know if she is close to her parents?"

"Yes," Madeleine replied. "She is. They will worry if they don't hear from her and she doesn't return home. I hope I can get her to commit to the extended format before she blows out, but I don't know if we can convince her to commit by then. A few more exposures to the morning sit might get her curiosity up enough to want to stay. We'll see. Otherwise, we'll have to make the call for her. We'll say that she's deep into a meditative retreat, and that she'll call in a few days. I will lay the Will along the line of that connection and it should work."

"I will send someone to temporarily disable her car. We don't want her remembering she has a car and fleeing in a moment of terror," Eva said. "And when she blows out I want to be the first one to her. So no matter what time, day or night, when you sense it, contact me."

In her room, Angelica changed quickly into loose pants, brushing her teeth again, and moving quickly so she would not have to think about everything that had just happened. Some part of her brain seemed frozen on the image of the light behind the Moon Halter. She didn't want to think and risk moving it from the throne of her attention.

She put up her hair, grabbed her day pack with its water bottle, billed cap (gray, with the word 'PINK' written in pink in small print on the brow) and sunglasses (wrap-arounds that wouldn't fall off when she bent over). She picked up her rolled mat and closed her door behind her. She bounded down the stairs, making everyone in the Mansion know someone was there with the sound of it. When she hopped out onto the veranda, and down the steps, it was as if a drum in the house had gone silent. Anyone near a window watched her go down the footpath to the Barns. As she encountered other people on the path, both coming and going, she found herself wondering how many people were on the property. She recalled having seen about twenty when she arrived, then perhaps another dozen this morning. These she was passing made the number close to forty, varied in type and race.

She looked down on the Barn. It was a long building, not very wide, with two squat grain silos at one end and a wider building at the other end, which had been labeled 'Kitchen' on the site maps. She snickered when she realized that from above it would look like a large phallus. A row of windows along its side in the second story sparkled in the morning light. There was a large round building just beyond it, which looked like it may have held an indoor riding ring. Uphill to the right where the dirt road came down from behind the Mansion, there were two large Quonset huts that appeared to hold equipment. There was a midsize greenhouse and some smaller outbuildings scattered among the larger ones.

She went down the path, crossed a bridge over a small stream and then continued uphill to the barn. A covered concrete sidewalk ran along the length of the Barn. Doors marked 'Entrance' in the wall at intervals in between the windows. She entered the nearest door and found herself in a small lobby with a staircase going up and another door leading to a short hallway which led to the central hallway.

She turned right, walking past closed doors and open spaces. One door said 'Office' and was ajar. As she passed she could see lights and hear voices. She followed signs to the 'Studio' and crossed what turned out to be a foyer with floor to ceiling glass she'd not noticed from outside. She went down a short hallway to the double doors of the Studio. It was a large open space with curtained mirrors and windows all around. It could have held perhaps a hundred people. Against the far interior wall was a small stage, back-dropped with more curtains. There were recessed lights in the ceiling and a hardwood floor laid out in a diamond pattern.

There were two people standing on the stage talking, one masculine and the other feminine. There were small bunches of people scattered about the room. It seemed clear that several people already knew each other. The feminine spoke to the group, "By tens."

The bunches of people broke up, some heading to the walls to retrieve stools that were stored there. The people sat in ranks ten across, putting their mats down with the stools on top, sitting behind each other in rows. Angelica chose a short four-legged round top stool and sat in the last row, bending her knees and putting her heels behind her like the rest.

The people sat and settled in. Some sat meditatively, while others looked at the Instructors, who had also sat down on stools, the woman slightly in front of the man. As Angelica watched, the Instructors centered their heads on top of their spines and lowered their eye lids, not quite closing them all the way, and sat still. So did everyone else. A few more people came in while they were sitting, taking up places behind her.

After about ten minutes, during which Angelica dropped down into remembering the imagery of the phallus that had appeared to her right after waking that morning, the feminine Instructor said, "Good morning." All eyes opened and focused on her.

"We begin with the Rules.

"We agree to be non-violent. There is a martial arts class occurring at the same time as this retreat, and they, too, must make the same commitment. Contemplate what this means as compared to your current definition of 'non-violent'. Allow your understanding to comprehend.

"We agree to not lie to one another. This is not the same as always being completely truthful. Much opinion masquerades as truth. It is wiser, sometimes, to keep one's opinions to oneself, mindful that they may change later when you know more. Sometimes it is better to remain silent.

"We agree to not steal from one another. None of us is so wealthy as to afford much loss, and, if someone steals from us they rob of us more than the thing. They rob us of the opportunity to be generous.

"We need to talk about sex. We are a mixed gender group, and we anticipate that many of you will do what the genders do. We ask that you restrain yourselves to having sex in private, mindful that there are others around you. Remember that nothing must happen without consent.

"We practice non-attachment here. This means non-attachment to outcomes and also non-attachment to our own expectations. Things here, and the way of this class, may not be as you expect them to be, and you will save yourself much useless suffering if things do not conform to how you think they should be.

"These things are what not to do. Later we will cover the rest; that is, what to do, what to practice affirmatively."

"Are there any questions? Is there any discussion?" the masculine Instructor asked the group.

"Would you speak more about non-violence and the martial arts?"

The masculine instructor answered, "A man, and I include women... Well, I shall say this. A person can be well-trained in self-defense, as well as in defense of others and be completely peaceable; completely at peace with themselves and the world around them. That is one meaning of non-violence.

"Another meaning of non-violence is predicated by skill. A person can have a level of skill that enables them to disable another person—but without violence. In that context, violence is an energy that is absent from the practitioner's spirit. The adept can even kill without violence, although the dead are unlikely to see it that way.

"An adept practitioner can accomplish whatever is necessary without the spirit of violence. There is, however, the need for power. The adept practitioner must be able to cultivate and use power in the non-violent way. In these practices of cultivation, the will to dominate, especially in men, can be sublimated into the will to power, and that power can be used in many ways, not just martially.

"Another question?"

"I get to a place on the slide toward having sex where I can no longer say 'No.' Is this bad? Or is it good?" a woman in the second row asked.

The feminine Instructor answered, "Yes." She paused for the chuckle from the group, then continued, "It is good in a way. You have learned how to embody the receptive, you have learned how to surrender. If this were a class in Tantra and you did not know how to embody the receptive and surrender, you would have to learn this. But it is also bad, in a way. Unless you are in circumstances that are absolutely safe for you to surrender, you must keep a part of your awareness separate, so that you can give consent and if a threat emerges you can say 'No' and act to stop what is happening in time to prevent something more not so good from happening."

"I have a question," one of the men near the front said.

"Wait," commanded the Feminine. To the woman she said, "You can learn to master this. Would you like to know how?"

"Yes," the woman nodded.

"You begin by inserting an interruption in the process of getting to the place where you normally can no longer say 'No'. Start anywhere, perhaps most easily stopping at some familiar place on the way, say, before a first kiss, or, more difficultly, between a first and a second. And alternate this with practice in slowing down and actually consciously saying 'Yes' to each place where you may have said 'No'. "

Several people chuckled at this.

"You can move in both directions from your start point. You can learn to say 'No' after the first glance, or even before—you can often identify where that glance is going to come from, and you can have a 'No' waiting for it. You can stop after making out, or after warming up with a little petting, or whatever. You can do it even in the middle of making love, which is where the real practice comes from, there in that engagement right before you lose your separate awareness.

"And there's an esoteric reason for mastering that moment, right before the dissolution.

"But the thing is, you have to mean it. You have to say 'No' and then really stop. You have to disengage. You have to get up and walk away."

"In the middle? Even in the middle?" someone asked.

"Yes. Even in the middle. Get up and walk away."

"But what about my lover?"

"What about them? If they're in training they already know what's going on, and what to do. If they're not, you can train them. If they're untrainable, what are you doing with them at all?"

"So, OK. What's the esoteric reason?"

"If I tell you, it won't be 'esoteric' anymore will it?"

Someone in the group said, "Aww."

"That's OK. I can speak the answer to this group. This group is already a mesoteric group, as evidenced by where you are, as evidenced by your being here at all. This is not an exoteric group. The answer to your question is this: By mastering those moments right before and just after the transition into the dissolute Pool of Undifferentiated Sentience one can take one's awareness back and forth across the barrier.

"At a certain point, especially in this work, a door opens into the Divine World. Then the Divine Feminine comes through it and, seeking Ecstasy, she inhabits the feminine body. It is better to be able to be aware of this Presence and have the memory of the bliss of the Pool, too. To become lost in the Pool, to have one's awareness subsumed into Ecstasy is great fun, but to come to know the Goddess in this form is spectacularly exquisite.

"And, by becoming able to keep one's awareness intact both crossing the boundary as well as in the presence of the Divine, then one becomes...well...I can say only a little more. One becomes empowered to become a Servant of Life in ways that are unimaginable. The feminine can even become a Priestess of the True Creator, the Divine Feminine."

The room was silent. Angelica felt like her mind was coming apart at the seams. She had a quick vision of her mind as a scaffold unfolded in three dimensions, with plastic sheets like wind screens filling all the rectangular openings. As she watched the scaffold came apart, cross-pieces fracturing, screens ripping, uprights collapsing. She even had an odd sensation of ripping inside her head.

She realized that all over the world the Creative Power was assigned to the Masculine. But not here. All the social systems across the world began with positing the Masculine as primary and hence validating the patriarchal as primary too. Although progress had been made in her lifetime, it was still the dominant world view, and the cause of much grief and terror, particularly for women.

Into the silence, as if she was speaking to Angelica, the Feminine Instructor said, "The Feminine creates, the Masculine makes." Angelica looked up and the Instructor was looking directly at her.

After a pause, the Instructor said, "You, I don't know your name, what was your question?"

Angelica froze, thinking the Instructor was speaking to her. But when she looked, the Instructor had turned her face toward the man she'd silenced so she could finish her teaching, even though her eyes were still on Angelica.

"Um, ah, I had a question about power and violence. Um, uhh, I can't remember it now."

"I remember your question," the Masculine said.

"But, uh, I didn't get to ask it," the student said.

"Nevertheless, I remember it," the Instructor said. "In your imagination you saw a woman below you falling into ecstatic trance and you felt an urge to dominate her in that moment, a moment when she could not give you consent. You thought about how to use this power to get your way with women. Take something, perhaps, you would not normally be offered, use it to control or manipulate her. You were gloating. The words were, 'Now that I've fucked her into submission...' But you quickly turned from going down that path, not wanting to look down that rabbit hole. The thoughts were very fast, but observable. Your question was, 'What can I take?' but that's not the question you were going to ask. That question was, 'How does power without violence affect sexuality?" Yes? That was your question, yes?"

"Um. Yes, I guess so."

"You guess so? Was that the question? Yes or no?"

The man blushed. "Yes." There was audible gasp in the room. The man paused, then asked "But how did you know?"

"Your thoughts," the Masculine replied, "your thoughts were flowing across your face like shadows from passing clouds. Your lips moved as you mouthed the words."

The ripping sound in Angelica's mind had stopped, to be replaced by a melting sensation. It was as if her bones had liquefied under the onslaught of what was, to her, a new kind of honesty and a new kind of Truth. She started swaying, uncertain of her bearings and her balance. The world had shifted, her worldview collapsed, and she badly needed to reorient herself. She almost fell off her stool. She looked up when the Feminine began speaking.

"The will to dominate is present in all men, as is the will to relate in all women. When men sublimate, consciously sublimate, their desire to dominate, especially women, this energy re-emerges as the will to relate. In this way, getting sex, and getting sex without domination, becomes practically guaranteed. This is especially true if a man is looking to have sex with a woman who is conscious of her own will, and willing to help a man sublimate his desire to dominate. These behaviors are, on both sides, the use of power without violence."

"We have an expectation," the Masculine continued. "We have an expectation that there will be no violence in the getting of sex here. We have that expectation of each of you. Do not, I warn you, disappoint this expectation."

"How does someone learn the sublimation of the will to dominate?" someone behind her asked. Angelica turned and saw a man in his late thirties leaning against the back wall.

"From a teacher who knows the working of it," the Masculine replied.

"That's the internal alchemical exercise he's talking about," the Feminine put her hand out towards him, palm down, to shush him. "There are three things that a man must do. The first is to be trained in that which is neither Creation nor Destruction. The second is to understand and accept the Antecedence of the Feminine. The third is the commitment to serve."

Angelica heard herself speak, but her voice had changed, dropping a register. "What was that?" the Feminine asked. Angelica raised her face to the room and tucked a strand of hair behind one ear. She repeated her question, "Why did the Feminine create the Masculine?"

The Feminine smiled. "That is the question, isn't it? The question will be answered at another time."

"When?" Angelica wanted to know.

"Right time, right place, right people. Right circumstance," the Feminine smiled at Angelica, and the melting sensation returned, except this time focused on her heart. She felt her heart melting, and she started to sway again, a little.

The Masculine indicated that they were to take a break now. There were refreshments in the next room behind the dais. Angelica felt like she had to go outside, stand in the sunlight; stand in the sunlight like it would harden her bones. As she came up by the man leaning against the wall, she looked down, so she didn't see that he was following her with his eyes, not moving his face.

When she thought it was safe, when, as she was passing him and 'saw' that his face wasn't looking at her, she risked taking a glance at him, and instead she met his eyes watching her. She felt a flash of light leap from him to her, felt it and palpably sensed it. It brought her up short. When her vision returned, she saw him smiling, perhaps at her.

He pulled his gaze away and looked toward the Instructors. This freed Angelica to continue moving past him, freed her to go outdoors into the light, a light the same color as the flash that had illumined her scant moments before.

When she stepped out into the sunshine the light hit her first, clearing her mind, and then the heat, clearing her breath. She stepped off the sidewalk onto the grass and sat down. Turning her mind to her breath, she slowly eased herself into slow regular breath. She'd been breathing so tightly and shallowly during the talk that her diaphragm hurt. She directed her attention to that place, willing it to slow and ease and breathe deeply.

She alternated between closing her eyes, registering how she was filling with light and then opening them halfway, taking in the green until her visual field shimmered. She felt light, almost empty and yet, somehow, her mind had a serious set to it. She felt focused, and not hungry. She returned to the studio.

The man who had been leaning against the back wall was nowhere to be seen. The masculine Instructor said, "What we teach here is based on an eight part royal yoga. In this portion of each class session we will practice postures, what are called by some asanas. We will also practice chanting, what are called mantras, and hand postures, otherwise known as mudras. The aim of all these practices is, as you know, to become free of the buffers that keep us from seeing Life as it really is, and each other as we really are. We seek release from these buffers, that we may become free to live Life as it ought to be lived."

The feminine Instructor continued, "Our thoughts, our feelings, our senses, even our awareness, is dulled and altered by these buffers. We, as we are, are diminished, and the energy held behind the buffers we never come to know. When the buffer is overcome our awareness will become different. We are going to try to make sure that everyone experiences a portion of this different kind of awareness, even if only for a moment. This awareness is of the energy of the heart, and it is a different kind of awareness of the heart. It is the next level of awareness closest to us in our daily lives. The buffer that is maintained by the trapped energy keeps us from experiencing our own true heart awareness most of the time, and we want to overcome that at least a little. We will see that this awareness will help us to preserve ourselves in the new subjective reality."

The masculine Instructor stood up and stepped down onto the floor. "So we will begin with doing everyday things in a different way. We will begin with sitting. Everyone make sure you have a stool or a bench, then sit. Sit with your knees in front of you on the floor and your feet behind you with the tops of your feet resting on the floor as well. Now listen."

The feminine Instructor stood up and stepped down to the floor also. "Everyone is different, in fact so different are we, as members of the same species, that we cannot all be expected to attain certain postures and positions. It is difficult for certain people, particularly long-legged people, and, in fact, impossible for some people to get into the sitting position known as the 'Full Lotus' or Padmasana, for example. It is also impossible for some people to get their sacra 'straight,' nor should they try. It is harmful for some. The sacrum in its natural state ranges from almost vertical to almost horizontal, and those who have sacra tending to the horizontal will never be able to get it pointing straight down, even if they should find a way to straighten out their lumbar curve."

"There is no one identical posture that all can attain. Our bodies are too mechanically different," the masculine interjected.

The feminine said, "Yes. But there is an ideal posture that everyone can attain, and that ideal posture is that posture which matches their body type. So we begin with a simple posture that all of you can do, but each of you will do it in a way that accords with your body type. We begin with sitting."

The Instructors walked between the files of students. The masculine picked up the thread. "Each of you rock slowly back and forth on your butts. Don't rock your whole body, just your pelvis, slowly back and forth, finding its full extension and flexion. Notice that you are crossing over your Ischial Tuberosities, your 'Sit Bones'. When you find them, stop. Now, hold your pelvis still and sit up straight with your thorax."

The feminine said, "From this position, rock your pelvis slightly back and forth until most of your weight is either directly on your sit bones, or slightly in front of them. This puts your primary center of gravity in the approximately correct place. Sitting up straight with your thorax puts your secondary center of gravity, located in the center within the heart, in its proper place, above your primary. Holding your pelvis still on its sit bones, rock your upper body slowly back and forth until you can sense this center of gravity moving into place and stop there."

The Instructors moved among the students, helping them with the exercise, adjusting a pelvic tilt on one, and lifting a thorax on another. After everyone more or less had the first two parts, the Instructors spoke again. The feminine began. "As you know, at the top of the spine are the so-called Axis and Atlas vertebrae. There is a column of bone arising from the Axis vertebrae and extending through the Atlas vertebrae called the Odontoid Process. Your third center of gravity is just above where this column of bone ends, in the space just inside your skull."

The masculine finished the instruction. "Slowly stretch your neck left and right. When you sense left/right balance stop and breathe. Then place your forefingers on your neck on either side of your skull just behind the bottom of your ears. Imagine a line running between your fingers. Slowly nod your head forward and back. All the way forward and all the way back. Do this a few times. Come to a stop when you sense half the weight of your head behind that line and half of the weight in front. This is your head on top."

Again, they went around the room, making adjustments. The masculine continued, "Use your eyes to orient yourselves in the room. Look up and down, then left and right." After a few moments had passed, the feminine said, "Close your eyes. Sense this posture." Then, after a pause to allow the students time to complete this task, she said, "Slump. Slouch. Let it go."

The students slumped, and slouched and leaned around, stretching, groaning, letting go of the tension caused by using muscles they were unaccustomed to using.

"Now," the masculine said. "Find the posture again."

When the hour for lunch arrived the class had worked on two sounds, meant to be part of a larger chant. One the vowel short 'o' sound, "Ah", and the other the consonant "Sh" as if 'shushing' someone, working with the breath in different ways while they sounded. The mudra, or hand posture, they practiced was the 'Straightened Hand', accomplished by leaning forward and pressing one hand flat to the floor with the fingers spread, then lifting the hand and holding it with the palm forward, and looking away from it to the other hand, flattening that one while trying to keep the first hand straightened without looking, trying to sense the position of the first hand without looking.

Lunch was light fare; salad, fruits, a deli selection for sandwiches. Angelica had been through the line, refilled her water bottle, and was going outside to sit in the late spring light when Janice caught up with her.

"Hey, mind some company?" Janice asked.

"Not at all," Angelica replied, sitting at a picnic table. "Did you ever get any sleep?" she asked, slyly.

"Eventually. After a late night date with Mr. Digit," she said, holding up her hand, palm forward with only the middle finger extended upward, waving it at Angelica, smirking. "No thanks to you."

Angelica laughed at her. "Hey! At least I let you want me."

Janice's eyes popped open in mock surprise. She couldn't hold the face and soon laughed, too.

After taking a few bites, Angelica asked, "So, what can you tell me about this place? You said you've been here before, right?"

"Right," Janice replied, wiping oil and vinegar from her chin. "Right. This is the third summer. My boss sends me. Sometimes it's this class, sometimes another."

"What other classes do they teach?"

"Different yogas. Tantra. And they have their own kind of martial arts, some mix of different styles with a lot of qi gong work. It's kind of a special school."

"Yeah, I'll say. What do you think of that Feminine Creator stuff they laid out in there?"

Janice paused, choosing her words. "Honestly, Angelica, I think they're probably right. My boss started sending me here because he thinks like these people. He studied here. I started taking classes with him at his studio and one thing led to another, you know?"

Angelica nodded that she did.

"And, when I realized what a good guy he was, and how well he treated me, I just kept going back for more. No possessiveness, in fact, the opposite. I got to keep doing what I wanted, see other guys if I wanted. But the more we talked, hell, the more we fucked, the more I came to believe as he did. It was in everything he said and did, devoted to the Feminine, and devoted to the Feminine in me," she said with emphasis.

Janice paused, then continued, "This is a different kind of school. I think they probably teach more here than they let on."

Angelica nodded that she understood. "Do you know anything about the other people in the class? All the other people I see walking around?"

"I know they seem to have a lot of sex."

"Really? A lot?"

"Yeah. You'll see. I think the whole second hour for lunch—what do they call it, 'Rest'?—is just a cover for 'Go find somebody to fuck for an hour'."

Angelica startled herself with her sharp laugh. "Unexpected," she said.

"Yeah, that's how I felt. It was unexpected. You can smell it. It's everywhere here. It'll make you horny. It made me. Most of the people in the class already seem to be hooked up, but I always find one or two of the staff, the interns who work here."

"One or two?" Angelica asked.

"Well, three or four maybe." Then with a grin, Janice leaned forward conspiratorially, "Maybe I should have said, "One or two at a time, once or twice.""

Angelica clapped her hand to her mouth and leaned back. "Seriously?"

"Seriously," Janice whispered across the table, grinning wickedly, still leaning forward. "It was great."

"Wow," Angelica shook her head.

They paused in their conversation to take a couple thoughtful forkfuls. Then Angelica said, "What about the Instructors?"

"Carol and Bob? They're pretty great. A little too serious, but then this is serious stuff. If things go wrong a person could get pretty messed up. But they talk like they can handle it."

"Do you think they're involved?"

"You mean, like, with each other?"

Angelica nodded.

"No, no I don't think so. I mean, I look, you know? They don't have that way about them. They don't incline toward each other. Know what I mean?"

"You mean, like, leaning toward each other?"

"Yeah, in that way that lovers do. It's like they bend toward each other, sometimes in subtle ways. Yeah, like that. I don't see them doing that, and they're so close to each other all the time I think I'd see it."

"And what about that guy who came in and stood in the back?"

"What guy?"

"Kind of tall, dark hair, looked to be late thirties."

"All his hair or was he losing some?"

"Looked like he had it all. Heavy about the chest and shoulders. Brown eyes."

"I think he's the one they call The Foreman," Janice said. "I think his name might be Marcus. He's responsible for all the maintenance of the buildings and the grounds. There's tractors and mowers over in the Quonsets. There's a whole crew who lives here and works here, the Interns, whose job it is to keep the place up. They alternate between working and taking classes."

"Where do they stay?"

"Here. In the Barn." Janice pointed. "The whole second story is bedrooms. Mostly doubles."

"Really? There must be 50 people here."

"Yup. Maybe a few more. They pack 'em in. Don't forget there's the third floor up in the Mansion. A lot of the senior people, like Marcus, have a room there. We're on the fourth floor probably because there isn't room down here for us."

"Well, besides sex, what do they all do around here? No TV, no internet."

"You mean in the evenings? There's more classes. There's meetings, and music, and reading. Sometimes people just hang out and talk. What do you think people did in the old days?"

"Well, I mean, not even a movie on Friday nights?"

"Nope. This isn't summer camp, you know? But there is a Friday night social."

"That'll be interesting. What kind of music?"

"Well, different nights it's different things. Sometimes it's just pick-up, other times it's practice. They're big on drums here; the Interns have to learn it. Other percussion. Some woodwinds. High and low, even didjeries."

"We can sit in?"

"Sometimes, for parts of it. There's even dancing on some nights. We can certainly go listen. It's how I singled out the Interns I went with. I just sat there, watched how they moved their bodies, and looked for a chance to talk to them. Once, I even got one on his way out the door, and he came with me that night. Man," Janice let the memory overcome her for a moment. "Man, what control."

"Control, you mean like in the power without domination they were talking about this morning?"

"Sort of. What he had was self-control. He had me coming the first time in less than a minute. He had me going like he wasn't going to come at all. In the end I had to almost beg him. I needed him to, like I'd needed nobody else to fill me to the finish ever before. And he relented."

"Relented?"

"Yes. He relented. It was power without domination. He said something in the end, whispered it in my ear. I'm still not sure I heard it right. He said, 'For the boon of you.' Who uses words like 'boon' anymore?"

"Wow. Umm, I don't know what to say."

"Neither did I, except 'Thank you, thank you, thank you. It's usually the other way round, don'tcha know."

"Yeah, I know," Angelica said. "The other way round."

They stopped talking then, wanting to eat and be thoughtful; Janice with her memories, Angelica with her musings.

They were coming to the end of the first hour of their lunch break. Angelica asked Janice what she wanted to do. Janice said, "Take a nap, I think. I'd hit on you, but I know you're just 'letting me want you'," getting snarky again with the quote. Janice smiled, and Angelica grinned.

"Yeah, you were up late," she said. "You can always get a date with Mr. Digit, you know."

"Yeah," Janice snarked back. "But you be careful. You won't always be able to get a date with Miss Tongue."

"Oooo," Angelica grinned. "Touchy. Well, no, not touchy exactly. More like licky."

"Oh, enough," Janice said, standing up and waving her hands. "I'm too tired for you. I'm going into the classroom and crash on a mat. If I'm lying on my belly, leave me alone. And you'll find out. You'll find out what it's like around here. You'll see. Come knock on my door some night, and I'll show you."

Janice went on into the Barn, taking Angelica's lunch plate with her. Angelica sat and stared off into the distance, scanning the up slopes into the different vales, studying the great rocks of what the site map had called Snake's Knob. She allowed her eyes to rest on the cool dark green of the Pine Eye. Her vision fuzzed and she closed her eyes. Her body remembered the melting state she experienced in class and she started to sway, so she climbed up on the picnic tabletop and lay on her back in the sunshine. She folded her hands over her belly and fell asleep quickly, sinking into some diffuse state of being.

She dreamed almost immediately. She was running along a trail in the woods, running easily, with a small pack on her back and over her shoulders. She was heading into the rocky land on Snake's Knob ridge. Just ahead she saw an odd zigzag stick across the trail. As she drew close she saw its mottled color and realized it was a snake pretending to be a stick. She thought about stopping but decided to leap over the snake instead. She hurdled it, extending her back leg almost parallel to the ground.

When she landed she ran a few more steps. Then she stopped, turned around and walked back to the snake, curious.

The snake had coiled in the trail, facing her, scanning the air with its tongue. Her vision fuzzed again and the snake suddenly appeared very close to her. She refocused and realized she'd stopped too close to the snake, and had actually bent down on one knee to get a closer look. The snake was rattling. She saw the pattern, the wide jawed head, and realized she'd made a grave mistake.

She knew the snake would strike, knew she was too big and too close to avoid it, and her life might depend on what she did next.

She became a snake, narrow and flat on the ground. The rattler struck and missed her, aiming for where the human had been. Snake Angelica withdrew into a coil and contemplated the rattler for a moment. There was a moment of recognition, without words. Then a moment of decision that was pure impulse. She uncoiled and slid along the ground towards the rattler. The rattler turned and moved off the trail in the direction it had been originally heading. Snake Angelica allowed herself to slide over its vanishing tail.

She allowed herself the full sensation, snake sliding on snake. Then suddenly she was in a well of snakes, all sliding on each other, immersed in the sensation of touch so completely that she became afraid her awareness would be lost in sensation. She came awake with a gasp.

In the Mansion, Madeleine came awake with the same gasp from the same sensation, snapping back from the touch of countless snakes slithering around and over each other in the cistern. "Bull snake," Madeleine wondered aloud. "How did she know it would drive a rattler away?"

Angelica sat up on the tabletop, hugging herself, cool even in the sunshine. She breathed, looking around for the sun. She saw a wall on the Barn kitchen that was completely in the sunshine. She went over and crouched down, leaning against it, letting the block wall warm her back. She closed her eyes again, reviewing the dream, remembering it so it would stay fixed in her mind. A bell rang, signaling the time to return to class.

PART 2 AFTERNOON

Angelica rose from her spot against the wall, went around the building and in the foyer entrance to the Studio space. People were assembling and she found her original spot and stool and sat down. Janice was just rolling over, and sitting up. She let down her hair and shook it out, then pulled it up on top again.

Janice looked around for Angelica and smiled when she saw her, getting up and taking a place next to Angelica. Angelica felt into that, felt it was OK, but resolved to speak to Janice if her energy became too distracting. Angelica was here for more than witty dialogue about unsuccessful seduction.

When the class resumed most of the students were in fresh clothes, some had showered even. It was obvious to Angelica that many of the people had been having sex, and not at all obvious who had been having sex with whom.

Janice leaned over and said, "See?"

Carol and Bob came in, talking to each other, and assumed the same seats, Carol in front, Bob behind her and to the side.

"Sit," Carol said. "Rows and files."

"Except this time," Bob added, "Sit forward on your stools so that your sit bones are on the front edge and your genitalia are over the edge, situated in free space. You'll understand why later."

The Instructors looked around the room with their eyes narrowed and faces relaxed, scanning. When they saw some who were still working on sitting properly they got up and walked around touching one in the mid back, another on the sacrum, several on the head, adjusting their postures. When they returned to the dais and resumed their seats they sighed in unison and settled in to sit. The Feminine said, "Sense your Centers of gravity."

Angelica allowed herself to sink into her low belly, sensing her lowest center of gravity, rocking slightly. Then she sensed her second and third centers, rocking. It occurred to her that she should be trying to feel the centers to see what emotions might come up, as well as relax her mind and pay attention to any images that came.

She withdrew her senses from the room; she no longer heard even Janice's breathing. She focused on the lowest center and suddenly she could smell the sex. Her clitoris twitched. Then it started to move. She could feel warmth and blood fill her pubis and swell. It made her vagina wet and her clitoris seemed to be slipping out of its hood. She thought to herself 'That's enough sensation for now'.

Aroused, she drew her awareness up to the next Center, her heart, and sensed it beating, tracking it. Then she became aware of another pulse, perhaps an echoing pulse of blood in her arousal. Her clitoris pulsed with the same rhythm as her heart. The sensation was great and she knew that she couldn't focus on it without getting wetter and maybe even orgasming a little; she was afraid that she would make a sound and that then everyone would know.

So she pulled her awareness up to her third center, past her heart to the base of her skull, letting her awareness rest there. The pulse of her heart pooled there, then. She felt herself smiling. Then her awareness of hearing suddenly returned and she could hear the people in the room breathing. Some were breathing hard, almost panting. She could hear Janice's stool creaking ever so slightly as the young woman rocked on her stool and struggled to hold still. She suddenly realized that several of the people, both men and women, were caught in a web of arousal. She laughed out loud, suddenly, a short string of hahaha's and opened her eyes. She heard Janice snort.

When she opened her eyes she saw that the Instructors were looking at her, smiling. They sighed in unison and the Feminine said, "Enough" to the class. They looked at different people, and watched the class. Several men and a few women adjusted their underwear, squirming. A few people actually reached inside their pants and moved things around.

The Instructors sat there, smiling, watching all this, and the Masculine said, "Now you understand why you were instructed to sit as you are."

The Feminine said, "Yes, but do you really understand why? Do you really understand what just happened here? This is the first of the things we do here, it is the first of our pro-active engagements with the world around us and the world within us. We seek to understand, and we practice this seeking. What do you think happened?"

"You cast a spell on us," someone said, provoking laughter. "You manipulated the field," said someone else.

"We did nothing," the Masculine said. "So what do you think happened?"

"Entrainment," Angelica said.

"Say more," the Feminine said, leaning forward.

"It started with the unusual position. Everybody's awareness was shifted to their sex. It was a new position and the mind was noting the novelty," she paused.

"Go on," said the Masculine, smiling.

"OK. And then there was the smell," Angelica said, hesitating again.

"What smell?" someone said.

"The smell of sex. Some of you had sex after lunch. Maybe sex instead of lunch. The smell of it goes all over the room. Suddenly all of us were reminded of sex."

"Perhaps even more than that," the Masculine said. "In our olfactory system there are odors of which we are conscious, and odors of which we are unconscious, including some pheromones and other large molecules. This sensing can influence our behavior as well as supply information."

"Really?" someone asked.

"Wow. Unconscious influence, eh? Wow," someone else said

"OK. And what then?" the Feminine asked Angelica.

"It all contributed to entrainment. When we started breathing together that was the last element. Our senses and our feelings aligned with each other, and then our awarenesses did, too. That's all it took. Then it was like tall grass in a breeze. If one moves one way then pretty soon the others are moving that way, too, under the influence of the wind. Back and forth the field moved us until we were all entrained with each other. Then the power of it built, one feeling or sensation pulling other awarenesses after it," Angelica replied.

"What would have happened eventually?" the Feminine asked her.

"Eventually? We'd have all been aroused. Some of us would have had orgasms," she said.

Someone said, "Ick." Someone else said, "Sloppy."

"And what about the energy pattern?"

"Oh. I see. In a closed space it would have started swirling. Could have formed a whirlwind, I guess. I don't think I know what might have happened then." Angelica finished.

There was a momentary silence while the class took that in.

Then the Masculine said, "Imagine what could happen if, instead of sex, the dominant feeling in the room was one of fear, or rage. Imagine."

After a moment the Masculine said, "This is one of those phenomena we seek to understand: influences on us of which we are normally unconscious."

The Feminine said, "Things normally don't happen so quickly at this intensity. Usually it takes a few days before the class builds up enough energy for psychic phenomena of this order to occur. What else could have caused this?"

"Hypnotism, maybe induced by neuro-linguistic programming," someone else up near the front said. Angelica recognized him as Max from the previous evening in the kitchen. With this recognition she remembered the sensations from their experiment with Del, and her entire skin suddenly came alive as one organ of sensation. She could feel the different fields she had felt the night before; not just sensation but whole categories of sensation.

Suddenly, she found herself sensing the room in three fields. She felt Janice, felt her swollen root and giddy top, felt the fields on the back of the man in front of her. He turned around and looked at her, but she didn't see him. She extended her sensation to other people in the room feeling the energies roll like clouds around the students. Beyond them she saw the Instructors, columns of golden lights stacked up on each other, and a golden lotus flower open above each of their heads supported on two silver threads spiraling cylindrically from the floor below them. Sitting on each flower was a small image, one Feminine, one Masculine. The Masculine was looking at her intently. Then the Feminine turned her gaze to Angelica, and smiled. Angelica heard the words from Feminine image, "Too soon."

Then Angelica's mind exploded in pain. All her sensation turned into pain. She felt she was bleeding from her gut. She went rigid, her breath coming in hyperventilating gasps. Her vision went black and she felt herself falling. The man in front of her, turned around already watching her, fell forward toward her. He caught her as Janice came off her stool and reached out.

Her first awareness on return was of the rustling of leaves in the treetops, and a tactile sense of the warmth of the afternoon. She then became aware of lying on a line of pillows, with hands and fingertips at her temples, pulsing. Then she felt someone at her feet, her legs on a pillow and her feet pressed into flesh, a man's belly, she realized, also pulsing.

Angelica opened her eyes, looked up, and saw Carol's face inclined to her, eyes closed, smiling. "What happened?" she asked.

Carol opened her eyes, too. "You saw Her. You heard Her. Too soon. Are you OK now?"

"Yes, I think so. Let me sit up."

She pulled her feet from Bob's lap, sat up, and rolled to her knees, sitting on her heels. She felt firm, solid, her senses normal and steady. She sighed. "Yes, I'm OK." She looked around, saw the class standing in a circle around her. Rather than be embarrassed, she smiled at them. In a second, almost beyond her control, she started to beam at them, flashing her teeth, exuding gratitude. They smiled back. "Too soon," she said. Suddenly she rose up, moving smoothly from her knees to her feet, unfolding, and came completely into a steady stand. "Let's go back to work."

"Yes, let's," Carol said, coming smoothly to her feet in the same way.

"You demonstrate the next principle of active engagement with the world. Perseverance. In all things, especially inquiry into the nature of the esoteric, the arcane, and the mysterious, we endeavor to persevere." She turned to the circle of students. "Do you all understand? This is the exemplification of perseverance. Now go sit."

When she looked around, Angelica realized that she had been lying on a line of pillows set up for her by the open window. She must have been carried there. She glanced up at the trees, tops blowing in a breeze, hearing the sound that called her back. As she turned her head to look back at the class, she saw the flash of something that looked like a person, a woman with thick straight red-blonde hair standing on the leaves of the tree tops, dancing with the wind. She looked back and image was gone.

The class returned to their seats, as did the Instructors. The Masculine spoke. "So that is our second principle of pro-active engagement. Perseverance. The third principle for action is the Pursuit of Perfection of the Higher Self, and the development of Conscience. What does this mean?"

No one spoke. It was as if they weren't ready to return to work, as if their minds were still distracted by the breeze in the tree tops. They settled slowly, becoming clear. When they were still, the Instructor asked again. "What does this mean?"

Still nothing from the students. Angelica watched, and said nothing. This was not a subject she knew much about.

The Feminine began. "It means, initially at least, that we, each of us, are two people. If I posit the existence of a Higher Self I am implying that there is a Lower Self. And if I posit the possibility of the development of Conscience I am implying that there is an absence of development of Conscience. Consider, then, what this means for you." She gave them time to consider it.

"There is nothing wrong with the Lower Self," she continued. "It is simply your everyday Self, and you need it to get along every day. It handles things and carries your awareness around all day so you can do whatever the machine needs; eat, breathe, feel what passes for feelings, think what passes for thoughts. It's what makes you look both ways before you cross the street. It's what keeps you from being run over. But it's also what keeps you asleep to the reality of the Higher Self, the True Self, the full awareness that is yours if you are willing to work on yourself.

"And your Conscience is undeveloped because your Everyday Self doesn't need it to function. In fact, it would probably get in the way. An Awake Person, awake in their Higher Self, would never do many of the things we do every day; the small crimes that would be against Conscience, like rubbernecking at an accident on the highway, or passing a beggar on the street without recognizing their existence. And this would interfere with our everyday sense of ourselves. A Conscience would not let us pretend that another human did not exist."

She stopped. Some people in the class were blushing. Others, including Janice, had quiet tears running down their cheeks. Angelica simply watched. Then she felt out into the room, keeping her eyes open but not seeing. What she felt was that the class was in a very tender place. The idea occurred to her that this was deliberate on the part of the Instructors. It made her curious as to what they would do with the tenderness: treat it tenderly or harshly? The answer came quickly.

"Hey!" the Masculine shouted at the class. "Hey! Knock it off! Your self-pity over your past sins is useless here. Pity those you have wronged!"

That was all it took. Almost everyone in the class broke into open weeping. Angelica watched, almost serene.

Into the trough after the first wave of grief both Instructors said in unison, "Now that is the function of Conscience."

Some laughed out loud, some redoubled their sobbing briefly. Others wiped their noses on their hands, and wiped their hands on their pants. Angelica smiled at something, but she didn't know quite why. An inner voice said, "The human condition," to which Angelica had a reaction. She jerked slightly and out loud sounded, "Hmp."

Janice looked at her sideways, wiping her nose on the back of her hand.

"What?" Janice asked.

Angelica replied, "This. The human condition."

Janice "Oh" and nodded like she understood, but Angelica could feel that she didn't understand. She decided against saying anything more, preferring to leave ambiguity intact and let Janice think whatever she would.

When Angelica looked back at the dais to see what was next both Instructors were looking at her, not smiling, but looking to discern. The Feminine spoke. "Which brings us to the fourth principle of pro-active engagement in the world: The use of ritual to access and cultivate a relationship with the Divine. We will engage in ritual later, under different circumstances. For now, understand this: there are, under normal conditions, four kinds of time and space. These are the Profane, the Mundane, the Sacred, and the Divine. Your Everyday Self goes through the world in Mundane time and space. Sometimes we come into contact with the Profane, sometimes the Sacred. Sometimes we are so unaware in the Mundane that we don't even recognize the presence of either the Profane or the Sacred.

"About the Profane, you need to know nothing at the moment. But you do need to know that by using ritual to access Sacred time and space you give yourself a platform from which to access the Divine."

The Masculine took up the instructions. "There is a fifth principle of pro-active engagement with the world. We will withhold this principle for now. What I want you to spend the rest of the afternoon thinking about is a simple question: Why would anyone want to wake up? Or have a Conscience? Or why would anyone want to leave the Mundane and its comforts and learn the initially difficult practices of the Sacred?"

The Feminine said, "Now take a break. Go blow your noses and wash your hands."

Angelica stood and went out the back. She took a seat on the edge of the porch and put her feet out in the grass. After a short while Bob came out and sat down beside her. Angelica felt a quieting presence emanate from him, no changing interactions in the fields. She returned her attention to the grass under her feet. After a moment she asked him, "Will that happen again?"

"Maybe," he replied.

"Why was it so painful?" she wanted to know.

"Because it was too soon. Because you weren't ready yet. Too much sensation overwhelmed your nervous system. Too much energy was running through the pathways, like too much water in a pipe. The pipe can expand if it has enough time. The pain was the water pushing on the pipe walls."

"I'm not sure if I can do it again. That was too much. And this is only the first day. Is every session going to be like this?"

"No. But you can learn to manage your sensation and energy levels. There are things that you can use around you, like your feet in the grass. And inside you there are 'valves', I guess you could say. You don't have to open them all the way. You can keep them closed, either partially or totally. But you're not here to keep them totally closed. You came here to learn how to control things that were probably already happening to you."

Angelica nodded, wondering how he knew. "So tell me about these valves."

"There are different kinds for different kinds of energy. Air and water are very different substances. Magnetism and electricity are very different kinds of substances, so there are different things that control their motion and flow."

"How many?"

"Well, we'll see. In your body you have your diaphragms. The first one you know about—that one that controls your breath. It's why we start there. In addition there's the pelvic floor, the thoracic outlet, and the tentorium. And your senses are valves. So are the chakras, the wheels, and there are different kinds of those."

"How do I stop the pain?"

"Prevent it in the first place. Establish boundaries. Develop Will by learning control over yourself. You can withdraw awareness from anything in an emergency."

"But I could die!"

"Yes, you could."

After he let that sink in, Bob said, "Awareness requires a surrounding form to become Self-Aware." He paused. "Tomorrow we will do an exercise in withdrawal from sensation. I think you know how to do this already. It is why you blacked out. The thing is, we don't want to do that. That is a reflex that happens when certain things get out of control. If we can learn control, we don't black out, and we don't die."

They returned to class. The Feminine was waiting on the dais. When enough people were in the room she said, "Sit. Breathe. Just breathe normally for a while. Settle."

After a few minutes Bob said, "We move. We move quickly between a start point and a stop point, usually without paying much attention to the movement itself. Today we pay attention to all of it. Notice where you are right now. Are your centers of gravity lined up? Now, slowly lean forward until your head touches the floor. Rest there and notice the new location. What effects do you observe?"

After space for 8 breaths, Bob said, "Rise. Come back to your initial position, paying attention along the entire way. Sit."

Carol spoke. "Well, y'all certainly did that every which way. Some of you bent at the waist. Others used your arms. Your heads were on the mat this way, that way, no way. So we do it again. Sit. Genitals over the edge. Spread your knees so they make more of a triangle with your feet instead of parallel lines. Find your centers of gravity. Sense the line of it. Put your hands on your hips.

"Now, lean forward at the hip, not at the waist. Keep the line straight as you slowly—paying attention completely—lean forward. All the way forward, putting your forehead on the floor. Sense the floor. Now sense your backs, and then your backsides.

"Now, what feelings does this position bring up?"

Someone, a woman, said "Oh…my…gawd."

"You OK?" Carol asked.

"I'm vulnerable here."

Someone else started crying.

"Enough!" Carol said. "Sit up. Come back as slowly as you can, keeping the line if you can. Don't use your arms, keep your hands on your hips!" They sat up. Carol went over to the woman who was weeping. Angelica could see that some of the men were wiping their faces again.

Bob said, "What was it like being vulnerable? Good or bad?"

Carol, who had reached the crying woman and put her hands on her shoulders, asked the class, "If you were vulnerable behind, what were you in your head, down there, on the floor?"

The woman started crying harder, put her hands to her face and folded forward, sobbing. Carol got down on her hands and knees next to her ear. "Do you know why you're crying?"

The woman nodded.

"Are you remembering something?"

Again the woman nodded.

"Something that happened to you?"

Again the nod.

"Are you OK with what's happening to you? Do you want to move through this?"

"Yes, yes," she said. "Please help me."

Carol reached around behind her and pulled out the stool, gesturing for the man behind to take it away. "Roll over on your side," Carol said. To someone else she said, "Bring me a pillow."

Bob had stood up and was herding the class into a loose circle around the two on the floor. Angelica and Janice stood in the back of group. Janice reached out and took Angelica's hand. Angelica allowed her. Janice was already weeping silently, tears dripping onto her cheekbones. Angelica watched the Instructors.

Carol leaned over the woman's ear again and said, "So, here you are, lying on the floor, curled into a ball. You were younger than you are now. Something happened, something bad that you didn't like. It pushed on you, and it pushed you into this place, where you are right now. It pushed you here. What do you want to do? Do you want to stay here like this? Yes?"

The woman, in a small voice, said "Yes."

"Yes, yes you want to, but you know you can't stay here. So what do you have to do to get out of here? Remember, it pushed you. What do you have to do?"

"Push back," the woman said.

"That's right, you have to push back. So that's what I want you to do." Putting one hand against the woman's back, she said, "Push back."

The woman pushed tentatively against Carol's hand. Carol signaled people in the circle to come forward and put their hands up near, but not touching, the woman's back. Carol leaned forward and whispered again, "Push back."

The woman did, and quickly encountered the hands of the others, resisting her push. Carol coached her through getting to her hands and knees, weeping and screaming and shouting, the people in the circle alternately weeping or shouting encouragement. Then, eventually, the woman stood up, reclaiming herself with a final cry of "Get OFF Me!"

After beaming her triumph around the circle, the woman stood still.

Carol, standing beside her, said to her, "You OK now? Breathe. You OK?" The woman nodded. "Good," Carol said. "What's your name, hon?" knowing full well what it was.

"Joy," the woman replied.

"That's right, Joy. Now Joy, I'd like you to pick two people from the circle to go sit with you for a few minutes over against the wall. I want you to pick one of them as a man who can serve as your Protector. I want you to breathe, and share any impressions you have with the other one, your Friend. Then come back over when you're ready."

She picked two, and Bob gave her a blanket in case she got cold. They went over by the wall and the man sat a few feet from her with his back toward her, facing outward to the class while the woman sat down next to her.

Then Carol said, "Sit." And the class went back to their stools. When they were seated, she said, "Does everyone understand what just happened?" There was no response from the class.

Bob said, "She pushed the imprint of an oppressor out of her body, her feelings and thoughts, and her energy. Perhaps it was a bully, perhaps worse."

"A rapist," Joy called in from the wall. "A gawdamn motherfucking rapist."

"That's anger. That's the next piece of work. Can you hang on to it or do you need to deal with it now?" Bob asked.

"I can hang on to it. I want to feel it. I want to eat anger," Joy growled.

"Good," Bob said.

Carol added, "There will be more work that will be needed to be done, but it is not necessary at this time. Thank you all for your help and support." She nodded at most of the group, looking at all of them, raising an eyebrow when her glance fell on Angelica.

Angelica couldn't make up her mind whether or not to acknowledge Carol's implicit question; doing nothing or nodding back that she was OK. She decided to simply break eye contact and look down. She felt that should convey enough information about her internal state. She was beginning to feel disconnected from the class, from the Instructors. Her internal dialogue was starting to go something along the lines of "This is too much. Too much weirdness. Too much information. Too much suffering" and when she got to that final word she had to stifle the urge to sob. She simply wanted to move on with the postures.

"Alright then," Carol said. "We do it again. Except this time you are to use your arms to form a rest in front of you. Use your thumbs and forefingers to make a triangle, like so," she showed them. "When you come to the end of the bow, which is the name of this posture, let your forehead rest in the triangle."

On the dais, Carol assumed the position as an example. Bob walked around the class, spreading knees, lifting butts, spreading elbows until the forearms were continuations of the triangle. Carol raised her head and said, "Now, arch your backs, and slowly draw your thorax back until your elbows touch your knees. Rest there."

Bob, still moving around the group, said, "What feelings come up in this position?"

"Why do you ask about feelings and not sensation?" Angelica asked, a little irritated.

Bob replied, "So, irritation. That's a feeling, isn't it? Or is it a sensation?"

Angelica sighed audibly, choosing to pay attention to herself, her sensations, feelings, and thoughts all on her own, and withdrew into herself.

It wasn't long before someone spoke, "Again, I feel vulnerable," a man said.

"Me, too," said a woman.

Suddenly someone farted. A few others giggled.

Bob said, "So, who else is sensing the need to fart? Go ahead and do it."

Two more people farted in quick succession. Then a third, taking his time. Then someone else farted and this one sounded wet. Two more farted, one of whom had been among the first to fart.

Bob, in mock dismay, standing among the farters with their butts in the air, many of whom were now laughing, "Oh no! My unconscious mind is being assailed by large pheromonal molecules! I can't detect them! What is happening to my unconscious mind? My nose is under assault, too! I'm feeling faint!" He collapsed on the floor. "The air is better down here. Nothing but feet," he mock confided to the woman closest to him.

By this time everyone, and including Angelica, who had found that she couldn't withdraw with all the outgassing, was laughing.

Except Carol. "Get it out, y'all," Carol said, seriously. "Get it out. You can't relax into a posture if you're squeezing it in. Or squeezing it out. Farting is allowed here. By the way, this posture? This asana? It's called the gas-assana." She couldn't keep a straight face anymore, and started laughing herself.

Angelica, in the midst of laughing, found herself watching herself laugh. Her awareness was somehow disassociated from the part of herself that was laughing. This disassociated part didn't think it was at all funny. It wasn't judgmental about the laughter—that would have been a different part of herself that she could go to if necessary. But this part, this split off part, just wasn't interested in fart jokes. As near as she could tell, it was interested in the posture, the asanas, and exploring what would happen in terms of different sensation and feeling.

Then she realized it was mostly interested in sensation. Sensation seemed real compared to feeling. Warmth and coolness, stretch and rest, inhale and exhale. Pay attention, she told herself, to odd sensations, energetic flows from one place to another. Let feelings go off into the pot of chaos that seemed to be filled with not just her feelings, but the feelings of those around her. She felt she didn't have the boundary control to protect herself from that. And if feelings were a pot of chaos, thinking threatened to become a maelstrom of madness. She didn't want to think either.

Her split off awareness was calmly disinclined to think, and she felt content to identify with it.

Bob got to his feet and sniffed the air. "Air raid over," he said. "All clear."

Carol continued with the instruction. "Now drop you butts until you're in neutral, neither straining to raise them up nor force them down. Rest here for some breaths." She paused, waiting and watching while the class made the adjustment.

Carol said, "Now slowly, slowly, tuck your butt under and arch your mid back toward the sky. Then return to neutral" Again, she watched and waited. "Now do it again. When you have done this two more times, for a total of four, extend the posture back to the original, with your back arched toward the floor and your butt up in the air. Then go through the full range of positions, slowly, six times. Slow your breathing so that each rise is one inhale and each fall one exhale. "When everyone had flexed their hips in this way for the required number of times Carol said, "Rest".

After a brief period she said, "Hook your toes into extension and place them bottoms down on the floor. Slowly push back and come to a squatting position. Spread your feet if you have to. Rotate your legs if you have to. I want your heels on the floor."

Bob said, "This is a mandatory position for you to master. In other countries people are able to do this their entire lives; it is the position for elimination. If you can't do this your guts don't work right."

Carol continued, "Keep your torsos forward, bring your shoulders in front of your knees. Now, shift side to side." Then after a time she said, "Now rotate your hips clockwise." This continued for several circles, then Carol said, "Now counter clockwise."

Bob said, "This is joint lubrication." Some in the class groaned with the effort. Not everyone could do it; some fell backwards.

After several cycles Carol told them to rest. "Sit on your stools but keep your feet under you and your knees in the squatting position. Rest there. You can put your hands or elbows on your knees, and rest."

Bob came back to the dais and conversed quietly with Carol. He stepped back and Carol said, "Sit. On your stools, knees down. Resume what we call the 'Sit' position."

Bob said, "Find your centers of gravity. Rock your pelvis, stop when you find the first one. Then your thorax, then your head. Stop when you have them." Some people found them quickly, others took more time, slowly rocking back and forth. When all had stopped, Bob and Carol moved through the group again, making adjustments. They arrived at Angelica at the same time, standing on either side. Angelica watched them with her peripheral vision.

Carol, from Angelica's right side, got down on one knee, putting a hand on her low back and moving it slightly forward, tilting her into more of an arch. Angelica felt her mass begin redistributing itself toward her perineum. It felt as if her pelvis was spreading.

Bob put his hands lightly on either side of her thorax one in front, one in back. "Make the space between my hands greater with every breath." The effort put a natural rhythm of tilting forward and back in her pelvis, rocking her perineum on the stool; forward on the inhale, back on the exhale. Where they touched her she felt little sparks of energy

Angelica's awareness turned inward, sensing her own motions and losing awareness of the Instructors' hands. She heard the rustle of their clothes as they walked away and returned their attention to the room.

Arriving back at the dais, Carol sat, Bob remained standing and said, "Bring your feet forward and your knees up to the last position you were in, keeping the line of your centers of gravity straight. Hands on your knees, for now, lean forward at the hip not the waist, keeping the line straight, and come to a stand."

When this was done, Carol said, "Keeping the same distance between your feet, step forward. Rocking back and forth at the ankle, check your line."

"Unlock your knees," Bob said. "Just out of lock is top dead center. Find that spot."

Carol got up again and they walked through the group, checking positions, working often with the students' head positions.

"It's hard," one woman said about getting her head on top.

"Yes, it is," Carol said. "Women have been trained to keep their faces down. It's a deference posture in primates. But you must keep your faces forward to the world. You must learn how to do it. Put your face down only when it serves you in the moment. We are not supposed to walk around like that, and talk to each other like that, all the time, especially when women are talking to men."

The woman Joy, having rejoined the class during the Sit, started laughing out loud. Others joined her. Angelica closed her eyes to better sense the balances, and a kind of ecstasy began pouring over her, head first, like she was standing under a water fall. Bob noticed scintillations in the light around Angelica and, catching Carol's eye, nodded toward Angelica. Angelica started laughing and shaking herself in the flow of the energy. Several people in the class turned toward her; others seemed lost in their own ecstasy.

Angelica heard Carol's voice as if she was standing right next to her as her shaking calmed to shivers. Carol said, "This is the baseline with which we should daily go through life."

Bob said, "This simple joy is our birthright, which has been lost to us and to which we have returned. You need only stand up straight to begin to recover it."

"Unlock your knees," Carol said. "Rock back and forth from your ankles, keeping the line."

When everyone more or less had the posture, Carol nodded at Bob, and Bob said, "Sit."

Everyone returned to their stools and found the sitting position. "Bow," Bob said. And they did. One breath later he said, "Arch down." Another breath and he said, "Arch up." Then he said, "Neutral."

Carol said, "Come into the squat." There was some awkwardness as people moved their stools back.

Bob said, "Next time we come into the bow come a little farther forward from the stools."

Carol continued, "Rock side to side. Eight times." Then, "Circle clockwise eight times, then counterclockwise eight times. Then sit."

There were sounds of breathing hard, then calming breath as the students sat again and found their line.

Then Bob said, "Stand." The students swung their feet forward and came standing in many different ways. Bob told them, "Tomorrow we will work on how to do that.

When they had all stood still and upright for a moment, Carol said, "Finish."

There was an audible exhale and visible slumping and shaking of shoulders.

Bob said, "Time to go get ready for dinner."

PART 3 EVENING

The class broke up, people going up to one another and conversing; Bob and Carol talking to each other in the front, then turning to students who came up to speak to them. Now that she was looking closely, Angelica started recognizing faces in the class. In addition to Max, she recognized Emmalia and Jackson from the Gate House when she arrived. As she looked, her vision seemed to have developed a clarifying effect. She was recognizing new detail: a man who needed to shave, a woman who had not washed her hair in a of couple days. The smell of bodies in the room began to grow acute, and threatened to overwhelm her.

She started to breathe shallowly, through her mouth. Janice turned to her and said, "Don't wait for me. I brought a change of clothes with me this morning. I'm going to eat down here with some friends from before. Then I'm going to stay for the evening. There's a poetry reading after supper. Don't wait up for me." She winked. "I may be a little late getting in."

Angelica was surprised by her contrasting emotions. She was a little offended that Janice was abandoning her, and offended also that Janice didn't invite her along, as if Janice were somehow assuming that she wouldn't like poetry. In contrast, she also felt relief to be free of Janice for a while and have some time to herself.

She realized that the smell was suddenly making her claustrophobic, so she smiled and shrugged. Turning, she grabbed her pack, put her cap on her head and left the room without looking around again, and without looking back.

Janice stepped to the window and watched her go. She waited until Angelica reached the edge of the lawn and disappeared into the woods, down the path to the footbridge. Janice picked up her stuff and went down the hall to the Manager's Office, where Eva Gardner was waiting for her, sitting in the office chair.

Janice knocked. Eva swung around and motioned her to come in. Eva asked, "So how did she do today?"

Janice recounted the events of the day, Eva nodding and saying "Good, good" or asking questions for more detail. Janice was at the point in the story where Angelica fainted when Carol appeared at the door behind her. Taking a seat, she listened as Janice continued the tale. When she'd finished with that episode, Eva turned to Carol and asked, "What do you think she saw? What was 'Too soon'?"

Carol explained, "Well, when we got to her, she was completely de-polarized. We repolarized her and she woke up and seemed able to participate in everything. Bob went out to talk to her on the break and she complained about how painful it was."

"That's it?" Eva asked. "Painful? Nothing else?"

"Nothing else, according to Bob. Nothing about what she sensed, or saw, or felt."

"Well, what did Bob say to her?" Janice asked.

Carol and Eva startled a bit, almost as if they had forgotten her. Carol answered, "He told her that she had to grow her capacity for large amounts of sensation and perception. He told her that her nervous system got overwhelmed. She seemed to accept that as an answer."

Eva pressed the issue, "What was "Too soon," do you think?"

"I don't know," Carol replied. "She was staring at me, staring at us. I know she saw something, but I don't know what. The Goddess spoke through me, seeing her also. It was the Goddess who said, 'Too soon.' So she saw something, but I don't know what."

"So, she saw something it was too soon for her to see." Eva stated.

"Yes, as far as I can tell. Perhaps the Seeress can see more." Carol concluded.

"So, go on then, Janice. Finish the tale of the day."

Janice described the rest of the afternoon, and included her impressions. Eva thanked her, then asked, "And how did it go last night?"

Janice blushed a little, and Carol laughed. "Blushing, are you?"

"Yes, but not because of why you're thinking. I blushed because I got turned down!" And at this, both the other wen laughed while Janice made a mock pouting face. "And then she had the balls to tease me about it at lunch!" All three laughed at the anatomical mismatch.

"Tell me what happened, both last night, and at lunch today," Eva prompted.

When she was finished with these tales, Eva asked her, "So. That was good work, Janice. And how are you feeling with all this? How are you with this assignment? Are you OK?"

"Yeah, yes," she said after a moment's contemplation. "It's a little hard, sometimes. I worry about the trust issue. I'm pretty sure she won't see through me, but I'm also pretty sure she's not going to trust me. And it bothers me some that I'm actually not trustworthy in this case. She's a very smart woman and I don't see how it will be long before she stops sharing anything with me, including questions. She'll know something is up."

"Well, then you'll just be an observer. And I agree, she's a very smart person. Carol, anything else from you?"

"No, not yet. I'm sure some impression or judgment will surface tonight and I'll share them with you tomorrow," Carol responded.

"Good enough, then. Thank you both. Go get cleaned up and get something to eat. We'll talk again tomorrow," Eva concluded, and turned toward the desk to make some notes in a leather bound journal.

As they passed back through the foyer, Carol saw that Marcus was waiting outside, looking up toward the Mansion. Carol said goodbye to Janice and went to stand beside him, slipping her arm into his.

"Whatcha looking at, big fella?" she asked.

"Her," he said. "It took her a long time to get through the woods. Maybe she stopped at the footbridge, I don't know."

"Maybe," she said. "Did she make it to the Mansion yet?" squinting her eyes.

"Not yet. There she is, walking across the lawn," he said.

Carol squinted again. "All I see is a blob of colors against the green grass."

"Yup," Marcus said. "That's her. The blob."

"Soon," Carol said. "Soon, that's what she'll be, if we're not careful."

Angelica, for her part, had stopped at the foot bridge. It was unusual but she couldn't quite put it to herself why. She went upstream and looked at it, studying its beautiful glowing wooden arches. She asked herself, "I wonder where they found curved trees like that? Two of them, even." Then she realized that was impossible. Tree just didn't grow that way, especially in pairs. She got down under the bridge and looked closely. She saw the joint, cut at an odd angle and the ends of the logs sawed down to create the illusion of a curve. Then she examined the hand rails and saw that they were joined in the same way. She was astounded at the perfect fit, and the amount of time it must have taken, hand-sanding to make it that way.

She stood in the cool stream and marveled at the beauty of bridge, in awe at the effort in must have required to build it. She heard the grind of an old electric golf cart starting in the distance at the barn. She heard the sound of a running step on the dirt of the path and froze. Two women she recognized from class came running down the path and over the bridge, followed by two men. Angelica guessed they were Interns, running to the Mansion for kitchen duty. One of the men was the young man she'd seen the first night learning how to wash the outside of cooking pots. The women did not look to the side as they crossed, but the men did. The first one looked downstream. The last one, the one she'd seen, looked upstream, his eyes passing right over her, giving no sign that he'd seen her.

Angelica crossed the bridge after picking up her shoes from the stream bank. Barefoot, she made her way through the narrow woods holding down the flood plain, old willows mostly. She looked up when she crossed into the meadow.

She was already in shadow from the setting sun but the Mansion stood out on the promontory, so white it seemed to glow. This glow fed into a blue white glow that outlined the whole thing, the main building, the circular Ballrooms, the long wings at odd angles. Her breath stopped and she stopped to catch it, let her breath catch up with her. The Mansion seemed to pulse, and she couldn't tell if the visual effect was because her pupils were pulsing in dilation and contraction as well.

She drew in a breath of determination, and set her mind to the path ahead, knowing in herself that her resolve was a metaphor, not just for the footpath up the hill to huge house. When she reached the veranda she stopped and felt a pull to turn around and looked back, surveying the land, noting the variation in the shadows. She identified a light spot in the shadow of the barn.

Below, in that shadow, Marcus turned to Carol and said, "I wonder if she felt us."

"Maybe," Carol replied. "I can't tell much about her, except there's chaos and no way to tell what's going to happen next."

They watched as Angelica took the broad steps up to the deck of the veranda. Angelica turned and looked back at the barn. Some trick of the light and the humidity made her appear to light up in the westering sun. "Whoa," Marcus said, leaning back. "Is that her?"

"Maybe," Carol said. "I'd be surprised."

Angelica stood, drinking in the light. Then she turned and went in through the high narrow French doors, through the library into the great hall, up the stairs. Slowing on the fourth flight, she arrived at her room exhausted. She opened her door and stepped in. Leaning on her wardrobe, she closed the door, closed her eyes. She realized she was swaying and pulsing. A third tactile sensation, a kind of shiver, ran through her, although she was not cold. She decided the best thing to do was take a nap, since she had an hour before supper. She fell face first onto the bed, sighed deeply, and fled the world into darkness.

Eva had arrived at the Mansion in her golf cart while Angelica was walking up the hill. She'd gone into her office, the office reserved for the High Priestess, at the end of the West Wing of the Mansion. She stopped when she came in through the veranda, sighing at the sight of it. She loved the office, the high back leather covered chairs with brass studs at the seams, the old tables, the fireplace, the light pouring in through the windows.

She sat down at a table, leaning on it with one elbow and put her chin on her hand. She began to run through her mind the trouble that might come up if Angelica went into full blowout. Angelica might become completely disassociated, taking a long time to come back, if ever. She might become suicidal. She might run screaming and naked into the outer world, putting them all at risk.

Angelica was the first person in a long time to be admitted to Stonehaven and its arcane adaptations of various practices. Eva was happy with the choice of Janice to shadow Angelica. Janice's lack of seriousness, combined with her ability to prevaricate, was useful. She hadn't asked Janice to lie about anything, just be close to Angelica, in case Angelica needed to talk. "Be available," Eva had told her. Pulling her off-duty for the night was a good idea, too. It gave Angelica breathing room, as well as the chance to interact with some of the senior people.

Eva had assigned several men to be prepared to respond to Angelica, should she decide to approach them. Some were only to talk, others were to be available for seduction and intimacy if Angelica were to approach them from that direction. All of the High Consorts were, of course, free to exercise their own judgment in the matter, should they be approached, but none of them, when the issue was discussed in the planning sessions, seemed eager to take on the burden. Angelica was beautiful but someone raw, untrained, and possibly crazy was not something that called to any of them. Any of them would help, if asked, she was sure, but she wanted to hold them, and their power, in reserve; use them if things went very badly. Nevertheless, even with all precautions in place, she still felt some uncertainty.

She went over to the water altar in the corner of the office, sat, lit a few dried leaves of the appropriate Artemisia, dropped them in the tiny brazier and washed herself in the smoke. She lit a votive candle. On the third level of the altar were statues of various sizes, and painted icons on stands, of various water Goddesses and Deities, some fresh, some salt, spring, and storm and rain Goddesses.

She activated her gaze and let it drift over the various forms, feeding each idea with attention. As her attention moved slowly around the field she saw one small statue appear to move, some ripple in her vision. It was a smallish, reddish hued statue of a Goddess of sweet water, streams and springs, kin to the water spirits that lived at Stonehaven. She was young, and beautiful, this statue, gazing into a small mirror held in one hand.

From a collection of small bottles on the second level of the altar, Eva took a bottle and put a drop of rose oil in a very small cup. From a very small pitcher, she poured a small amount of fresh water into the cup and placed it in front of the statue. "Thank you," Eva said. "Thank you for coming. We are in need of your blessing."

Eva held in her mind the image of Angelica on fire, burning from within with the new fire about to be released in her. Eva summoned the feelings of fear she had for Angelica and the possible outcomes. In her mind's eye, Eva saw Angelica consumed in the fire, dissolving into sparks and ashes. And no new Angelica resurrected itself from those ashes. "Do you see, Goddess? I am afraid. Please, I ask you, help me help this one. She will turn wen back to you."

Suddenly Eva heard the sound of rushing water, saw herself walking through a meadow to a small stream, getting down and looking into the water. There, in a small eddy of stillness, she saw herself and the sky behind her. Then, looking deeper, she saw the face of the Goddess replace the image of her face. "I will help," the Goddess said, her voice as light as the sound of the water. The Goddess smiled. "Bring her to me, when the time is right. Bring her to me and I will cool her so she does not burn away."

Eva smiled, she knew the stream. It was one of the ones that ran wholly within the boundaries of Stonehaven, protected in its watershed and sacred. Eva bowed her head, raised her arms and hands toward the statue then raised them above herself. "I love you, Goddess," she said, and sent waves of love out through her hands. Then, lowering her hands palms up, she filled them with gratitude and sent it showering out over the entire altar, feeding everything.

Eva sat back, closed her eyes, and sighed. Suddenly she was transported back to the stream bank, looking at her reflection again. But the Goddess of Sweet Water did not appear in the reflection. Instead she saw in the reflection above and behind her, in the sky, neither cloud nor kite, but a sheet, its points waving in the air, drawing closer, then suddenly rushing her, covering her, her vision disappearing under its blackness.

Eva withdrew from vision space as quickly as she could. In the distance she heard a crash. Disoriented, she turned her head, and focused her hearing. Her mind reconstructed the sound into that of a silver tray holding a tea service in the dining hall having been dropped. She could hear the noise in the distance, and voices, as the crew moved to clean it up.

Suddenly the door to her office burst open and there stood Madeleine, breathless, leaning against the door frame. "Something is coming," she said, with an edge to her voice.

"Yes, I saw something of it just now. Does she draw it to us?" Eva inquired, knowing that Madeleine would know who 'she' was.

"Yes. No." Madeleine shook her head. "There is more than one. Help comes, but help is being followed by darkness. This darkness draws another darkness, and this other darkness is very bad. I cannot see into either darkness, yet. This latter darkness draws yet another darkness, masquerading as light."

"Does Death come with the darkness?"

"It may. I cannot see. We will do ceremony, the Madeleines and I."

"I must prepare the trap for Death, then."

"Yes, in case it cannot be averted." Then Madeleine paused. She rushed quickly over to Eva and went to her knees next to her. Madeleine took Eva's hands. "Are you sure you want to do that? Can we not attempt a diversion?"

"We could," Eva answered, smiling sadly, looking down. "What I am shown indicates that, if the diversion fails, there will not be time to set up the trap. So I shall follow Her indications, and prepare."

Madeleine took Eva's hands fully in her own. Her tears fell on the backs of her hands, and Madeleine leaned forward and kissed those hands. Standing up, she turned and left the room without looking at Eva again.

Some echo of the crash reached deep into Angelica's mind. It drew her back to her body, to her bed, where she lay sweating with a damp spot of drool on the mattress under her cheek. Gone, she'd been. She knew there were dreams out there on the edges, but nothing very light. People talking, fighting, arguing, but perceived through a dark veil. Things were shifting on the edges, some moved by a great power, others countered by a great power. Her last image, as she pushed herself up, sat, and focused on the room, was of sparks rising from a fire.

She looked at the time on her phone, all it was good for here in the valley. She still had a few minutes until supper and she wanted desperately to take a shower. She turned on her fan and set it on the chair by the open window. She opened the door and blocked it open so the room would air out. She grabbed her towel off the back of the chair and went down the hall to the bathroom. She checked for her kit; it was still there.

She set the shower to hot. She was burning up inside, but not like a fever. Her belly was hot. Her back was hot, more like a sunburn. The hot water couldn't manage to penetrate her far enough to bring her relief. Her mind began to see images of fire. After all she'd been through this day—her mind melting, fainting dead away, the extraordinary dreaming and sensations—she became angry that her body wouldn't do what she wanted. She'd had enough. She turned the water to fully cold. She began to shiver under it, and although the heat withdrew to a small center deep in her belly, right on top of her womb, she couldn't make it go away. It was then that she saw the huge green phallus again, veined and throbbing. In her mind, with one hand on her clitoris, she reached out to the phallus and touched it. Immediately the shivering stopped.

She reached a kind of balance, her heat radiating to just the surface of her skin, where the water cooled it. The cold drew the heat to the surface, the heat moving in a slow, smooth, continuous flow. She sensed particular streams of heat, arising from within, dispersing along different pathways. The spots where these streams reached the surface remained warmer than her skin. She could cool these simply by willing the stream to slow down, to move slowly between the river banks of her greater warmth.

In her mind's eye, keeping one hand on the phallus, and in this world one hand on her clitoris, finding the balance between her inner heat and the outer water, she suddenly had a revelation and a sensation at the same moment. The thought came into her mind, with an accompanying felt sense that descended from the top of her head, that the phallus and her clitoris were one; one thing, and the same thing. Her clitoris was the spirit of the phallus.

The revelation made her laugh out loud. She thought she heard a masculine voice laugh briefly. She was unsure about doing what the next image in her mind was. She did what she was shown anyway. She aligned the giant green phallus with herself and visualized the two merging. She became the green phallus and it became her, but not in a permanent way. It was an energetically interpenetrating way, the head of the phallus overlaying her own head. When she stepped out of the cold shower and toweled off, she could sense the testicular heaviness bouncing on the tops of her thighs. She could feel that the greenness was balancing her own heat.

She wondered what would come of this merging, and her vagina pulsed, heavily, once. "I don't know what that means," she said aloud. "I don't know what any of this means." Then she stood completely still, naked in the room, hair down her back, and turned her palms forward. She summoned herself into one awareness and said to the world, "I don't know what any of this means. Who can help me?"

A still voice, quiet, a whisper of no clear gender, said, "Help will come." Then she had an image of Eva, then Madeleine, then, emerging from a light behind them, a short form bent forward, intent on her, the walking image of the Moon Halter. The whisper said, "Start with these."

Angelica, realizing that the world had spoken to her, not knowing that this could have happened, slowly fell to her knees, legs trembling, overwhelmed with a wave of gratitude. Her gratitude made her weep. She fell slowly forward so she was on her hands and knees. Her hair slid forward over her shoulders making a curtain, reducing the noise of the still running shower. The sound of the plopping of her tears brought her awareness back to the present, and when she opened her eyes she saw the floor through a field of green light. This reminded her of "Who She Was," a giant green dick that could go anywhere. The thought of it made her giggle.

She sniffled and sat back, wiping her face and nose on the backs of her hands, still giggling. "Big green dicks don't cry," she said aloud, and laughed.

She picked up the towel, wiped her face again, stepped to the shower, and washed her hands off in the cold water, enjoying the rush of heat down her arms. Then she turned the shower off and walked naked down the hall to her room.

She stood naked before the fan, brushing her hair, thinking about what to wear for supper. She'd seen the Madeleine wearing slacks the day before so she pulled out a pair of black jeans and pulled them on without underwear, "Too hot for that," she thought. She pulled on a thin strapped pale blue tank top and chose a flowered shirt over a white one, "Black and white, too butch."

She stopped, her inner dialogue surprised her. She thought, "Why'd I say that? What does that mean? 'Too butch.'" Then she answered herself, "It means 'Unfeminine'. Is that what I don't want? To appear too unfeminine? Shit, I'm a giant green dick. Yeah, I think that's what it means. It means I don't want to look too much like a dick, I need to keep it hidden."

She paused. Then another revelation struck her, a felt sense about what it means for a woman to love a woman, and then another sense about what it meant to love a woman in a certain way, to feel, perhaps, what the masculine feels when it loves a woman. "Oh my Goddess," she said, and said for the first time in her life, "this is how the Feminine loves. She loves each, and can become each, and loves both as She is, and can love both as the other."

And she heard a feminine voice say, "Four loves for the Feminine at this level, yes." She realized that she had yet to work that proposition through in a logical way, she didn't understand it yet, but knew the puzzle was solvable.

Angelica put on the flowered shirt, and tied a pair of red Converse high tops on sockless feet. She pulled her hair back in a scrunchy, and left her room, bounding down the first two flights of stairs, stopping to compose herself on the landing before the last flight. She walked down the last flight in a normal fashion. She made the last turn and looked up.

There was the Moon Halter, standing square in her path, looking up at her with an expression in which Angelica honestly detected no meaning. She raised her eyebrows in quizzicalness.

The Moon Halter was wearing loose black trousers and a white tunic that came to mid-thigh. She narrowed her eyes slightly and said, "It's too big. The green dick thing. Make it about this long," she said, and she held her hands to mid-belly. "Make it about this big around," she said, holding her hands curved to about the diameter of a grapefruit. "That's about how much space it occupies in the masculine brain. You'll learn a lot from it."

The Moon Halter suddenly grinned at Angelica, nodded her head toward the dining hall, and stepped aside to let Angelica pass. As Angelica crossed by her the Moon Halter said, "Remember, about this big," making the gestures. "And think about that color, while you're at it."

As she walked Angelica tightened her lower belly and the phallus shrank to the prescribed size. She suddenly realized she was having trouble keeping it 'tucked in'. "Interesting," she thought. "Leading with your dick. How much does that explain?" she wondered.

Suddenly she felt a small open palm slap her on the back of the head and Moon Halter's voice in her ear, "You're supposed to have a dick, not be a dick."

Angelica stumbled into the Dining Hall, saying "Hey!" back over her shoulder, but the Moon Halter had been several feet away and was already laughing herself up the stairs.

Angelica stopped and took stock of the room. Everyone she could see was looking at her. Some smiled and she smiled back, others returned to their food and conversation. She walked over to the buffet. There was no line so she went through quickly, taking rice, a chicken breast, served cold, that had been marinated in olives, figs, capers, and vinegar, and put that on top of the rice along with a spoonful of the marinade. She found herself having to turn sideways as she moved because when she bent forward the dick would get in the way. She found it frustrating. She got salad at the end of the line and put over it a small dipper of some oil based dressing whose name was in a script she couldn't read. This ticked her sense of frustration up another notch.

She turned and looked around the room. The dick swung past where she stopped and then swung back, oscillating slightly. There was no one from the class in the Hall, and, she noticed she was the youngest in the room. She couldn't find Eva. At one table sat the Madeleine, with a man she guessed was in his forties, sitting next to her. Across from them were three people, two women and a man, all in their thirties. The man caught her eye, smiled and nodded her over, indicating the seat next to him. She sat, bumping her dick against the table. This put her opposite the man sitting next to Madeleine.

He spoke to her, dark hair cut short and smiling. "Hi. I'm Thomas Johnson. This guy next to you is also a Thomas, so I just go by Johnson." Thinking of his name as a slang term for the phallus ("Hi, I'm Thomas and this is my Johnson") she had an image of the two of them, sitting on either side of her, with their dicks bouncing against the edge of the table, as hers was. Then, she saw the women suddenly have erections that matched hers, and the room suddenly became deeply absurd in her mind. The women, stopping their conversation, turned and looked at her.

She shook her head, clearing the vision, smiling at the ridiculousness of it, and said, "Hi, I'm Angelica," directly to Johnson and nodded at the others.

"Nicky and Paulette," Johnson said, indicating the two women on the other side of Thomas.

The Madeleine said to them, "So, OK, you have your instructions. Be careful and cover your tracks."

Johnson said to them, "Let me know, and he and I will watch your backs," including Thomas with a gesture.

The three nodded and got up, taking their dishes into the servery and washing them. Angelica watched them go, swinging dicks leading the way, and shook her head again. Madeleine indicated that Angelica should move over across from her with an invitation of the hand.

Angelica moved over, being careful not to knock her dick into anything. She sat down and looked up to find the Madeleine smiling at her, looking at her intently but not at her eyes. Madeleine brought her eyes down and leaned conspiratorily across the table.

"They can go away, you know. Erections always go down. They always go away" she said, grinning sideways at Johnson, who snorted. And with that, Angelica sensed the erection disappearing, contracting to the size of her clitoris, draping itself through the extended related tissue under her mons and down the inside of her thighs, outside the edges of her vulva. She went still. It was one of the strangest sensations of her life.

"Hard springs…" Johnson said.

"What?" Angelica asked.

"Hard springs eternal," he replied.

Madeleine laughed at the confused expression on Angelica's face. "Oh, I get it," Angelica said. "Hard springs, hard—hope."

"It's a place, too." Johnson said, smiling. "Hard Springs, that is."

There was a pause and into that silence Angelica spoke. "What's your position here?"

"Ok," Madeleine said. "That's where we start then? I'm Madeleine.

You could say I'm the Assistant Director.

"And the other one?" Angelica continued.

"The other one?" Madeleine smiled. "You mean Eva. She would be the Director. Are these really the questions you want to ask?"

Angelica shook her head. "What is happening to me?" she asked. At that moment there was the sound of a bell.

"This is Grace," Johnson said as they turned in the direction of the source of that clear call.

A woman, wearing a hag's mask, a gray wig with stringy hair, and dressed in rags, walking with a cane, came into the dining room from the servery. She was holding a bowl in her free hand. She was followed by a man dressed in a torn and bloody tunic that covered him to mid-thigh, a bloody mask and wig, carrying a butcher's knife. He placed a bit of food of each kind in the bowl as they moved along the line.

At the end of the line and near the door she raised the bowl over her head and said, "These died so that we may live."

The man said, "All die so that Each may live."

The old woman responded, "Each dies so that All may live."

The rest of the people in the room responded then, "We call upon the True Creator, Goddess of Life and Death, to accept our offerings."

A form, a whirling smoky-white cylinder, appeared over her outstretched hand. It whirled into a long elegant feminine arm and hand descending to the bowl. A golden smoke, scintillating with bright flashes, rose up from the bowl and into the hand and disappeared. Then the arm itself disappeared.

The people intoned, "AAAoom."

The old woman and her assistant departed through the solarium and out onto the veranda, going down to one of the stairways leading to the lower level.

"What was that?" Angelica asked, a little breathless.

"That was the fourth thing we do. Use ritual to access and cultivate a relationship with the Divine," Madeleine said.

"That was Grace," Johnson added.

"No, what was that? That gold stuff that went up into Her hand?" Angelica insisted

Madeleine said, "That was Love. The Love that goes into the food and all we do here."

Angelica sat silently, looking down into her food. She found herself weeping again, tears sliding softly from her eyes, dropping onto her plate. Madeleine and Johnson watched her sympathetically. Madeleine reached across the table and put her hand on Angelica's forearm.

"You had a question?" Madeleine asked, encouragingly.

"Yes. A different one. What is going on here? I mean, all this," Angelica said, looking up and waving her other arm around. "What is going on? What's with all the magic? It all seems so normal to you. And then, can you tell me, what is happening to me?"

Madeleine looked at Johnson, inviting him to speak. He said, "What's going on here is that this is a school. We teach certain things here. Some of what we teach are the same things that are taught elsewhere. The difference between us and those others is that what we teach occurs in the context of the Antecedence of the Feminine. She came first as life evolved. The masculine derived from the feminine. It's the combination of what we teach with the core idea of the Antecedence that makes the magic possible."

Madeleine continued, "What's happening to you is different. You're different, I don't know why yet. You're engaged in a process that was already happening to you. Your yoga instructor back home, Jonathon, noticed this and referred you to us. He knows that we know and understand what you're going through, and how difficult it will probably be.

"You're going through a process that's historically known among yogis and yoginis as the Release of the Kundalini Serpent. What is happening to you is that your buffers and filters, those parts of yourself that keep you from seeing the real world as it truly is, are falling away. Sometimes they melt, sometimes they flame out, and others break or tear. And there is a great buffer, the buffer that traps people in their egos and keeps them from their true selves. When this barrier is broken down it is like a damn bursting and the energy that had been trapped is released and rises up from the low back along the spine in a vortex shape."

"So, that's what's happening to you," Johnson continued. "You can see the magic that's there already, there already because of what we do here, because your eyes are opening, and your ears will open, and your sense of smell and touch will broaden. It can be painful, like having the myelin sheath that protects your nerves melt away, and everything suddenly becoming a raw nerve, and the intensity can be more than your everyday mind can bear. It can be maddening. It can be maddening until you figure out how to regard the world and your own suffering in it from the place of your sacred mind. And you have to develop your sacred mind in a hurry now because the breakdown of the last buffers is coming on you quickly."

"It's why you're here," Madeleine said. "We know what's happening to you, and we can take care of you while it's happening."

"What will happen to me afterward?" Angelica asked.

"After what, exactly?" Johnson replied.

"After all this release, all this overcoming, what will happen to me?" Angelica clarified.

"It's difficult to say. That depends on how much you can integrate all your new perceptions. We can help you with the integration, if you decide to stay. You can stay as long as you need to," Madeleine said.

"Seriously?" Angelica asked.

"Seriously," Madeleine replied. "If you're interested, you could probably get an internship here. But you might want to at least plan on staying for another two weeks. Your parents are expecting you back after this two weeks, yes?"

Angelica nodded.

"Then you should call them, and tell them you've decided to stay for an extended retreat," Madeleine said. "There's a landline phone in the office you can use. Call them tomorrow. Call them while they will accept it as a natural thing."

Angelica nodded again, and lowered her head. When she looked up she was clearly afraid. "I'm afraid," she said.

"Who's afraid?" Eva said, sidling up to sit next to Angelica. "Food no good? You haven't eaten a bite. So was I, by the way. Afraid, that is."

"You went through this?"

"Yes. In a different way from you. But through it, yes. I met a man, once. I wanted to sleep with him, badly. Well, to be honest, I just wanted to fuck him. I was drawn to him like iron to a magnet. But he wouldn't, not least because my boyfriend was passed out in the next room. I backed him up against a wall and kissed him. He kissed me back, and it was like I was thrown into a pool of the most exquisite water. I became immersed in pleasure. Pleasure poured through my lips from his and pooled in the root of me. A pounding pulse started between my legs. When he broke the kiss he just held me. We stood there, the two of us pulsing into each other, up against the wall, until my legs started to shake. I stepped back. He nodded in the direction of the bedroom and shook his head 'No.' Then he left. I have to tell you, he really rang my bell. I was vibrating, hearing a high tone in my head, and I was so wet I masturbated four times, until I was too exhausted to pay attention to anything. But the tone kept playing in my head all night.

"In the morning I had a yoga class, just a regular old hatha class. But, wow, young lady, let me tell you, the results were different. The sensation level was through the roof. Everything was intense and sensuous. Then, standing up at the end of class there was this little squirt, a little whirlwind of energy at the base of my spine and I felt it rise up like heat, and when it hit the base of my skull it was like my face and brain flooded with blood. I had to sit down against the wall before I fell down. When I opened my eyes again everybody was gone except the instructor, sitting cross-legged in front of me. She smiled at me. 'You alright?' she asked. But I could see into her, see her motives, you know? I could feel them. She'd already thought about hitting on me. I told her 'I can't move.' Which was the truth. I was paralyzed. Couldn't move a muscle. And then I could. My jaw fell open and I said 'No'. And tears started rolling down my cheeks. Then I blacked out, slowly, sliding along the wall until I lay on my side. The last thing I saw was a look of alarm on her face.

"I woke up on a mat, lying on my back, head on a pillow, and covered in blankets. The instructor was sitting in a chair nearby, reading and drinking tea. "I've got to go," I said. "I have to get to work." "Too late for that," she said. "Day's done. Don't worry. Your work number was on your information card from the first night. I told them I was your sister and that you were really sick and that I was taking care of you." Then she smiled a smile that had just a little bit of a predator to it, and I rolled to my side and threw up."

Eva laughed aloud. "You should have seen her face. Much worse than yours is now," to Angelica. "Go on, eat!" Eva nudged her.

"I can't," Angelica said, looking down.

"I know," Eva said, this time with some gentleness. "Anyway, I let her take care of me. It was two days before I could move reliably enough to go back to work. But everything hurt, hurt all the time, and everywhere. Eventually I had to quit, though. I could see the motives on everybody's faces. It was venal.

"And I let her continue to take care of me. My boyfriend was an investor, and he was venal too. Eventually I let her become my lover and we were together off and on for a few years. During that time we checked out the Craft some, went to some workshops, including a couple on Tantra. That's where I discovered the Goddess, the Divine Feminine.

"But those little breakthroughs, those little tornado-shaped squirts of energy, kept happening, about once a year. And I'd be down, sometimes for a few weeks, overwhelmed by absolutely everything. I stayed with the yoga, though. That's how I ended up here. The rest of it blew out near the end of my first class here. I've been here, or out on assignment, ever since."

Eva smiled. Angelica didn't, instead she stiffened. "I'm afraid. I feel like I'm being indoctrinated. And that feeling makes me angry. Look. All of you. One of me. What am I doing?" she said, backing away. The paranoia intensified into a fear that quickly became a terror that made her shake. She was staring at Eva wide-eyed. The blood rushed into her ears, and she could hear nothing but its pounding. The room seemed to close down to a dark, narrow tunnel with only Eva's face at the end of it.

Angelica could see Eva mouth the word "Breathe," and pantomime a panting breath. "Breathe," Eva repeated. Angelica panted, slowly coming back to herself, still alternating between trembling and shaking.

Suddenly a man walked up behind Eva and sat down. He was wearing cotton summer whites with sandals, but when Angelica looked at his face she could see the remains of camouflage grease paint striping across it. She could even see some up in his hairline, once brown hair now in a short gray cut brushed back. The image was disconcerting enough that it made her shake her head.

He leaned into Eva and kissed her on the shoulder. "Hello, my dear, what's going on here?" Eva nodded at Angelica. The man looked and said, "Oh."

"Hi," he said to Angelica. "It's better outside. Would like me to help you get there?" Angelica nodded.

"Can you walk?" he asked. Angelica put her hands on her thighs and tried to stand, but she couldn't get her legs under her. They trembled too much.

"OK," the man said. He came around the table and dropped to a knee at Angelica's side, ducking a little so her head was higher than his. "My name is Robert Craft. I'm the Outdoor Activities Director here. I would like to carry you out to the veranda. The setting sun will be perfect about now. Would that be OK with you?"

Angelica nodded again. He slipped an arm behind her knees and another around her back under her arms. Holding her, he stood up in one motion without a sound, and turning with her in his arms, he carried her toward the veranda.

Madeleine had already gone ahead with Johnson, holding open doors. Eva followed behind.

The deep red light and evening warmth enveloped Angelica like a cloud. She sighed in Robert's arms and stopped shivering with an exhale.

"Put her on the top step," Eva indicated.

Craft set her down on the deck, her feet two steps below. Madeleine draped her shawl over Angelica's shoulders. Madeleine sat next to her, and Eva sat down on the other side. Johnson sat on a chair behind them, and Craft went down below them a few steps to sit with his back to them.

After a few moments, during which everyone breathed consciously, Eva spoke. "You know, dear, everything that's happening to you now would have happened to you wherever you were. Maybe not as fast but just as surely. You wouldn't have seen much magic out there, just madness. And there's a good chance it would have driven you mad. You intuit the truth of what I'm saying to you, yes?"

"Yes," Angelica said quietly. "Are you leading me into saying 'Yes'?"

"I suppose that's possible. I'll stop. And do you also intuit you're safe here?" Eva continued.

"That's harder to feel," Angelica replied. "I don't know you. I don't trust you. I can't believe this place exists. I can't believe you people exist. I can't even believe this is happening to me."

"That's what you get when you live in the world of belief," Craft said, over his shoulder.

"What he means is," Madeleine explained, "Is that belief, as a function of human nature, isn't the appropriate function to approach all this with. Belief is not enough. Trust is not enough."

"You know what you know. When you don't know, you don't know," Craft said, over his shoulder again.

"And what that means is that you have to hold out for knowledge. Someone taught me that long ago," Eva took up the thread. "What's happening to your body—that's empirical knowledge. You know it. You know your feelings for what they are, too. Even as chaotic as they are, you can still track them. What you don't know is what's happening to your mind. You don't know what's going to happen to your body and your feelings tomorrow. Your mind is in flux, that's all. And, if you think about it, you never really know what's going to happen to your body and your feelings tomorrow. You just assume that things will go on as before. Except now you can't make that assumption anymore."

"Why are all of you here with me now?" Angelica asked, eyes adjusting to the horizon, the dark shadow line of sunset advancing toward them over the ground.

"Because you are here," Craft said.

Angelica smiled, laid her head on Eva's shoulder, and Madeleine leaned over and put her hand on Angelica's arm. Angelica closed her eyes, and dreamed. She saw herself, as if she were off in the distance, walking across a grassy pasture with a girl, clearly her daughter, holding her hand. When she looked up again she was looking through her other self's eyes. She was looking up a hill, still holding her daughter's hand with some kind of basket on her other arm, its contents covered in a cloth. She was looking at a stone wall that appeared to be a part of a house on the top of the hill, with a sod roof, grass on top waving in a breeze. There was a stone bench built into the wall and a woman sitting on it next to a polished copper bowl.

As Angelica got closer, the woman looked up at her and smiled. The woman was clearly Madeleine. Angelica handed her the basket and Madeleine pulled back the cover cloth to reveal a clutch of eggs, with a black snake wrapped around them. The snake leapt out of the basket without startling them. They looked at each other and laughed as the snake slowly crawled away into the grass.

Madeleine indicated that she should look into the bowl, which was half full of very still water, reflecting what seemed to be an evening sky.

She looked into the bowl and was suddenly inside the house, alone, holding a candle in one hand, tracing spirals and zigzags carved into the stone walls, walking down a central hallway to a round room open to the sky. There was an old woman there, on the far side of the room. A hallway behind her was shrouded in darkness. She was seated on a three-legged stool with a leather seat, a candle on a plate sitting on the ground at her feet. Her thick, straight hair, gone to steely gray, framed a square face with vivid blue eyes. The woman's eyes locked on Angelica's. Thunder rolled.

Angelica woke up on the veranda to the same thunder rolling across the landscape, giant thunderheads under lit with orange, pink and gold from the setting sun, rising to tower over the mountain. She reached out and patted Madeleine's hand with her own. "You were in my dream," she said.

Madeleine said, "I know." Then after a pause she said, "She is a beautiful daughter."

As if on cue, Johnson stood up behind them and came to sit on the top step next to Madeleine. At that, Craft turned, walked up the stairs and sat next to Eva. They watched the light fade and the fireflies rise up in the yard, breathing in the warm beauty. For a moment it was so quiet that Angelica heard a faint hiss, and she couldn't tell if it was from the fireflies rising or the stars coming out.

In the Mansion a piano began to play in the music room. Angelica turned her head to look in that direction and saw the silhouette of Moon Halter, leaning on the railing, watching the west along with them. Angelica sighed and looked back to the west with them, also.

Then there was a bang of metal dropping and peals of laughter from the kitchen coming from the other side of the Mansion. The men got up and moved off. The wen sat for a few more moments, then they also rose. "You're welcome to stay and listen to him play," Madeleine said, moving to the open French doors.

Angelica shook her head, choosing to stay on the porch and watch the fireflies. The others went in, Craft remained standing in the door frame, able to turn and keep an eye on her, if needed. A young man emerged into the light, walking west along the brick walk from the kitchen courtyard. He stopped just inside the light when he saw Angelica sitting on the veranda steps. She recognized him as the young man who'd been receiving instructions in pot and pan washing the night before.

He looked along her sight line, seeing what she was looking toward, and sat down on the bottom step. He spoke into a long silence.

"They're only doing it to have sex, you know."

For some reason Angelica found an incongruence, something absurd, that made her burst into a peal of laughter.

"It's true! It's true!" the young man insisted. "They fly to the tops of the trees to have sex. They find their mate by the flashing of their lights."

Angelica had stopped laughing and was smiling at him now. "I believe you," she said.

"Then, when they're finished, they fall gently to the ground, and burrow in among the grasses, to rest and hide from the birds, then climb out to do it again," he finished.

"I heard they eat nothing, after they emerge as adults. They have sex, mate, and die." Angelica offered.

"Perhaps you are thinking of the mayflies."

"Perhaps. I shall have to look the question up."

"You an intern?"

"No, just taking a class. But I'm thinking about it. Are you?"

"Yeah. First year."

"You like it? I mean, it looks like you interns do all the work around here."

"Yeah, maybe it looks like it. But it takes a lot to keep it running. It's got to be kept up and working for the guests like yourself."

Angelica was taken aback by the thought that all this was focused on taking care of guests. "Really?"

"Yeah," he said. "Our focus in the program is always on service to others."

"Oh, yeah? Well, then, who's in service to you?"

"Right now, I don't need it. But if I did, then all this service, especially the attitude I keep now, will come back around and take care of me."

"I wish that's how the world worked."

"Maybe."

"What do you mean, 'maybe'?"

"Well, the world works on a version of it. Big fish eats the little fish, and all that."

"Yeah, but the little fish doesn't think of it as service!"

"True. But I said it was only a version. People, too. But that's only a version also. You're just as likely to get ripped off out there as have it come back to you. But that's out there, where the world is usually just mundane, if not profane. In here, it's different. In here, it's the rule, and not the exception. In here, it's Sacred. And safe. And it's set up that way. It's in the rules."

"You trust the rules?"

"Yeah, here, I do."

There was another pause as they both contemplated the night, and the music.

Then the young man said, "I have Friday evening off. Would you like me to take you around? Give you the tour?"

"That'd be great!"

"Alright then! I'm off at 3:00 and the class is over by 4:00. Plenty of time. I'll meet you at the corner of the kitchen courtyard. Alright, then! Cool! See you then." The young man got up and walked off west into the darkness.

"Hey, wait a minute, what's your name?" Angelica wanted to know of the darkness.

But the darkness had no words, only the pulsing beat of the tree frogs and the inconstant rattle of the early cicadas. And there was music in the light.

Craft had been watching Angelica off and on; he knew she had been talking to someone, but he couldn't see whom. So he was looking at her when she stood up and wobbled a little. He covered the ten feet in two steps and took her by the arm. It wouldn't do to have her pass out and fall down the steps. "You OK?" he asked. "You want to sit back down?"

"Yes," Angelica said. "I'm so tired." Sitting there, listening with her eyes closed, she leaned into Craft for support. "Why are you here? I mean, why do you work here? Stay here?"

In his simple and direct way, Craft replied, "I am a Servant of Life."

"I don't know what that means," Angelica responded, sleepily. "I don't know what that means."

"If you want to, you will," Craft said.

"It sounds like it means so much, like it means the whole world. And it sounds like it means one very specific thing," Angelica said.

"That's true," Craft allowed.

"I can't think. You don't say much, do you?" Angelica yawned and laid her head on Craft's shoulder this time.

Craft, appreciating the irony, didn't say anything. Angelica smiled to herself and fell asleep.

Craft picked her up in his arms. He stuck his head in through the French doors and got the attention of the first person inside. Craft had her get Johnson to come help him. He caught the pianist's eye, a third year intern named Gregory, look focusedly at Angelica and smile. He thought, 'She's just like a dream'.

Craft made a mental note to tell Madeleine to put Gregory on Angelica's list. Johnson appeared a moment later at the doors and Craft said, "I need your help. Go open the elevator."

Johnson nodded. The Mansion had two sets of elevators, one on the east end involving the dumbwaiter from the kitchen, and a series of smaller elevators used to bring supplies to the upper floors. On the west end, in the west wing just near the entrance to the offices, was a freight elevator that went only to the third floor. Johnson headed that way, opening doors, and, when they arrived there, he opened the doors on the freight elevator.

"Come with me," Craft ordered.

Johnson rode up with Craft in silence. The men had known each other a long time, and, although they went through the world in different styles, they went the same way through the world. When they reached the third floor, Johnson opened the doors and they went up the stairs to the landing of the fourth floor over the main part of the Mansion.

Johnson asked, "Which?"

Craft said, "South side, middle."

Johnson went on ahead and opened the door to Angelica's room. He turned on the light, turned the cover down and went to the window to look out. Craft put Angelica down on her side on the bed and covered her up. Johnson turned to him. "The view is spectacular," he said, walking towards the door.

Craft stepped over to the window, leaned on the sill, and looked out. He could hear the music roll out from under the second floor veranda roof. The moon shone all through the billions of firefly lights, creating a blue-white backdrop for the golden flashes. The moon lit the whole landscape, all the way to the mountain, except for the dark pine eye. There were no fireflies there. He sighed, and turned to the door.

"You know, she's hot," Craft said.

"Yes, I could feel it radiating off her. Qi fevers, I suspect. She'll have a lot of them," Johnson commented.

"Yes, it's more than that. There's an energy swirling in her already. Not the Kundalini; this swirls in a circle within her, then it straightens out and writhes."

"Hmm. We should tell Eva and Madeleine," Johnson said, thoughtfully. Craft nodded assent.

Johnson stepped out into the hall. Craft turned the light off and pulled the door closed behind him. He caught up to Johnson and lightly bumped Johnson's shoulder with his own. Johnson smiled and they went downstairs to enjoy what was left of the evening.

In the dark, Angelica stretched. Her awareness drifted up and she could feel the fields of the men receding down the hall. She stood up and undressed, throwing her clothes on the floor. In the dark, she went to the window naked and looked out. It was magic, the evening breathed, the lights in the trees breathed, she breathed. She wiped sweat from her brow with the back of her hand, stripping it from her eyebrows. She tied up her hair in a soft knot on top of her head. She sighed and breathed again with the night.

Her mind still prior to words, still below thought, she put the fan on the chair and turned it on low, setting it to oscillate over her when she lay down. She lay down on her belly, feeling the circling swirl slow down, and become a slowly writhing line that ran from her face to her base. She slid one hand between her legs, cupped it over her sex, and laid her head down on her other arm.

The writhing within her stopped, and, drifting downward, slowly settling to the bottom, she slept.

14

ALAM ARRIVES

Time, as it naturally flows, here a seep and there a river, is different for immortals. Well, actually, there is no immortality. Gods die, ideas die, Love dies. Everything is mortal. What matters is not so much the moment when mortality is encountered, but the quality of the path leading to the moment—the taste of the water—until one hits the rock in the stream and splatters everywhere.

Some things live a long time, some do not. Time for gods passes so slowly compared to ours that they seem to be immortal and live forever. It is a seeming only. Mortals, called so relatively, live lives that last so short a while that our lives are seen not even as a season, but more like a moon; one moon cycle or less. And, in truth, more than half of us live not long enough to see our full Lunar return.

So, in order for an immortal to interact with a mortal in 'real time' the immortal must speed up. And for a mortal to interact with an immortal, the mortal must slow down. The forms of the immortals become blurred into the background because a mortal moves too fast with respect to them, and they are unseen. The forms are there, emergent, but only when the mortal slows down enough to see them and hear them.

If, in the meeting time, the mortal slows down, not much is lost—perhaps the time in which to accomplish some task more likely unpleasant, than not. But the immortals must speed up; it is costly to them, energetically. They have more momentum, and it is possible for the energy of momentum to leak through from the immortal to the mortal, like an effulgent descent seen from below.

It is simple physics, which means that it is simply Nature. It is the implications, as it is with Nature, which seem complex. That interaction, and the sum total of interactions, helps produce the complexity that fills the world with Life, as over and against Nothingness. It is astounding. All Beauty thus comes from Life, and it is all alive.

This flow across time lines acts as the material basis for the 'blessings of the gods,' filling the space around the mortal. The mortal, slowed down, is able to perceive—see, hear, be touched by, and feel—the immortal, based on the reality created by this material.

However, the gods must receive something in return for this blessing; otherwise too much energy is consumed and their lifespans are affected by living faster than they normally would. Ideally, it is the mortal that supplies this energy by cultivating the feeling of devotion. It is a Love that Nurtures the Divine.

And where the Divine is fed, the Divine returns.

Alam was thinking about this problem, the problem of feeding the Divine, holding an offering up toward the mountain She usually came over, when he felt the antlered god behind him. The great stag 'whumpfed' once, and Alam froze in mid motion.

He could think of nothing to say, for a moment. Then he said, for reasons he wasn't quite clear about, "I am that on which I feed, I am that which feeds on me."

"Ahh," the stag man said. "Turn around."

Alam turned, holding the offering of wild sweet basil in his hand. The stag man snuffed at it, and said, "Indeed." Alam looked up at him, looked up at his magnificent antlers, smaller replicas of the ones he carried in stag form. They seemed to change shape and orientation as he watched them, focusing forward, then turning outward, like antennae.

Alam spoke. "She told me She has no power over you, though the herds are Hers to command."

"Tell Her I want my doe and her friends. Release them to me and I will leave the mortals alone. That includes you."

"I will," Alam replied.

"Did you learn what you bargained to learn, Mortal?"

"I suppose so. I know I have not learned all I imagined I would learn."

"Who does?" the stag man asked, displaying a rare philosophical mood. He stood silently, gazing over Alam's head, as if waiting for something.

"I would," Alam said, almost under his breath.

The stag god looked down at him. "Then we are not finished, you and I."

Alam's anus clenched involuntarily, and it showed in his entire body.

The stag man laughed out loud. "Don't worry, mortal," he said. "You paid in more than you received. I have no interest in being indebted to you."

Suddenly there was a burst of heavy wind, lifting both men's hair, the air began to crackle and spit sparks of blue fire. Then, suddenly also, there She was, hovering in the air ten feet away, cloak spiraled around Her, hair blowing free above Her head. A line of red light shot from Her hand, reaching under the stag man's ass and focusing on his testicles. After jumping in the air, he went very, very still.

"You," She said, with force. "From now on you come to me first. You come to me before you come to see him again. You see him with my knowledge and blessing, or not at all. Disobey me and it will not go well with you. Am I understood?"

"Yes, Storm Hag," the stag man said.

Calley threw back Her head and laughed, squeezing the stag man's testicles. The heat of it made him begin to grow hard.

Alam had been observing this interaction silently, with very wide eyes. He did not know how much She knew about his history with the stag man, and how much of what he'd learned was applied in tracking Her down. He did not know that she'd visioned it all.

The Goddess, still gripping, pulled on the stag man's testicles again. "You know I know how to hurt you."

"Yes, Storm Hag,"

"Even now, arrogant," Calley said. "Believing yourself my superior. Be gone!" She said. The red line grew into a lightning strike and the air split with its thunder. The stag man disappeared, replaced by a cloud of smoke.

Alam, knocked to the ground, couldn't look up at Her. He heard Her say, in a gentle voice, "Look up the mountain."

Still avoiding looking directly at Her, he looked as She commanded, and saw the giant stag form loping up the mountainside, limping on a rear leg. When he looked back he noticed that She had settled on the ground. He stared at Her feet and stood up.

"You will come to my house," She said. "On the day of the next full moon. I will send you a black ram as a guide. Look at me."

Alam slowly raised his eyes. She was smiling at him, light in Her eyes, full lips pulled back. She shook Her head slightly. "You are something, aren't you? Did you think I didn't know? Why are you still alive?"

"By your leave, Goddess," Alam said, looking down again.

"No, no," Calley said. "Keep looking at me. By my leave, yes, but why? Why have I granted you this leave?"

Alam looked within himself, eyes darting left and right. He couldn't decide if it was a trick question or not. He closed his eyes and stood still, waiting for an answer to come. He heard Her say again, "Look at me. Open your eyes and look at me."

He did. The words came to him, "Because I love you." But he couldn't say it. He was afraid to tell Her he loved Her, afraid She would find it presumptuous. He was staring at Her while he was thinking all this.

"Say it," She said. Then, after a moment, again, "Say it!"

And Alam continued to stand there, mute. Calley tried to look into his mind, read his thoughts, but She couldn't, thinking he was too well shielded. She didn't realize that he had actually stopped thinking, and there was no thought there to be read.

Alam, mute, put all of his concentration into simply looking at Her, holding Her gaze, impassive, showing no outward signs.

Suddenly She looked down, breaking the gaze, and smiling. "That's right," She said. "You don't know, do you? How could you have known?"

All Alam could do was slowly shake his head, "No" when She looked back up at him.

She told him, "You are alive because of your devotion."

In that moment he knew it to be true. He was devoted to Her in some way that went beyond love. He nodded slowly, indicating "Yes," but there was no way he could speak about the understanding.

"So, since you are devoted to me, what was he doing here?" She asked.

"He came to try and get out of our deal," Alam said, slowly finding his words, not thinking about saying anything other than the simple truth.

"Did you let him?" She asked.

"No. Although I did not mean to. When I am finished learning what I bargained for it will be over. He said I'd paid for more than I received."

Calley thought, "I'm certain you did," but She did not want to let him know that She had seen everything that had happened. Instead She said, "Then you will see him again."

Alam nodded again, "Yes."

"Is there any devotion in you toward him?" Calley asked, already knowing the answer.

Alam opened his mind to all his memories of the stag man, and found nothing, no felt sense of any devotion to him. Then he said something that confirmed what She suspected. "I didn't do it for power. I was dreaming about you. I did it so I could learn to find you. If I was in a different form you might not see me, and then I could get close to you and change back."

And then he said something She didn't know. "I saw you once. It was the third winter I was here. I was in the sheep pen, I had taken on the first form I learned, the ram."

She raised an eyebrow.

"No, no. It was nothing like that. They were acting spooked in the morning, and I wanted to understand what had done it. I changed shape so I could understand them. A wolf had come by, and peed near the tree line. They could smell it."

"Uh huh," She said, teasing him.

He said, "No, no. I never took a form to fuck an animal."

She knew this already, but She was relentless today. "Uh huh," she said again.

"I never fucked one in human form either."

"Uh huh."

"I was in the pen…"

"Uh huh."

"Stop it," he said, and She giggled. He knew then that She'd been teasing him.

"I was in the fold, looking over the wall and I saw you form out of the fog on the trail that led down to the water. You formed there. I saw your cloak. You turned your head, and looked back over your shoulder. It was as if you felt me looking at you. You looked right at me. Well, you looked at the ram anyway. In just that moment, just from that profile view of your face, I fell in love right then," he finished.

"You hadn't seen a woman in years. That's why you fell in love." She continued to push at him, wanting to know it, wanting to hear it from his side.

"No, I'd seen women. I'd been to the village in the foothills. But no woman is going to come out here. No woman is going to live in this much isolation. But you have to understand how beautiful you are," he continued.

She humpfed in indignation. "I don't have to understand anything."

He stopped, raising his arms palms up and shrugging, not knowing what else to say. Suddenly She was gone.

He heard a whistle and turned. There She was, standing in the doorway to his house, with Her back to him, looking over Her shoulder at him the way She had that morning three years before. She slowly dropped Her cloak. Her nakedness revealed itself slowly, flashing in the sunlight. When She dropped the cloak She stepped inside his house, into the shadows.

Her cloak lay heaped on the threshold. Rather than stepping over it, he picked it up and hung it on the hook embedded in the wall. She smiled. He was passing all the tests today.

The house was dark, and cool. Alam stirred the coals in the fireplace and put fresh wood on them. He lit an oil lamp fueled with rendered sheep tail fat and set it on a stand near the foot of the bed. It illuminated Calley, naked, lying back on a pile of sheepskins and wolf pelts, her long thick hair splayed about Her.

Alam pulled his tunic over his head, unlaced his boots and dropped his kilt. He kneeled on a sheepskin on the floor beside the bed. Sitting on his heels he let his gaze travel Her body. He stopped on Her face, simply smiled into her eyes, and held her gaze in return. After a moment, She raised one knee then dropped it to the side opening Herself to him. Still holding Her gaze he leaned forward as She slid her hips closer to him.

He grazed over Her skin, inhaling, then he let his lips fall lightly, grazing again. From the top of Her opening to the bottom he let the tip of his tongue slowly open the furrow. From the bottom of Her well he sipped. So wet, he thought, then he paused at the top to fasten his lips upon the budding of Her.

He held still there, keeping the kiss intact, until Her breathing increased its pace and She began to squirm against him. She made little sounds as the shuddering started, making small buckings with her hips against him. She "Ohhhh"'d at him and her panting slowed. He rose, fully erect, and She lifted her other knee for him. He put one knee up on the bed and picking up Her hips he brought Her to him and entered Her.

Her back arched, She arched it more, then, in a swaying upwards motion, She pulled Herself upwards and wrapped Her arms and legs around him. He picked Her up, turned and sat on the edge of the bed with Her facing him. She brought Her feet up to the bed and thus poised, She rode him.

She rode him harder and faster, their bodies slapping against each other with such force that a wind blew on the lamp. At Her peak, She reached up and grabbed his hair at the back of his head with both hands, stood up, and squirted on him, while he groaned with the impacts and grinned. He lay back soaked and soaking. She stepped backwards down off the bed and bent to finish him with Her mouth.

He didn't take long. She took the first blast in Her mouth, hard up against Her palate. She took the next on Her throat, then the rest on Her breasts and caught in Her hands, rubbing it on Herself, laughing. "So sweet!" She said, licking Her lips, "And so much!"

"You inspire me, Storm Eyes," he said, as She slipped him back inside Her. "Your eyes are storms, clouds passing in the sky."

She closed Her eyes and intoned, noncommittally, "Ummm." She lay down on him, squishing all the rain from between them. She waited, knowing he would get hard again. She used her envelopment to massage him, concentric rings of rippling motion pulling him into Her, elongating him and pulling him back into erection. If She worked quickly, She knew she could keep him almost hard and start again from there.

The manipulation worked. Knowing that the immediacy of his need was past him, She moved slowly now, taking Her time. First She rode him laying down on him, but he started to trot. She sat up then, slowing him down, finding the long undulating rise and fall of slow gallop. She rode like that, building Her own pressure, Her own charge, Her own 'head of steam'.

She began to make a sound like the rumble of thunder in the distance. Soon there were sounds like thunder rolling along the landscape, then thunder breaking close by. She made a booming sound, it came out as a "Whoom" sound, then in quick succession, a "Whoom-ooom" sound. Her hair was standing straight out from Her head, forming a radiant light in the darkness.

All of Alam's hair stood up straight, his skin prickled with both sweat and gooseflesh. She "Whoom'd" again, then another "Whoom-ooom," in a marvelously deep voice. She extended Her arms and lightning began to crackle at Her finger tips and toes. Alam could feel the charge building in his own hands and feet. He raised his knees so his thighs were behind Her and supporting Her.

Suddenly She bellowed a "Whoom" so loud she shook the walls of the house. Thatch fell to the floor. The lightning arced between their hands, and between their feet. Alam's back arched off the bed as he came. Calley's back arched over Alam's knees, rigid with ecstasy. With another "Whoom" that seemed to come not from Her, but from the world around them itself, Calley lit up, then disappeared, winking out, imploding out of this plane of existence—this time and space—and into Her own world.

Alam collapsed on the bed, and faded into unconsciousness, staring at the guttering lamp.

Calley reappeared in Her timeline, Her world, landing with a sliding bump on her backside, in the meadow just below the Wolf's Head rocks. She sat up dazed, trembling, and laughing. And there, sitting next to Her in a bed of wildflowers, was Mom, Her Mother.

Mom appeared in any form She chose but Calley could always recognize Her. "Hi, Mom," Calley said, laughing, naked, shaking out Her hair. Today Mom chose to be dark-skinned, a brownish-red, with long thick black hair. She was sitting cross-legged on a red cloak, a shawl over Her shoulders on the windward side, breasts, and belly, and thighs soaking in the late spring sunshine.

"Hello, Daughter. What are you doing? These days...," Mom said with a grin.

Calley stood up and brushed off Her backside, examining the twin skid marks Her butt made in the meadow when She landed. "Hmm," She toned. "You've seen."

"Yes, I've seen. What you're doing is fun. Trust me, I know. And what I'm not clear about is what you're thinking," Mom stated.

"You're asking?" Calley wanted to be clear.

"Yes."

"I'm thinking everything, to be honest. I'm not like Bree: I don't go down among the people, and I don't have all the responsibilities she does. I don't want to leave here. I feel like I want children."

"If you have them with him, they will be demi-mortal. Could you watch them die?"

"I have watched Death many times; I could watch theirs, I'm sure. What I'm uncertain of is how I will feel."

"There are some feelings that cannot be known before the experience."

"I know you have watched the death of your children before," She said.

"I have held them in my arms, and felt them go, felt them fall apart, separate, even their spirit dissolving as it rises," Mom said.

"Well, perhaps I shall not see it. Perhaps I shall die first," Calley replied.

Mom looked far away to the West. "Perhaps."

"I see myself giving my children my responsibilities. That will extend their lives. And I will be free of them—the responsibilities; free to leave this land, even."

Mom closed her eyes, waited, and eventually smiled. "That will shorten your life."

"I know. I also know that in the long life I have already had, I have experienced all there is to experience in this way of living. I know this land, every bit of it. I know these seas. I have rained on all of it. I know the cycles of it. If I want different experience—more experience—I will have to live differently. My responsibilities keep me here, keep me to this land. This means my life here has to change," Calley said with resolution.

"He will make a good consort. You will have to disabuse him of any notions that he is what they are already calling themselves, your 'Husband'. Indeed, as if we were animals to be herded and controlled. You may have to keep him in his place."

"I may. So far the only thing he arrogates to himself is the presumption implicit in his love for me, a Goddess, an immortal."

"That's hardly arrogance, beloved daughter. That may be something more simple. It might even be Hope. And remember, there are ways in which he cannot help himself. He knows you are the most beautiful Feminine he will ever encounter."

"Why did you do it? Why did you make them?"

"Men? To extend time. If they increase the variability in Life then they increase the duration of Life. They extend time. When it was just us—just the Feminine—we started to decline in time. When the diversion was created—by which I mean the creation of the Masculine—even those that stayed in the Feminine-only line were enriched and enlivened. The Masculine was created as a diversion, not in the sense of entertainment, but as a way to divert Death.

"Do you think he will make a good father?"

"He is not like the others, already I see that. It depends on his relationship to power, and how he uses it. His children will be greater than him. Will he see them as a threat, or as a gift to be nurtured? I believe he will be a good father, and he will have the respect of his children. He will be spending a lot of time with them while you are out fulfilling your responsibilities."

"Yes. It will be interesting. I shall have to figure out how to nurse."

"I am the Mind of Life on this planet. You are my daughter. I shall help. The prospect of being a grandmother again makes me smile," Mom said, as She reached over and patted Calley's knee. "I shall help."

Calley felt a wave of warmth wash over her; she felt both loved and appreciated. She sent a wave of love to her Mother in return.

"So, how's your sister?"

"Bree? Oh, Bree, She's so sweet, She's teaching me how to read!"

"She's resting, is She? Resting up for Her turn, come summer?"

"Yes. Her people grow more numerous every day. I hear their plans for Her festivals. On Imbolc the people made the boghas out of rushes and hung them over their doorways. You see them everywhere in the villages, even on the outland homes. She gets so busy this time of year, preparing for Beltane. You should come by the house, Mother. She would love to see you."

"I've already been, Daughter. I stopped by on my way up to wait here for you."

"Oh, good! So you just wanted my opinion, right? If you've already been there, you know how She is. She complained about needing to get out more just the other day." Calley went silent a moment, considering what She wanted to say next. "Mother, there is something I wish to give to Her, and I may need your help with it."

"Yes, I wanted your opinion. And what is it that you might need my help with, Daughter?"

"I wish to give Her my Rulership of half the year. I wish to retain only my responsibilities for the storms."

"Oh, my. I shall have to think on that, how it can be done. Hmm. That is a big thing. Have you talked about it with Her?"

"No, I haven't, Mom. But if I'm going to raise children I have to cut back on something. Rulership is fine, but it takes a lot of attention to detail and I find I'm having trouble keeping up the energy to deal effectively with the people. She's actually helped with that this winter past. To be honest, the people don't care for me the way they do for Her. I am their weather, and not high on their list of subjects for praising." She laughed. "She is in their Hearths, and that puts Her in their hearts."

Mom looked closely at Calley now. It was a difficult fate, handed to Her by Her father. "You were the one who was always outside. There was no keeping shoes on you. You would barely keep a tunic on, let alone a skirt. Your bare butt would be showing as you ran off into the fog. It is why the weather came to you. Your sister took to the inside, watching what the people did, rather than the wind.

She continued. "I remember your first cloak. You were standing in the rain, looking down the path that came by the house. You would not come in. You just stood there, staring, the rain spattering off your head and shoulders. You just would not come in. So I took a cloak off the peg, went outside and stood beside you, sheltering you. Do you remember?"

Calley nodded and said, "Yes, I remember."

"What were you looking for, Daughter? What were you looking for?"

"I wasn't looking. I was listening. I was listening to the sea."

"Ahh," Mom sighed. "I understand. Do you remember suddenly becoming aware of me? It was like some shock passed through you and you shook yourself and leaned back into me."

Calley shook her head.

"You let me usher you into the house. The next time you wanted to go out you reached for the cloak on the peg. I let you take it and the hem of it dragged in the mud. You didn't care at first, but after one day you let me hem it for your height. After that we couldn't keep the tunic on you either, unless you were in the house. You would run all day naked under the cloak. That's when you started learning to hide. You became quite good, quite invisible. You could be a rock or a tree or a wall. I remember when you disappeared in plain sight, standing right in front of me in the path." Mom was smiling happily at the memories.

"I remember it all, now, Mother."

"Even when you became a young woman you'd run naked under the cloak. I don't know how you could do it. I mean, I know how you did it, but it was marvelous to watch. A smile, a flash of white flesh, and you'd be gone."

As Her Mother talked, Calley sent Her thoughts to the cloak, hanging on the hook at Alam's house. Slowly she turned the cloak to a fog, then whisked the fog to where She was sitting, and re-materialized the fog as Her cloak around Her.

"Good," Her Mom said.

"You took off early. Your father was happy to let you go, and He gave you weather powers even before He was killed. Then, after His death you received the rest. What He'd given you control over became your responsibility.

"Your Siblings all got something, too, when He died. But it was your sister who took all the things that the people love that your brothers and sisters didn't want. What Bree got are some of the things that He loved the most, too. But you have to know that it was when We were out here, just He and I, earth and sky, that all of you were conceived."

"Thank you, Mother. This is good to know. It helps me understand why I feel the way I do, and what the right decisions are."

Mom looked around, tucking a strand of hair behind Her ear as She turned her face into a freshening wind. She looked up at the rocks of Wolf's Head and smiled. She looked back at Calley, grinning. "What do you say? Shall we go home now?"

Calley nodded and they rose up together, skirting the rocks, and crossing over the top. They paused, just over on the other side, and surveyed the vast landscape before them. The shouldering mountains of the highlands, sides covered in timber, tops open in grass, almost empty of people.

They watched the westering light a moment, the breeze blowing back their cloaks and their hair, two magnificently naked women lit up like beacon fires on a sacred day, or stars that shone even in daytime.

Mom said, "I think you are doing the right thing. Up here you will be able to raise your family, even though all this will change. More people will come. Those people are not our people. They will bring change that many will not survive. It will be hard on your sister because the people, except for a very few, will no longer remember Her. It will become unsafe to even mention Her name. People will even forget me, the one who truly made them. Already we have been invaded. I have been invaded, and I do not have the defenses we need to keep them from overrunning us here. Even the land will change. The trees will be cut down and the sheep will rule. But we will survive. For you to disappear in these mountains is a good strategy. You can raise your family and live with your man and train your children safely, in obscurity."

"Yes, Mother. I have felt change coming. We will retreat and endure, even though it take a thousand years for these strangers to arrive, and another thousand for the trees to return."

"Yes, Daughter. It will be that long, perhaps a little longer. We will retreat, retreat to the heart of these mountains, and endure, yes. And that will, you know, give us more chance to spend time together—we shall not be so busy."

Calley smiled at that—Her Mom, always looking to spend time with grandchildren. "Will you find a way to repel the invaders?"

"Yes, but it will take awhile, as you say—thousands of years. They will poison half the planet, and confuse the minds and steal the hearts of the people. The natural order will be turned upside down. I am the Mind of the World, and I do not know how to do this, stop this; I only know how to do what I do. And I tell you, child, that although we shall live—you and I and your sister—many of the people will die, their bodies piled up unburied, because of this invasion, and I cannot stop it. It will use the people, use the people to rape me, and then when their days are done it will suck up their souls, because souls are that upon which it feeds."

"Why Momma?" Calley asked, close to tears. "Why can't you stop it?"

"Because I do not yet know what I need to know. But I will. Because they come from another world, Baby Girl. They come from another world, and they come as gods. And they seek my rape."

Calley sat down hard, to keep from falling down as her mind began to fill with images of the future her mother was describing.

"They will rape us too, won't they? It's already starting, isn't it?"

Her Mother sat down, and put her hand on Calley's shoulder. "Yes, it's already happening. They won't get to you if they can't find you. Therefore, my dear child, you must not be found. But beware, Daughter. It is going to be very hard on the Feminine everywhere. The people's women, themselves, shall become subject to the rape, as well. It will go hard on your sister, particularly."

There was a silence between them, surrounded with the sound of the wind in the rocks. Mom spoke into it. "Do not look at it, Daughter. It came from outside, from beyond the Sun, but now it is within me. The rape has begun. It is within me, and without my consent. Remember, I will survive it. So will you, and so will your sister."

There was a sudden rumble, and the ground shook a little, dislodging a rock from the Wolf's Head. It came cracking down, making a sound like ice breaking. They watched as the shaking passed as a wave out through the mountains, making trees sway, until it disappeared over the horizon.

"Come on then, Little Girl," Mom said, standing up. "Let's go see your sister, and make sure the house hasn't fallen down."

Calley stood, and flapped the sides and bottom of Her cloak like wings, shaking off the grass and dirt. Mom stood and did the same. When She flapped Her cloak, She came off the ground, levitating. Calley smiled and did the same. Together They floated, red and black, gray and gold, down from the Wolf's Head, down into the ancient forest, and disappeared.

Alam woke in the gloaming. He rose in the last light, found his kilt and tunic and put them on. He walked barefoot out into the yard. The dogs had brought the sheep down from the hillside and were sitting sentinel at the entrance to the pen, waiting for him to put the stile in place. He walked past them with a sideways "Good dogs," and they whined and thumped their tails with pleasure.

He went to the edge of the yard, lifted his kilt with one hand and took up his phallus in the other. He peed a long steaming stream into the weeds, breathing out with a sigh of pleasure. When he was done, he shook it, then shook it out in the general direction he was facing. Suddenly struck with an inspiration he turned, shaking his pecker in the four directions. When he came round to where he started, he leaned back and shook it at the sky. He spoke to it, "You, my friend, are the lover of a Goddess."

He dropped his kilt, went back to the pen and put the stile logs in place, dropping them into slots left for that purpose in the stacked rock wall. The dogs, freed of their duties, ran for the river.

He picked up an armload of wood and re-entered the house. He built up a small fire from the coals and moved the gruel pot closer to warm up. He thought he felt a draft so he stood up and turned around to check the hide covering the door. There was the stag man, standing there, horns laid back, erection in one hand, leaning against the wall with the other.

"Tell me what you want, mortal. You can have some more of this for free," he said, shaking the erection at him. "Tell me you want this, and I'll tell you what you want to know."

Alam stared at it, the erection, his mind filling with memories of all the things he'd had to do with it, the trade-offs for what he wanted to know. He said, "You'll tell me what I want to know in any event. I remind you I spared your life."

"An action you may live to regret, mortal. Now what do you want?"

the stag man retorted, letting go of his erection.

"I want one more shape."

"And what shape is that?"

"Wolf." Alam replied.

The stag man's eyes grew large, reflecting greenly in the fire light. "You will never beat me. I cannot be taken down, no matter how powerful you become," the stag man said with such quiet sternness that Alam knew it to be true.

"I wouldn't try," Alam said.

The stag man looked at him with one of those clear pauses that left no doubt, turned and went out the door, gesturing for Alam to follow him. They walked over to the tree line where the wolves had established a territorial marker. As Alam had studied it, he couldn't be sure if it was marking a boundary or simply a warning to a traveler that the sheep in the pen belonged to these wolves.

The ground was damp at the edges of the marker. The stag man, with his flair for drama, ordered Alam to his knees—the stag man's pecker twitched at the sight of it. He reached down and scooped up a handful of urine dampened earth. He rubbed it all over Alam's face, particularly on his upper lip, and stood back. He used more damp earth to fashion Alam's hair into a rough approximation of a wolf's ears, making him look ridiculous.

Alam waited on his knees, his eyes closed. The stag man smiled, slowly drawing up the dirt to make the mass of his huge stag form. When the transition was completed, still seeming to smile, the stag turned and kicked Alam with the injured hind leg in the middle of the forehead, a quick, slashing strike. Laughing, chortling really, the stag bounded off.

The blow knocked Alam unconscious, backward into to the excrement pile of the marker near the base of a tree. Blood flowed from his forehead into the dirt on his face, and slowly Alam started to come apart, shedding mass and form into the pile. When what was left of him had about the size of a wolf, the new form began to take shape. Alam slid sideways, taking on hair, sprouting a tail, extending a sharp-toothed snout. The wolf was black, and between the ears was a white blaze on the forehead, a scar from the last act of the stag man's hoof. It was a sign, a reminder, that the wolf should take care, and not confront its superior.

Alam, now completely in his wolf form, twitched his legs, dreaming he was running. The sensation of four legs brought him back to consciousness, images of hunting red deer, scattering a herd, scanning for a pick, still haunting the back of his mind. He sat up off his side quickly, scanning the immediate area for threats. He tried to smell around him but the stink from the marker was too overwhelming. He stood and quickly stepped away from the pile.

He sniffed the air, looking for the stag. He could tell which way the stag had gone, and that he was nowhere around, long gone. The sheep in the pen bleated, frightened at the new scent. The dogs came to the threshold and growled. Alam decided to leave things with them as they were; he'd familiarize with them later. Instead, he turned and bounded down the path to the river, eager to figure out his new tongue.

On the appointed morning, the morning of the full moon, Alam rose early to step out into the yard to urinate. Scanning the yard he noticed a huge ram lying on the rock fence. The beast, far larger than his own shape-shifted ram, regarded him with one expressionless eye from a disdainful profile view.

Surprised, Alam speculated that the earliness of his guide's arrival presaged a long walk. When he returned to the house he dressed in his cleanest kilt and tunic, thought better of it, and went down to the river to bathe. Dressing again, he packed a small loaf of bread. He was going pack a fore shank of mutton, then he thought better of that, too. He didn't want to risk offending his guide.

The walk was long and difficult. The ram did not stop. When Alam tried to look up to keep his bearings, he found himself tripping and stumbling every time. After a while he stopped trying to keep track of where he was and focused on the ground in front of his feet. The day became overcast, with the clouds low on the mountains, obscuring the peaks, and, shortly after he lost his sense of location, he lost his sense of direction, as well.

They arrived outside a small farm with an enclosed yard. When the ram stopped, Alam stopped and looked around. He was on a small hill above a stream that ran down from the hills and through the farm yard, with a gate on one bank. There were no animals visible in the yard. Smoke was rising from one chimney. He stood there, looking, alternating between fear and joy.

When he and Calley were together, their interactions were quick and action-filled. They had hardly spent time together in any other context; never had a long conversation, never eaten together. The longest time they'd spent together was once when he was working at the forge. He'd turned around and found her standing there, watching him. He couldn't know for sure how long she had been standing there, but he intuited it had been a while.

He didn't know how to behave. He decided he would just smile a lot.

He saw Calley's head appear through a doorway, and then suddenly she was standing beside him. She nodded to the ram, took Alam by the arm, crossed the stream on the rocks with him, and took him through the gate. He realized when he was through the gate that he could look up and around at the view again, noticing the cloud cover was lifting. When he looked forward he saw another woman standing in the door-way. He paused.

Calley said, "That's my sister, Bree. Bree, this is Alam."

Alam bowed, which Bree acknowledged by inclining of her head. Alam grinned. Bree returned the smile reservedly and stepped back into the house.

The weather cleared during the rest of the afternoon. The conversation consisted of Calley asking Alam questions about his life while Bree was listening. Bree noted that he had eyes only for Calley, and that he cast just one inquisitive glance at her when he first entered, looking at her in the same way he looked around the room, taking it all in, nothing untoward in him. Calley left out any questions related to his wanking routines.

They ate a stew for dinner. At sunset they all went outside to watch. The moon rising at the same time kept the landscape well lit. Bree returned to the house and Calley took Alam to the edge of the yard. When Bree looked out a few minutes later she saw her sister bent forward with her skirts pulled up and Alam taking her from behind, swirls of energy at his temples, threatening to become spiral horns. She laughed out loud.

Calley heard the laughter and started laughing, too. She couldn't continue and pushed Alam through the gate with his kilt tented. "I will see you again, soon," she said. She pointed toward the hill where the guide was waiting.

Returning to the house she looked at Bree and asked, "Well?"

"A deep subject," Bree said, grinning broadly. Calley snorted in response.

"Bring him back in a month," Bree said, indicating her acceptance of his presence. "We'll see what more there is to him."

Several years later the way to Calley and Bree's house still could not be easily found. Although Alam had been there many times to see Calley, he always required a guide. He'd noticed that the way required him to look down, staring at his feet, and the path ahead and the guide, not looking up or studying landmarks. When he'd gone back, trying to find his way there he would only get so far and then lose the trail.

It seemed also that they went by different trails on different occasions. Either that, he'd thought, or the place moves around. Which, it turned out, it did. The house didn't move, the mountain where the house was situated moved from place to place. It was always at the end of a series of false tops, requiring him to rise to ever higher and higher vistas. And, no matter what trail they took, they always approached the house from the same view.

The mountain behind the house was steep, rising to a top with three rock outcroppings, the tops of which were covered in grass. The outcroppings on either side extended down the mountain veering left and right. The central rocks were set off from the others by short widths of meadow, coming together in a V-shape below the outcropping. From below it looked like the tops of the thighs and the mound of a woman. Halfway down to the house a spring burst from the end of the meadow, cutting a rocky bottomed stream that ran into the compound. The stream emerged from the compound then turned off to the side, where it appeared to go over a short falls.

There were two long stone houses with thatched roofs set at right angles to each other, surrounded by a yard and then pens with sheds backing up against a completely surrounding stone fence. The gate through the fence was a dolmen; two large flat standing stones set on edge and a larger flat stone set on top of these two. Alam knew that the top stone would fall forward to close the entrance, then, miraculously rise along the edges of the support stones back into place to open it again. There was always a cloud , or a fog, along the ground that separated the gate from the knoll where Alam and the guide would come out from the trail.

It was again the morning of the full moon. When Alam emerged at first light from his house, the black ram was waiting there, resting on top of the pen wall, head with massive curling horns set nobly in profile. It didn't move the whole time Alam prepared for the trip. He had a small pack with a change of clothes, including a nice tunic to go over a clean kilt. Over one shoulder he strapped a short sword and over the other his bow with a few arrows wrapped to it.

On a previous trip to the house Calley and her sister Bree had made him bathe in the stream and wash his clothes before they'd let him in the house. He'd sat out naked inside one of the sheds, avoiding the rain, trying to dry off. They'd left him there for a few hours, until there was a break in the rain to bring him a newly fashioned kilt. They'd taken him to the house then, and left him shirtless while his clothes dried near the fire.

Bree was often not present when Alam came. Calley would only say that She had work that would take Her away. When She was there, Bree would tease him about the encounters that he'd had with Calley, often with the bawdiest language. Remembering all this made Alam laugh. The ram jumped down off the rock, went over to the head of the trail that led to the river and looked back over its shoulder at Alam. Alam started after it at a jog, the ram leading the way.

It was a long trip this time. Sometimes it seemed that they would arrive after a morning's jog. Today they stopped at noon to rest. Alam always had a small loaf of bread with him. The ram disdained it when Alam offered him a piece. Alam used the opportunity to study the ram's horns. They were massive, curling out in a four turn spiral that extended to a very polished and sharp looking point which could be swung hard enough to break a wolf's ribs. As he thought about a wolf the ram stood up immediately and snuffed the air, searching. Now that it was standing, it refused to lie down again; instead it stared at Alam, willing him to get up and resume the journey.

As they rose from the river valley up into the mountains, time seemed to slow down, as did their pace. There was no more jogging. The higher they went the harder it became for Alam; at one point lifting his feet felt like travelling through a bog. Even the ram's pace had slowed, and his small steps seemed to take a long time. The effort gave Alam a headache.

Suddenly, at what felt to him like the last step he could make without resting, Alam came to a full stop and took a long, very slow breath. The inhale and exhale seemed to go on forever. He felt his heart rate slow, slow way down until it seemed that he could discern the sun move between beats. His breath slowed to match that beat. With a rush Alam's head cleared and he felt like he had entered another world, like a dream world, where he could walk normally again. His next step felt normal.

It was always like this on his way to the house. He would come to some spot where he could go no further, and it seemed to him that the whole world slowed to a stop. Then he would step out, or step through, and the world would seem normal to him. Calley explained to him once that the way time flowed had to change for him so that he could stay safely and easily in Her world. He knew it to be true and when he returned to his regular life there would always be a reciprocal change when he left. He would find himself speeding up, often running downhill. When he stopped, his heart, slowing from pounding with the effort, would put him, and his breath, back in the Mundane world that was his home. The transition back to his world would hurt his heart, and his guts would knot into a terror he couldn't understand.

Calley framed it as a price he had to pay if he wanted to be with Her for any length of time. For his part, it was an easy choice to make. Being with Calley, making love to Her, brought him to places of such mind and heart soothing ecstasy that he longed constantly to be with Her.

One day he lay in bed, moaning the entire day. Now, he refused to become so love-sick that it incapacitated him, but it was hard work to keep his feelings in line. In the years they had been lovers, he had come to an inner resolve that if there was some way he could stay in Her world, stay with Her, he would do it, and do it in less time than his own heart took to beat.

He had resolved to tell Calley about this desire of his, and his need for Her, even though he was afraid that his confession would lead Her to send him away. Arriving on the rise opposite Her house, the ram lay down while he stood there, contemplating his resolve and his devotion to Her. He would be Her servant if She would only let him. He would be Her servant in all things. His heart answered only to that prospect, the Mundane world no longer held anything for him.

He looked past the foggy cloud at the gate into the compound, and saw that She was standing there in the yard by the door to one of the houses, looking at him. He waved at Her, and She, in turn, waved him to come on in. He went toward the place where the stream bent and entered the cloud, emerging with his hair damp with small beads of water. He headed toward the gate, his heart filled with joy and terror and, surprisingly, lust for the beautiful woman dressed only in Her long hair, by whom he had just been beckoned.

15

CURRICULUM

PART ONE PREPARING SACRED GROUND

Beverly Washington stood watching the sun rise from the ground floor office window in the East Wing of Stonehaven. The sun was coming over a ridge, making the rise an hour later than true horizon. "It's so beautiful," she thought to herself, blowing the steam from a cup of tea before taking a sip. She heard the door opening behind her. Rachel came in, carrying another pot of hot water, which she hung on the swivel hook attached to the fireplace.

It was winter, and Beverly had been thinking about the children, her own and Rachel's son David. She was wondering about all the changes that were happening now that two college graduations were coming— her oldest daughter's and David's. Both had applied to law schools in the northeast. Her other two were still in college. She had always hoped that David would get together with her daughter, but they were both too independent. She'd caught them together once during one of the Christmas visits. Naked, on top of the bed, with their heads toward each other's feet, in the too-warm room, fire blazing. She'd smiled and closed the door quietly. She'd always wondered if they'd seen her, because she never caught them again, and they never seemed to get closer. They were determined, it seemed, to create separate lives.

Rachel came up beside her, carrying her own cup of tea. Rachel said, "I miss them."

"Me, too," Beverly sighed. The children, along with some friends, had come for Christmas but had now departed for other houses to celebrate the New Year. For the moment, the four of them—Rachel and Craft, herself and her lover Paul—had the place to themselves, although the managers were expected to arrive with their support staff at the beginning of March for the annual retreat. Then there would be the Meeting of the Sisters, a precursor circle to the Council. It would be 1960 next year and they had to work on the new decade plan.

Paul Manfred was the head accountant at Rachel's trust corporation and, along with Beverly, helped to direct her various enterprises. Paul had been tasked with beginning to set up the corporate diversification process. Rachel wanted to be completely out of arms manufacturing and had a number of ideas about the kinds of businesses she wanted to set up. Beverly had been helping her fantasize about it.

More importantly, Paul had come to understand the nature of the Divine Feminine through the wen and from many talks with Craft. He was thoroughly on board with Rachel's vision to establish a school to train Priestesses and Consorts for the return of the Diosa. He was brought into all the planning of this—necessarily hidden—enterprise, as well.

Beverly was curious about some new additions to the Sisters meeting. A wen named Amanda MacGregor and her daughter Regina had been invited and it was Beverly's job to make sure the travel arrangements were in place.

Beverly leaned over and kissed Rachel on the cheek. "So, tell me about Amanda and her daughter—what is it, Regina?"

"Amanda was one of the wen in the group trained by the Lama Dzordze to do his sacred temple dances. She is also one of the wen who had a child with him, like I did. Regina is his daughter, like David is his son.

"They escaped France in 1939, right before the invasion. I don't know if Regina was born then, or born after Amanda returned home to Scotland.

"We've been in touch by mail since the war ended. Like me, she didn't attend the funeral when the Lama died in 1949. The Lama taught her a great deal about his tantra, but I don't know how much she's done with it. She's been pretty isolated. I do know that she has been studying the practices of her people's old ways—the Celtic ways—and, according to what she's written, has established contact with the Diosa in Her face as Brighid.

"She wants to bring her daughter here to study, and her daughter wants to come. Imagine that!"

Beverly laughed. "Imagine it not!" she replied, and Rachel laughed in reply.

"Seriously, Rachel, what are we going to do? Your vision is so grand, and sometimes it frightens me."

"We're going to do it as simply as we can. We follow Diosa's advice. We both see Her. We agree with Her, and with each other. That's how we do it, at least.

"As to what we do—we take Paul's advice on how to implement the ideas, both in the business and in the Order."

"Why do we have to call it an Order?" Beverly wanted to know.

"What else *is* there to call it? A circle? A council? Of course, we may use all those patterns, but an Order has discipline and requires a commitment. It requires an initiation, which is the only way I know of to permanently change the organization of a person's sentiments. And maybe it sounds corny, but the simplicity of the name *Order of the Fleur de Vie, the Flower of Life*, leaves room for a lot of meaning. Not just the commonly understood concepts, but the inner Flower that both you and I know about. It is what will set us apart, and that apartness, that different flower, must be one of our secrets."

"Yes. On some level I know this. It is thrilling, but thrilling is also scary. I remember the first time I saw it. I...well...that we carry it within us..." Beverly's voice trailed away. She took a sip of tea.

"Yes, I know," said Rachel, taking a sip. "Maybe in the future they will change it. But for now, we have to have secrets within secrets. That world out there," Rachel pointed through the window, "will not let us function in the open. Like concentric rings, like some city of old, with gates only in certain places, we shall organize. We shall train the wen, and we shall train the men. It is not my vision alone; it is Her's. I have Faith."

"I have Faith, too," Beverly sighed. "I suppose it is Trust I do not have."

"Trust does not belong here," Rachel replied. "We must rely on discernment and knowledge."

"And Faith," Beverly added.

"And Faith," Rachel agreed.

After standing in silence for a moment, slitting their eyes as the sun topped the far ridge, bathed in its red gold luminance, communing, feeling into each other, supporting each other in the felt sense of Faith, Beverly sighed.

"So, what do you say, Beverly? Shall we go eat?" Rachel asked. "The men have been in the kitchen since late dark, making breakfast."

When they arrived in the kitchen both men were carrying trays to the dumbwaiter. They were wearing aprons, big rubber boots, and nothing else. It was also clear that, under the aprons, they were erect. Rachel laughed out loud when she realized it.

"What are you two doing?" Beverly asked.

"Bringing you breakfast," Paul replied.

"I can see that," Beverly stated. "I suppose I mean what were the two of you doing, I mean, look at you. Hard as hammer handles.

"What? Why?" Paul stuttered.

Craft said, "Doing? Nothing. Why? Oh, these...well, we were talking about the two of you and it just sort of happened. It got uncomfortable in our clothes so we just took them off, had this crazy idea to bring you breakfast like this."

Paul, still trying to wrap his mind around Beverly's implication, asked, "Why? What did you think we were doing?"

Rachel laughed out loud again.

It was Paul's third winter visit to Stonehaven. The first year Beverly had brought him along in both his role as chief accountant for Rachel's firms, and as her lover. The winter visit lasted a month and near the end of that time Rachel and Craft had switched lovers with Beverly and Paul. Craft, who had already been a lover of Beverly's, with Rachel's encouragement on previous winter visits, had been delighted. Paul, to whom this was both new and an indication of the path to a blissful life, had adapted and taken on the role of Consort to their Priestesses. Rachel had a practical philosophy about sex and she wanted to test the fundamental hypotheses.

In the week since the children and the farm help, including Morton and his wife, had all departed, the four of them had taken to sleeping together in the same room, often on the same bed. Although the sex was still hetero, the shared intimacy had begun building bonds among the four of them. A deep sense of being comfortable had established itself. The men in particular had become close, at ease with each other, comfortable with touching each other, although the sexual attraction was for the wen.

In a teasing mode, Beverly and Rachel had openly speculated the previous night about whether or not it would stay that way. The men, only slightly embarrassed, had teased back that if it did happen—if they did become sexually involved with each other—they might like it so much they wouldn't come back. Then where would Rachel and Beverly be? Rachel teased back that she and Beverly had been roommates in college and wouldn't they like to know what they would be doing if the men became too fond of having a cock in their mouths.

The teasing brought a lot of emotional and sexual tension into the room. Both men had had sexual encounters with other men earlier in their lives. For each, their first sexual experiences had been with other boys and had involved masturbation, oral sex, and orgasm. They had internalized a fundamental ambivalence about the encounters that persisted despite their grown identification, not just preference, as heterosexual men. Bisexuality didn't appeal to either of them.

The tension in the room over the unspoken past was palpable. The teasing had ended and a smoke-like silence had settled into the room. They were sitting in high back leather chairs around the fireplace in the ground floor office, sipping a nice scotch. Rachel broke the silence by taking a sip of whiskey and sighing. "Now, I know things aren't being said."

Beverly moved to speak but Rachel put a hand on her arm to silence her.

Craft started speaking.

"I was young, perhaps thirteen, and had been invited to a neighbor boy's house to play. I forget what. We ended up in his basement, again I forget why. He was a year, perhaps two, older, and while there in the basement he asked me if it ever got hard, and said that his did, and he wanted to know if I ever played with it. I said I didn't. He said he'd show me how and asked if I wanted to see it. I must have said yes because the next thing I remember is that it was out of his trousers, and hard and in his hands. Then he said that since I had seen his, now I had to show him mine. So I did.

"Mine had gotten hard as soon as he had asked me the question. I took mine out, too. Soon we were stroking ourselves, then we were stroking each other's. He said he'd put mine in his mouth if I would put his in mine. We went over to two old wooden chairs against the wall and dropped our trousers to our knees and sat down. He said, "You first," and put his hand on the back of my head and pushed it down to his cock. It was larger than mine and I hesitated, wondering how much of it would fit. He pushed a little harder and then I had him in my mouth. He told me to suck it, so I did, like I was drinking something through a straw. He told me to move my mouth up and down, so I did.

"He said I wasn't doing it very well, and to let him show me. I got up on my knees on the chair seat beside him. I arched forward toward him and he took me in one hand and steered me into his mouth. He leaned sideways so I was facing the back of the chair, and he had me move my hips back and forth, face-fucking him. He was pretty good at sucking and moving his head, too. I figured he had done this before.

"After a while he sat up and said there was something else, that we could both shoot stuff with our dicks. He said, 'Here, I'll show you.' Then, sitting next to each other, we masturbated each other until we orgasmed, coming on our bellies and thighs. I believe I went first, because I remember him insisting that I had to finish him. When we were done, we used a handkerchief he had to clean ourselves up.

"That blast of pleasure I had was the most intense experience of my life. I wanted to do it again. I was kind of shook up, though. I remember being surprised at how much come there was, and something happened while I watched him coming, watched the ejaculate coming out, some shock hit me.

"I told him I had to go. He made me promise not to tell anyone—not that I would have—and told me that if I came back we could do it again and he would show me other stuff. I told him I would come back and walked home. The first thing I did was go inside and to the bathroom and I sat there and masturbated again. I masturbated a lot after that, although I never went back to his house. It hurt his feelings, but I wanted to stay away from the shock. I'd take all the pleasure I could get from my own hand, but I didn't want to do it with him. I had a few other experiences with other boys and young men. These troubled me, too."

"Why did they trouble you, John?" Rachel asked.

"Well, I wasn't really worried about being a homosexual. Girls did it for me, and I would do it for them as often as I could get close to one. I became a really good petter. But I was worried about being seen as a homosexual, or about becoming one. Eventually, I just wouldn't let myself get in the position, you know, get into the situation where it could happen."

Craft had drained his glass while he was talking and he stood up to reach the bottle.

Rachel said, "It made me wet, listening to your story."

Beverly said, "Me, too. What about you Paul?"

Paul said, "It made me want to get hard while he talked. It started to, but then I frowned at it, and it went away."

Everyone laughed. "No, not that, fool. What about you, what's your story?" Beverly wanted to know.

"My story?" Paul started. "My story is similar. It started early for me, though. About age 6, same thing, an older boy said, 'I'll show you mine if you show me yours.' I don't know why that line always seems to work. We didn't do anything else, we didn't even have a clue about what to do. I got to do that with little girls a couple of times, too.

"With guys, though? Yes, there were a couple times. I was in a youth corps group before the war. I was thirteen or maybe fourteen. In the summer they sent us out into the woods to build trails. Some of the guys were bragging about how much pubic hair and how much experience they'd had. One night the older men who were responsible for us went to town to get drunk. They left the older ones in charge of the camp. The bragging started up again and some of the younger boys dared the older ones to show or shut up. So they did.

"They went over by the fire, dropped their trousers, and showed off. Some of them, of course, got hard, and they'd play with it, dancing around, but nothing really happened. None of them touched each other, although they talked about girls doing it. After a while, everything calmed down and we all pretended to sleep. But a little later, once someone started to snore, you could hear voices in different places making sounds, sounds like they were masturbating. Sometimes you could hear sounds, even whispers, from different places, and I kind of knew what was happening. Some guys weren't just jerking themselves off, they were jerking off the guy in the bedroll next to them.

"Listening to the sounds and whispers made me hard, certainly. I whispered to the guy next to me, a shy guy who always kind of held back. I could hear him breathing hard. I think I said something like, 'Want help?' and he turned to me and lifted up the edge of his blankets. I could just make it out in the darkness, his penis was out of his shorts, in his hand, and pointing at me. I could see why he was shy, he scarcely had any hair. I was on my side and I bent forward and put him in my mouth and sucked on him for a minute or so. Then I laid back, expecting him to do the same, but he wouldn't. So we just pulled on each other's cocks until we came. He came mostly in my hand, I shot out all over the dirt. I think I even landed some in his blankets.

"I think I may have had dreams before this, dreams where I woke up ejaculating into my pajama bottoms at home, but that's probably the first time I had an orgasm with another's help."

Craft brought him the whiskey bottle and refilled his tumbler.

"Thanks," Paul said. "You know, it was kind of like it was with him," he continued. "Eventually the compass pointed to girls, and it's been that way ever since."

"Yeah," Craft said. "The one-eyed snake is blind."

"What?" Rachel asked, laughing. "Say that again."

"The one-eyed snake is blind."

"Oh, Diosa, I love it," Beverly laughed also. "But what does it mean?"

"It means that the dick doesn't care where it puts itself. And it will put itself anywhere it can once you get a rise out of it," Craft answered.

"Exactly," Paul agreed. "It doesn't care. At least in the beginning. I'm the one who developed discrimination, it didn't. In the beginning it was just exploration, that's all."

"So, you feel OK about it now?" Rachel asked.

"Yes. For the most part. Something still feels odd about it. I'm not ashamed of it, exactly, but I'm not proud of it either," Paul answered.

"What, and you're proud of your conquests of wen?" Beverly asked, with a little mock outrage in her tone.

"No, it's not that, exactly," Craft picked up the answer. "Getting close to a girl, getting some kind of access, was something to be a little proud of; guys bragged about it. At least until they grew up a little bit and learned better. It's really a private thing, and girls who are generous at a young age always get a bad reputation if they go with a guy who talks about it. That gets him cut off. But it's like it he said," indicating Paul, "I'm not ashamed of it, but I'm not happy about it."

There was a pause. They all sipped at their whiskey while they let this understanding settle in.

Rachel opened the conversation again. "So, you never took it in your ass? Never put yours in another guy's ass?"

"No," Paul said calmly, looking into his glass, stirring the whiskey, watching it drain down the inside of the glass, studying its legs.

"Nope," Craft answered quietly as well.

"Well, I certainly have," Rachel said, with more volume. "There are whole sections of the tantra that are about ass work. I know. I've been through most of them. It's what we were required to do at the temple when our fertility prevented us from coitus. Now, that's something we have to make sure we include in the program: teaching the wen how to know when they're fertile. But," she said with emphasis, "there's ass work for guys."

Then, grinning, she watched their faces, looking to see how they reacted. The men composed their faces, revealing little. Some of the composure was clearly feigned indifference. They cared—they clearly had an emotional reaction to the prospect, but they weren't yet ready to talk about their feelings. There was some sorting to do, and some naming of what those feelings actually were.

Craft's face was passive, Paul's was pensive, so she decided to start with him. "What are you thinking about, Paul? You seem concerned about something."

Paul held his breath and sat forward, putting his elbows on his knees. "I'm not sure. I suppose my question is, 'Are you going to include them'?"

"'Them,' who?" Rachel asked gently.

"You know," he replied. "The homosexuals."

"Yes, Paul," she replied simply. "The Mother made all of us. We were all born of mothers. Generally speaking, mothers love all their children. I cannot turn away some of my siblings because they are different than I am or different than you are. If even the stones are safe here, then so shall they be. Of course, they will be included."

Craft watched the exchange closely.

Paul said, "Are you sure?"

"What a strange question. Of course, we are. Now let me ask you one. Are you sure?" Rachel responded.

"Am I sure about what?" Paul asked, considering. "Oh, I see. Am I 'sure' about my commitment? Or am I 'sure' about my sexuality?"

"Yes," Rachel said. She gave him the time he needed to consider his answer. After near to a minute of time passed, she said, "I'm waiting. So is She." Rachel leaned forward and put her hands in a mudra with the fingers pointing in opposite directions, up and down.

Paul said, "I am committed to Her, Rachel, and to this enterprise. Of that, I am sure."

Craft, from the side, saw the flash of the Diosa within Rachel. He tensed, knowing something of Rachel's power and knowing nothing of what might happen next.

"But about my sexuality? I don't know, honestly. And if I say I don't know, that means I'm not sure, doesn't it?" Paul finished answering the question.

The tension in Rachel's hands eased, and she returned one to her lap, and took a sip on her whiskey. "Maybe," she said. "But wouldn't you like the chance to find out?"

"Again, Rachel, I don't know. I'm not sure," Paul answered.

"Well, you think about it. Feel into it and see what comes up," Rachel said.

"So to speak," Beverly added, giggling.

Paul sat back, sighing with relief.

"And you, Mr. Quietude?" Rachel asked, directing her attention to Craft.

Craft sat up and took a long pull on his whiskey. "I'm with you," he said, toasting Rachel.

Beverly said, "Ass work. My, my."

There were no other topics of conversation that evening.

Later that night Rachel arranged a special tantric ritual. She told the men, "Look, we don't know yet what the Diosa intends for us. But there is always a way to find out. We ask Her. Let's ask Her together, shall we?"

They retired to the East Wing office and built up the fire. They pushed two ottomans together and the men sat on them, naked, back to back, back leaning into back, full contact.

The wen had pulled their hair up on top of their heads, tied in place with white silk strips, and left it to fall, like the tail of a proud horse. They changed into winter robes, open down the front. While they changed, Rachel told Beverly what to do.

The wen started by going to their knees, taking the men into their mouths, lightly, sucking. They used their hands, stroking the testicles, then lower, across the perineum. They kissed there also. They sat back on their heels, leaving a finger of one hand, moistened, rest on the anus. With the other they stroked the erections, feeling the twitching from the asshole travel all the way into the shaft. They contemplated their handiwork for a moment smiling while the men struggled to control their feelings. The men's reaction to the finger, the impulse to withdraw from it, had pushed both of them closer into each other's backs.

The wen brought their heads forward again. The ritual almost ended when Beverly gagged on a pubic hair. She gacked several times, cursing, and was able to clear it, but the moment was almost lost. Rachel laughed at it, and that made them all relax.

The wen rose in unison, stepping up across the men's laps, settling their forearms on the men's shoulders. The men, as trained, were holding their erections straight up and a little away, allowing the wen to ease themselves down onto the rods.

Slowly, the wen eased themselves down, then they rocked in unison, orgasming, and holding onto each other over the men's shoulders. Keeping their right feet on the ground they hooked their left legs around the Consorts and over each other's right leg. They breathed this way for four slow breaths and summoned the Goddess, the Diosa.

The Diosa came and abided in both of the wen. The men, the Consorts, had seen this before and knew that nothing was required of them except to look into the eyes of the Priestesses, to hold their gaze, to allow Diosa to look out and see devotion and love. The Priestesses gave the Diosa time to know and feel the pleasure, the ecstasy, the feeding.

Rachel leaned in and said, "She wishes to speak."

Then, in unrehearsed unison, both wen spoke as one, "I may ask you to do something you do not want to do. But I will never ask you to do something that goes against your Nature."

And then both wen, Priestesses, threw their arms open, up toward the ceiling, and started laughing and orgasming, riding, bucking on their men, their Consorts, hard and fast. Then the Priestesses put their hands on the shoulders of the Consorts, leaned forward and said, "Now."

Thus released, the Consorts used their arms to raise up their hips, planking, upper backs leaning into each other hard, lifting the Priestesses off the floor, freeing the wen to truly ride. Release came to the Consorts at the same time, and, connected to each other at the shoulders and then at the backs of their heads, they felt each other come. Almost, it seemed, each feeling two comings at the same time.

When the Consorts finished pulsing from their planks they held the position for a moment. The Diosa lofted Herself out from Her Priestesses, blessing them with love as She withdrew. The men sat back down. The wen, newly free of the Goddess, leaned forward into the men, hanging on, and hanging on to each other. Slowing, slowing, Rachel asked, "How did you know to plank when you did?

The men answered in unison, "I saw it in my mind." That night they slept in separate beds in the great guest room on the second floor, as instructed by Diosa. So much time together could become too much time together. It could become binding. It was necessary to balance the time together with time alone.

All these memories flashed, faster than could be caught and examined in stable images, through Rachel's mind as she stood there in the kitchen laughing. It set her mind on a platform of consideration. She knew the Diosa, or her helpers, facets of Her will, would work on people when they slept. They usually preferred to work on someone with their energy field intact and isolated, rather than entangled with a sleeping partner.

Her thoughts returning to the current morning, she regarded the two beautiful men, pantsless behind aprons, holding up breakfast trays, and wondered if they needed to spend some time alone.

Beverly had moved and taken Paul's tray and set it on the counter behind him. She'd pulled aside the apron to look at what was under it. She sucked in her breath when her eyes fell on Paul's erection. His hair had been cut. His pubes were trimmed down close to the skin, as close as scissors could get it.

She looked up at him. "No more gacking," he said. She smiled, and got down on her knees, holding his erection, examining his scrotum, stroking lightly. She looked up and over at Craft. "You, too?" she asked.

"Yes," Craft said. He turned and set down his tray, turned back and pulled the apron aside so that Rachel and Beverly could see. He, too, was close-cropped, starting at his lower belly. Rachel was suddenly determined to seize the moment.

"It's cold down there on the floor. You two," she said, indicating the men, "get your butts up on the counter." The men did so. The wen moved in, Beverly reading Rachel's mind. Very slowly they grasped the men's erections with both hands, pulling upward, raising again the poles that had begun to flag.

Rachel looked at Beverly and said, "Practice." In this context, practice meant that they were to practice the art of orgasm simply by feeding on the masculine. This was attainable by establishing an internal energetic connection between the tongue and palate to the clitoris. With time and practice, this connection could be triggered almost instantly, and the wen could begin the cultivation of the state of continuous orgasm.

By using the phallus to connect the tongue and palate, rather than the tongue itself making the connection, a charge was introduced into the internal energetic loop known as the microcosmic orbit and forced the circulation of energies to increase. The clitoris becomes erectile in response to the erectness of the phallus. It will light up sometimes as it swells, radiating energy that pulses a wen into a field of blissful stimulation. It becomes possible to even journey, eyes rolled back in the head, to the palace of a thousand lights.

Soon, holding their heads still, circulating the energies, the wen's legs were shaking. In not too long a time, they had to return to being present to keep their legs from collapsing beneath them. Rachel lifted up her head, as did Beverly. "Good one," Rachel said. Beverly looked at her and nodded, saying "Uh huh. Let's eat."

So they stood at the counters and ate, the men in their shirts and aprons and rubber boots, erections falling, letting the wen feed. The wen stood with their robes open down the front, showing their breasts and bellies and thighs. The men, for their part, were doing their internal work while the women ate. For the men, the tantric goal was to learn self-control, eventually learning to separate orgasm from ejaculation, enabling them to become repetitively, if not continuously, orgasmic. Part of the training involved having sex without release repeatedly, release no longer being the goal. Another part was that this enabled them to practice the 'big draw' exercise and practice the energetic circulation of the 'microcosmic orbit' with a completely activated nervous system. The men, who knew they would be having sex again later, were completely comfortable and pleased with the program. It enabled them to become better lovers, better Consorts, making love and having sex more often, and for longer periods of time.

Rachel said, "It's a good idea, I think."

"What?" Beverly asked around a mouthful of sausage.

"Trimming up down there. It reveals a different kind of beauty. I like it."

"Me, too. Shall we?"

"Yes, I think we shall. This morning let's let the men go down and handle the horses. You and I, we'll stay here and handle this," Rachel said, sliding one hand into her crotch, toast with jam in the other.

The men smiled. "Trail riding," Craft said to Paul, who shook his head in assent. Leaving the dishes until later, if the wen didn't do them, the men went upstairs to change for the barn. As he left the kitchen Paul turned back, pulled his apron aside, and shook his pecker at the wen. They laughed and waved him on. "Later," Beverly said.

While they were upstairs changing they decided to ride over the mountain and check the boundaries along the roads. The weather was dry, no snow on the ground except in the pass along the shoulder of the mountain, and not too cold. Craft liked night riding and this night's full moon would provide enough light for the final part of the trail back. They told the girls that they were going to prepare to spend the night out just in case something delayed them or they decided to go further out with the boundary riding. All the supplies were already at the barn, except the three flasks of whiskey, one for each and one for 'finish', which Craft had filled and put in his pockets.

They started up the ten-year-old Chevy pickup and rolled on over to the barn. The horses they were going to take were grained and curried, the rest were grained and hayed and let out into the paddock, winter coats shaggy in the morning light. They were going to ride two Connemaras and use a gentle Arabian for the packhorse. Rachel had been experimenting with different breeds over the years, although she still kept the Thoroughbreds she used for trick riding.

They changed clothes, pulling wool pants and shirts on over their union suits. Wool socks and lace-up boots, with toes that would fit in the stirrups of the western saddles, completed the basic layers. They both strapped on six-shooters and Craft took a 30-30 Winchester lever action for his saddle scabbard. Both men had old fashioned oil-skin dusters and wool felt hats for the top layer, and thick well-worn gloves with wool liners. They packed one horse with heavier clothes, food, and a simple kitchen, planning now to spend the night in a rock shelter down near the bottom of the west side of Piney Mountain. The horses were saddled, bedrolls behind, and a long lead line was attached to the halter of the packhorse. They saddled up and headed out of the barn doors and up the cove, planning to make the north boundary in three hours. The wen would bring the other horses in before dark.

In the Mansion the wen had finished eating and piled their dishes in the sink. They went back upstairs to the bathroom by the great bedroom. The steam plant kept the room warm, and, most importantly, provided plenty of hot water for bathing. They bathed at the same time, singing to each other through the partition.

Back in the bedroom, in their robes and brushing out their hair, Rachel threw more wood on the fire. "It needs to be warmer in here if we're going to do this."

Beverly agreed. "I don't want to be working on a shrinking purple bearded clam," she said.

Rachel laughed out loud at the image. "No, I expect not," she said. "So how shall we do this?"

"Let's start with combs and scissors. Let's trim it down that far, and see what it looks like. We'll need hand mirrors, too, I'm thinking," Beverly answered.

Sitting on the end of the bed, Rachel pulled up the back of her robe and sat on a towel. Beverly sat on a towel on the top of a cedar chest at the foot of the bed opposite, and looked down at her copious bush. "Girl friend, this is crazy," she said to Rachel. "Look at all this. Are you sure?"

Rachel cocked her head and closed her eyes. Beverly knew she was accessing the Diosa when she did this. "Yes," Rachel said. "She smiled and nodded Her head."

"Alright then," Beverly surrendered, and started combing and snipping inward from the tops of her thighs. When they were working on their lower bellies down as far as the pubic bone everything seemed to be going well. When they came around the corner and started having to work with their mirrors Beverly said, "Good grief. I have hair growing inside the outer lips. How can I? Couldn't we just have given it a good brushing and leave it at that?"

"No," Rachel said, staring hard into the hand mirror between her legs. "She gave the men the same idea, too. Let's do this. Now that we've started, let's see this through. Good grief is right. Looking at this now, the hair goes all the way around past my asshole."

"Yes, mine too," Beverly lamented.

"Well, we're just going to have to act like good sisters and help each other out. Here, I'll help you first," she said, standing up. "Lie down and spread them, sister. I'm coming to the rescue."

Beverly flopped back on the foot of the bed in mock surrender. "Oh. If you must, then you must," she said turning her face to the side and covering it with one arm, her gestures filled with faux drama. "Oh. I cannot bear to watch."

Rachel got to her knees and used Beverly's comb and scissors to work diligently for half an hour, having Beverly hold her legs up as she worked all the way around. Several times, while snipping along the edges of the vagina, both wen held their breath. When, at the end, she saw how hairy Beverly still was, she was struck with an idea. "Come with me, back to the bathroom."

When Beverly got there Rachel was rummaging around in Craft's shaving kit. She held up his safety razor with a triumphant smile. "Let's save ours, and use his."

"No," Beverly said, with a commendably small amount of dread.

So Rachel commended her. "Brave girl. Now go sit on the edge of the tub." Rachel made up a batch of lather and applied it with Craft's brush. Slowly and carefully Rachel shaved around the tops of Beverly's thighs. Then from the bottom of the pubic bone Rachel very carefully shaved down, and even inside the outer lips, using her free hand to pull the flesh one way then another, she stretched the skin tight, making not a single nick.

By the time she was finished, Beverly had become a juicy mess. The close attention, the unusual sensations, even Rachel's breath, had all combined to create a kind of dazed altered state of mind. Rachel, too, was in an altered state, but a clear and contemplative one. That much time up close and personal with the sacred of sacreds, the holy of holies, was new to her. The image seemed to burn in her mind's eye, and then, as she watched, it seemed to burst into flames, flames that didn't burn the flesh, but enlightened it instead.

"Squat down in the tub, dear. Wash off and then you can do me," Rachel said, gently.

Beverly did so, but when she went to squat she found her legs were shaking so badly that she had to sit down. As the warm water rose she started twisting, saying, "Oh, my Goddess, how this feels. Oh! Oh!" and thrashing her legs, she orgasmed, discharging all the acquired stress and excitation.

Rachel leaned on the tub and patted Beverly on the shoulder, then paused. Still in an altered state, she was trying to see what Diosa was showing her, trying to see what she, herself, was thinking, and the images were coming fast. She sighed deeply as Beverly's legs stopped shaking and she calmed down. Then the images slowed.

"This is ritual," Rachel said. "This is ritual that could be made sacred."

"What do you mean, Rachel?" Beverly asked, wanting nothing but to relax.

"It's ritual. Look, primates groom each other, right? They spend lots of time combing each other's hair, stroking each other. We don't do that, but we could. And we could elevate it to the level of ritual, make it sacred," Rachel paused to gather her next words.

"What happened to me while I was doing it, going into an altered state from spending so much time and concentration on the sacredness of your vagina, I found myself in both deep concentration and contemplation at the same time. I was lost in a deep concentration of the sacredness of life and the sacredness of what I was doing. The power of it, the power of your vagina, I believe, pushed me into this state. And I'm still in it," Rachel continued with a calm and steady tone.

"OK, I get it. This, something like this, needs to become a part of what we do. The symbolism of this, the preverbal impact, was amazing. And it wasn't particularly sexual, was it?" she concluded, helping Beverly get out of the tub. "It was so intimate, but it wasn't sexual, you know? Was it sexual for you?"

"No, not really. It wasn't sexual at all for me personally, but I think it may have been sexual for my pussy, know what I mean?"

"No. Say more."

"My pussy responded to all the attention, all the stroking and touching. I was afraid, but my pussy wasn't. It was odd, an internal state of division of awareness. But all that sensation is why I orgasmed the way I did."

Handing Beverly a towel, Rachel leaned back, putting her hand on the sink for support, she said, "I'm having a vision now. I am contemplating the door of a temple. That's what it was. That's where the power came from. I was contemplating the door of a temple."

"A temple of what?" Beverly asked.

"A temple of Life," Rachel answered, and in her mind's eye she saw Diosa smile. They both stood silently a moment, lost in reverie. Beverly came out of it first.

"OK, your turn," Beverly said.

"Wait," Rachel said. "I want to do this differently. I want to be able to fall back and journey while you're working. Would you mind terribly getting one of those big bowls from the kitchen and bringing it back up here? Bring a pitcher, too, and you can fill it with hot water when you get back up. I will move everything back to the bedroom."

When Beverly returned Rachel had set herself up on a chair so she could slide her sex forward where it would be easier for Beverly to reach and work. Also, if called into vision, Rachel could just lean back and journey.

"You're going to have to do it twice, Beverly," Rachel said. "It has to be a very close shave. And my instructions are that you are to take it all off. I'm to go bald."

Beverly said, "I'm walking funny."

PART TWO BOUNDARY RIDING

The men rode easily along the path up the cove, stopping occasionally to remove deadfall, heading for the north boundary. The property extended for a thousand yards beyond the dirt county road. For this ride, however, the intention was to ride as far as the road and then travel along a path set back off it in the trees, so that anyone passing on the road would not see the riders easily, yet the riders could see the road through the trees. The path had been made over the years by the riding classes and all the boundaries of the property had this kind of path.

The road ran roughly northwest to southeast after climbing the ridge on the back side of the mountain from the north. The men followed the path, crossing the ridge three peaks north of the Pine Eye peak. Near the road in the northwest corner they found a deer carcass on the edge of a clearing. The shoulders and haunches had been cut away by someone. They studied the tracks. One of the skills Craft wanted to continue to teach was tracking.

Circling around before they closed in on the carcass they found human footprints, two sets that approached the carcass from the road, where they found a set of tire tracks in the dirt. "When did this happen?" Craft asked.

Paul studied the tracks. "Two days ago. At least two nights. "

"Why do you say that?"

On the edges of the tracks, in the dirt, there are two lines of frost and thaw. That means two nights, three days before today."

"Check your math. If this morning counts as one thaw line, that leaves yesterday. Day before today I think. Night before last night, to be exact," Craft corrected.

Circling back in to the carcass they found several sets of tracks around it, which they studied slowly. Craft asked Paul what he saw. Paul identified the smaller tracks as skunk and raccoon. There was a larger set of paws with claw points out in front. He correctly identified these as bear, but he was surprised, and asked Craft about it. "It's winter. Shouldn't it be asleep?"

Craft replied, "Usually. But it's been a warm winter, no big snows yet. It could have gone to sleep on time but woke up. And it probably woke up hungry, so it wandered around, looking for food. You know what it means, right?"

"That its den could be near."

"That's right. And it could still be awake, or not very far asleep. We'll have to be careful. There's no reason for us to look for a cave, but we still have to be careful about rock shelters."

"Okay."

"But look deeper. What do you see?"

Paul looked closely for a few moments. Then he said, "Dog."

"Yup," Craft confirmed. "Keep looking."

"Two dogs. One came around but didn't come up to the carcass. The other just dived right in. And the second one's prints are on top of the first one's. Big dog, that second one."

"Yeah, big dog. Maybe not a dog," Craft mused.

"What do you mean?"

"Can't be a coyote. Could be a wolf."

"No. Not possible. There's never been a coyote sighting around here. And years since there's been a wolf."

"Oh, I don't know. You're right, it's too big to be coyote, but they're going to come, trust me. But it's a really big dog, or a wolf, maybe working its way down from Ontario. They've been known to swim the St. Lawrence River. In any case, it warrants watching, don't you think?"

"Yes. Either way, a big feral dog or a wolf. But the hunting by the locals needs watching, too, don't you think?"

"Yes, we'll watch it. But we don't want to stop the hunters. They came here to hunt this meadow, knowing the deer would come out here to graze. Maybe even they spotlighted it. And you know what? We want to keep good relations with the people around here. We don't want to draw attention to ourselves. Most likely they came out here to hunt because they knew it was easy, and they were hungry. It's winter, there's not much work, and not much work anyway. It was two days ago, judging by the crumbling of the tracks. The bear came the next day, the wolf came last night," Craft said.

They stood quietly for a moment, in reverie.

"Yeah," Craft drew it out. "Yes. Dogs almost always run in packs. Wolves, although pack animals, kick their young males out and they have to go it on their own until they can build a pack, or they die. I think it's a wolf. And it's big. We need to make sure we take the horses in at night, and hobble ours close to us and the fire tonight. If it was here last night it could still be around. Or it could be 15 miles away."

"Ok. Have we learned enough? Shall we saddle up?" Paul asked.

"Not yet. There's one thing we can do. Come with me."

They walked over to the edge of the road. Craft said, "Alright. Now pull it out. Take a leak."

"What? Why?"

"We're marking our territory. The hunters were interlopers. We need to leave a psychic sign that we know it. If they come back out and spotlight in the next couple days they won't get another deer. The deer will smell the pee and stay away. But they're hungry; they'll come in despite the corpse. There're too many of them. And we want to keep the hunters hunting. Honestly, we need the wolves and mountain lions back. It worries me. We should eat more venison at the Mansion. If I cross paths with one I'll probably take it down. How's your butchering skills?"

"Nonexistent."

"Good. I'll teach you."

They unbuckled their gun belts, slinging them over their shoulders, opened their trousers and pushed them down their thighs. When they finished pissing, they buttoned back up and walked around the edge of the meadow to the horses. They mounted and Craft clucked at his horse. Paul, with the packhorse tied to his pommel, followed him off to the southwest. The lead rope burned into his thigh as the packhorse resisted. "Ouch. Fuck," he said.

"Yup," Craft said, laconically.

The men rode for three more hours on the path running parallel to the road, then cut back east on smaller paths heading for the shelter. In some long ago time, a stream had created a slump on the mountainside, exposing some large rocks which had fallen on their sides, creating natural chambers. Craft and his riding students had long ago cleared a space in front of the chambers, dug them out, and built small fire pits in three places close to the edge of the shelters for cooking and heat. Over the years several such shelters had been identified and the ground prepared. All were kept stocked with wood. These shelters were hidden in deep woods, invisible from below and above.

Arriving on a path that had followed a stream, they dismounted. They let the horses drink and tied them off in some willows. Craft looked around, smelled the air and drew his rifle from the scabbard. He stood staring up hill in the direction of the shelters.

"You think the bear's up there?" Paul asked.

"Nope. But I don't like surprises. Keep your pistol holstered until we get closer."

There was a deer path leading uphill away from the stream and the men took it, stepping quietly. When they arrived at the edge of the small clearing they stopped and scanned the camp.

Paul exhaled audibly, "No bears."

"Yup," Craft agreed. "Can you bring up the horses?" Paul turned and went without comment.

Craft took off his slicker and hung it from a branch end on the side of a tree, left that way to form a convenient hook. From behind the tree he brought out a small rake, placed there years before, and began to rake the leaves out of the shelters, ever mindful of snakes.

When he finished he set to making a fire. Using kindling and small wood stored in one of the shelters, he had the fire laid and lit by the time Paul arrived. While Paul unsaddled and curried the horses, Craft took the pack off the last horse. Opening the canvas he withdrew a pot and a package of dried meat and berries and a couple of potatoes. He took a canteen with him over to the fire and made a stew of the pemmican, setting the potatoes on the edge of the fire to roast. He went back to the pack and pulled out the sack with the breakfast bacon. He tied it to a rope leading from a pulley, and suspended the meat out of the reach of any bears. He brought a coffee pot and some coffee back with him, along with the other supplies from the pack and put them in the shelter with the firewood.

By the time darkness fell, Paul had finished and tied the reins of the horses to a hitching rail that had been strung between two trees. He brought the bedrolls from the saddle backs over and pitched them into separate shelters. Craft grunted his approval and bid Paul to sit down with him near the fire.

The men sat in silence until the soup boiled. Craft turned the potatoes so they would cook evenly. Paul set out metal bowls and spoons. When the dried meat was soft and the potatoes done, Craft used his glove to pick up the pot and pour the stew. He slid a potato into each bowl. Paul rummaged around in his slicker pocket and brought out a salt shaker he'd taken from the Mansion kitchen. "Good idea," Craft noted.

Paul picked up his bowl and attempted to take a spoonful of the stew.

Finding it too hot, he set it down again on a rock. "Do you see Her?" he asked. "Really see Her?"

Craft, both laconic and curious, replied, "Yup."

"Oh, come on. You can say more than that. How come you can see Her, too? And will I ever be able to see Her like you do?"

"I can see Her because She wants me to."

"That's not what I mean. How do you see Her then? In your mind's eye, or out here? In the world?"

"Oh, so you want me to talk, do you?" Craft pulled out two flasks of whiskey from his slicker pocket, passed one over to Paul and took a drink. Paul took a sip, too.

"Yes."

Taking a moment to gather his thoughts, Craft said, "Put some wood on the fire, will you?" Paul built the fire up high enough that they had to sit back. They both took another sip.

"Well," Craft began, "I started seeing Her by seeing Her visage slip over Rachel's face. Rachel's eyes would go dark. Not just her pupil and her iris, no, the whole thing, white and all, would go black. I would watch it, wondering what I was seeing, and I realized I was seeing the pupil of the eye of a very large being. So I saw Her out here, in the real world, first.

"Rachel explained to me that it was Her, looking to see if I was paying enough attention to Rachel, you know? That I wasn't selfishly absorbed in my own pleasure, and was paying real attention to Rachel.

"Once I could see Her come in reliably, I learned how to…to hold space, I guess, is really the best way to say it. I had to become a container for the container that was Rachel, for the Diosa. I learned the rhythms, and postures, and set and held a boundary, so that into that space the Goddess could compress Herself, kind of shrink down, you know? And then Diosa and Rachel could be as one. Not one mind, I don't mean that. Rachel was always there, but then sometimes the Goddess would be in front, and speak."

Craft fell silent and Paul waited.

Then Craft said, "She sure likes sex."

"Yes. Both of them do, it seems,' Paul responded.

"No, I mean the Goddess. The more attention I paid to Her, the stronger Her presence became in Rachel. And then the Higher Heartbeat started. The power of Love started it, one very intense and loving, oh, I don't know how to say it. Suddenly we both felt the presence of another heart, and this heart beat would circulate within us and between us. The more we loved each other the more we loved Her. And the more Love we made, the more Love we created, the stronger the heartbeat became and eventually it became permanent in both of us.

"And somewhere in that process, when I would think of Her, an image of Her would appear in my mind, and the image would move, raise Her hand or shake Her head. It had self-will and was operating beyond my imagination. It was particularly vivid when I would focus on my forehead."

Craft went silent again, gathering his thoughts and memories.

"I would direct questions toward the image, and She would respond. Yes or no questions were good. And then there were the gestures and expressions that would convey meaning, Her hand held a certain way, blessing, lifting, declining.

"I also began to hear Her voice, although at first it wasn't synchronized with the image. That happened later. Now, if I'm too busy to see Her, I often hear Her voice. Sometimes there are other manifestations, things that appear outside my mind, out here in the real world.

"Hallucination or not, Rachel and I always have the same visions and voices when we ask the same question. This is how we check out what we perceive; we verify it with each other. It's all we can think of to do. If the same things happen to you, then maybe you could be part of the verification. I think it maybe happening to Beverly soon, if it hasn't already. If you see anything like what I've said, pay attention. Create a container. Hold space. Do what you've been learning to do."

Paul started to ask another question "What does She..." but Craft interrupted him, holding up a hand in a 'stop' sign. Craft said, "Contemplate the answer to that in your own way, in your own mind. Maybe better if you think about the Higher Heart."

After a while, Paul started to ask another question. Craft looked at him and raised an eyebrow in an expression on his face that could be translated as "Really? Are you actually going to talk again?" kind of way, and returned to gazing at the fire. Paul remained silent for a while longer then. Suddenly he said, "Who is She?"

Craft looked into the fire. "She says She is an image of the First One, who is the one that made the One before Her, and then that One made Her. And from Her the thousand faces of the Divine Feminine here on this earth derive. It may be that She is Life itself, Life here on the planet, maybe the planet itself. I think sometimes that the entire planet is alive, and that Life, as we think of it, is the proof.

Craft finished for the moment, watching Paul watch the fire. "If you want to see Her you have to pay attention to the wen. You cannot be self-absorbed and paying attention only to yourself. Understanding that is the point of all I have just said. Your mind is off wandering, and instead you should be thinking on just this one thing: Pay attention to Her. Put Her first, and then you shall see."

Here," Craft said, waving his arms to indicate the land and the life around him, "Here, everything else is taken care of so that you can do one thing. Pay attention." He took another drink.

After a long thoughtful pause Paul spoke again. "You remember last night? When we talked?"

"You mean the night we talked about our pasts?" Craft asked, wanting to be clear.

"Yes," Paul replied.

"Yes," Craft said. "Yes, it was just last night. What about it?"

"Didn't it make you feel strange inside? A little weird or something?" Paul asked, taking off his hat and running his hands through his hair. "I almost felt embarrassed about it."

Craft said nothing, watching the man's discomfort, taking another sip from the flask. Then another, watching the emotions run across the man's face, letting him work himself up to speaking again.

"Maybe it's the whiskey talking. But I'm afraid. What if She, what if the Goddess told us to do something. I mean, we're way out here, alone, what if She told us to have sex with each other?"

"Well then, by gawd, we'd be going down on each other, coming in each other's mouths. We'd be all up inside each other." Craft watched the other man's face carefully again. He saw fear and confusion, but no disgust. A good sign. Craft decided to push him further.

"Yeah, I'd get some grease from tomorrow's bacon and really put it to you. Yes sir," Craft drawled.

Paul went very still, seemingly paralyzed with fear.

"Look," Craft said in a kind voice. "Look. What did She say last night? She said "I may ask you to do something you do not want to do, but I will not ask you to do anything that goes against your Nature." Do you know why? Because She is Nature, and She is disinclined to go against Herself. As are you, disinclined to go against yourself."

He paused to let that sink in. "You must understand that homosexual people are Her children, too. Like any good mother, She accepts and welcomes all Her children. There is no stigma here, there is only compassion for the difficulties they experience that we don't have to go through in life." Craft looked closely at Paul in the fire light to see how much he was hearing.

"If She told me to do that with you, I'd have to think about it," Craft continued, feeling, across the fire, the new surge of fear run through Paul. He continued, "I'd have to think about it, because that's not my Nature. I'd have to ask myself, 'Now, why is She asking me to do this?' and I'd figure it out that She was asking me for an act of Service. She would be asking me to rise from my Basic Nature to my Higher Self, my Higher Nature, in my Service to Her.

"And you have to understand, Paul, my Higher Nature is my Basic Nature now, this is what She's taught me; this is how She's taught me how to be. And I, being completely free to choose, choose to serve Her."

Craft decided there was not much more worth saying, but then he checked in with Her about it. In the vision She stood with her hand in front, palm down, and slowly lowered it, smiling. Craft smiled, too, and took another pull on the flask, draining it. They'd been sipping all along while talking. Paul, semiconscious, semi-lost in thought, reflexively pulled on his flask, tilting it up. Craft got up and went over to the pack, fished around and brought out the third flask. "Hey!" he said. When Paul looked up Craft tossed him the flask. Paul caught it with both hands.

"Here. Always be prepared, Scout," Craft said.

"Yes, Master," Paul responded. "I mean, 'Yes, Scout Master.'"

Craft smiled, although Paul couldn't see it. He went back to the fire and squatted down to pick up his slicker. He turned and went to his shelter, rolled out his bedroll, removed his boots and then his pants, rolling them up and putting them in the back of the shelter with his slicker. He sat in the bedroll, took off his shirt, rolled it up, too, and stuck it in the back, as well. In three breaths he was asleep.

Down the mountain at the Mansion, after supper, the conversation continued. "No, no, Beverly. That's not it. We can't trust people. We can hardly trust anybody at this point. It worked with Paul, and it's working with some others, but if we want to grow it, expand it, we have to have more people. But they all have to be able to keep a secret. And we have to make sure they can keep a secret before we even give them one. This is too important to let the enemies of the Goddess know, and these enemies surround us for hundreds of miles, I remind you. They will be relentless if they ever discover us or understand who we are and what we are really about. And how, how can we verify trustworthiness?"

After a moment Beverly said, "We could do what the enemy does."

"What?"

"Hypnotize them."

"No."

"Yes. Hypnotize them. Put them in an altered state and hypnotize them into keeping a secret. They'll love it."

"That's very cynical, Beverly."

"Yes. And necessarily so, if I'm to believe you. You say you cannot let them betray us. Then do not let them. It is your vision," then after a brief pause, "Excuse me, I have that wrong. It is Her vision."

"You're right. This has to be secret. And in order to keep it all secret we have to use suggestion and reinforcement. We have to exploit their suggestibility," Rachel finally concluded.

"Good. Now we're getting somewhere."

"Have you studied initiation ceremonies at all? No?" Rachel asked, as Beverly shook her head. "The ceremonies always induce an altered state of consciousness. This altered state is always hypnogogic. The state of mind I was in after shaving was hypnogogic. Ever studied hypnosis?" as Beverly slowly shook her head again. "Well, we shall study that also. While in a hypnogogic state the Code, the Code of Conduct, is delivered, the demand for loyalty to the group. There must be a vow that the Secrets will be kept upon pain of terrible death." Rachel stopped, hearing herself.

"Death?" Beverly asked quietly. "Seriously, Death?"

"Yes," Rachel, also quietly, replied. "Death, or something like it. A great forgetfulness, perhaps. This really bears a lot of thinking."

Rachel went into the library and pulled some books for Beverly to read.

The relevant passages were marked.

They worked deep into the night, taking notes, constructing the initiation, and the levels of initiation, and the vows, and details of the ceremony that induce the kind of Devotion required to hold a Secret, even unto Death.

When Craft woke up in the morning light before sunrise, Paul was still sitting by the fire, cross-legged, head down, not moving. Surrounded by smoke from the fire, and a softly swirling light snow just beginning to skiff along the ground, Craft could tell Paul was still alive by the cloud of breath that was regularly added to the mix. What had been a well-stocked wood shelter now had a serious dent in it.

Craft sat up and stretched, stifling the yawn. Paul didn't move. Craft got up and sneaky-pete'd over to Paul. When he got close he could see the flask fallen from Paul's hand, and hear him snoring quietly, sound asleep. "Damn," Craft thought. "Follow the Way. We'll make a good Taoist out of him yet."

Craft built up the fire and set coffee water on to boil. He lowered the bacon from the tree and put it in the pan to start frying. Then he broke camp quietly around Paul, and saddled his horse. Soon the coffee was done and he was squatting down, turning the bacon. Paul still slept.

Sipping his coffee, Craft offered the cup to the sky and poured a little on the earth. When the bacon was done he laid it on a brushed off rock near the fire to cool. He took the grease to the edge of the clearing where he dumped it and wiped the pan with a handful of leaves. Paul still slept.

When he was finished eating he wrapped half the bacon in an unused handkerchief and left it on the ground near Paul's leg. He left the coffee pot, too. He led the horse down the trail to the stream, where they both drank. He mounted up. The horse snorted and reared once, looking back up the hill at its companions being left behind. Craft headed up the valley for the top. He knew a place where a buck usually bedded down, in the brush near the top of the ridge on the Stonehaven side. He'd watched it with binoculars the previous autumn. He figured if he was careful and prepared, he might get close enough to get a good shot when the buck spooked, assuming it spooked. As he started picking his way upslope, guiding the horse with his knees, he pulled the rifle out of the scabbard, levered in a round, gently lowered the hammer, and laid it across the pommel.

Downwind of the camp a black wolf with a white blaze on its head had been lying back in the trees. The bacon was an item of extreme interest. But there was a man sitting there, very still, and two horses still tied off to the trees. There was no fear in the wolf, but it was cautious. It could smell gun oil. It decided to creep along the ground to the edge of the clearing. The man still hadn't moved and the horses hadn't smelled him yet, nickering, alternating between wanting to move out and boredom.

Crawling on its belly, the wolf moved slowly into the camp, creeping then pausing, creeping then pausing. The bacon was getting closer. Slowly it moved, step by step, inch by inch, and its nose was less than a foot away from the cloth when a shot echoed down the valley from above. It froze.

Paul woke up immediately when he heard the rifle report. He startled the wolf, who leaped away, which startled Paul so that he threw himself back, landing on his gun. By the time he remembered he was sitting on his pistol the wolf was gone. With the bacon.

At the Mansion, Regina, daughter of the Lama, stepped out of the hired car as the driver turned the motor off. The next sound she heard was the faint echo of a rifle shot. She said to her mother, Amanda, "Did you hear that, Mum? A gunshot, a long way off, echoing down the valley like they do back at home."

Her mother, irritated by the long drive on dirt winter roads, said, "Lovely. A one gun salute."

"Either a good shot or a bad shot, there was only one. I wonder which," Regina mused.

"That's enough wondering for now, dear. Let's pay attention to what's in front of us," her mother counselled, "and not some random noise off in the distance."

Rachel and Beverly, who'd been up late exploring their new 'bald" sensations, weren't dressed yet, although they had water on for tea, when they heard the car door slam. Beverly said, "Go invite them in. It's your house. I'll get dressed quickly."

Beverly pulled on a work shirt and pair of heavy work pants with suspenders. She shook her hair out with her hands and ran barefoot down the stairs, holding her socks, trying to catch up with Rachel. Too late, Rachel had already opened the door and shouted, "Amanda!"

Rachel ran down the steps in her morning gown and robes, "You're early! When did you leave Richmond?"

Amanda answered, crankily, "As soon as I could no longer stand the stench of blood in the town."

And then Rachel turned to the driver. "Hello. You're not my regular driver. Who are you?"

The driver answered, "Sam, ma'am. Sam Jamison. Just a driver. She called my company, you know? They called me at 6:00 AM yesterday. Didn't think it was this far."

Beverly appeared in the door behind Rachel. When she'd heard Rachel engage the driver as a stranger she knew something was wrong. She redirected and ran down the stairs to the kitchen level in the basement. She came up through what had been the servant's entrance behind the car.

She'd managed to find a pair of muck boots on the way and put them on. "Hey, hi, howdy!" she said to the driver, waving her hand to take the attention off Rachel.

Amanda turned, Regina didn't. She insisted on staring off into the woods. Beverly came up behind the trunk and opened it. Inside were two suitcases; Rachel had promised Amanda everything she would need, and Amanda and Rachel were of one mind on what that meant.

Rachel said to Amanda, "Oh, do. Oh do come in. All is prepared except myself."

Beverly took the bags from the trunk and, walking around the set stone raised from the surface of the brick walkway, the set stone that people used to step down on from horse drawn carriages. She set the valises on the lowest step, and walked around the front of the car to the driver. She introduced herself, leaning on the fender, looking at the tall, rangy man standing there, stamping his feet to get grounded again, Beverly judged. "Look," she said. "Are you looking for work?"

"Who ain't?" he said.

Beverly knew in that moment she had him. She looked at Rachel and nodded.

Rachel nodded slightly, flashing Beverly a real smile in an interruption of her smile at Amanda. Rachel waved her arm, signaling. "Come on, come on, Amanda. Come on in, it's cold out here."

Amanda looked up the fourteen narrow marble stairs. A person could weave side to side and scarcely avoid touching the wrought iron railings drilled into the marble. Amanda came stiffly up the steps, worn in the middle with the passage of feet, up onto the colonnaded porch.

Amanda noticed that the door was wide enough for two large, fully armed men to exit and take up positions behind the eighteen inch wide columns. She became curious with herself, wondering why she thought of it as an exit, rather than an entrance. Then she remembered seeing similar close-in defensive planning at home. Men, already spotted, might be advancing. Men from the house could open the door and emerge two at a time and fire at the advancers, and then back easily up into the house and close the doors.

As Rachel held the doors for her to walk past she said, "You must be tired. Let me show you to the powder room."

Amanda entered and turned to look at Rachel. Rachel had already turned to look back outside toward Regina, and didn't see Amanda. Regina was still standing and staring out into the woods. Rachel said, "I don't know what to say! Come in when you want to!" and closed the doors.

"Seriously," Rachel said. "Come see my powder room." Rachel invited Amanda to follow her around the square spiral staircase down into the lower level. There was a heavy, wide access door opening to the staircase down. They passed the intersecting staircase from the servery and went down to the stone-lined basement floor. At the bottom of the stairs they turned right. Several yards down the hallway they went down a few more steps to a flat iron door set in the wall, held fast by a steel pin through an iron hasp. Rachel opened the door and they stepped into a brick walled circular room with a brick hemispheric ceiling.

Amanda's consternation was evident. "Look!" Rachel said, smiling. "It's my powder room. They used to keep the gun powder in here. This way, if it exploded it wouldn't blow up the house; the shape of the room directed the explosive force back on itself."

Amanda turned to see Rachel smiling broadly, eyes twinkling. She realized Rachel had been teasing her, having a go, and she laughed. Rachel held out her arms and the wen, friends from twenty five years past, fell into embrace.

"Come," Rachel said. "Let me show you to your room." Rachel led her out through the kitchen and into the courtyard. Amanda stopped to look out through the arched gateway onto the lawn. "Come on," Rachel said. "It's cold." They went around the stone foundation wall of the circular east ball room and entered the east wing at the ground level, then up a flight of stairs to the main floor.

"We close down most of the house for the winter. On this level we have offices, with the main office down at the end of the hallway here. Bedrooms are the next level up. Come see." They went up another flight of stairs, turning in the stairwell and emerged onto the landing. The long hall had four doors on either side, with a large door at the end. "These first two rooms on the right are for you and Regina. There's a southern view, with lots of good sunlight during the day. The next door is for Paul Manfred, my chief accountant and the next is for Beverly Washington—you met Beverly, yes?"

"No, not really."

"She's out front taking care of the driver. She's my business manager. Paul is her fiancé. The last door on the left is for my farm manager and head teacher, John Craft. The room at the end is my room. Come with me and I'll show you yours. We can look at how I've supplied it and you can tell me what else you may need."

"Yes. Where is the loo?"

"Down the hall behind us in the main mansion. Let me show you," Rachel offered. She took Amanda by the elbow and steered her toward the broad short flight of stairs that took them up to the level of the Mansion's second floor. "Here. Generally, men are to the right, wen on the left. "

"Wen?" Amanda asked. "Ah yes," she said, figuring it out. And then she said, "Generally?"

Rachel ignored her and held the door open. "When you've finished just come back down the hall. I'll be in your room, making sure the heat is on, the curtains open, and that everything is as it should be."

Amanda entered the bathroom and chose the commode by the window and the radiator. She sat, and looked out the window, allowing the vista to help her relax. She had finished when the radiator banged, startling her back to the present. She looked around. She was in a stall, almost a private bathroom with its own tub and sink, and a door she could have closed but had been in too much of a hurry to bother with.

She finished, washed her hands and admired the monogrammed 'S' on the hand towel. She emerged and looked at the larger room. On the other side of the wall from the tub was a bank of three commodes in individual stalls, and opposite them a bank of showers. Against the wall toward the hallway was a bank of three sinks set in a countertop with a large mirror over them.

"Quite the set-up," she thought to herself. She went back down the hallway to her room. Rachel was there, leaning against a window frame, looking out. She turned when Amanda entered and smiled. "In the wardrobe are shirts, and wraps and robes. There are slacks there, too. And some dresses. Around here in the winter we mostly wear work clothes, heavy shirts and pants, thick socks. Winter hosiery.

Boots. Socks and gowns and underwear, including camisoles, are in the dresser. I think everything should fit. If it doesn't, we have more choices. If you'd like, we can go have tea in the office until Beverly has a chance to feed the driver down in the kitchen. We can bring your valise up later."

"Certainly. Tea it is, then. I would like to take my shoes off, however. Have you any slippers?"

"I do. Look in the bottom of the wardrobe. Try the wool socks with the leather soles. They won't be slippery. Here, let me get them for you. Give me your coat and I'll hang it up and fetch you a wrap."

Amanda sat down on the bed and fell back. Very nice. Rachel returned with the clothes. Amanda sat up and sighed when she kicked off her shoes. Already she was feeling better. "Lead the way," Amanda gestured. She thought, "This is very nice. I think Regina will do well here." Walking down the hall, she asked, "I assume you and Craft are lovers?"

"Very much so, Amanda. I am very blessed. He is devoted to me. It is as if I were a Priestess and he my Consort," Rachel said, smiling to herself at how true that was.

 Out front, Beverly was leaning on the fender with the driver. "Can I interest you in some coffee before you go, perhaps a bite to eat? Why don't you come down to the kitchen with me and I'll fix something up?" The driver, thinking of the long ride home, agreed. They picked up the suitcases and came up the steps into the main entry room and set the cases down. "The kitchen is this way, follow me."

The kitchen still worked with two cook stoves, one burned wood, the other was newer and ran on natural gas. Beverly had the driver sit on a stool at a counter, poured him some coffee, lit a flame under a frying pan, then she scooped in some lard to fry eggs. She put toast in the toaster, and got out butter and jam from the cooler.

While she worked, she had the driver talking. She learned that he worked for a limousine service in Richmond, and the woman, Mrs. MacGregor, had contracted to be driven here with her daughter the day before. It was an unusual request but the woman was able to pay in advance with a local bank note. For various reasons none of the other drivers could go, and as the company went down the list they came to him. They'd had to leave at 7:00 AM the day before to arrive here before noon, which was what she specified. He said the lady got him his own room for the overnight stop, but had them on the road again in 5 hours.

While he ate, she asked if he knew anything about their regular driver, and he did not. He asked about the operation at Stonehaven, commenting on how big the Mansion was, and Beverly told him they were horse-breeders. She asked him if he knew horses and he said only at the track.

When he had eaten Beverly took him outside to his car, directed him over to one of the farm's fuel tanks, and used the hand pump to fill his car. When they shook hands she pressed a $100.00 tip in his hands. He said, "You folks sure are good people." He departed a happy man, in a hurry to beat the light snow out of the mountains.

Beverly, who had been practicing some of the hypnogogic techniques she had studied the night before, deemed her efforts a success. The man would carry no strange tales nor any resentment back to his life in Richmond. And, in fact, because of his felt sense of fondness for Beverly, he might become a useful asset to Stonehaven, in the future,

Walking back to the house, Beverly noticed that Regina, who had still been standing by the parked car when they'd emerged from breakfast an hour later in the January chill, must have gone inside when the car moved off to the fuel tank.

When her feet had finally become cold Regina had gone inside, but not for long. She picked up the suitcases and carried them through the dining hall to the circular ballroom. It was one of the most quietly exquisite spaces she had ever seen. She paused and turned slowly. Then she heard voices through the far door. She opened it and found herself on a landing for a set of stairs and heard her mother's voice from a room at the end of the hall in front of her.

Intuiting the bedrooms were upstairs, she confirmed which room was hers when she found a pair of new work boots in her size in the bottom of the wardrobe. She loved the new sheepskin lined work jacket that fell just to mid-thigh.

She dressed for the outdoors, taking gloves and a wool hat. She stopped in the office where her mother and Rachel were laughing over some old story, and told them she was going to the horses.

"Off she goes," her mother said.

"So, tell me about her. And let's go down to the kitchen and eat. Your driver has gone, now, and the three of us will have the place to ourselves."

Rachel dressed for the day in work clothes. Amanda did the same. They met in the hallway and together they went through the ballroom and the dining room to the stairs and down to the kitchen. Beverly had breakfast made: bacon, eggs, and toast. They sat, the three of them, and made some introductory conversation between Beverly and Amanda. About halfway through the meal Rachel again asked Amanda to tell Regina's story.

"Well, I was eight weeks pregnant with her when I left the Lama in Paris in 1939. We knew, he knew certainly, that it was time to go, and, of course, he wouldn't come. We returned to my parents' place in Edinburgh. They passed off the pregnancy as being from a fiancé who'd been sent overseas, which they knew they could later change into having been killed in the War. They were always debating how much to include me in their lives. I volunteered a lot. And raised Regina, of course. I kept her with me as much as possible. And I read a lot, eventually focusing on the history and mythology of the Goddess in Britain. Oh, and I continued the internal work as the Lama had instructed. And I masturbated…a lot. You know, the path of solitary cultivation."

At this last remark all three giggled. It was Amanda's test comment. By it she was able to judge something about these two women, and her judgment was positive. Rachel had written to her about the educational experiment she was considering, and by their open and easy reaction she felt hopeful that what might come to happen here was real. After eating a few bites, during which time Beverly offered her more tea, she continued:

"In the summers, we would go to the estate in the Cairngorms. I don't recall how many sheep my father had but it was at least a thousand. There was a notable difference in how well Regina would sleep between the two places. In the city she would be fitful all night. In the mountains she would rest, even smile in her sleep. All in all, I kept her close.

"Her hair came in fast, and lots of it, thick and strong. Her coordination developed quickly. She walked early, barely pausing to crawl. I taught her French along with English, and by five she was fluent, both speaking and literate, in both. I also brought her up in the ways of the Goddess as I was uncovering them.

"I began teaching her yoga, also, at an early stage. As I went through the asanas she would be right there on the floor with me, practicing. I learned a lot from you, Rachel, in that year we were there together.

"She would sit with me also, before the altars. There were many things that happened to me with the energies, and for much of that she was in my presence, near me, and unavoidably entangled with what I was feeling. When I would tremble with ecstasy, so would she. She says she doesn't recall, exactly, but it seemed to me that she, too, was also caught up in Visions, as was I. Only sometimes the Visions were obviously different.

"As I cultivated my relationship with the Divine Feminine, so did she. I was working mostly with Her ancient divine face for my people, Brighid. But Regina, it seemed, was seeing many faces and having many conversations. She would tell me these stories as if she were telling me stories about an imaginary playmate.

"On the estate she could wander. She would play with the other children but she became bored easily. From about the age of seven she would go off on walks in different directions. I would go with her on these early walks. We would pack a lunch and see how far we could get and still be home by dark. As she became older and more sure of herself, I would let her go on her own. She'd come back knees all dirty and hair all wind-blown with grass in it. Quite the wild child.

"In the winters we would head back into the city. We tried school. We sent her with other children of our station—you know? It didn't work.

One of her teachers, whom she bit when the teacher grabbed her arm, called her utterly feral. She often took off her shoes as soon as she was inside, for example. She would remove clothing if it bothered her.

"It was a very difficult time for us. One subject that kept her attention was math. She has some kind of gift with numbers, able to factor and multiply large numbers. And she has continued to do well with the higher math also. Another subject that worked well for her was music. I had been playing the piano with her by my side since she was an infant, and as soon as she could sit up safely, she'd sit beside me while I played. In school that was what they'd do with her when she behaved badly. They let her play because any kind of normal punishment didn't work.

"By the time she was nine, the situation became intolerable. Her behaviors could not be tolerated by the school, and neither she nor I could tolerate the behavior of the teachers and the headmaster. He tried to use corporal punishment on her and she fought back. She leapt on him and tried to scratch out his eyes."

Amanda paused, allowing the memories to recall her feelings from the time. She took the pin out of her hair and shook it out, running her hands through it so it fell below her shoulders.

"That was my fault, actually. I had told her to do that if anyone ever tried to hurt her. She had no idea about the standard that allowed adults to discipline her like that. She told me later that he'd held her hands together behind her back, laid her over his lap, pulled her pants down—she wouldn't wear skirts—and spanked her bottom. He was leaning over her, so when she arched her back her head hit him in the nose. Blood was everywhere, including all over her back when I went to retrieve her.

"For her, it was the end of formal schooling. She would gladly learn whatever I would teach her, but she was done with the rest of it. In any event, I may not have been able to get her into any school, once the word went out. Eventually, I was able to get her to agree to tutoring in special subjects, like biology and anthropology, but tutoring was as far as she was able to go.

"It wasn't just western science either. I was determined that she wouldn't be one of those spoiled wealthy girls that it had been my fate to become. I had learned that I had to be able to do many of those things that, as a child, I had counted on servants to do. Doing the cooking, for example. I learned to cook. Thank you, Beverly, by the way. Excellent breakfast. Laundry, cleaning, seamstress work, all the tasks of routine management of every day, the mundane—I had learned to do these things in the group where I met her father. I made sure she knew how to do all these.

"Speaking of her father, I took her to meet him in Paris as soon as I could after the War ended. It was a complicated time."

Amanda paused again, recalling her feelings, then began again.

"We had our own apartment, of course."

Amanda paused again, letting some of her memories revitalize her. She started to glow with pleasure. When Rachel and Beverly saw this, they looked at each other and smiled.

"We danced together, the group of us. It was so good for just over two years," Amanda continued.

"He was so old, you know. No one knew for sure. He would admit only to eighty. It is a wonder to me that I conceived from him when he was in his seventies. I had no way of knowing then, there was nothing in his appearance that showed his age. His work on himself had a magnificent result in Regina. I am always so grateful to him.

"But the War had aged him greatly. The dual life, doing hypnosis shows for the invaders, while hiding or helping perhaps hundreds of people. All these people had been attracted to him after the war and were around him all the time. Many others from the time before the war came back and made demands on his attention. He was kind to Regina, and she so wanted to please him, her father. But he had so little time for her."

Amanda sighed, paused again, and considered. Then, with both the other wen riveted in attention, she said, "Of course, you know who had taken over his affairs. There were no longer affairs with others either, to be clear. I'm not so sure he chose her, exactly, to be his chief mistress when she returned from Switzerland, more that he allowed it. He knew his time was limited.

"But it was wonderful to move, to do the dances, again. And Regina learned."

Amanda paused again, recollecting.

"It was required of me that I return to Scotland. So I was not there when he died. We did not go to the funeral."

Then she stopped talking. Everyone sighed. Beverly was the first to break the spell when she placed her palms on the countertop. "We're done here, I think. Finished eating, I mean. Let's clean up, you and I. Give Rachel a chance to go handle some business matters."

Rachel smiled with gratitude toward Beverly, pleased to be considered. "Why, thank you, dear," she said.

Amanda stood up at the same time as Beverly. She put her hair back up and stacked the plates. "What do you say, Beverly? Shall we clean up?"

"Yes, let's," Beverly replied.

When Regina arrived at the barn she found a halter and the grain and set out to make friends with one of the horses. A second level in the herd hierarchy mare had been watching her closely and was already at the fence. Regina was impressed that she willfully shared with the other horses, backing out yet staying close. When the grain was gone and the other horses left, the mare came back over and responded to petting, leaning into the boards of the fence. Regina showed the halter and the mare stood still for it.

Having found the horse, Regina led her into the barn. She studied the tack, looking for the right bridle. She chose a saddle that would fit her. When the horse was saddled, she rode out of the barn into the western pasture. After dismounting at the far side to open, go through, and close the gate and remount, she took off up the trail in the direction of the shot she'd heard, looking to investigate, reminding herself of the differences between Western and English style riding.

When the dishes were in the drainer, the counters wiped down, and Rachel had returned to the kitchen, the three piled into the front seat of a second truck and took the dirt road over to the barn. Rachel noticed right away the missing saddle. They put on muck boots and cleaned the stalls. On a break Amanda resumed the story.

"We spent as much time out on the estate as possible. Regina had all that great land in which to wander. She was always pretending, talking to imaginary friends. It turned out, though, that some of them were not so imaginary. One day, I think she was twelve, she had travelled far into the uplands. She encountered a house she had never seen before, in a place she was sure she would have known about. There were people in a fenced-in yard playing music.

"As she gazed at the house, menarche came upon her. She felt that first flow, she told me, and simply sat down. Eventually, she said, someone noticed her and a young woman, about as old as Regina is now, came out of the yard to the little knoll she was sitting on and asked if she could help her. Regina said, 'I'm bleeding.' And the young woman said, 'Ah, come with me, then. I'll help you'. The young woman took her to the house and found clothes for her. She helped her clean up, and gave her clean cloth for a pad. At the end of the day, they sent her home, letting her ride on the back of a plow horse, and, she told me, the path home was much shorter.

"And that was the beginning of a quest to which she became fiercely devoted. But it began in a very strange fashion. The next time she wanted to go their house I went with her, to meet the family, and make sure the child wasn't being a nuisance. And, you know? Regina could not find the house again. She was very upset. She could find the knoll, she thought, but there was no house. She returned, she told me, many times to that knoll and just sat there, looking at the space where the house had been.

"This initial contact, with a house that she could not find again, became a long and obsessive mystery for her. I will tell you more about this later. But, oh my, the sexual side of her life became so active. She began to masturbate. A lot. Some days she was like a boy, doing it three or four times. And I knew when she was doing it, too, bless me. My nipples would get hard. In the morning, yes, and at night, and often in the middle of the night. And then once or twice during the day. And as sore as my nipples got, she must have been more so, more sore. She'd be off somewhere, doing something, and suddenly they'd crinkle and get hard and I'd look around and say, "Where is she now!"

"We had our own house there in Alandale, but there were still people around the house employed by my father. I wondered what they would think if they caught her with her hand up her skirt—so, together, Regina and I took over their tasks. They were still employed, but we cared for our own house and laundry. It was a good thing too. I hadn't intended to talk to her about it, but one day when she'd gone off riding early, I went to change her bedding, thinking I was doing her a favor. I found a polished thigh bone from some long butchered sheep under her pillow and stains all down her sheets from when she'd come.

"I figured it was time for us to talk, so I kept the bone. She was a good girl, she always came home before dark. That day I'd told her I wanted her to come home in time for supper, so when she came in she went upstairs to finish changing out of her riding breeches, a nicely tanned pair they were, and I heard a wail from her room. And then 'Mother! Mother! What did you do?' and she came running downstairs, her shirt untucked and her pants open, she was in such a rush. Her face was filled with embarrassment and fury, one shade of red competing with the other.

"Oh, I had to smile, I did. I was standing at the stove, the bone covered on the counter and a pot of boiling water on. "What did you do with it, Mother?" she demanded, and then she saw it under the towel and her eyes grew wide. "Why, I was just going to boil it up for soup, my dear? Is there some issue?" and she said, "Indeed, there is." So I said, "Indeed, it would seem quite some issue, judging by stains on that bedding of yours." And her eyes went wide and her mouth made such a comical 'O' that I couldn't keep a straight face any more. As the light of comprehension of the pun dawned across her face, I couldn't help but laugh, and my laughing made her laugh with me."

All three wen were laughing openly now, also.

"It opened a door between us. We could talk about it, now. In fact, now that we could talk about that, we could talk about everything. And we did, honestly and without fear. We talked about her plans to take a lover. Well, to have sex, anyway. We talked about who might be appropriate, and who wasn't. It was such a small settlement, that everyone there, every possible choice, seemed unwise, and it would have been intolerable to her had anyone spoken of it. In the end, she settled on the Postman for her first. It was perfect. He came through only twice a week, and he didn't live anywhere near, so she wouldn't have to deal with him in any other context. She planned to seduce him by walking down the road when she knew he would be driving along. He'd stop and ask her if she needed assistance, and she would take matters into her own hands. So to speak. I thought it superbly ironic that he delivered the box of condoms through the post that I'd ordered from a friend in Aberdeen. And that, eventually, these were what she would use on him.

"Not at first though. And this was one of the best things about our new relationship. She would tell me what she intended, and what she did, and what she'd let him do. And she made him work for it, made him play and explore just like it was young love with another man her own age."

"Wasn't it dangerous?" Beverly asked. "Weren't you afraid for her?"

"A little. But it was highly unlikely that he would harm her. And I asked the Goddess to watch over her. She did, closely as it turns out. Sometimes I would see through Her eyes what Regina was doing. So I knew the Goddess was as with Regina as She could be, right there, with her and around her and within her."

Amanda paused and sighed. And then lapsed into silence.

Rachel, breaking the silence said, "We know something about this ourselves, in our own lives, don't we, Beverly?"

"Yes. We do," Beverly agreed.

"This is why I began corresponding with you, Rachel. You had spoken of this possibility when we had known each other in Paris before the War. You had told me about this, this visitation of the Divine Feminine, when you were teaching the yoga. Then the Goddess began to spend time with me, teaching me, and leading me to other women who felt about Her the way I did. So, with Her help, I have created circles of men and women devoted to Her, and practicing the Divine Union. But I have to say that those early experiences, watching and feeling and sensing what my daughter was doing in this first seduction, well, it was disconcerting, and a little embarrassing, almost incestuous. Once I overcame that, once I let my gratitude for her safety abide with me, then the experience became very sensual, and ultimately beautiful."

"I tell you what, Amanda," Rachel said. "Let's finish up here and go back to the house and make some lunch. Then you can tell us the rest of the story, and why you've come to us."

The wen spread hay around in the stalls, changed back into work boots and piled into the truck. Rachel and Beverly chatted, pointing out various features to Amanda as they drove up the hill.

PART 3 VISITING THE TEMPLE

Paul had to dismount as he neared the top of the shoulder on the south side of Piney Mountain; it was too difficult to ride his horse leading the pack horse on the narrow trail through the rocks and scrub vegetation. As he crossed over the high point he looked up and saw Craft bent over a deer, stripped down to his union suit top, knife in hand. He'd lain the deer, a doe, with its head hanging over a rock, throat slit, bleeding out.

"No buck, eh?" Paul asked.

Craft replied, "Nope. He was in there, though. He just didn't panic. Eventually, after the shot, I heard him scrambling away through the brush, even though I couldn't see him. Wily old bastard. Come up here and help me."

Paul tied off the horses and took off his coat. Making his way up to the rock he studied the trails Craft left through the brush. When he got to the rock he paused. He looked at the threads of thickening blood hanging from the doe's throat, and lips, and nose, and shuddered.

Craft was looking at him. "You get used to it," he said. "You want to eat, you get used to it. And, we should probably expiate it, anyway."

"What do you mean?"

"Atone for it, I guess. Perform a ceremony, do something ritual. In some way. A man can get blood-guilt from doing this. At least make certain to give out gratitude for Life that allowed us to take Life in order that we may live. It's one of the great paradoxes of being alive.

"So, come on up here. Got your knife? We're going to just take the shoulders and haunches, like that carcass near the road."

Paul got out his knife, then made a step toward climbing up.

"No, not that way. Put your knife away. Don't climb rocks with it in one hand."

"Sorry."

Paul got up on top, and Craft showed him how to find the joint at the hip and how to lift the leg and start cutting in through the groin. Craft stood there, watching him pierce the skin and start sawing.

"No, not like that," he said. "Like this. Slide the blade with short strokes, so that the next stroke slowly reveals itself. Pull it apart as you go."

Craft moved toward the head and took the shoulder off, then went back to help the struggling Paul. He pulled the leg back revealing the joint and told Paul how to use the point of his knife to cut into it, cutting the ligament in the middle. When they had it completely off they rolled the doe over to its other side. As they rolled it the doe's belly rolled heavily over, like there was a large stone inside. Paul looked at Craft, questioning.

"Yup," Craft said. "Pregnant."

"This feels bad," Paul said, the smell of blood overwhelming him suddenly, and he retched, a dry heave of whisky slobber.

"You smell, too," Craft said.

"Fuck you," Paul responded, wiping his hand across his mouth, leaving a smear of blood and fur across his lower face. He stood up and wiped his brow with his other hand, leaving another smear. Craft grinned at him, but said nothing.

When Paul realized what he'd done he got angrier. "Fuck, fuck, fuck," he said, looking around for something to wipe his face with, and finding only his shirt. This served mostly to smear the blood and hair around.

"That'll teach you," Craft said. "Never touch yourself while you're butchering."

"Fuck you twice," Paul replied.

Craft smiled again. "Let's get this done," he said. "I'll take the haunch this time, you take the shoulder." Then, after working at it awhile he said, "You know, the native people would have used all of this, even the fetus."

"How would they have used that?" Paul asked.

"They'd have eaten it," Craft answered.

Paul retched again, this time wiping his mouth on his sleeve.

"You hungry?" Craft asked.

"Yes," Paul answered. "A wolf got the bacon."

"Oh, ho!" Craft responded. "So there is a wolf! Amazing. We'll leave everything right here except the legs. Oh, and if you're hungry I could cut the liver out for you. That you can eat raw."

Paul almost retched again.

Craft said, "You know, you're going to have to get past this. Hunting, butchering, these are things we do. It's a part of the archetype of the Provider. These days maybe a man could go his whole life and not do what you're doing now."

Paul lifted the leg and gingerly started cutting. Craft was almost finished when he said, "Seriously, Paul. There's enough meat here to feed
more than twenty people. Would you not hunt and let them starve?"

"No, I'd hunt," Paul said. "I'd even kill, but I don't think I'd butcher.
I'd just take it back to camp."

"Well, friend, no guts, no glory," Craft said, and slit open the abdomen,
spilling the fetus out onto the rock along with the intestines beside the
kneeling Paul.

"Oh, no," Paul wailed. Overwhelmed by the smell and a sense of horror
at the unborn fetus he started dry heaving again, and began weeping at
the horror of it all.

Craft watched him without mercy. "You'd have to gut it before you
took it back to camp."

Then, after watching Paul weep for a couple minutes, Craft said, "You
have to master this. The lives of other people depend on it." And then,
as Paul calmed down and began to breathe without sobbing, Craft said,
"You have to learn to hold the paradox."

"Hold it how?" Paul asked.

Craft considered his answer. "Hold it on the one hand—that Life feeds
on Death, and on the other—that Death feeds on Life, at the same time.
And hold it until it resolves itself in you," he said, looking out over the
distance, the blue mountains, his home valley below.

"Look, Paul, you know this. In order to function as a Consort, you
have to be able to hunt, and to fight, and to be able to both respond to
and share leadership in the making of critical decisions. You have to
manage. You don't just get to fuck. You have to practice devotion to
the Divine Feminine. You know these things. Fuck your fear and your
delicate sensibilities. You, my friend, have to toughen up. Hungover or
not, you finish this."

"Fuck you, I'm an accountant, not a biologist. I'm not a hunter. I hate
blood."

"Too bad, buddy. Confront yourself. Use your knife to open that amniotic sack."

"What?"

"Do it."

Paul started weeping again, but he did as he was told. He pinched a bit of the sack and stuck the point of his knife in it and made a cut. The fluid ran out and covered his hands.

Craft said, "Use it to wash the crap off your hands. I don't want that hairy muck on one of my bridles."

Paul listlessly wiped his hands, using his shirt to dry them. He stopped weeping, and surrendered in silence, kneeling by the dead fetus.

"You have to understand," Craft said quietly. "Without a top predator, soon there will be so many deer we won't even be able to keep a garden. We take this life not only for ourselves but for everything these animals will destroy. By killing we are saving Life. And that there's another paradox for you, a paradox you can hold."

Then Craft leaned forward and spoke quietly into Paul's ear. "You were born in blood, boy. As were we all. Get used to it."

After a pause to let that all sink in, Craft said, "Grab your half and let's go load it on the packhorse. I want to get back while we can still get some lunch. We leave the rest for the wolf."

Greatly subdued, Paul did as he was told. They hung the meat over the pack horse, hooves up, tying a line through a slit cut in the space between the bones and the tendons.

When they mounted, Craft turned in the saddle and said, "You have to learn to control your Self, not just your pecker."

From higher up the wolf watched and licked its lips.

"Now tell me about the wolf," Craft said as they picked their way along the trail.

Down below, making her way up the same trail, Regina heard Paul talking. She reined the horse off into the woods beside the trail, dismounted, calmed the horse, and waited.

Craft's horse stopped on the trail when it pulled even with Regina's horse, hidden in the woods, and snorted, tossing its head. Craft sat there a moment, then reached into a pocket of his slicker and pulled out a pouch. Taking off his gloves and putting them on the saddle in front of him, he rolled a cigarette in true cowboy style. From the same pocket he pulled a lighter, flicked the lid open on his thigh, and rolled the striker wheel across his pants. He lit up, exhaling in the cool air. Finally he said, "Supper time is around six. Try to be back by then. I'd like to meet you. And I don't want to come out tonight and have to look for you after dark."

Then he geed up the horse and proceeded down the path. Paul followed, flexing his hands inside his gloves, sticky with dried fluid, looking around to see to whom Craft had been talking.

When the pack horse passed her hiding place, the head of a thigh bone flashed whitely in the light. Regina's eyes grew wide as she recognized the shape, and the use to which she'd put one similar. She realized she'd been holding her breath and released it. "A good sign," she whispered.

After the men and horses passed, Regina climbed up into the saddle, and, ducking around branches, she returned to the trail. Almost two hours later she was at the top, standing on the shoulder below the peak, looking west and south into the mountains, holding the reins in her hand. A breeze from the northeast brought the smell of offal to her, and she turned to look for it. When her scan found the rock there was a blackness, a shadow almost, at the carcass. It flickered and disappeared behind the rock. The horse shied. She smiled, thinking of the secrets she carried in her luggage.

In the kitchen, "Where do you get greens this time of year?" Amanda wanted to know, washing a colander full at the prep sink.

"From the greenhouse over in the formal garden," Beverly replied, returning with a block of cheese from the walk-in refrigerator. "We'll probably head over there this afternoon. We do succession planting through the winter so we'll have these."

"You all seem really busy. Why don't you hire help?"

"We do," Rachel said, backing through the swinging doors with the tea service on a tray. "It's winter break here; no classes, no students or interns. We send the help off on vacation. They're in Florida. They may retire there soon. They're local people. We have to be careful, and we've not yet found people from Her Path that are willing or able to stay here full time. Speaking for myself, I am happy to have a few weeks alone."

"Why didn't you use the dumbwaiter?" Beverly wanted to know, indicating the tray.

"Because it's full," Rachel replied.

"Baking tomorrow," Beverly said, as she laid out the last loaf on the counter.

"OK," Rachel said, as they sat at the counter. "We can add it to the list." They ate in silence for a moment.

Then Rachel said, "So, Amanda, go on with your story."

"We were close, Rachel," Amanda began. "You and I, well, at least I felt very close to you. Someone wiser to whom I could tell everything. I still feel that way. You opened my mind to the nature of the Divine Feminine and I have lived upon that flower ever since. So, She bids me tell you what it was like, sharing Her mind and my daughter's mind while she seduced the Postman. So that you know that I know, She tells me."

"Go on," Rachel said, and Beverly nodded.

"The first day, it was raining intermittently. I was meditating at my altar in the late morning, being in a place of prayer to Her, as I knew there was some danger. It actually thrilled me a little, that this was going to happen for Regina. She picked out a dress and heavy hose and boots. No knickers, though. She chose a spot on the road where there were no houses for a good way. And suddenly I saw the tableau as if I were a camera making a film.

"The car slowed to a stop as he drove alongside her. He asked her if she was in any trouble and she replied that she was just on a walk, and could she trouble him for a lift farther out so she could walk back. She had a huge smile on her face, and he couldn't help himself but to respond with a smile, also. He had good teeth. So she went around the car and got in.

"As he drove they introduced themselves. About a mile down the road there was a pull-off for traffic coming the other way, and, just as she was going to get out, there was a bit of a downpour. Into the silence while they waited for the rain to let up, Regina pulled up her skirt to mid-thigh and simply said, 'Fancy a bit?'

"'Wot?' the Postman replied, turning to her, his eyes widening.

"'Yes', I'll take that to be,' and then turning to him in the seat she said, 'Look first. Do not touch.' With one knee up on the seat she leaned back and pulled her skirt up over both thighs, letting him see the top of her bush. Then she said, 'Want to see more? I've shown you mine, now you show me yours.'"

Rachel and Beverly laughed out loud, remembering the conversation with the men two nights prior.

"What?" Amanda asked. "What did I say?"

"Oh, dear, that's because of another conversation with the men, not you," Beverly said.

"We'll tell you about it later. Please continue, dear," Rachel said.

"Well. Then," Amanda said, shaking her head. "He didn't hesitate. He turned in his seat, unbuttoned and pulled it out. It lay there, just the phallus, soft and shining in the dim light. And as she watched, it grew. She didn't do anything, didn't move except to sit forward and look more closely. It grew to its full extent, and hard.

"'Touch it,' she told him, and he did, wrapping his hand around it, he started wanking. 'No,' she told him. 'Just hold it. I want to see.' She came forward on both knees along the seat, and bent forward to look closely, it being the first one she'd seen on a man. She blew on it, and he twitched. 'I'm told a man needs to spill his seed, especially in this condition. Is it true?' she asked.

"All he could do was nod. 'Show me,' she said. 'Would I pull it like you did?' He nodded again, slowly wanking. Then she said, 'Let me.' He removed his hand and she reached forward, drawing the nail of her forefinger along its length, from the base to the tip. She slowly grasped it, and slowly squeezed it, feeling how hard it was. Slowly, too, she stroked him. She marveled at how the skin moved, the foreskin slipping over the head and then revealing it, like some flower opening to reveal its crown.

"It didn't take long before he squirted with such force that it struck him in the chin—gob smacked him, it did—and laid a trail along his shirt. She, too, orgasmed, a shiver of ecstasy starting in her face and travelling to her sex. She told me later that the pulse of energy that came off him as he ejaculated was what caused it. She even squirted a little herself, her juices running down her leg and into the hose.

"The last pulse of thick whiteness rolled down over the head of it and across her fingers. She sat back on her heels and sniffed it, then she tasted it with the tip of her tongue. She looked up at him and smiled. Then she reached back behind her with her other hand and opened the door and backed out. 'You will see me on the road again,' she said, and gave him a big grin as she closed the door.

"She licked his juices off her fingers before the rain washed it away as she walked back toward the settlement. She savored the tastes—salt, with a hint of sweet and a little metal, almost like licking a knife. She disappeared downhill into the woods along the river, and then the vision of it disappeared as well."

"Well, that's some story," Beverly said, one hand pressing into her lap. "How do you...?"

Rachel interrupted, "Did you come, too? Did you orgasm, also?"

Amanda nodded, "Yes, I felt hers as she came."

"Her's, not yours, differently?" Rachel asked.

"Yes, her's. Does it make a difference?"

"Yes. What you experienced was some kind of sensible telepathy with your daughter, not just your own excitation. That is very powerful and indicates something. I'm not sure what it means. I shall have to meditate and ask Her."

"Is that how you remember them so vividly?" Beverly asked, having already heard her answer.

"Yes," Amanda repeated. "When the portal opens, I experience what she experiences."

"And how was she, how was Regina with it all?" Rachel wanted to know.

"She was fine with it. When she arrived home she was flushed with it, flushed with a sense of happiness and success. The whole gambit was her sixteenth birthday present to herself."

Everyone sat, hands or elbows on the counter, heads at different angles, the story having triggered reflection in all of them, and contemplation of the memory of their own first encounters.

Rachel was the first to move, slapping her hands on the counter. "Well," she said. "Let's get this organized and go back to work."

In the greenhouse the heat had been turned up. The sun shone and the wen sweated. Rachel had slipped out of the top of her union suit, unbuttoning the front, and pushing it to her waist, tying the sleeves around her belly. Her suspenders held up her pants, and she was working bare breasted, preparing a seed bed, mixing in fertilizer with a shovel.

Beverly was showing Amanda how to plant the spinach seeds using a chicken wire grid laid over the soil. "Tell us about Regina's first time," Beverly said to Amanda.

"Alright, yes, well," Amanda said, glancing sideways at Rachel. "From the first, Regina maintained total control. She initiated all contact, all touching. She told him what to do, and what not to do. After not long she had him asking permission to do anything, even the things she told him to do. And he, poor man, did it all the way she wanted, from a place of humility and gratitude. Any time she thought he might have forgotten how fortunate he was, she would remind him.

"She'd go down to the road at least once a week except when she was on her monthlies. By the way, how do we deal with that here?"

Rachel replied, turning over a spadeful of dirt, "In an old way. You get the days off. End it with a special bath. You'll see."

"What counts for vacation around here," Beverly mock snarked.

"Well, then. I guess I shall. And so," Amanda, not sure she understood the exchange, picked up the story line again. They stayed with masturbation for a while—she doing him while she did herself. She made it a game, how quick could he go, how long could he last, learning for herself the ways of the phallus. By the end of that first month she progressed to kissing it, then sucking on it for him, discerning what could make him stay up, what would make him go.

"She spent time along the river, building little shelters, little bowers near the pull-offs up on the road above, so that they could get out of the car and walk to them. She'd show them to me on walks we'd take together and tell me the stories of what happened there, as if I didn't already know. Once, when they were down by the riverbank, someone had stopped and hallooed the Postman, making sure he was alright. She made him pull his face from between her thighs and halloo back, then made him get dressed and go out to reassure the farmer that he had only stopped for some lunch. 'A bit to eat' she told him to say.

"The hardest part for her was letting him touch her. She'd inspect his hands, make sure they were clean, making him wash them in the river. I had to laugh when she learned how cold that would make them the first time she let him touch her upper thighs. She'd give him a peppermint before she'd let him kiss her, and she soon found out the effect of that the first time she let him kiss her down there!"

All three wen laughed and squeezed their knees together, imagining the sharp tingling as the essential oil took hold of their labia. "Ooo! Ooo!" Rachel said, leaning on her shovel. "Ouch! That must have hurt," Beverly chimed in.

"But he was sweet about it. He didn't laugh when she suddenly jumped up and ran down into the river to wash it off. He was all concern and sweetness, but Regina was angry about it. She noticed, however, that he didn't lose his erection, standing there pantsless on the riverbank. Pretending to use it as a handle she got out of the river and got down on her knees and sucked him off right there, kneeling in the moss, the sound of the rushing water filling her head, the wind in the trees swelling her sensation as his cock swelled in her mouth. I remember it as if I was there." She paused and touched two dirty fingers to her lips, leaving streaks of topsoil on her chin.

Beverly thought it was almost unbearably cute; she almost fell in love with Amanda in that moment, but she smiled and said nothing. She knew then that Amanda would work out here, fitting in with them and what was happening.

Rachel stopped digging and looked up, watched the entranced wen for a moment, and smiled.

Amanda shook her head, strands of hair coming loose from her bun and falling on her cheek. She brushed these aside with her fingers, making more streaks of dirt along her jawline. "The first time they did it was in July. You could reliably count on a few sunny warm days then. She was always a little uncomfortable on her back. She'd let him go down on her a few times, and discovered she preferred sitting on his face. So that was how she did it, sitting down on him, on top.

"She made him hold it up for her, and she eased in just the tip at first, spreading her lips around it with her own hands, letting it snug in. She discovered the working of her muscles and almost brought him right then. But then she stilled, until their breathing steadied. She took him slowly past the bone-pierced wreckage of her hymen, the tight petals hooking like a ring behind the head of him, locking him in. Then she took him in a little farther and leaned slowly forward and back, finding the contact for the little walnut behind her clitoris. The pressure made her squirt a little and she smiled. Then she sat all the way down."

Amanda shivered at the memory, and the shiver was contagious; Rachel and Beverly shivered, too.

"She didn't move for a while. She just sat there, sensing everything, the long filling length of him, her own inner movements of accommodation. Then she leaned forward on her hands, her hair falling in a curtain hiding her face, and began to move. She'd trained him over the months to control himself, so he lay back and relaxed. She lifted herself a little way, feeling the lock around his head, learning which muscles controlled that. Then she lifted her hips a little more, taking him back past that sweet spot, and came off him entirely. Then she went through the entire thing again, fitting him in, then sliding down on the shaft, filling herself and stretching over it all. She sat back and rocked on it. She took his hands and put them on her breasts, and squeezed her hands over his. Then she shivered her first full orgasm, from her shoulders and spine shaking down onto him, successive waves coursing down from above, it seemed, pouring around him into the earth.

"When it stopped, he said…he said, 'I'm feeling like some kind of tool here.'

Regina shook her head and laughed. "A screwdriver in the hand of the right wen is an amazing thing to see. Hmm. Perhaps here we have the hammer of Thor, eh?"

"And laughing, she rose and fell, posting on the Postman, orgasming as many times as she could, hair wild, shaking her head from side to side, and riding, until he finished."

Amanda looked up and smiled at the others.

"The affair continued for over a year, until the Postman was replaced with another driver."

"How many of those stories do you have?" Beverly asked, a little breathlessly.

"Perhaps one hundred. I remember almost all of them," Amanda answered. "Do you like them?"

"Yes, I do, very much. I can see it, maybe perhaps even as you see it. At the least, your telling is powerfully evocative," Beverly said.

"I, too, like them very much. Will you tell us more when we ask for them? They make me feel powerful. As well as horny," Rachel asked.

"Certainly. I don't know if I can tell them in front of her, but when it is just us, I will tell you."

"Thank you."

"Yes, thank you."

"Well, briefly, on with the rest of it," Amanda said. "After the affair ended Regina kept her composure about it, but the loss hurt her. Not her feelings, so much, as her longing; her physical, sexual, longing, bordered on the painful. We moved back into town, in the hope that on the social circuit, or perhaps in college, she could meet someone appropriate. All the eligible men were looking for wives, and it was taking a long time for Regina to cultivate friends. I started introducing her around the Brighid circles but it wasn't until a holiday that I could get one to accept her on the condition that she played the Divine Feminine in the Union Ceremony. But she was a little too much for the man, and it was a struggle to complete the Hierogamy. We had just about determined to begin looking for a lover for her among the help when Regina was contacted from Paris.

"As you know, yes? Her father had a book published the year after his death."

"Yes, I have it. Typically impenetrable," Rachel said.

"Yes, well, some of his heirs wanted to pick up where he left off. Some of his other students do, too, establishing themselves as separate lineages from each other. The main group was searching out all his children, seeking to bind their allegiance, or if not, get them to sign a document releasing the estate from all claims. The other lineages were after the endorsement of any of the children they could find, seeking legitimacy.

"It became frightening. There were multiple threats from different groups, even. Threats against her safety—and mine. She fucked a couple of the emissaries for her own amusement, cultivating false hopes. But when it was realized she was just using them, mocking their pale imitations of her father, it became ugly.

"This is why we came. Here, I believe, she will be safe. And, I think she will be supportive of your plans and work hard for you. She already believes much as you do, but we have nowhere else to turn."

"Sister, you are welcome here," Rachel said. "And your daughter. For as long as you need."

Craft and Paul unsaddled and curried the horses, and hung the venison in a cool room near the freezers to be butchered the next day. Craft made Paul wash at the stand pipe, although it didn't make much difference when all he had to dry his face with was his already bloody shirt.

They drove the truck to the house and changed clothes. In the kitchen making lunch, Craft noticed that Paul had tried to wash again but there was still blood in his hairline. Craft smiled again and said nothing. He decided that it was best to let one of the wen point it out to him. Craft decided to wash the dishes in the sink before they ate. When they finished they made sandwiches to take over to the greenhouse, where they knew the wen were scheduled to be.

They went out through the courtyard and on out past the east wing to a set of terrace steps, and turned left toward the power plant. The greenhouse, glass and metal framed, was just to the south of the plant. As he came up to the door he could hear voices inside. He opened the door with one hand, went through it eating a bite of his sandwich and came to a dead stop.

Paul, following too closely, bumped into him and dropped his sandwich in the pile of aged manure just outside. Craft saw an interesting thing: Rachel was standing naked in the middle of the greenhouse, leaning on a shovel. Kneeling before her were Beverly, her back naked but for her suspenders and a wen he took to be Amanda, with her union suit unbuttoned to the waist and breasts exposed.

Rachel had one leg extended to the side, knee bent, foot resting on a chair. The other wen were examining her sex, Beverly with one hand on her lower belly and another on the inside of Rachel's thigh, opening the flesh for a better view. She and Amanda were leaning in to look.

Craft followed her look and discerned something very special. Something very bright and smooth. He let out a low whistle. The wen turned and looked at him briefly and went back to their examination. He moved slowly in their direction, taking in each change in perspective.

Paul stood in the open doorway, regarding his manured sandwich with dismay.

"Come in, idiot," Rachel said, looking up at him, smiling. "You're letting all the heat out.

Later in the afternoon, Regina came through the green house door and was stopped suddenly in her tracks by the tableau before her.

The woman, Beverly, was bent over a work bench, resting on it with her elbows. Her hair had come down and hung alongside her face in sweaty strings. Her union suit was unbuttoned down the front, her breasts swinging freely, and her back flap was unbuttoned, leaving her bottom exposed. The second horseman had mounted her from behind, his pants around his ankles. He was moving in and out steadily and Beverly was making grunting sounds when he buried himself all the way in.

Farther in, laying on her back on another bench, naked, was the woman Rachel, and the first cowboy, also naked and on his knees, between her thighs.

Her mother was standing on the far side of them, naked from the waist up, one hand on Rachel's lower belly, another on the man's head, leaning in, looking.

Beverly, hair loose and sweat soaked, with hooded eyes, turned to Regina and said, "Close the door, you'll let the heat out."

Regina did, stepping back out the door and closing it, laughing. Leaning against the door she resolved something in herself and turned, opening it again. She went inside and closed the door behind her. She bumped Paul on her way by and did it deliberately, pushing him into Beverly, whose nipples dragged across the rough wood table.

Beverly said, "Hey!" Regina laughed, and Beverly growled at her.

She went over to her mother, smiling, unbuttoning her shirt as she went. "Whatever is so fascinating down there, momma?"

"Come look," Amanda beckoned.

The cowboy, still naked on his knees between Rachel's legs, said "I am gazing at the doorway to the Temple." Regina heard him say this as she stopped at Rachel's side, across from her mother. Rachel's clitoris was swollen and visible, emerging from beneath its hood. Her vulva was engorged and distended, and she was open below. Clearly she'd been having sex already. Then Regina realized what she was seeing—that she was actually seeing what she saw because Rachel was completely shaved. She drew in her breath and whistled in a low and quiet tone.

The cowboy stood up, fully erect, and placed the head of his glistening phallus against her opening and moved it slightly, spreading evenly her now visible lips. He said, "To contemplate is to adore, to enter is to worship." He slowly slid himself in, Rachel shivering as he did.

"Watch," Amanda said. "You can see it all. It's beautiful." They did more than watch. Both Amanda and Regina put a hand on Rachel's belly and leaned in to watch, the cowboy careful to not obscure the view. In and out, they could see the unfolding and the folding, see the embrace of the lips, hear the sliding, and inhale the smell. Soon their breathing synchronized with Rachel's, their excitement built with hers, and they came when she came. Moaning when Rachel cried out, they went to their knees no longer able to stand when Rachel's legs began to shake in her seizure of ecstasy.

That evening, after dinner and clean up, the six gathered in the office sipping whisky, they brought Amanda and Regina up to speed on their planning for how the Order of the Fleur de Vie would function, what its rules would be, and how the members would be trained. For the wen, Rachel and Beverly had the basic idea of teaching everything Rachel knew about the tantra, adding it to a necessary devotion to the Diosa, the Divine Feminine. But it was clear to them that the men would be different. They would receive training in the tantra, but for Rachel that was not enough. The sublimation of the need to dominate must lead to devotion and service—devotion and service not just to the Divine Feminine, but to the Priestesses themselves. It was to be a Priestess-run operation, no priests, only Consorts. "There are enough priests in the world," Rachel had remarked.

Rachel believed that it was through the power of the idea of the Antecedence of the Feminine that this conversion could be effected in men. Giving up the idea of masculine antecedence and the ensuing presumption of universal creative control, and giving up the idea that masculine dominance of the feminine was the natural order. These ideas had to be made manifest in practice. Rachel believed that a new kind of equality could be generated; the strength of the men being balanced by the understanding of the Antecedence of the Feminine and that genuine respect would come to be the norm. In an atmosphere of natural and genuine respect Love would have room to breathe. The Divine Feminine would assume Her natural place and Her natural rule.

Rachel and Beverly spoke of the vows and the stages of initiation for the members, both men and wen. They told of their speculations about the inclusion of altered and hypnogogic states of consciousness that would alter the systems of sentiments from the old order to the new, and how to build safeguards into that process. After laying all that out for Amanda and Regina, Rachel said, "We...we have to create a place where men have what they want, so that then we can work on men becoming what men can best become."

"Well, what is it most men want the most?" Regina asked.

"Pussy and Food," Craft answered.

"Really," Amanda commented.

"Well, at least most men," Craft amended.

"Yeah," Paul picked up the thread. "When they have enough pussy—I wonder, is that even possible?—when they have enough sex, their mind is freed to think. All that desire clouds the brain, and they can't think, really, about what they should do."

"And food," Beverly added.

"Yes. If they're fed well enough they can be outside, running around in all kinds of weather, doing whatever else it is that needs to be done. Gets them out of the house and out from under foot," Paul added.

"Sex and food. And I'll thank you for not continuing to say 'pussy'," Amanda said.

"You're welcome. When men get their need for sex and food met they can work. Most importantly they can work on themselves, work in their inner world, fashioning themselves into better men: more mature, more responsible, more accepting, and more beautiful. In short, it frees them to become Good Men," Craft said.

"It also frees them to work on the outer world," he continued. "Men who alternate their focus from the inner world with the outer world can see what needs to be done and do it. They can work the land, hunt, study, make things and be creative.

"Enough sex and food, combined with the right inner and outer work, leads to men being both self-disciplined and kind. These men are able to understand the need to be in service to the Feminine," he finished.

"Well, you'll have to teach them to lie," Regina said.

"Why?" Beverly asked

"Because nobody would believe this, and what this place is, unless they're the kind of people you don't want to believe in it. Those kinds of people you don't want to know about it. Bad people. Bad people will come and hurt us," Regina replied.

"Yes, I see. Well. Acting maybe. Teach them acting," Beverly said.

"You could simply teach them loyalty," Craft offered.

"Maybe. But what happens if somebody goes bad who already knows about this. What are we going to do?" Amanda asked.

There was a long pause. Then Paul, resonating with his bloody experiences of the day, said, "Kill them."

"What?" Rachel said.

"Kill them. Kill them as fast as you can. Before they can tell anyone. And never, ever, tell anyone that's what you do," Paul continued.

"I still need to think about this," Rachel said, hesitantly and with reservation.

"What's to think about? If this is important enough to lie for, important enough to lie to protect it, it's also important enough to kill for," Paul argued.

"I agree," Craft said. "I don't want to agree but I have to. There are bad people who will hurt you, who will hurt us—people who must be prevented from doing that."

"But what about Her? Won't She protect us? Won't She keep us from that?" Amanda asked.

"Maybe," Craft said. "But I don't think we should count on it. Look at what happened to Her cities. To Her Priestesses."

"Look what happened to the women accused of witchcraft. Where was She then?" Regina added.

"Where *was* She then?" Craft asked.

"I don't know. So we have to ask Her," Rachel replied.

"What if She is just an archetype? What if She is just a dream?" Paul asked, his doubts surfacing.

"We can ask Her to protect us now, while we are still small," Beverly said.

"Yes, we can ask Her to work through everybody's dreams," Amanda offered.

"It will take more than asking," Craft said, in a serious tone of voice.

"No, seriously, where *was* She then?" Regina wanted to know.

"If She's just an awareness, what could She do? What power does She have outside the human mind?" Paul continued his train of thought.

"Then it's through the human mind She must work," Amanda concluded.

"What about their god? Is he just awareness?" Regina continued.

"Not according to their oldest books. According to those texts, he's an alien. He and all his kind came here from another star," Beverly said. "Either that, or he was one of us that became immortal. It would explain how he looks."

"Maybe. But the form can be manipulated through the image of the form. She looks like us, too. If She looked like something else, well, actually She looks like anything she pleases," Craft offered, looking at Rachel observing the room. Trying to refocus the conversation he said:

"We have to kill if need be."

"No, we may not have to kill. But we do have to able to kill." Rachel conceded.

"We have to be prepared to kill," Craft interpreted. Rachel nodded in assent.

Everyone was silent, letting this idea settle within themselves. Craft put more wood on the fire.

"If we're not going to call it 'pussy' what are we going to call it?" Craft asked, sensing everyone was lost in their own thoughts. Everyone smiled and recentered.

"I've been working on it, just like I began to use the word wen for women, sometimes in the singular, too," Rachel answered. "I think I have a word, I've been searching for it, looking for a word that can be the equivalent of phallus, a word I like very much. I have been working with the word 'phulva.' I think it has the right sound. Phulva and phallus. Say it slowly. Try it."

They all took turns saying the word.

"I like the way it feels in my mouth," Regina said. "The word, I mean."

They all laughed, Paul saying, "Me, too."

In a serious tone, Amanda said, "The word has no weighted connotations in my mind, no associated meanings. It's clean, to my mind."

The discussion turned to the possible content of vows. Near nine o'clock, Rachel said, "It's time. Let's get cleaned up and meet back here in half an hour. I can feel the ritual coming on. We shall ask Her what happened, where She was."

During normal times they would have bathed before supper, but with no help to prepare the food they had all waited until this moment. In the hallway from the kitchen to the stairs Rachel pulled Craft aside and asked him, "How are the Asswork Negotiations going? Is he receptive?"

"Very funny," Craft said. "The fucking negotiations are going fucking well enough, thank you very fucking much," he continued, his voice loaded with sarcasm.

The wen went upstairs to wash while the men arranged the furniture according to Rachel's instructions. Negotiations between them continued. When they finished with the furniture, they, too, went to wash and change clothing.

Beverly told Amanda and Regina where in their rooms to find the most appropriate gowns, robes, and slippers, and to then meet them in the bathroom.

The men were getting ready to shave, cleaning up two days of beard when Craft noticed a long hair, clearly a pubic hair, in his shaving brush.

He went across the hall to inquire as to its origin and found the wen engaged in a lively conversation. Rachel and Beverly were sitting up on the sink counter, feet on the edge, their legs up, and spread for Amanda and Regina to see. The wen were comparing notes on the details of the differences between the two phulva. He stood there, watching this remarkable scene, brush in hand, until Rachel looked over at him, and gave him a wicked smile of acknowledgment. He grinned goofily and shook his naturally enlarging phallus at her. He went back across the hall to shave and found that the blade was so dull as to be useless, and he had to change it.

They assembled in the hallway outside the office doors, the wen in gowns and doubled robes, the men in nightshirts and robes, everything opening down the front. Paul led the way through the double doors, followed by Beverly, then Regina, Amanda, Rachel, and Craft. Beverly stopped just inside the door, putting Regina on her left and Amanda on her right. Rachel stood behind Beverly. Paul and Craft closed the doors.

They contemplated the room in semi-darkness. The fire burned steadily, casting rich light on an open carpet with an ottoman at either end. Moonlight flooded in through the high southern windows. They breathed in silence. Before them on a small buffet were candles in candle holders made with handles on the side. Beverly handed one to each of them. Rachel, accompanied by the men, went around to the north approaching the fireplace. The wen did the same to the south. There were long thin pieces of kindling on the mantle, used for lighting candles. Rachel lit the men's and Beverly the wen's. They set the candles on a row of low tables along the western side of the carpet.

The wen kneeled on the carpet in a line from east to west, Beverly in the middle, Amanda to her left and Regina to her right, nearest the fire, their palms resting on their thighs. Paul went to the southern ottoman, and sat, leaving one foot on the floor and the other tucked under his thigh, his back to the windows, facing the carpet. Craft took the northern ottoman and sat in the same fashion, right foot on the floor and the left tucked under the right thigh. Rachel stepped to the edge of shadows on the north.

After a pause to settle, Rachel began to tone in a low voice, "Oh woe, woe, woe, woe, woe." After seven repetitions the men joined her for four, then were silent for three. When the men had repeated this pattern seven times, Beverly took up Rachel's chant on the same note. With a hand to each of the other wen, she indicated they should join her. After they'd sung it once, Rachel switched to a higher note. Three times they cycled through, each time Rachel singing a higher note. Suddenly she stopped and stepped forward into the light. There seemed to be some sort of wavering shadow over her face that the light could not penetrate. She whispered, "Ohay, ohay, ohay, ohay." All repeated it.

Rachel stepped forward and put hands on either side of Craft's head and laid him slowly back until his upper back and head were parallel to the floor. Rachel opened her gowns, her belly flashing in the light. She stepped over his face and squatted down. There was a visible reaction on her face when she made contact with his tongue. The expression sorted out into a smile. She moved on his mouth, a slow circle of her hips in one direction, then the other. Then, rocking her pelvis, she leaned forward and opened Craft's robe and shirt, exposing his full erectness, and gazed at it.

The wen raised their hands in the offering pose and lowered them again, opening their robes also. Paul, completely erect now, too opened his robe and pressed his palms together at heart level in alignment with it.

Rachel leaned forward and took him in her mouth, Craft still supported himself on his arms, to keep his mouth in touch with her. She just held him there, using her tongue to lick across the ridge, using it to make connection with the roof of her mouth. Then she stood up and stepped forward until she was standing over his erection. He held it up for her and slowly she settled on it, making contact, slipping over the head, and sliding down the shaft easily, feeling her insides unfold and stretch and suddenly she was down, sitting on him, breathing.

The others had all been watching the union with close attention, captivated by its beauty. Regina sighed.

Rachel raised and lowered herself completely four times and then sat still, raising her arms out to the sides, palms up, leaned her head back and whispered to the ceiling, "Why, why, why, why." She rocked her pelvis slowly back and forth until she spasmed, like she'd been shocked with electricity. Four times this happened, then she started to scream, a rising "AH" that tore through her throat. At the peak of it she came forward and off of Craft, coming to her knees in front of Beverly. She screamed at her, "I had no defense."

Three more times, each with less volume and more sobbing, she said it. "I had no defense, I had no defense, I had no defense." She laid her head in Beverly's lap and fell to her side, back to the fire, sobbing. The wen were sobbing now, too.

Craft sat up and closed his robe, Paul did the same. They raised their arms in a circling gesture, and sat, holding the space for the grief and the fear.

Outside, a blast of wind came down off the mountain and rocked the house; they could track the wind's progress by the creaking of the windows. When it whumpfed past the east wing, Regina, wiping her tears on her sleeve, turned and put more wood on the fire. When she turned back Rachel was sitting up on her knees, her hands folded, palms together, in her lap. The wen did the same. She looked up, the tracks of her tears glistening on her cheeks in the firelight.

"She had no defense," Rachel said. "They came and She had no defense. She has had to evolve, evolve a defense. It has taken time. We are a part of that evolution. We are a part of Her defense."

16

CHESTER AND THE TATTOO

Lulu had the shower running, thinking it might afford her some privacy. She stood in the bathroom admiring her new tattoo in the narrow full length mirror screwed to the back of the bathroom door. She tilted her pelvis, forward and back, turning into quarter profile. "It's cute," she thought, the red heart rising from the blue whirlwind racing across her pubic bone. "Or falling," she said out loud. It was just small enough to not rise to her bikini line.

When she'd shown it to Missy, Missy had leaned forward and examined it closely. "I got to get me one," she'd said, smiling up at her daughter. Lulu smiled at the memory.

Then she remembered: Chester was in the habit of coming into the bathroom to pee when he thought she was in the shower. The broken lock on the bathroom door, one that he somehow never got around to fixing, required her to be vigilant. The noise of the shower was what kept her from hearing Chester's weight making the floorboard in the hallway creak.

When she saw the door move she panicked, fear rising and dropping at the same time so quickly it almost paralyzed her. "No, wait! Wait!" she shouted, pushing at the door. The distance to the tub was too great, and as she turned to pull the curtain closed, Chester came through the door. She stood in the falling water, shivering, wondering if Chester had seen the tattoo.

He had. Chester had seen the tattoo, but was pretending he hadn't while he peed, thinking up what he was going to say and do. Clearly, this was a large challenge to his authority and an affront to the Laud. The girl had to be punished, but how? He finished and put himself away in his pants.

Lulu was about to ask him why he always did that—come in while she was showering—ask him like she always did, but Chester flushed away her voice.

He turned suddenly and ripped the shower curtain back, startling Lulu so much that she almost slipped and fell. She acted instinctively, covering her breasts with one arm and covering her pubes with her other hand, concealing the tattoo. She screamed.

"Gawd amighty, girl, what have you done? You have desecrated the holy temple of your body, in violation of the Laud's word! You have damned yourself for all eternity," Chester bellowed. He reached out and grabbed the arm covering her breasts and pinned her to the wall, then shook her back and forth by it, yelling, "What have you done, girl, what have you done?"

Missy heard the scream from in the kitchen and came running down the hall, banging the door open. Chester turned, saw her, and pulled Lulu to the edge of the tub. He said to Missy, "Look what she's done, look, look at it!" while he batted away the hand Lulu was using to cover the tattoo.

Missy shouted at him, "Chester!" and when he turned to look at her, Lulu slapped him in the face with that batted hand. He turned back to hit her. Missy stepped forward and grabbed that arm, pulling him away from Lulu. "That's my child! Not yours! You don't get to punish her. I do! Leave her alone! Get out! Get out!" she shouted.

She pulled him out into the hallway and pushed him away, then rushed into the bathroom. She closed the door and leaned against it with her back, bracing in case he tried to get back in.

In the shower Lulu collapsed to her knees, sobbing, her tears lost in the falling water.

In the hallway, Chester was confused. He wasn't used to being pushed around by a woman, especially one that made sense. Parents owned their children; that's how he was raised to believe. It's how he was raised, and how his Daddy used to justify beating him when he was a boy. It was Missy's right to beat Lulu, not his. But clearly Lulu was a sinner and needed to be beaten for her disobedience and lying. All he could do was preach the word to Missy and offer to hold Lulu down.

He hollered through the door, "Well, you just make sure you do. You punish her good, Missy, and I'll help if you need it. You think on this, you think on the way of the Laud. If you have to, you have to beat the Laud back into that girl's soul. If you don't, you'll be damned along with her for the same reason. Hellfire, Missy. Hellfire forever. You think on that."

Chester went down the hall to the kitchen and the phone, shaking his head to clear it of the image of Lulu: her nakedness, her youth, his fist mashed against her breast when he shook her. In his mind, he stared at her again, her mound, the heart riding the tornado, now, forever, painted there. In his mind's eye he magnified it, filling it with detail until it became all he could see. He bumped into the counter, blindly, hand out, searching for the phone. He called Mickey.

"Mickey, come get me," he said into the answering machine. "We got to go put out flyers in Bellefort today." He hung up the phone and went outside to sit on the steps and wait, bumping into the door frame because the image blinded him again.

Missy relaxed when she heard the door shut, grabbing a towel and going to Lulu, turning the shower off. She knelt down and put the towel over her daughter, still weeping into her hands.

"It's a beautiful thing, honey. Don't you listen to him," Missy comforted her.

"It ain't what he said, Momma. It's what he did. It's what he did!" Lulu replied. Then she yelled, a long shout of anger, and frustration, and outrage at what had just happened.

Chester heard it, and nodded his head, thinking that Missy was punishing her somehow. When he closed his eyes he could still see the image, a silhouette in white, as if the image had been burned into the surface of his eyes, as if it was all that he could look at, all that he could see.

"I know, baby girl, I know," Missy whispered to Lulu. "But you got to be quiet. You yell, he may come back in here."

Chester raised his hand to his cheek, suddenly aware of the mild burn from the slap. It made him angry. He stood up, turned and banged the door open. He walked down the hall, taking his belt from his pants. He pounded the bathroom door open, belt in hand. He saw the two kneeling women and he stopped to look at them, huddling and afraid.

Missy raised a hand to protect herself from the inevitable blow. But Chester suddenly couldn't see her, blinded by that white-out of an image. When his vision cleared he found his gaze focused on Lulu's face, her eyes now blazing at him with fiery hatred. Something in her look stopped him.

"Slap me again, girl, and I'll take this belt to you," he growled, slapping the belt into the wall for emphasis. "I'll beat the devil out of you. I'll whup you so you never do it again." He turned on his heel and went on down the hall to the bedroom.

Missy stood up and closed the door. "Get up, Lulu. Get up and get dressed before he comes back."

Lulu stood up, letting the towel slide off her shoulders, still feeding on her anger. Her naked form, standing erect, her fists clenched, all showed a resolve to do it again: to fight Chester, belt or no.

"No, no, no, baby girl. You can't do that. You can't win," Missy hissed at Lulu.

"I don't care, Momma. I don't care. I just want to hit him. Hit him again and again," Lulu hissed back.

"Get dressed, Lulu," Missy quietly and sternly said. Lulu picked up the towel and stepped out of the tub. She wrapped the towel around her, tucking it in over her breasts. "I got nothing else in here, Momma," Lulu said.

Missy made a sound, "Hssst!" as she reached for another towel to drape over Lulu's shoulders.

In the bedroom Chester had quickly packed an overnight bag. Coming back down the hall he banged on the bathroom door with his hand. "I need my stuff," he said.

In the bathroom the startled women jumped and cringed. "Go buy it new, Chester," Missy said. "Just go buy it new. Take the money from my purse. Just go."

Chester went on down the hall, opened Missy's purse on the counter, and took out her wallet. He thumbed through the cash, pulling it all out except the one dollar bills. He fanned it, guessed there was almost a hundred dollars there, folded it and put it in his pocket. He humphed in triumph, and went outside again.

Mickey was watching a porno on his VCR and masturbating. When he heard the answering machine tape rewind, he finished what he was doing and ejaculated into a dirty towel. It took him longer than he thought it would, and the friction made his penis burn. He dropped the towel on the floor and stood up, unable to put himself back in his shorts. Pausing the videotape with a greasy remote, he went over to the answering machine, pressed 'Play' with a greasy finger, and listened to the message, his detumescing dick hanging out. He dropped a last drip of ejaculate on the table. He stuck a little finger in one ear, wiggled it around, and examined the crud that came out. Then he ate it.

He turned off the TV and VCR. He smoothed some of the off-brand vegetable shortening he used as lube onto his burning penis. He went to the refrigerator, took out a beer, and chugged it down, tilting his head back. He belched when he finished, looking down at his shrink-ing tool cooling in the air from the open fridge, pleased with himself. He went to the bathroom and peed. When he finished he put himself away, ignoring the little drops of yellow dampness that added to the already stained front of his shorts.

He brushed his teeth like Chester had told him. Then he spit, rinsed, and grinned at himself in the mirror. He put some gel in his hair to stiffen it in a messy look. He got dressed in his least dirty jeans and shirt. Pulling on his black engineer's boots, he noticed a big hole in one of his socks. He put the boots on anyway, grabbed a jacket from the floor by the door and went out to his truck.

On the way, he stopped and took the axe he'd been sharpening yesterday from the vise bolted to the picnic table in the front yard. He stuck it under the spare tire in the back to keep it from sliding around. He put the drill he'd been using to hold the grindstone under his seat, then checked behind the seat to make sure the baseball bat was still there. He started the truck, humming some theme song from a cartoon.

When he arrived at Missy's, Chester was sitting on the steps of the trailer, staring into the distance in a way Mickey knew meant Chester was having a vision. He put the truck in 'Park' and waited.

Chester stood up, shaking his head, and put his bag in the back. "What's the bag for?" Mickey asked as Chester got in the cab and closed the door.

Chester sucked at his teeth. "Gonna be gone overnight. Let's get to the Mill-o-mart, I need to buy some things."

Mickey backed out of the driveway and they drove off.

"Why don't you ever comb your hair?" Chester asked.

Inside the trailer, the women had sneaked over to Lulu's bedroom, which had a door that locked. Lulu had put her hair up in one of the towels and was defiantly taking her time getting dressed while her mother talked.

"You've got to understand, baby girl. You can't do nothing about it. He's just the way he is."

"No, Momma, I don't. I don't understand. I don't have to understand. I don't understand why you're with him, why you let him ruin our lives this way," Lulu responded.

"It's because I need him, Lulu. I'm ashamed of it, I am, but I need him. I got nobody to stand up for me. I need him for that," Missy said.

"I'll stand up for you, Momma. We don't need him," Lulu replied. "No, baby, it's my job to stand up for you," Missy corrected her.

"No, Momma, we'll stand up for each other. If we do that we can stand up to him," Lulu asserted.

"That's right, baby. We'll stand up together. But there's some things you need a man for. I need a man to stand up against other men. Nobody's gonna bother me if they know Chester is around," Missy explained. "So I need him. Just for a while, maybe not long, but you have to understand."

"Alright, Momma. I don't understand. But I'll stand up for you. And I'll stand up for me."

"Be careful, honey. Just be careful. You draw attention to yourself, then you get paid attention to, and sometimes in ways you don't want."

"I'm not afraid," Lulu stated firmly.

"I am," Missy said. "I am, and maybe you should be, too. I'm afraid of all men, what they can do, and how barely in they control they are."

"What do you mean, Momma?" Lulu asked, starting to comb out her hair. "They control everything already."

"Not that kind of control, honey. I mean control of themselves, I mean self-control. Most men seem to have barely any."

"Oh, yeah, you mean like Mickey."

"Yes, I mean like Mickey. You have to watch out for him, never be alone with him. A man like him, he's thinking about doing stuff all the time, stuff he doesn't get to do. And he's thinking about things he would do to you if he had a chance. You can bet on it. You need to understand something about men, honey."

Lulu sighed, "What, Momma?" thinking that this would be another sad old lecture. But what she heard next surprised her.

"Men are thinking all the time about stuff they want to do, but shouldn't do. All the time thinking and considering; considering this woman or that job. Considering this car or that TV, all the time blaming somebody else for what they can't do. It drives them crazy, mostly. And after a while they can't deal with it so good, and it all comes exploding out— all that unfilled desire. And if they think they can get away with it, they'll do it sooner rather than later."

"And you know this how, Momma?"

"Chester told me once. He was explaining to me about sin, and why men do it. And, watching him, watching Mickey, watching my boss at work, I believe it. And, besides, I've been a woman all my life."

This last remark led Lulu to look up, grinning, at her smiling mother.

"Chester said that if it wasn't for fear of the law, or fear of the Laud, most men would be animals."

"Well, I guess he'd know, now, wouldn't he, Momma?"

"Shush, child. You think about Mickey and you know I'm telling the truth."

"What's Chester have to say about women, Momma?"

"You know what he says. He says women are the root of all evil, and have been since the days of the Paradise. He says the difference between men and women is that women are inherently evil, and men become that way at their Momma's breast."

"That's terrible, Momma. What a terrible thing to say!"

"It is terrible, honey. More so, if it's true."

"Do you think it's true, Momma? Do you think we're inherently evil?"

Missy paused, choosing her next words carefully. "No, baby girl, I don't. But he does, and they do, and they're in control."

"So, why does he get to have all those other women, Momma? All those other 'wives'."

Her mother blushed. "He said that, for him, it's like it was in the days of the patriarchs of old. It's a special dispensation. A kind of grace he gets to have because he's doing the Laud's work."

"Aww, bullshit, Momma."

"The Laud works in mysterious ways. You and me get lots of time when he's not here. And watch your mouth."

Mickey watched Chester pay, in cash, at the register in the Mill-o-mart. He'd bought clean-up supplies, including deodorant, and a new set of clothes for Mickey. Mickey knew that Chester didn't pay taxes and didn't use banks, so there had to be a stash somewhere and he was always on the lookout for it. But Chester was crafty, if nothing else, and Mickey had never been able to figure it out.

"Oh, well," he thought to himself, shrugging. "It'll turn up. One day he'll piss me off for the last time, and when he does..."

"What're you shrugging at?" Chester asked, folding his change into his pocket, and indicating that Mickey should pick up the new clothes in the plastic bag on the counter.

Mickey said, "Nothin'," and looked away.

Chester narrowed his eyes and squinted at Mickey. "Don't be thinking too much. It don't pay."

"Don't be doin' that, Chester. Don't be looking at me that way," Mickey protested, turning the other way.

Sometimes, he knew, that when Chester looked at someone in a particular way he was trying to see into their minds, read their thoughts. Mickey had seen Chester do it many times from the back of some church or tent, reading somebody's secret sins and telling them out loud, sometimes whispering in their ear, sometimes shouting them out to the crowd. Mickey feared this power. So did many people, and they would confess their lesser sins to him up front, keeping their darkest secrets hidden. Folks would come just for the show—to watch their neighbors squirm. And, he knew, to never let Chester touch him. If Chester got his hands on both sides of a man's face then no secret could be kept.

On the way out of town, they stopped at a copy store, Chester dictating the flyer for the tent meeting to the young clerk, making sure she correctly spelled the names of the men with whom he'd be sharing the stage. Chester probed her mind, looking to see the last time the girl had sex. He snorted, trying to catch the scent of it. "Ah, there it is," he said out loud.

"Pardon, sir?" the girl asked, looking up from the computer screen. Chester caught her eye, and grinned. Suddenly the girl's mind was filled with the memory of having sex with her boyfriend, earlier in the dawn twilight: head turned to avoid morning breath, making little cries of pleasure with each pounding stroke, her boyfriend eager to come, forcing it through the morning wood of his erection. She loved morning wood; it made him work so hard to make his nut. Chester saw that, too.

She focused on Chester's grinning mouth and blushed. "I think that's it," she said, shaking her head. She printed out a copy for Chester to see, and when he nodded his approval she took it to the copier.

Chester stood at the counter, watching her from behind. He projected himself to a spot on the floor within arm's length of her and kneeled down in his mind's eye. He ran one hand up the inside of the girl's thigh, sliding it into her crotch, and slowly applied pressure, then gently rocked his hand back and forth.

The clerk, feeling this pressure, became excited and leaned into the copier, picking up its vibrations as it churned out a hundred copies. By the time it was done, her knees were starting to shake and there was perspiration on her upper lip.

Chester, who had been about to imagine inserting a finger, was shocked from his reverie by her voice and scowled. The girl looked up at him, and he turned it to a grin, although not fast enough. She dropped her face, and blushed deeply, knowing he had seen something of her excitement. She boxed up the copies and looked up at Chester when she handed it to him.

"Here, honey," he said. "You've got something on your lip." Chester wiped the sweat from half her lip with his thumb, and stuck it in his mouth. "Hold still, you got a little more on this side." The girl stood still, in thrall, as Chester wiped that other half and put his thumb in his mouth again. Chester grinned and backed away from the counter, then turned toward the cashier. The girl stayed frozen to the spot, paralyzed by the paradox of terror and desire so juxtaposed.

In the parking lot, sitting in the truck, Mickey was fuming. Chester had told him to stay in the truck while he went into the copy store. He'd said, "Son, you smell bad. Don't know if it's you or your clothes. I'll get these made up, and you wait here. We gotta get you cleaned up, boy."

Mickey couldn't smell himself unless he lifted his arm and sniffed his pits. He figured this was good enough, and Chester could just roll down the window. It made him angry that Chester felt that he was better than Mickey because he was cleaner. Feeling put down, he began a fantasy about finding Chester's money. For Mickey, the problem was one of keeping his fantasy and his designs hidden from Chester and his ability to see into people. He practiced erecting a wall in his mind that not even he, Mickey, could see through. While he was practicing he decided to move the truck to a different spot and see how long it took Chester to figure it out. The deception made him happy.

Chester came out of the store whistling. He looked around for the truck and his gaze fell on it immediately. It took him a second to realize it had been moved farther away, not so much hidden as moved. He wondered what that fool boy was up to now.

He walked out to the truck and climbed in. Mickey was grinning. "What foolishness you thinking about now?" Chester asked.

"Just wanted to see," Mickey said. "See how long it took you."

"Took me to do what? Walk another 30 yards? You some kind of knucklehead?" Chester said as he cuffed Mickey twice on the back of the head.

"Ow, ow Chester! Knock it the fuck off, man," Mickey hollered.

"Then don't fuck with me," Chester said. "Drive. One more stop to make, then we go post these in town. Head out the highway here and turn off when I tell you. And, Laud gawd a'mighty get a breeze going through here, cause you stinking up the cab just settin' still."

They drove the next fourteen miles in silence, until Chester said, "Turn here." They turned onto a dirt road, raising a trail of dust for three miles. Then Chester said, "Turn here," again. There was a dirt car track leading to a trailer with a car and a truck parked in the yard near the door. "Stop," Chester commanded, holding up a hand. "That truck ain't hers. Back up and pull over in the road where we can see who it is."

They didn't have long to wait. A middle-aged African American man came out the door, and looked around, putting something in his pocket. He backed his truck around and came out the driveway, pausing at the entrance. Seeing Chester and Mickey sitting there, somewhat dumbfounded, he grinned and nodded at them, turning out the other way on the dirt road, and heading deeper into the countryside.

Chester told Mickey to pull on into the yard. He got out, told Mickey to grab his new clothes and supplies and follow him. Chester bounded up the stairs, pulled the door open and hollered "Becky! Where you at, woman?"

Elizabeth Watkins, "wife number four" was right in front of him as he stepped inside. Startled, she screamed, then said "Shit, Chester! You scared the crap out of me." Mickey, not paying attention, bumped into Chester from behind, forcing him to reach out to steady himself. He grabbed Elizabeth by the shoulders, pushing her back against the kitchen counter before he was able to steady himself.

"Fuck, Chester, stop it! What the fuck do you think you're doing?"

Chester slapped her across the face. "Watch yer mouth woman," he growled. "You profane me, you profane the Laud."

"Ow, Chester. Shit. That hurt." She said, putting a hand to her stinging cheek.

"Cuss at me again and I'll slap you again," Chester said, seriously. Mickey stood grinning goofily in the doorway.

"Mickey here needs to clean up. Mickey, go use the bathroom in the hallway. Shower up good, hair, nails, everything. I need you in the congregation tomorrow night."

Mickey nodded, still grinning, plastic bag rattling as he turned and went down the hall. He kept moving past the hall bathroom and into the master bedroom at the back of the trailer. He threw the bag on the bed, stuck his head in the master bathroom and looked around. He smiled and inhaled deeply. Girl stuff. He loved it.

Becky watched him disappear into her bedroom and pointed, making a sound of protest, "But, Chester…"

"Pay him no nevermind, woman. I got questions for you. Who was that man?"

"He hays my daddy's old fields. His name is Joe Widder."

"Did you consort with him? Did you have sexual relations with that man? You doing a black dick when I ain't around?" he said, grabbing her shoulder and pulling her toward him in a shake.

"What? No, Chester. No. Like it's any of your business."

Chester slapped her again. "I'll have none of your insolence, woman. I ask you a question, you answer it."

"Ow, ow, ow, Chester. Laud, stop it," she said, putting her hands on both sides of her face now and shaking her head. "No, Chester. He mows the fields, then runs his baler over them. He came by to pay me my share of the sale."

"You take his name in vain again and I'll punish you. Show me the money," Chester said.

"It's behind me on the counter."

Chester pushed her aside, and saw a short stack of cash laying on top of a check. He moved to pick it up, but she fought him then.

"No, Chester, no. I need that money. No, Chester, no." She struggled with him, pushing him, and trying to take the cash out of his hand.

He set the money down and grabbed her by the shoulders. He slapped her across the face again, then grabbed a handful of hair and twisted it. She cried out. He used the hair to force her head, then her body, onto the floor. He put one booted foot on her back and held her down there, saying "Laud a'mighty, woman, what's got into you? Dark meat? That's what got you all uppity?"

"No, Chester, no. Please don't. I need that money," she whimpered, her voice muffled by her arm. She started weeping.

Something in what was happening got to Chester; something about the act of counting money with his foot on the back of a weeping woman got to him, and he grew erect inside his pants. It happened quickly, so quickly he had a hard time counting the money. There was a check made out to Becky for a thousand dollars and about five hundred in cash. His erection became so uncomfortable in his pants that he had to stop counting. Throwing the money along the counter in frustration, the whole pile slid over the extended countertop and onto the floor. He needed both hands to get the erection out in the air. He took it out, along with his testicles, through the hole in his boxers and then through his zipper.

He reached down and picked Becky up by the hair, again, as far as her knees. He bent over toward her, holding her face in his hands, looking in her eyes. "Look at me," he commanded. "Look at me and let me look into your soul. I will know it if you're lying."

She looked at him, eyes red-rimmed and teary, blinking, afraid.

"Did you do it? Did you have relations with that man? You been miscegenatin'?" Chester asked in his commanding preacher's voice.

"No, Ches—" Becky started to say, but as the energy from Chester's hands poured into her mind, she fainted, leaving Chester to hold her lolling head. But he had seen enough to know she was telling the truth. When her awareness returned from some place filled with white light she was gagging. Chester's erection was already in her mouth. Chester was using her like she was an inflatable doll, and he wouldn't let her pull away.

In the bathroom Mickey checked the medicine cabinet first, finding some kind of something that had the word 'codeine' on the label and took the bottle, throwing it out on the bed by his clean clothes. He sat down to take a dump, and looked around. As the smell rose from the bowl, he took a mister of some kind of floral scent and sprayed it around, which made the room smell like a manure covered field. Soon, his feet started to feel slimy in his socks inside his boots, so he kicked them off while he was seated. The smell that rose from his feet, mixed with the manure scented flowers, was too much even for him. He threw his boots and socks out in the bedroom and switched on the ventilation fan in the ceiling. Sitting back down, he smeared feces on the seat.

Looking around again he saw a laundry hamper within reach, so he dragged it over and opened it. On top was a pair of Becky's panties. He took them out and examined them, holding them to his face and sniffing at the crotch. Done moving his bowels, he tried to wipe himself, but standing up to turn on the fan had smeared the stuff around between his butt cheeks. Paper was hopeless to cope with the task so he used the panties. He was going to flush them, too, but thought better of it, not wanting to block the line. He threw them on the floor, but, since he was on the path to sanitary high ground, he picked them up and threw them in the trash instead. He looked in the bowl and realized the mountain that rose above the water line was too much to flush anyway, so he closed the lid.

With his new razor and can of foam he stood naked in front of the mirror to shave. Looking at his phallus in the mirror, he pushed it between his legs and closed his thighs in front of it, making himself look like a girl, a hairy girl. He wiggled his ass side to side and was suddenly struck with an idea. He dug around in the hamper and came up with another pair of panties. He put these on, tearing the waistband elastic as he pulled them up as high as he could. The tight thigh holes held his flaccidness back in place between his legs.

He contemplated this image as he began to shave. The erection that came up while he was watching became quickly uncomfortable and he pulled it out, first through a leg hole, the tight elastic of which threatened to decapitate it. He cut himself while shaving and trying to adjust it at the same time. He got blood mixed with shaving cream on his hands as he tried to stanch the cut. Then he pulled his erection up through the waistband, nicking his face with the new razor again, cussing, getting more blood mixed in with the shaving cream. He got the shaving cream mixed with blood on his erection when he moved it this time, the alcohol in the cream making it burn again for the second time in the day. Cussing some more, he put down the razor, slipped the waistband under his erection and washed it off.

Then he kept washing, washing the snake, looking at it in the mirror, blood and shaving cream running down onto his chest. He'd about worn out his penis for the day. It was burning again. He found a bottle of moisturizer that smelled pretty good and poured it all down the length of him, continuing to stroke it. When the inevitable moment arrived, he splooged in the sink bowl, and over the faucet and handles, splatting it up against the splash board in back.

He made a cursory attempt to splash water on the mess, then went back to shaving. He felt very satisfied with himself. Standing there in his ruined panties, he watched his favorite stuffed toy, as far back as he could remember, lay down to rest on the counter top.

In the living room Chester was struggling. He had dropped his trousers, pulled Becky's jeans to her knees and was mounted in her from behind. He was working way harder than he wanted at, as he called it, making his nut, and he didn't want to get his slacks dirty. He also was in a hurry to finish before Mickey came out of the bathroom, so he was distracted by looking over the counter and down the hallway. The unsourced fury with which he had begun his assault on Becky had abated, and he was tiring.

Trying to figure out why he had been so angry brought him to a pause. He couldn't make the connection to what had happened earlier with Melinda and Lulu, but his next thought made him snort with repressed laughter. He chalked up his inability to figure out why he had been angry to a man's infamous inability to think and have an erection at the same time, due to the blood loss in the brain.

Becky heard the snort and it made her think of pigs. She imagined Chester as a pig, rooting around, and it made her giggle.

Chester heard the giggle and knew he was done. Being laughed at made him flash with anger momentarily. In that flash, his vision filled with the same white silhouette he'd been blinded by before and he couldn't place it. He shook his head to clear it. He reached forward and grabbed the hair on the back of Becky's head and pulled it toward him, forcing her to arch. He redoubled his efforts at pounding away and quickly faked an orgasm just so he could stop.

Becky held still on her knees even when Chester got up. He pulled his pants almost all the way up, penguin walked over to the couch and sat down. "Get up. Get me a towel or something," he ordered, leaning back and closing his eyes.

Becky stood up and pulled her jeans up over her hips, wondering what had just happened but not daring to show it. She went around the counter extension and saw the money scattered on the floor. She bent down and scooped it under the rug in front of the sink as she pulled out a drawer where she kept clean dish towels. She took the towel over to Chester and stood there, jeans unbuttoned and stared at him, waiting for him to open his eyes and take the towel. She watched him as his breathing slowed. Soon she realized he was asleep, pants almost to his knees, and she laid the towel on the couch beside him, frowning at her good fortune.

She could hear the shower running so she knew she had a moment alone. She returned to the kitchen, gathered the money from under the rug and put it in the drawer under the towels. She went outside, sat on her steps, and put her chin in her hand. Contemplating her life, she wondered why she allowed things to happen to her all the time; why she couldn't just do something, make something happen with her life that wasn't just waiting for another truck to pull into her driveway. "He's the truck and I'm the driveway," she said aloud, and sighed. She might as well start drinking now, she decided.

She went in the house and retrieved a beer from the refrigerator, restocking it from the case she kept under the sink. She pulled a pound of ground meat from the freezer and put it in the sink to thaw. She went around back to the shed and got the bag of charcoal and the bottle of lighter fluid. She would grill outside tonight, avoiding being in the house with the men too much.

She sat back down on the steps and took a long pull on the beer. She thought about Chester, and why she put up with him. She thought about the white light place he took her to when they were having sex. Nothing but white light, and she couldn't feel anything, or sense anything, or even think anything. The white light place where nothing mattered, and she was no longer in her dead daddy's trailer on a back road in Alabama, on a squeaky bed. It didn't matter what he did to her, she just wasn't there. She'd take it if it was the only way to get out of her life.

She realized then that she could take the money from the first cutting and go, just go somewhere, and stop when she ran out of money. Live there, wherever there was, and maybe he wouldn't find her. She'd miss the white light, but since she couldn't live in it all the time, what good was it in the end anyway?

She thought of him, sitting there on the couch, pants near his knees, his limpness lying on his belly, head back and snoring. Yes, she hoped he'd forget about the money. She'd have to keep him distracted. The thought of what she might have to do to accomplish that task made her sigh again. She took another long pull to fortify her resolve.

Later, on her way back to the kitchen she covered Chester's limpness with the towel. She was in the kitchen when Mickey came out of the bathroom, smelling of flowers, manure, and toe cheese. Her stomach convulsed. Mickey grabbed a beer. Glancing at Chester still napping, the dish towel covering his nakedness, he smirked. He slammed the door on the way out, waking Chester with a snort. Chester looked around, threw the towel on the floor and stood up, tucking in his shirt and fastening up his slacks. He smacked his lips.

Becky said, "Beer in the fridge. Burgers gonna be on the grill in a little bit." She went back to her bathroom to assess the damage.

The room might have been in better condition if a real pig had been let loose in there. She stepped across Mickey's filthy clothes to open the window. She turned back to look, taking it all in. She realized she couldn't take it all in and that she shouldn't try. Just focus on one thing at a time, she told herself. She decided not to try to imagine what had happened in there. In the end, she had to use an empty plastic macaroni salad container to scoop out half of the dump in her toilet so she could flush it, twice.

During the night, aroused by the noises and the bed squeaking from the back room, Mickey masturbated into the dish towel Chester had thrown on the floor. He fell asleep, angry again, and worried that tomorrow he might have a self-inflicted scab somewhere on his penis from all the friction.

In the morning he drove Chester into town. They distributed the flyers, socializing with the store owners on the main street. At the dollar stores, one on either end of town, they got permission from the managers to tape them with blue painters tape to windows.

They stopped by the tent where Chester was sharing the bill with two other preachers. There was a small stage and at least fifty folding chairs already set up under the tent. For light there was a scattering of tiki lamps stuck in the ground. There would be no band, but there would be a soloist that Mickey had his eye on impressing enough to get with her behind the tent after the show. Then he and Chester went to lunch at a small diner-convenience store-gas station on the edge of town.

The waitress was charmed by Chester, of course. Mickey couldn't understand it, couldn't understand how Chester could do that to women; draw them in and make them smile at him. Loneliness and jealousy sparked in him so hard it made him grind his teeth. The jealousy gave way to anger that he couldn't seem to have what he wanted.

Chester touched Mickey's arm, reading him. Chester said, "Nobody really gets what they want, anyway." They sat in silence then, looking out the window, waiting for some car to pull in, waiting until the food came, waiting for something to come that would change their lives, waiting for something that would never come.

That night in the tent, filled to standing room only, Chester was third up. He started his sermon with "Yes, brothers and sisters. Yes, that brother just told you the Truth, the Truth about immortal life. And you shall know the Truth and the Truth shall set you free. Forsake the sins of the flesh, brothers and sisters, that you shall attain the kingdom of heaven."

In the back, Mickey waited for Chester to call down the holy spirit. Then he could go into his act, limping through the crowd, holding his back, pretending he had sciatica, so the laying on of hands could start, so the healing could begin. Chester would lay a hand on him and he would confess to lying, and drinking, and womanizing. He would confess to covetousness, thinking of Chester's charisma, then he would fall down, thrash around, and sit up 'pain free.'

There was now nothing to stop Chester as he called down the holy spirit. Flashes of light popped over the heads of some of the people. People fainted. People cried out. Some spoke in tongues, babbling deliriously.

"The Truth, brothers and sisters, we shall know the Truth! Your sins shall be laid bare and you shall be forgiven."

The holy spirit of irony had fled the tent in horror long before.

17

BLOW OUT

Angelica's next few days in class moved her to a mind-filling calm. The work was hard. It made her sore and tired. The meditations were restorative, combining efforts toward unitary awareness and internal energetic manipulation. These were all aimed to loosening the bindings of ego with its traps of attachment caused by the restricting condition of the Kundalini barrier. The resulting emotional work was liberating.

Angelica looked for the young man who offered to show her around, but didn't see him again until Thursday morning breakfast.

She felt a pull to him from low in her belly. Working at the coffee table, he felt the pull, turned and smiled at her, nodding. She went up to him, intending to refill her cup.

"Hi, I'm Angelica."

He said, "I know. Hi, I'm Jake," looking up at her.

"You work here, right? And live here, too?"

"Yes. It's a kind of apprenticeship, an internship."

"I want to know more about it, and about this place. Is your offer of a tour still good? Would you like to show me around the place?" she asked, feeling the pull low in her belly grow stronger.

"Yes, I would. But I can't make it by three. How about if I meet you at the courtyard kitchen door tomorrow at four?"

The pull in her belly pulsed with pleasure. "That should work. If class runs until four, like it's scheduled, I may be about a half hour late. I want to clean up and change. Is that OK? I'll be there as soon as I can, I promise."

"That will be fine, Angelica. Four thirty. I'll be there, waiting. It's fine." He smiled at her, and took the hot pan that had held scrambled eggs into the servery. Angelica went back to her table, sat down, and sipped her coffee. She squeezed her knees together and shivered with excitement and anticipation.

During the day, her anticipation continued to build, such that by nightfall she could barely stand to be in her own skin. So, that evening she attended the drumming practice session held in the great indoor riding ring, now repurposed as activity space. The talk was that there would be homemade ale for everyone, and there was, chilled, in reusable glass bottles. The drummers would be allowed to start drinking themselves at the second break, when a jam session was scheduled to start.

There were a lot of people there, waiting to dance on the raised wooden floor. Her new friend Jake was sitting on bleachers with the drummers, both men and wen, reviewing and practicing what seemed to be a composed piece of music. She saw her Instructor Bob sitting on a wooden folding chair near the coolers with the beer. She went over and sat with him.

When the first session got rocking the people danced until some mistake would cause the conductor to stop the work. The dancers would all turn and clap anyway, yelling out praises, cheering and whistling, making some of the drummers blush. Bob and Angelica got up to dance together, letting their bodies move however they wanted, finding a groove in the beats. Angelica stayed near Bob, but not close enough to make it look she was dancing with him. She did notice, however, that Bob had a fluidity to his moves. Even when he was hopping up and down his entire spine would rock.

The djembes, their heads tuned to different notes, found that place low in her belly and rekindled the desire and anticipation she'd been struggling with all day. On a break, the two of them, Bob and Angelica, stepped outside with fresh brews to cool off. It was Angelica's third beer. Her defenses were down and her desire was up. In a move that surprised even her, she turned to Bob and said, "Can I invite you to make love to me tonight?"

"You could," Bob said. "But I don't think it would work out well. I'm gay, you see."

Angelica blushed. "I'm sorry. That was so out of place. I feel like I should have known, or something. I'm so embarrassed. Please, accept my apology."

"Why should you be embarrassed? How could you have known?" Bob replied.

"I just assumed, you know, this is such a hetero place. Or it seems to be," she said, suddenly remembering the attempt made to seduce her the first night she was here.

"Oh, it is," Bob said. "Very hetero. But, unlike some belief systems, here we are all children of the Goddess. She created us all and claims us all. We are all Hers and She accepts us all."

Bob paused, allowing that precept to sink in for Angelica.

He continued, "You must also understand that I am under assignment. As a man interned in the path of a Consort, most of my engagements are assigned to me. I go with the person, masculine or feminine—most often when I'm here, I go with a couple—but I go where I'm assigned."

"Who assigns you?" Angelica asked.

"There is a team of Priestesses and Consorts. There are Seeresses in training among them, women, and occasionally a Seer, a man, who look at the people here. They see in some way what it is that a person needs, and create assignments for them. Sometimes what a person needs is something they don't want to do, but the Goddess never asks anybody to do anything that goes against their Nature. That's one of the truest things about the Goddess I know," Bob explained.

"And you would have to be assigned to me?" Angelica wanted to know.

"Yes. At the moment I am not free, even if I had the natural inclination. You're brilliant, and I like you a lot, but I am assigned. And I don't want to break my assignment. I like it, actually. The other Consort is also engaged in something he does not want to do, but it does not go against his Nature. We are in service to the Feminine together, and it is quite something."

He rolled his eyes back in his head, then looked at her sharply. He said, "You already have a date. What are you bugging me for?"

Angelica smiled at him wickedly. "If I don't have to wait, why should I?"

He grinned wickedly back and they returned to dancing, Angelica thinking, "Priestesses and Consorts? Wow."

Friday morning she awoke from a dream of her parents. They were worried about something, although she had the sense it wasn't about her. Still, it made her decide to call them and tell them she'd decided to stay the additional two weeks for the advanced course. Eva let her use the sole land line in her office after breakfast.

The day in class was much like the others. The external work, the postures, continued to create the space in her for the active inner work. She continued to become more aware of the energetic phenomena happening inside her, sensations of motion, heat and vibration; feelings of sympathy and empathy and compassion for the suffering of others; and visions arose, sometimes of suffering far away, sometimes of constellations of divine beings assembled to witness her work, and the work of her classmates.

The duress of the work continued to trigger emotional breakdowns in her classmates as they overcame past trauma. This led her to feel gratitude for her parents for being so surprisingly normal and good to her. Toward the end of the day she began to have visions of having sex—not just herself, but visions of others having sex as well. This included visions of Bob having sex with whatever couple in which he was an assigned partner. She found it too distracting to meditate in the midst of these visions. She allowed herself to stop trying to clear her mind. She felt disgust with her weakness, and her inability to master the sensations within that the visions caused. She surrendered to sensation, and just let the visions flow, her feelings suddenly becoming focused on her desire.

That afternoon Jake was waiting for her, wearing a pair of tan cargo pants and a white linen shirt with big rolled up sleeves, and over that a brown vest with a lot of pockets. His hair was brushed back and clean, as were his hands.

He gave her the major buildings tour. They stuck their heads in the kitchen, where supper preparations were in full swing. He introduced her to the people there. Then they walked across the lawn and over the bridge trail to the barns. He showed her the dormitory hall in the Great Barn, explaining that it had once been a hay loft, but could now sleep more than one hundred people. He took her to the other barns, large Quonsets, one for machinery and another for livestock. There were a few head of sheep and goats, several horses, a few cattle, and some pigs. The goats licked her hand.

He showed her the greenhouses and explained that most of the food they ate was from several other working farms that Stonehaven owned. There were deliveries two or three times a week. He also explained that two or three times a week the non-compostable trash and recycling were taken in to a commercial property Stonehaven owned near the edge of town and put in the dumpsters in the parking lot. He said that the trash run included the rental houses up on the county road to the north of the Mansion. He took her back to the Great Ring, where the drum practice had been the previous night. Then he showed her a building she hadn't noticed before, on the far side of the ring with a sign on it called the Laboratory. There was another small building marked Recovery. He explained that the latter was the medical station. When asked about what went on in the Laboratory, he said he didn't know.

While walking back to the Mansion for supper, she looked up one of the draws and saw the roof of a building. She asked about it, and Jake told her it was what they called a chapel. He said it was a pretty interesting building, built over a stream. There was no time to make the hike before supper. However, he agreed to meet her on the steps of the veranda after supper, near sunset. He promised he would take her up to the chapel.

She was surprised to find herself not particularly hungry, so she took a small serving of Greek salad and ate quickly. She had only the briefest interactions with others. When she took her plate back to the servery and left without looking at anyone, there were some surprised faces in the dining room. Others smiled knowingly–knowing, that is, that she was focused on attending a rendezvous.

Someone was playing the grand piano in the music room. The house had been set on the side of the hill to catch the cross-draft breezes of sunrise uphill and sunset downhill. The curtains of the tall glass doors were wafting in the wind. She sat on the lowest step of the veranda and waited.

He met her on the steps, as promised. Looking down at her he extended a hand, which she took as she stood up. Her low belly throbbed when she touched him, and again when she drew near him. She knew that she'd be doing what Desire wanted.

They took a path up over the ridge from the north side of the mansion, coming down to the main path to the chapel. He let her lead, so she could look at the landscape and set the pace, only pointing out which way to go when they came to a fork in the trail. They passed a stone bridge wide enough for a cart that went over the stream. They continued up a narrowing path to the chapel house. She could see that it was actually built over the stream, with an arch in the foundation that allowed the water through.

Jake pushed back the heavy wooden door. To one side there were some shelves and a trunk; to the other, some stacked wooden folding chairs.

At the far side of the chapel, opposite the door was a plain altar, composed of a large wooden block set on stone work. There was no adornment on the wall behind the altar. Angelica ran her hand along the smooth wood, looked at Jake, and said, "Here."

Jake, understanding exactly what she meant, nodded. He took a thick blanket from the trunk and laid it over the wood. From the shelves they got candles, and built a ring of them around the altar. They stepped into the ring then, and kissed.

The sense of the sacredness of the place, cool and formidable, made them slow down, as if it put a weight on the trajectory of their course. In each other's arms, slowly touching each other while still in their clothes, they built heat within as the candles warmed the air around them. Drawing back, they gazed at each other and she nodded.

He put his hands on her waist. Together they picked her up, she hopping up and Jake lifting, and she sat on the edge of the altar. He went to his knees and removed her shoes and socks, then she unfastened her jeans and scooched them over her hips so he could slide them down her legs as well. He stood up and they kissed again, bodies pressed against each other, Angelica's legs wrapped around him, holding him in close. She undid his trousers, which slid to his feet, and he stepped out of them.

They embraced again, sex pressed against sex, gasping on first contact, his desire evident. They unbuttoned each other's shirts, belly heating belly, chest breathing into chest. He went to his knees again and pulled her forward to him, burying his face between her thighs, his tongue becoming another heated source of pleasure. After assuring himself of her readiness, he stood up again. He entered her slowly, alternating between pause and motion, until he was completely ensheathed.

They paused then, she sighing great sighs, struggling to steady her breath. The sighing did not stop for a long time, repeated gales of breath that evolved into panting, all while he held still inside her, watching, learning. Her panting slowed, and became a moaning as she began to move her hips, slowly and slightly, rocking on him. Still, he held still.

The moaning became panting again, a different pant, an audible inhale that drew in more air than she released, building a pressure that she voiced, which then sped up to a sound that almost became a song. Then she clenched around him, shivering her orgasm with her whole soma, her whole body, shivering around him. Still, he remained still.

The wave of shivering passed on. She moved on him again, wrapping her legs around him, locking her ankles. She sat up and pulled him down to her, kissing him, rocking her hips in time with the movement of her tongue. Soon she came again, growling into his mouth. She broke the kiss to raise her face and shout toward the sky. She collapsed back, laughing. The rhythm of her laughter rocked her hips against him and she came again, laughing all the way to orgasm. Still, he held still. And he marveled.

She conceived the desire to hold him in her mouth, to savor what she was sure would be delicious. She slid herself off him and to the far end of the altar, signaling him to come around to the other side. Still on her back she hung her head over the altar, dropping her head, opening her mouth, grasping him with a hand and feeding him in. Still, he held still.

She noticed clearly how well trimmed he was. She looked closely and saw that he was shaved, the thin line of hair on his belly going only to just below the belt line. His lower belly, his shaft, his testicles and perineum, all shaved, and smooth and lovely to the touch. "Slowly, fuck my mouth," she whispered. He moved slowly out of stillness.

She tongued him, coming to know his contour. She drew him in with her hand, then pushed him back, controlling the pace, rocking him back and forth, and taking him slowly ever deeper within. Deeper and deeper she took him, her mouth and her phulva connecting, sensation transferring itself from one place to another, melding into one long line of white ecstatic light. Untouched, except by where she touched, she moved toward orgasm, rocking her hips with the pace of his stroke in her mouth.

She took him all the way to the hilt, and triggered her gag reflex. The reflex triggered a memory. In that moment she remembered gagging before, but this time on her uncle's cock. With her cousin she had been playing 'Show me yours, I'll show you mine,' when the uncle had caught them touching each other. He mouth raped her, terrifying her into compliance, threatening to tell, making her cousin watch. In the moment just at peak ecstasy her awareness flashed from memory back into her body and her spirit broke under the paradox of ecstasy and rage.

It felt like some wall or dam, some kind of barrier in her lower back broke down and a force rose up her spine in a spiral, spreading out as far as her shoulders. She pushed him away and screamed, going completely rigid with the fire of it rising up her spine, seeming to catch her hair on fire and then dance along her scalp in a ring of burning fire, a crown of burning fire. Then the fire banked itself, became subdued, and her skin stopped burning. Her body relaxed. She wept. She felt the core of her torso start throbbing.

She felt something expand outward from her, making a popping noise like a sail in the wind. It seemed a different kind of sense, like touch but somehow more felt, almost like a feeling; an emotion of calm, almost neutral receptivity. Then, through this sense, she became aware of thousands of living things, things all around her. This awareness blew past Jake, out into the woods. She could feel the night creatures; the frog in the basement, then the frogs on the trees, the millions of fireflies, the tens of millions of emerging cicadas, their scritching noises from lower in the trees as they searched for mates, then the humming of them up high, fulfilling the purpose of their thirteen-year sojourn underground.

The feeling of these lives seemed to trigger in her a seeing of them in her mind's eye. If she focused, she could hear them individually in her mind's ear. Her awareness drew close to someone, wrapped in a fog of concealment. As she watched, the fog parted and she saw it was Eva. Then past Eva she saw a woman kneeling, sitting on her heels, in deep meditation before an altar, a large bowl of water on the floor between her and the altar. In her mind's eye she touched the water and ripples appeared in the vision. She recognized this woman to be Madeleine.

Madeleine's eyes popped open, and looked directly at her, frightening her. The fear was instantaneous and overwhelming, penetrating every cell of her being. For an instant she saw everyone around her, where all the people were, in the Mansion and down by the Barns, so fast that it seemed she saw them all at once, her mind becoming a field. Some of them turned their faces toward her, surprise, concern, and in two cases, smiles.

Then her awareness contracted back to where she was, lying on the soft blanket and the cool wood of the altar top. She had a sudden image of other women, a long line of other women, lying right here where she was and she felt-sensed them. She felt-sensed the echoes of their ecstasy, images flashing backwards in quick succession. Underneath it all she felt a connection with something, something both deeper and higher. And then she felt herself dissolve into it, both dark and light. Then she lost consciousness, head and long hair hanging over the edge,

Jake's erect phallus hanging over her, her eyes closing to the sight of its beauty.

Jake watched her, slowly slipping away, her body twitching. He realized that she had lost consciousness, and, concerned, he raised her head in one hand and then walked around the table top and slipped his hand under her lower back, picked her up in his arms and slid her back on the table. He covered her with another blanket, and stood by her, holding her hand, not yet knowing that what had happened was far more than it appeared to be.

Eva was sitting in her suite, reading in the Queens Book. She felt a nudge at her shoulder and recognized the touch of the Madeleine. Maddie had reached out to her before like this, sometimes in dreams, bidding her to look with the second sight, examining the psychic field of Stonehaven. Eva closed her eyes and relaxed, journeyed to Madeleine and saw that she was at her altars with the Scrying Bowl before her. Madeleine was seeing not a dream, but the Stone Chapel. A field of power had flared around the building, electric spark blue, and pulsing. Eva journeyed inside and saw Angelica writhing naked on the altar and Jake standing above her, holding his hands out over her. And Eva saw the Vision that Angelica was having. Angelica was Returning to the Source.

There is a descent. A deep descent, a descent to the bottom of the Soma, to the door out through the bottom of the Soul. She just fell, and kept falling, not quickly enough to frighten her, but too quickly to relax. Down she went, down to the bottom of space and the beginning of time. Her breathing steadied, but stayed at a hurried pace. She stayed in her Spirit and fell out into a world.

In this world she saw a form; immense, dark, heavy, spherical, going around and not wearying. Drawing closer she saw it was solid. She reached out her hand and saw that there was slow, swirling motion inside. She knew intuitively it was the First One, the First Being, sole and solitary, aware, but not self-aware.

And then something moved. The movement seemed to come from outside, but she couldn't tell for sure. It could have happened on the far side, a movement that caused a screeching sound, a terrible sound like sheet metal or steel being torn apart. She wondered everafter where that motion came from. Perhaps it was a response to her having moved into that First One's world, like a wave, a shock wave of interrupting presence.

The dark sphere of the First One cried out in response to the sound, shuddering. Crying out, the cry went out into the empty space around it, and there was no echo to that cry, for there was nothing there to reflect Her voice. Angelica felt this cry and the vacuum of no response, and then a wave of fear rolled through the First One, sole and solitary, followed by a wave of despair and loneliness. These together pushed the First One into self-awareness.

Angelica realized fully that this was the First One, and that it was feminine; all Life was contained in Her, all suffering, and She was alone with Everything that Is within the womb of Her.

Angelica felt the resolve form. She felt the newly created Self-Awareness resolve to not be alone. Suddenly Angelica was drawn back, pushed back along the path she'd travelled, watching the Sphere draw into Itself a little and then expand, growing faster than her eye could see. Then she saw the Light of its explosion. Angelica understood she was witnessing the beginning of the Universe, and the beginning of the World.

Angelica knew somehow that, in the True Creator's resolve to not be alone, She would give Herself almost entirely to Creation, and that when it was done the First One would have kept only as much for Herself, for Her own being, as a Stone.

Across the land, Eva came to her present, having felt-sensed, and seen, what had happened to Angelica. She had felt the wave of release roll across the land. She knew what release that was; the release of the Kundalini Serpent. And she knew that Angelica's loss of consciousness was because she had become overwhelmed by the sensory experience, her brain's ability to take in and process a logarithmically increased number of impressions was overloaded by the input.

Eva knew that when Angelica awoke she would be in agonizing pain.

Eva was still in the suite, the Queens Book on her lap. She was wearing her evening silks. When the vision ended she stood up, put the book to the side, sent a blessing of being cared for to the Madeleine. She went to the door and slipped her feet into a pair of rubber sandals. She took her summer duster off the coat tree and shouldered it on, flipping her hair outside the collar, patting the pockets to make sure her medicines and sacreds were there. Last, she grabbed her cowgirl hat, a gray felt Stetson, and put it on her head. She stepped outside to the electric ATV, unplugged it, and drove off, muck boots and tree spade bouncing around in the cargo bin, loose hair pinned by the hat swaying to the side when she rounded the corner of the North wing.

She drove the path to the access track that ran up the narrow valley to the chapel. She went up the access track, stopping near the bridge over the stream, and put her muck boots on. She slid down the bank and looked at the arch through which the stream flowed, making sure the passage was open and debris free. She ducked under the arch holding her gowns and duster hems gathered in one hand, her hat in the other, and emerged into the cellar below the main floor of the chapel. She went to the space under the floor where the altar stood, and looked up into the hollow echo space beneath the closed altar. She stood there, and breathed, extending her senses upward into the cavity, feeling what drained down, and then sending her light upward, from below, she built a cloud under Angelica, supporting her, buoying her.

Standing there, Eva realized that something extraordinary was happening. There was almost twice as much palpable energy echoing through the altar than there should have been.

She took one of the iron spiral staircases up to the main floor, almost sailing up it, emerging to one side of the altar table.

Jake was standing alongside the Altar, forearms extended and palms faced upward, praying to the Goddess to help, to help her Servant, and help this new birth happening in front of him. He had studied this, and although it hadn't happened to him, he knew it for what it was. He was stunned to helplessness at what he saw above him, glowing in a cloud of red and white light. He dropped his head and was about to drop to his knees when he was startled by the sudden apparition of a wild-haired cowgirl crone sweeping out of the staircase onto the floor next to him.

Candles had been lit on the floor and the sideboards, flickering, their light broad and penumbras broader. But most of the light came from above Angelica. There, hovering in the cloud of red and white light was the form of a sleeping dragon curled up with its nose resting under its tail. She couldn't tell what type it was, but she was glad it was asleep.

Angelica came back to awareness of the room. She was panting, moaning, and rolling to her side. She cried, then gasped, then sobbed, sobbing at the beauty and pain of what she'd witnessed. She sobbed and wept like she would never stop weeping.

A darkness seemed to gather in the room, closing in on the light. Eva spoke a word of command and the darkness drew back. She lit a stalk of an herb and held it aloft like a smoking brand and waved it over her head, sparks flying off, driving the darkness back further.

Angelica rolled onto her back, then started breathing fast. She arched her back, belly straining for the ceiling, drew a breath and screamed, "Aaahhh, the Fire! The Fire! I'm burning, Aaaahhhh!"

She flailed her arms, then sat bolt upright, panting, wild-eyed, looking around the room, not recognizing it. "Where am I?" she panted. Then her eyes rolled back in her head. She seemed to pass out, and collapsed back on the altar.

Eva said, "Om Tara, tu tare ture, svaha." She touched Angelica's feet. Angelica's body jerked, spasming entirely, then she smiled and relaxed.

Eva told Jake, "It's time. We take her out on the stream." Jake scooped his arms under her and carried Angelica back along the open floor to the stairs from which Eva had emerged.

Angelica weakly writhed in his arms, whispered now, hoarsely, "The fire, the fire, oh, I am on fire. Put me out. Put me out!"

Jake carried her down the stairs and out onto the stone floor of the basement of the chapel. He carried her to the back where the stream had been dammed up to form a pool, about eight feet by four. The raised edges were rounded mounds, lying along the circumference like snakes, higher in the back. The water poured through a gap at the bottom end where the heads of the snakes would be. A board could be slipped into this space, damming the water higher, to a depth of two feet. A person could lie down and bathe in the cold running water.

It was into this pool that Jake waded and put Angelica down. She gasped again at the cold, and whispered, "The fire...the fire!"

Eva put the board in place and the pool began to fill. Under the light of the dragon, she sprinkled Angelica's naked body with certain essential oils and rubbed them in. The pool filled quickly. At one point, Angelica appeared to stop breathing, the cold preparing her body to shut down. Jake was holding her head above water now as her body began to sway in the current running past her over the dam. The dragon light above her began to sway also, in the current of some different stream.

She gasped and sat partway up, realizing she was in water, coming consciously back into the room. Eva looked her in the eyes and said, "You're here, yes?"

Angelica replied, "I'm here." And then a spasm grasped her entire body, spine bowed back, a full kriya, so quickly it choked off her scream of pain. Jake had to work to keep the back of her head from hitting the bottom of the pool as her head flew back.

Angelica's body realized her head was under water before Jake lifted her up. Her eyes flew open and she realized she was locked in the kriya. She was terrified. As her face broke the surface the spasm eased a little and she took three breaths. The bath was doing its work. Then she kriya'd again and Eva said, "Roll her over."

Jake rolled her in his arms, so her belly was down. When the kriya relaxed she was on her elbows and knees in the water, gasping.

Eva said, "You must go. You must be born. You must return to the world." She reached down and lifted her about the ribs, pushing her toward the dam. "You must go."

And Angelica started to crawl over the edge, watched over by Jake, holding his hands and arms ready. As her hips came over the edge, her hands slipped and she planted the side of her face in the sandy bottom, but she'd recovered by the time Jake reached her shoulder to make sure she could get her face above water.

Angelica pulled herself forward, her knees slipping down the walls, feet trailing. She crawled forward on all fours, then another kriya seized her on the edge of the sandy stretch, before the stream descended into a rocky, mossy channel. Her hands retracted and her knees extended, and a long scream tore out of her throat. She rolled to her side in the water, head pressing against a rock.

The stream rushed past her now, into a short falls. Eva and Jake slipped her rigid form over the edge. As the spasm passed her body relaxed. She sucked in a mouthful of the cool sweet water and coughed explosively. Eva told her "You have to crawl," and rolled her back over onto her belly.

Eva stood up and reached across the stream, both pushing Jake back and leaning on him for support. He stood up slowly and reached one arm under Eva's. They stood over her, watching her crawl over the slick and mossy rocks, out toward the arch.

Angelica crawled, skin scraping over the rocks, her finger tips clawing, elbows raw, nipples and knees scraped raw. Scrapes on her belly sent shooting sparks of fire deep inside. Her dragon woke up and crawled with her.

Eva whispered hoarsely, "Stop," before Angelica was fully through the arch. "Look!" Eva said.

Angelica stopped, holding completely still, and paid attention to everything she was sensing and feeling. Then she rose up on her elbows, water streaming hair bunched and straggling over her cheeks and shoulders. Raising her eyes, she saw the rising moon illuminate the valley below her, the small valleys opening opposite her still in shadow. She saw the hayfield, waving in the pale light, little breezes dancing across it, ripples of shadowing. The dragon, awake now, stood still with her, and looked out also.

She shivered, and kept shivering. "Go out," Eva said. "Go out."

She slipped farther down, over another short falls, moss under the spreading pool slipping her along into another small, sand bottomed pool. She tried to claw herself to a bank, and out of the water. Suddenly Jake and Eva were alongside her, pulling her up the bank. They turned her around and sat her up. She crossed her arms over breasts and sat there, shivering.

Eva took off her duster, and draped it around Angelica's shoulders. She told Jake, "Go get some blankets from the chest by the door."

While he hoofed it up the bank and in through the chapel door, she leaned forward, put her arms around Angelica, and hugged her, telling her, "I'm proud of you."

Angelica's response was to twitch harder, twitching in recognition. Eva put the Stetson on Angelica's head and said, "There you go, cowgirl."

In a moment, Jake had returned. Eva placed a blanket on the ground. They turned Angelica around to her side and laid her down, tucking the duster around her. Eva threw another blanket over her. Then she noticed, while she was on all fours, that Jake had moved around behind her.

She looked up and back at him over her shoulder and smiled. She said, "Release?"

Jake said, "Not yet."

Eva said, "Don't be so serious," and reached back, slowly pulled her evening robes up over her backside, exposing her tautness to him in the shadows of the moon.

He fell to his knees and with his hands on his thighs, leaned forward, putting his nose right up against her sex, he inhaled, and exhaled. Then he inhaled again and blew. He inhaled a third time and put his mouth on her, slowly letting his tongue slide out and downward, reaching the tip to her clitoris.

She spasmed, the first small orgasm of many. He ran his tongue back up, slowly separating her lips until he reached the opening of her, inhaling and blowing, lightly, feeding on the scent.

One hand on Angelica's shoulder, Eva reached back between her legs with the other, looked between them along the path her hand had gone, and looked to see Jake's condition. "Here," she said, beckoning him with the hand between her legs.

Jake rose up on his knees. "Come here," Eva said. He knee-walked a little closer, until Eva could grasp him with that hand between her legs. "Come here," she said. She pulled on him, on his maleness, a few times, stroking it to full erectness, then let her fingers play lightly over it.

Then, using a finger, she ran it, splitting the phulva, opened herself, folded herself open for him. Then all he could see when he looked down were her beckoning fingers, calling him forward into her opening. He put the head of his phallus against her, pausing, then slowly moved forward, and leaned in.

She sighed as she felt herself parting for him, deeper and parting deeper. She exhaled, leaving room for him, leaving room for everything, to enter her from behind.

She leaned forward, grasping him with a contraction of her inner walls, pulling him along behind her and whispered in Angelica's ear, "I am the Receptive. And someday you will be, too."

Jake started working, not troubled at all by the nearly forty years of difference in their ages.

Angelica smiled, feeling the power of the coupling ride down Eva's arm and hand into her, filling her with warmth and ease.

Warmed by this, Angelica fell asleep and dreamed. As she went, the dragon and the cloud of light settled upon her, and dissolved within.

In this dream she saw that there were many faces of the Divine Feminine, True Creator of all that is. Searching through these faces she looked for those that were eldest. Eldest not in appearance, because she couldn't tell by the appearance of age. They all seemed relatively ageless, unless they were supposed to look aged. What she was looking for was who was born first, remembering the vision she'd had on the altar.

In her search backwards through time, into the line of succession and manifestation, she finally arrived at a young, dark haired woman, laughing, having fun with a man. Then she saw her having some serious fun with him, riding on him cowgirl style, arms raised above her head, head thrown back, laughing.

Behind that, as if through a wall, she saw someone else, another Goddess; a Mother of that Daughter still riding the man hard. The Mother was smiling, her hands palm out in blessing. Or perhaps in a gesture of helplessness to intervene.

Then she saw that Mother having sex with someone, some man who looked like a man she had seen on the grounds of Stonehaven.

Suddenly it was as if she was looking at Stonehaven in the present with different eyes. She saw many of the people she had seen in her time there as solid and real. Other people she had seen were more vaguely outlined, as if they had not enough substance, and were temporary.

She also saw other forms, not exactly ghostly, but apparently insubstantial. These were the forms of the Divine Mother, and the Divine Daughter she had already seen, but there were others, faces of Goddesses and Masculine faces as well. She saw these other forms engaging with the substantial people of Stonehaven, talking to them, no, talking with them. Then she also saw these forms lining up with the people, and experiencing their ecstasy when they made love.

She saw the Daughter form aligned so perfectly with one woman riding some man whose face she couldn't see, that they both threw their hands up, their heads back, and laughed at the same time. They laughed as one.

She saw that Eva had a relationship with both of Them, longstanding, and they acted like friends; Eva, the substantial one, chatting with the insubstantial Divines. She saw that it was Eva's relationship with the Mother that informed her that Angelica was caught up in the blow out, that she was in the Chapel, and maybe in trouble.

Then, looking beyond the Mother, she saw there was a third face, the face of the White One, the Crone. Somehow she knew the White One came forward rarely, and even more rarely for sex. She stood on the Path to the Source, the First One. She is the Grandmother, at least that is what She is now. She was the first formed container for the awareness of the First One outside Herself.

This awareness, the White One, was the Mother of the Divine Mother that created the Daughter. Then the Divine Mother created a first Son, creating both the Daughter and first Son out of what She was, as she had been created by the Grandmother.

The ovum that will became each of us was made by our Grandmothers when our Mothers were conceived in our Grandmothers' body. And so this is how it has always been.

She saw then that the Divine Masculine exists in the Son and the Brother first. Only after that do the Lover and Sexual Partner, the Consort, come into being and manifestation. But, given the limitations of the family unit, with whom would he have sex? She wondered this in her dream. There is only the Mother, and his Sister, the Daughter.

Then she sensed that the pulse of the Universe is exogamic. It is expansive, and outward looking in its trajectory, seeking to create difference. Therefore the Faces of the Daughter and the Son fracture into a thousand Faces each. And each, so to speak, is a mask. It is in these fractured forms they mate, they have sacred sex, they fuck. They create and they make. All Form comes from this, all forms come from this.

It is into these fractured fragments, this forest of facets, that a person steps, slowly moving to the Source. She saw that a human can even become a Consort of the Mother.

Then she saw some of the men at Stonehaven in consultation with each other and with an insubstantial being that she thought of as the Divine Masculine. There was contention between the men, and between the men and the insubstantial.

She saw then that the relationships were not just about Pleasure, but that there were elements of Power to it. She saw the vibrations and colors around them shift as the people and insubstantials shifted from Pleasure to Power and back again. She saw there were troubles among the alliances and the kind of help that was offered. She didn't understand it. It gave rise in her to a kind of caution, and a knowing that trust was irrelevant here.

Suddenly, she felt she was in the presence of some kind of Grace. Something benevolent was smiling at her, and she felt love welling up in her in response. The love continued to rise up in her until she was shaking with it. Then she realized she was being shaken as well.

She felt herself return to the present, lying on a blanket, wrapped up in a duster, on a stream bank, with an old woman having sex beside her, so close they were touching. The woman was shaking, shaking with an orgasm and that shaking was passing into her. She knew the woman was having sex with the man she had just been having sex with. She knew it by the smell, and she began to cry. Something in her seemed to break and Angelica wept and kept weeping, and shaking, going from feeling helpless to feeling shattered, almost to her heart, and then feeling loved. She slept then, knowing she would not remember her next dreams. Nor did she want to, anymore.

Eva, having tracked Angelica through the whole dream, knew what almost broke her heart. Eva knew what had been in there, and knew what had to leave, even if it meant by breaking. It meant the passing of a naïve one-man-one-woman idealism, at least as Angelica had believed in it. Eva knew that had to go, and knew that Angelica would come to a new understanding of that relationship, and what her possibilities, her real possibilities for attaining that ideal would be when the time was right.

When Angelica fell asleep, Eva removed her hand. Jake had been finishing, deeply in need of the release. Eva had been taking it all and feeding both Angelica and the Divine Ones who had gathered around to watch. Eva raised her face and turned it to each of them, not quite seeing them but sensing they were there, and smiled at each and every one, extending her arms to them in both gratitude and power.

Eva began the internal alchemy, drawing the energetic signatures deep within her, and quickening them, nurturing them into the energy of new life. Then she beamed it out from her heart into a field—an expanding field that washed over all around her: the Divines, her Consort Jake, Angelica, the stream, the grasses and trees, the bugs, and the frogs, and the birds, and the altar in the Chapel.

She lay her head down on the grass for a moment, thanking the Earth, then rose up on her hands, looked over her shoulder at Jake and smiled at him. He, sweating, still catching his breath, slowing his pulse, smiled back.

Jake pulled out, slowly, then sat back on his heels. Still smiling, then grinning more broadly, he leaned forward and planted a big kiss on both cheeks of Eva's backside. "Thank you, High Priestess," he said. Then he stood up, pulled his pants up and tied the string.

"Here, Beloved, let me help," he said. He stepped to her side and with his forward hand, offered her a hand up, while his other hand pushed the robes down over her back.

She stood up, turned to him, smiling, and planted a kiss on his lips. When she finished she leaned back, still smiling at him, and asked him, "Can you carry her?" nodding toward the ATV.

"Yes."

"Good. Then let's take her to Recovery."

Eva stepped out of the way and let Jake bend down and pick up Angelica. He carried her up the bank and stepped into the ATV on the passenger side. Eva picked up the last blanket and followed them. Climbing in on the driver's side, she pressed the start button.

Looking over her shoulder, backing down the path, she flashed a smile at him. "You were pretty good," she said. "Want to do it again?"

Jake smiled and said, "Any time."

They unloaded Angelica at the Recovery, already staffed, alerted by Eva's hand radio. While Jake carried Angelica inside, Eva called the Base again and told them, "Someone go get Craft and ask him who knows cars the best. There's a red Honda Accord in the Guest lot. I need him to temporarily disable it, but in a hidden way. The keys are in the..." she looked at Jake and he gestured with two fingers from the hand under her legs, "...second room on the fourth floor of the Mansion".

Jake went into the Recovery carrying Angelica. There was a wen there named Diana, about ten years older than him, and a wen closer to his age named Margo. He had not met Diana yet, but knew from the week-ly briefing that she would be arriving and that she was an initiated Priestess. Margo, he knew personally. She had been there almost a year as an Intern and worked hard. She did what she was told, and then some. She seemed to carry herself a little too tightly, but when it was the right time, she could unwrap like a coiled spring, and curl around a man like the lash end of a whip.

Margo held open the door for him, and Diana led him down the hallway to one of the Recovery rooms. The sheets had been folded back so he laid Angelica down, and Diana and Margo covered her up. Margo sat down on the edge of the bed and put a hand on Angelica's shoulder. Angelica, in her sleep, started to weep.

When Jake emerged from the Recovery, Eva turned to him and smiled. She asked, 'Did you mean it? Anytime?"

Jake smiled back. "Yes, ma'am," he said.

"Can't break that habit, can you?" she asked.

"The 'ma'am' stuff? No, I can't seem to."

"Look, just stand there. Grin if you have to," she directed him. He grinned like a fool.

Eva, feeling merciful, grinned back at him. "Now, listen closely, and answer cleanly. What do you intend with those words?"

"I intend to convey respect," he said.

"I get what you intend. But it has an impact different from what you'd expect. I'm not put at ease by it, for one thing. It makes me a little suspicious. I lean away from you and look at you askance. Like this." She showed him the gesture of her reaction."

He said, "Really? But I'm safer than that. I'm in a good mood. I mean no disrespect."

"Yes, but to be honest, I feel a little disrespected. What do you make of that?"

"I don't know," he said.

"So," she said, "Stand there and be the respect. Feel the respect. But keep your mouth shut."

Starting in his mind, his eyes rolling up in his head, he allowed himself to feel the feeling that was intended to go along with the words 'ma'am'. He dropped it out of his head, and the feeling slipped down past his heart and settled behind his solar plexus. As it settled there, he took the time to feel it.

He saw that there was no disrespect in him. As he continued to feel into it, he began to feel something else. The certainty began to rise in him that the behavior wasn't about her. It wasn't about respecting her. It was about him. It was about him and how he wanted to behave; the behavior wasn't really about respect at all. It was about what he wanted to show about himself, not about what she needed, nor about what she deserved.

It wasn't really respect at all. Rather it was just barely a sign of respect. He looked away from her, off toward the mountains.

She watched him process all this. Then she said, "Let that old behavior and feeling dissolve." She watched him stand there in confusion. Tears almost came into his eyes. The longer she let him hold it, the closer he came to shame about his behavior. She watched his cheeks begin to flush. This is a good thing, she thought. He draws nigh to a Conscience.

Then she said, "Good. Now imagine what real respect feels like. Imagine that you really respected me, and allow the felt-sense of true respect to arise in you."

He turned and looked at her again. He saw her eyes looking at him, clearly and directly, almost with what he read as a sense of expectation, but not quite. She was holding neutral space for him, a space that promised reconciliation.

He closed his eyes and a series of scenarios passed before his mind's eye: an old fashioned courtier's bow. Getting on one knee. Kissing her and pulling her into his arms. He let all these go. When there were no more scenarios passing his vision he directed his awareness back to his solar plexus, finding the third chakra and inquiring of it "What is true respect?"

Slowly a feeling began there, a pulse of energy that buoyed something up in him, lifting his heart. He felt his heart chakra open with that buoying energy, felt it spill out of him and down, down to her feet.

She felt it curl around her ankles, felt the lift of it coming up her legs, up her thighs. She noticed it particularly on the back of her thighs, lifting her, lifting her buttocks, as if she were being picked up. She leaned into it a little and felt it go up her back, lifting her. The sensation was one of being held up, rising even to the back her head. She tilted her head up a little to look more down her nose.

She allowed the lift to curl around to the front. It held her phulva. She thought I should stop him, so he learns. Otherwise it will go further than respect needs to. For now anyway.

She said, "Yes, that's it. Hold that sense of lifting. By showing me this feeling of respect in you for me, you support me. You make my life easier. I feel I can rely on you more, maybe even trust you. But you have to hold it. You have to pull it back, even, a little bit."

She watched him do it, felt the curl withdraw and the support at the back of her head drop.

"When you respect me you want me to feel supported. Do you see? Now withdraw it further. Withdraw it until it is just in your field, and hold your heart open. Can you do this?"

He could. He didn't want to, because he could feel the way in which respect for her would get him laid. He wanted to play with it, but he did as he was told.

"Now open your eyes and take a step back. Hold this feeling." Again he did as he was told. "Hold this feeling," she said again. "Take another step back."

"Now sense what happens when I bring my field into contact with yours."

He felt a flare of his energy reach out toward her. She said, "I felt that. In my third and fourth. It makes me want to pay attention to you. Respect for me is a source of strength; it strengthens my soul.

"And there is a reward for respect. There is a reciprocity." Smiling at him, she slowly sank to her knees in the dirt. Pushing her cowgirl hat back on her head, she reached out and untied the drawstring on his pants, letting them slide over his buttocks and down to his knees.

She looked at his phallus, drew close and breathed, smelling the sex they'd had, smelling the sex he'd had with Angelica, drawing it all in deeply. He began arousal without even being touched, simply by being inhaled. Eva drew her nose in close, smelling the root of him against his clean shaven skin. Touching her nose to him, she extended her tongue and licked slowly, just one slow, hot lick, inhaling and exhaling.

"So easily," she thought. Jakes erection had grown fully, so she had to duck under it and hold her hat on the back of her head as she moved to the other side. She nosed him, then licked him again. Then, pulling back, she crouched lower, looking up at it, standing tall and curving upward above her, seeing what Angelica saw last before she went out. Again, holding her hat on her head she nosed and licked at the bottom of the shaft, trailing her tongue along his length from below, then at the tip, circling her tongue once around it. She could feel Jake working the pump deep in his root chakra, watching it wave up and down over her, seeing it silhouetted against the moon. Then, putting just the head in her mouth she inhaled again, then exhaled, bending her head back so his phallic head touched the roof of her mouth. She licked the underside then, little rapid flicks that drew a groan from Jake. She made an "Umm" sound, moaning against him, vibrating her mouth on him.

Jake held the space around her, holding himself still, pelvic floor contracted, keeping his ejaculation closed off, allowing himself to shiver with orgasm at the promise of release, easier now that he had already come once. He had been working the floor pump while she had been nosing him, bringing blood in, establishing control. Now that he had it, he folded the energy into a roll and spiraled it upwards, feeding his guts, then his feelings, then his heart. He pulled the charge of it up into his head, and out his arms. These he flung upward, arching his back, and he shouted with ecstasy, laughing as he felt the spirits of the land draw close.

The shout brought Diana and Margo to the windows under the porch beside the door. Slowly Diana edged over to the door and slid through, beckoning Margo to follow. They slipped outside and stood in the shadows under the porch roof in front of the window, getting a good view of the couple in profile. "Watch this," Diana whispered. "It might be something special."

Eva stood, backed up to the seat of the ATV, pulled her robes up over her waist and sat down. She kicked off her muck boots, placed her left foot on the dash board and reached up with her left hand to hold the frame of the canopy. She lifted her right leg and with her right hand she reached between her legs and stroked herself, then spread her lips for him, and said, "Come here."

Jake stepped out of his pants, said, "Yes," and stepped toward her.

He's learning, she thought. No 'ma'ams' now. Much to her surprise and delight he fell to his knees and kissed her on the clitoris: a long slow loving kiss with just his lips, and in a moment, with the tip of his tongue. Still keeping his upper lip over the hood he let his tongue slip down to feel the wetness of her, and taste the traces of himself. She was flowing with juices, so he took the middle finger of his hand and placed it against the opening, allowing it to get wet, then slipped it straight up inside her, right along the pubic bone, and gently massaged the swelling he found there.

With her free hand Eva pressed his head harder against her and put her free foot up on his shoulder. She could feel it starting, feel the pressure building, feel the need to let go. She pushed his head back and let go, the mysterious fluid pouring out in a thick jet on his face and into his open mouth. Once, twice, she squirted on him before she pulled his head back to her, and then she squirted twice more in his mouth, he swallowed, the volume so great he couldn't take it all. It ran down his mouth and chest and dripped onto the ground.

When she finished bucking her hips against him, he resumed his kiss and slowly moved his finger, still inside her, again. Suddenly his heart flared with the respect and love he had felt earlier. As it flared up and rose out, it embraced her, embracing her sex with a pulsed caress. Eva felt it and gasped. This brought Eva to two more explosive ejaculations, and the ground beneath Jake's knees grew muddy.

On the porch, Margo was bent over, holding onto Diana's arm with one hand, her other between her legs, caught up in the energy of what she was seeing and feeling, mouth open in an "Oh!" of silent exclamation. Diana was standing erect, free palm upraised, drawing the energy in through her root like breath, pumping internally and coming. Soon Margo began to shake in body orgasm herself and Diana resonated with that quiver and felt the pulse begin inside her.

Out in the lot, Jake stood, apparently harder than before, casting a phallic shadow in the moonlight. She looked down at it, her whole body beckoning him to come forward, and rocked her pelvis up toward him. He stepped up and lodged just the tip of himself inside her, waiting for her to open.

When she opened, it was as if she were sucking him inside in slow pulses, pause, suck, pause, a half an inch at a time. When he was fully in, he bent his knees slightly to angle himself up, and gently stroked that spot within. At the seventh stroke he paused, and feigned his own ejaculation, quivering his whole body in orgasm. That brought her again. The force of her contraction pushed him out, and she covered him from the waist down in rain.

She threw her head back and laughed, and laughed, and finally the cowgirl hat fell off her head, landing on the driver's seat and rolling off onto the ground on the other side. She felt the Goddess slip in, descend, and match her position.

On the porch, Margo was on her knees, gasping. Diana still stood, breathing with her sex, exhaling with her mouth when it inhaled, drawing up the power that was lying all around, inhaling with her nose when her sex exhaled. Eyes closed to a slit, she saw the energy swirl about them both, seeing shapes forming in what looked like mist. She was shivering constantly, syncing with Margo's shiver, and adding to it the pulse of the resonance to keep it steady.

With the huskier voice of Diosa, Eva spoke, "Again." So Jake, slipping in the mud, came forward, and entered as before, except he had to curl his toes to grip when he bent his knees. He held the position, both hands on the frame above him and let her ride. She rocked until she came again, one last burst of rain. But this time she locked him inside and held tight while she shook—her entire body jumping like she was connected to a live wire—which, in a way, she was.

She collapsed back on the seat, breathing hard, laughing, and said, "Thank you Goddess," as she felt the presence leaving.

Over on the porch, Margo had collapsed onto all fours, head hanging, panting like a dog in the summer heat. Diana still stood, palms upward, smiling, eyes hooded, face enigmatic, as she watched the forms in the mist disperse and the air around them, once gold and silver, fade to moonlight.

In the Recovery, Angelica shouted; a sustained shout that rose to a scream, then a cry, and then sobbing that could be heard through the open screen door. Diana tapped Margo on the shoulder and turned for the door. "It may be a long night," she said.

Eva and Jake both turned their heads at the sound, realizing they had an audience, and laughed. Jake withdrew slowly, while he gripped the canopy frame. Still hard, no longer needing release, he sighed.

Eva sighed, too, and reached up to scratch her head, felt the tangle of her hair, and wondered aloud, "Where'd my hat get to?"

"On the other side," Jake said. "I'll get it."

Eva sat up, and pulled her robes down. Jake, still gripping his toes in the mud, turned and picked up his pants. He walked around the front of the ATV, picked up Eva's hat and handed it to her. Then he slipped into the driver's seat and sat on his pants, his erection poking up and banging against the steering wheel until he tucked it out of the way with a pants leg.

Eva put the deformed hat on crookedly, her hair coming out wild at all angles, and said, "Home, James," as Jake put it in reverse, and turned to look over his shoulder. When he turned back around to put it in drive, he grinned broadly. "Yes, ma'am," he said.

She barked a laugh at him, and punched him in the shoulder. "Asshole," she said, in what may have been the most loving tone of voice Jake had ever heard.

Around 2:00 AM Diana looked out the window and saw the image of two muck boots, one standing upright, the other on its side, at the edges of what looked to be a puddle in the parking lot; a damp spot where Jake's toe tracks had churned up the mud like claw marks. She wondered what some stranger might think, coming up on that sight. She smiled at the thought of how few people would actually guess correctly. She went out, picked up the boots, and put them on the porch.

18

THE BLISS AT HOUSE DOMESTIC

Calley stretched as She sat up from the sleeping furs. The sun, almost unbelievably, was shining through the window. As a Goddess of Storms and Thunder, She found it ironic as She rested from the ardor of the May Celebrations. She withdrew Her power so far into Herself it left not even the possibility of clouds in the sky. As She stood up and stretched through the delicious sorenesses, couched here and there throughout Her body, She stopped suddenly.

She felt the slightest and smallest of motions deep in Her belly and She knew that the efforts of the past days had resulted in a fulfillment: the fulfillment of Her plan to conceive. She knew it to be a daughter. Although She could have willed Herself into pregnancy, She was proud that Her long planning with Alam had achieved its purpose. It was their child, their creation together, that She carried.

She could hear him outside, hammering stone that would be used to continue the extension of the two-room house She had shared with Bree all those millennia. It had taken a long time to slow Alam down enough that he could manage his aging and abide with Her. It had become necessary that he leave his world, and return to it only in his animal forms of ram, stallion, bull, and wolf And even then, not often.

She remembered watching the day Alam's father's men had shown up at the remote farm to which he had been banished. It was five days travel from the closest village using their two-wheeled cart and pair of oxen, and it had been four years since they had come. Alam's father had been involved in a battle of tribes allied against an incursion from the south and had been slain while defending the lands. Alam's brother had succeeded as chieftain of their clan, performing the rites of mourning and the work of succession. He had completely forgotten about his younger brother. It was only when it was remembered that Alam should be sent word of his father's death that the father's annual habit of sending the cart with supplies was also remembered.

She, and Alam in wolf form, had followed the slow course of the men. Calley happily drizzled on them all day, withdrawing only at night to couple with Alam, allowing the rain to stop and the clouds to part, revealing the moon—the moon to which Alam would call, howling, forcing the four men to rotate watches through the night.

Alam would sneak downwind through the woods, crawling on his belly the last yards through tall grass, just to bark at the slumbering oxen and startle them into snorting defensively and lumbering to their feet.

As amusing as it had been, he stopped when he was spotted as he ran away after just such a spooking, and caught a well-thrown rock on his backside. He was the largest wolf the men had ever seen. The men were filled with consternation and fear, magnifying the size and closeness of the great wolf in their retelling of the events. The wolf soon become known as the haunter of the Highland hills.

When the men finally arrived at the farm, they found the animals had scattered and not returned. Even the pigs were gone.

One of the men, got down off the cart and went quickly from building to building, knife drawn, looking for Alam. He was intent on gaining his new chieftain's confidence by carrying out his secret instructions for assassination. When the man climbed up on the roof to look at the land about the house, a bolt of lightning slammed into him, causing him to a collapse and fall, landing on his head and breaking his neck.

The remaining three men fell immediately to their knees and cried out to Calley's sister Bree for protection. For their devotion, they were spared the same fate. Calley blew a warm wind on them, startling them into smiling. They took it as a sign that their prayers had been heard.

They rose up and walked about the farm, looking for signs of occupancy. There was a thick layer of dust over everything, and the hearths in the house and forge smelled only of old damp ash and coals. One man found what could have been Alam's footprints going down the path leading to the river. But nowhere, as they circled the farm, could they find any signs of a returning trail.

They speculated that he had been taken by the huge wolf. Alam, listening nearby, grinned, tongue lolling at the irony. "If they only knew," he had thought to himself, Calley thinking likewise.

"Did the wolf take me? Or did I take the wolf?" he inquired of Calley in thought.

"Do you feed the wolf or does the wolf feed you?" Calley asked in return, amused, Her voice slowly filling his mind. She knew that Alam still needed practice with this mode of communicating.

Alam smiled, "Yes," was his sole response. He left the men then. Trotting off into the woods, he turned his back on his last contact with his father's people.

Calley remembered then. She remembered thinking how smooth it had been, this transition into Her world with no regret on his part. Nor had there ever been, She knew, in the centuries since. Alam loved Her, and was devoted to Her as no other. This had been good enough for him to begin his transition from his time to Hers.

It had also become necessary that She give up control of Her half of the year to Bree. The six months for which She had been responsible were, in a way, the clock of Her existence, bringing Her into the timeline of the mortals. Now, a year of their time could pass without making Her vulnerable to the passage of their time. The energy She saved thereby could be poured into Alam, like rain into his upturned face, fueling the alchemy that would extend his life.

She knew that later She would, if Her longer range plans were to manifest, have to pour even more into him—life force that would cost Her some of Her own life's energy. But not today. Today was a day of rest, in their land and house far above the earth, where that sunshine would last for as long as She cared to abide it. Then She would lower the house into the shadow of night and they would couple again, and rest again.

Now that She was responsible for the entire year, Bree had chosen to remain below, close to where She could hear the prayers of Her people and answer them. Her mind diffuse among the people, Bree could feed upon their offerings and maintain Herself. Bree now only rarely returned to the house, visiting during those times when Calley would bring the house to earth.

Calley's mind turned again to the night She'd conceived. She and Alam had worked out the details of how they wanted the children to grow into power and maturity. Calley had decided that each child should have provenance over Her power in different landscapes; one child should have the care of the Highlands, another the Lowlands, and the third should have power over the Seas. Each would have a full suite of Her abilities.

Alam offered that he could possibly pass on the powers of his different animals; ram to the Highlands, Bull to the Lowlands, and Stallion to the seas. Calley thought this was a brilliant idea and together they worked out a plan to achieve it. Since their plan was to have three in the order of girl-boy-girl, they needed to make sure that they could pass on the ability to change gender when in animal form. The idea was that he had to be partly in animal form when he orgasmed. In that way his contribution would contain the imprint of a form—the capacity to appear in the general form—and they could teach the children to manifest the form through a full range of possibilities.

Alam had been in his horns that night. She remembered being on Her back, legs wrapped around him, ankles locked behind his back. She had reached up and stroked his horns, wrapping Her hands around them, stroking them. They seemed to grow longer as She stroked them, spiraling out. She gripped them and used them to pull him in closer, joining their mouths in the slow kiss of spiraling tongues. She had begun to roll then, long waves of rolling power, long waves rolling like the sea. He rose above Her, breaking the kiss, feeling the waves roll over him like he was standing in the surf, the waves not breaking on the shore, but passing by him, over him, lifting him up, until they passed onto the shore and hissed away.

Then the thunder boomed. The lightning struck. The rain poured down, pounding on the roof, guttering the fire in the hearth. Alam willed it to recover, and it blazed up. It seemed that he himself almost became fire, fire riding on the water. He glowed with heat and power and when the power had blazed up in him until he could stand no more he released himself, letting the fire fall into Her waters, going out, nearly extinguished, except the littlest sparks.

She felt these sparks, these sparkly little lights, spread throughout the waves of Her, lighting Her up like fluorescence on the seas. Her mind filled with light. She gasped as She, too, could see no more for a moment. When She returned, She touched the sides of his head, and stroked the curls she found there.

She slipped from reverie at her table. She wrapped a satin cloak over Her shoulders and went to the door. Alam was working in the stone yard, shirtless and sweating in the sun, with sheepskins kilted around his waist to catch the flying shards as he chiseled a block into the form he wanted. His plan was to build a square compound, one stone at a time.

He had two walls and the chimney built, and the yard was growing short of stone. Their plan was to return the house to earth today, landing at first light by the mountain he preferred, so that Alam could gather the stone he needed. She called him to come eat when he was finished with the stone at hand, and turned to move the stew closer to the hearth fire.

After they ate, sitting thigh to thigh on the edge of the bed, Calley reminisced about how crowded the house had been with the three of them, before She had given Her half of the year to Bree. It was winter when Bree would stay at the house, and the weather, of course, was almost always typical Calley: atrocious. Although Calley could change the weather over the house and yards, most days She left it be. Returning at night after a day out being the weather, Calley and Alam would pile furs on the floor by the hearth fire, leaving the bed to Bree.

No matter how quiet they were in their lovemaking, they would always wake Bree. She would sit up on one elbow and watch them until they caught Her attention. Laughing, embarrassed almost, they would hide more deeply in the furs. One night when the furs had slipped away and Alam was spooning Calley while he was still inside Her, and they were both glowing in the light, Bree had slipped down behind Alam, and spooned him. Stroking Her hands along his back She whispered, "Sleep with me."

They had planned this moment in advance, Calley and Bree, unknown to Alam. He then leaned forward, stroked Calley's hair away from Her ear and whispered to Calley, "Your sister is here. She has asked us to go to bed with Her." Never once did he think that Bree was speaking only to him. This was the test Calley wanted him to pass—did he think of their partnership together first. From that moment on they shared the bed whenever Bree came home. Alam's capacity for gratitude grew to be commensurate with the genuine love and generosity Calley and Bree felt for each other, rare sisters back to back in metaphysical defense of their very lives.

An omen, a warning of the times to come, occurred when Calley lowered the house to earth. The house and land settled over the mountain like a transparent sheet, forming land in front of the mountain and below it, creating an image of a landscape that belonged with the land around it. She landed, flowing around the earth's curvature, appearing to the few who saw Her land as if She were a falling star. She settled on the Highland peak just before local dawn.

They made love on the grass below the outcropping Alam wanted to mine. Their passion created small tremors in the earth that extended upward into cracks in the rock, breaking them apart a little more, opening the earth for the wielded chisel. Alam had climbed up the face, tapping here, hammering there, letting the rock fall into the yard below. Calley went back to the stacked rock fence around the lower yard, below the house, to watch.

Suddenly a sense of danger filled the air. In the moment right before the buck god's hooves would have struck the back of Her head, She felt his oncoming presence. She bent forward so fast She came down off the wall and landed on Her hands and knees on the earth. The buck god landed on his feet several yards in front of Her. He back kicked at Calley swiftly several times shedding clods of dirt from his hooves, which struck Her face and head. Calley ducked his kicks, evading him in those first terrifying disconcerting moments, then She recovered Herself and went mist on him.

He stopped and bugled his frustration and rage, the sound so pow-erful and surprising that Alam lost his footing on the rock face and dropped his tools; the hammer and chisel clattered away. He clung to a point of rock with one hand to keep from dropping to the ground below. Swinging, hanging, he saw the buck god, snorting, make several more kicks in the direction where Calley had been, staling and shitting on the wall. The buck god bugled again, raising its head to Alam. Its eyes, filled with a red-black fire Alam had never before seen—eyes of madness—stared at Alam and seemed to grow larger the longer Alam gazed, the flame threatening to reach out and engulf him.

"I am god," the buck raged. "I am coming. Your time is dead." The buck bugled again, raising the timbre until it became a scream.

As Alam watched, the ground beneath the buck god's feet started to crackle and spark with blue fire. Soon the ground seemed to be frying, sparking, the electricity travelling up the buck's quivering legs and making every hair on its body stand straight up. With the last bit of its presence of mind the buck sprang up, bending backwards, and back flipped over the wall.

Alam dropped to the ground and bounded over the walls to the spot where Calley had been. He leaned over the shit spattered wall look-ing for Calley. The buck god was gone, hoof prints smoking in a trail of burned grass. Calley formed out of the mist alongside Alam, and leaned forward to look also. Alam turned to Her and brushed dirt from Her hair.

"It was possessed," She said. "An army comes, my Mother said. He is the scout. They come from out there," Calley indicated the sky with her hand. "They have invaded the Mother, taking what they can, tak-ing that for which they have not asked. It is the rape of the planet. Sometimes they come with the madness you just saw, the madness of Murgos. It was insane for him to come here, but he had no choice; he was possessed. Sometimes they are very beautiful, causing men to fall under their spell and believe what they're told. Men even believe in what they know to be untrue. In the east there are already armies forming, warring with each other. The wars will come here, too, but not for a while. We are safe, and we will be safe. Our children will be safe. I will see to that."

"How?" Alam asked.

Calley shrugged a shoulder and continued the prophecy. "It will take a thousand years for them to win, to destroy the old ways, to dominate the Sacred Feminine, and to grind the Sacred Feminine into the dust. For that is their goal, and the enemy will rule the hearts of men in darkness for a thousand years more. We will follow my Mother's advice. We will retreat. That is how our children will be safe."

Calley paused, eyes gazing at the future. "It will go hard on Bree, the Brighid Queen. Her people will die under the relentless assault. Even Her name will be almost forgotten, for it will be a crime to even speak it. My name will be forgotten. So we shall be safe."

"Is there no hope?" Alam asked, dismayed.

"There is always Hope. There will always be Love. In perhaps another thousand years, She will show Her face again, show Her face to the people." Calley turned to Alam and continued. "These people coming, they will plant seeds. They will cut down the forests. They will become legion, hearts embodying the contradictions of their new Masters. They will fight and kill each other, warring out their new god's self-hatred until the hearts of men are so blasted they can no longer be herded like sheep. When the time is right..." Calley paused and stopped talking, looking far ahead, then closing Her eyes to shake away the visions. "When the time is right," She said, and left it at that. "The future is not guaranteed, even though it may seem so. The outcome is in the balance, and we shall see to what side the balance comes down."

"What is the madness of Murgos?" Alam asked.

"What you just saw. It is the possession by a demon intelligence. Murgos is the name the Mother has given to the invader. De Murgos, She has come to call him. Those intelligences of madness, along with the beautiful ones I mentioned before, all came here with him. Perhaps they are all insane."

"What shall we do about him?" Alam asked.

"Him? Nothing. We hide, we retreat until the time is right for us to re-emerge. He would imprison me if he found me, steal my power and use it as his own. You he would kill. About him we do nothing," Calley replied.

"Then what about the buck? He trespassed. Him we can do something about," Alam offered.

"What do you have in mind?" Calley asked.

Over the next few days Alam gathered all the rock that the yard would hold while Calley meditated with the new life within her and communed telepathically with her Mother. When the moon was full, at sunset, they set off in search of buckman-god. As they stepped out of the magic land Calley transformed into a fast moving fog. With a leap, Alam went wolf.

They had a good idea where to start looking for their acquaintance: the meadow by the river where Alam had spared his life many years before. There they found him, mounted behind his favorite doe of the moment, grunting and snorting, making bugling and whistling noises, locked mentally in the sole pursuit of his pleasure, confident in his safety. The doe, also, was lost in pleasure.

Calley set up a wind blowing into the couple's faces, waiting until Alam took a long circle around the buckman-god and had started sneaking up behind him. From low in the grass Alam could read the vibration of their pleasure by lowering his belly to the ground. Several yards behind them, Alam rose up and was running at full speed by the time he came up behind them. He nipped at the buckman-god's fetlock, breaking skin and grazing the tendon.

The buckman-god leapt into the air, driving himself deeper and forward into the doe, who bent her forelegs just as Alam passed her nose. Alam barked at her. She leapt back into the buckman-god, triggering her locking reflex around his phallus. Then she took off, kicking and thrashing at the buckman-god's legs, knocking him off his feet. She galloped as well as she could, churning up clods, dragging him by the phallus, kicking at him when she could.

Calley formed up next to Alam and together they listened to the buckman-god bugling in pain until the sound vanished in the distance. The Alamwolf sat grinning with Calley's hand on his head, Calley smiling broadly above him.

"Let's go, beloved. Time to go," she said. And they ran home under the moon.

19

CURRICULUM TWO

The next few months passed quickly. Rachel gathered to her four more wen whom she felt, and the Diosa confirmed, she could trust: wen who had worked on themselves and studied life to the extent that they were certain that the Divine Feminine was antecedent to the Masculine. They believed wholeheartedly in the rectification of the disparities between the wen and men. With Rachel's help, each had worked to bring men into their lives who believed this also. Including Amanda and Beverly, this brought the number of wen in the first Council to eight.

At the first extended meeting of the High Council of Stonehaven, Rachel outlined the educational program; the establishment of the Order of the Fleur de Vie; the disposition of her properties, such that the Council would also be the ultimate Board of Directors; and the business development plan that would take Stonehaven into businesses where the members of the Order would be employed. Rachel decided that she would hire Regina as the Secretary to Council. Regina was to record everything, and to make sure all was arranged for the care and feeding of the wen. Rachel paid her very well, and made it clear that she thought it was necessary that Regina have her own money and her own means of acquiring it.

It was during this first meeting of the Council that Men's and Wen's Circles were established. The men stepped in to handle all domestic tasks—preparing food, house cleaning, and laundry— in order to provide for the wen during their meeting. It came to be clear, during these times of working together, that the men had very different levels of understanding about what was happening. They decided to meet in circle and teach each other what they knew. This enabled them to work together toward a common understanding of a common purpose: Service to the Divine Feminine.

A part of every day was dedicated to performing the necessary work of maintenance on a farm as large and complex as Stonehaven. Then, a part of every day was dedicated to spending time in circle. Soon a low level of hierarchy evolved, with Craft and Paul taking the lead and the five other men sat in a semi-circle around them. Instruction was provided in the yoga, the tantra, and the qi-gong and the internal processes of alchemy. In the afternoon was a session on martial arts and self-defense.

Life began with a daily sit: the eight wen with Regina in a circle in the middle, the seven men encircled the circled wen. The wen joined the men for the martial arts practice in the afternoons, receiving special instruction that accounted for gender based differences.

It was on one such morning sit that a revelation came through Regina, and she spoke it aloud to the group in the middle of the sit. "That men are seven, you know, XY, seven legs, and wen are eight, XX, eight legs, is not a sign that the masculine came before the feminine. The universe, and life itself, expands by octaves, doubling what was: one, two, four, eight. Something was broken away from the feminine at eight to make the masculine, making it seven."

And Craft, his mind awed by the simple profundity, responded, "Blessed are you among wen and men. Any religion that doesn't have the Feminine at the source and center of it is a bad religion." Then he paused, struck by the fierceness with which he had spoken. He said, more calmly, "The feminine creates, the masculine makes."

A shot of terror ran through several people in the room, caused by the impact of Regina's revelation and Craft's fierce response. Rachel immediately ended the sit. She commanded silence, saying, "No one speaks until I say so." She had everyone stand up, leave the room, and go outside into the cold fourth moon air. Then she swept out the sitting room; it was the only thing she could think of to do that was different from standing still and shaking uncontrollably until she fell down. Before she was finished, she did stand in the center of the room and shook uncontrollably. Then, she sat down. After a few moments outside, Craft led everyone into the kitchen.

Rachel remained sitting and speechless the entire day. No one else said a word the entire day either. In the evening, as the setting sun cast a long light across the floor through the tall west windows, her awareness returned from her distant communion to find everyone sitting in a circle around her. She rose, walked over to Regina and kissed her on top of her head, calling her by her middle name, "Blessed Sophia", and walked out of the circle. In the doorway, she turned and said, "You may speak now."

After Amanda and Regina had arrived at Stonehaven and before the beginning of the Council, Amanda had begun having sex with Craft under Rachel's direction. They practiced the Tantra, and sometimes Amanda practiced with Rachel and/or Craft. Rachel had chosen to begin Regina's further education with the cultivation techniques of the solitary path.

"In this path, in this tantra, the work begins with the path of solo cultivation. When the basics are learned, the devotee will choose between continuing the path of solo cultivation or beginning the study of the path of dual cultivation," Rachel told Regina one morning while Craft and Amanda were practicing.

"Wen can go very far along the path of solo work, almost all the way to completion. For men it is much more difficult. The substances, or energies, that are used in the alchemy, the energies required to create a higher body, are much more difficult for men to create and extract from within. Wen create enough energy to not only create this form almost entirely within themselves—they create enough beyond their own needs that they are able to share with men this extra substance, if you will, and help them with their work.

"When I first began doing this work in Windia, I was taught the solitary path first. This enabled me to gain control over my internal functions, including my monthly cycle, and also, therefore, my fertility. The control I developed did not eliminate these permanently. Nature demanded that I allow my body to become fertile and bleed periodically. So, if you wish to become free and independent, this is something you must learn, and you must work hard to learn it.

"Service to the Diosa, service as Her Priestess, may require that you have a great deal of sex when you begin working in the path of dual cultivation. It will serve you, and serve Her, to know your Self so well, and to have developed such Self-control, that you will know when you are fertile and when you are not. In this way, you will be able to choose to become pregnant when it is appropriate and wise.

"You will also discover that this energy can be used for power, or for healing."

"What kind of power? Power to do what?" Regina asked.

"Power to manifest, for example. Watch." Rachel held out her palms, cupped together. As Regina watched the cupped hands filled with water, and then, amazingly, a small yellow flower appeared, floating in it. Regina's jaw dropped.

Rachel folded her palms together and the whole thing disappeared. "Now, here's the question: was it real or an illusion?"

"That had to be an illusion," Regina asserted.

"Really?" Rachel asked, smiling. She flicked her fingers at Regina, and drops of water flew off, striking Regina in the face and chest. Regina backed away, closing her eyes against the drops. "Illusion, eh? And was that illusory water?" Rachel smiled.

Regina said nothing, and sat in silence, contemplating the mystery of what she had just observed.

"It takes energy to move energy," Rachel said. "It takes power to use power. One must only learn how."

Wiping her cheek, Regina asked, "Alright, then, where did the flower go? Was that sleight of hand?"

"It could have been. You, as you are, cannot tell yet. But I will say this: what you see is the reflection of light, whether it was a real flower or a phantom flower, both are reflections of light. That being said, how could you tell which it was? And which takes less power?"

"The phantom flower takes less power. So, by using reason I can deduce that, if the flower was real, it was most probably produced by sleight of hand. It would take less power, but a lot of skill, to place it there, in your hands. But it would take less power, by orders of magnitude, I should suspect, to create the illusion of a flower. The question remains, how?"

"Very good, Regina." Rachel took one palm and held it up, vertically facing Regina. Rachel made a pushing motion with her hand from over a foot away and Regina moved back, feeling the push of it. Rachel then closed her fingers part way, like she was making a claw. She pulled her hand back. Regina felt pulled toward Rachel and felt compelled to lean in closer. Rachel did it again, pushing Regina back, then pulling her forward. The third time Rachel did it, Regina began to feel alarmed, as fear spread through her belly. She put her hands down on the floor, and resisted the power of the push and pull.

"Stop it," Regina demanded.

Rachel stopped it, dropping her hand to her lap. She turned her head to one side. When she turned it back toward Regina she saw that Regina had gone still, eyes staring at Rachel, with a track of tears beneath each eye. Rachel smiled, and looked down.

She said, "You are sitting in my field. You are sitting in the field of my power. I daresay I could have made you see anything. I sent you the word 'flower'. You heard the word, 'flower' in your own mind, and thought quickly to yourself, 'a flower belongs there' floating on the water."

Regina gasped, remembering.

Rachel continued, "You conjured the flower yourself. Or rather, you conjured the image of the flower."

Regina nodded.

"But I was the one that made it yellow. I'm fond of that family of flowers," Rachel concluded.

They sat in silence for a while.

Then Regina asked, "What about the water?"

"Ah…I thought you were going to forget. That was real. Or rather, some of it was. That was a situation where you need a little bit of something to make more of that thing. One of the powers I developed in my work on myself was the power to bring water to my palms, not something humans can usually do. One would not think such a thing could be so useful, yes?"

Regina nodded again.

"But you must understand, I could have made you see the whole thing. You could have even touched it. If I'd had enough power up, the power would have made you even believe it was wet."

"Did the water come from you?" Regina asked.

"Good girl. You are keeping your presence of mind. The answer is, yes. Some of it came from me. Later, I learned how to draw water from the air around me. That took less power than forcing water to my palms. As I'm sure you can imagine, that, too, would be a very useful skill to have."

Regina nodded again. And then, slowly, she leaned backwards, leaning all the way back until she lay flat, and face up on the floor, her legs still crossed at the ankle. Rachel could see her eyes were still open; that she was still thinking.

"Could you hold me, here, on the floor like this?" she asked.

"Yes. I could both hold you there, and make you hold yourself there, as well," Rachel replied in an even tone of voice.

Regina lay there in silence. After a while, eyes still open, she uncrossed her legs, sat up, then crossed them at the ankle again under her skirt. "You said it was more difficult for men. Why is it more difficult?"

"Because men are always trying to give birth to a baby, the one thing they cannot do. And almost everything a man does—an everyday man, that is, not one on the path—almost everything a man does is some version of the attempt to do the one thing he cannot do: that is, trying to do the impossible."

"No, that's not what I mean. You said something about substances?" Regina clarified.

"Oh, that," Rachel said, smiling. "I can explain that to you later. But it's all explained in your father's teachings. Do you know them?"

"Did I know him?" Regina asked, misunderstanding. "After the war he only lived a few years. I guess, added up, we spent perhaps two years there, with him. And with everybody else who was hanging around him all the time. He paid only a little attention to me, although my mother reminds me every so often of the times I've forgotten. Everyone else required so much of his time—that, and his book." Regina paused.

"Well," Rachel asked. "Have you read it?"

"I tried. I really did, but I couldn't get past the first few pages," Regina replied.

"Then I want you to try again. You will have plenty of time here. And the answers to that question are mentioned in there. I want to see if you can find them."

"Christened on a cracker, Rachel. Not that. Anything but that," Regina objected.

Rachel laughed out loud at the imagery. She said, "No, no, you have to do it. So much of your inheritance is in there. There is so much that you can come to understand, not just about the world, but about him. And you deserve to understand it."

Regina went silent, verging on a pout.

Rachel said, "Now, let's talk about another difference between men and wen. In this way, especially when she is engaged in a path of solitary cultivation, a wen is supposed to practice masturbation." Rachel paused to see Regina's reaction.

Regina smiled. "Really," she said. "Do tell me more."

"Well," Rachel began. "There are whole volumes written on the sub-ject."

"Any of them by women?" Regina asked. "I mean wen?"

"Yes, there are. But there are none translated. That is why you are going to write one, too. You are going to write down what I am going to in-struct you to do. You can even record your observations. In fact, I want you to write down a great deal. Ideally, we'll get it typed up, but we can start it long hand. For now, let's call it Regina's book. No, let's call it the Queen's Book. That's what your name means. I have blank hard bound journals for you to use.

"I need you to write it all down, Regina. That's why I'm going to pay you to be my assistant and secretary. In this way, what you learn and what I know will be preserved and passed down for all the wen who are coming. And it will be used to prepare the men for their arrival."

"And then, after masturbation we can talk about self-denial. Well, that's another difference. Wen are supposed to learn to orgasm and ejaculate as much as possible. Men are supposed to learn to ejaculate rarely, if at all."

"Wait. What?"

"What what? Well, that's not fair, either. Look. You do know about masturbation, yes?"

"Yes."

"Let's start over. You are aware that there is a difference between or-gasm and ejaculation, yes?"

"Yes. I have orgasm often without ejaculation."

"Yes. And you do ejaculate, yes?"

"Oh, yes. Sometimes the volume is embarrassing. I'll make a puddle. Or soak the sheets."

"Oh, fortunate wen. Most wen don't do it at all, you know."

"No."

"Yes. The first time, it happened to you automatically?"

Regina nodded.

"Most wen have to train themselves to do it. It doesn't happen naturally for them. It takes practice. That's why the manuals—for instruction. And men, well, men, they don't require much instruction do they? It happens all at once for them, automatically. Well, it usually just happens all at once, almost immediately, yes?"

Regina laughed and nodded her head again.

"Men require a different form of instruction. Men have to learn to not ejaculate, unless it's under controlled conditions, and by their own choosing."

"Men need to get control over themselves."

"Yes. Men need to get control over themselves. And once they establish the power of self-control, then they must learn to separate orgasm from ejaculation. Men, like wen, can learn to have as many orgasms as they want, just like wen. In fact, one the stages of development in this tantra is that men and wen both can become almost continuously orgasmic. That's because orgasm is primarily neurological, and men and wen are wired up sufficiently similarly. The difference between wen and men, then, is with ejaculation. Ejaculation is physiologically different for wen and men. It's not neurological; it's glandular. Wen and men have the same glands, for the most part. Men have testicles, and another gland wrapped around the ureter that together create ejaculate. It's palpable through the anus. Wen's ejaculate comes through this gland as well, and it's palpable behind the front wall of your phulva, yes? You know the spot?"

"Yes," said Regina, fascinated. "I know it."

"Good, then" Rachel smiled. "You'll require less instruction. Even finding it is a problem for some wen. However, as you've noticed, wen don't have testicles. And with men, you've noticed, also, I'm sure, that with men, it's basically 'one and done'. Almost all men need to rest, they detumesce after ejaculation. And it takes a while for them to be able to regain tumescence, and even longer before they can ejaculate again. Which, incidentally, is a part of their training; they can learn not to detumesce. They can even learn to stop ejaculation, even when it's once begun."

"What? Wait," Regina held up her hand. "They can stop it in the middle?"

"Yes. And we wen also become erect you know. Our phulva's swell, and the little rod—you know, your clitoris—it swells. It is erectile also, our own little phallus. Neurologically speaking, it's easier for wen to become continuously orgasmic."

Rachel paused, thinking about continuous orgasm and what she wanted to say next.

"So, then, from where does the difference in volume come?" Regina prompted.

"The intra-pelvic spaces," Rachel answered, distractedly. "The bladder is permeable in one direction, not so in the other direction. We draw it in from the intra-organ and even the intracellular spaces in the pelvis. Then we orgasmically squirt it out, pushing it through our own glands, and then out the urethra, same as men. Why are you smiling?"

"When you said 'pushing' I heard 'pussing', pussing it out".

Rachel laughed out loud. "Sit like me," she said. Rachel sat up on the cushion, folding her legs under her and sitting on her heels. She paused, allowing Regina to do the same. Rachel breathed, alternating her breath in the Four Elements pattern: first through the mouth, inhaling and exhaling both. Then inhaling through the mouth, exhaling through the nose. Then inhaling through the nose and exhaling through the mouth. Finally, inhaling and exhaling through the nose. Regina breathed with her.

Then Rachel said, "Do as I do." She shifted her weight to her right leg and brought the other leg up, bringing her left knee to her chest and putting her left foot flat on the cushion, bringing it in as close as she could, and leaning slightly forward. Regina started to do the same thing in mirror image.

"What, are you left-handed? Oh, yes, that's right, you are. This will be interesting. Do as I do," Rachel commanded again. "But continue with the mirror imaging."

Rachel raised her skirts so Regina could see. Still leaning forward she brought her right foot inward until she could actually sit on the ball of her foot. "Can you do this? Bring it this far?" Rachel asked. "No? Then practice. Some wen, some men as well, can actually set their sex on their heel. Bring it in as far as you can, then."

They sat, again. Rachel started the cycle of breathing again, except extending the amount of cycles of each kind of breath. After a moment she said, "Think about what kind of present I must have left for you under your pillow."

Then they were off, Rachel showing Regina how to breathe to orgasm. A few moments in, Regina was having a hard time following Rachel. She opened her eyes to find Rachel looking at her, eyes narrowed in examination. "Do as I do," Rachel coached.

Then Rachel slid her right hand into her underwear down along her belly and touched herself on her own little phallus, and gasped. Regina did the same.

Later, after changing her wet clothes, Regina looked under her pillow and found three phalli, made of polished wood, each different in size and conformation. They were beautiful. Each could stand upright on its base, the base being short legs, crossed into the siddhasana position, testicles hanging over its heels—an erection with legs.

"Lovely," Regina said aloud. "How like a man. A dick with legs."

20

RETURN OF THE PRODIGAL

Sally reached over Quinn to turn off the alarm. He never seemed to hear it, breathing undisturbed by the sound that made her jump, a sound she hated deeply. Quinn swore that he didn't need one; all he had to do was program his mind to wake up at a certain time, and he always did. Well, almost always. Except when he was drunk.

When he was drunk he was good for nothing, except a sleep from which he couldn't be awakened by anything. It was as if he were dead. He said that he'd been tied down asleep in the back of a flatbed once, and the truck had been pulled over for hauling the dead without a license. His friend driving and the cop had had a hard time waking him up. 'The sleep of the dead,' he'd said. That's what he guessed people meant when they said it.

But there was a certain point during the descent to what he called 'the mud at the bottom of the pond,' when he could get a massive hard on and fuck Sally for a long time with a thumping assertiveness, pummeling her clit with his pubic bone. It would scratch her deepest itch and leave her languid and exhausted, smashed flat by love, and ready to fall into the deepest and most restorative level of sleep—sleep where she never dreamed and was glad of it.

Generally, she didn't like that kind of sex, that pile-driver sex, except that Quinn didn't do it like a jackhammer. He did it more like at the speed of the pile-driver she'd watched from the window at the diner, and with a softer contact, more like a whoomp than a bang. It didn't hurt and he was paying attention to her the whole time, not completely absorbed in his own sensation. He wasn't using her like a bathtub, like the men she'd usually had, who were masturbating into the tub during their shower in the morning. She knew that's what was happening, because she'd check the tub when she got home from work. There was always splatter.

"That's him," she thought. "No splatter."

Quinn was the dishwasher on the second shift at the diner where she waitressed. She'd been there long enough to be the counter girl as well as the cashier when it wasn't too busy, so she didn't have to do all the walking the other girls did. It put her closer to the kitchen. She was on first shift days and had to be there for the breakfast crowd.

She thought, getting into the shower, "Maybe I'll have him switched to first shift and then just see if he can wake up without a fucking alarm."

Quinn opened an eye when he heard her turn the water on. He felt an urge to pee and sat up, sighing rather than yawning, sagging rather than stretching. Using his hands on his knees he stood up. No dizziness, no wobbling, no hangover. He remembered he'd drunk a lot of water before he went to bed.

He bumped into the corner of the bed on his way to the bathroom and jammed his toe on the frame leg, pushing the bed back into place against the wall between the nightstands.

"Gawddamn," he said. "The fucking bed must have moved." And it had. During the previous night's "frame test for sturdiness," as they called it, the wheels must have come unlocked and the bed had shifted about 15 degrees.

He went into the bathroom and lifted the seat. Soon the noise of his urination was louder than the shower. Sally pulled the curtain back, looked at him, then looked down at him holding himself in his hand, aiming for dead center. The bowl made a rumbling noise deep in the bottom and she said, "Laud, Quinn, it's so loud I can feel it through the floor."

He shrugged, and said, "Thunder Cock the Rock Splitter." He finished while she watched; then he flushed and put the seat down, making an elaborate mockery with his hands of inviting her to sit there, and grinned at her.

She said, "Asshole." He grinned and went down to make coffee, not even bothering to close the bathroom door.

When she went downstairs dressed for the day, he was still in the kitchen, naked, butt leaning against the counter. He looked old in the dim light. It irritated her.

"How clean's that ass of yours?" she asked.

"Clean enough to eat off of," he replied. "You want some?"

She said, "Yeah, why not? Hard to get good sausage these days." She pulled a chair over, sat down in front of him, took his phallus in her hand and put it in her mouth. "You have to hurry," she said, around the floppy mouthful. "And don't mess up my hair."

Five minutes later she sat back, satisfied, with only a few strands of hair hanging forward of her ear, and a slight smudge of eyeliner down her check. She loved the way he tasted, sweet and salt. She'd go down on him anytime, and she had made sure he'd known it. Her jaw would ache, her tongue would feel swollen, and the roof of her mouth would feel bruised, before she would stop.

That was how she'd gotten him, not that he was much of catch. She'd been out back on her last break before the end of her shift having a smoke. She'd suddenly felt a presence, turned around and saw him sitting there on a milk crate, staring at her. She could feel that he was attracted to her—feel the desire welling up in him, the pull of it having been what she'd sensed. She'd allowed it to pull her around.

"What're you doing out here?" she wanted to know.

"Looking at the sky," he replied.

"And what're you looking at now?" she asked, feeling suddenly a little hard toward him.

"Something just as pretty but a whole lot closer," he'd said with a smile.

The smile got to her. The smile was a little shy on the surface but with a deeper flexion that showed he knew he was feeding her a line, and at the same time, he meant it. Knowing that he meant it brought her back to meet him when he came out the back door at the end of his shift. It didn't bother her that he was white; she'd had them all come through the diner at one time or another, and she'd had them all. It didn't bother her that he was a wanderer, maybe even a bum or a hobo, because he was clean. He always changed clothes when he came in and changed back out when he left.

So, she'd taken him to a roadhouse on the edge of town, an integrated bar where she was known. Over bourbon and beer she'd asked him if he wanted to dance and he said, "Yes." And from that first contact of their hands, she knew. The first time he'd pulled her in close she'd felt his erection pressed up against her, so she knew that he knew.

She'd done him in the back seat of her car, a dusty red Plymouth sedan that she'd pulled around behind the bar. She'd finished him by going down on him then, after she'd straddled him for a while, enjoying him 'til she had come a few times. She'd sat back, wiping her chin, going "Mmm, mmm, mmm!" like he was a commercial for something tasty. "That was good! I'll be doing that some more."

"You will, will you? I'll be happy to help," he'd said.

"Bet your ass you will," she said, pulling her skirt back down and buttoning her blouse. "So where can I drop you off? I'll need to know where you're staying."

That had been eight months ago. It had turned out that he'd been staying in a room over the roadhouse all along, swapping clean-up for rent. She'd punched him on the shoulder when he told her; all along they'd been cramped up in her car when they could have just gone up the stairs to his bed.

After two months, enough time for her to be sure he wasn't some kind of serial killer, she'd taken him home—not every night—but often enough he knew she trusted him, and, at that level, he trusted her. He didn't talk much about himself, but it became clear he didn't trust anybody much. And when he did, he didn't trust it. When he'd drink, he would be honest about what he felt and thought, but never anything about where he'd been. She figured he was running, but it didn't feel like he was running from a crime. Bad love, maybe, or some bad shit, but not a crime. It made her wary, but it didn't make her want to fuck him any less.

Once, she'd been there to his room, and he'd let her look around and touch whatever she wanted, watching her from the bed. She'd opened the drawers in the small dresser, checked in the small closet, checked the medicine cabinet in the bathroom. She picked up the book on the nightstand, a dog-eared paper back with the smiling face of an old Chinaman on the cover, and opened it. It looked like poetry of some kind and her eyes fell upon the words "uncarved block". She put it down. She liked life simple, no contradictions or paradoxes. She never asked him to move, so she could have looked behind the headboard and seen the Glock 9mm in a holster he'd velcroed behind it.

This morning, sitting back and rinsing her mouth out with coffee after she'd given him a leg shaker of an orgasm, she grinned and said, "I'll see you later. And bring that Thunder Cock with you. I might have need of it."

Then she picked up a sweater off the back of the chair, grabbed her bag and checked to make sure her phone and keys were in it.

She kissed him square on the lips and he didn't flinch. She slipped him a little tongue and he still didn't flinch. It was one of the things she liked about him. He didn't mind where her mouth had been. He accepted her, all of her, the way no one else ever had. He was sweet water for her soul. Well, sweet with a dash of minerals thrown in.

She turned and stepped out the door. He smiled, looking into the swirling coffee in his hand, and said, "I'll be sure to. It's not like I have a choice," as it closed softly behind him.

Six hours into her shift Sally glanced up from the counter, rag in hand, and saw the Crown Victoria sedan pull into the lot and up to the parking rail. Two men got out. The passenger went back and opened the door for a woman in a black business grade pantsuit. The driver went back and got the men's jackets off the seat. It was then that she noticed both men wore shoulder holsters. "Cops," she thought, then, "No badges," when she couldn't see any. "Could be plain clothes," she muttered, looking down again as they scanned around and through the window. "Could be bounty hunters; trouble, anyway."

They walked to the front and the driver handed the passenger the other jacket over the hood while shrugging into his own. The woman took the lead and led them down the sidewalk to the door. Sally stayed where she was, putting the rag under the counter.

"Afternoon, ma'am," she said as the woman came through the door. The woman smiled tightly, nodded, and came over to sit on a stool at the counter. The two men took a booth behind her.

"Pie?" the woman said.

"Key lime, coconut, and blueberry. Don't nobody ever eat the coconut," Sally replied.

"Key lime, then. And coffee."

Sally poured a cup and put the coffee down. She grabbed two menus to take over to the men, who took them with barely a glance at her. She went back behind the counter and got the pie out. She stepped away after serving it and said across to the men, "Let me know when you're ready."

The woman pulled out her phone and checked for messages, ignoring Sally's sideways assessment of her gray hair, pulled tightly back in a bun, the thin lines of turkeyneck, the pressed lips, the stark blue eyes. Judging by her eyebrows, her hair had been black when she was younger. One of the men waved her over.

While the men were ordering sandwiches and soft drinks she watched them, too, looking for the folds in their jackets, seeing if she could catch a glimpse of any badges. Nothing.

She put the order in through the window and went back to leaning against the counter, crossing her arms and looking out the window.

"Excuse me," the gray woman said. "Let me ask you something." And, reaching into her suit pocket she pulled out a small photograph of a man about passport size in black and white. The picture itself looked old and was sealed in laminate. The man may have been in his early twenties with long hair pulled back tight and a short beard. She looked at the writing beside it and realized it was a union card. But there was no mistaking the eyes.

"Have you seen this man before?" In her other hand she held up a sketch. "It's an old photo. He may look something like this now."

Bunny, the bus boy, was walking past with a tray of dishes. He set them down on the counter and said, "Sure, I know this dude."

"Oh, yeah?" the woman asked.

"Yeah, sure," Bunny said. "He took $20.00 off me in a bet."

"Yeah?" the woman encouraged him.

"Yeah, he did. He bet me where a fly was gonna land next," Bunny said, still resentful.

"Really?" the woman asked, disbelieving him. "How'd that go down?"

"I took some dishes back," Bunny said. "He was standing there scraping the garbage off before he put them in the washer. There was a fly, a big one, flying around, landing here and there and taking off like none of the food was good enough for him. Then he circles around and Quinn says, 'I know where he's gonna land next.' And I says, 'No way.' And he says, 'Twenty says I do.' So I says, 'Twenty on' and we shook real slow and quiet like. He says, 'It's gonna land right there between those two plates.' And I says, 'Naw.' And he says, 'Watch.' And it does. It lands right there between two plates and disappeared down between 'em. Man, I was sore. So I asked him, 'How'd you know?' And he waggled his goofy fingers grinning at me until I paid up. Once he had it he lifted the plates and there was one of them used up honey packets stuck there. 'Flies to honey,' he said. 'Flies to honey.'"

Bunny picked up the tray of dishes and backed through the swinging doors. "Name's Quinn. He works here, washing dishes," and he sniffed triumphantly.

The gray woman looked up at Sally, who'd been standing there paralyzed but managed to succeed at looking simply indifferent. "That true?" she asked of Sally.

Sally nodded. "Yup, that's true. Name's Quinn, works here, washing dishes." She wasn't going to volunteer more.

"Here, now?" the woman asked.

"No. Day off," she lied.

"Nah," Bunny said, coming back through the doors with an empty tray. "That ain't right. He'll be in at two today. Either that or Lester's gonna be real mad at him, cause he's got a date this afternoon."

The gray woman looked at Sally, who shrugged. "My mistake," she said.

"Where's he live?" the woman called after Bunny.

"Roadhouse. Out by the highway," Bunny called back.

The woman turned around and nodded at one of the men. "Go see if he's home." He got up, went outside, and drove off. She turned back around and said, "Now about that pie," and picked up her fork.

The sandwiches came out and Sally took them to the table. The remaining man took both plates and arranged them equally in front of him. "Good for me," he said.

When Sally realized that neither of them were paying the slightest attention to her, she backed away, turned the corner, and headed for the Ladies room. Once inside, she locked the door, then reached in her dress pocket and pulled out her cell phone. She speed dialed the number for the little burner phone she'd bought Quinn as a present so she could sex talk him during the day.

Quinn was getting out of the shower when he heard the phone ring. He hopped over to the nightstand, trying not to drip. He got there just when it went to voicemail.

When he listened to it he sat down. The message Sally had left him was hurried and hushed. It was "You got to go, baby. They've come for you."

Quinn had his hot bag with him; it went where he did. But if he was going to run he needed his go bag and that was back at the roadhouse. It was almost two hour's walk cross country there and six hours til dark. He dressed quickly and looked around to make sure that nothing of his remained behind. Then he had a thought. He sat down and typed something into the phone, then closed it and laid it on her pillow.

The man at the table ate his sandwich and then started in on the other man's by the time the gray woman had finished her pie. He said, "Don't you think we should call him back?"

"Yeah," she replied, wiping her mouth with a paper napkin. "If he's there, have him check it out. Then come back."

The man called the man driving the car and said a few words Sally couldn't hear. She was thinking, "Go, baby. Go."

Two hours went by. The man with the car had come back, having checked out the roadhouse and found no one. Quinn didn't show up for his shift, and they all got up and left together. No tip.

Quinn arrived at the roadhouse and scanned the parking lot. The afternoon was hot and sunny. There was no sign of anyone. He went through the woods until he was across from the staircase. He quickly scooted across and up the stairs. He could see foot prints in the dust where someone had looked in the window and left.

He grabbed his bag and was throwing in some unpacked stuff he thought he'd take. While he was reaching for the book he heard gravel crunching in the parking lot. He shot a quick look out the window and saw the Crown Vic. "Never a good sign," he thought. He grabbed the Glock from behind the headboard, pulled it out of the holster and levered one up into the chamber.

He went over and locked the door. He threw the bag in the closet, pausing to remember whether the door had been open or closed. He closed it just down to where it snugged against the frame, and left it that way.

He went around to the far side of the bed where a section of floor big enough to hold him came up. He lay down and covered himself with the floorboards.

One night drinking with Frankie, the owner, Frankie had told him about it, and promised him to secrecy. When the three climbed the stairs and looked in through the windows, the room looked the same as it had when the driver had been there earlier. They turned and went back down the stairs to wait in the car, still running with the AC on. They'd backed up and parked the car where the passenger could just see the bottom steps and the driver could see the front entrance.

About 4 o'clock Frankie pulled into the parking lot and saw the car, obviously full of dicks, parked at the edge of the lot. As he opened the doors they all three got out and walked toward him.

"Hey!" the driver called out. "You open?"

"Not yet," Frankie replied, muttering "Dick" under his breath.

"Well, we'd like to talk to you a minute," the other one said. The woman followed behind, but she was clearly the one in charge. She set the pace, and the men didn't walk too far ahead of her.

"Well, you better come on in then. Too hot out here," Frankie said, holding the door open. Expecting one of them to take it, he almost bumped into the driver trying to go in alongside him. He stood back and turned aside as they all went in ahead of him. Pulling the door closed plunged them into darkness. He went to the light switch, muttering "Dicks. All three of them."

A flashlight came on, and then the lights. Frankie saw the woman had pulled it out of a pocket.

"Waddaya wanna talk about?" Frankie asked.

Quinn waited until he could hear all four voices through the floor. He eased up the floorboards and quietly made his way around the room, avoiding the corner of the bed this time. He opened the closet, grabbed his bag, and the book off the nightstand. Carefully closing the door behind him, he snuck down the stairs, avoiding the ones where the nails squealed.

He knew Frankie would stall them as long as he could, just on general principles, but he didn't know how long that would be. Frankie was just saying to them, "Have a drink?" when Quinn made it to the woods and disappeared into the shadows.

When Sally got home—late because she'd had to work an extra shift to cover the missing dish washer—she turned on the lights, set down her things, and paused. Breathing into the house, she tried to feel if he was still there. She heard no sounds, felt no movement of either air, or presence; no one coming toward her like he had whenever she'd returned from being out.

She went on further into the house, feeling a terror and a grief rising in her belly, as she turned on the light in the bedroom. She saw the phone on her pillow and recognized it.

She picked it up, opened it, and it lit up immediately. There, in an unsent text addressed to her number and one other, was typed a single word: Love. She took the phone to the kitchen, tears running down her face, got her phone out of her bag. She hit 'Send'. Both phones buzzed at once, and that's when Sally Oshune knew for sure that he was gone.

The people looking for Quinn stayed at Frankie's bar until nine o'clock. After that, they the drove over to the hotel near the exchange with the interstate highway and booked two motel rooms. The woman showered to get the dust and disappointment of the day rinsed away. She kept a bottle of decent scotch whiskey in her suitcase, and she thought she would take it down the hall to the room where the men were staying and strategize about their next steps. The trust fund she was running on was running out, too.

They weren't in the hunt for philosophical reasons, like she was. She considered vengeance a philosophical enterprise. They were hired men, private investigators. Loyal, but it was paid-for loyalty. They were not driven, as she was.

She took out the bottle of scotch and poured herself a half shot in a plastic drinking glass. She went down the hall to the men's room and noticed that the door was not completely closed. She listened but heard only a muffled sound she couldn't quite make out. Drink in one hand, bottle in the other she leaned into the door and it opened.

She stepped down the short hallway and paused, remaining mostly out of sight. And the sight, truly unexpected, that met her eyes was of the two men having sex. One of them was lying on his back across one of the beds, his pants down around his ankles, and having his cock sucked on by the other man. The other man had his cock out through the zipper in his still belted slacks, masturbating.

He was too big to lean over so far and lost his balance, falling on the other man. The woman laughed out loud.

The Top man rolled to the side, his jaw agape. The Bottom sat up, and tried to hide the erection with his hands, unsuccessfully,

The Top said, "Ms. A.!"

The Bottom said, "We can explain!" A. laughed again.

"I can do that better than either of you. You do women, too? Or just each other? Women, yes?" she said.

They both nodded their heads at her.

"Well, good then," she said. "You do me. Both of you. And I'll show you how."

The men simply nodded.

"Well?" she asked. "Stand up, both of you, and take your clothes off." She took the drink she held in her hand and poured it back, down her throat, in one shot.

She watched them get undressed and stand there, trying to cover their erections with their hands, and, curiously, their erections failed to flag.

She smiled at this futility, and said, "Come here. You," she said, indicating the Top. Then she said, "Get a couple of those plastic glasses and pour us all a drink," holding hers out. "Oh, and bring him over here, too. Pull him along by his cock, will you?"

Top took Bottom by the phallus and pulled on it, pulling him along. "Stop!" A. said. This had the effect of Top's hand gripping and sliding back along Bottom's cock. "Like that," A. said. "Pull him along over here, jerk him off as you come."

She set the bottle down, and when Bottom came up next to her she forced him to his knees. "Undo my skirt," she said to him. Then, "No, never mind. Just put your hands up under it, and put your fingers under the edge of my panties."

Bottom followed the directions, sliding his hands up over her hose, pushing her slip up under the skirt, and the skirt followed. He crossed the tops of her hose, and slipped up alongside the straps for the garter she wore to hold them up. He found the edge of her panties and slipped his fingers under the edge.

"Slip them around. Find the edges. Take them off," she said, her hands gripping in Bottom's hair as she spread her legs and leaned back. Bottom slid them off and she, still holding his hair, pulled his face in between her thighs. She tilted her pelvis to him, bringing her sex right up against his mouth. "Lick," was her simple command as she held out her glass for a refill. She threw back the entire shot again.

She set down her glass and told Top to take her jacket off, then her blouse. She pushed the straps of her slip and slip down over one shoulder, fished out a breast and offered it to Top, who took it greedily. It made her smile. She undid the zipper on the side of her skirt and slipped it off. She slipped the strap over her other shoulder and brought Top's head over to the other side, offering that breast to him. She'd never had children and her small breasts looked much as they always had. In her seventies now, she knew she still had a good body, but age will eventually tell and she chose to keep the rest of her clothes on.

She pulled up Bottom and guided him onto his back on the bed. She climbed on, pulling Top by his shaft. She turned around and sat on Bottom's face, counselling him to do what he could. Top she brought around and had him lean over so his face was at Bottom's cock, and told him to suck. Then, after a moment, she told him to stop. Then she showed him how it was properly done. Top watched, then practiced for a while, using his hands as well.

After a short while, she changed the men up and lectured Bottom on the finer points of cock sucking while she sat on Top's face. She told him to use his fingers.

Then she did something the men had never heard of, let alone seen. She had the men lie on their backs, balls to balls, with each having the right leg raised at the knee so the other man's left leg could lie extended under the angle.

She climbed on top and squatted down over the two phalli. She slipped them in, one at a time, getting the sense of the feel of them separately. Then she held the two tightly together and slipped them in the same hole simultaneously. She settled down with a deep sigh.

"Don't say anything. Don't move unless I say so," she said.

She proceeded then to do them, using their knees as arm rests, squatting over them, using them until she drained them. Both men came at the same time, she drawing the power in, working her inner energetic channels, coalescing the forces in her belly, pulling them into her crown. At the moment of her orgasm she raised her arms skyward from hugging herself, and toned an awful deep tone of 'AWW'. She released, through her hands, into the world all the energy she couldn't use to feed herself. A wave went out from her hands, a pulse out into the energetic world.

Almost ten miles away, camped down in the woods for the night, Quinn felt that pulse wash faintly over him. The hairs on his arms and the back of his neck stood up for a moment. He had a brief vision of the source of the pulse. He shook himself.

"Spooks," he said aloud.

21

RECOVERY

Angelica awoke in a room she didn't recognize. The walls were pale green, the color of a katydid. The curtains were dark, dark purple, and heavy. The bed was firm but the linens were soft and lovely and caressing.

And then she remembered. With the memory came a kriya, a full body spasm, so swiftly that she couldn't stop her spine from snapping back, her arms and legs contracting, her fingers and toes clawing at nothing but the empty air.

Into this emptiness she cried, "I don't want to be alone."

"You're not," said a voice from a dark corner. "I'm here."

Angelica sobbed. The spasm passed and she folded herself forward, contracting in to a full fetal position.

"Who are you?" she asked.

"I am Diana. I am assigned to watch over you."

"Well, fuck." Angelica said.

"Yes? Really?" Diana asked.

Angelica could sense the smile spreading over the face of the invisible woman. "No, fuck you. Not really. Oh, so not really," Angelica said.

Diana said nothing. Into that silence Angelica finally said, "Where are you?"

"You know." Diana said. And suddenly she did. Diana was sitting in an easy chair in a corner of the room, behind her. She sensed a closed door. Suddenly she sensed the dimensions of the whole room without even opening her eyes.

Then she asked, "Where am I?"

Diana said, "You know."

Angelica expanded her awareness outside the room, then outside the building the room was in. "I am in the Recovery."

"Yes."

"What happened to me?" Angelica asked.

"You know," Diana said.

Angelica gasped, sat up and shouted. Then she fell back and screamed, and spasmed again into a full kriya. Her mind flooded with memories, in a time distorted jumble, with the most intense experiences first.

She remembered the blow out sensation in her spine while she was on the altar, then the vision of the phallus looming over her face. She remembered the rape by her uncle. Then she remembered the pool, and the journey down the stream. The kriya released her, and she fell into shivering. With each new memory she wailed. With each memory diminishing in intensity, she cried out, then sobbed starting with an expelled "Oh! Oh. Oh."

The shivering slowed down and became twitches with longer times between them.

Then a remarkable thing happened. The twitches began to pool to-wards her belly, gaining slowly in speed and intensity. The center of the pool moved to her hips and slowly built, accompanied by sighs. The slow building of intensity as she bucked her hips compelled her to put her hands between her legs, covering her clitoris and opening. She felt she was protecting herself, but the bucking against her hand led to greater pleasure, pleasure with protection.

In a last effort to slow the wave she was riding, she cast her mind about her and looked wildly over her shoulder to see Diana sitting in the chair, upright with her hands palms together in the prayer position, eyes narrowed only to slits, and smiling mysteriously. Angelica felt safe and allowed herself to let go into the wave.

At first she sobbed. Then she wailed again, but the wail was not one of grief. It was a wail of ecstasy. She arched her back again, but this time not with a kriya of agony but a great arching explosion of orgasm. Again and again she bucked her pubis against her hands, and then she started laughing. At first, she laughed out loud for joy and she surprised herself. She wanted to become self-conscious but the laughter wouldn't let her. It just kept coming and coming, much like she was, coming in riding the waves.

The waves became spasms, then twitches, and her cries slowed to become a chuckle, then a sigh. Then three more sighs as she slowed down, arriving in the present. She breathed, simply breathed, and paid attention to that, sensing her heart, sensing its slow beating.

"The lights around you were beautiful," Diana said.

Angelica stirred at the sound and sat up. Her hair had gone wild, the tangles from the stream water having dried. And now, from her thrashing in the bed, these had grown stiff and stuck out at wild angles, making her look like a mad woman.

Diana laughed out loud, and told her so. "You look like a mad woman."

Angelica's response was to turn toward her, widening her eyes and lips in a horrible face, raising her hands like they were claws. She stuck her tongue out at Diana, making "Hah! Hah!" noises and slurping sounds.

Diana laughed out loud and jumped up, clapping her hands once. "Oh, good!" she said.

Angelica rose from the tangled sheets and made for Diana, suddenly screaming, leaping just before she got to Diana. Diana braced herself, and caught her, hugging her in toward herself from outside Angelica's arms, using the momentum to turn around in a full circle and pin Angelica on the near side of the bed.

Angelica kept screaming and began pounding and clawing on Diana's back. Diana slowly slid her arms down over Angelica's arms, pinning her. Pelvises pressed together Angelica bucked and struggled, kicking at Diana's calves.

Once her arms were pinned, Angelica tried to head-butt her but Diana was waiting for this and easily moved away.

Diana sent a pulse of energy into Angelica's pubic bone which divided into two, shooting down her clitoris into her vagina and upward into her dan tien below her navel.

"Stillness," Diana said. "Stillness." With a breath filled with power, Diana breathed over Angelica's face, and she went still. Her eyes closed.

"If I let you go now will you be calm?" Diana asked.

Angelica nodded yes. Diana then planted a kiss on her, right on the lips, and jumped back. Angelica's eyes popped open, so filled with surprise she couldn't do anything else. Then the feelings passed through her: of anger, of shame, of joy, then pleasure. She had seen an emotional off-ramp leading away from what would have been grief, or possibly despair, following the shame, and then hatred following grief. But she chose to step out of that cycle of negative emotion, to break it, and feel into the positive because that was where life was.

Sitting up, the image of her rape came to mind. She could hold the image of it only briefly, and remain safe. She knew she would have to work through it sometime but not now. That contemplation led from shame into grief. She saw she could sink into despair because of it. But the ultimate despair would be a kind of death to a feeling in which she could feel the possibility of a desire to continue living. She didn't want to run away, and she didn't want to sink.

She flashed on what followed if she chose grief and despair. It would be hatred and loathing, and she would begin to want to cause pain to those who had hurt her. She would live for that. That would become her desire, the desire to cause pain in someone else.

It became clear to her why she had to take the other path. By stepping away from despair and its inevitable descent to hatred, by stepping toward Love, she would feed her desire for pleasure, and that would feed her desire to live.

She saw a circle then in her mind's eye: a circle where the Love would turn to a sense of Pride. True pride in a good accomplishment well done, not a pride that would feed her vanity but a pride that would feed her soul, feed her feelings. She saw that this would lead round to Happiness. From Happiness she would move on to Joy; a joy that would be the opposite of the grief and despair into which she might otherwise fall.

She wanted to continue to live. So Pleasure and Love it was. But the kiss still pissed her off.

Diana, watching her, asked, "Figuring it out?" Angelica nodded yes.

"Come on then," Diana said, and held out her right hand. Angelica took it with her left hand and stood up. She moved to slap Diana but the other woman countered it, blocking it but not forcing Angelica's hand away.

"Look, Angelica, I know what you're going through. I've gone through it myself. So I am not your enemy, I am your friend. I am your older sister. I know the way."

Angelica relaxed visibly. Diana said, "I know. Come. You get to take a hot shower and wash your hair. You can eat something, too."

Angelica's stomach rumbled with hunger at the thought of food. Diana smiled. Angelica looked at her sideways, and couldn't keep a smile off her face. Then she covered it up and set her lips in an expression that looked to be mock anger. She shook her head. "You pissed me off."

Diana laughed again, "Yes, I know. I told you. I know. Now, the shower's this way," nodding her head to the left.

Angelica's wild hair brushed Diana's arm as she walked by, bouncing with the sway of her hips as she stepped. On a sideboard on the wall opposite the bathroom door were two peaches sitting on a bed of mint in a small bowl. Angelica looked directly at it. "I'll bring it," Diana said, following her.

Walking into the bathroom Angelica sat down on the toilet. Suddenly she realized she was naked. She put her hands between her thighs and leaned forward, rounding her shoulders and squeezing her thighs together. She peed a little while Diana turned the faucets on and got the water warm.

She looked with some interest at what Diana was wearing. She was barefoot, wearing a blue sarong with some sort of Celtic print over what appeared to be a full slip in midnight blue. A tan alpaca shawl was draped over her shoulders.

"There's a seat inside you can sit on. Come here, let me help you in," Diana turned and held out her hand.

Angelica moved to get some paper. Diana said, "Just come here. You don't need it."

Angelica got up, and accepted the hand. Diana led her to the shower and said, "Test it. Good for you?"

Angelica came close to the other woman, and could feel the energy when she got close. Something like heat, but not just warmth. She felt something like a field she could relax in, so she did, and held out her free hand to test the water. "Just don't kiss me this time," she said.

The water was fine to start. Angelica stepped in and stood there, water pouring on her head. Then she lifted her head, so the water landed on her throat, and then her breasts and heart. "Ouch. Ouch, ouch, ouch," she said, pulling back and crossing her arms to cover her nipples, still raw from the excursion down the stream. The scratches on her belly and thighs burned, and she had skinned one of her knees pretty good dragging it over the rocks.

Diana said, "Turn around then, and sit down. Let the water work on your back." Angelica did as she was directed. Diana turned from the door and folding the shawl, put it on the counter next to the food. She removed the sarong, and laid it there also, draping down. She pulled the slip off over her head, keeping an eye on Angelica all the while. She dropped the slip on the sarong and stepped in. "Now who else would wash your hair," she said, anticipating Angelica's objection.

"There's a new toothbrush and some paste on the shelf in a cup. They're for you." Diana said. Angelica looked up and reached for them. As she brought them back down she glanced at Diana, whose pubes were at eye level and noticed that Diana shaved. She glanced down, then up and realized that Diana shaved everything but her forearms and head. Her beautiful chestnut colored hair was now wet at the tips, clinging to her full breasts.

Angelica turned her head and dropped her face again. "Pretty," she thought. Then she thought she heard Diana's voice in her head saying "You, too."

Diana smiled at her, "Relax, sister. Let me care for you now, because there is more to come. Don't worry about it, but rest, so that you will be prepared." Angelica looked down again, focusing on putting the paste on the brush, smelling the fresh mint, and realizing her mouth was filled with sour tastes. Brushing, she remembered the stream, and swallowing water as she descended. Then she remembered before that, Jake's beautiful phallus in her mouth, and his sweet kisses.

She twitched, and in that twitch her soma cut loose and she was suddenly spasming. Diana put her hand on Angelica's head, grabbed a handful of hair, and pulled her head back. She grabbed the toothbrush from her mouth. "Stop it! Breathe! Stay present!" she commanded.

Angelica spasmed once more, her sensation orienting to the pulled hair on top her head, and gasped, leaning forward. Diana let her, keeping hold of the hair. "Are you here? Say so," Diana said.

Angelica nodded and said weakly, "Yes." She spit, toothpaste falling out on the shower floor, and held out her hand, "I'm not finished," she said.

"Where'd you go? Back to the Chapel?" Diana asked. Angelica nodded yes. "Don't go there again, yet. There will be time later."

Angelica wondered to herself if Diana meant "go there" as in "go there for real". Diana said, "No, of course not, silly." Slowly the awareness dawned on Angelica that Diana heard that thought in her head, without her speaking. Diana handed back the toothbrush and said, aloud, "Of course I did."

A second wave of awareness rolled through Angelica and she turned and looked up at Diana, eyes filled with wonder, toothbrush paused in her mouth.

"Hold still," Diana said, smiling with such love that tears came to her eyes, "Let me wash your hair." Angelica felt tears welling up in her, too. She turned her head back and looked down. Tears dripped onto the shower floor as she finished brushing her teeth, determined not to cry.

But, even as she finished and spit she knew she wouldn't be able to help it. Diana held the cup under the water, filled it, and passed to her. She rinsed and spit again, the tears still flowing. So she raised her face, hair hanging back into the water, and just let the tears roll silently down her cheeks, mixing with the water like rain falling on the sea.

Angelica sat like that, head back, hands on her knees, while Diana shampooed and rinsed her hair. Diana then laid in a conditioner that smelled of some flowers she couldn't identify.

When she was finished, Diana crushed some mint under Angelica's nose, and said, "Here. Eat, while we wait." Angelica brought her head forward and opened her eyes as she turned toward Diana. She saw the hand holding out a peach. Hers eyes followed the forearm, and she noticed Diana's belly. In the shimmer of water she noticed a faint pattern of scars, stretch marks in ovals like tiny feathers, rising up from her low belly and spreading out to the sides, rising up like a tattoo of a pair of matched silver wings, the tips disappearing somewhere higher on the sides, higher than her navel.

Angelica took the peach and looked down again. "Where's your kid?" she asked, almost dully.

Diana replied, "With their Dad. We take turns working."

Angelica was surprised and asked, "This is your job? You work here?"

Diana, taking a bite of the other peach, said, "In a manner of speaking," and motioned with her hand to Angelica to take a bite.

She bit into it, and it exploded with juice into her mouth, "Oh my gawd," she said around the fruit, as the juice rolled down her chin and down her thumb into her palm.

"Diosa," Diana said, and began combing the tangles out of Angelica's hair with her fingers.

Angelica was still reacting to the magnificent flavor and juiciness of the peach. It was at the perfect moment of ripeness, skin just taut enough to hold it together until the edges of her teeth broke through, releasing a fruit that was almost pulp already, flesh and juices rolling into her mouth, folding around her tongue, forcing her to swallow. But, still around this, holding up her free hand to her chin to catch the juices, she said again, "Oh my gawd, this is sooo good, oh my—what?"

"Diosa," Diana repeated, continuing to rake through the tangles.

Angelica shook her head, and said, "What? What are you talking about?"

"Her," Diana said, nodding at the peach. "Her. Around here we don't say 'gawd' much. We say Diosa, or Goddess." Nodding again at the peach, she said, "Her. Eat your peach," and then Diana one-eyed winked at Angelica.

Slowly, thoughtfully, Angelica turned and took another bite. The flavor filled her mouth again, saliva swelled to meet it, and she swallowed, the fruit so sweet and tart it bit at the back of her throat.

She looked at the peach falling apart in her hand and wondered silently, "These people worship a peach?"

Diana laughed out loud, almost a bark of laughter. "That's funny,' she said. And then, "One could do worse than worship a peach."

Angelica turned and looked up at her, one eyebrow raised, the question not even needing to be thought, let alone spoken. Diana smiled, "It's a symbol, dear. Every part of it has symbolic meaning. Can you read it?"

Angelica looked at it: the skin, the color, the little valley that ran from the stem to the bottom, the fruit, the seed. She shook her "no", and said, "I don't get it."

"You will," Diana said. "Lean back again and let me rinse."

Angelica did, leaning her head back into the flow, letting it pound on her skull, hearing the water drop from both inside and outside. She let the water cascade through her hair like hanging vines in a water fall. Diana spread the hair out, holding it in her hands, making sure the tangles were gone.

After a minute she said, "Stand up, and turn around, let me see those scratches." Angelica did, suddenly both self-conscious and proud. Diana made a serious face, almost a frown when she looked at her nipples. Then she looked at the scratches on down her belly and her thighs. "Here, she said. "Put your foot up on the seat so I can look at your knee."

Angelica noticed how it suddenly hurt to bend it, and put a hand out on Diana's shoulder to steady herself as Diana bent down to look. "You'll be OK," Diana said. Then she stood up, opened the door, and stepped back out of the shower. "There's a bar of soap in the corner. Be careful but wash yourself." Diana grabbed a towel as she closed the door and started drying off.

Angelica did, rubbing the bar under the water with her hands to make it lather, and turned away. She washed her hands and elbows first. She carefully washed her breasts, then under her arms and down her belly, pausing at each scratch and nick. She hadn't realized how dirty she'd gotten, crawling up the bank through the mud. The dirt washed off and pooled down the drain. She washed her face then, and her neck, holding her hair up with one hand. Then she washed her pubes, and down the crack of her butt, bending over to rinse off and start on her legs.

She felt something seem to roll over inside her, and then she cramped, low in her abdomen. She wondered if her period was coming. If so it would be five days early.

"I don't think so, not yet," Diana said. Angelica shook her head, thinking, "How did she know?" and heard Diana respond out loud, "You know. Keep washing."

She did as she was told and finished washing down her legs and feet. Even the tops of her toes were scratched, her nail polish was scratched and chipped, the ends of some of the nails ragged. She remembered again the old woman, encouraging her, even pushing her once, or was it twice? down the narrow freezing stream. "What was going on there?" she asked to herself, but out loud this time.

Diana, from out in the other room by the bed, said, "Not yet. Later. Finish up now."

While she was bent over, washing one foot up on the seat, Angelica wondered why she wasn't irritated with all this mental hearing of her by Diana. "Because you like it," Diana said. "Remember you said you didn't want to be alone?"

Angelica said, "Huh," under her breath and decided to stop thinking. So she did. In the other room, Diana smiled.

Angelica finished rinsing and turned off the water. She stepped out, picked up one of the two towels lying on the counter and wrapped up her hair. She toweled off her back with the second towel. When she rubbed down her front she snagged her nipples again. "Ouch, ouch, ouch, fuck me, ouch." Diana's smile grew broader.

Angelica walked out into the bedroom still scowling. While she had been washing, Diana had dressed, gone out into the waiting area, and brought in some cashews from a cabinet in the small kitchenette. Angelica grabbed a handful from the bowl as she passed by.

Diana was on the other side of the bed opening the heavy curtains, revealing a slat blind underneath. She turned, pointed to the bed, and said, "There's a jar on the bed. Open it and rub some on your cuts and bruises. It'll help."

Angelica went over, picked it up, and opened it. She sniffed it suspiciously. It smelled like honey on the surface and then of something deeper, heavy, almost bloody. "What is it?" she asked.

"Arnica, among other things," Diana replied.

Angelica sniffed it again. "Smells like old sneakers. Toe cheese, or something."

Diana said, "That's the Valerian."

Angelica didn't really know what these herbs were, but she acquiesced. The ointment felt cool on her skin, and her knee seemed to just soak it up. She spread some on her toes and the tops of her feet then dabbed some on her other scratches, especially her elbows. The relief was wonderful. She gently dabbed some on her nipples, which immediately crinkled up and got hard. The almost electric charge of it connected straight to her clitoris and she made an involuntary "Ooo" sound, shivering once. If she paid attention to it, she realized it would start to grow hard itself, so she decided not to think about it, and pulled her mind away from the sensation of growing warmth. She noticed her nipples were warming, too.

Diana had opened the wooden slats so that daylight came in to the room. She turned off the light standing in the corner and came around from the window. She went to a closet off the hallway on the other side of the bathroom door. She returned with a thin pile of clothing; a black satin thigh length slip, and a sarong in deep green with a black Celtic pattern that matched Diana's. Underneath that was another light weight alpaca shawl, a darker tan than Diana's and it had an embroidery edging of pretty white flowers, flowers that she thought she recognized.

"Angelica," Diana said.

"What?" Angelica replied, her mouth remaining slightly open, thinking Diana had addressed her.

"No," Diana said, shaking her head. "The flowers. They're Angelica."

Angelica closed her mouth, shook her head and looked down. "This is getting to be too much. I don't like you hearing me in my head. I don't understand it. It makes me feel guarded."

Diana replied, "But you can hear me in your head, too."

Angelica objected, "Yes, but only when you're in my head. I can't get into yours. I don't hear your thoughts in your head."

Diana laughed. "There aren't that many." Then, "Come on. Get dressed. We have some things to take care of."

"I still don't like it," Angelica repeated, then she moved to comply.

She unfolded the slip and pulled it over her head. She noticed it had a broader strap across the shoulder than she was used to, but when she stood up to pull the slip down she noticed that it felt good. It spread out the weight of the dress. She slowly lowered the slip, easing each breast into its place one at a time. The slip felt light and cool.

She stood up and wrapped the sarong tightly around herself then rolled the top edge of it down as she pulled it up to tighten the cinch. Diana handed her a long cloth belt to tie below the roll. Angelica picked up her shawl and followed Diana down the hallway to the waiting room. No one was sitting at the desk. Her sandals, and Diana's, were on a mat next to the door. She turned to Diana and asked, "What day is it?"

Diana said, "Tuesday. You're supposed to leave in four days. You've been out since Friday night." And then she added, "You were dreaming a lot. You made a lot of noise. You were lost in the waves of energy. You would wake up some times and a couple of times you even talked to us. Do you remember any of it?"

"Yes. It's all there, and I think I can access it if I want. But I don't want to, yet. There are some things in there I need to look at."

"Yes, it looked like you were re-living some things. We can talk about it when you're ready. Is there anybody you need to call? Anybody who's expecting you?"

"No, I called my parents. I told them I was staying on for the advanced class."

"After this, you can tell them you've decided to stay for yet another class."

"Is there really another class?"

"Not really. But you can stay. We can always find something for you to learn. There's a program. I think it's a good idea for you to stay. You need to understand what happened to you, and why. You need to be able to control your energies, and we can teach you how to do that." Diana watched her closely.

"Stay out of my head," Angelica said. "Let me think."

"I am," Diana said. "Check in with yourself. You won't be able to feel me there."

Angelica did, looking down, then closing her eyes. She saw only a pale green field of fog in her mind, she felt nothing else. She felt she might just step out into the field, and started to sway on her feet. Diana reached out and touched her on the shoulder.

"Come back," Diana said, gently. "Come back. I could see you go, and I don't want to have to try and catch you before you fall."

Angelica opened her eyes and straightened up. "I need to sit down," she said, and reached out for the nearest chair.

Diana tracked her intently. "You see now about how you need to control your energies? You need to be able to control your awareness, and where it goes. We can help you. Will you stay?"

It was clear to Angelica that she wasn't ready to go anywhere. Even the short time she had been out of bed had tired her. She knew she was in no shape to make a long drive. She looked up at Diana. "I have no real reason to go anyplace. I was just going to go home and start looking for a job, or an internship somewhere. I just finished college and I came out here sort of just to take a break and get my head together and reattached to my body." She paused, then said, "I didn't foresee any of this, though," gesturing with her palms up. "I'm starting to feel a little lost."

"Stay, then" Diana said. "You will need time to re-orient, and integrate.

You won't feel lost, anymore."

"How much?" Angelica asked, dropping her hands, and looking squarely at Diana.

"How much what? You mean money? None. Nothing. You're a guest, our guest. You stay for free."

"Are you sure?" Angelica asked.

"Yes, I'm sure, Angelica, for as long as it takes," she said.

Angelica knew this was an easy decision, an easy place to stay, and she felt safe here. Even though they didn't know her, really, she felt they knew about what was happening to her. And that talking with Diana completely inside her head stuff was amazing. Some part of her wanted to know, and understand.

"I'll stay," she said.

Diana thought, "Wise" and Angelica heard it, but not like it was in her head, but like it was in Diana's head.

"I heard that," Angelica said. "You said, 'Wise'".

"Now who's in whose head?" Diana laughed.

"Yes," Angelica replied.

"Good one," Diana said. Then "Come," and she gestured. "Let's try going for a walk."

They both moved to the door, shawls in hand. They both bent over together to slip their sandals on, and pull the straps up over the heels, Angelica thinking, "Someone brought these over here for me."

Diana pushed open the screen door and they stepped out into the world, Angelica counting thresholds.

22

CHILDREN

It was an unexpected benefit from the crossing of Calley's and Alam's lines that the children grew out of infancy quickly. They acquired motor skills and communication skills more in the way of Alam's animals.

They learned to walk and go about almost immediately. They learned to feed and take care of themselves, and they learned to communicate in understandable language. The pace of development slowed down as they aged, but there was accelerated development all the way into young adulthood.

The birth of the children was spaced 500 years apart in mortal time. When She was two thousand years old, the eldest daughter, Torey, had long completed her developmental growth. The middle child, the son named Balan, at fifteen hundred years had finished growing and was treated by his parents as a young adult. The third child, a daughter, Maray, was finishing her adolescence.

It was over these two thousand years that the awareness, worship, and understanding of Brighid was almost completely destroyed. The children were angry about the fate of their Aunt, and all She suffered. She suffered what Her people suffered. The persecution, the incarcerations and tortures, the burnings at the stake, all at the hands of the forces of the alien invader; all these Brighid suffered, right alongside Her people. When the lives of Her people were taken while they were in belief of Her, She would soothe their souls and escort them to the fields of the afterlife, where they could dwell, for a time, in peace and plenty.

Calley helped Her as best She could, hiding people in fogs, raining so hard that wagons and horses would become mired in the roads, and generally making the lives of the invading soldiers miserable. The memory of Brighid survived a long time; long enough to be written down, and the record of Her name was preserved. Even Calley's name was preserved here and there, somewhat to Her dismay.

Brighid grieved for their loss for a long time. But for the children, it was a blessing. Their Aunt spent much more time with them growing up than She could have otherwise. They learned the skills of their Aunt. She taught them to read and write, how to care for animals, and how to cook and be helpful around the house. When they were a little older, She taught them healing and music.

She worked sometimes in the smithy with their father, making small items and toys. The children would watch them, Brighid and Alam, working closely, laughing together. She was happy there, and it made the children happy to be around them. Their mother was also happy when Her sister was around. The children knew, of course, that the three of them would sleep together most nights, even though their Aunt had her own house. It was built for Her by their father, there, in the compound in the Hidden Lands.

As they moved into adolescence Calley would take them, individually, with her on her journeys, for training purposes. It was necessary that they master the magics of the storm and manipulation of their appearance. It was extremely inconvenient when the children practiced storm magic in the hidden compound. Laundry, for example, would never dry hanging on a line or lying out on the rocks. practicing had, more than once, turned the yard into a pool of mud. This was fun for the children to play in, but problematic when they wanted to come in the house. A good, hard, cold rain, summoned by Calley, soon taught them that there were consequences to inappropriate application of magic.

Torey, the new Goddess of the Storm in the Highlands, was both wild and stern, as eldest daughters often are. With her, Calley had to work on cultivating mercy. Pounding animals and men into the ground with rain, causing them to hang onto something to remain in place in the wind—these things were funny in the beginning to Torey. She added anger to her experimentation when the clear-cutting of the ancient forest started. Calley had to reprimand her about killing the soldiers with lightning strikes. Torey came to understand that killing was to be reserved for especially bad people, although She disliked it. The argument that finally persuaded her was that too much killing would bring the attention of the enemy's priests and magicians. That could then reveal that some of the old powers were still active and alive. And according to Grandmother's instructions they were to remain hidden and forgotten.

Balan understood this readily. For some reason he took an interest in plants and flowers at an early age. A keen observer as a child, he would sit and marvel at the way plants would respond to rain, how they grew and unfolded. His focus became how to bring the right amount of rain, and when—especially since he was responsible for much of the rain. It had to rain nearly every day somewhere in his lowland territory. Sometimes the best he could do was to hold the water back slightly, so that it fell in ways that weren't damaging. He worked the same way with the prevention of damaging winds.

Maray, the youngest, would be responsible for the storms on the seas surrounding their island. When She was little She was unhappy about this, because the storms would, of necessity, harm and kill people. She eventually came to understand that storms at sea were a necessity, and that, as long as She was fulfilling Her role, any harm that came to people was the result of their own choice to be where they were when the storm came. There were other inducements as well: there were Goddesses in the water. In time, Her propensity for making friends, as She would with Regina, and later, Amanda, led Her into deep friendships with those Goddesses of the Waters. In particular, one, still alive, who emerged from the water in the time of the Titans and was dedicated to Love.

Destiny and fate play a greater role in the life of Divine and Sacred Beings. It is a paradox of their existence that, while on the one hand they seem to be subject to fewer natural laws than mortals, on the other hand they are more closely and strictly bound to the remaining laws. They have both more freedom, and less freedom than mortals.

It was in this regard that special arrangements had to be made to preserve and protect Calley and Her family. All life performs its functions through the transformation of energies—from lower to higher, and higher to lower. And all must eat to live.

Since the most ancient times, those Divine and Sacred Beings that were favorites of the people were dependent on the worship of the people for their food. Deities of the elemental or natural principle types were less subject to the vagaries of human projections. They could be, when properly invoked, invited to be present, even if they chose to remain invisible.

Calley, more so than Bree, was one such deity, as elemental as a storm and as much a natural principle as the wind. Bree, being the patroness of several human arts, found it more difficult to survive. At times, She had to lean on Calley for support. The children did, too. They were half mortal, and that half needed occasional mortal sustenance. But Alam was a problem. He had already lived far longer than his mortal lifespan and could only enter the mundane world shape-shifted into one of his forms. The nutritive support he required was always in the process of discovery and adjustment.

In the compound yard in the Hidden Lands there was a vegetable garden and a few sheep in the paddock. But it was a scant resource they managed and it became Calley's responsibility to figure out how to feed Alam, so that he would continue to live. Calley worked out some solutions to the problem: the largest component was to feed Alam rain. She knew that She could alter the composition by thinking about it, and so was able to get many of the minerals and nutrients in it that he needed. But Alam, and to a lesser extent the children, needed bulk. So Calley became a herder, taking the children along with Her. Even Alam could come along, so long as he did not stay too long away from the Hidden Lands.

For Bree, with Her more insubstantial needs, Calley allowed Her to receive devotion from Alam, on the condition that Alam remained truly devoted to Calley. It was not as much devotion as that to which Bree was accustomed. But, it was more available and better fashioned than a lot of what She had received from the mortals of the mundane world, given Alam's unique nature and status.

One day the entire family had been outside the Hidden Lands, working on herding some cattle into a pen. Alam had tried leading them. But Balan, in bull form, was best at it. However, he was slow. Maray worked the strays with Her horse form, and Torey and Calley stood and watched, commenting and shouting advice, most of it errant, much to their amusement and the frustration of the others. Bree had tried to walk along beside Balan but found that made the cattle even more shy, so She went and stood by Her sister and niece upslope from the path the others were trying to move along.

The troop, with their cattle, finally arrived at the wall of the compound. Sitting on top of it was, to everyone's delight, Calley and Bree's mom, the children's Grandmother. She did not visit often, as she was afraid of revealing the existence of the Hidden Lands. She was laughing at the difficulty the family was having herding the animals to their pen.

She said, "Look, silly ones. Look at what you can do." She, with Her mind, called the cattle to attention. They formed a line, looking at Her. She made a clear image in Her mind and sent it to the cattle. Then they all turned as one and filed into the pen. Grandmother was laughing the whole time.

"Look, you all can do this, too. Even you, now, Alam. The work Calley has done with you about communicating with Her applies to these animals, also. Project the image to the right part of their heads, right between their eyes, and they will do what you show them to do. Come children, come. Try it." Grandmother used Her mind to make a half a dozen cattle leave the pen.

"Now you try it," She said. The cattle looked at the family expectantly. "Come on," She encouraged. "Each of you pick one."

Calley and Brighid sat on the wall with their Mother and watched as one cow turned and walked back in the pen, another lay down, another started turning in circles chasing its tail. Yet another started hopping from side to side. Everyone laughed. When these latter two started protesting Grandmother said, "Enough, enough already. Try to make them do only things they understand. Alam, how imaginative of you to make the cow lie down. It probably would have done that anyway, out of boredom if for no other reason."

The cow that was lying down rolled over on its back and waved its feet in the air. "That's more like it," Grandmother said. When the laughter died down, She turned to Her Daughters and said, "Let's go inside now. We need to talk. Bring him with you," She indicated Alam with Her head.

The four of them came together in the dining hall, over mugs of stout and a board of bread, butter, and cheese.

Over the years, Alam had built a series of rooms, some with doors between them and others only sharing a wall. Hearths were usually back-to-back, one in each room, sharing chimneys. The dining hall was open to the kitchen, which was open to a pantry room on the other side. Under this pantry was a cellar where ale, and other food, was stored. These rooms and buildings were all standing away from the compound wall, now chest high with the main gate on the east side, and smaller gates in the other directions.

The bedrooms were at either end of the line, the children's on one end, and Alam and Calley's on the other. Just beyond that, in a separate house, were Bree's quarters. There were several other freestanding buildings—the barns and animal sheds, the smithy, and storage buildings. Even though none of this was necessary from Calley's perspective, She liked that he had done the work, in case, as he put it, someone ever saw the Hidden Lands. In that case it would look like a normal homestead.

Grandmother, "She who is the mind of all the life on the planet", began simply. "My family, I love you. I am happy that you are all safe, and happy yourselves. Here I can smell the sweetness that makes life worth living.

"You know," She continued, "That the face of the world has changed very much in these past few thousand revolutions around the light. You must know that we are here for a reason.

"I am here because I will be wherever there is life. But you also know, although I will state it, I was unable to stop my rape. I made an attempt to counter the foul influence of De Murgos on the minds and feelings, on the spirits and souls of the people, by using his own weapon, what they call religion, against him. In a land not too far from where his people dwelled I arranged to have my own people make ceremony. They made ceremony on the high hills, around huge fires, dancing, drinking, eating my sacred plants, and chanting. They would chant until one of my consorts would come. And he would love them, love them all. Men and women would fall down in ecstasy. I selected a special group of women to do this ceremony by themselves. The chant I gave them was the reverse of the secret name of De Murgos. His unconscious mind was summoned, and these women would love him. He could not, this unconscious part of himself, resist them. He loved them all, and since I was in all of them, my hope was to turn him from the madness of my rape with the power of Love.

"It almost worked. Under the influence of Love he neglected those poor souls he had first hypnotized into obedience to him. His people were even sold into slavery. His helpers, even his enemies, could do nothing to rouse him from the somnolence to which Love had reduced him. And then one day he awoke. Some cry for mercy from one of the slaves pierced his sleep and roused him. He arranged to send a son among them, who led them from slavery, and back into lands where the people remembered me first. They slaughtered my people, all the men, and enslaved the women and children themselves.

"In time he figured out my ruse. He came to understand the spell that sent him into somnolence. He sent a second son to make a people to destroy my people, my chanters by the hilltop fires. It took a long time, but his people murdered almost all of my people, murder in the most horrid ways. Then he sent a third son to destroy the children of the people who originally enslaved his, and then to destroy all the people that could be found who had even the faintest notion of who I was, and who I am.

"I have survived the brutality because there is life, but it is not the life that was. It is no longer natural in the way it was. What is natural now is confined to what they call parks and the few wild places that the people do not live. Among the people it is almost impossible to find anything natural about them and the ways they live. Most of the people are simply surviving, if not struggling desperately to survive, one day to the next, and they scarcely have any time or energy to fulfill their duties, let alone remember Me.

"The invaders, De Murgos and his minions, are almost finished with the rape. He has sent his sons repeatedly to herd the people into his maw. He has feasted so long on the souls of most of the people that his palate is beginning to crave something new, some other planet perhaps. What worries me is that he will introduce some new form of suffering for the people, something that will send him new and different energy. I worry that he will send some new, more horrible son.

"So, in this moment his grip is loosened by his distraction, and it is time to begin a counter move. He has retreated to the far side of the moon and is not paying such close attention. Hopefully, we will get them off this planet, and off of me."

Both daughters were sitting with their hands in their laps, looking down and crying. Alam, one fist held in the other palm, looking out the window so no one would see his tears, said, "So, Mother, what would you have us do?"

"Misdirection. Trickery. Sleight of hand. Direct action when the moment is right, and not before. And whenever possible, we will use proxies in this fight. We will use those humans who have chosen to ally themselves with Me. They will do this, they will make whatever sacrifice, out of love for life.

"A young woman has appeared outside the gate, yes?"

The daughters nodded their assent.

"A human, but she was born able to see, and she has seen this place. She will also know it is magic. You are to help her, and befriend her, particularly Maray, since she is closest to her in appearance.

"On a visit soon after this one, she will bring her mother with her. You should know, Bree, that her mother already loves you. She has sought out all the writing that remains about you. You may already know her, you may have felt her prayers. It is her most fervent prayer that you recognize her as your servant. I suggest you do so."

"I will, Mother," Bree replied. "It has been a long time since I opened the portal to receive the prayers of the people. I will do so, for you. When I come to know her, I will let you know about her fitness as a servant."

"Spoken like a true Goddess, child," Grandmother responded.

"Calley, your assignment is different. This is because, so long ago, you wished so fervently for a different life. You shall have it. Even your immortality will come in play. We don't know what will happen; I don't know what will happen. Your assignment will be in the new world. This is why we need the human child. We will need to ask her to find her father, long dead, and use him as an emissary to clear the way for you.

"Alam, also, I tell you, your life could be easily forfeit."

Alam replied, "Yes, Creator, I vow to die honorably in your service."

Grandmother laughed. "Yes, you do. And we can hope it will not be necessary."

Grandmother looked at Calley to see Her reaction, and wait for Her response. Calley had stopped weeping and had gone very still, an inscrutable expression on Her face. Finally she spoke: "Mother, I will do as you say. We talked about this long ago; we spoke of this possibility and I made a commitment then. Because I was willing to serve life, I understood that my own life was at stake. And I am deeply grateful that, with your help, I have had a family, I have had love, I have had a good life, a sweet life. And now there are my children to take over my duties and set me free—and the purpose was always to set me free. I thought perhaps it would be true freedom, freedom to live or die completely on my own terms. But now I see that I still have a higher duty, the duty of service to life in all that I do. I will follow your indications."

Grandmother sighed. "Good, then. I am pleased you understand now, my wild storm-riding child.

"So, now listen. This is what you will do when next the human child appears at the gate."

23

CURRICULUM THREE

"Do you really think that if you give a man enough sex and food that, once those needs are met, he'll suddenly become a good man? Isn't it true that once he has enough of those his other desires will rise up and he'll be off and making trouble now that he has some spare time? Making stuff, yes, but also making trouble, hoarding stuff, fighting over stuff, fighting with other men? Inventing religions? Isn't that how it's always been?" Regina, angry, asked her mentor Rachel, her mother Amanda, the business manager Beverly, and a new addition to the core group, an accurate psychic named Madeleine.

Rachel responded, "Yes. It has always been that way. Providing the sex and food is just to get their attention. Once we have it, the men have to be educated. They have to be educated about particular things, and about how to get along. They have to be educated about how to work, and, more specifically, what kinds of work.

"Remember, the Feminine Creates, the Masculine Makes. There must always be something for making, even if it's only making sacred art.

"The other factor you are not considering about sex is that we're not talking about giving a man enough sex to satisfy him. For most men, it's one and done, as your mother, I think, put it. Then their attention wanders off to food, or trouble, or making something. I'm talking about enough sex.

"Some men think that's three times a day. For other men, it actually is three times a day. But all men can respond more often than that. When a man can't get it up anymore for the day, that's it. I mean we have to fuck them into exhaustion. That's enough sex.

"When we can get them to that point, we let them sleep. When they wake up, we fuck them again. We do that, over and over, until they get it, somewhere deep down in their little lizard brain, that there is enough sex."

"So, that begs the question: what about enough sex for us?" Amanda asked.

"Yes, that is the next question. What about enough sex for us? Our capacity for sex is greater than a man's capacity. Would you agree?" Rachel returned the question.

"I don't know. Sometimes I just don't want it. I don't want to be pestered. Sometimes I'd even prefer to masturbate rather than have to deal with men," Amanda replied.

"I understand. And men often feel the same way, but we are more complicated than men in this regard. You are speaking on the emotional level now, rather than on the purely physical. You are speaking about emotional desire rather than physical desire. Or rather, I should say, the emotional component of desire. And, although we both, men and wen, relate to our physical sexuality in very intense emotional ways, these ways are different.

"So, think carefully about the physical component of desire for a moment. Is our capacity for sex greater than a man's or not?" Rachel's question filled the air.

There was a quiet pause for contemplation.

"I think," Regina responded, "that my capacity is greater than a man's, at least based on how much I think about it and want it, but am unable to act on my wishes, constrained as we are."

"Yes, you are correct, generally," Rachel said, "But understand this also: there is a difference. Most wen, most of the time, want more time to be spent in the sex they are already engaged in. Most wen want to have sex until they orgasm, and, often, until they orgasm several times. This takes time and work, and most wen are never given that opportunity.

"And understand also that, whereas wen generally want more time in any given tryst, men want more frequency, and generally do not care to spend a long time getting a wen to orgasm. Did you know that many men, especially when they're younger, could have sex three times a day and then masturbate three or four more times? And they would, too, if they could find the privacy.

"So this is why our training must address these behaviors. Men must be trained to control themselves, extend their erection time, and the time they have available to pay attention to the wen. This training will eventually allow them to separate orgasm from ejaculation. This will grab their attention and hold it. The reward in this kind of training is access to ecstasy, and there is a higher neurological circuitry involved in this that overwhelms the limited attention span of the lizard.

"And then, too, the chivalry involved in paying attention to the wen will appeal to that part of their emotional brain. Once they learn that it is in caring for the wen, and the wen's needs, a different circuit in their emotions comes into play. In their own minds, they become a kind of hero. This is the core of the emotional education of men. It is for the wen to realize that and respond appropriately.

"The wen's pleasure becomes part of the reward, and the wen, even if she must work for it, needs to learn to surrender to pleasure. She needs to learn the arts of her own ecstasy, also."

Rachel paused to let this sink in for Regina. After a moment Rachel said, "You used the word 'constrained' earlier. To what constraints were you referring?"

"Pregnancy, and particularly the fear of becoming pregnant. That whole bloody moon thing. What others will think," Regina answered.

"Yes, these are all true constraints. And constraints that men don't have. So what if the wen have everything they need? What would it be like if a wen could become pregnant with the certainty that she would have all the food and care and support that she might need until the child is grown? How would that affect the fear of pregnancy?"

"Would she also get all the sex she needed?" Regina asked, with a grin.

"Yes, of course, child." Rachel chided.

"Then yes," Regina said. "It would affect my fear. The idea of insecurity is what frightens me, even more than the fear for myself should the pregnancy be difficult. I can find the thread to that place in myself where I can be brave facing the natality. But it's much harder to extend that courage into a place of not knowing I will be cared for by others."

"Well, with us, you and the baby will have everything you need. So will the man, if you want to recognize him as the father. We encourage you to do this. Loss of paternity is one of a man's strongest fears. If you are incompatible with the father, too incompatible to live together, for example, we would support alternative living arrangements that would ensure he would still get to participate in the raising of the child," Beverly said.

"Speaking of which," Amanda interrupted. "What about the role of the grandmother?"

"Again, that depends; that depends on what's in the best interest of the child," Madeleine said.

"And how would you know that?" Amanda demanded, clearly triggered by the idea of Regina becoming pregnant.

"You know my position here, Amanda," Madeleine replied. "I am the Seeress. It is up to the decision of the mother and the High Priestess. I merely advise."

Somewhat mollified, Amanda backed down.

"Speaking of which" Rachel picked up the thread, "How is it coming, Regina, developing the self-knowledge necessary to know when you are fertile?"

"I am now able to sense when I ovulate." Everyone applauded. "Most of the time," she continued, and the applause stopped. "I mean,

I can sense something. I just wish there was a way to validate what I'm sensing."

"There is, child. Both Madeleine and I can do this—she because she can see it, and I, because I am trained to detect it. And I want you to be able to detect it, too," Rachel revealed as Madeleine nodded.

"It seems that when I detect it, the ovum takes some time getting to the uterus. That's true. Yes?" Regina continued, both confused and in pursuit of the resolution of the confusion.

"Yes. Four days, perhaps. So, unless you want to risk getting pregnant, which means no sex, or at least no coitus, from ovulation until a few days after your mucus is thinnest and most slippery. You're working with your basal temperature, too, aren't you? Keeping a chart?" Rachel continued.

"No, not really. It's such a pain in the arse," Regina complained again.

"How like a child you are, or still are, in this way," Rachel said.

"You don't have to insult me. We have condoms now," Regina said.

"Look, I wouldn't want to risk it. Refrain from coitus. No excuses. Practice the solo path. Find someone willing to have other kinds of sex with you," Beverly joined in.

"That's what we do. We all have consorts that act within the boundaries we set," Rachel concluded.

"And when will I have my consort?" Regina whined again.

"Soon, child, soon. Patience. The right man must be found and prepared. Our search is underway. It is not as if a trainable man can be found on every block, or even in every town."

On this note, Rachel asked the other wen to retire, leaving Rachel and Regina alone.

"So, tell me, Regina, how goes it with the circulation of the energies? And the path of solitary cultivation?"

"I have spent my mornings, after meditation, and my evenings after our meetings, in moving the energy of the second pulse as you have shown me. I set the sphere around me at first and then, beginning always with the small centers in my hands and feet, begin the circulations. The vibration starts quickly now. I have only to think it, and I am able to hold the awareness of the first four simultaneously. When the beat doubles I move the energy to my knees and elbows, repeating the pattern. Then my hips and shoulders. By the time I reach the core, I have lost my awareness of these, the first twelve points of focus. My breath is slowed. My heart is at rest.

"I summon the pulse to my opening, my phulva, and let it dwell there, expanding and contracting, coordinating with the breath. My tongue is on the roof of my mouth. I focus in the large centers, front and back, as you have shown me. As you said it would, the whirling has stopped, and now there is only the pulse. When the pulse doubles, I move to the next pair of centers above. When I arrive at the crown, the pulse drops straight down through the center of me to connect through my womb to my phulva. It is ecstatic, as you said it would be, and I work to keep my awareness present, present to this entire pulsing cylinder that has become my core.

"Then I insert the phallus, and run the pattern again. Only this time the image of the Diosa is there, in the central cylinder, sitting on my womb like it was a throne. Some version of this vision appears at each level of this pulse. At the top, in my head, behind my forehead, She is almost unimaginably bright, and smiling at me. I am happy to have pleased her, and I have come to think that it is Her pleasure that She is allowing me to feel.

"I change phalli, in accordance with the pattern you've told me, marking and focusing on the differences in sensation, feelings, and imagery. In each pattern I allow my awareness to move into the different points of presence, and pay attention, without trying to change anything about what is arising in my awareness.

"By the end of the third pattern I am trembling. My mouth floods with a sweet taste. Sometimes, still, I faint, returning to awareness as a heap upon the floor.

"Then, removing the phallus, I run the first pattern again, except in reverse, ending with my awareness in my hands and feet, and collapsing the sphere."

"Excellent, Regina. Oh, you are so good! Thank you for not fighting with me over these exercises. Just remember to focus first on sensations, then on feelings, then watch your thoughts as you go through the sequences. So tell me, what changes have you noticed when you are not practicing the cultivation?"

"Rachel, I'll be honest. I have become almost completely sexualized at the tactile level. Even a breeze can make me tremble with ecstasy. The things I touch, the things that touch me, even my clothes, all take me on the path to orgasmic ecstasy. It is hard to pay attention to anything mundane, anything other than this exquisite sensation, and the feelings of deepest joy at being alive and in the world.

"In only a few months you have shown me how to live the whole day in the Sacred, communicating with the Divine. There are no words for the Love I feel for Her, nor to describe how Her Love for me feels. And no words for my Love for you. I am blessed," Regina concluded, looking away shyly, and making a hand sign for gratitude.

Rachel sighed. "Go, child. Practice. And remember this: sex is a prayer."

Regina got up, turned and bowed at the door, and went to her room.

Rachel rose, turned out the light, and she went down the dark hall to her room, noticing a faint light from under her door. Craft was with Amanda that night, so she was expecting no one. Slowly she opened the door, and saw Madeleine, dark hair down, wearing a robe over a gown, reading by lamp light from the table beside the bed.

"Hello, friend," Rachel said.

Madeleine smiled, a little tightly at the end of it. "Hello, friend. I have missed you."

"And I you. Welcome home."

At this Madeleine looked down and then to the side, raising a knuckle to her lips, pressing them closed, fighting the need of her face to break into a sob.

"Talk to me," Rachel said, starting to undress. "Just talk to me."

So Madeleine talked, sobbing when she needed to. Rachel undressed, then dressed for sleep. Rachel sat at the vanity and brushed out her hair for the night, listening, watching, as Madeleine told the story of her long journey away from home.

In the end, Rachel rose, put Madeleine's book on the floor, kissed her hands, pulled back the cover, and sat in the middle of the bed, pulling Madeleine to her, and into her arms. "Come to me, beloved, and let me hold you while you rest."

Madeleine came into her arms, without resistance.

At the group meeting the next evening, Rachel was almost impossibly angry. Alternating, it seemed, between anger, then rage, then silence. "Madeleine, tell Regina the story you told me last night," she said.

Madeleine Crowe looked at Regina, her eyes at first piercing and focused. Then she softened them, gazing at Regina, her face solemn. "You'll go a long way," she said. Regina shivered.

"I was born in 1927," Madeleine started. "During the war, when I hit adolescence, things started to happen around me. Things would move, sometimes flying through the air and breaking when they landed. I started speaking in strange tongues and could spend whole days in trance. I wouldn't wash or care for myself in any way. I resisted being around people. When I was around people I would say things to them, about their private lives, or their health, that I couldn't possibly have known about.

"I had long spells of lucidity, so my parents didn't think I was insane, but they were at a loss about what to do. My mother heard about Rachel, and her travels, at a social event of some kind and became prepossessed about finding her.

"Rachel agreed to come and take a look at me. When she came, she just sat on the edge of the bed and held out her hand toward me, palm up. I could feel her there, even though she wasn't touching me. I opened my eyes and saw a woman on fire. I screamed but then I noticed that the woman wasn't burning; the flames were all around her, but like a halo.

"She held out an object toward me and said, 'Tell me the history of this'. I took it, it was a comb made of ivory, hand carved, with the teeth far apart for untangling knots. I told her it was her mother's—I saw her mother using it on her when she was a little girl. I told her it was old. She asked how old. I told her a hundred years. But no, I saw something else. She asked me what it was made of, and that one was easy: ivory. And then that something else came through. It wasn't an elephant, it was a hairy elephant, an elephant from long, long ago. I told her this, but I began to faint. I never heard any more questions; I was lost in the land of long ago elephants."

"I could confirm all this," Rachel said. "That it was fossil ivory was a surprise. But, it turned out, completely true. At the time, I just checked her pulses and confirmed she was journeying, that all was well, and that she would return. What I marveled at was that I had just met a genuine psychometrist—someone who could tell the history of an object by holding it her hand. I had only met one other, a lama from Tribhat. Your father."

Madeleine gasped. "Her father? Regina's father? Your David's father?"

"Yes. It was one of his Siddhi powers, psychometry," Rachel answered.

Regina spoke, "I did not know. About the power, I mean."

"He kept his powers largely hidden, except when it would serve his work. Sometimes, though, he would use them to create spectacles. Along with attracting the attention of people genuinely seeking the truth, the spectacles would draw out his enemies from hiding, where they could be dealt with. I will tell you more as we spend our time together," Rachel said. "Please, Madeleine, continue."

"Rachel agreed to work with me. My parents were only too happy to let me go. They had been fearful that I would have to be institutional-ized, maybe lobotomized.

"She brought me here. The poltergeist phenomena stopped. And there were others here. It was a sort of boarding school for odd children. More arrived. There were odd teachers here, as well; people who knew the things that Rachel learned in her travels.

"When I was grown, I was completely in control of my ability. And I knew a great deal else besides that almost no one else knew, except my sisters from my time here.

"Rachel asked me to undertake a mission for her. Many years before, when she had stayed with the Trants in Flora, she had heard the leg-ends of the Seven Sisters. She asked me to try to find any evidence of them; their temples or their worship. She arranged for introductions and guides.

"I stayed with the Trants for a long time, almost two years. I studied the ways of ecstasy, and how to bring the enlightenment near, for they be-lieve in finding the enlightenment through sex. I helped them move the whole tribe. It was after the war, and people were on the move all over. There were many opportunists, many warlords, and many seeking to establish their new ideas of order. The Trants had chosen to move deep into the jungle of a neighboring country where they would be tolerated and there would be less civil disorder.

"With their help, I returned to Flora to continue my work looking for the Seven Sisters. I was kidnapped by bandits, and raped, of course. My men scattered. I used my Trant skills to survive. Rachel arranged to have me ransomed, and by that time the bandits had even begun bringing me items they believed might be from a temple of the Seven Sisters."

"Who are the Seven Sisters?" Regina asked. "Or, rather, were."

Rachel looked sharply at Regina. Regina caught the look, and revised herself. "Perhaps later, you could tell me about the Seven Sisters. Tell me, were any of the objects brought to you real? Really from a temple? Could you tell?"

Madeleine smiled. Regina noted that Rachel was smiling also. She realized that this was part of a training in how to track what was important
in what was being said and ignore that which was a distraction from
the salient.

"Yes. There was one. The bandits were robbing graves at an old Temple
site deep in the jungle. They realized, looking at the grave goods, that
all the graves were for wen. This confirmed for me that it was some
kind of wen's Temple. There was not a lot of precious metal, almost no
gold or silver. There were some items, awls, knives of stone, pots that
must have held herbs or food. In every grave they found identical small
flowers of polished shell inlaid in wood that seemed to have hung on
silk cords. I had them bring me some to sketch, then return them. I kept
one to show Rachel.

"In one grave, however, they found an ivory egg. They brought it to
me. When I touched it, I could tell how it had been used. It was for
vaginal insertion, to gain control of the muscles. When I was alone I
turned it a certain way and the egg opened, revealing a golden ball
inside. The ball would roll around in the egg as the wen moved and the
sensations could be picked up from inside.

"When I held the ball in my hand I became overwhelmed with impressions from the time of Temple. The wen who lived there, their training
in devotions and sacred dances, their sexuality and relations with men.
All these were shown to me in visions. I also saw how the teachings
of the Trants were derived from the Temple teachings. I saw into the
source, into the mind of the Divine Feminine deity that guided and
inspired them—the energy they fed, and that fed them. The energy extended to the villages around the Temple—the villages that supported
the Temple.

"These wen were an orgiastic cult, I suppose you could say. On festival
days they would have sex in the villages, go about naked and seduce
the everyday people, right in public. They behaved sometimes as crazy
wen, or wild wen, or manifestations of the exorcised demons of the
unconscious mind.

"All this I saw holding the egg and the golden ball. The egg was in the
ground when the soldiers came, an army that destroyed the Temple
and chased the people away, or killed them. I could feel the feet of

the soldiers as they ran over her grave, the thumping of their footfalls imprinting into the trembling little ball. I could hear the echoes of the screams.

"When I was ransomed, I took the egg and ball with me, hiding it inside. I've brought it with me."

Rachel looked at the table between herself and Madeleine. Regina followed the glance and noticed a small pillow with a cloth covering what was clearly an egg shaped object. "You may look," Rachel said.

Regina raised the cloth and looked. It was the egg, the ivory so yellowed by age and use that it glowed golden in the light. She sighed at the beauty of the thing and covered it again.

Madeleine continued, "I went further north, into Windia. There were people Rachel wanted me to visit, teachers and temples. But the War changed things. Of the people to whom Rachel had given me letters of introduction, many were dead or retired, with other men running the temples and schools.

"Practices had changed, and wen were treated differently, even in the schools that practiced Maithuna"

"Maithuna?" Amanda asked.

"Maithuna. Ritualized public group sex," Rachel answered.

"Yes," Madeleine continued, watching how the idea of Maithuna affected Amanda and Beverly.

Amanda, she could see, countenanced the idea easily, based on her experience of the Hierogamy, the ceremony of the ritual marriage of the Divine Feminine and Masculine principles. Regina, Madeleine could see, was working to resist falling into the idea stream. Rachel watched closely also. Regina, eyes closed and focusing, asked, "So, tell me please, what happened as a result of the changes?"

"I was raped, again. And assaulted another time. The rapes took place at the schools, by the teachers. They weren't overtly brutal. I conceded; I simply did not give my consent. Do you understand the difference?"

"Yes, I think so."

"Worship of the Divine Feminine in all Her forms had declined across the country. Western ideas of the second class nature of wen had reinforced local patriarchal practices. There was a rise nationwide in the worship of the Destroyer, Skreeva. And among the practices of the people of the third son of De Murgos, the role of the wen had become more constrained.

"After that first time, the teachers took me without agreement, and without negotiation. They took me as if it was their right. They got to fuck me simply because they allowed me into their presence. There was no Sacred. No worship of the Divine. The flowers of respect had all died. It was simply a price—a price to be paid in order to learn, a price in addition to the menial work assignments—carrying waste to the public cesspools, for example. And there was very little teaching."

Madeleine paused, choosing what to say next. Regina took this as an invitation to ask a question.

"And what about the assault?"

"In one city, I had to rent a house and walk to the Temple every day. After the incident with the bandits, I kept body guards. One would walk ahead, one would trail behind. I was grabbed by a group of men while passing the entrance to an alley. They confronted the lead body guard and kept him from me when I screamed. A filthy hand came down over my mouth. By the time the trailing guard drew his pistol and made it down the alley, I was almost to the end, with a turn into an even darker alley. The rapists had already exposed my breasts, and were pawing at me. They already had their hands between my legs, holding them apart. A finger had already bruised its way into my anus.

"The guard fired a shot in the air. Men ran. Three hesitated, thinking that if they got me away they'd have to share me less, I suppose. The lead guard was freed and came into the alley when the men assaulting him ran away. This was too much for the last three, they dropped me and ran.

"When the guards came to my side they helped me cover my ripped blouse. I had lost my sandals, and I was afraid to stand up and walk until they were brought to me. When I arrived at the Temple I was summoned. The teacher commanded me to bend over in front of him and he proceeded to fuck me in the ass."

Madeleine paused.

"I couldn't move when he finished, I simply collapsed and spent the next half hour discharging, shaking violently on my belly. Eventually, I rolled to my side and pulled my knees up. I regained control of my breathing, and ceased my sobbing. He, of course, was nowhere around."

Into the silence that followed, Regina asked, "What did you do?"

"I met with the teacher one more time. I wanted to tell him that I had figured him out, what all his obscure aphorisms were meant to convey, why he taught by degradation. His response, when I started off by telling him this, was to grab my breast and squeeze it hard. He said, 'This is what you want, yes?' I rose up and walked away. I returned to my house, packed my things, and left Windia on the first steamer available for me to book passage."

"And would you like to know why I'm angry, Regina?" Rachel asked.

Regina could only nod.

"You have to understand: all this so-called science, the internal work, the tantra, the alchemy—all these orders and disciplines and religion—have held the Feminine to be the inferior gender.

"These men doing all this inner work, conserving substances, circulating energies; they all held that the men's practices should work equally well for wen, ignoring the screamingly obvious differences between wen and men. And then when the men's techniques didn't produce the same results in wen, they concluded that wen were inferior. Inferior!

"For example, in the men's work they focus a lot on the root chakra. There is theory that states this has a necessary impact on the endocrine system through the prostate gland, and that this endocrine system change is a necessary part of the process. Stick a finger up a man's ass and you'll find the prostate soon enough."

"No, thank you," Regina said.

"But why do you think these techniques don't work for wen? Because there's nothing there! No gland! Stick your finger up a wen's ass and there's nothing but space! If you look at it neurologically, the internal local nerve distributions are completely different.

"The biological analog of the prostate gland in wen is somewhere completely different: it's the little spot on the inside of the phulva, just behind the clitoris. It's called the paraurethral gland, the good spot, and sexually wise wen know all about it. Trust me, this gland produces substances as well—it's just that our ejaculate comes through it, picking up those substances as the fluid comes from a different place.

"And if focusing attention on the region is a critical part of the work for men, it better damn well be true for wen also. That means that in all that work, the wen were focusing on the wrong place.

"And, while it may be true that the anatomical analog of the testicles in men is the ovaries in wen, there's another screamingly obvious biological fact. Wen have a system for which men have no equivalence. Do you know what that is?"

"The womb."

"That's right. The womb. Men have nothing equivalent to the womb, and they, those high-faluting masters and yogis, usually pay this fact no attention. When they do, they consider it an annoyance, or worse, a sign of feminine inferiority. Men don't bleed once a month; icky wen do."

Rachel paused to take a breath. Amanda realized she had been gripping the arms of her chair, and relaxed her hands. Madeleine stared at her hands, folded together in her lap. Regina adopted a mudra.

Rachel spoke: "Look, it is not just the degeneration of the men of Windia into worship of the Destroyer, Skreeva. Every good thing the religions of the Three Brothers, the religions of the Three Sons of De Murgos, the good things these may have done does not yet outweigh all the bad things they have done. Slaughtering each other by the thousands, hundreds of thousands, and millions is not the worst thing they have done. Slaughtering hundreds of thousands and millions not of their own kind is not the worst thing.

"The worst things they have done are the bad things they have done to wen. Much worse than killing each other, much worse than hacking each other apart, much worse are the things they have done to wen. Much worse, the denigration of wen. Their men die, but their wen die worse, and even living as a wen among them may be worse than death."

A sudden thunderclap shook the windows, the French doors to the veranda blew open and the sky burst with rain. Rachel got up and walked out onto the veranda and down the steps, standing in the downpour, silhouetted in the lightning when the others followed her outside.

Rachel screamed. Rachel screamed her rage into the storm and the storm screamed back, the air making a ripping sound before the sky opened right in front of her, blinding the others, making them duck and cover their ears, the shock wave making them reach down for the ground.

Only Rachel still stood, screaming into the storm.

24

PATROL

From the time of the first Craft, the residents of Stonehaven maintained patrols of the property. The property could be traversed through a series of hidden trails and camps. These patrols could last from overnight to a week in duration: the boundaries could be checked, the valleys and coves could be inspected, and the patrollers could practice tracking, wildlife management, and survival and evasion skills.

It was policy to have at least one patrol out at any given time, year-round. Extra patrols were added at High Holiday times, and during the scouting and hunting seasons. Depending on the paths taken, the trip around the property's six thousand acres was twenty to forty miles. For tax and protection purposes the ownership of the contiguous properties was listed as various real estate and rental management companies for the boundary houses along the county roads, and timber and holding companies in addition to the lands of Stonehaven proper.

Patrols were almost always in pairs—usually co-gender, but not always. Patrol time was coveted by the residents because of the privacy it afforded. A week alone with a lover was prized time for all affinities. There was never a shortage of volunteers. Scheduling was handled by the Administrators and confirmed by the Seeresses. Priestesses on patrol were not always accompanied by their Consorts, but often by assignments. Even a Senior Consort could be assigned to a young Priestess or a Candidate. In cases where the Consort possessed the greater experience, the Masculine would lead while maintaining proper deference to the Feminine. Exceptions to this rule of leadership by the most experienced were granted in the instructions that came with the assignment.

Gear varied, depending on the season: every patrol member carried at least a small pack with a rain poncho, emergency blanket, fire starting kit, and extra ammo for the pistol worn on the belt. Emergency food, water and water purification equipment were carried in a separate section of the pack, even though there was no danger of starvation and the water on the land was all contained in controlled watersheds and was safe to drink. Other gear was either carried or worn, except for longer trips when one of the old horses would be brought along to carry extra gear.

Firearms proficiency was expected. Under the Laboratory was a subterranean firing range where both pistol and rifle skills were fostered. In addition to 9mm handguns there were telescoped collapsible stock .223 semiautomatic rifles that could be concealed in a back pack. New developments in materials technology had contributed to experimentation with crossbows instead of rifles on patrols.

Jasmine Delta was nearing the end of her training as a Priestess, and had been informed that her initiation as a High Priestess was to be soon. She had returned to Stonehaven with her Consort, Wade Oberstrom, for additional training and preparation. The pair had been running a martial arts training dojo, owned by Stonehaven, in a mid-western city for three years, while they practiced the urban training techniques of stalking, evasion, and escape.

Several months prior to her return, Jasmine began to receive impressions from the Madeleine, successor to the original Madeleine Crowe. She would see the Madeleine in her mind, watching her, or she would be in the position of observing the Madeleine as she went about some task. Sometimes, the Madeleine would turn and look at her and smile. Eventually, in Jasmine's vision, the Madeleine held up a written note that said "Call me." The note specified the date and time and provided the number to call. So Jasmine called.

Madeleine answered. She was laughing. "You got it! You got it! I'm so pleased! How is your conjuring practice going?"

Jasmine said, "What? What? What?"

Madeleine replied, "How's your conjuring and telekinesis going? Can you move anything yet?"

"Yes," Jasmine replied. "I have moved a couple things, not very large. Some of the statues you gave me to work with seem to have moved, at least a little. And I've been able to move myself. Why?"

"It's time, my dear," Madeleine said. "It's time for you to come home and finish your training. The next Initiation awaits you. The next octave in the skill set awaits you. Come home."

"Yes, ma'am. Yes, Seeress. We will be there in three days," Jasmine had said.

"Good," Madeleine had replied. "Your replacements will be there tomorrow. You can show them the ropes. Come home, dear. I've missed you. There will be a new assignment."

So they had come home, she and Wade. She wondered what the new assignment would be. She didn't think it would be replacing Wade; she thought it would probably be a new job.

Since she had come home, her abilities, under direction and with energetic assistance, had increased logarithmically. She had actually been able to move Wade several times—at first during sex, but later, also, when they were at some distance across the room. And she learned that she could move him in two ways: first, by sending him a command telepathically with compulsory undertones. She could stand across a room, tell him to raise his hand, and he would. The other way to move him, she discovered, was to simply will him to move.

This was, she understood, high Siddhi power. Madeleine assured her that these abilities were normal, so to speak, and that she did not have to worry. But Jasmine thought that she detected a detriment to Wade's will when she used him that way. Madeleine confirmed this observation. Jasmine found it disturbing, and declined to continue to use Wade as her guinea pig.

Madeleine told her that was fine, and that she should pick someone else on whom to practice. Madeleine encouraged Jasmine to use Madeleine's apprentices in the position of Seeress, the Crows. Madeleine said it would be good practice for them: first, in terms of them increasing their awareness; second, in terms of their ability to erect better shields and protect more people at one time. Madeleine told her to practice her arts as if she were in a battle to save not only her loved ones, but to save all the wen who were captive by the enemy. This energy would provide the clarity necessary for the Crows to begin to function at a higher level, in response.

So, Jasmine had attacked. Nothing she flung was death-carrying. In fact, she reserved the fear that comes from "scaring someone to death," for emergencies. She was clear that she could make the Crows terrified long before they figured out what was happening to them and created countermeasures. Psychics could be so stupid. They ignored their own vulnerabilities too often.

She beset them with phantoms—nothing that would harm them, just something that would give them pause, and make them work to figure out what was going on, then fix it. For Jasmine, the fun was in creating the phantoms purely as acts of her own imagination. The trick was to project that imagination into the external psychic field of the collective unconscious and then to imbue them with sufficient energy and direction to appear to the apprentices as emergent forms.

Shortly after her return, three additional consorts were assigned to her, for her use. Her instructions were to continue with her Consort and add these three men to her routine. She was to use them as an energy source, almost a food, in order to hasten the alchemy.

Always someone with some gymnastic skill, Jasmine had been following a training regimen that required her to run up walls, first in a harness and later free style. The goal, as Madeleine saw it, was to train Jasmine to run horizontally along a wall. In order to accomplish this, Jasmine had to become less dense. They both considered it an experiment in the alchemy, endeavoring to produce results along the lines of the Taoist Masters of old, some of whom were said in the legends to be able to fly.

Jasmine came to Stonehaven as a legacy, which is to say that both of her parents had been initiated members of the Order. Her parents, both artists, had created a mixed race daughter of such beauty that, unless she veiled herself in an invisibility projection, Jasmine turned heads wherever she went by the time she was fourteen. With her invisibility intact, Jasmine could pass for someone from most of the races of people, which enabled her to move among them. She had also, from an early age, been trained in the ability to learn new languages. Most recently, she had become fluent in Nutch and Windonesian.

The time spent with the additional Consorts had placed a strain on her relationship with her Primary. Wade had been assigned another Priestess, a Novice, with the instruction to begin to further this new wen's skills at the tantra. He found it intriguing, and allowed himself to devote his attention to it. That they each, Jasmine and Wade, were paying less attention and devotion to each other put a distance between them that had made them inexplicably irritable with each other, until they figured it out.

When the chance to go out on a four day patrol alone with each other came open, they jumped at the chance to spend the quality time together.

Wade was also a legacy, through his mother. She had been assigned to his father, who was not a member of the order, but seemed like he might have been a prospect. He was patient and curious about Wade's mother's beliefs, and approached the whole subject from a place of neutrality, combined with benign amusement. Before he had been able to fully understand the idea of the Antecedence of the Feminine, he was killed in an explosion at the chemical plant where he worked. Wade had been four.

Wade had some memories of his father. The memories where fragmented but they included sensations of being held, and his father's smell, and the emotional sense of security in his presence. They were good memories, although sometimes Wade sensed that smell at odd moments. It always made him stand up and look around.

Despite the distraction of training a novice Priestess, and the other distractions the Crows provided for him while working with Jasmine, he was also left alone much of the time. This gave him time to think, which he wasn't quite as fond of as actually doing something. Even digging a hole would have been a relief. He knew they were watching him, to see what he would do. He volunteered in the kitchen and spent a lot of time reading.

His thoughts would invariably turn to the hardest internal struggle he had ever faced. As he thought of it; here he was, he had everything he needed. All the sex, and food, and money he could need. All he had to do was to do certain things for it. And here was what irritated him: he got all the sex he wanted, but he had to do what he was told. Well, he didn't have to, but if he didn't do what was expected of him, the sex would be withdrawn. Food and money, too.

But the sex thing bothered him the most. There was still some part of him, deep inside, some part of him that believed that all he had to do was take it—take the sex.

And then his rational mind would kick in and he would suppress the impulse with the certain knowledge that whatever sex he could get by taking it would certainly be inferior sex. What he had was not just sex that he was taking, but, by far, superior sex, freely shared with him.

But the impulse continued to rise up in him and it always, automatically, triggered a resentment. The resentment was that he had to do anything at all.

His rational brain would kick in again and he'd ask himself: 'And what age was I when that resentment came up?'

It was as if the part of himself that wanted food, as well as the part of himself that wanted money, both these parts, had learned the lesson that he had to do certain things to get what he wanted—even things he might not have wanted to do. Only the sexual part of himself still seemed to have this unreconciled and unintegrated impulse and concomitant emotion.

He took the issue to the icons of the Sacred Masculine. He sat before the altars in the Men's room and held the question in his mind: 'How do I surrender what I want to what I have to do?'

The answer came back: 'You surrender what you want, in order to get what you really want.'

It seemed it was there one minute and gone the next, this understanding. Wade found that he could not even hang on to the understanding without losing his initial desire to not do what he didn't want to do, and the idea to take it instead. When that desire would renew itself, he would tamp it down with this new—for him—understanding. But it didn't stop the problem with the desire itself.

It made him want to experience, at least, a taking. To be the one doing the taking, it seemed, would satisfy something deep inside him, some urge that, once manifest, would never need to manifest again. It did not occur to him that what he might really want was to be taken, himself, in a way he did not want.

Wade vowed to talk to at least the Madeleine, if not the High Priestess and her Consort, on his return. On second thought, maybe he would just start with the High Consort.

And so they prepared. Since it was a four-day patrol, they opted to carry only two days' worth of supplies and rely on the caches hidden around the property. If it was to have been a quick patrol, they would have had to cover only fifteen miles or so around the six thousand acres in a day. But on this longer patrol they would be walking back and forth along the coves, along the ridges and through the vales.

Into the small packs they put rain ponchos, radios, food, fire starter kits, and extra ammo for the Glocks and the .223 collapsible that slipped inside the pack. Covering as much ground as they planned to cover increased the odds of contact with bears, mountain lions, the occasional coywolf, coyotes, and snakes. On a few patrols over the past several years there had been encounters with feral dogs. It had been necessary to put them down. Which, in part, was the reason they chose to leave Homer the dog at home. He was too old to be in a fight.

A small water pack was integrated into the knapsacks. Water purification straws were also included. They knew that the entire watershed of Stonehaven was contained in the boundaries of the property, and therefore protected, and it was generally known how clean the streams were, but anything could have happened somewhere upstream.

Also packed was whatever clothing change they thought they might need, plus a bedroll each. In addition, they packed Jasmine's shawl and Wade's stole, which was long enough to cover his shoulders and wide enough to go more than halfway down his back.

They reached the first shelter at dusk. It was composed of a high ceiling rock that laid over and extended out over two large, flattish boulders that had clearly tumbled down from the rock wall higher up. The floor had been excavated many years earlier, and replaced with hard packed dirt. There was a small clearing facing the east with two small fire pits.

They took small wood from the pile stacked at one end of the shelter and made a fire, putting a tea kettle for hot water on the flat rock nearest the fire. They rolled out pads and lightweight blankets. Jasmine undressed and redressed in her shawl and a sarong.

The water boiled and tea was made. The rest of the water poured on a dehydrated rice and stir-fry mix. Jasmine sat on a log opposite Wade and opened her legs, exposing her sex to the fire while she ate. She talked about how it was for her knowing that she was in training for a particular assignment. She chose this moment to let him know that she knew where she was going: Wallid Island, an outpost of Winduism in the archipelago of Windonesia. Her recent training in Windonesian now explained, she was told by the Madeleine two days prior that a part of her next assignment was to also learn Wallisi, the banned language of the native people there.

Wade waited to hear if he was going to be assigned to go with her. She said nothing. He wondered what that would be like. Registering his disappointment, the impulse to take flared in him, unexpectedly.

He remembered the voice of the Sacred Masculine: "You surrender what you want in order to get what you truly want." Then, suddenly, the meaning of it flipped in his mind and he thought that, since what he truly wanted was his own way, that everything that he surrendered should serve that end. It was a different end, his own way; different from what he had truly wanted before, which was to be in right relation with the Feminine.

The impulse gave him an erection.

Jasmine said to him, setting down her bowl, "Take your clothes off."

He untied his boots and removed them. Then he stood up and dropped his pants, kicking out of them, revealing a rising erection swinging in the firelight. He bent over and pulled his shirts off over his head, looking like a man being born feet first, and stood up.

Jasmine, heedful of the Madeleine's instructions on how to deal with him, and, sensing the need—Wade's need for animal appeasement—crawled forward to him on her hands and knees. Stopping a step shy of him, she sat back on her heels and inclined her head, waiting.

Wade exhaled, and closed his hands into fists. He took that step forward, and, bending at the knees, caressed her face with the head of his phallus, dancing it on her cheeks and her forehead, then her lips. He dropped lower to her throat, and continued to dance his cock across her throat, then along it, lifting her chin with it. She raised her face, but kept her eyes lowered, not looking up at him. Yet, still, through hooded eyes, she looked at him.

He paused with the head of his cock resting on her lips. He made a motion with his hands. She saw it, and pushed her tongue out of her mouth, holding him up with it from below. He took a half step back, pulling her tongue along with him, made clear by his "follow me" gesture. As he continued backwards, Jasmine's face dropped to perpendicular to the ground, facing straight ahead, just the tip of him resting on the tip of her tongue.

Then he pressed himself slowly against her mouth, in the gentlest way possible. But, still, without her consent. Without her invitation.

She allowed it, this being the Dance of Appeasement.

He wasn't painful to her, but he did require that she take all of him in her mouth. When he finally took her, he took her from behind. He turned her away from him and bent her forward. He raised her sarong until her buttocks and the backs of her thighs were exposed. Her hair and shawl hung down, concealing the rest of her. He took her that way without her agreement. He grabbed her by the hair and pulled her head back. He rode her to the ground, his legs outside hers, pinning hers together.

And that was his taking.

When he fed her, in the end, he fed her two times, below and then above, powerful food that was drawn into her, the essences mixing quickly. It charged her spirit. And her spirit was charged with victory. She had, of course, used him completely, letting him ride her to the ground while she was screaming out her pleasure. Now she was smiling.

Wade stepped back and went to one knee, putting his head at her level. He leaned forward and kissed her, kissed her thoroughly, and said, "Thank you."

Then he stood, stepped back, and went to one knee again. He put a hand down, leaned into it, and lay down. He looked at her sideways, then fell asleep.

She let him sleep for a while. She smiled again, fingering the short blade sewn into the hem of her shawl, just long enough to reach a jugular. She smiled because the victory of the Dance of Appeasement had saved her from having to take up the Way of the Cut Throat. She sat, cultivating the inner alchemy. Drawing it higher, she entered a state of full-blown ecstasy, shivering into the dirt, and making it vibrate in response back to her. The vibration of the dirt alone rose her up, rose her up above ground level, by almost an inch.

After some time in this state of active contemplation she returned to earth. She rolled Wade over on his back and started sucking on him, bringing him hard at the same time she brought him awake.

She built up the fire and told him to grab the pads and a blanket. She led him by hand up on top of the roof of the shelter, where she had him lay out the pads and the blanket. She laid him down on his back, and feeling the strength of his erection, pulled the sarong aside, and revealed herself to him. She opened herself with one hand, held him vertical with the other, then slowly settled herself on him.

Jasmine rode him until she felt the onset of the consciousness of the Divine Feminine. She leaned back, still joined, but leaning back far enough that she could rain on Wade. She squirted around his cock, out along his belly, squirted as far as his face, where he drank her in. This had the desired effect, well known to Jasmine, that Wade expanded his erection to its largest possible stretch of girth and length. Jasmine could feel the expansion, and she sighed. She felt Wade engage the

Lock, as it was called, which would let him orgasm while keeping him from ejaculating and allow her to ride him for a long time. Then, head bowed, she allowed the Goddess entry.

Jasmine became the embodiment of a Goddess while orgasming. Her legs grew longer so that she could pin him down at the shoulders with her knees and still remain impaled upon him. What his eyes saw was Jasmine slowly turning black, her face surrounded by an elaborate black headdress emitting blue sparks, eyes turned blue, and fangs visible on her lower lip, flashing in the fire light.

What his mind's eye saw was her opening to him. The head of his phallus emitted a pale light, illuminating his vision. His mind's eye, inside her, saw the inner flower of her, and he watched it open, the teeth of closure morphing into the petals of openness.

His mundane eyes saw her stick her tongue out at him. He sensed her licking him, and then, it seemed clear to him that multiple pairs of hands were holding him down and holding him to her, all at the same time.

In the after-spasms of his orgasm he knew, then, knew with a certainty that the reason he had what he had, all that he had, was that he was made to be had.

In the morning, Jasmine was feeding the need for ecstasy. She was sucking on Wade's phallus, taking advantage of the morning wood and heading toward the palace of a thousand lights. Then they heard a metal click, then the rasp of a file wheel on flint. They froze, Jasmine's mouth on the head of Wade's cock.

Then they heard the crackling sound of rolling paper on fire and smelled the faintest hint of weed burning. Wade rolled out from under Jasmine and then rolled again out of the shelter. Coming to his feet, he looked up on the top of the shelter rock.

He saw a stranger sitting there, apparently on one heel, with his other knee upraised, his feet obscured by the angle. A Caucasian, the stranger was bald, with a fringe of long white hair falling to his shoulders, and a long white mustache. He was wearing some kind of camouflage tunic over tan canvas pants. Secured by a tie around his neck was a bamboo paddy hat, pushed back off his head, giving the stranger a pale green halo.

Wade, naked, his erection bouncing and swinging, glistening in the morning sun, gestured at him aggressively and said in a loud voice, "Hey you! Asshole! Who the fuck do you think you are?"

The stranger closed the lighter with a flick, and replied, exhaling smoke, "I am, in fact, the Bodhisattva of Assholes."

Wade said, "Bullshit!"

The Stranger said, "That would have been my preference, but the Bodhisattva of Bullshit was already taken."

In that moment, Jasmine stepped out from under the edge of the shelter with her shawl draped over her shoulders, holding it closed across her breasts with one hand. It was a red shawl, made of light wool, embroidered with flowers in gold, and green, and blue.

She smiled up at the Stranger, taking in his appearance, what she could see and couldn't see of him, just his knee and upper body, and said, "Good morning, Bodhisattva. How are you today?"

He said, "Good enough. Getting better." He squinted against a flash of sunlight off the top of her mound below the hem of the shawl and took another hit on the joint. "Here," he said. "Have some. I got it out of a garden a few miles back." And he tossed it toward her.

Still holding the shawl closed, she bent to pick up the joint with her left hand, watching the Stranger the entire time. The Stranger watched her in return. She stood up and drew on the joint, holding it in for a moment, exhaling up, watching the Stranger's eyes track the clouds. She turned to Wade and extended the joint toward him, saying, "Here."

Wade stared at her, somewhat dumbfounded, not knowing what she was doing. She nodded at him again, saying, "Take it. It's a peace offering."

"Smart girl," the Stranger said. Wade took the joint, staring at the Stranger, and in that instant when the Stranger's eyes locked on Wade, Jasmine slipped her right hand under her shawl and drew one of the

Glocks from the shoulder holster she'd slipped on before rolling out from under the shelter.

She pointed it at the Stranger and said, "Don't fucking move, Mr. Bodhisattva." She grinned broadly, "Or is it Mr. Asshole?" The Stranger sat perfectly still, except for narrowing his eyes again.

She squatted before Wade, keeping her eyes on the Stranger, and with her free hand fed his flagging manhood into her mouth and moved her head back and forth a few times.

Wade stood there, joint in one hand, trying to stare fiercely at the Stranger, but not succeeding. The Stranger didn't move.

Jasmine looked at the Stranger, deep into his eyes, over the barrel, and smiled at him around a mouthful of Wade. She said, "I've always wanted to do this." She held the gun up to Wade, and said, "Here, take this. I'm going to finish what I started before this new guest of ours interrupted us."

Wade took the gun and Jasmine dropped her newly freed hand between her legs and moved it back and forth there, too. Wade was now completely dumbfounded. Joint in one hand, pistol in the other, he was trying to glance down at the top of Jasmine's head, but not take his eyes off the Stranger at the same time. The Stranger smiled at him and slowly shrugged his shoulders. Wade understood and shrugged back, now almost helpless to change the standoff.

His legs started to shake as Jasmine moaned around him, working it, sucking it. Then she stopped, the head of it against the roof of her mouth, making the energetic connection. Her eyes rolled back in her head as her mouth filled with saliva. She saw the field of the garden before the palace of a thousand lights. In the field was the Stranger, completely surrounded in an ellipse of pale green light. Then ecstasy closed over her senses, and she trembled completely, and dropped to one knee. Then she slowly sucked on him without moving, once, twice, three times drawing and releasing, and Wade, responding to the cue, legs almost buckling, released in turn. Filling her mouth, more than she could swallow, and she, still in ecstasy, shivering with each blast from him, dropped to her other knee, swallowing.

Wade closed his eyes, and in that instant the Stranger leapt down from the rock, holding a long staff that had been resting in his lap, hidden below the line of sight. As he landed he brought the staff down hard on Wade's wrist, causing him to drop the pistol, and before Wade could recover, the Stranger clocked him on the back of his head with the butt of the staff.

As Wade backed away, falling, Jasmine scrambled backward and pulled the other Glock from the second holster in the harness, and, resting on her back, trained it on the Stranger.

"This one's chambered," she said seriously. Then she smiled as a drop of Wade's release slipped off her chin onto her chest. "The other one wasn't." Then, sitting up, she motioned with the gun. "Sit." she said. "I always wanted to do that. Hold a gun on one man while I suck another one off."

Now, smiling broadly as the Stranger sat down cross-legged, settling the staff across his lap, she said, "I suppose I should thank you. That was pretty good!" The Stranger smiled and nodded.

She said, "Wade, you OK?"

He sat up rubbing the back of his head and said, "Yeah. Fuck! Yeah."

"Then pass me that joint, and let's get to know our guest a little better," she said.

Wade passed her the joint, and she pulled on it, motioning for Wade to retrieve the other pistol and sit. Wade chambered a round as he sat just out of her arm reach, balls and detumescing phallus settling in the dirt. She eyed the staff, and said, "That's unusual. What kind of wood is it?"

"Diamond willow," the Stranger said.

"Ah, may I look at it?" holding her hand out.

"Sure," the Stranger said, and proffered the bigger end toward her. Jasmine holstered her gun, took the butt, and hefted it. "Nice," she said. "Long and hard, but not real heavy. It almost lifts itself. Kind of like a metaphor." She giggled.

Then she stood up, whirling the stick. Shawl falling from her shoulders, she leaped off, doing staff katas across the clearing, striking at the nearest trees, running four steps up a tree and back flipping down, leaping and turning; a gorgeous nude in a shoulder holster, hair flying, dappled in the morning sun.

She came to a stop in front of the Stranger, chest heaving, breasts rolling with each rise and fall, sweat running between them and then down her belly. Slowly she squatted, showing herself to him. The Stranger could see her quiver when his eyes fell to her sex. She smiled and handed him the staff, butt end first. "Have you eaten yet, Mr. Bodhisattva?"

The Stranger took the end of the staff, and she leaned forward, not letting go of the other end. She came forward onto her knees and crawled the last few feet to the Stranger. Pushing him onto his back and eyeing the swell of his trousers as she crawled over him, she came to her feet directly over his face, straddling his head, tall, sweating, and naked, still holding the other end of the staff.

She stared down at him, hazel eyes dark and serious. He grinned up at her. The veil came over her eyes, and suddenly She was looking at the Stranger, too. Sweat dripped from her phulva onto the stranger's face. Diosa smiled, and Jasmine smiled, too. Jasmine looked down at the stranger again and, feeling his gaze of awe and longing, sensed her para-gland swell. She had to control herself or she would rain all over him right there.

The Stranger couldn't believe his eyes as he watched her relax something and her labia extended toward him, then she tightened it again and the lips withdrew. She had actually pulsed a palpable energy at him, a pulse that he sensed landing on his heart. Then Jasmine laughed, and Diosa with her, head back, face to the sky. "I meant food," she said in a deeper voice, and, releasing the staff, stepped over him and away into the shelter.

The Stranger sat up, eyes alight and laughing, and looked at Wade, who shrugged first this time, and reached to pick up the joint. The Stranger said to Wade, "I know what food is. She is good food."

Wade nodded, and responded, "And she feeds."

The Stranger nodded his head to the side and contemplated the ambiguity of that remark. He asked, "Do you mean she feeds another or feeds on another?"

Wade replied, "Both." Then he said, "My point is that you will be both fed and fed on. You need do nothing, all will be given you, and as you give you shall receive."

From the shelter Jasmine called out, "Are you dangerous, Mr. Bodhisattva?"

"Yes," the Stranger said.

"Are you a danger to us?" she asked.

"No," he said.

"Do you think I'm dangerous?" she asked.

"Yes," he said.

"He's alright, Wade. Diosa said so. Let him be." Wade lowered the gun into his lap. When the stranger raised an eyebrow at the proximity of the pistol to Wade's 'pistol', Wade said, "It's a Glock. It won't go off."

The Stranger said, "I know."

"Here," Jasmine called out, tossing a pemmican bar at the back of the stranger's head, bouncing it off his hat, and another one over his head to Wade. "Make some tea, would you?"

Wade said to the Stranger, "You make it." Then to Jasmine, "I'm going down below to the spring to wash up. He interrupted me. I ejaculated but I didn't get to finish my orgasm."

Jasmine tossed him a radio and said, "Call Base and tell them we have a guest. Then call Craft and have him come pick up our guest and take him to the Mansion. Tell them it is the Bodhisattva of Assholes. And we still have three more days of patrol, so be patient, lover."

He grabbed his stole and a sarong. The path down to the spring from the shelter was cleared, and hard packed dirt, safe for bare feet. He removed fallen twigs and leaves as he went.

As soon as he was clear of the shelter clearing he stopped and turned the radio on. He called Craft but couldn't get him. He needed a better line of sight to the repeater.

High in the trees around the land were small, solar powered, antennas, using the trees as towers. Radios could be aimed toward these from across the deeper coves. The low powered system was only turned on by a steady signal activating the once-a-minute scan function in the receiver when a patrol was out and close by. A part of a patrol's task was to check these antennas when they came upon them, depending on their path.

Wade looked around, trying to remember where there nearest receiver was. Spotting it, he aimed his radio antenna to it, and raised the Base. He told them Jasmine's message and their location. Then he asked them to call Craft to come fetch the Stranger.

"Hello Base, this is Rover 4. Come in," he said.

"Hello Rover. Good morning. What's up?" the young wen on duty replied.

"We have an intruder. Repeat, we have an intruder, over," Wade stated firmly.

"Say again? What? You have an intruder?" Base came back.

"Yes, repeat. Yes, we have an intruder. Someone calling himself the Bodhisattva of Assholes."

"Copy that. The Bodhisattva of Assholes."

"He has been secured. Call Craft to come fetch him."

"Your location?"

"Rock Shelter 2. Repeat. Rock Shelter 2," Wade stated.

Hidden just off the paths were special areas of plantings where the people on patrol could relieve themselves. These latrine locations were known and were visible from the trails. There was a schedule for using a different latrine on any given day. Wade stepped into one such thicket to relieve himself, then made his way to the bathing pool.

The pool was below a spring, which erupted from the side of a hill, moss dripping, into a clear natural stone gravel and sand pool. At this time of year the spring was still running at a gallon a minute. By late summer it could go almost dry, as the water was all being pulled up into the trees. The pool opened through a crack into a falls, over a boulder, and sheeted down over the boulder's face. The drop was four feet of rise over a three foot run, giving the place a sacred and Pythagorean symmetry.

The first pool was to remain untouched by humans. There was a bucket to the side of the pool below the first pool and further off to the side was sand spread over gravel for someone to wash themselves away from the pools. There were many such washing stations off the side of the different streams. Once washed, someone was free to step into the flowing water.

The water was cool to the touch, but not so cool that the body couldn't adjust and begin to feel warm. Wade laid back in the pool and floated. He loved to go to that pool whenever he was on patrol; in the winter he would sit by it for a long time, watching the water flow around the ice, staring at the dripping icicles. In the summer, he would lie back and dream in the waters. He always dreamed of the same thing: a water colored wen with chestnut colored hair. The wen would come to him, watch him bathe, and when he laid back, she would slip into the water with him, and caress him—the caresses feeling the same as the waters caressing his warm skin.

Usually, in these dreams the Naiad—for this was all she could be, to Wade's way of thinking—would stroke him to an erection, at which point he would remember the prohibition on having sex in the waters.

This time, in his dream, she kissed him. And the kiss was filled with more longing for his lips and tongue than he could have ever imagined. His erection was harder, in his dream, than he could remember having in a long time. It lived as an urgency between his thighs—an urgency to find entry, and to find release.

The chestnut haired wen smiled at Wade through their kisses, and laid off caressing him with her hand. She raised a leg over him, and inserted him. It was as if he was on fire and the Naiad was the only water that could put him out.

She rode him for a few moments, then leaned forward and kissed him again. Then she turned him so that she was under him, still kissing him. She sucked upon his mouth with such need that Wade became unaware of how long he had held his breath. He breathed out, and was so relaxed that he started to do two things at once—orgasm and inhale.

Suddenly he remembered the prohibition, and pushed himself up in the shallow pool on his hands. His head broke the water, gasping for air, and he realized he was in full release. He could still feel the Naiad wrapped around him while he was coming. He could still see her faint image under the water, her eyes closed in ecstasy and her lips pulled back in the broadest of smiles.

He could feel her twitching around him, and he pulled out, still ejaculating, coming into the water.

He shouted, some almost untranscribable sound between Ohhh and Arrggh and Aww, and pushed himself up and out of the water. His last image of the spirit below the water was of her open eyes, staring at him, shimmering, and an almost wickedly satisfied smile, and then the boundaries of her outline collapsed into water. The remains of his orgasm swirled away over the rocks.

Jasmine looked up from watching the Stranger make tea when she heard Wade's bellow. She paused, waiting to see whether or not there would be another cry. When, after a moment, the only sound was the resumption of the bird talk, she shrugged slightly.

The stranger had poured water in the pot and set the pot on a rock, putting the handle on a hook suspended from a tripod over the fire. He raked in coals, and set two cups on the edge of the rock ring. Jasmine had dressed, the Stranger was sitting on his tunic, having retrieved his pack from the rock.

So they talked, Jasmine sitting on a folded blanket, sarong loosely running down her thighs, only barely concealing her sex, her shawl hanging in such a way that the Stranger could see her breasts swing with every movement, rise and fall with every breath.

The Stranger: "Am I where I think I am?"

Jasmine: "Where do you think you are?"

Stranger: "I may be home."

Jasmine: "Probably not."

Stranger: "I have been led here, almost like some kind of compass, pulling my heart in this direction."

Jasmine: "Then we shall have to find out why."

Stranger: "You will allow this?"

Jasmine: "That is our instruction."

Stranger: "From whom?"

Jasmine smiled at his English: "We were told someone was coming. Some old man. And then She confirmed it to me."

Stranger: "She?"

Jasmine: "You know She of whom I speak. And you have seen Her."

Stranger: "I have seen Her."

Jasmine: "Then you know what we're dealing with here. Relax and be patient. And try to do what is suggested to you."

Stranger: "Like what?"

Jasmine: "Like go with Craft when he gets here to escort you. You are here now, so be here. And that means learning the order of things here and fitting in. You know, be a good guest. And we shall be impeccable hosts."

Stranger: "No one knows what that means anymore."

Jasmine: "We do. Your needs will be taken care of. I was told to say that to you, because you know what it means."

Stranger: "Is She talking to you right now?"

Jasmine: "Yes. And another."

The Stranger started to ask her 'who?' But she smiled and shook her head, long hair still down, swinging side to side, signifying, 'No, don't ask'.

They paused, looking at the fire, and the water coming to a boil. The Stranger lifted the pot handle off the tripod and set it on the stone ring, open to the west. Jasmine lay the strainer ball in the pot.

Stranger: "So you're a Priestess then."

Jasmine nodded.

Stranger: "I'm remembering...Oh, it was that dream. I remember where I am now. Some of it, anyway."

Jasmine leaned around the fire and put a hand to his temple, her fingers slipping back into his hair. She just left her hand there a moment, flooding herself with compassion, and sorrow for his suffering. Then she opened herself to empathy, feeling what he felt. While his head was cooling, she opened the higher door to telepathy, and saw his suffering.

She had inhaled quickly through drawn lips as she felt it, then sounded a short, sharp 'ah' as she saw it, and withdrew her hand.

The Stranger had closed his eyes at her touch. He opened them, eyes brimming, and saw a lone tear run down Jasmine's cheek.

He said, "I may be home." And he sighed into the relief he felt.

Later, Craft and the Stranger walked up the hill from the shelter single file, the Stranger putting his feet where Craft did, sliding his feet into the track like putting on an overlarge slipper. This freed some of his attention to study Craft's back and the crossbow slung over it on a strap. He studied the bolts lined up in a belt around Craft's waist. From there, his cerebellar automatism took over the placement of his feet, freeing his attention even more. He extended his awareness of his peripheral senses and caught a flash of dark movement off to his right.

Turning his head quickly, he caught the motion stopping.

So he stopped, turned his body, and stared. Craft moved on several steps, having long since accepted the silence, and the silent stepping, of the Stranger behind him. His acceptance had caused him to stop paying attention to the Stranger.

The Stranger stared openly at what appeared to disappear, chameleon-like, becoming the colors of the rock on which it was lying. Craft suddenly became aware that the Stranger had stopped. He turned and looked at the Stranger, then toward the direction the Stranger was staring. There was a momentary sound, like the dull roar of a distant waterfall, then the spot on the rock wavered like heat rising for a split second, then the rock returned to being just a rock. A rock reader would have seen it smiling.

"What was it?" Craft asked.

"A lizard," the Stranger replied. "A big-ass lizard."

"Did you see it before it camouflaged?"

"Yes. For just the briefest image."

"Would you recognize it if I showed you a picture?

"Yes, I would," the Stranger replied.

"Good. I have a book at the house. You'll look at it and tell me what it was."

"I will, will I?" the Stranger asked drolly.

Craft looked at him, directly, seriously, and yet somehow lightly, with nothing dull in his gaze. That ended the conversation. Craft turned and resumed walking, listening to make sure the Stranger followed, keeping his attention high.

As they stepped into the backyard of one of the houses on the county road, the Stranger felt a tingle at the level of his knees. They bent slightly, and would have buckled had the tingle been any stronger. But he kept moving, and said to Craft, "Nice wards."

Craft said, "Yes, and I want to know how you got past them."

"If you're polite to me, I might tell you," the Stranger replied.

"Fuck you," Craft thought, but he simply stared at the Stranger. "Then I'll figure it out myself," he said.

"Let me know what you figure out," the Stranger smiled back. "If you're polite, I might tell you if you're right or not."

The wards along the road were set back from it into the forest. They were not as strong and well defined as the wards around the yards. Finding a weak point near a ward mark where a thunder storm run-off had created a gully, the Stranger had slipped under the line, and then strengthened the ward after he got through, concealing any trace of himself so that none could follow. Not that he believed anything was after him; he simply wanted to be sure. He knew that meant that Craft would probably never find the spot, because there was no break, nor weakness. It pleased him to know that Craft would probably be driven crazy trying to solve the puzzle.

Their meeting at the shelter had not been the best. He had appeared on the rock where the Stranger himself had been sitting, and stared down at Jasmine and the Stranger having tea, the Stranger smiling and Jasmine just laughing into her hand. Craft's face lapsed into a scowl, which the Stranger appeared to feel. The Stranger looked up, and mimicked the scowl, then smiled.

"Tea?" he asked, offering his cup.

Jasmine said, "Yes. Step down and join us for some tea.

Craft, much like the Stranger earlier that day, leapt down from the rock, landing in a crouch to absorb the shock. The two men began appraising each other as Jasmine stood, bowed slightly to Craft, and offered her cup. Craft accepted it, but did not sit.

"You'd be Craft, then," the Stranger said.

"And you'd be the Bodhisattva of Assholes."

"The very one," the Stranger nodded.

"Indeed."

They stared at each other then, and continued eyeing each other over the rims of their cups. The Stranger saw a man in his late thirties, hard and fit, dressed in the colors of the forest, bark brown, dull green, and rock gray. He carried a crossbow over his shoulder and extra bolts on his belt. The Stranger saw a man of deep and steady presence.

The Craft saw an older man, balding and dirty, looking like a forlorn hippie with a ridiculous and slightly smashed paddy hat on his back. He would have smiled at the clownishness of him, but he could feel the image was a distraction. What was beneath it was opaque, and he couldn't see through it. The lack of transparency made him feel suspicious and cranky.

"No time to sit," Craft said. To the Stranger he said, "Let's go."

The Stranger had stiffened. He took another look at the camouflage clothing, the crossbow slung over a shoulder with one hand on the fiberglass stock.

Jasmine had noticed the stiffening, laid a hand on his arm, and nodded that it was OK to do what Craft called for. The Stranger came up on one knee as he drained his tea cup. When he put it down Jasmine reached for the Stranger's face and pulled him in. She planted a kiss, a sweet and lingering kiss, on his lips. The Stranger, surprised but not off his game, kissed her back.

Craft cleared his throat and said again, "Let's go."

So they arrived at the house, both men cranky, curious, and feeling the slightest edges of fear. Craft was afraid because the wards had been breached. The Stranger was beginning to be fearful of his immediate future.

They entered an unlocked sliding door of the house and went into the kitchen. Craft told the Stranger to sit down, that he would go get the book—and to not touch anything. The Stranger sat, but then he noticed a half-bath just off the kitchen and went in, took a leak, and washed his hands and face.

He looked at himself in the mirror, saw his age, saw fleeting shadows of hope dancing across his face, and shook his head at the folly of hope.

When he emerged, Craft was waiting at the table with a book on the Reptiles and Amphibians of the Mountains. The Stranger flipped through the pages to lizards but didn't see anything resembling what he saw in the woods. He looked at the salamanders and the image was immediately obvious to him.

The Stranger said, "It was a Hellbender."

Craft looked at it over the Stranger's shoulder. "The fuck you say." In all his years in the woods, he'd never seen one. And now there was one on Stonehaven as big as an adult alligator. He would have found an alligator easier to believe.

"Go ahead, be rude then. I don't much give a fuck, myself. If I say it looked like a Hellbender, it looked like a Hellbender. I notice how much luck you seem to have had seeing it for yourself," the Stranger replied.

"Yeah, you're right. I apologize," Craft said. "And now that I know, I'll have to do something about it. Now that I know we have a salamander as big as an alligator that can camouflage itself, I'm going to have to know more. I mean is it dangerous? What does it eat?"

The Stranger closed his eyes. "I don't know," he said. "It knows that we've seen it. It will be watching us. Where are we going next?"

"To the Mansion," Craft answered. "The Leaders want to meet you as soon as possible. They tell me they've been expecting you. It would have been nice to have had some detail."

"You're whining," the Stranger said. "How are we getting there?"

"There's a cart in the garage."

"We should walk," the Stranger said, his eyes still closed. "It's waiting for us."

"What?"

"It won't eat us," the Stranger continued. "I sense no aggression from it. And it isn't hungry."

"How the fuck would you know that?"

"I can feel it," the Stranger replied. "I feel a soft pressure around my head, and the pressure kind of resolves itself into words. I don't think the thing can lie, either."

"Unbelievable," Craft said.

"Yeah. Never-the-less…" the Stranger shrugged. "Afraid?"

"Not if you aren't," Craft stated, aggressively. "So, let's go then."

They went out the backyard and headed out at an angle toward the woods at the edge of the lot. The Stranger realized that this would conceal the trail from the road. He thought to himself, "Pretty smart, these guys".

Entering the woods, they took a trail that turned from one direction to the other, until they were far enough back that the road could not be seen at all. Then the trail went downhill, using only natural switchbacks in the landscape. The Stranger could see that the trail was smooth, hard-packed, and well cleaned.

Then the pressure wave hit them, and brought them to a complete stop. They felt it in their solar plexes and diaphragms, and in their guts. It felt like a sub-audible rumble, a voice too low to hear, was telling them to stop.

They came to a complete stop, and both crouched down, the Stranger rocking slightly on his feet. Craft touched the ground for balance and to see if the pressure was in the earth as well. It was. Neither reached for a weapon.

"Whoa," the Stranger said, then "Whoa," again, the second time more slowly and quietly. He went to one knee.

"What is it?" Craft hissed at him.

"If we agree to hold completely still, he'll show himself to us," the Stranger said.

"What?" Craft hissed again.

"Well, do you?" the Stranger asked.

"What?" Craft hissed yet again.

"Agree to hold still," the Stranger answered patiently.

"Yes," Craft agreed, also dropping to one knee.

"OK. Wait for it," the Stranger said.

They watched as the air at the top of the narrow rock ridge started to oscillate and bend. It seemed to bend with the colors of sunlight and dirt, and then an image resolved itself, lying along the rock.

It was, as the Stranger had identified, a Hellbender, but very, very big. The Stranger estimated twenty feet long. Its mouth was so broad that it could fit a human torso in it. When the Stranger thought this, both men felt an energy, a change in the pressure, which felt like a smile. Then the Stranger heard slow words in his head, slow as in an entire exhalation for one word. The word was "No."

Then they felt another smile, and the Stranger, translating out loud for Craft, heard the next word, "Perhaps."

Then another smile, and the words, "But not you."

Craft asked, "What are you?"

And the Stranger spoke the Hellbender's words, "I am King of the Salamanders."

At this, the Stranger bowed low, put his forehead on the ground, and said, "Greetings, Your Majesty."

Craft looked at the Stranger, askance. The Stranger said to him, "Don't be a fool."

Craft bowed, almost to the ground, and said, "Your Highness," with neither facetiousness nor fear.

"Why are you here?" the Stranger asked.

"Safe," was the reply. "Safe here."

"Why are you showing yourself to us?"

"I see much. I hear much. My people bring me tales. Troubles come, not safe. Not you. Trouble comes."

"Can you help?"

"I warn." Then the pressure of the field of mind emanating from the King eased, the image waivered and again the giant salamander disappeared.

"I wish I could do that," Craft said.

"Hear giant amphibians talk?"

"No, don't be a fool. Disappear."

They stood up. The Stranger shook his head and said "Whoa," again. Craft exhaled, low and long.

"What do we do with that?" the Stranger asked.

"We tell the Madeleine."

"What's a Madeleine?"

"She's our Seeress. She told us you were coming."

"Me? Me, me?"

"No, not you, you. Someone like you."

"That's similar to something that Jasmine said."

"Yes, patrols have been instructed to keep an eye out for a Stranger. And not to shoot him," Craft added.

"Armed patrols. Seeresses. What are you people?"

"We are an Order here. And the Seeress is an archetypal power in that Order."

"Order?"

"Order of the Fleur de Vie, the Flower of Life."

"Order of the Flower of Life. You a member? Or do you just work for them?"

"Both. I'm a member, I work for them," Craft said. "And I'm proud of it," he added, in an attempt to divert judgmental questions.

"Where do I sign up?" the Stranger asked.

"What?" Craft replied.

"Where do I sign up?" the Stranger repeated, grinning now.

"You don't just sign up. It's not an army."

"Looks like one," the Stranger said, nodding at Craft's weapons.

Again, trying to sustain a diversion, Craft said, "Look, we just met the world's largest lizard and he talked to you. And you're questioning my weapons?" He stopped to let that sink in and said, "No more questions.

Let's go to the Mansion and all your questions will be answered there."

"Salamander," the Stranger said. "It's a salamander."

The rest of the walk down from the ridge top to the Mansion was uneventful. The Stranger noted the careful hand of humanity on almost everything, so that it looked both cared for, and wild.

They came down out of the woods into a pasture overlooking what seemed to have once been a very long barn and two large Quonset buildings. They went into the nearer north end of the barn, turning immediately into a stairwell and going down one level, then out into a long hallway that ran the length of the barn. They turned into a room with a push button key code combination.

When Craft turned on the lights it was clear they were in an armory room. There were assault rifles, hunting rifles and shotguns. There were handguns hung on hooks behind glass front cases, and locked safes which the Stranger assumed were filled with ammunition. One wall was partially cleared and several crossbows hung there.

Craft turned to the Stranger and said, "You can leave your weapon here. I'll put it in a safe if you like. No one goes to the Mansion armed. Not even security." Craft said this, turning to disarm himself onto the desktop.

"If it's in a safe, how will I get it back?"

This was not the question Craft thought he was going to be asked, so he simply said what he was prepared to say: "I could tell you were armed by the weight swinging in your bag."

"Oh," the Stranger said. "Don't put it in a safe. Put it in a drawer. I can't get in here. Let me keep the ammo," releasing the clip, and clearing the chamber. Handing it grip first to Craft, he dropped the clip back in his bag. He pulled a multi-tool out of his bag and offered it to Craft. "This OK?" he asked. It was a classic bait and switch, adding to the confusion Craft's mind was already in. Getting him to agree with the 'voice' the Stranger was using was important.

"Yes," came the reply.

The Stranger smiled at his success.

They left the armory and headed for the Mansion, plainly visible, set back from a cliff in the distance to the east.

"Big place you got here," the Stranger said.

Craft said nothing. Craft maintained silence for the entire walk to the Mansion. Eventually, the Stranger gave up asking questions.

When they arrived at the Mansion, they went up the north steps to the main hall. There were several people there, standing still. Some had been talking, obviously, but all seemed to have been waiting to get a glimpse of the Stranger.

Craft led him down a hall to the right, through a high portico and into an office where several people were seated in easy chairs, leatherbacks, and couches, their backs to a fire place on the north wall. They were arranged in two semicircles, men behind the wen.

They stood up when Craft entered the room. They remained standing when the Stranger entered. Craft moved around and took up a position behind one of the wen near the center.

One wen stepped out from the center of the line, and then another. Together, they walked toward him.

"Nice stick," one said.

"I know him, Madeleine" said the other.

He looked at Madeleine and their eyes locked so quickly they did not have time to stop them. They both saw each other's eyes go black, then golden. By then the other wen was so close to the Stranger that she almost brushed against him. She was sniffing at him, noisily.

"Yes, I know him," she said again. And then, "From where?"

"From where, indeed?" the Stranger asked.

Hearing his voice, she startled. "A long time ago," she said. She moved across his field, coming close. Side-to-side she looked at him, not yet touching him.

"I know you. A long time ago. St. Louis. I let you drive my car, and you drove around corners on two wheels, wrong way on a six-lane, one way street. We took you back, me and my boyfriend, to my place. We drank more beer. He passed out.

"I wanted to fuck you. I wanted to fuck you so bad. I almost threw myself at you. I was as close to you as I am now. You were leaning up against the wall, watching me as I tucked his passed out ass into bed. I remember, I leaned in, pressed myself against you, and kissed you, and the top of my head blew off.

"I leaned in and kissed you, like this," she said. She kissed him. She kissed him and then the top of her head came off, she made muffled sounds of bliss, not letting go of his lips, hopping up and down a little bit on her toes.

She broke the kiss and said, "Yes, I know you. You're Quinn."

"I remember you. What's your name?" Quinn asked.

"Oh, you asshole. Of course you'd forget," she said, and punched him in the shoulder. "Most important kiss of my life, and you'd forget." And she punched him in his other shoulder with her other fist.

"Yeah, but I remember you. I told you I had to go. I couldn't stay there and fuck you with him sleeping in the next room, after he'd been so cool to me all day. See? I remember you," Quinn said.

"That's right. I know you, Quinn," she said.

"Yeah! But what's your name?"

"I'm Eva."

"Yeah. You had a perm back then," he recollected.

And she punched him again. "Yeah! You asshole! You would remember that!" and she punched him yet again.

"Ow," he said.

And she leaned in and kissed him again.

Then she took him by the hand and said, "Come with me."

She led him through a door at the far side of the office and into a hallway that had rooms with doors on either side. She went to the end room and let them in. There were three sets of tall windows on the three sides of the room. There was a bed on the southwest side of the room and a great fireplace on the northwest wall. The room was divided by sunshine and darkness. They stood in the middle, she holding both his hands and turning them three times round, alternating through the darkness and the light.

She said, "You blew the top of my head off. I spent my life searching for the answer to how you did that. I started with yoga, and ended up here. And here you are. What do you say we…"

By then, Quinn, having leaned the stick up against a wall, had grabbed her by her shirtfront and pulled her toward him as he stepped toward her. He kissed her.

"I'm sorry," he said, breaking the kiss. "Can I try to make up for it?" he asked.

She pulled him toward her by the waist of his pants and with her other hand rubbed his crotch, seeking anything firm. She found it more quickly than she thought she would, as he had become aroused by just a kiss. She rubbed it slowly, leaning backwards, making him lean forward for the next kiss; and he put one thigh between hers.

They had sex for a long time, she on either her belly or her back, legs hanging over the edge of the bed; he, both feet on the ground, limited by the reach of his pants stuck around his ankles, feet restrained by his lace-up army surplus boots.

Eventually, she let him go long enough for him to sit on the edge of the bed and untie them, and get his pants off.

Also, he eventually realized that she was controlling his pleasure levels; she was controlling the pace of things and he had fallen into it, suddenly feeling like Alice going down a rabbit hole. He became aware of a pattern in what she was doing: every so many strokes, she would stop, have a small orgasm, and squirt along his phallus, keeping everything slippery.

So he stopped what he was doing. Just stopped. She moved her hips a few times then stopped herself and looked at him. She smiled. He smiled back. She laughed, and then laughed a little longer. He started laughing and then he said, "I'm sorry. I wish I had known."

"Known what, Quinn?" she asked.

"What you'd become. This place," he answered.

"You couldn't have known. And, I couldn't have found it if I hadn't met you."

"And who are you, Eva?" he asked.

"I am the High Priestess of Stonehaven." she said without comma, hesitation, or pause.

25

WALKING

Angelica and Diana stepped out onto the porch of the Recovery building. The old dog was sitting there on the porch, looking out. "That's
Homer," Diana said. "Come on boy. Let's go for a walk."

"I remember. He was at the bottom step of the porch when I arrived,"
Angelica said. "I could swear he said 'Hello' to me. It was long and
drawn out. It sounded like 'eh-woh'."

"That's right. He says a few other words in English, too. Like 'ow' for
'out'. You'll see. He's very smart," Diana said.

There was an opening toward a view where the lawn sloped away,
down from the porch. The road in came around from the left and ended in the gravel and dirt parking lot. A canopied golf cart was parked
there. In her mind's eye, Angelica saw around the low ridge to her
right, up the steep, narrow valley where the Chapel was perched across
the stream.

Down near the bottom of the lawn was a small grove of trees with a
gazebo in the shade. "Let's head over there," Angelica said, pointing.

"Good choice," Diana said. "Come on, Homer." The dog got up and
trotted slowly over. Tying her shawl around her waist, she turned and
headed, bare-shouldered, for the grass. Angelica did the same. She fol-

lowed her, stepping around what appeared to be an old mud puddle in the lot.

The gazebo was unusual, Angelica noticed. The posts, that held up the roof, shaped like columns, kept presenting odd symmetries to her eyes as they slowly walked a path that switch-backed down the lawn. This disorientation made her cautious, watching her step, pausing on uncertain feet. She looked at the image while she was still, to see how a changing perspective affected what she saw. They crossed a little foot-bridge over a seep that led to a small pond. It had cattails growing in it and what looked like some water lilies.

"Lilies and lotus." Diana said. Then, "Sorry. I didn't mean to listen in, but you are broadcasting, actually. It's one of the things you'll need to control. Sometimes the blast can be so loud that even the animals can hear it."

They walked up a slight rise toward the small wood. The birds singing up in the leaves went quiet. Angelica looked up and paid attention to the strong young trees, some forty or fifty feet tall. They had serrated leaves, but she didn't know what kind they were, maybe beeches. They were blooming, a kind of long conical flower with lots of little flower-lets arranged to make points on the cone's surface.

When they walked into the woods a heavy scent enveloped them, a scent that smelled exactly like the aromas of sex. She breathed deeply, feeling both oppressed and empowered by that scent at the same time. She felt the smell of sex. It made her flare her nose, and breathe deeply again.

Diana went up the steps to the gazebo first, pausing at the top to wait for Angelica. There were four chairs around a small table. Looking at it, Angelica realized the table was seven-sided, and set at counter point to the angles of the gazebo itself. So, that was it, she thought. Seven sided: that's why it was so disconcerting.

Diana sat on a chair to the side, untying the shawl and draping it over the back of the chair, leaving the chair with the longer view open for Angelica. Diana sighed. "You have to stop broadcasting," she said. "You have to learn. I can shield myself from you. Yes, it is seven-sided. But right now you have an enormous field around you, and when I'm in your field I have to strike a balance between openness and being a closed door to you. I need to be able to read you, but not have the book of you slam itself over my ears whenever you have a thought. And the trees are chestnut--blight resistant American Chestnut."

Diana paused and breathed in the intoxication of the scent. Then she said, "They are the most endangered native tree on this continent. A long time ago they developed a blight from the introduction of a foreign species, the Japanese Chestnut. Even cutting the trees down didn't stop the blight. Understand, the Chestnut was the climax tree of the forest. It was the dominant tree. Sometimes the foliage would spread over an entire acre, and the trunks of the eldest were fourteen feet in diameter.

"So they were all cut down, all logged out. And the entire forest has been changed. Other species have grown to take over the forest. What the scientists at the time didn't know was that some of the trees can develop defenses against blights and other attackers. Some chestnuts, by chance not cut down, didn't die from the blight. When they were attacked they fought it, getting sick at first, and then recovering. They developed a resistance to it and passed this resistance on to some of their offspring. That's these trees, here. This grove comes from a mother long gone, but these are her offspring.

"Chestnuts were a major food source for the life here, including the Native Americans. They made milk from it, and flour.

"Some trees, isolated and remote, like some planted by immigrants in Kansas and Wisconsin, watered by hand, survived untouched by the blight because they were outside of the normal range. These days there are people working on blight resistant trees, and they're succeeding. As long as the trees live, the spirit of the tree looks on."

Diana paused, inhaled deeply, and turned to look all around her. Angelica couldn't tell what she was looking for, but then Diana settled on the long view. One of the men was driving a tractor, carrying a load of compost in the front loader bucket around to the garden. "You know, sometimes in the evening the air turns blue. It is as if the sky descends, somehow, and fills this valley." She sighed.

"You remember the peach, right?" she asked. Angelica nodded. "Well," she continued, "it's symbolic in all the ways you were looking for. But you need to do the work on it to really understand. And there's another level, a mythic level to the symbology. You remember the story of the Fall from the Garden, right?' Angelica nodded yes.

"So, you know the symbol of the fruit of the tree of the Knowledge of Good an Evil is usually the apple." Angelica nodded again.

"Well, do you remember the other tree in the Garden that the First Pair didn't get to eat from?"

"Yes," Angelica said. "The Tree of Immortality. They were kicked out 'lest they eat of it.'"

"That's right," Diana said. "Many cultures describe the fruit of the Tree of Immortality as a peach." She paused to let that sink in. She watched as Angelica's mind retreated to literalness, and spoke before she could get there.

"And no, you don't develop immortality by eating peaches," she said, scowling with such fierceness that Angelica was a little shocked. She even said, "But..." meaning to say, "But how did you know?" but Diana raised her hand and cut Angelica off. Angelica felt it as an uncontrollable need to shut up.

"You must understand what a peach is, in order to understand what it means."

"Will you teach me?" Angelica asked.

"No. Not that, anyway. Someone else will." Diana replied in a flat tone of voice, which settled on Angelica like a presage of anger.

She asked, "What are you angry at?"

Diana, still holding her hand palm up, said, "Nothing, yet. But I could be, at you. You retreat into literalism when your mind senses the imminence of revelation. It's protecting itself; I understand that. But in your condition, everything you struggle to protect yourself from realizing will become harder later. You erect barriers to understanding that you will have to tear down later. Sometimes that's a lot harder than putting the barrier up in the first place. Cement is a lot easier to move before it dries. Be quiet now. No talking."

They were silent together then for a while, sitting in the grove of chestnut trees, breathing the scent of sex, watching the long view, the tractor. They watched the sunlight move across the valley, shadows turning to point east, and then lengthening as the planet turned toward night.

Angelica thought about barriers. She tried to think quietly.

Diana started in, "You asked me about my children. I have two. Their father also works here. He works at Stonehaven sometimes, but also for one of the companies Stonehaven owns, when he's not here. We met here when we were in our twenties, and it sometimes happens that we fall in love and get to start a family. We both still belong here, only with the kids we usually can't be here at the same time. Except for Family Camp time, this really isn't a place for children.

"So, I'm here for six months or so. I go home on the weekends sometimes, and I talk to them a lot on the phone. It's a five hour drive. They think I work for the government, and that my job requires assignments overseas, which it sometimes actually does. I miss them, but I trust their father. Sometimes I have long periods at home, and then he'll be able to come here for a few weeks. Stonehaven also owns a few import businesses, so when I come home I've always got presents, which they love.

"When they were little I was with them all the time, and he worked. It was great. We loved each other and pretty much had the strong and loving happy family experience. We only came back here for holidays. Because the family experience was so strong, and the kids were so well developed, I was instructed that it was time for me to tell them I had to go back to work. The assignments began when the oldest was about seven, and the younger one five. I would be brought back here for a week or two at a time. That was five years ago. Now that they're older I'm brought in for longer stays. It's a lot like a military deployment, except we're not killing.

"I love him, and he loves me. The times we have together are profoundly happy. The times with the family intact are great times. But what we know is that the only reason we have that life, the only reason we met, the only reason we were blessed with two great kids, is that the Divine Feminine, the Diosa, wished it for us. The life we lead is based on Her indications, and on the providence that Stonehaven provides."

"Why are you telling me this?" Angelica wondered.

"Because you asked. And I am assigned to you, for now. You need some sense of security in the world around you right now. By telling you about the normal side of my life, you are reassured. I can feel it in your heart-rate and in your posture. You have calmed down. Your nervous system is learning the tones of my voice like the neonate knows the sounds of their mother's voice.

"You will need this link with me when the cycle starts up again for you."

"What cycle? What is going on with me?" Angelica asked, and her calmness surprised her.

"You had the experience commonly called the Release of the Kundalini Serpent. But that's not what we call it. We call it Overcoming the Kundalini Barrier. The experience creates a huge shift in the psyche. Before, you were one kind of person; after, you're another."

"What kind? What kind of person?" Angelica wanted to know, anxiety rising in her.

"A better kind, usually. If it doesn't all drive you crazy. That's my job," Diana said.

"It's your job to drive me crazy?" Angelica asked.

Diana laughed. "No, it's my job to keep you sane. Which might look like driving you crazy. Right now we are in a sacred place. The energy of this grove is helping to keep you calm and not become lost down the tracks of your inner journeys.

"The kind of person you were before, did you have any strange abilities? Any psychic powers?"

"No, none that I can think of. Sometimes my dreams were pretty powerful. I dreamed about having sex with someone from here who came and visited me before I came to the class."

"Have you seen him here? Have you recognized him?"

"No. I'm not sure I would. It was more a form, a form composed of energy, and it looked more like a cloud than a person."

"Interesting," Diana said. "Very interesting. Was the sex good? I mean, did it make you feel good or did it scare you?"

"It was good. I don't remember a lot of it. It started with him going down on me, kneeling at the edge of my bed. Honestly, when I woke up I thought it was a dream. I slept a long time afterwards, but when I woke up, I was just lying there—as if we had just finished—relaxed and happy, like he'd left me only a moment before. I wasn't scared at all; I just chalked it up to my imagination."

"I wonder..." Diana left her wondering unfinished. "If you run across somebody whose energy reminds you of that night, you tell me, OK?"

"He won't get in trouble, will he?" Angelica felt anxiety again.

"No, but we need to know who he was."

"I think I may have heard him playing the piano in the Mansion. In the dream I came here first, and he followed me home."

"Well, that narrows the list some," Diana said. "You know, this is all significant. It all points to what you might become. Clearly, you had a talent for journeying. You maybe thought it was just a dream, but it may have been real. Psychically real. Tell me something else about you. What did you study in college?"

"I like people. I studied ethnology in college. I look for patterns in the different myths that people believe in. I speak a couple languages. I feel bad for a lot of the suffering people go through and want to do something effective to help them."

Diana nodded affirmatively at Angelica, gesturing to her to go on.

"Right before I left to come here I started having strange sensations, and strange feelings. I started to feel like I owed something back to the world for all the good things that had happened to me in my life." Angelica paused, remembering. "One morning the shower started to feel like little needles. When I got out I looked in the mirror and my eyes were spinning. They were whirling around in spirals. It looked like little tornadoes were coming out of them."

"Interesting. That's very interesting, too."

They fell into a reflective silence. Then Diana resumed.

"Before the Overcoming people tend to be more focused on themselves, even if they're engaged in helping others. They are, in many ways, buffered from reality. Afterward, after it happens, they tend to become more 'other-focused.' That's because, at least for one reason, they find themselves more open to others.

"Their lives and experiences aren't just isolated in themselves anymore. Their relations with others aren't just about casual friendships and sympathizing with others. Instead, afterwards, you begin to actually feel what others are really suffering. Sometimes realizing the contradictions in others, the contradiction between what they're doing and saying, and what they're really thinking and feeling is huge. It can be terrifying and crazy-making.

"But another thing that happens is that you will feel all your own feelings more intensely. All your sensations will be more intense. It's like trying to put too much water through a pipe, or too much electricity through a wire. Pleasure can turn into pain.

"With time and practice you will learn to make the pipe bigger. And the wire will handle more current."

After a long silence, while they listened to the wind in the trees and the rustle of the grass surrounding the grove, there was a faint sound of a stick breaking, just a little click. It startled Angelica out of her reverie about the feeling of this place.

Diana spoke, "There are spirits in this land. Some have always been here; others have been driven here by civilization. Still others have been brought here by the Priestesses. They know they are safe.

"Every species, except humans, has a mind, one mind that represents all of its individual members. With training, it is possible to acquire the power and the quality of development that will allow you to see them; sometimes even to talk with them. They have their own purpose: to keep the species alive and care for its welfare.

"Learning how to talk to them begins with learning to listen, spreading out your sense of hearing into the world around you, into the subtle sounds that we never hear in civilization. This is a wild place," she said, gesturing around toward the mountains with her hand.

"After you learn to extend your hearing, you must learn to extend your feeling until it encompasses the same range; let your feeling flow out to the sounds you hear. Rest there, waiting, perceiving. Something might show itself to you.

"You heard that stick snap. Now follow it out with your feelings. See if you can feel what's there. But don't look directly. If it wants to show itself, it will appear in your peripheral vision."

Angelica did what she was told, exhaling, sitting up straight, folding her hands in her lap

She listened toward where she heard the noise, extended her feeling, and waited. She turned her head slightly toward where she heard the sound. In that moment, on the edge of her vision, emerging from behind a tree, she saw what appeared to be a small, thin, brown elbow. Then she heard a short, quiet barking sound that registered with her as a sound of surprise at discovery. Then she heard another stick snap, and the feeling of presence fled out of the field of her awareness. Homer stared intently in that direction.

After some time, Diana spoke again, "There was a myth once: the myth that the sun went around the earth. Almost everyone believed it. But it wasn't true. What you will learn will be no less significant than learning the opposite: that the earth goes around the sun. It will involve a perspective shift that is just as huge, and just as difficult." Standing up, she said, "Let's go." She walked down the steps, heading out of the grove toward the valley. As she went, she picked up her shawl and threw it over one shoulder. Homer padded after her, down the steps.

Angelica followed, silently—mentally silent, at least, because she tripped and fell trying to keep up with Diana. "Gawdammit," she muttered under her breath.

Diana spoke back over her shoulder from ten yards away, "You shouldn't say that around here, either," without offering to come back and help Angelica up. Angelica rolled to a sitting position and started picking burrs and seeds out of the fringe of the sarong. Then she realized that Diana had hiked up the bottom of her sarong as she emerged from the grove and into the pasture.

"Too late," Diana said, turning around. "Just hitch it up and tuck the hem into the waist." Diana showed her how to do this, turning the sarong into a mid-thigh skirt, revealing how strong and tanned her legs were, gleaming in the sunlight. Impatient, she started waving the bottom of the skirt, fanning herself with it. "Come on," she said. "It's hot standing here." Then she turned, and walked on, crossing the face of the ridge in the pasture, just below the tree line.

Just inside the edge of the woods on the ridge line was a small open front shed with a bench against the back wall and a small old table with two chairs just under the roof line. Leaning up against a wall were some axes and splitting mauls. There was an old broom for sweeping the hard packed dirt floor. The space smelled of sawdust and chainsaws. Hanging from hooks on the wall were bow saws, wide-brimmed straw hats, a chainsaw chain, and a canvas bag containing sharpening files.

On the bench, next to a pile of used work gloves, was a case of bottled water in real glass bottles, and an old metal cooler used as a small dry food pantry. An overturned metal bowl sat on top. There were whole wheat crackers and hard candy in the cooler.

Diana stood looking out over the valley while Angelica nosed around inside. "Get yourself some water and bring me one, will you? Help yourself to anything in the cooler, too."

Angelica took two pieces of the candy and the bottled water, went over, and sat down by Diana.

"Look," she said, opening her bottle, then waving her hand. "We own this whole watershed. Nothing comes in here without us knowing about it. You can drink the water from any one of these streams, except below the livestock and the little stream just below the driveway. We'll go down to the one below in a bit. That's the one you came down. Maybe I'll find a little bit of you in it."

Angelica opened her bottle and poured some in the metal bowl for Homer. She looked around the watershed and counted ten steep valleys coming into the bottom land. She guessed that they probably all had small streams in them that merged into the creek running near the foot of the ridge. She looked over her shoulder to the left, toward the Mansion, and saw there was a very small stream coming into the creek. There was a driveway coming down alongside it, leading to a bridge near where the creek disappeared into the woods on its way out of the valley. The road from the bridge climbed up onto a flatter pasture and led around to the barns and dormitories.

She looked again, back at the ridges that came down into the valley, with the big mountain in the west brooding over the whole thing. It looked like the shoulders of a gigantic being with many arms rounding in toward the center. It reminded her of something, an image of a many-armed Goddess she had seen. They were sitting on one of those arms, with the Mansion on a broad flat arm behind them. Judging by the rock outcroppings, the Mansion spanned two arms. There was another beyond that where the driveway came down from above. That rock outcropping was sheer, and went down to the edge of the creek, the water flowing onto it and around its base. One of the other ten arms came down to match it across the creek. There was a broader floodplain in the valley bottom on that side, cultivated now and planted in corn.

She looked back to the west, where the first arm of ridge came into the valley and ended in a rocky crag. The buried rock strata pushed up into vertical walls by the ancient volcanic explosion were sharply exposed there, looking like a sheer sided tower; and the collapsed sections on top looked like the crenellations of an ancient tower. She turned to Diana and asked her about it.

"We call that Snake's Knob. It looks interesting, doesn't it? You could climb up there, but it isn't advised unless it's winter. It's called Snake's Knob for a reason. Only certain of us go up there, and you wouldn't want to go alone, or without training," Diana said. "There's a cave up there, too."

"Snakes? Really? What kind of snakes?" Angelica wanted to know.

"Black snakes and Blue Racers, mostly. Some Corn Snakes, and Garter Snakes, too. Sometimes a King Snake. Occasionally you'll find an Eastern Diamond Back, or a Copperhead, especially further back in the woods. There used to be a big Rattlesnake den up there, but they've moved on now, and the Black Snakes have moved in. Like I said, don't go there alone. The rock is dangerous," Diana said firmly.

Angelica nodded. "I've already dreamed I've been up there. It was dangerous." She looked around at the other valleys, noticing that a trail went up each one. "What about those other trails?"

"They all lead up," Diana replied. "There's something special along each one of them: chapels—but not exactly like the one you were in. Campsites, Sacred Circles, Graveyards. There are paths around the edges, connecting from one ridge line to the other. We patrol out there, tracking the wildlife, and the game. Sometimes hunters wander onto the property, but we keep a perimeter on the watershed to protect it."

Diana stood up. "Let's walk down by the stream. See those Elderberry bushes over there? There's some shade there and a little footbridge over the stream. The fruit's not ripe yet, though. Grab one of those hats off the wall for me, will you? And get one for yourself."

Angelica stood, went back into the shed and picked the prettiest two hats off their hooks. They made their way out to the field, stopping at the wood's edge to look down over the pasture, pausing in the dappled light. The grass was knee high, sprinkled with wild flowers, waving, then going still in the intermittent breeze. It looked like the little winds were dancing, skipping from place to place, the tall grass bright in the afternoon sun.

"This is all an experiment here," Diana said. "This grass, I mean. Mostly it's wild Einkorn with some Emmer, mixed with native grasses and flowers. We try to cultivate only native wild plants, but Einkorn was maybe the first wheat. It's OK to cultivate things, enhance some quality of a thing so that it helps make our lives better. It's OK; we just have to be careful doing it.

"Things can go wrong and there can be unforeseen consequences. One of the things we do here, this endeavor to communicate with the plant spirits, seems to foster positive outcomes. We lose very little to pests, for example. We consider cultivating this ability to be a part of how we work on ourselves, and we do it in service to life."

Angelica stood quietly, taking it all in. Diana held out a hand for a hat and Angelica passed her one. Diana smiled at it, put it on her head, and stepped out into the light. Angelica followed, smiling, but for some reason she couldn't explain to herself.

They crossed the sun gilded grass, walking back and forth along the hillside rather than directly down, as if they were following some old, overgrown switchback path. To someone looking up from below there would be no sign of a trail, no marking of their passage. They flattened the grass in only the narrowest ways, Angelica stepping almost in Diana's footsteps. They arrived at the bottom in a small meadow filled with a different kind of grass, next to the bridge under the Elderberry.

Diana walked into the shade under the trees to a small path along the foundation of the bridge and went directly to the stream. She squatted down, cupped up a handful of the water and drank it. "Yup," she said, turning to Angelica and smiling. "It tastes like you."

Angelica hurried down beside her and said, "Wait, no way," and bent down, cupping up a handful herself. When it tasted just like water, sweet water, she turned to Diana to say, "No way." But she found herself staring at Diana's smiling face, almost breaking into a laugh under twinkling eyes. She knew she'd been had, that Diana had been pulling her leg. Angelica had to smile back in return.

They sat down on the grass that came to edge of a small bank to the stream. Angelica asked her, "This thing—this thing that's happened to me—did it happen to you?"

Diana looked thoughtfully up at the Elderberry trees close overhead. "Not like it has to you. It has happened to you all at once. It looks like what we have learned to think of as a 'full-blown' event. The barrier is overcome, and all the buffers destroyed, simultaneously. The energy latent in the stored fluids all gets released in the system, into the river of you, all at once. It is more common for parts of the dam to go, not the whole. Partial releases, maybe a floodgate fails, something new and energetic happens. In partial release, the systems of you open to the real world more slowly, often just one subsystem at a time.

"If some of the same things hadn't happened to me we couldn't have heard each other think. I think that's all you need to know about what's happened to me so far, though. It's one of the reasons I'm assigned to you."

"But what was it like, what happened to you?" Angelica asked, leaning forward to swirl a hand in the stream. It was broader here, and more shallow. Since it had spread out some as it came down into the valley, it was warmer too.

"You're going to just keep pushing on this, aren't you?" Diana asked.

"Yes," Angelica replied. "I have to know."

"Alright," Diana said. "One at a time, all of my senses became amplified. And being amplified they became more sensitive. The sense of touch was particularly overwhelming. Everything became pain for a while; clothes, caresses, sex. Even eating food became pain. Smell became horrible, especially when it would trigger memories that weren't my own. I had to go naked everywhere for two months because I couldn't stand the feel of anything touching me. I am grateful I was here. The work on overcoming my embarrassment was easier.

"Hmm," Diana said, and laughed. "I learned to masturbate. The only thing I could stand to have touch me was my own self."

Angelica asked, "Were you my age?"

Diana replied, "Some senses went earlier: vision went when I was a teenager; hearing went when I was about your age. The touch thing didn't happen until I was twenty eight, though.

"Ha ha ha ha!" Diana laughed again, in a rising voice. "At the same time I couldn't stand for anybody to touch me I got crazy horny. My sensitivity to sexual sensation went through the roof. I could stand outside naked and have an orgasm just from the caress of a breeze. Wandering around naked in front of everybody just added to it. I learned I could orgasm just from being looked at. Being looked at became an experience akin to touch.

"It's how they brought me back. Once we figured it out, they had a ceremony for me; a ceremony where everybody looked at me, and all imagined themselves doing things to me. I learned to catch those visions, catch them in my mind, feel them, and sense them in my body. I'm telling you, all that pain and sensitivity became fun."

She laughed again, a single, "Huh." Then she looked down into the flowing water. "We had some serious fun." Together, they stared at the water, resting in the contemplation of motion.

"Come on," Diana said, finally. "Let's cross the bridge and go up the other side. There's something I want to show you when we get to the top of rise."

They reached the top of the rise and stood there in the hot afternoon sun, listening to the echoes of the cicadas. The sounds were crashing off the ridges and rolling back at each other, their twinned noises giving the world a simple orchestration of the drawing power of sex, creaking like an old spring mattress, humming like some alien ship from another world. The grasshoppers clattered by. Somewhere, an early cricket chirped.

Diana looked around for a flat spot she knew was there, left over from the foundation of an old smokehouse. They picked spots next to each other, and they sat down on their shawls.

As they sat there, a dancing wind, a whirlwind, formed. It came down from the hump of the mother mountain, swirling the tops of the trees, coming straight for them. Homer stood up, faced into it, and growled.

A displaced breeze blew around them, like the bow wave of an immense ship. Diana said, "Get up on your knees, like me. Sit on your heels. Face the sun, look to the southwest, like me. Do like me." And then she made a low 'O' sound.

When they were both sitting on their heels, making the sound, Diana raised her arms, palms forward, arms angled up at forty five degrees. They were kneeling together close enough that Diana's hand brushed Angelica's hand. Diana slid her hand in front, so Angelicas fingers were touching the center of the back of her hand.

Diana said, "Feel what I feel."

Angelica felt what she could only describe as a whoosh and then a quiet boom sound that rocked her gently. Suddenly she felt connected to Diana, feeling what she felt. Diana said, "Open your heart to the sun."

Angelica did that, focusing her awareness on her heart. Sensing and feeling what Diana did with her heart, she did the same. Then she was suddenly filled with golden light; golden light, like a cloud inside her, filling her up from within. Her field of vision became suffused with gold.

"Send it through you," Diana said. Angelica felt Diana open her root, and, like opening a floodgate, draining into the earth, the golden light poured through.

She felt-sensed Diana moving the focus of her awareness a little higher, to her womb, and then divide the light into three channels. Angelica saw her intention to send the lines separately to different parts of her pelvic floor. Angelica tried to do this but couldn't quite follow it, the new sensation of her womb catching her, and her focus, by surprise. It was as if she were sensing her womb for the first time. The power of the sensing drew her attention down in a slow contracting sensation.

Diana sensed this and shifted the energy instead to her legs, then down along the ground to the energy centers, the chakras, at the souls of her feet. Angelica's attention and energy followed along. These centers opened and the golden light poured out upon the ground, spreading it out in a rising circle around them.

The whirlwind they'd seen arrived and formed a standing column of wind whirling around them. It lifted off their hats, as if it wanted to see their upturned faces more clearly. Angelica felt the lift of it, as if it wanted to see what they weighed. It swirled up their skirts, exposing the tops of their thighs to the sky, lifted their hair. And then it was gone.

Left with blissful faces turned toward the sun, Diana said, "Close your heart." Although she didn't want to do it, Angelica did as she felt Diana do.

Angelica collapsed forward, forehead in her hands on the grass. Still kneeling, hyperventilating, shivering in the sudden cold, she started to weep. A faint cloud of reddish light began to form over them.

Diana touched her shoulder and said, "Here. You can keep some of it for yourself. You can take some back and keep it for yourself."

Suddenly, Angelica felt the light and the heat gather at her behind. She reached back and pulled the slip up over her rump as the light slowly entered her and filled her up.

It stopped, and, knowing now that light and warmth inside her, she started to orgasm, her whole body quaking.

"This is one of the ways we serve," Diana said.

When it finished, and with a sigh, Angelica's arms and legs slowly extended. Straightening out, she lowered her body slowly to the earth. She fell deeply asleep, sinking through the lake of dreams and settling in the darkness on the bottom. Diana picked up one limp hand and set it down. She pulled the slip down a little to cover Angelica's backside, and straightened out the shawl with the little white flowers she was lying on. Diana covered Angelica with her own shawl, sat down next to her, watching the sunset.

She put her hand on Angelica's shoulder, feeling the tremor of a high speed pulse, about two hundred forty beats per minute, rippling through her skin, in addition to, and in counterpoint to, her slowing heart. She patted Angelica's shoulder as the red light over them faded.

"Sleep, baby girl," she said.

Diana stayed with Angelica. She retrieved their hats, and sat down to watch the afternoon fade into evening. She sat in the sun, adjusted the brim of the hat to shade her eyes, and breathed it all in: the scents of grass, and dirt, and water, and sweat. She faced the sun, closed her eyes, and allowed the sweat to run. She loved the heat and relaxed into it fully.

After a half hour, she heard steps on the foot bridge and then a rustle in the grass heading her way. She extended her senses, trying to feel who it was. She realized it was two people; one not caring about noise, the other being very quiet.

She knew it was Eva when they were twenty feet away. By ten feet she knew it was Raphael, a good looking legacy in his mid-twenties. His skin was dark, a heritage of African American parents, but his eyes were hazel and his hair brown, worn in dreadlocks. Eva came up behind her, dropping a bedroll she had carried over a shoulder. Clearing her throat in the polite way, she touched Diana on the shoulder. As Diana turned with a smile to look at Eva, she felt the thump as Raphael dropped something heavy on the ground. She took Eva's extended hand and stood up, next to the still sleeping Angelica.

They had both brought backpacks, Eva's had food and water. Raphael's pack contained their standard woods travelers pack with tools, fire starting kit, and small weapons, including bear spray. They laid down their packs and Eva said, "He's been assigned to her, too, now. He's your relief. We need you in the ballroom tonight. You're one of the seconds. Maybe first, if you're ready."

Raphael smiled at her, good-naturedly and with a little shyness. He turned to start working on the big bag he'd been carrying on one shoulder and she realized it was a portable canopy. He pulled the red canopy out of its bag and began to set it up.

Diana raised an eyebrow, "Really?" she asked.

Then Eva gestured at the sleeping Angelica, "She may be here awhile. How is she?"

"Easy. So far, at least," Diana said. "She slipped out in ecstasy after the modified Hymn to the Sun and she's been asleep for about an hour now. Hasn't stirred at all. She can probably hear us, so I want her to understand. She's doing really well. She's accepted that something has happened to her that's pretty extreme, without a trace of self-pity. She feels safe here, even though I haven't told her much about who we are, other than that our expertise in the yogas has given us the experience to help her. So far, not much pain. But you and I both know that we can't predict what it will be like. So far it looks to be extreme sensitivity to all the normal sensations, and a vulnerability to other telepaths."

"I saw the wind," Eva said. "Why'd you do the Hymn?"

"It called," Diana replied. "It showed up, so I went with it. I had her touch the back of my hand and she followed me. She followed me really well, actually, and did exactly what I did. When I tried to move into the lower Division of Three she got caught up in her womb so I jumped to the end, Feeding the Grass."

Eva nodded. "Did you see the Dragon?"

"Yes. Not in much detail, but the cloud was there, over her, during the feeding."

Raphael, who had been listening while setting up the canopy, cut in, "Seriously? A Dragon?"

Both wen turned and stared at him. He became embarrassed, stopped working, and looked down.

"Listen, Raphael," Eva said, letting him off the hook. "As an Intern in the program, you've been taught the Protocol for Good Manners, yes?"

He nodded.

"Then don't interrupt when we're talking. It's not a conversation that involves you; it's a conversation that you have the privilege of witnessing. If it's something that you need instruction about, wait until you're recognized before you ask. If it's something like this, that doesn't involve you directly, wait until you're in the Circle to ask it. I don't anticipate having to remind you again."

He nodded again. "Yes, High Priestess. My apologies; my surprise got the better of me." He paused and then said to Diana, "My apologies, Priestess."

Diana nodded her head in acceptance of the apology, and said, having mercy on his deepening embarrassment, "Remember, the Protocol changes, should you become Consort. By then, your surprise won't be getting the best of you. Now finish setting up the canopy."

Eva didn't nod. The Protocol of Manners did not require it.

Raphael did as he was told, berating himself internally. The work schedule and the practice schedule were so full for the Interns that he'd barely had the chance to hear Eva talk outside of Lecture. He'd never even been this close to Diana before, and he felt the power of her like warm syrup all round him. He was startled by the sudden realization that she was doing it to him on purpose, making him feel that she was sweet when being sweet to him was really the last thing on her mind. He took a sideways glance at her and saw Diana was looking at him sideways, too—down and sideways under hooded eyes, while she was listening to Eva.

Then he realized suddenly that it was a test; a test to see if he spoke out of place again, using the sense of sweetness he felt as an invitation to open his mouth again. He felt a sudden flush of gratitude toward Diana that her field was so sweet, but he kept his mouth shut. He looked away, back to the tangle of stay-lines for the canopy in his hands. He knew that if he looked at the tangle of her hair, instead, he would be a goner.

Eva had continued, "Well, we'll have to watch out for it. I'm surprised she has one, frankly. She's so new it might drive her. It may shield her from Diosa, but it will also shield her from other things. We'll see. We haven't had a new dragon show up like that in a long time. It could be a limitation. We shall have to see what it wants."

Raphael was listening to all this, setting up the canopy on the flat piece of ground just below and east of the rise in the ridge. He knew that he would come to understand exactly what was so special about this one girl, but he was also dissatisfied that he didn't already understand.

Diana stood there, proud, looked over her shoulder at him, and told him, "Take the collapsible bucket and go get some water. You'll need it."

When Raphael stopped what he was doing, he showed no reaction or resignation in his body. He showed, instead, the posture of the sensation of complete neutrality at the personal level, and they all somehow managed to sigh at the same time.

They all thought the same thing at the same time, too, although perhaps for different reasons.

That thought was, "Finally."

Raphael picked up the bucket and went to get some water.

As he came back the wen were getting ready to leave. They had laid out the bedding under the incomplete setup of the canopy and they were in the process of rolling Angelica over and waking her to semi-consciousness so she could help them move her over to the new location.

Later in the Men's Circle Raphael would say he heard Angelica say, "Oh, oh. Fuck you. Leave me alone. You don't know."

Both of the other wen leaned forward to her and quietly whispered, "Yes, we do. We do know. And, you know," He saw Eva smiling, particularly broadly. They had just put her to bed, so to speak. She rolled over to her side and snuggled in. She had moaned, "No," with her arms crossed over her chest.

Eva had leaned over her, in Raphael's hearing, and said, "There, girl. There will be surprises. Rest until then. Remember, you will become the Receptive."

She stood up, took Diana by the hand and led her away, back over the footbridge, leaving Angelica and Raphael alone.

Raphael stood there, watching them go. His jaw almost dropped, watching them, and then he remembered the Protocol of Manners. He closed his mouth, yet again. One could never tell; they might look back and see him standing there with his mouth open, looking stupid, in the presence of a magnificence he might never be able to understand.

No, he knew that wasn't true. He wouldn't be where he was unless there was a chance he would understand it. But he wouldn't risk creating the impression he didn't understand, not in the face of that much magnificence.

Being in the presence of magnificence was the feeling Diana left him with. The feeling that Eva left in her wake was undetectable, as if she was never there, a deep quick swish of memory, a Goddess whose footsteps were beyond his power to track.

He watched them go. Then he turned and finished zipping in the mosquito netting, and then the solid wind screens on the sides of the canopy. He had a sudden intuition that he should lower the canopy, closer to the ground, below the ridgeline, down to about four feet. He intuited that there would be wind later. And maybe a storm. It would be stupid of him to not anticipate this, and then, through his stupidity, expose Angelica to it.

That was not his purpose. His purpose was to serve, and to Serve Life. That was his promise, the promise he made at Induction.

And it wouldn't Serve to be stupid.

26

REGINA AND THE LAMA'S GHOST

Amanda, Beverly, Rachel, and Madeleine were sitting near a low fire, meant only to drive away the chill of the spring evening. Lamps and candles were being used; no one cared for the electric light. They were half way through a bottle of whiskey when Rachel turned to Amanda and asked her to tell more of Regina's story. Regina was off, out of the house on a ride. The moon was full and the woods, not yet fully leafed out, were filled with light.

Amanda began with a sigh, and a reluctant shake of her head. "Madeleine, I don't know if Rachel has told you, but I have told her and Beverly many stories of Regina's early sexual life. Something in me is moved to talk not of this, but to tell another story, one that may bear much more relevance to this place and what we are trying to accomplish."

Turning to Rachel and Beverly, Amanda continued, "I mentioned a story earlier that I would tell more of later, a story about Regina going off into the Highlands and finding a house that she hadn't known was there. Menarche came upon her while she stood there looking at it, looking at its buildings and its walls. The people there took her in and cared for her. She fell very hard for their youngest daughter, the one who came through the gate and took her in. The people sent her home on their horse.

"And that was the beginning of a friendship to which, for Regina's part, she was fiercely devoted. But it was very strange. The next time she wanted to go their house I went with her, to meet the family, and make sure the child wasn't being a nuisance. And, you know, Regina could not find the house again. She was very upset. She could find the knoll, she thought, but there was no house. She returned, she told me, many times to that knoll, and just sat there, looking at the space where the house had been.

"Perhaps a year later she was sitting on the knoll when the young woman appeared behind her. She sat down and they talked. The young woman, whose name was Maray, explained that they were all—mother, father, two daughters and a son—magical beings associated with the weather, and that they were kin to Brighid. And that, through that kinship, they knew about me, and my developing devotion to the Goddess. Maray also said that, in time, they would let her bring me to the house. She said to wait, though. The house moved, she told her, like a cloud along the ground. Usually it couldn't be seen at all. But the reason Regina couldn't see it now was that it wasn't there; it was somewhere else. Maray told Regina that she was special and that was why she had been able to see the house in the first place. Maray told her she had the second sight, and that many things would become clear to her that were obscure to others. Maray told her she was gone often, working for her mother, but that she would meet her there, on the knoll, at that same time every year. Maray also told her that her older brother and sister would watch over her, and not to worry if she didn't see their house.

"I tell you this story now because much has happened in the years since then, much that I did not understand at the time, and now I am worried that, since things have happened that I never believed would happen, these are things I must tell you all, also.

"Once this young woman, or Goddess, or whatever she was—Maray—told Regina to come back every year on the same day, and the next time to bring me, her mother, with her, I must confess my credulity was strained to the utmost. Magical beings, kin to the Goddess Brighid. How could that be? Long gone was Brighid, long gone also must have been all Her kin.

"Yet despite my doubt, nay, my disbelief, I went with Regina the next year. We went back to the knoll where we had been before. To my amazement, there was the house, with buildings, surrounded by a large fenced-in yard. It was an old house, built in the old style, with thick walls of rock and a thatch roof. There was a loom in the yard. I could not believe my eyes. And sitting at the loom was a young woman.

"Regina whistled at her. She whistled back and waved. She got up and came toward us. She was beautiful, with a long dress, and she seemed to float over the ground. She stopped at the wall and leaned on it. 'Hello, sweet girl, how good to see you.' It was hard to understand her, her accent was so thick. And Regina replied, 'Hello, sweet girl, how good to see you, too.' They touched hands across the wall, and a wind came up. 'And this is your mother, Amanda, yes?' and Regina replied, that, yes, she'd brought me as instructed. 'Mother, this is Maray,' she said. Maray made no move closer toward me, and, indeed, I felt a push from her that kept me in my place.

"She made a gesture with her right hand, two fingers up, in a swirling motion. 'This is my mother,' she said. And a column of gray mist whirled down from the house and stopped beside her, the whirling slowing down and resolving into a tall form, the eyes intent, the smile slight. 'This is Cai-ya-lee-ach,' she said. 'She is called Calley, for short. She's my mom.'

"This Calley looked at me, Her eyes stern, Her smile enigmatic, and turned to the left, gesturing for me to follow Her along the wall. We passed by an arched gate, under part of which ran a stream. On the other side of the gate She stopped and turned to me. She leaned forward over the wall and said, in a voice no louder than a whisper in the wind, 'This is She for whom you long,' and disappeared. Simply vanished. Behind her was a form, another woman. She was exactly as I had imagined Her; chestnut hair and rowan lips. I trembled so hard I went to my knees, for I knew it to be Her, the Brighid, focus of my studies and prayers. I lowered my face, too afraid to look up. I wept, I sobbed, I have no idea how long. When I fell into silence, I dared to look up, under my brow, and there She was, leaning over the wall, grinning at me. 'I know you,' She said.

"I will leave this part of my story for now. Rachel, I have told you part of it, but much of it still abides in me as being too much for me to put in words. There are parts, though, of Regina's story which I feel compelled to share. I am so grateful that you have made a safe space for us, and that it includes the opportunity for me to talk to you all about the deep, and the dark. And the hopeful."

Pausing to take several thoughtful sips of her whiskey, Amanda gathered her thoughts. Setting aside the overwhelming memory of her encounter with Brighid, she focused on the events of Regina's life.

"Before we left to come here, Regina went back to the Highlands House one more time. When she returned she was possessed of a determination that would brook no talking. No questions garnered any response but the shaking of her head.

"She had been given an assignment by this Calley person, I mean, the Storm Goddess Calley. I had never heard of Her before, and, when I looked, I could find only a couple place names, sea side cliffs, and locations of that sort. Nor had I found any evidence that She was Brighid's sister; Her older sister, actually, according to Regina.

"Regina was disturbed by this assignment, deeply disturbed. Shaken even. She asked for my help. When I asked her what it was, she told me that she had to find her father in hell. She had to go to him, find him and ask him to do a favor for her and the Goddess Calley. What the favor was, she would not say. She said only that she was to enter a trance state, induced by some herbs that Maray had showed her, think of Calley, and that Calley would guide her to the hell her father waited in. It would then be Regina's task to find her father in hell by thinking of him, longing for him, recalling her love of him as a child, and that would lead her part way to him. Once in, she was to stop, and wait, and keep her longing for him pure, and that this would call him, call him to her."

"Hell?" Rachel asked, leaning forward in her chair, whiskey cradled in both hands.

"No, not really. That was not the name Regina used. She used the word 'Bardo'. It's a word I am not familiar with."

"Hmm," Rachel said. "That makes more sense. He was a Lamaist, and the Bardoes are where a soul spends time between incarnations. There are levels depending on the density of someone's spirit when they disincarnate. There is a level where one can wait until one is ready to choose what they want to do next, but this level is only for the most evolved."

"I assume he was not at that level," Amanda said, edgily.

"That's not a safe assumption to make, Amanda," Rachel said, just as edgy.

Madeleine leaned in also, looking at Amanda first and then Rachel. Holding up a hand, palm down, then palm up toward Rachel, but discreetly, so Amanda couldn't see it. She indicated that Rachel should wait. Amanda became introspective, her eyes became puffy, and she took a long pull from her tumbler.

"Go ahead and cry, hon," Beverly said. "I know you loved him."

"Yes, but I'm so gawdamned angry!" Amanda beat her fist on the chair arm and jumped up.

"Why are you angry, honey?" Beverly stayed on track.

"Because I wanted more, and I didn't get it. I didn't get it for Regina and I didn't get it for myself," Amanda answered, sitting down again.

"But you always had everything you needed," Beverly pointed out evenly.

"But no powerful man in my bed in the winter. No powerful man between my legs at night," Amanda bemoaned.

Beverly said, "I understand," in an empathetic tone of voice.

"Yeah, well," Rachel cut in, pronouncing 'well' like it had two syllables, and in a tone dripping with false sympathy. That made Amanda cry and then become angry again, except this time directly at Rachel.

"Look, Sister, what are you really angry about?" Madeleine asked. "Rachel just deliberately provoked you, and you fell for it."

"Because Rachel—," and then she stopped. "Because Rachel—she—,"

"She what?" Beverly prompted, while Rachel sat still, erect and regal.

"Well, look at her," Beverly gestured, palm up.

They turned and looked. As they looked, Rachel began to grow dark. A dark fog formed around her, and Rachel simply disappeared into it. They could see the wall and window behind her through the darkness, but all image of Rachel had disappeared.

"Can you do that?" Madeleine asked.

"No, I can't," Amanda said, sniffling and not really appreciating what she was seeing in front of her.

Madeleine said, firmly, "When you can do that you can have what she has."

"But, no," Amanda wailed. "I need it. I need it now!"

"Oh, bullshit," Beverly said.

Madeleine said, sharply, "Brighid! I need to see you now!"

Amanda's head dropped immediately, her chin resting on her chest. A deeper, still feminine voice, issued from Amanda.

"How may I help you, daughter?"

"Your child here is in trouble. Not me, the one you are speaking through."

The Goddess said, "Her people are breaking down."

Madeleine responded, "She is breaking down."

The Goddess said, "Of course. Would you like me to stop her?"

Madeleine said, "Of course. Her people are one thing. She is another. Cut the ties to them if you must. But her mind is needed here, free from her attachment to her own suffering. Perhaps you could show her some of yours."

"You think you know," the deeper voice said, no longer talking to Madeleine. "Let me show you."

Amanda's face rose, her visage contorted, and she screamed in pain.

The darkness in which Rachel sat concealed wavered. Amanda's head turned to Rachel, and the deep voice from Amanda said, "Be sure you understand, I see you."

The darkness parted to reveal Rachel's face, "I see you, too, Brighid."

Amanda laughed out loud, then screamed again. Her chin dropped at the end.

Into the silence the voice said, "I am not done with you yet, servant."

Amanda continued to scream, shadows flickering around her head. In the kitchen Paul and Craft heard it and came running upstairs. Madeleine halted them with her hand when they slid back the door to the library where the wen were sitting. Regina, up on the mountain, thought she heard a faint echo of a woman screaming, but told herself it was probably a bobcat.

Paul bumped Craft with his shoulder. "Let me see," he whispered, trying to see over Craft's shoulder. "Let me in."

"Maybe never," Craft whispered back, harshly, sliding the door closed.

The wen sat, with their hands in their laps, listening. The flickering shadows above Amanda's head showed red flames at their roots. After a few minutes, Amanda's voice gave out and the screaming stopped. Amanda's head fell back against the rise of her chair; she was panting. After a few seconds her head dropped forward, and the voice emerged again.

"That was what it feels like to be burned alive. Do you understand this happened to me many times? Do you understand?" the voice asked.

Amanda nodded, speaking out a faint "Yes," in her own voice.

"Yours is no complaint," the deeper voice said, and then there was a palpable rush of air leaving the room.

Suddenly Amanda began panting again, and shouting like she was in childbirth. After a couple minutes, or so, the panting stopped.

Amanda raised her head when she was finished. Calmly, she said, "There."

Everyone sat silently. Slowly Rachel reappeared, sitting in the same position, looking impassively at Amanda. Amanda opened her eyes, looked directly at Rachel and said, "I apologize."

"For what, precisely, do you apologize?" Rachel responded, giving no hint of impending softness or mercy.

"I apologize for my lack of gratitude. Your generosity with me has been both impeccable and extraordinary. I refer not just to material generosity. You have treated me like a sister. I refer also to your generosity of soul and your generosity of spirit. The feelings with which you have comforted me have led me into a dwelling in the sublime. You have taken my understanding past the liminal, past the threshold and into the place where the pediments of nature have been shown to me in ways I could not have imagined, even though I found myself walking in the midst of them when I arrived here. Your generosity has been extended, without holding anything back, to the whole of me."

Into the silence, Beverly leaned forward, smiling wickedly, and said, "Don't forget. She let you sleep with her Consort."

Amanda let a single sob burst out, almost a laugh, and sat back smiling through tears running down her cheeks. "Yes. She has been generous, even to that furthest extent, in her care for me."

Rachel finally spoke, unsmilingly, "There is the matter of your daughter."

Amanda looked at Rachel then. Unflinchingly, she said, "Yes, I know."

"She will not be leaving with you when you return to Scotland."

"Yes, I know. This has become clear to me. I will leave her in your care, safe in the generosity of your spirit, that she may learn from you. She knows what I know. She needs to know what you know."

Rachel said, simply, "Yes."

Madeleine said, "Tell the story, Amanda. If you're ready to resume," and took a sip at her whiskey. In response, in silent recognition, the other three wen reached out and took a sip of theirs.

"And so," Amanda began again, with a sigh. "Regina was required to journey to hell to find her father."

"And how did she do that?" Beverly asked.

"Her natural skills, enhanced with an infusion of poppy and other plants. She couldn't just go. She had to be buoyed by something. The instructions came from her friend, Maray. For most of her life Regina could dream. She could set her mind before she slept then dream of some place, and bring back details she couldn't have known otherwise. This was different.

"She needed a guide. She needed a guide to the gate, to the threshold of the Bardoes. She'd never done anything quite like this. I've been told, by you, Rachel, that there are living people who know the way, who can find the way. He could, you've told me. But we didn't have access to that training. So, as Brighid told me, Her niece would serve as a guide.

"From her bed, then, with a fire on the grate, Regina slipped out of this world into the underworld of dreams. She slipped her skin, she told me, like a snake, and was gone. She went to a place far up in the Highlands, a rock outcropping she knew, where she had agreed to meet with Maray. Maray took her hand and they walked awhile. Then they stepped off an edge together, and they flew.

"They flew to the east, Regina told me. They arrived at a high plain, and flew along it to an isolated hut. Smoke was rising from the top. Maray stopped at the door, a skin door with heavy hair. Maray smiled at her, indicating with a nod that Regina should open it. She did, and had to get down on a knee to enter.

"She leaned in, let the door fall, and allowed her eyes to adjust to the darkness. The only light was a few coals, and the light reflected from someone's eyes. Then she fell, fell forward into a darkness that lasted only a moment, and she was there."

"Where is 'there'?" Beverly asked.

"In a realm, a realm both outside of time and space but not a realm so far from here as to be beyond the sun. She said it was a realm of this place, this earth, but one higher and lower, as it were, at the same time.

"There was another landscape, under the moonlit night. Before her was a cave, with torches burning at the entrance. She stepped in and saw, shortly across the threshold, a set of steps going up. She took them. She said the journey took her as long as she took to think about it. When she thought there might be many stairs, there were. When she thought there would be fewer stairs, there were. When she thought she was at the top, there she was, standing in sun light. Before her was a canyon. The walls of the canyon were bands of different colors of light. Each band of color, when she looked closely, had a platform balcony and a roof over it of the same color of light; colored, light infused, rock.

"She heard music. When she paid attention to it, she recognized it as, what do you call it here? Big Band Jazz. The saxophone seemed to be the instrument that caught her attention, so her attention took her there. She arrived on the balcony of the top story. She realized she heard other songs of the same type being played on the levels below her.

"She entered, walking around the tables of outdoor seating, and entered a bar. There, sitting on a stage in the back of the room, was her father, the Lama. He was playing sax in a bar in a Bardo Band. He was engaged in a high-note swing solo.

"She heard a man behind her say, 'Quite something, your father is. He plays in the Bands on the other levels, too. At the same time. Playing different songs. Quite something.'

"She could sense that her father was aware of her presence telepathically. She heard him say, 'I'll be with you shortly, child.'

"When she heard the word 'child' she felt the love she had for him the last time she'd seen him in 1949. And she felt herself shrink, like Alice, she said, to the size she was at that age, perhaps ten or so. Same dress, same pigtails even, she said. And she allowed herself to swell with the ten year old's love for her father. She could feel it when he felt that love and took it into himself. It swelled within him, and he played so that everyone started to weep, helplessly.

"And everyone in all the Hells felt this terrible ache of Love, the love of a parent for a child, yes, but particularly the love of a daughter for her father, and the difficult love from a father in return.

"It was panging, poignant and heartbreaking in its intensity, when the unreturned and unfulfilled love note was played. Abandoned love brought them all low. The undiscovered love of organic pride in a daughter's accomplishments brought them high again. When he finished, a note on a calm ocean of freedom, out of the sigh of it, the sigh of all the souls in the Hells, there arose, like the sun in an opening below the clouds at the horizon, a brief moment, almost, a flash of Hope.

"In the ensuing chaos, he set his instrument on its stand and walked from the stage to her. She stood still and watched him approach. She held still. He got to his knees in front of her, but she held still. He leaned in toward her, but she did not incline toward him. She held still. Then she reached for his hand. He stood up, and she turned, and led him out of Hell.

"When they arrived back at the hut on the high plain, the light reflected on two sets of eyes in the darkness. Maray spoke and said 'Welcome. We go.'

"They crawled out onto the high prairie. The Lama looked around him, and smiled. He recognized it as home country. "Hold hands," Maray said, and they flew to Hidden Lands. They arrived quickly, landing in the yard, inside the stone fences. Regina told me she could feel the land moving beneath her feet for a moment.

"The family was gathered to meet them: Brighid and Her Sister, Her Sister's Children, and Her Sister's consort. They all went into the house together.

"Regina was there for most of the talk, she said. But the energy required to stay in that world was fading in her. So were the effects of the draft of poppy. She said she doesn't remember the details. Maray brought her back home. I saw it happen. A brightening, a cloud filled with light entered the room, and from it emerged a smaller cloud of light that settled into Regina. Her breathing changed, and she sighed. I knew that she was returned, and sleeping.

"I don't know what else to say," Amanda said after a pause, and fell silent.

All four wen stood as one, easily and naturally. No one said anything. They turned, and went to bed.

On this same night the Lama, for his part, had completed his mission and was sitting in the Gatekeeper's hut. They were having a deep conversation about what changes to the Karma, and the impact on the Dharma; that is, what changes had happened to probability as a result of his actions, and whether their might be some impact to Natural Law.

He had, of course, agreed to do what the Goddess asked him. While he was listening to the plan, he found himself thinking that this was only a small portion of a larger plan. When he allowed his mind to travel out into the realm of possibility he felt the floor start to rise under him, and he received a clear image of a man adrift at sea. A giant sea beast, perhaps a whale, but perhaps a dragon, rose up under the man. He felt the mind of the beast, a greater mind, greater and more calm than his own. He tried to fathom the extent of it, but he could not. He took this as a warning, and stopped the exploration.

He had gone east, to the ocean there, and boarded a canoe for the western lands. He felt the great beast again, under the boat. He kept his mind still. When the boat landed on the western shore he began to walk. He climbed high into the mountains until he found a slump on the shoulder of a great peak, where the land had fallen in on the top and the great spruces and pines had collapsed into it, making a tangled nest. There was a great bird there, dark like a thundercloud, with small white spots, like hail sweeping toward him. The bird stepped to one side for him, and nodded, bidding him to enter the nest.

The bird looked east and then south, and they waited. The Lama felt that this was what they were supposed to do. Into his waiting practice a tall, thin, graceful column of wind came. Behind this column he could see another column of wind, taller, thicker, larger, and another wind, more of a whirlwind, came around the nest, circling once and settling in the south behind the graceful column.

In from the north came two columns, bent like the old sometimes are.

The graceful column came into the nest and resolved itself into a naked feminine form, in a rendering so beautiful and bright he had to look away. When the light dimmed he turned back and saw her sit, clothed in white. She nodded at him.

She said, "I am Falling Star. Behind me is my consort. Over there," She said, nodding to the giant black bird, "is one of my brothers-in-law and the young one over here peeking out behind me is my nephew. In the north is another of my brothers-in-law and his wife. My brother-in-law from the east will not come here."

She paused, then said, "I know who you are. I know why you are here. Do not speak."

The Lama nodded in the affirmative, once, to show he understood.

"There will be deeds done in return for what you ask," she said. "When you return you will have to tell Her. The first deed is to meet the requirements of my brothers-in-law. The deeds must be done so that they will make room for Her here. How shall I put this? In order to accommodate Her, She must accommodate Them. It is the only way to make room for Her storms and thunders here, in this land, which is already filled with storms and thunders. Do you understand?"

The Lama nodded.

Falling Star continued. "There is a deed to be done for me as well. A long time ago a piece of Me fell to Earth far to the east of here. The people found me and took me to their village. The Priestess there had me built into a wall. She would come and sit and listen to my voice. In time, the men of De Murgos came and my voice was stilled there. I shall want it to be restored." She stopped, contemplative and listening to something, a voice the Lama couldn't hear, the voice of the mind of Her Mother.

"Do you understand?" She asked. He nodded again.

"Your daughter shall bring Her here. She will convey the instructions and deliver the means. Do you understand?"

And, for the last time, he nodded.

"You may go," She said.

The Lama departed the nest the way he came, and then continued travelling east and north, crossing over the ice. When he arrived in the region of the Hidden Lands he sat in a high place and waited until someone found him. Brighid's sister, the Storm Goddess Calley found him, and the instructions were passed on. Calley laughed out loud when she heard them.

The Lama had then continued east until he found the hut on the high plain. When the Lama finished telling his story to the Gatekeeper, they sat in silence for a while. Then the Gatekeeper cleared his throat, long unused, and said, "In the moment that the Gate was closing after you a black flag came through, following in the wake of your departure. It was moving fast. I did not catch it. Beware of it."

The Lama thought about this and said, "Well, that means the Karma has been affected. I suppose I will stick around, then, make sure the Dharma remains as it should be." The Gatekeeper nodded and passed him the mouthpiece of the hookah.

27

CURRICULUM FOUR

In the weeks after the meeting of the quadrivium, when Rachel stood screaming in the rain, in the weeks after Amanda was burned, the wen met and laid the plans for the future of Stonehaven. It was to become a haven for a special kind of learning, a training center for wen and men to find psychic and spiritual evolution under the reorganizing principle of the Antecedence of the Feminine.

The school was to remain hidden from common view. The men and wen who received training were to be integrated into society through a network of business enterprises owned, eventually, through a series of holding companies, by the Order of the Flower of Life, the Fleur de Vie.

The Order was to be international, owning property globally, wherever possible, that could be used as bases of operations for whatever tasks the Council of the Order deemed necessary, and as refuges for agents of the Order.

During the almost nightly meetings of the founding group, there was time taken for teaching and the telling of stories. One of the stories Amanda told the group was the story of the establishment of her relationship with Brighid, High Queen of the Old Ways of her people. She resumed the story where she had left it, with the two, Brighid and Amanda, on either side of the wall around the compound of the Hidden Lands.

"Brighid knew me, you see, because She'd felt the pull of my study of Her history at the edge of Her Mind," she said. "I'd read everything I could find about Her, and meditated on Her many times, searching for Her, making myself susceptible to Her, and Her influence. She was reluctant—She explained to me there—reluctant to return Her attention to the mortal world.

"'Let me touch you,' She said. She reached Her arm over the wall and I reached up for it. A 'whoosh'—I don't have any other way to describe it—a whoosh of power poured down my arm, and She disappeared—I could no longer see Her in front of me.

"My head fell back and my eyes rolled up. Then I saw Her, as if suspended on a cloud, inside my head. As I watched, the cloud became a throne and She sat down. A reflecting pool appeared beside her and arrayed around her throne were her signs. She smiled at me, then She said, "Here is where you shall find me; think only of this image, and I will be there.

"'And for this boon I shall ask one thing of you.'

"'Name it,' I said.

"She laughed at me. 'Do not be simple, child. I shall show you what I ask before you agree to it.'

"She stepped down off Her throne and into the pool. When She did I felt Her foot become my foot, Her leg become my leg. She stepped deeper into the pool and both my legs, then all of me, became Her.

"I felt Her face settle into my face, and Her eyes looked out onto the world through my eyes."

Amanda paused and felt the memory. She closed her eyes. When she opened them the other wen saw four eyes looking back, then the green eyes of the Other settled over Amanda's blue eyes, and the words emerged, "Hello, daughters. Close your eyes that you may see Me at the pool."

The other three wen did as commanded. They saw.

After a moment of lovely contemplation, where they were all aware of each other, and all saw Amanda sitting at the pool, naked, dangling her legs in the water, smiling at them and nodding, the Goddess said, "Open your eyes, that you may see Me manifest."

The other wen did as commanded. When they opened their eyes they saw the green-eyed One looking at them, smiling at each individually. The eyes shifted briefly to Amanda's blue. "I'm here, too. Right behind Her." The eyes shifted back to green.

"I see you, Mother," the Goddess said, laughing. "Lurking there. Show yourself!"

Rachel began laughing, then grew dark as a shadow entered the room, seeming to expand from Rachel herself. Rachel's eyes seemed to become large, and her face became a mask as broad as her shoulders.

Beverly and Madeleine watched it all through slitted eyes. Suddenly, the shadow turned to light, soft, backlit so the face of the Mind of All Life remained in shadow.

She made a sound, through, but not through, Rachel, "Shh," long sustained. Then the light collapsed and it was only Rachel present in the room.

The three wen regarded Amanda and Brighid, sitting there, looking out upon the world, gazing at the room, gazing at them.

"Would you like to go outside perhaps, stand on the veranda and look out?" Rachel asked the paired mind.

She smiled, and nodded affirmatively. Using the arms of the chair She slowly stood. Beverly and Madeleine stood beside Her, unsteady at first through Her legs. Rachel cleared a path to the veranda doors, opened the screens and smiled as She walked through. A newly waning moon lit the deck. The Goddess glided to the edge, looking up, smiling, hands on the railing, leaning out and looking up. She went to the steps and sat down on the top one. The other wen joined Her. Rachel sat beside Her, the others two steps down, looking back and upward to gaze at Her.

She sighed. "So beautiful the lights. So beautiful the sound."

"I do not know what to do," the Amanda/Goddess eventually said.

"I am caught between the need to be free and the need to manifest. In my home land, by Amanda's hand, I am now returning. And I fear the torture. Yes, we feel," She said, answering an unasked question.

"There may be no torture, Queen," Rachel said. "No one has burned for a long time. And we remain hidden, here, for now."

"The groups there, those people, they are in trouble. An evil comes, I can feel it coming, I cannot see it," Madeleine said.

From under the shadow of a lone chestnut tree in the yard came a voice. Regina spoke: "I hear you, Queen, I hear you, Mother. I am told the problem is with the men. You have priests, and there should be none."

The shock, the silence on the porch was profound. Deep it went, until their feet touched the Mind in the Deep. Rachel smiled. "Yes, it is the men. You have priests. There will be no priests here, only consorts."

"Those men there are certainly not superior in their relationship with you. They are not equal, even, and yet they presume superiority," Madeleine said.

"Daughter," the Amanda/Goddess said, "Why do they not aspire to the status I would accord them?"

"They presume they already have it," Madeleine answered.

"Ah," the Amanda/Goddess said, and fell silent.

The Goddess departed then; left Amanda. They all felt it, as a lifting. Amanda said, "Come daughter, sit up here with us in the moonlight."

Regina came to the steps and sat down, putting her chin in one hand, elbow braced on a knee, thinking.

The wen sat on the steps in silence for a while, watching, listening.

"It's all about sex, you know," Regina said, finally. "Well, maybe not just about sex, but gender also. Gender complicates it."

"How so?" Beverly asked.

"The Masculine is usually bigger than us, stronger and more power-ful. We need this, we need that for ourselves, that's why we created the Masculine in the first place. We displaced our aggressiveness into them, in order to use it outside ourselves, so that without that within ourselves we might better bring forth Life onto the Earth.

"We can give them sex," she continued. "Indeed, that was part of the design. We designed them to have sex with us, for the most part. Lots of sex. But we cannot overpower them. I am afraid that this is an inherent inequality which we cannot overcome. That's what I mean by gender."

"But what can we do?" Beverly asked.

"Love can overpower them," Rachel said. "We must find a way such that their love for us keeps them from using power over us."

"Love alone is not enough," Regina said.

"Nor are Hope and Faith," Madeleine added.

"I, too, despair, sometimes, that not even all three are enough to inspire the Masculine to aspire to Service," Rachel added.

"When She touched me the first time, when She came into me, I felt power. I felt a power I could learn to use. I believe this power could also be used to overcome those who hold power over us. Or, if not overcome them, because that may not be what we are supposed to do, at least persuade them to hold that power in check, use it in Service to us, rather than using it to reduce us. If we use the power of sex and combine it with the power of the Goddess, then they might be drawn into Service," Beverly said.

"Then the power that will induce them into Service is the power of the Goddess, the power of the Diosa, embodied in us and revealed to them. She created them. She created Him. Perhaps He can make them," Regina offered.

"Him, whom?" Amanda asked.

"Does the Goddess not have a Consort?" Regina responded.

"No longer," Rachel answered. "He was destroyed by the invader."

Everyone went silent at the mention of Him. Their first thoughts were images of horror from the rape by De Murgos. The old image, the old archetype of the Divine Masculine was destroyed, crumbled even as the Colossus of Rhodes was gone, even to the stones. The old values of the Sacred Masculine had disappeared, or where preserved, were preserved in such a form as to keep the Feminine subservient.

"Can they even understand the difference between Service and subservience?" Regina asked.

"I'm not sure," Madeleine answered.

"Nor I," said Rachel.

"Nor I," Beverly and Amanda said, almost simultaneously.

"They have to be trained," Rachel said. "They have to be educated, not just mentally, but physically and emotionally. The Lama was right about this. Only by educating these three—the Soma, the Soul, and the Spirit—can the Sacred Heart be activated, and become the fourth possibility.

"Right now, men have no other possibilities than the first three kinds of lives. We must give them a new possibility, and that is Service to Her. And, Service to us as it supports Service to Her. Our Service to Her shall be the embodiment of Her, the True Creator, in all Her Faces, and we shall show these Faces to the men."

Everyone was silent again.

While this silence held, there was a man, a man who had met the Lama but, because of his magical tradition, was not allowed to study with the Lama by the Lama's own command. This man was standing in the Shadows of a gate on a country road in England, contemplating how it would feel to motor up the drive of the estate to the main house. While he waited for some sign, out of the darkness a black flag drifted down from the sky and settled on his shoulders. He shivered, and suddenly felt a strengthening of his resolve. When the silence ended he drew a sigil on the gate post, returned to his car, and departed into the night.

At Stonehaven, Amanda resumed her tale at the same time the dark man moved. Beverly asked her to wait, went into the sitting room and returned with a tray of glasses, and the bottle of whiskey. Walking down the steps, distributing glasses, she poured first at the bottom for Regina, then poured small amounts for the others, topping off their tumblers.

"Do you think we can train enough wen to be able to train the men?" Amanda asked.

"I do not know. At a certain point, I believe men will help train men. The men I am imagining would be men that others would naturally want to emulate; strong, confident men. But I am certain that it is the Divine Feminine, manifesting in front of them, through us, that will hold their attention long enough for the prospects of devotion to be made clear," Rachel said.

Madeleine added, "I can see this. It can happen in the world. But our plan must span decades; it will be beyond our lifetimes that we will begin the assault on history. It will require a shift in a large culture, more than one, even. And we must plan for that."

Amanda spoke, "That was Brighid's idea. Small groups, a few travelling teachers. She said She would guide me, and guide us, Her teachers. For the most part it has been so. Some groups we started around couples. Sometimes one of my students would serve as the carrier for the consciousness of the Goddess in ceremony. We would bring leaders of the groups together for meetings. Build slowly.

"The Goddess would point out people for us to strike up conversations with, exchange invitations for tea. There are a dozen or so groups now, studying, conducting ritual together as much as we could reconstruct it with the help of the Goddess. The groups are all in small towns, and cities. But still we must take great care. It is not safe that we be known." Amanda sighed. "I have received letters describing troubles in the groups. Some of the men, serving as priests within the groups, supposedly teaching other men their ritual roles, have begun challenging their Priestesses, and in front of the group.

"I suspect that the arrogance comes from that lack of understanding of the Antecedence of the Feminine. These men believe that they came first, and that they still ought to come first in the leadership of the group. They seem to be unable to show the deference to the Feminine in a way that makes Brighid Herself hesitate to embody.

"I don't know what to do," Amanda said quietly

Madeleine said, "The Diosa says to wait. She will show you what to do more easily if you can learn to embody Her as well. I am told She will tell Brighid what Brighid must do also. She is, after all, the daughter of Diosa. And, one more thing: I am told you are to confirm this with Brighid Herself, later tonight."

In England, the man to whom the black flag had attached itself decided that he would launch the final stage of destroying one of the Lama's lineages. The house behind the gate was owned by the head of the lineage. To the mind of a magician—a dark mind operating under a black cloak, which the black flag slowly became, spreading out upon him—it was now but a simple thing.

Everyone who passed the gate would be impacted by the sign he had made, left vulnerable to the extension of his mesmeric powers; left vulnerable to hypnosis. And hypnotize them he would. He would induce them to serve him. Serve him rather than their Teacher, student of the Lama who had rejected him. None of them were good enough for him, and he would kick them all away eventually. But the ones who wouldn't serve him would be ruined, unable to think, or really do much at all. The weakest would be reduced to staring vacuously at the walls. He was, after all, an accomplished magician.

He established himself with the Teacher of the Lineage as a person of some merit via his reputation as a scholar of the arcane. He presented letters of introduction from other people known by the Teacher, of whom it could be said they may not have had much choice in the writing. Thus, he appeared two weeks later at the gate.

Had anyone been there who could see when he emerged from his car, they would have noticed him moving under a film of black. As he came up the steps, his demeanor shifted to a charming man, teeth bright and eyes flashing, hat, suit, scarf, all in the latest style.

He charmed the woman who let him in, then the man in the hall who directed him to the Teacher's Study. Taking a chair offered him while the Teacher finished transcribing some thought, he took the moment to size up his quarry. When the Teacher set down his pen, stood up, and came around the desk to shake his hand, the dark magician had him. He knew how to direct the Teacher's focus away from his handiwork, the manipulation of the energetic field, for just the moment required to plant the suggestion, the trigger word, an ancient word of command.

He executed his strategy. When the word was spoken, the old Teacher said, "What?" and then shook his head as the dark magician shrugged and smiled.

Over the course of the next two weeks the dark magician was introduced to nearly all of the lineage students, eating with them at meals, especially the communal ones. During these meals he found ample opportunity to solicit their complaints about their Teacher. He was invited to give several talks and lectures, which served to set the eyes of the students on him as a source of authority.

He manipulated all he could, and only a few could resist. These, the ones who could resist, gathered close to the Teacher, serving as his inner circle. They shared their frustrations with each other when it seemed the Teacher wouldn't listen, and wouldn't drive away the dark guest.

The Teacher refused to listen, or seemed to refuse. It was as if he was deaf to their words, unheeding of their concerns. As the charm of the dark magician grew among the students, the Teacher seemed to fade. Two weeks stretched into a month, the dark magician beginning to teach the students the joys of the life of a bon vivant, opposing the austerities and self-discipline the teacher had adjured to them.

During this time the inner circle, fearing that the Teacher was fading and becoming a shadow of his former self, made arrangements for the Teacher's possessions, his library and his notes, and all his wife's possessions to be moved to a different location on a day they could foresee but not yet specify.

They realized that the Teacher would have to flee if he wanted to preserve his life, even though the Teacher himself could not yet foresee this. The Teacher's wife was the one that finally got through to him, quietly informing him of the dark guest's sexual escapades with the students.

It was very early on a Saturday morning when the lorries showed up to take away the possessions. As the workmen moved things out of the front hall and down the steps, people gradually came awake and watched, speculating. The estate was full of students who had arrived for a large gathering over the weekend.

Eventually, the dark guest felt the disturbance, and, disentangling himself from the arms of the previous evening's partners, rose quickly, threw on a robe, and went to stand in the hall, watching. He went into the dining room, gauging the tenor of the room and its confusion in the absence of the usually prepared breakfast.

Around noon, the group was called together, some standing in the hallway, others on the porch surrounding the teacher, others on the steps below and to the sides. The dark magician, not by accident, stood in the doorway.

The Teacher stood there, gray, almost ashen, and said, "I am closing the school and giving the house to our guest. You are all free to go with him, study with him, learn from him if you can. I know only that I am done here."

Many reactions could be observed. Some cried out inarticulately, others cried "No," and "What will we do?" Others smiled or showed no expression at all.

The Teacher turned, went down the steps and entered the back seat of his waiting car and drove off into a sudden rain.

The black magician stood in the doorway and smiled. He had been smiling through the whole thing, except once when he allowed his expression to become one of exaggerated, even mocking, concern.

Turning to the people crowded around him, he smiled, and exuberantly shouted, "Let us go find something to eat!" He was cheered by some. Others he touched, and they smiled.

Two of the men he touched in that moment were priests in Amanda's Brighid groups.

Then began a period of debauchery at the estate house. The black magician created orgies like Caligula, directing the hypnotized participants into acts beyond their imagining. Pornographic films were shown on the walls at night.

Order broke down: some people moved away when it became clear that the magician did not have the funds to support the lifestyle; and some of the people were unwilling to donate their fortunes to him, although some did. These monies kept the debauch going for several weeks.

At the end, bored, the black magician sold the property, the entire estate, broken windows, filth on the wall, the soiled laundry, the rotting food, to investors with plans of building a neighborhood of new townhomes. There was speculation this had been the magician's intention all along.

Perhaps a quarter of the students found their way back to the Teacher, a quarter remained loyal to the Magician, and the rest disappeared into the fogs of the life of everyday people.

The other lineages of the Lama thought this Teacher's line to be cursed, and made it an outcast. Those students who stayed with the Magician, were, by their enamored support of his charm, trained in the dark art of compelling others to do what they wanted. Worse, he trained them in how to feed upon the souls and spirits of others. Those that did, allowed him to feed upon them.

Among them were the two priests of Amanda's Brighid groups. They returned to the groups, and used their perfidy to work the magics, hypnotize and use the people, reducing them to subservience and sexual toys.

The others the magician turned loose on the world, where they established themselves as the progeny of a secret Lineage of the Lama, one that was supposedly formed in secret with instructions to reveal itself after the Lama was gone. Thus they, too, were guaranteed a long line of seekers that could be used as food.

The ghost of the Lama watched all this, watched the destruction of this lineage, and the evaporation of his teachings in some odd distillation of what the Teacher took from the Lama's teaching. He re-organized the material in a way he thought of as being better prepared.

The ghost chose not to intervene, knowing that his action had created the opening that allowed his spiritual descendants to be attacked and eviscerated so thoroughly. Instead, he foresaw a future that would wreck the black magician's false lineage, bring it low and scatter death among its adherents.

It was this lineage that Quinn was to encounter many years later, as a young man, and the last leader of this lineage—the magician long gone to whatever hell to which his ego drew him—the lady A., that pursued Quinn, even as far as Stonehaven.

28

QUINN AT THE MEN'S CIRCLE

When Quinn emerged after three days and nights with the High Priestess he was a changed man. They'd had room service, three meals a day. Lots of sex and alcohol had Quinn feeling his best. He'd even rolled up a couple joints for the High Priestess, and they'd had themselves a blast—much to the consternation of the other thirty-seven men and 'wen' (Quinn had been told) that were the staff of Stonehaven, not to mention the other fifty-some people living and studying on the grounds.

Quinn's first overheard speech when he emerged with Eva on their way to breakfast in the Dining Hall was a reference to somebody called the Dragon Angel. His thought was that, from here on out, it was only going to get weirder.

There was a brief moment of silence when they entered the Hall. It felt for a second that people were going to simply resume their conversations but then someone, some man, stood up and began to applaud. Sincere applause.

Then everyone stood up, applauding sincerely, stepping up to Eva, even to Quinn, shaking hands and giving kisses to cheeks. Even the Madeleine stepped up, hugged them both at the same time, and kissed each of them.

Then, as they sat, someone said, "Bravo! Bravo!" For a moment, everyone was saying it. Then it stopped, and everyone resumed their seats and their conversations.

A man sitting next to the Madeleine said, "What would you like? I'll go get it."

"Coffee first, please. Black," Eva said.

"Me, too, please. Thanks," Quinn said.

"Madeleine, meet Quinn. Quinn, meet Madeleine," Eva said.

"We've already met, dear," Madeleine said.

"Really? Where?" Eva asked.

"While you were sleeping. While he was sleeping, too. He's quite an interesting person. Not very trusting," she said.

"Do you blame me?" Quinn asked.

"No. You've never found anyone you can trust. Well, almost," she finished.

"And how was I supposed to know that?" Quinn asked.

"You weren't. There was no 'supposed to' there. There was only that you didn't," Madeleine answered, with a bleakness that she quickly covered. Then she smiled, "What do you suppose the applause was for?" she asked.

"I don't know," he said.

Eva smiled. "It was for our performance. We made a lot of noise. The windows were open."

"People ended up having sex on the lawn under the windows," Madeleine said, and laughed out loud. "They would sneak up there to listen and become so horny that they behaved like they couldn't help themselves. People would sleep there when you slept just to have wake-up sex when you had wake-up sex."

"Ugh," Quinn said.

"True!" Madeleine said. "All that crusty, first thing in the morning camping out sex. I could hear that, too! Pulling stuck bits of flesh apart," she said. "Delightful. I'm surprised you stopped to wash at all."

"Madeleine's bedroom is next to mine," Eva said to Quinn.

"Ah," Quinn said, almost knowingly. "But really? They came to have sex while listening to us have sex?"

"Yes," Madeleine said. "Like moths to light, flies to shit. Skeeters to blood. Take your pick."

"Not that bad, come on, now," Eva said.

"True, not that bad," Madeleine replied. "There were times when I fell asleep on rising tides of sighs. Sighs and squishes. Oh, yes! And 'Oh's'."

They both smiled, Madeleine and Eva. Watching them smile, Quinn smiled uncomfortably, uncertain that he was allowed to smile. "Fuck it," he thought. And smiled with them.

Then, asshole that he was, he asked, "Who weren't you fucking?"

Madeleine said, "Oh, baby. All you need to know is that I wasn't fucking you."

Eva said, "You want him?"

Madeleine nodded slowly, smiling.

"He's all yours," Eva said.

Quinn's smile froze on his face. He then made one of the best, most Taoist, statements of his life. He said nothing.

When he emerged again, after two days with the Madeleine, he was again a changed man. Whereas before he had simply been feeling shagged, now he was positively sore.

He remembered things that he already had known, and had forgotten. This time, he vowed to remember them. His time with the High Priestess had been magnificent—all action, all doing. His time with the Madeleine, the Seeress of Stonehaven, had been enough to take him to the threshold of enlightenment again but draw him back, just in time. Instead, he learned how to hold space for her to journey into that land, bringing him back understanding that he needed to have. All being.

He sighed, as he hitched up his pants, re-tying the drawstring. These people wore comfortable clothes, he'd give them that. He was completely unused to it—the clothes, not the people. Although he was unused to that, too. People.

Madeleine had told him that he'd have to meet with the men. The next meeting of the men's group was that night, Thursday night, and they'd asked to have him present. The High Priestess had assented.

She hadn't even asked him, although she notified him after it had been done.

Quinn had a reaction. "How come she gets to make up my mind for me? Without even talking to me?"

Madeleine asked him, looking away, "And what else would you do? Say no? Run away? Leave?"

"No, I would have done none of those things. I'd have gone to the meeting," he said.

Madeleine looked back at him. "Yes, exactly. She knew that already. She simply saved you the time and energy of thinking about it."

"Wait, wait. I should still have the choice," he said.

"You still do," she said.

He said nothing, again. He was learning.

He went down the hall and through the office, buttoning the top buttons on a tunic type shirt he'd been given. He stopped at a door in a circular wall, and opened it.

There were men inside, milling about, talking to each other. The men were of all ages, and, it seemed to him, ethnicities. Someone saw him and came to him, indicating the pile of shoes to the right. Quinn slipped off his new 'house shoes' and followed the man to a place on a dais, three steps above the rest of the floor. "Please sit. Others will be here shortly." Quinn noticed that all the men were wearing comfortable clothes. Some were even wearing what looked to be modified Asian monks robes. Others were wearing long cassocks, with a loose cut, like a long riding coat, but made of cotton, or perhaps linen over loose cotton pants.

Two men, who had been sitting and talking on the step below him, turned and introduced themselves to him. They said, "Hey, hi. We're two of the cardinal elements here." Then they turned and laughed at each other at the simultaneity of what they'd said.

"Whoa, that was creepy," Quinn said, and he refused to talk to them anymore, preferring instead to look around the room.

There was a shelf running around the room that held objects and statues. The statues were classically masculine, including several of warriors from different cultures and periods. There were statues of wrestlers, men carrying tools, men riding horses, or elephants, or camels, men in embrace. There were phallic carvings, including a classic lingam embedded in yoni carving. There were carvings and casts of men and wen in embrace. There was a statue of two men clearly in a sexual embrace. There were other statues of men he presumed were historical or religious icons that he didn't recognize at a distance. There were two signs: one said 'There are no Priests here', and the other simply a word 'SAFAW'. Quinn had no idea what it meant. In the back were several drums and horns. Everywhere there were carpets, and pillows, and stools.

Three men walked in together, one of whom was Craft. They stepped up onto the dais and seated themselves around Quinn. The other men in the room, perhaps nearly forty of them by this time, milled around briefly, agreed to finish their conversations later, and found seats.

"Brothers," one of them began. "This is the Stranger that the Madeleine told us to look out for. His title is, well, the Bodhisattva of Assholes. His name is Quinn. He came in through the barriers and sneaked up on Wade, there, and his Priestess Jasmine. It seems the High Priestess knew him from before." Then he stopped.

"Well, 'sneaking' isn't hardly the word for it, all the noise they were making," Quinn said. And several men laughed. "You know her, do you?" And more men laughed, until a man in the back hissed. Quinn recognized him as Wade.

Quinn decided in that moment that he might, just as well, just jump right in.

He said, "Look, they told me all about it. Eva and Madeleine. You guys have all the Pussy and Food you could possibly need. Once those are taken care of, what are you doing? What are you doing for them?"

"We cultivate the availability for relatedness," someone said.

"What the fuck does that mean?" Quinn asked.

"We share in all domestic tasks—cooking and cleaning, even the toilets," someone else said.

"Great. You're dishwashers and janitors. I've done that, and it never… well, never mind, it did actually get me laid. What else?"

"We maintain," a third man said.

"You what?"

"We maintain," the third man said. "All the hard stuff, the making of new stuff, that's already been done. We don't have to build that tractor down in the barn, casting the metal and winding the stator on the generator. But we have to maintain it. We don't have to build new buildings, they're already built; although from time to time we've talked about tearing something down and building something else in its place just for the work of it. But we do need to maintain what we have. And we do. We take care of the buildings and grounds. So do the wen, by the way.

"And we farm, even though we don't need to. And we train. We train in tracking and hunting and martial arts. We run, and work out, training for strength and endurance. The yogas we practice here are demanding. We train in energetics, too. We work on the internal disciplines—the circulation of the energies, the alchemy and the arts of self-control. And, in all these, we practice the cultivation of availability—availability to the Feminine."

"And don't forget music," came a young voice from the middle.

"Oh, yes. And we learn how to play music. Our rituals and ceremonies require music, and everybody learns to play when they're not participating directly in the dance."

"You're the luckiest guys in the world," Quinn said.

"Yeah, we think so. And nobody gets in here who doesn't think so," one of the men who called himself a 'cardinal element' said.

"But what about the other things men live for? What about Power and Control? You get enough Pussy and Food and what are you going to do? Just exercise? Learn the flute? Fuck each other?" Quinn asked.

"I resent that. Fuck you, asshole," the same cardinal element replied.

"Remember, you're dealing with the Bodhisattva of Assholes," Craft said.

"And, no. We don't fuck each other. But there's the Assfuck Tantra, if you want to take a look at it."

Men laughed at the shocked expression on Quinn's face.

"Wait, wait, wait. Some of us do fuck each other, let's be clear. Some of us are gay, and some are bi-sexual. It's welcome here, we are all Her children," the other cardinal element said.

"And the metaphorical part of that 'not fucking each other' is that we don't fuck each other over. That's what we don't do to each other," someone in the back chimed in. "And fucking over someone is about, and only about, power and control."

"And knock off the P and F bullshit. We call it sex here, because it's not just about pussy," someone else said, angrily

"Yes, that other stuff is about pleasure. Your question was about power and control. I, for one, have all the power and control I need. That's a part of the training. Recognizing that I have all that I need.

"I can do whatever I want to do, and, for the most part, when I want to do it. What more could I ask for?" the second element concluded.

"And what would I want power and control over? Owning this place? Running this place? Managing everything else that Stonehaven and the Order does? Why the fuck would I want to do that? Let the wen do it. I'll give them my opinion about something when they ask, and I know they will; they always ask, and that's because they respect my opinion, and what we men do for them. If they do something I don't like strongly enough, I can leave," Craft stated.

"Can you?"

"Yes, I can. But that won't change the core of why I do what I do. All that power and control energy that I have, that all men have, all that desire for power and control goes into self-discipline and service. Service to the Feminine, that is. That's where all my archetypal Warrior energy goes.

"And if I'm not doing that here, I'll be doing it out in the world."

"Yeah, yeah," Quinn said. "You guys are so great, so-oo developed," he said, resorting to sarcasm. "What about jealousy. Don't tell me you didn't feel the pang of it when Eva recognized me, and gave me that kiss. Don't tell me it didn't bother you when she took me off to bed for three days."

Craft grinned. "One of the things we've learned is that we have to be mindful of things like this. Negative emotions like jealousy, can sneak up on us unawares. We also learn that we can eliminate it from ourselves. We work on it, expose ourselves to it every day, then work to eliminate it from our feelings. If it comes up, all you have to do is sit with it, and refuse to do or say anything that arises from it. And then the feeling will disappear. And then the capacity for it disappears.

"It's like becoming fearless—that works the same way. But becoming completely fearless is foolish. You eliminate some part of the instinctive warning system, and eventually you make a mistake, you didn't see something coming, and your survival is, how shall I say it, negatively impacted.

"So we've learned that it's a mistake to eliminate something like jealousy or fear completely. These feelings have evolved for some reason, and that means they must have some kind of survival value. We've worked on this problem for years and we've found that, once you understand what the survival value is, you can work to meet that value, fulfill that need, in a different way.

"And then the jealousy, or fear, or anger, doesn't get triggered."

"Wait, wait. Don't tell me you didn't feel even the slightest pang of jealousy," Quinn stated.

"I looked," Craft said. "I have artificially kept alive the possibility for jealousy. But there wasn't any."

Craft paused, cocking his head to one side as if he was listening. Then he said, smiling, "Besides, you have no idea what I was doing, and with which of the wen, while Eva was busy with you. Perhaps you should consider asking him. At this time, he's the High Consort." And he grinned, indicating a man sitting on the other side of Quinn.

Quinn thought about it. "High Priestess, High Consort. Yeah, I get it." He turned to the other man.

"Hi, I'm Peter," he said. He leaned forward and shook Quinn's hand. "I was busy elsewhere, also." And some men laughed at that.

"What I did feel, and I want to tell you about it, is fear. Your appearance here is potentially threatening to our survival," Peter said.

"Everybody here has been invited, and before that happens they are thoroughly vetted and trained in all the preparation required to actually be here, and be a man," Craft said.

"Except you," Peter finished the sentence.

"Yes, except you. Nobody invited you, nobody vetted you, nobody knows who the fuck you are," the third man on the dais said, with some heat.

There was a pause. They were all staring at Quinn.

"So, what the fuck do you want from me?" Quinn asked, beginning to feel a little, well, 'tetchy' about the whole encounter. "You want to fight, or something?"

Craft said, "No, we don't want to fight. Although I heard about what you did out at the shelter. Maybe sometime you'd like to spar with one of us on the mats."

"Fuck sparring," Quinn spit out emphatically. "Waste of an old man's time."

"What does that mean?'

"You guys make me angry. And you frighten me. What does a frightened and angry and cornered animal do?"

About half of the men in the room felt challenged and made it known through their grunting and groaning and shifting around in their positions.

Quinn had maintained what he called the Warrior's Rest pose, sitting on one heel with his other foot bottom on the ground under a bent knee, so he could stand quickly on one leg. He rose up a little bit and made a slight gesture with one hand.

Peter said, "Enough. He's a guest. And an Elder. No bad manners allowed. Fuck with him and I'll fuck with you. The Madeleines and the Seer have vetted him and so has the High Priestess. Any issues you have with this are personal issues. Which means it's a personal problem. Deal with it."

Quinn remained sitting awhile in the ensuing uncomfortable silence. Then he stood up, rising smoothly and quickly from his pose. He looked around the room at the other men and sat down again. He said, "If I want any shit from you people, I'll invite it out of you. Like I told your man out there in the woods, I am the Bodhisattva of Assholes. Fuck with a lion long enough and there's gonna be missing limbs."

Several men laughed. The aggressive ones seemed confused. Even Craft cracked a smile. He had seen the little energetic bolo Quinn had thrown into the middle of the room. He guessed it was some kind of defusion bomb.

"Alright then, now that we're all friends again," Quinn began, "What about the Divine Masculine? I have heard all this stuff about the Divine Feminine. Where's the Masculine counterpart? Where's the equivalency?"

Peter answered, "The equivalency, right now, is in functioning one level below the Divine. It's functioning in the Sacred. We are, the wen and the men, still working out the details of what Sacred Relatedness looks like. So far, it looks like partnership in all things, with the one exception of the Antecedence of the Feminine.

"Most people who practice an earth-based—or earth conscious, paganism, I guess you'd call it—like to look at the earth as feminine and the sun masculine. We don't, we take the sun as feminine, and the planets, symbolically, to be Her children. Our entire orientation is different. We look at all phenomena as having the Feminine in the Antecedent.

"As for the Divine Masculine, well, it's still emergent. Take a look, for example, at the Windu Divinity, the Trimerid. You have the Creative aspect, the Drahma; the Maintaining aspect, the Wishnu, and the destructive aspect, the Skreeva. Nominally these all have equal roles in the universe, but these days the Skreeva is worshipped as a god of transformation, not as a god of destruction. The creative and maintaining powers of the other two, and the fact that they are also both powers of transformation, are ignored and consequently life is out of balance. Destruction—planetary destruction—is an imminent threat.

"If you wanted to classify us by that system—and I suggest you don't—then what we do, as men, we are primarily engaged in the Maintenance of All Life, which we consider the greatest task. Creation and Destruction tend to happen pretty much all on their own. It is in Maintenance that true Will can be grown and developed."

"But what about the Divine Masculine?" Quinn asked.

"That is something that is, as I said, being grown and developed," Peter answered.

"I don't understand," Quinn said.

"Clearly," Peter said. "Wait, I didn't mean that to be as smart-assed as it sounded."

"Yeah?" Quinn said, on the verge of sarcasm. "Say more then."

"Four kinds of time and space: Profane, Mundane, Sacred, and Divine. That's it. There may be others, but that's basically what we have access to here. I mean, those are the only kinds of time and space to which we have access."

"OK," Quinn conceded, "I think I get you."

"That's it then. The old imagery, the old ideas of the Divine Masculine, as our culture was handed it, are out of balance. It is re-emerging. But the Divine Feminine is emerging first, because She is Antecedent. She's coming first, and the Divine Masculine, the one that is capable of sustaining life before taking it, is emerging behind Her. We can't quite see Him yet."

"Ok, ok, ok. So what is this Divine Feminine?"

An 'Ah,' sigh rolled around the room, as if the men were receiving something they'd been waiting for, some fundamental concession from Quinn.

Peter said, "Sit!" and the men lapsed into meditative silence. This went on for five minutes. Quinn, barely able to sit still for it, looked around the room when he thought others weren't looking, and they weren't.

The last man on the dais, an older man who hadn't said much, said, "This is the Antecedence of the Feminine originally composed by the First Craft, John, with new fact added as it has become revealed:

"I awoke this morning under the influence of a dream I could not recall. I knew only that it was bright. I awoke to the dark, warm and comfortable and listening to the sounds of my own heart pulsing and my beloved's breath gentle and steady. I awoke feeling at ease, but also feeling that I did not know where I was. I could not remember where I was. The question, 'Where am I?' soon led to 'Why am I here?' and this one led to 'How did I get here?' Finally, circling around, stalking questions like I'd stalk a quarry, I asked myself 'Where did I come from?' and my answer to this last question was, 'I came from something greater than myself.'

"And in the darkness, I sat up. I realized that I was a part of all that lived, animate and inanimate, yes, but I had a sense of something else, the origin of myself. I felt the part of myself that came from my mother. All the stuff, all the substance of me, came from my mother when she bore me in her womb.

"It was she that created me, created the parts of me, sustaining me within her until I was complete enough to come into the world. All that I am, as I appear before you, was first created by her. And so it is for all of you. Your blood, your sinews, your bones; all made by her. We know this to be true. It is she that first sustains us.

"We are born from her."

And then much to Quinn's surprise, the assembled circle of men responded with, "We are not born from our fathers."

The old man continued, "Our fathers supply instruction. Our fathers contribute to our form by altering the instructions on how the substance of ourselves is made. The contribution of our fathers is small, invisible to the naked eye. But the substance of ourselves comes from our mothers.

"And this substance is antecedent to any contribution of our fathers. The substance that is us was born with our mothers when they were born. This was the egg, the ovum, the massive. We now know that a wen is born with all the ova she will ever have, and that these ova are made, not by her, but by her mother. The mass that became us was made by our grandmothers."

The group responded, "The feminine is antecedent in time."

"The feminine is antecedent in evolution as well. We have learned that sexual dimorphism is an evolutionary development. For eons the cells of life replicated themselves through division, each cell a mother cell that would split off a daughter cell from herself. In this way it can be seen that Life itself began in the Feminine, and the Masculine evolved out of it. In this way it can be seen that…" the Elder paused.

Again came a response, "The Feminine is antecedent and the Masculine is consequent."

The Elder continued, "We now know that species as developed as sharks and snakes have retained the ability to reproduce without sex, making live, healthy, copies of themselves. And some mother snakes have even retained the ability to make males without sex.

"And even in ourselves, ourselves as Masculine, it turns out that we develop in the womb initially as Feminine, our masculine gender characteristics appearing only later in our development. This means that…" the Elder paused again.

The chorus spoke, "The Feminine is antecedent and the Masculine derivative."

"I had risen from the bed, the floor was cold under my feet, and gone to the table to make notes of my revelations, and a new question came to me. What does this, what do these facts have to say about the relations between the sexes? About the meaning of my relationship to wen? What does it mean to say the Feminine is Antecedent?

"And sitting there, a blanket thrown over me, chin on my hand, I fell into a waking dream, looking out the window at the autumn colors. In this dream, I was pursuing something, something bright in the darkness, running through the woods. So bright it was that it illumined the path beneath my feet, stopping when I paused for rest. At those times it seemed to come closer, teasing me, drawing me further on.

"Then I realized that, if I let it, it would come to me."

"And what came to me was this: an understanding of the Proper Accord, what my relationship to wen should be."

All said, "The Feminine creates, the Masculine makes."

The Elder asked, "And what is the relationship of a Maker to a Creator?"

The men answered, "I was created by the Feminine and in my life I am a Maker."

The Elder said, "The Feminine sustains, the Masculine maintains.

"Without the Sustainer there would be nothing to maintain. Therefore everything the Maintainer does is in Service to the Sustainer, for without it there would be nothing to maintain."

The men said, "The Feminine is the Sustainer, the Masculine is the Maintainer."

The old man continued, "And then therefore the Masculine is in service to the Feminine.

"And this is what I was told by the voice in the light that came to me as I stood in the Forest of my Dreams. As I stood still, still and waiting, the light came to me and those are the words the light spoke to me, the words I heard within me when the light touched me.

"The Feminine is Antecedent. Serve Her upon whom you depend."

The men, then, intoned the following invocation:

"Oh, Great Sustainer,
Keep me Well 'til the end of my days.
Sustain me Well that I might be Good.

"Oh Great Maintainer,
Work me Well 'til the end of my days.
Work me Well so my Would is the Should."

There was a long silence, where only the sound of men breathing could be heard. There was a palpable pressure of feeling in the room, regulating the breath.

Into this, Quinn sighed. "You really are an Order."

"Yes," Peter said.

"And you do put the Feminine first," Quinn said.

"Yes," Peter said.

"But why?" Quinn asked. "Especially when you don't have to?"

"Because it's the Truth!" one of the men in front of Quinn blurted out.

"Yes," Craft said. "Because it's the Truth. Everything we said is biological fact. It's the basis of our values; biological truth, not beliefs from an ignorant past. Recognizing the Antecedence of the Feminine is simply a logical consequence of biological reality."

"This is correct," the old man who'd led the call and response said. "And we extend the logical consequence into as many areas of human experience that we can. There are psychological consequences, for example. A psyche tuned by generations to seek dominance and control must be re-tuned to seek it in ways reflective of that reality. If a man needs to deal with feelings of inferiority, we help. If he feels impelled to lash out and take, we help. Since the Feminine came first—and for all of us it did—then we put consideration of the Feminine first in our deliberations. We put Her first, what serves Her best, into our decisions."

"And it is because you believe that if you do this then you will have everything you really need," Quinn said.

"Yes. And, it turns out, it's true," the Elder said.

"Then there is the spiritual dimension you must consider," Peter said. Men around the circle acknowledged this in general agreement, as if general agreement about a spiritual dimension happened among men every day.

"You see," Craft said as he picked up the thread. "It turns out that the Divine Feminine is interested in manifestation, being among us here in life. The wen are trained to allow Her to manifest through them. And She does."

"Yes," Peter said. "She is not really interested in Divine Union with just one facet of the Masculine Principle, one Divine Male, a God. She is interested in Union with every man, which is each of us who seeks Her. And insofar as we, as men, embody the principles of the Sacred Masculine, She, through Her Priestesses, and the other wen who serve Her, responds to and manifests for us; She will manifest to us."

Peter continued, "And you have seen Her, yes?" Everyone said yes, including Quinn.

Peter turned to Quinn and said, "And that is why you are here. And allowed to be here. You have seen Her. And, according to the wen, She loves you."

Quinn smiled, and said, "Well. Imagine that. And how do you know I'm not still a threat to you?"

"Asshole," Peter said.

And, for the first time in a long time, longer than he could remember, Quinn blushed.

Peter patted him on the shoulder, and said, "Here." He produced a wooden bowl from behind him that contained some small dark balls that looked like rolled up herbs held together by molasses.

"What are these?" Quinn asked, sniffing the bowl suspiciously.

Peter answered, "Immortality pills. I've been working on the recipe."

"I've heard of these. What's in them?" Quinn asked, grabbing a handful as he watched other men doing the same from other bowls circulating among them.

"Certain longevity herbs and mushrooms, a little ground dried venison, trace minerals, honey and molasses both, rain, and a secret ingredient. That's been the experimental part."

"A secret? Really?" Quinn asked.

"Yes. I've found one old text—a part of my training was to learn to be literate in Tribhatan. I found one, and only one, reference to 'rain' on the list of ingredients. Rain must have been left off the other lists because it was so commonly known as to be thought superfluous, or it was left off the lists because it was the secret. And it was commonly known that there was, in fact, a secret ingredient. So, I've been experimenting with 'rain'. Tell me, what do you think?"

"What've you got, a little cloud chamber in the basement?" Quinn asked as he popped a few into his mouth. "Hey, these are good," he said around the mouthful.

The little balls burst with flavors in his mouth, flavors so poignant he began salivating immediately. He swallowed as quickly as he could. An involuntary 'yum' sound escaped his throat, resonating down into his belly as he swallowed. Then he shivered with pleasure.

"See? I thought you'd like it. You know this already?" Craft, who had been watching him out the corner of his eye, asked.

"This what?" Quinn mumbled around the mouthful, noting for later an irritation arise in him for what he considered to be Craft's persistent obliqueness.

"This sensation. This shiver of ecstasy. You know it, don't you?" Craft explained.

Quinn closed his eyes, and concentrated. He swallowed again, and shivered again. "Yes, I know it. But I don't recall from where at the moment. There've been so many."

"Ah," Quinn heard the old man behind him say.

When Quinn opened his eyes again it appeared that the men were taking a short break, one of those 'water in, water out' breaks. He stood up and followed some men downstairs to a bathroom that had an old, extended stall, a single trough urinal along one wall. Quinn bellied up to the trough with the rest of the men. When a wen emerged from the doorless stall behind him, pulling up a pair of pants, he turned involuntarily to watch, and peed over into the stream of the man next to him, who yelled at him, "Hey!"

Quinn startled, pissed up and down, pulling closer to the man. He yelled again, "Hey! Don't piss on me, old man!"

"Ah, hahaha!" Quinn laughed like a mad man at him. "Hell, boy, I'll piss over you, all the way over your head," Quinn bragged, and turned back to piss in thundering resonance on the back wall of the metal trough. Just as he was turning he saw the departing wen look back over her shoulder at him, and smile. "Ah, hahaha!" Quinn laughed again. "Thunder Cock the Rock Splitter!" and peed hard, making the metal plate oscillate with a low note. Quinn thought he saw a glint of flashing teeth in a large grin as the wen turned profile to go down the hall.

The men on either side scuttled away from him. "No splatter," Quinn mumbled to himself, and settled down for the last few seconds, deliberately controlling the stream until he was the last man finishing. Finished, he shook himself and pulled on it before he put it away with a sigh. Everyone had seen the Madman, the Sacred Clown, emerge, and none of them really knew what to do with it.

"Hey!" Quinn said. "It's an Archetype!"

The men shuffled away, some bumping into each other at the door. Some mumbled, then a few laughed out loud.

The men re-entered the circular room and resumed their seats.

Peter said to Quinn, "In this part of the meeting we invite men to speak to a theme we've all been working on since the last meeting. This week's theme was simple: 'Share your observations of how something you did in Service to the Feminine made you feel.'

"Introduce yourselves to our guest when you speak," the old man yelled out at the group.

A young man started off with "Umm, hello, Mr. Quinn. I'm a Journeyman, here. My name is Jake. I was assigned to be available to the new girl, Angelica, if she sought out companionship, and sex. You know how it goes. Hold the space for her possibilities, and follow where she leads. In this case, it led up to the Stone Chapel, and to sex on the Altar.

"And she freaked out. I mean, I knew what was happening, I thought so, anyway. But I've got to say, she freaked out. Full body spasms, I thought it was orgasms but there was a lot of pain.

"About the time I ran out of ideas the High Priestess showed up. The girl had a blow-out, right there, just like we are taught it could happen.

"We, me and the HP, took the girl downstairs and the HP sent her down the stream naked. Oh, man, by my balls I was seized with the sensation of it. I don't know what to say, except it was magnificent and awesome. We followed her down and got her out on the bank. And well, I guess that's it."

"Not a girl," Craft said.

"What?" Jake replied.

"She's not a girl, Jake. You kept calling her a girl. She's not a girl. What is she?"

"Umm, I don't know. I'm sorry."

"Yes, you do know. Sit with it until the answer comes."

"You didn't finish the story, Jake." Peter said.

"Umm, I don't know how much further I should go."

"Everything that happens in the presence of the assignment is part of the story. Go ahead, finish it," the old man said.

"Umm, OK. Well, there was this, uh, dragon."

Men stopped still, even Quinn, to hear this next part.

"There was this dragon that appeared in the air over her. And it stayed there for a long time. It stayed over her the whole time she was in the stream. We, uh, me and Eva, that is, followed Angelica down the stream and got her out on the bank. Then Eva, the High Priestess, that is, offered me Release. And I took it."

There was a stir among the Hands and other Journeymen. One sucked in his breath, another let out a low whistle. The Consorts smiled and the High Consorts grinned.

"The dragon," Craft asked. "Did it have wings?"

"Not that I could see," Jake answered.

"Wait, just like that? She offered you Release?" Quinn asked.

"You can stop there," Peter said.

Jake nodded, knowing now that Peter and Craft, and probably the Elder, knew the whole story.

"So how do you feel about it?" Craft asked.

"Honestly, I was shocked. On the energetic level I was both exhausted and exalted at the same time. She fed the World, Eva did, and I helped. That, and we brought someone through.

"She made me understand about a behavior that I thought was showing respect was actually disrespectful. Now I'm looking at everything.

"I've had some of the release from the buffers happen to me, but never this much all at once. I feel amazed.

"And my mind feels like it's been hammered. Sometimes I can't think… but that's not a feeling.

"My last feeling, I guess, when I sit still for it, is gratitude."

"Good," Craft said. "Who else?"

A man stood up. Peter said, "This is a Consort. His name is Wade. He is currently handling several assignments, primarily to a Priestess named Jasmine. Jasmine, well, we consider her to be a Wild Wen. She's an expert in security, martial arts, and survival, in addition to being totally dedicated to the experiment of hierogamous alchemy. Her training is dedicated to producing higher results."

"I may not know what that is. But I know who Jasmine is. And I've met Wade. How are you, son?"

Wade smiled, suddenly grateful to Quinn for not making any comment about anything that happened out at the rock shelter.

Wade began, "Jasmine and I were on patrol; we were the ones who found Quinn. Well, Quinn was the one who found us."

"They were pretty noisy," Quinn allowed. The men laughed or smiled. "But really, it was the smoke that led me in."

Wade smiled, too, then continued. "Sometimes this is difficult for me. Not just the talking—talking's not much my style. But this thing about assignments. It feels like it takes too much out of my control. I don't have to do any of it, I know. And I want to do what I'm assigned to do. But I don't want any of you to get assignments, at least not any that require me to share wen. I thought I was past all this, but it still comes up.

"And I know that the techniques of sublimation turn that energy—the energy I would spend in bringing those desires to the surface, or in mentally obsessing about them—into another form that I can use for other things. I can feel the change, I can feel the extra energy. Mostly, these past few weeks, I put it into sex, rather than practice the techniques for crystallization.

"I've been doing that because, since Jasmine's been assigned to acquire enough life force from a bunch of you," he said, indicating the men sitting around him, "I've been struggling with being assigned to help her do it. It's not that I haven't been given other assignments, some fun ones, too, that are supposed to help me balance it out. I spend the energy on sex with the assignments; it helps them with their development. It feels good to help them, but then I slip into Shadow, and I realize that I have a power over them in those moments.

"And then, as she gains more power, and she has been, as some of you know, that power in her attracts me more, and makes me want to control it. Both her and that power she has, control it more. And I get angry when I can't.

"The other day, for example. I was walking across the lawn at the barn, carrying her clothes as she went from one Accumulation Ritual to the next. She had decided that it was too much trouble to put her clothes on and take them off again, so she just went to the next assignment naked. Walking behind her, carrying her clothes, something started to happen in my second and third centers. When we got there my job was to watch, just watch, and monitor my responses, physical, emotional, and mental. I got hard watching. And it made me want to reach out and pull her off him. And it made me want to take from her what she was getting as soon as she was getting it.

"I get that part of the reason I'm there is for protection, but the situation doesn't require that kind of vigilance in these circumstances, so I just paid attention to what was happening in front of me.

"I know that I'm supposed to be working, or to develop my ability to sense and palpate the fields that she's generating around her. I know I'm also supposed to learn how to manipulate those fields myself, so as to facilitate the tantra in both of us. But that doesn't, or I'm afraid it won't, fill this desire for control.

"Sometimes She comes to me, the Diosa comes to me, through Jasmine or one of the other assignments. She smiles at me and tells me She loves me. The awe and the ecstasy of this, being loved by Her, is the only salve for this desire for control and my anger and frustration at not having it.

"And then, of course, this starts a new struggle with wanting more of that awe, and more of that ecstasy."

"We are appetitive, we men," Craft said.

Everyone smiled and nodded their head.

"So, something happened to me," Wade continued. "Jasmine did something to me."

Men leaned toward Wade, eager to hear. Craft, Peter, the Elder, and Quinn did something remarkable. They all four raised their hands simultaneously and beckoned to Wade in the exact same way and at the same moment; identical gestures beckoning Wade to come sit on the first step of the dais.

"She did something. Jasmine performed a Ritual on me. I didn't know it was one at the time; I was just in it, but the Madeleine told me later.

She said I could talk about it. She said what was important was not that you men would hear about it, it's not a secret. It's just not an experience to be coveted. She said you wouldn't even know about it at the time.

"It's called the Ritual of Appeasement. What happened was that Jasmine had learned how to take my anger as food. And at the end, held down by many arms, she showed me the Goddess of Death."

Wade, and everyone else, held the ensuing silence in stillness, each contemplating his own images of what it would be like to have congress with the Goddess of Death.

"I went to the Madeleine to tell her all this, since the assignments are approved by her. This is what the Madeleine told me: 'Understand, when you put the desire for pleasure into the desire for power and control, you create two effects: on the one hand you create the desire for the imposition of order, and the desire for virtue. And you also put your desire for pleasure into opposition with the desire for release; you put sex in opposition to death. You see, sex and death are really the same door, the difference is one is the way in, the other is the way out. You can see what I'm talking about with couples in restaurants. You want to see them side by side, not in opposition to each other, where the wait staff will keep running into each other. So, you see, as long as your newly generated desires for order and virtue come to rule your conduct, you'll be fine. Just remember, now, it's not Sex or Death. Now it's Sex and Death.'

"Well, honestly, I didn't see. So she drew it out for me."

Men laughed.

"Here's the drawing. I brought it so I could pass it around," Wade concluded, pulling a folded piece of paper from a shirt pocket.

When the paper came into the hands of a younger man, he glanced at it, passed it to the man next to him and stood up.

"I'm new here. I'm just a Hand. I cannot believe how fortunate I am."

Craft said, "Do not believe it. Belief has no real place here. We either know or we do not. What we do not know, we endeavor to understand."

The Hand replied, "She is beautiful. I write poetry about her. I am falling. What do I do?"

Craft said, "Fall if you wish. Learn that suffering."

"Oh, no," the Hand said. "I'll embarrass myself."

"That's part of it. Fall, and learn how to overcome your embarrassment. Give the wen the chance to practice Grace," Peter said.

"Grace?" the Hand asked.

"Yes," Quinn and Peter said at the same time. Peter deferred, letting Quinn speak.

"Yes," Quinn repeated. "It is by an act of Grace that she will respond. And it will be Grace whether she grants you a boon or not."

"Yes," Peter took his turn, "And it is by Grace that she will choose not to rebuke you in your embarrassment, that, perhaps, by Grace, she will accept your attention, and the poems. Tell me, are you any good at poetry?"

Everyone laughed.

"If so," Peter continued into the laughter, "Can you write some poems for me? I find myself falling. Falling all over the place."

Men laughed even harder as Peter fell over on his side. Suddenly they all fell over on their sides, still laughing.

To Quinn, still sitting upright, it looked like a field of hay had been mowed down, like a squad of soldiers had been laid out in a spray of weapons fire. But instead of violence, Quinn noted, they had been laid low by Love, helpless, laughing about it, and sighing.

The Hand was still standing in the middle of this, looking around him, not quite getting the joke.

"Sex and Death," Quinn said to him. "Sex and Death."

Craft sat up. "Imagine you are writing a love poem to the Goddess of Death."

The Hand's eyes went wide, showing the whites, frozen in Fear.

Then Peter, sitting up also, said something merciful, something full of Grace, "Even Death needs Life in order to live. Write about that."

Everyone else sat up, adjusting their clothes to accommodate their crotches, settling the prominences of their gender into comfortable array. That is, they shifted their cocks and balls around until their clothing wasn't binding. Quinn shifted which leg he was sitting on, watching it all, and wondering at the animal nature of what he was seeing.

"So," Peter said, when they'd all settled down. "Do you all have your assignments for the next week?"

"Let me revise that. Is there anyone without an assignment?" Peter clarified.

No one raised their hands, or gave any sign that they were unassigned.

"So tonight, because we have a guest, we're going to interrupt the sequence and repeat the first lecture on Tantra and Alchemy," Peter began.

"You have been trained in anatomy. You have studied gross anatomy in general and sexual anatomy and neurology in particular. You have been introduced to spiritual anatomy and have been exposed to the general theory of tantric and alchemical practice.

"The creation of higher energetics requires at least the energetic signature of the opposite gender, just as was required for natal conception. This is in accordance with the yin/yang unification symbol. For much of what was required, it was simply required to spend time in a resonant state with the opposite sex. However, a small amount of material was necessary to be introduced at the appropriate moment in the process—hence the supplement we passed around.

"Make no mistake, homo-erotic energies are welcome here. They are considered to be duplications, that is, a doubling of the energies generated during solitary practice, and this doubling is very powerful, and very intense. When they arise you are to be prepared, and use these energies for yourselves, as well.

"You must understand that the first goal for you men, the initial goal, is the attainment of self-control. Self-control begins with the ability to Will oneself to have an erection, or not have an erection, at Will. You are all relatively young, so it is easy to Will yourself to have an erection. But what will you do with it once you have it?

"In the beginning, you are to do nothing at all with it, nothing physical that is. You are not to touch it, but learn to keep it erect using only your thoughts, feelings, and sensations. While it is erect you are to practice certain muscular contractions, learning to gain voluntary control over certain muscles groups. You will learn how to coordinate the breath with muscular activations, and to use the energetic paths, established by your breath, to move energies along certain paths in certain sequences. Eventually other paths of circulation will be shown to you. Certain stops, certain stopovers, as it were, in these paths will be concentrated on.

"Eventually you will be ready for Phase Two, where you will practice, without touching, with a partner. For the first sessions you will remain clothed, that is to say, you will keep your erection covered. You will be allowed to be as close to your partner as is comfortable for both of you—no closer—and without touching and without speaking. Your communication must be by gesture and eye. You will be monitored. While in this situation you will practice your prescribed energy circulation exercises.

"In this way you will begin to learn to separate arousal from the need for completion. One of the goals, as you know, is to separate the masculine orgasm from ejaculation.

"Next you will be allowed to open your robes and look at each other. When you begin to do the circulation exercises you are to look at each other thoroughly and completely; and then to continue these exercises while looking into each other's' eyes.

"You must learn how to make love to the wen, to bring her to orgasm and satisfaction as if you were a wen, and you must do this without expecting any return of attention on her part during this introductory stage.

"At the third Phase, therefore, one of you may, with the use of your fingers touch the other, but only one may do the touching for these first session of the Phase. The wen will make the choice. At the next session you may use fingers and lips, and again, the choice will be the wen's. In the third session the wen may invite the man to choose. If he declines, she must choose. Only on the fourth session may you both touch each other at the same time, and then, only if the wen agrees.

"At this point, it is imperative you men understand that you are not to allow yourself release, nor will you be allowed to use your phallus for any type of penetration. You are to master the arts of making love to a wen as another wen would make love to a wen. Specific postures will be shown to you.

"At some point, depending on your progress as determined by your mentors, you will be assigned a partner with whom you will be allowed to practice the Union. As you know, your first practices will always be conducted with the proctors present. Only after that will you be allowed to practice in private.

"These rules apply to all attractions and genders. The body does not matter here; you are making a new body. Your feelings do not matter here, you are learning to access higher emotions. And what you think about it is irrelevant, simply because you do not yet know how to think about these things. Later, you will.

"Understand this: There is a power that the wen learn—the power to force a release in a man. Also, the power to keep an erection from happening, or make a man lose it if she wants—even before penetration, as well as at any point in this process. It is a matter of survival for them. In your practice with the wen, you will not know when she is trying to work this power on you, so you must learn to recognize when she is trying.

"Understand: this is a matter in the development of Will. Feel free to resist."

With that, Peter smiled, and the lecture concluded.

"This is enough for the evening," Craft said.

"Free Wen," Jake said. "That's what Angelica is. A Free Wen. And not to be presumed upon."

"That's a good start," Peter acknowledged.

"Remember," Craft said. "Tomorrow night is the Dance of the Crescent Moon. You are all expected to be there, unless you have a different assignment. Musicians: your assignment in the afternoon is to practice."

The Elder spoke: "The Feminine is Antecedent. Serve Her upon whom you depend."

The men, then, again, intoned the following invocation:

"Oh, Great Sustainer,
Keep me Well 'til the end of my days.
Sustain me Well that I might be Good.

"Oh Great Maintainer,
Work me Well 'til the end of my days.
Work me Well so my Would is the Should."

And then there was a humming sound, the last vowel sustained.

Quinn found himself in a place of sustained quiet, and sat there until he felt a hand on his shoulder. The other men had almost all filtered out, and Craft had leaned over to bring him back.

Craft beckoned that Quinn should follow him. Outside in the hall, Quinn found his bag was on the floor, over by the wall, next to his staff with his paddy hat hung from the chin string. Quinn looked at Craft, questioningly.

"You have a new room. Upstairs on the second floor. Room Ten. It opens on the veranda; you'll like it," Craft said.

Quinn shook his head in the negative. He still didn't understand why his things were out in the hall and what it meant.

Craft shrugged. "You don't have an assignment. And no one is assigned to you."

Quinn said, "Now, there's something you can explain to me. What is this 'assignment' business?"

Craft sighed. "We are assigned to different people, assigned to become their lovers—well, really, to have sex. That's more accurate. And we're often assigned which tasks we're supposed to work on. You heard the lecture; all those men will have assignments given to them. They'll be having sex next week, probably with someone different from whom they were practicing with this week. Sometimes they'll be having sex not necessarily with one at a time.

"It all depends on what the Goddess communicates to the High Priestess and the Master Consort. These communications are such that, as a person becomes trained in accessing the Divine Energies, they can learn to confirm the assignments themselves, or even receive them first, but then have them confirmed.

"Assignments could be such that, on one day, someone was assigned as a lover—a practice partner—with one person. Sometimes twice in a day, sometimes two different partners in a day. Those wen who are willing have lots of sex. Sometimes no sex on a particular day. Sometimes sleeping together, sometimes not.

"You have to understand. The Goddess loves the sex. It is her opportunity to manifest.

"The Goddess never asks anyone to do anything that goes against their nature. It may go against their wishes, or their inclinations, but never against their nature.

"Assignments, and whatever happens during them, are not talked about casually. They are sacred events that occur in sacred containers. If something were to come up that needed to be discussed, it is usually discussed with someone higher up, one's immediate mentor. Everyone has two mentors, one same sex, one complimentary sex. Some assignments we talk about in the circle.

"Inside the Program, assignments are an expected part of the routine. The person with whom one practices is changed, depending on the interpretation of the wishes of the Goddess, as communicated to the High Priestess and confirmed by the Master Consort.

"You're not in the Program, Quinn. You're a guest. I'd be surprised if you had any assignments at all," Craft concluded, holding Quinn's bag out to him.

Quinn took the bag. When he turned to take up the staff and the hat, Craft asked a question that had irritated him since he first laid eyes on Quinn. "What's with the hat?"

Quinn looked at it, turning it over in his hand. "I took it from a garden shed near the woods line about 20 miles north of here. Same place I stole the weed. Ticks had been dive bombing me from the trees. The hat kept them off. The big ones I could hear when they landed. They made little 'tick' sounds. The little ones I could pick off. Better off the hat than me." Fatigue was evident in his slumped shoulders and gravelly voice.

Craft looked at Quinn with an observant eye, wondering that this man had survived so long on his own. "I've been told to tell you, also, that you need rest. And pay attention to your dreams. Even Thunder Cock the Rock Splitter needs to sleep sometimes," Craft finished, smiling, and pointed Quinn to the stairs.

He walked up the long double-flight and down the hall looking for Number Ten. He heard someone coming up the stairs on the wen's side. She stopped on the landing and turned to look at him. Recognizing who he was, she smiled, understanding a blessing from Diosa was before her. She walked toward him.

"Ah, the new guy," she said. "The Stranger. I've heard about you. And I was under the window one night, too."

Quinn smiled, following her gaze toward his phallus. "I'm probably unable to help you with what you heard," he said, patting himself. "All worn down."

"I have something for that. Something that will help you heal. I'll be right back," she said, turning to go back to the stairs, smiling back at him over her shoulder, checking to make sure he was watching, and that he was watching her ass move under the robe.

When he heard her go upstairs he turned and opened the door to his room. He was surprised by how nice it was. A queen-size bed, lamps on nightstands on either side. A set of French doors framed the bed on either side. Over the bed was a rendering of what seemed to him to be Aphrodite reclining on a hammock tied between two trees at the edge of a beach, the huge shell on which she ridden from the deep nearby, and still foam covered.

He leaned his staff on the wall just inside the door, put his pack on the top of the small dresser and removed his shoes and pants. He threw the pants over the back of one of the chairs next to a small writing table. He unbuttoned his shirt, stepped out on the veranda and looked out over Stonehaven on a summer night, watching the brilliant syncopation of the fireflies from tree top level.

He heard a soft knock and turned, poking his head back through the open veranda doors and said, "Enter."

She came through the door with a towel over one shoulder and a cloth bag hanging from a strap on the other side. She smiled at him.

"Come here," she said, taking the towel and laying it out over one of the two chairs, turning it to face outward, away from the table. She indicated he should sit there.

He came into the room, naked from the waist down, cock extended, hanging down, fat and lazy.

She smiled, and said, "Sit."

He did, and she settled to her knees before him, laying the bag to one side, shrugging out of the top of her robe while keeping her shawl over her shoulders, leaving her arms and belly bare, her breasts covered with the ends of the shawl. Quinn could see the outline of them, moving softly when she moved. She pushed his knees apart and leaned in for a closer look.

"Is this an assignment?" Quinn asked.

"Oh, no, honey," she replied. "This is opportunism. Besides, I've been told to watch everybody on the upper floors."

"Then why are you doing this?" Quinn wanted to know.

"I just love cock. I want to see them all taken care of. You could think of it as my mission," she said, and giggled. "I have something for this."

She reached into the bag and brought out a white ceramic jar painted with pink flowers. The lid was heavy-duty glass, held down by a wire spring. She slipped the keeper off and opened it. The smell that inundated the room was immediate, a smell of roses and something deeper.

Quinn realized that the odor was too complex to analyze, and focused on her dipping the fingertips of one hand into the jar, watching her remove a dollop of cream-colored gel and rub it between her hands.

She leaned in between his knees and blew on his cock. It shifted in response. "See?" she said, gently. "There's life in the old boy yet."

Smiling, she put both hands, palms forward, on him, cradling him as if she were praying. She held still, letting him absorb all the sensations of the salve.

The first sensation was one of cooling. Not a cold that would make him withdraw, just a coolness that made him hold his breath. Then, as it warmed, he relaxed into it, growing larger in her hands. When the head of it extended past her palms to her wrists, while her finger tips rested on his belly, she shifted her hands slightly, rising a little higher. She wrapped her fingers down and around his balls, pressing on his perineum, holding all of him.

She pulled forward, pulling his scrotum out gently, stroking from there, down the length of him. And when she let go his erection sprung up, and bounced in the open air.

"What is that stuff?" he, for some reason—perhaps in awe—whispered.

"It is healing, is what it is," she whispered loudly back at him, grinning. "This is what healing is like."

She stroked him gently, rubbing in the salve, from root to tip, alternating hands, making a circle of her fingers as she came up around the head, pulling him, drawing him onward, outward, and up.

Finally, the rim of the head of him tingled, then sparkled with little flashes of light. He had slid forward on the chair, striving to reach for her. Now he leaned back, holding the chair with his hands at his sides. He realized that he'd been reduced to his orgasm, a beautiful orgasm. She, feeling it, came up higher in her kneel, holding her mouth open and off the head of him, where he could see her, holding him, stroking him lightly, keeping him pointed where she wanted.

He came, a long pulse that shot to the back of her throat. She smiled, around her open mouth, pooling him in the front where he could see his contribution. He squirted again, and several times more, the last twitches simply oozing out, rolling down his shaft until they met her hand. She removed it, bringing it to her mouth, still smiling, gazing at his eyes. She had held her other hand under her chin, and now she brought it up and licked off a drop that had escaped.

She held his ejaculate in her mouth, eyes closed, letting her saliva mix thoroughly with it. She put the tip of her tongue on the roof of her mouth and an electric shock went through her. Her eyes rolled back in her head and she looked upwardly inward into a field of golden light that filled her heart with joy and awe.

She opened her lips into a very small 'o', and made a sipping sound, mixing air into the contents of her mouth. She brought her eyes back to the room, opened them slightly, and gazed at the still half hard erection. She touched it again with both hands and swallowed, an electric spark travelling through her, into her belly, and then down to her root. She twitched with her own orgasm, then shivered. She looked up, and saw him gazing at her under lidded eyes, a slight smile pulling up the right side of his lips. 'This one's special," she thought to herself, "Very special."

She stayed there for a while, bathing in the golden light that fell down on her from above. Finally she heard the breath of sleep, coming from the old man. She smiled, put the ointment jar back in her bag and rose to her feet in one smooth motion.

Slowly, bowing at the hip, she backed up to the door, breasts brushing lightly against the soft fabric of the shawl, smiling, gazing, at the lovely image she wanted to imprint in her memory. The old man glowed in the light.

Janice opened the door without looking at it, slid out, and then closed the door without looking at him again.

29

MAITHUNA, STORMS, AND THE MOON

"As you might have supposed," Eva began as they walked over the footbridge, "you have been selected as a candidate for the next status. If you survive the initiation you will be blessed as a High Priestess. It's not clear yet, but your initiation will probably come after Jasmine's. This doesn't mean you'll be receiving an assignment as one, not right away. And if an assignment comes, it probably won't be here, at least for a while. There are others who are more likely, and have the wisdom you have yet to earn.

"You need to learn a few more of the higher functions, and master these. So you will be close to me during your stay here, and you will probably stand in for me in ceremony, maybe even at the Equinox, or perhaps, also, the True Midsummer Ceremony.

"But I need you here for a different reason. There is something happening, something about to happen out in the world. It is creating tensions here and I need your support. Nothing overt, I just need the support of your presence. I need to call upon our love for each other and your friendship. I need you here."

"What is about to happen?" Diana asked.

"That's the thing: we don't know. We can feel that it is impending, but we can't see it. It's driving Madeleine a little crazy. She is spending hours, sometimes, in a day, looking at the lines in trance, but she can't see the event. We know that means it's not fixed yet, too many variables, but it is under a cloud of darkness so we can't be sure.

"What we do know is that it's going to affect us here. We see people coming. We saw some things about that young wen there, Angelica; images of her. Both Madeleine and I recognized her when we monitored that last class. One of the new Hands, Jake, was assigned to be one of her potential choices, in case she made a choice.

"Then there was the matter of the Stranger showing up here, making it through our defenses. If I hadn't known him from my past, who knows what would have happened to him.

"But the big thing, we don't know. We can't see it. And She isn't being very helpful. She smiles, and nods, and tells us to wait. 'Go on as you are,' She tells us. 'Wait for this. Wait for me,' She said. We don't know what it means. I have journeyed with Madeleine, so I know what she sees.

"She sees war. She sees a magic war coming. And we're in it. I need you to spend time with her, so that you can see what she sees when she's scrying.

"Some of it was set in motion long ago, even back in Rachel's time. But we don't know what yet. There are evils hidden in the darkness and they've been lying there, waiting, growing. And in that darkness we can't find them, not without revealing ourselves.

"And then there's the matter of Her Return."

"Her Return? Is it close?"

"Yes. We think. We know it is coming in stages, though we don't know what stage we're in and when the last stage will be, nor what it will be. Not even the Order knows. But it looks like one of the stages will unfold here.

"I need you to be ready. I need you with me. And tonight, will you stand in for me? Are you ready? Do you remember it?"

"Yes, dear. I remember it."

By this time, they had reached the gazebo. They climbed the steps and turned around to gaze at the view. The valley was golden, lined with lengthening shadows as the sun moved toward setting. They could see Raphael still tightening the lines on the canopy. They could see the thunderheads building beyond the mountain.

Eva reached for Diana's hand, and held it. Diana felt the wave of emotion wash over Eva, and turned to look at her friend and mentor. There were twin lines of tears running down her cheeks.

Diana reached out and touched the tears, bringing her finger back to her mouth. After a second of tasting it, she took the finger, kissed it, and lightly touched it to her friend's temple. In another moment Eva wiped her cheek with her free hand, and said, "It is too beautiful. How could anyone ever leave?"

Diana wondered, "Leave? Has Madeleine told her something?" but said nothing.

"Come on then. Let's go pick up the cart at the Recovery and get to the Mansion. We've got a lot of preparations to make before the Ceremony starts at sundown."

They turned, went up the hill to the parking lot, picked up Diana's small bag from the Recovery, climbed into one of the carts parked there, and whirred off to the Mansion.

They parked the cart in a lean-to shed built on the edge of the woods just north of the northwest wing. They emerged, and paused to look up at the high wall before them: a massive chimney, three pairs of narrow golden mean-proportioned windows on either side of it, size changing to match the different heights of the stories, but the proportions staying the same; Pythagorean windows matching the roofline at the top for the attic. The effect was to make the building seem impossibly tall.

They entered through an arched doorway in the Shade Garden wall on the east side of the wing, and made their way down the walk alongside the building and up the stone steps to the patio that spanned the entire wall all the way to the curved double doors of the Ballroom. They entered through the closer double doors that served as an entrance to the main office. The first floor here was completely dedicated to offices for the Stonehaven Council members. They ran on either side of the hallway with the office at the end running the entire width of the wing belonging to the High Priestess. Cut-back stairways at the Ballroom end of the wing led to the second and third stories, with a last narrow flight leading up to the dormitories.

Eva's chambers, with a private bath, were directly above her office suite, accessed by a private stair. The third floor suite, less deep, also ran the entire width of the wing, but had two beds. The dormers above that, in the attic, were divided along either side of the hallway, as they were in the main part of the mansion but shorter in the wings due to the lower roof line.

The rooms just before Eva's, on either side, belonged to the Madeleine and the Elder, both of these also had private baths. The rooms closer to the Ballroom belonged to the High Consort and The Craft, and were at the near end of the hall, adjacent the stairs.

Diana's bags had been brought to the room above Eva's and left on the floor of the room. Before she separated from Eva on the landing to the second floor, Eva said, "Unpack only what you need for now. Get cleaned up and prepared to dress. I'll see you in a few minutes." Then she made her way down the hall to her quarters.

Diana had slept on the second and third floors of the Mansion before, but never in the suites. She opened the door, faced the fireplace, and felt amazed and relieved by the room's beauty. The queen-size beds on either side of the room, near the windows, were made up and lovely. An antique table sat in the middle on a beautiful oriental carpet. On the table was a small covered tray of sliced meats and cheeses, with a loaf of fresh bread and a small bowl of olive oil and a plate of salt. Beside it was a pitcher of cold water, left there at the order of the Hearth Keeper. Closets lined the walls on either side of the door.

Diana kicked the door closed, heeled off her shoes, went to the table, poured herself a glass of water and dipped a slice of the bread in the olive oil and salt. She had just taken a bite, glass in hand, when she was startled by a voice behind her. "Hi there!" The glass almost slipped from her hand. She turned, bread hanging from her mouth, free hand slipping behind her to make a fist, eyes wide. She saw Eva standing there grinning in front of an open closet door.

"Didn't know about that one, did ya! Come on, when you're ready, you can clean up in my bathroom instead of trekking down the hall." Eva laughed, turned, and disappeared down the hidden staircase in the back of the closet. Diana came to the door and looked down the narrow stairs after her as she disappeared.

Diana set down the glass, went back to her suitcase, picked it up and tossed it on the trunk at the foot of her bed. She popped it open, bread still hanging below her chin like a long brown tongue. She grabbed her kit bag, stepped over to the table to swirl the bread in the oil and salt again, stuck it in her mouth, grabbed a couple slices of meat and cheese with her free hand, and slipped into the closet. She bent and stepped sideways down the narrow staircase.

She emerged into Eva's room. Her bed was under the west windows, head against the north wall, with the tall casement windows open. A breeze was blowing the curtains out in advance of the impending storm. Diana knew that the shutters on the outside all worked and could be closed against the sun if needed. There were two easy chairs facing the fireplace, with a work table behind them. Against the east casement windows behind a floor-to-ceiling curtain were altars with a small stool before them. There was a bathroom with a sink set in a four-foot counter below a lighted mirror, an old clawfoot tub with a suspended curtain, and a commode alongside the tub under a case-ment, all under the space occupied by closets in the room above.

The normal term of a High Priestess as head of a local Council was six years, with two year extensions available after that. Eva had been liv-ing in this room for 9 years already; the room was clearly hers. A wall alongside the altar hung with pictures of beloved people, including former spouses, children, and grandchildren.

Clothes and shawls were scattered about, and her table was covered with books and papers. When Diana entered the room, Eva was laying out her costume for tonight's Ceremony on the bed.

"Come on," Eva said. "Get in the shower. That will leave some time for your hair to dry," she said, tying her own hair up on her head. Eva went into the bathroom and started the shower, warming it up. "Want help washing your hair?"

Diana dropped the shoulder straps of her slip over her arms and wiggled her hips until it fell to the floor. Diana said, "Yes, please," playfully hip-butting Eva out of the way before she stepped into the tub. She adjusted the temperature one final bit and pulled the lever to direct the water up. She laughed when the first cold spurt hit her.

She wet her hair and Eva lathered it up for her while she stood relaxing in the heat. She rinsed and conditioned, piled her hair up, while Diana soaped up and rinsed, then asked for her razor. She shaved carefully, while Eva watched and smiled. Diana smiled back; theirs was an easy and comfortable friendship.

Eva asked about Diana's kids and her consort and husband Bill. Bill had been given an assignment to maintain a relationship with a particularly difficult wen. This wen had developed naturally as a Priestess, able to relate to and receive assignments from the Goddess herself, but she had not received the training necessary to behave as a true Servant of the Divine Feminine.

Inside the Order, this wen was seen as something of a rogue and on more than one occasion some mishap had occurred in larger events because she hadn't done her part on time, or worse, substituting what she thought needed to be done for what the Goddess had instructed. The Order was under instructions to not reveal itself to her, but to help her stay sane. That looked like Bill maintaining an affair with her, basically, no matter how badly she treated him. And sometimes it was difficult, because it was clear that Bill wouldn't be leaving his family to set up a live-in relationship with her. It was, for Bill, an exercise in behaving in such a way that he was her true friend. The hope was that, in time, she would generate that capacity to become a friend and develop wisdom about herself, and would assume the part in the Return that the Goddess wished for her.

Shower finished, Diana put her hair up in a towel, and they sat by the vanity with its mirror and lights near the altars. "Come, sit," Eva said. "Let me do your eyes."

The body of Ceremony practiced at Stonehaven, and called by them

Maithuna, was a highly ritualized group movement, a dance, with everyone performing certain postures in a pre-determined sequence. It was, in appearance, a sexual ballet and ritual theatre. It was also more than that, giving the participants access to tantric states of consciousness. When performed in a group setting, it created an energetic field in which transformation and transcendence became possible. This transformation worked for the participants in alchemical and evolutionary ways. The field worked on those watching, and created possibilities of consciousness for them directly. More importantly, it created a Sacred field for the manifestation of the Divine Feminine and Her Consort. In this field of manifestation the affairs of the world could become ordered in such a way as to lead to Consciousness of Her Antecedence, and other states of awareness that were capable of producing change in the world.

The main corpus of movements consisted of twenty-one separate sequences—thirteen for each lunar cycle in the year and eight for the holidays of the annual solar cycle. There were known to be at least twenty-eight others, each for specific purposes. Each Ceremony required different positions creating geometric patterns on the floor of the Great Ballroom, along with different costumes for each. Some required everyone to be doing the same thing in the same rhythms, others required different movements by different couples at different moments and points in the Ceremony.

These were all recorded on video and in a special choreographic script. They all required special clothing, make-up, and scents. Each had their own music, recorded and played back so that the entire performance became a dance. Knowing each Ceremony was required curriculum for both Priestesses and Consorts. Daily practice of the movements was encouraged sans costume and make-up, if possible, for all Interns, Consorts, and Priestesses. This provided the chance to master the arts of self-control and internal circulation of the life-force energies in accordance with the different tantras of various cultures, including the Windu, Taoist, Buddhist, Egyptian, and Hermetic modalities.

The schedule for the year was set in advance, and which Ceremony was performed depended on where the Moon was on the day the Ceremony was to be performed. Each Lunar Ceremony was performed every year. The Ceremony this night was the Sixth Moon Ceremony, also known as the Veiled Moon.

In addition to different robes, all of which opened down the front, both Masculine and Feminine wore a veil over their lower faces: the Feminine veil a sheer white; the Masculine a length of opaque white cloth that looped over and around the top of the head, then across the mouth, with the free end thrown over the shoulder. Both Feminine and Masculine had their eyes and foreheads painted in specific ways. The body was also painted in an image of white smoke rising from the pubic bone to the heart, which was symbolic of seeking Enlightenment through Sex.

For tonight the eyes, visible above the veil, were to be painted in tri-color eye shades with eyeliner and shadow. The forehead symbol was a vertical vesica piscis in red for the Feminine and a horizontal vesica piscis in green for the Masculine.

Eva and Diana did each other's make-up, brushed each other's hair, and pinned each other's hair up in a coil held in place with long beaded hairpin sticks; the beads dangling freely off the ends. Diana's hair was still damp and it coiled tightly. It reflected and glowed in the evening light.

While they worked on each other, they talked of family, children and grandchildren, nieces and nephews. They updated each other on various assignments and assignations. In the end they painted each other's bellies in the smoke symbol, one standing still and the other kneeling, blowing on the paint to help it dry.

Then it was time. The call to assembly song was played. They dressed each other in the full sleeved, pale gray, floor-length silk robes with pale pink liners. They drew the ties to mid-close so that their breasts and hips were covered but the robe was open down the center, exposing the coils of smoke paint rising from their mons. Tonight, they would be barefoot.

The Masculine would be wearing white robes with a gray liner, tied to an open front like the Feminine robes but with a single belt-like sash. Additionally the men wore a kind of apron covering the phallus made from the same material as the feminine face veil.

The friends emerged from Eva's suite together, arms linked. They were joined by the Madeleine as they passed her door, putting Eva in the center. The Elder's door remained closed. It was unknown if she would be joining them. There were few exceptions to attendance at the Ceremony, and the Elder was in the privileged position of choosing to attend or not. The High Consort and The Craft were already in the Ballroom. Diana led the way down the stairs.

Tonight's Ceremony would be held in the round Ballroom that normally served as the Men's Circle room. The North Wing hallway opened on the Ballroom from the northwest. The main Mansion Hall opened into the room from the east. Aligned on the north-south axis were two large fireplaces. The southeast quadrant was occupied by a three-tiered orchestra dais which extended into the room in two interlocking semicircles, like the curves on the top side of a drawing of a heart. In line with the intersection of the semicircles was a raised table on short legs on the main stage, creating a fourth level from the floor. Tonight this would be where the High Priestess and the High Consort sat.

Each set of steps was broad enough to hold a series of couples which, when occupied, would create two semi-circles of people around the main Hierogamy.

The room was forty feet across and three stories high. It matched the roof line of the wing, with an octagonal eight foot high cupola with sky lights at the peak. This was supported by eight interlocking beams, each resting on the other and tied in to the skylight frame. The spiral pattern was self-supporting and required no central column for support. Additional rafters extended from halfway up the walls to support these beams from below. The roof itself was supported by eight rafters attached to the top of the cupola to increase the rise for snow slip, and was made of tongue and groove planking in an octagon configuration covered by steel sheeting. In the rain the sound became thunderous. There was a balcony running the entire circumference, which filled with people during the High Holy Days, and from which people could look down at the pattern of the movements below. There were four large chandeliers on pulleys wired for electricity and backed up with candle holders.

On the mantle of the north fireplace was a statue that showed the victory of Salakta over Skreeva, and on the south mantle was a statue that showed Wishnu in congress with Salakta. Hung behind these were cloth paintings that depicted the same scenes.

All afternoon, Raphael had been aware of the rising storm. At sunset, standing there facing the west, making his evening devotions, he could see the thunderheads building—building higher in a slow boil, but not moving across the landscape. He speculated that when they started moving they would move heavy and slow, with lots of wind: a prolonged downpour that would soak everything, and maybe some hail. It could be a big one, what he'd learned to call a gully-washer.

He was glad he had lowered the canopy to four feet high already. He hoped that would be low enough. He had tied down each pole with two lines to stakes that he had driven deeper into the ground, burying the heads. He hoped they'd hold. He also tied down the walls, effectively turning the structure into a square red tent.

He had started a small cook fire on the bottle stove to warm up a special soup Eva had said to feed to Angelica if she woke up and wanted to eat. It looked whitish, a little thicker than water, with some onions and some herbs in it. It smelled nourishing and slightly astringent, bitter on the edge, with the promise of healing to it. He wanted to remember to ask what it was, and what it did. He was in the class on food preparation, and would be getting to medicine later. He hoped he would be invited to the second year without first having to go out on assignment before he could return. There were two cups of it in the container, but he knew it wasn't for him; that it had been made for whatever it was that Angelica was going through.

He'd been in heavy storms before, so he knew he'd survive. He was worried about his responsibility though, his charge, the young wen who'd been entrusted to his care. She was pretty much out of it, clearly dreaming. She was so feverish sometimes, hair plastered to her face with sweat, he was afraid she might be truly sick. He would stick his head in through the flap every time she moaned, or turned.

About an hour before sundown on the tent, Angelica had risen from the bottom of the lake of dreams, like a groggy frog in the spring time, disoriented but still knowing which way was up. She knew her mind had been dreaming; it seemed like several dreams at once, all arranged in layers. Sometimes she let some bubble of her awareness rise up from the mud, and the bubble would report back to her flashes of what was happening near the surface. She didn't want to pay attention to any of it, so she'd let the bubble burst and dissipate.

She didn't want to leave the mud, leave the darkness. She didn't even know why she was rising She only knew that the air had changed, and that she had to come up to sample it, smell it for what it presaged.

Her eyes arrived first. She opened them in a red glow, not perceiving the details of the red canopy with its zipped in red walls. The red was the color of hot embers, and it suffused the air around her. Before her body with its senses had caught up to her, her mind had thought heat, and her first feeling was fear. Her body arrived up and plugged into a very heated mind. She smelled smoke and a gas fire and her fear turned into terror.

She gasped, and screamed, "Fuck! Fire! Fire! FIRE! Fuck!" She rolled over on her belly and got her hands under her, looked quickly, left, right, and around, and saw nothing but red, red light; she was surrounded by fire.

She could smell the smoke behind her. She couldn't go that way. "Go right," she thought, the floor was darker there. She started to crawl on her belly, on her hands and toes, like a lizard or a salamander, like a dragon, then she heard a voice; a man's voice. She froze.

"Wait! Wait! There's no fire. It's just red." Raphael had jumped up when he'd heard her, parted the flap and stuck in his head.

Slowly she turned, turned until she could see him over her bent elbow; she stared at him, eyes wide in terror. Slowly, she relaxed her eyes as the details of him became clear. She snorted, smelling the smoke.

"Food," Raphael said, somehow reading her, knowing what she meant. When she collapsed, laying her belly on the ground, her relief was palpable in the space between them.

"Huuuuuhhhh," was the sound she made, from deep in her throat, an animal sound, almost angry. Suddenly, she realized there was a strange man silhouetted in the doorway, and she had another reaction. She came up on all fours, nearly fell backward, then scrambled to get her legs under her—defensive, rather than on her back, ready to leap or attack. Her low belly coiled and spasmed.

Suddenly Raphael was confronted with a caged, feral, animal. He had an instinct to withdraw rather than enter, but he got down on all fours himself and looked into the red box. It looked very red in there, redder than the light outside; it seemed like it was glowing red in there.

"Food," he said. "Friend." He paused. "Raphael," he said, and pointed to himself

"A...A...Aangie," she said. The red light seemed to dim a little.

He backed away, about eight feet away from the entrance, and sat down where she could still see him.

She crawled forward, on hands and knees this time, slowly coming to an awareness of her surroundings and recognized them for what they truly were. She paused with her head just shy of the entrance and looked around.

Raphael gestured with one hand, "Come out. It's OK. You can come out."

Angelica brought one foot up under her, stepped to the edge of the doorway, bending over as she came through and standing up as she emerged. She brought her other leg out behind her and stood there, swaying, knees bent, with one hand in a fist and the other out, palm down, in case she would fall.

Raphael sat there in awe at the disheveled barefoot wen swaying in a black slip before a red tent, heavy hair in tangles swaying with her, the ends lifting in a sudden slight breeze. The thunderheads behind her rose high above the now dark green mountains, changing as he watched, dark blues almost to purples and grays, and deep within an occasional lightning flash.

She looked at the little stove, a small pot sitting on a frame above a gas bottle, a cup sitting on the grass beside it.

"Food," Raphael said. "Sit. Eat."

She sat down. Raphael removed the lid with a flat hook, and picked up the pot handle with a short hook on the end of a piece of wood. He took the flat hook and fit it into a slot, tilted the pot into the cup, and carefully poured out the soup. He set the pot back on the stove, replaced the lid, set the cup down in front of him, backed away another four feet and sat down again.

Angelica stepped forward, bent and picked up the cup, and sat down. She smelled it carefully, not recognizing anything but the onions, and took a sip. It was good. She looked around, and tried to get her bearings. She recognized the little foot bridge over the stream, and remembered where she was. Everything that had happened to her in the past week came back to her, and suddenly her perception of everything became intense.

The sensation of her legs on the grass, her butt on the ground, her sore breasts sliding in the silk, the warmth of the cup in her hands—she bent her head and shivered. She exhaled hard, trying to gain control of the impending wave of sensation before it threw her into overload, and made her lock up like it had in the stream, or shake uncontrollably like she had been doing in bed. She set the cup down on the grass with shaking hands, and the energy she repressed dropped to her womb and roiled there.

Raphael said, "Let me get your shawl," and she nodded. He got up slowly and went widely around her; he went into the entrance and looked around while she sat where she was, head bowed, hair forward, holding her hands together in her lap to control the shaking.

He emerged with her shawl and stepped aside to shake the grass off it, then turned back to her and placed it over her shoulders, draping it forward across her bare upper arms. He took a step back and squatted down on his heels, scanning her as he had been taught to do. He looked at every inch, assessing what was happening, and what she was likely to do next.

He realized he couldn't put himself in her position, and a feeling of compassion for her suffering arose in him. He reached down and picked up the cup. "Here," he said. "Try again."

She did, holding the cup in shaking hands, wrapping her fingers around his, and trapping them there. He helped her raise the cup to her lips, let her control the tilt, and the sip; just holding it and following her lead. She withdrew the cup, held it in mid-air while she swallowed, eyes closed. It burned a little, but not from its warmth. The burn created a different warmth, like brandy.

She moved to take another sip. Her eyes still closed, she felt him move his free hand toward her hair and shied away, quickly opening her eyes and stared at him.

"Grass," he said. "Just some grass in your hair."

She froze, watching him closely, not moving when he reached and pulled the stems of grass away.

She looked down and the faintest of smiles tugged at the corner of her mouth. It made him look at her, and at the thin moustache of soup along her upper lip. He smiled.

She took another sip, and then a long drink, drained the cup, and pushed it, and his hand, away. He took the cup and set it down. She looked down at the bridge, almost expecting Diana to come across it, and knew in a moment that she wouldn't be coming. It made her cry, tears from the feeling of abandonment welled up in her. She looked at Raphael with an expression of dismay that left him baffled.

She shook her head at his lack of understanding. She turned away from him, crawled back into the canopy, and cried like she had just lost her best friend. She let herself fall down on the tangled bed and sobbed herself to sleep, leaving a confused young man to squat there, wondering if he had done something wrong.

He raised his head toward the sunset. The bright red-orange light reflected from the thunderheads and turned the air all over the valley a deep red shading toward violet and indigo. In the fading light, he could see the storms had been moving east, toward them. He turned east, looking toward the Mansion, and silently sent a plea for help in that direction; then looked up to watch the first stars, and the last stars of the evening, shine out for their brief time before the storm, while he listened to the faint strains of music coming from the Mansion.

She was almost 80, hair still long and black from many years of practicing Phoenix and Tigress qi gong, white streaks separating black sections like the main strands of a spider's web. Not tall, five-four, one hundred fifteen pounds, heavy breasts that still looked great in a bra but were starting to lie flat without one. Her body still looked young, her legs those of a wen in her thirties, belly flat, back muscled. Her arms and hands were still strong and flexible, like a wen in her fifties. Her face had begun to show her age, crow's feet curved around from her eyes, lines of skin showing on her throat, her nose thinning and beaking.

She was the Elder of Stonehaven. She had lived her whole life so that she could be here now, doing what she was doing; embroidering flowers along the edges of shawls, being sought out by younger Feminine and Masculine for what they thought of as wisdom. She smiled, lifting a thread to her mouth, and bit it off with her own teeth.

She heard the music of the Maithuna starting and felt the faint plea of the young man out in the field wash through the Mansion. She felt it dissipate against the energetic container set around the Ballroom.

She had not been planning to go to the Ceremony. Perhaps she would sit on the veranda by the tall open French doors during the coming storm, but now she was not so sure. The young wen in the red tent or the man set to guard her might need help. She resolved to wait and track it all in her mind's eye. "The mind has an eye of its own," she breathed the ancient mantra. "May I see clearly." She laid the shawl and the embroidery hoops to the side, prepared her breath, and moved her mind into remote viewing mode.

Raphael guessed seven hours had passed since Eva and Diana had left. It was now fully dark. He took a small electric tent light and hung it from the frame in the center of the canopy. Eva's last instructions to Raphael had been to sleep at her feet. He untied his roll, took out the rain poncho and laid it on the ground. He was in the process of removing his clothes when he heard a groan, a long deep "Oh" from inside. He bent and looked in.

Angelica had rolled over and sat, looking up at the light. Suddenly her face contorted in anger and she growled, "I am no moth to light. I will not die in search of your brightness." Then she punched the light so hard with her fist it broke off its hanger and flew out, bouncing off Raphael's peering face.

Angelica collapsed backwards and appeared to sleep again. Raphael shook his head and rubbed his face. He looked at his hand. "No blood" he thought. He picked up the light and checked the switch. It still worked. He finished taking off his clothes and rolled them inside the rain poncho to keep them dry. He picked up the outer roll and shook it out. It was an old, brown oilcloth duster, like Eva's. It was lined with flannel, with a carapace so the rain would roll away off his shoulders. He put it on with nothing underneath. He would sleep in it like a blanket when the time came.

He returned to sitting at the entrance. If he listened he could hear the music of Maithuna flowing through the windows of the Ballroom, open to summertime. From his vantage he could see thunderheads racing away to the east, lightning just starting to flicker over the edge of the canopy above him.

The first 'whump' of wind hit the west wall of the canopy. Then another a few seconds later. Then two in quick succession, snapping the fabric like a luffing sail. Then it went still again, and the thunder rolled from behind the mountain. He thought, 'It won't be long now." He enjoyed weather, watching it, predicting it by the shapes of the clouds.

He stood up again, and turned west so he could watch the storm come over the mountains. In a lightning flash he could see the clouds boiling up and over, crashing upward like a wave on a beach, back piling into the comber behind it. Lightning exploded horizontally all along the crest when the two waves crashed. Then the pressure of the larger wave overcame the resistance of the mountain, and poured, breaking down the face, racing to fill the valleys, pouring together, flowing toward him. Above it all, was the line of towering thunderheads, the tops still orange in the fading light.

He turned around to hunker down in the entrance again. Yup, we're in for it, he thought. He sat back just inside the entrance, so he could reach up and grab the zipper to close the flaps. The wind hit again with a solid whump, and then continued blowing, audibly straining the fabric and the frame.

The rain hit with a thunderous flow of fat drops, the time between the first drops and the crescendo of a near solid wall of water only the time of two heartbeats.

Into that roar he heard a voice, deeper than it should have been, say, "Come here."

He turned and looked behind him. Angelica was sitting up, cross-legged, leaning on one hand, straps of her slip down over her arms, hem up over her hips. She raised one hand in beckoning and said again, "Come here."

He turned completely around and crawled toward her, uncertain he had heard. She beckoned again as he got closer. She beckoned again. In a steady voice she said to him, looking him straight in the eye, "Come here. I have need of you."

He came in closer. She put her beckoning hand behind his head and pulled him in for a kiss. He could sense the energy that flowed through her: it started at her shoulders with a shiver and descended from there, narrowed as it went down, and arrived in her pelvic floor with a thump upon the ground; a trill descending and ending in a bass note, over and over.

She switched hands then, and put her left along the side of his face, gripping it slightly to keep it there while she moved her head, then her lips against his, sliding then opening. With her right hand she took his right arm and placed the hand on the ground between her legs. "Help me," she whispered to him, barely audible above the rain.

Raphael leaned away to break the kiss, moved his face downward to begin the help in that way, when she gripped his face harder and said, "No. Hand. Help me. Now."

Angelica's mind feared frenzy, but she knew she had to have release from the pounding on her pelvic floor. She knew that connection would channel that energy into a form that would liberate her from the incessant heaviness of her womb.

Raphael took his hand and placed it on her mound, and found she was already wet. He slipped a finger inside, hooked it under the bone, squeezed his hand shut, and held it still. She moaned and moved against it. "More," she said.

He moved his hand and easily inserted a second finger. She sighed as her eyes closed. She let go of his head, put her other hand down on the ground and moved against his; she slid, pushing, and growling. Her growls came from deep in her throat, rose and fell in rhythm to her hips as she raised and lowered them. Raphael had to work hard to resist her push against his hand. Angelica threw her head back, squeezed her legs together in orgasm, and howled; the howl rose until it was lost in the wind.

The rain continued to pour down, drumming hard. Lightning flashed and the thunder was so close it shook not just the canopy, but the ground beneath them. Angelica shouted, "You! Now!" Raphael withdrew his hand and positioned himself between her legs and sat on his heels, his erection pointing skyward.

Angelica reached up and put her left hand behind his neck, squatted on her feet and with her right hand guided his erection inside as she lowered herself. When she was fully down she threw back her head again and howled. She began posting on him, hanging on with both hands. Raphael extended his arms to the side, palms down, maintaining his self-control while the wild wen in front of him rode him toward abandon.

The space inside the canopy began to glow red. Angelica felt some part of herself separating off, coiling off and up and out her spine. She slowed a little, pounding down on his erection in the same pace as the pounding in her sex, rising up, holding her breath until the shivers started, then sliding down with them, landing hard on Raphael's thighs, pounding down on him in matching time to the pounding in her womb.

Everything between them was wet, down his thighs between his legs, around behind her, dripping from her bottom, up their bellies almost as high as their navels.

She pounded on him twenty eight times—Raphael counted—growling on her way down, grunting as she landed; the grunt rose to become a shout, the last four as loud as Raphael thought she could possibly voice.

On the last shout her head was back. It stayed there, swayed slightly, her hair drifting in the air as she stopped moving, and just sat on him fully hilted, quivering. Then her arms let go of his neck so he had to hold her in his arms to keep her from collapsing, and he laid her down.

She was gone, completely unconscious and limp. He turned around behind him and fumbled in the darkness for the little tent light. He flicked it on, looked down, and froze.

He was covered in slime, brownish bloody slime, some dark blood and some fresh bright red blood. His terror rose within him as he turned back, held up the light, and saw the same bloody slime all over Angelica's lower belly and thighs.

He wanted to shout. He wanted to run away. He was nauseated, and his stomach heaved. He was horrified at the prospect that he had hurt her, and he turned to reach for her, saying, "Oh no, oh no, oh fuck, no."

He heard a cough outside the tent. Then a voice he barely recognized, saying, "Young man, it is raining like the Babylonian flood out here. I have travelled a long way and it is unacceptably rude for you to keep a guest standing out here like this in this monsoon. Open this canopy immediately and let me in."

Raphael was stunned. The Elder was outside.

He pushed open the flap, put his head out in the rain, and looked up. There she was, standing in a gold raincoat that brushed the ground and a gold sou'wester hat, holding a deeply curved umbrella that came almost to her waist. She was wearing knee high muck boots with flowers painted on them. She had a small knapsack on her back over the raincoat.

Raphael had never looked up to her before; always it had been down because of her height. Now, naked and on his knees, she looked like the tallest wen in the world. His erection twitched.

"Get out," she said. "Stand up." He did as he was told, and stood up naked in the rain. She flicked a small flashlight on and cast it up and down, a steady light in a sea of flashes, pausing at the mess on Raphael's belly and thighs.

She looked up at him. Raphael noticed the dark eyeliner around her eyes and thought she looked ageless.

"Humph," she grunted. "Go stand out in the rain and wash yourself off. And ponder on your great good fortune."

She turned and closed the umbrella, then bent down and entered the canopy. Suddenly the pair of muck boots came flying out, bouncing off Raphael's legs. "Go," she said. "Before you cool off."

Raphael looked at himself. There was steam rising from his arms and shoulders, and he guessed his head, too, standing there in the dark rain. He walked a little way down the field toward the footbridge, turned to face the west, raised his arms to Thunder and started to laugh, great belly laughs rising from his throat like the steam from his back. He let the rain pound on his chest and belly, groin and erection. He washed away the blood and thick fluids ran down his legs. It pooled briefly around his feet, until the rain pounded it down into the grass.

"Moon Halter," he thought. "I have been saved by the Moon Halter."

Inside the red tent the Elder bent over the recumbent Angelica, head turned to the side, her hair spread out around her head, legs askew and arms akimbo. She turned off her little light to see what she could see in the dark. When her eyes adjusted she realized the tent was filled with a red glow—faint, but as she waited, more detail emerged: dark red highlights on a very dark black green background. Even the grass was glowing.

The rain continued. It came in waves, pounded across the tent and leaning the whole structure down-wind. The Elder could tell it was the center of the storm passing. She took off her pack, sat down on her heels, putting the pack beside her. She opened it, pulling two liter metal bottles of water from it. She took off her raincoat and hat. She shook out her long sleeved white linen dress, and rolled up the sleeves to her elbows. She took a cloth scented with sweetgrass oil, wet it from a bottle, and started to wipe down Angelica. Angelica took a small short inhale that quivered the pools of her breasts and gave a small groan as the Elder laid the cloth to her belly.

The Elder saw that everywhere she put her hand the red light would ripple, and wash around her hand as if she was moving it through a red pool. Then she saw it, a red and gold rope flashing to the surface and roiling away like the back of a fish, or an eel or, she realized, like the body of a dragon.

She continued to wash Angelica, and with each wipe the red-gold body turned and rolled. Angelica began to turn and roll with it. The Moon Halter continued to wipe and wash, eyeing the forms beneath her hand. Then she poured water all over the area, washing down with a wave of her arm, spreading it down between Angelica's legs, soaking the bedding below.

In the dark red light the dragon emerged, back first slowly rising from Angelica's lower belly, then her solar plexus and finally the head emerged. It turned slowly to look back over its shoulder at Moon Halter. Then it emerged completely, but for the tip of its tail, and turned its whole body. Hovering at the Elder's eye level, it drew near and stared at her. The Moon Halter stared back, firmly.

The Dragon spoke: "Ho gved stedets." It turned, diving back into the pool that was Angelica's energy. The impact of the re-entry caused the image of Angelica's form to break into three full bodies, one image shifted left over her physical form. The other, slightly farther out, shifted right. Angelica rolled slowly as the waves rocked her side to side.

Moon Halter said, for no reason she could explain, "Ing gved stadaht." She placed her hand on Angelica's low belly, below her navel. Angelica's three bodies started to roll faster, then faster, vibrating beneath her hand.

Then a white form, a bird form with a long tail, emerged through the tent wall. It settled at Angelica's head, leaned forward and placed its wings alongside her head, touching her shoulders and the vibrating stopped. The Elder saw an image of the dragon's face hovering over Angelica's, long mustaches tangled in her hair. From Angelica's mouth came the whispered words, "Ishk inezdah." Then the image faded.

The bird rested there, and the Elder recognized the phoenix. She said, "We are in deep mythos now." In agreement the thunder boomed in the East, and the lightning cracked close by as the storm began moving on. The pressure lowered and the rain lessened.

The Elder thought, 'Raphael' and turned from Angelica to peer out the open flap, but she couldn't see him. She crawled through the door and stood up. Raphael was down on the ground, and face down. In the dark light she couldn't tell if it was smoke rising from his head or steam.

She ran down the slope, at one point surfing on the wet grass, white dress spread out behind her. She slid to a stop against his body. He made a "woof" sound on impact. "He's alive," she thought.

She stood at his head, noticed the smell of burnt hair, hooked a shoulder and rolled him over. He was grinning, and tried to open his eyes, which were rolling and looking in different directions. "Wow," he said, and tried to laugh. He sat up holding his head. "My foot hurts."

"Good thing it didn't come out your pecker," she said, noticing it was still half hard.

"I didn't get the whole thing. I was dancing to the thunder beings. Maybe I was saying something like 'Over here! Over here!' It hit over by the bridge, and these little legs like spider legs came out from the explosion. One came over and hit me, about an inch wide. Hit me right in top of the head." He started to laugh and hold his head in his hands, shaking it. "Wow. Scrambled me good." Then he lay back down on the grass.

The Elder reached down, grabbed his phallus and pulled on it twice. "Feel that?" she asked.

"Yup," he said.

She reached further down and tugged on his balls. "Feel that?"

"Yup. Ow! Yup."

"Then at least your eggs aren't scrambled. Get up when you can. I need help." She let her foot drag over him as she stepped away, giving him a little kick in the side. "Idiot," she said.

She walked back up to the door of the tent and looked inside. Angelica was rolling side to side, moaning, lost in visionary dreaming, sweating into the now wet and bloody bedding. The Elder spoke over her shoulder to Raphael, "Go down to the barn and bring some new bedding. Before you go, bring me some fresh water from the stream."

Raphael sat up and immediately fell back again with a groan. He rolled over and got up on all fours, picked up his head, slowly looked around to test his vision and came up on one knee. It all seemed stable enough so he stood up—but too fast. He took a step. His leg went out from under him, his foot slipping in the wet grass. He collapsed on the ground, with an 'Oomph' when he landed.

"Idiot!" the Elder said, "Crawl, if you must. I need the water. She needs the bedding. Show up, even if it's on your hands and knees." She tossed the collapsible bucket at him. "Here!"

The bucket landed near him. He couldn't stand up yet, and he needed both hands to crawl, so he put the bucket handle in his mouth and slowly made his way down to the stream, looking for all the world like an old dog doing a long time favorite fetch.

The Elder turned, crawled into the tent and put her hands on Angelica's ankles. The images of the dragon and the phoenix had faded. She closed her eyes and created the mindspace to begin to track her. She found her, adrift in a sea of voices and images. Around Angelica were forming little openings into the personal worlds of other people. There was a chemical salesman in Kansas City, failing to close a deal. There was a little boy in Somalia squatting down on his haunches, eating mud.

Angelica appeared to be in some kind of tube or channel, bending away heliacally, drifting. She was reading a scene from each person's life she was passing, little tubes bending away in the wall, seeing into their world from one of the layers of dreaming. She would see, then feel the feeling in the scene, and would suffer what the individuals were suffering, almost helpless to let go herself, as she was pulled along by some kind of force or gravity.

The Elder looked ahead and saw an opening to the stars at the end of the long tunnel, past the coils in the walls, past the little windows in each coil. She didn't want to get drawn into one. The Elder looked back and saw that it began, or ended, in starless darkness, a barrier to whatever the origin of the tube might be beyond the beginning.

She knew that, in time, Angelica would journey to each end and out into those other worlds. For now, though, it was time to call her back. The Elder smiled as she remembered a couplet from a cartoon television show. "Hither, thither, whither roam, time for this one to come home." Then she pulled on Angelica's ankles, both energetically and physically, and sensed Angelica coming back into her body. The Elder opened her eyes and waited for Angelica to open hers.

Angelica had been floating. It felt like she could stick her head through a window into the lives of any one life she chose. She felt a tendency to just slip in through it, a pull to fall into any life and she could see into the past, and into the future as well, of any life into which she fell. Suddenly, she felt a pull on her ankles, and felt herself being dragged from the channel where she was and into the wall of the tunnel. She felt a moment of terror when she sensed that someone or something had reached out and was pulling her into one of the lives she'd been viewing, not knowing what life it was and what kind of being could do that.

Then the despair arose, a despair caused by the patheticness, the pathos, of so many of the lives she'd witnessed, the shallowness, the smallness of their concerns and the probability of nothing good ever happening to them. Her last view, the one across from the window she was being pulled into was of the image of a man in uniform torturing another man who was naked and tied down, with a car-battery jumper cable, attaching it to his testicles. Her last image was an image of the torturer's face as he bent to his task.

The grip on her ankles burned. She had a sudden image of having her ankles shackled, and that she was falling into a life of terror. She started weeping her despair as she felt herself slip into the present with a small popping sensation.

She woke up weeping, shaking her head, saying, "No, no, no, no, no," trying to sit up and reach for her ankles. She saw a form there, a small form, silhouetted in the light from a clearing night sky. She saw stars surrounding the outline. The form was whispering, "Shh, shh, shh, shh, shh."

Angelica sobbed and lay back on some kind of bedding, like a thin futon, and remembered where she was, and what had happened. She was cold and wet and started shivering. The wen, whom Angelica suddenly discerned it to be, lay down next to her and pulled some kind of raincoat, glowing with a dull golden light, over the two of them. She snuggled in close, putting an arm and a leg over Angelica, pulling her in closer.

"Here, I will keep you warm," she said. Angelica turned on her side, crossed her arms, and pulled up her knees, spooning against the wen beside her. Angelica's teeth began to chatter in her sobs, and soon it became so violent that her whole body began to shake, rising and falling in intensity between her sobs.

The wen held on, breathed a sweet breath over her, and the coat began to warm. The shaking, the sobbing, the chattering teeth all began to subside. When it subsided far enough for Angelica to draw a breath she said, "Who, who, who are you?"

The wen replied, "I am The Elder, and I am the Moon Halter. And you are having yours."

Angelica nodded, "Yes, yes. I feel it. I am heavy with it and I am shedding from inside." She remembered the Elder.

"Yes," The Elder said. "You are shedding from within. You will make a new layer, a new skin, a new coat for yourself. That which is new within will rise to create something new without, new on the outside." She placed one hand down on Angelica's, belly, low, and rested it there. The womb beneath her hand was trembling with small spasms. It was well, the Moon Halter knew, and she did nothing energetically, except to observe.

She wondered where that Raphael was. Then she sat up and saw the bucket of stream water near the door in the starlight.

Raphael had left the bucket when Moon Halter was still holding Angelica's ankles. He had made it down to the stream, carrying the bucket handle in his teeth. Washing his face, throwing the water over his head and onto his back like an elephant, staggered him and he had fallen forward into the rushing water, catching himself on his hands, immersed but for his lower legs and feet in the rain-swollen stream.

He let himself slide completely into the water, coming up on his knees, feeling the burned hair on top of his head. He looked down and saw some sort of luminescent fish hiding in the slip stream created by his body. He stood up quickly and the fish disappeared. When he stood up it was as if he could see a blue-white outline of himself resting everywhere on the surface of his skin.

"Momma," he said. "What a night!" He reached for the bucket on the bank and filled it. Realizing he was actually standing on his own two feet for the first time, he set the bucket up on the bank and crawled up, holding onto the longer grasses. He walked unsteadily up the rise to the tent, felt what Moon Halter was doing, and knew he shouldn't interrupt it even if he couldn't see what was happening. He had his assignment; he knew what to do.

He made his way to the upper bridge over Stonehaven Creek, his pace quickening as he regained coordination of his legs. By the time he hit the bridge he was jogging. He opened the central doors under the long hallway of dormitory rooms where the linen storage rooms were, next to the laundry. It was quiet. Everyone was still at the Maithuna. He pulled out what he needed and set it on the table in the entryway, checking it and making sure, then went to get an electric cart from the garage.

When he was there he met Micah, another young hand, working to make sure all the carts were charged.

"Hey man!" Raphael said, struggling to see him around the pile of bedding in his arms. "What're you up to? No Ceremony tonight?"

"Hey man, no," Micah replied. "I'm scheduled to go relieve you at midnight, so I decided to just take it easy. You look like shit, however." He grinned.

"Yeah, man, wow. Did you see that storm? I got hit by a piece of lightning."

"What? No way, man, no way. How come you're still walking around?"

"Like I said, it was just a piece. Here, look," he said, putting the bedding down on the carrier at the back of a cart. "It burned my hair!"

"Oh, no, really man, lemme see." And Micah craned to look as Raphael bent over and showed it to him."

"How come you're naked?" Micah asked.

"I left my clothes in the tent, wrapped up. I knew they'd just get wet so I took 'em off. The Elder was in there working with her, so I just left 'em."

"Are you hurt?"

"No, man. Not really. I couldn't walk so good for a while, and I've got a case of 'fat cock' that just won't go away," pointing to himself.

Micah glanced at it and laughed. "Up to something, were ya?"

"Yeah, yeah. The instruction was that I was supposed to do anything she needed, right? So she came to, and man, is she in it. She told me she needed it. It was spooky, but you know, man, I'm game for anything. So we're doing it and everything starts to glow red, you know? And suddenly I'm covered in blood!"

"Blood! Oh no man, she didn't."

"Yeah, man, she did. It just happened. Man, she blew out like it was bad, like she was hurt, you know? Like I'd hurt her. Man, I was scared. But suddenly The Elder was there, and she took over and told me to go stand out in the rain and wash off. So I did. But while I was out there I started dancing around in the rain, and then I started talking to the Thunder, you know? You know how it is here; it's almost like the Thunder can hear you."

"Yeah, man, I know. It's spooky."

"So I started dancing around, you know? Like I was sparring. And I started saying, 'Come on man, hit me' and it did."

"You're an idiot," Micah said, tying the bedding down on the back of the cart.

"I know. That's what The Elder said."

In the ballroom, Eva escorted Diana to the table. A man she did not know was seated there, veiled, sitting on his heels, and waiting. Men were seated in costume on the different levels of the dais, and once Diana was seated, sitting on her heels also, other wen took their places. They sat while the Veils settled.

The Music began as wind and distant thunder from the drums, and from the storm. The lights were dimmed. Quinn, in the back of the room, leaned forward to see.

In the evening light, the wen bowed forward, rose to their hands and knees, then lowered their faces to the laps of the men in one move. They nuzzled the aprons/veils with their cheeks, then bit the fabric, pulling them up and aside. The men's erections were revealed, and they were already all erect, much to Quinn's surprise.

The wen all drew back to their heels and squatted, pulled their skirts to the side, spread their knees, and put their other hand on their sex, using their fingers to expose themselves. The couples gazed upon each other.

The wen all stood then, and dropped the aprons back over the erections. They all turned away from the men. The wen at the top level stayed that way while the others turned and stepped in a circle that led them back behind the men. These wen then squatted down again, their bellies against the backs of the men and reached around, took the men's erections in one hand and stroked them in time to the music.

On the main dais the wen of each couple went to their knees, then leaned back, and laid on the floor between the legs of the men. All three men lay back to the floor also, but they held their erections pointed straight up with their hands. On the table, Diana still stood swaying in time to the music, and faced away from her man.

The wen on the dais simultaneously raised their hips off the floor and arched their backs. Hands on either side of the men's hips, they arched their heads backwards over the erections. On the table Diana did a fully arched back bridge from the standing position. Together the wen lowered their mouths slowly on the sky pointing erections, and held their mouths there, making swallowing motions, for the space of four breaths.

The wen on the lower levels stepped around their men. Never letting go of the erections, and coming around to the front, they went to their knees, bowed down toward the men and took the erections in their mouths.

On the top level the wen twisted out of their bridges, never letting go of the erections and went to all fours. Then they did a controlled hand-stand walk-over of the men, letting go of the erections as they landed with their feet coming down on either side of the men's heads. The wen looked down at the men.

On the table, Diana did a walk-over from the full bridge, let go of her man's erection at the same time as the other wen. She came down in unison with them, her feet on either side of her man's head, facing his feet.

In unison, they slowly lowered their sex onto the men's faces. Fluffing their skirts on the way down, they pulled aside the men's face veils with a dramatic gesture. On the lower levels the wen stood up, pulled aside their men's veils, threw a leg over their man's shoulder, and pulled their faces into the phulva, pulling them in from the backs of their heads.

Outside, the lightning flashed and the thunder boomed. The rain lashed the walls and windows of the Mansion.

Not from any angle could anyone see what was happening under the gowns, but soon it was clear that each wen was orgasming. On the table and dais the wen raised both arms to the heavens, bucking their hips against the covered heads of the men. On the lower levels, each wen raised one arm skyward, while they held the back of their men's heads pressed to their sex.

Then all slid, along for the wen on top, downwards for the wen below, onto the erections of their men, and impaled themselves in a single slow steady motion.

The lightning flashed, the thunder boomed so close that the air shook, and the lights went out.

The music continued in the dark.

In the dark, the wen gave voice to the sound of their ecstasy, one long note, sung out with an "Oo" sound that changed to an "Oh" sound, then to an "Ahh" sound.

The music swelled and pounded, and the wen sent out a howling sound, while underneath it the men hummed a single groaning note.

Then silence. Only breathing could be heard. The lights flickered back on and the wen were still impaled, leaning back, arms extended, hair falling, held up by the arms of their men.

Slowly the wen came forward, stood up and stepped back from the still hard erections. They resumed their seats opposite the men. They bowed and sat up again, sitting with their faces down. Then, as the music stopped, everyone turned their faces upward.

The lights went out, this time by design. When the lights came up again, everyone on stage was standing and hugging and saying "Thank you." The men awkwardly moved their erections out of the way, covering them with their aprons.

Half an hour had passed. In the back of the room Quinn closed his open mouth with one hand, and adjusted the erection in his pants with the other. He turned to the musician next to him, who was examining the bow of his cello in the light. Quinn gestured toward the dancers on the stage. He said, "But…the men didn't finish."

The musician said, "Yes, that's the way it is here. We train for that. Control. Orgasm without ejaculation. They may get release later tonight, maybe not. Our job is to serve their pleasure. Most of us, most of us men, anyway, will spend an hour or so meditating now, practicing internal circulation and alchemical crystallization."

Quinn said, "Uh huh."

The next morning, in the first light of dawn, Moon Halter woke to an awareness of the man spooning her, holding her in his sleep. There was just the faintest whiff of burnt hair. She felt morning wood between her legs. When she reached down to help it into her opening, she touched it with her fingers, and suddenly it glowed blue white, sliding into her.

"The electric trout," she thought. And she laughed.

30

CALLEY'S RELEASE

On this night, the night that Amanda was burned by Brighid in a test of faith, the night Rachel went black, the night the Lama decided to stick around, ghosting this plane, Regina rode the horse up the shoulder of Pine Eye Mountain to the trail that led over to the Eye. She dismounted, rummaged in the saddlebags for a moment, and set off on foot.

The moon was so large and full that she could see where she placed her feet. Soon the dirt, with its sticks and leaves, gave rise to moss; her footfalls moving into a whispering almost-silence. She saw herself as a wisp moving through the moonlit woods.

The pines got thicker, and taller, until she was walking well below the lowest branches. The wood opened up, allowing her to see far toward either side. She could see even the small trees bathing in moonlight.

She could see the clearing well before she arrived there, lit with a column of bright light. She stepped to the edge and looked around. The frogs went silent. The land here had slumped. The trees had collapsed into it, making a tangled nest.

Her instructions were to make her way to the middle of the nest. She climbed over the slippery trees, taking her time. One slip, one fall, could impale her on a broken branch or at least cut her badly.

When she arrived at the center, she stopped. There, beneath her feet, was a pool. She couldn't tell if it was melt-water, rain, or a small spring, gathered in the pit at the center of the slump. It was pale silver on the surface, and completely still, with dark blackness beneath, darkness she did not want to plumb.

She looked around the moonlit nest. She imagined she saw, emerging from the shadows at the edge of the clearing, the wolf she knew. It sat down on its haunches and leaned forward.

She removed a small vial from the shoulder bag she'd carried. She unscrewed the lid, which was fully half the length, then held the cork that the lid had enclosed. She held it with both hands, thinking, feeling, and sensing the moment. Time slowed down.

She had some understanding that what she was doing was incredibly important; her feelings led her to believe that its importance was so great that she couldn't feel the extent of it. The frogs resumed singing and she opened the vial. More frogs joined the chorus.

She leaned forward, making sure her aim was free of snags, and poured the vial of the Thunder Goddess rain into the pool. As she watched, it spread out across the waters. She exhaled into a state of relief. "What's done is done," she thought.

While she watched the pool, a spiral of mist, white as smoke in the moonlight, rose from the surface, turning blue then silver, rising up and expanding until it was larger than her. Then it stopped.

The mist turned into a form, and the form became clearly that of Brighid's older sister, Calley, hanging there in the air.

Calley shook herself like a dog coming in from the rain, stopped and gazed at Regina. "Thank you, child," She said. "Good to get out on a moonlit night, you agree?"

Regina found she couldn't speak, so she nodded.

Calley asked her, "Do you like the horse?"

Regina found her voice, "He's steady."

Calley said, "He's a trick horse. Try to find out what he knows," and smiled.

Regina laughed.

"Alam must return with your mother," Calley said. "It is not safe enough here yet for the wolf. And there is yet work to do with the children. The magic is still intact; all she has to do is carry the bundle, and not open it, until she returns to the Highlands."

The wolf lay down completely, and whined. Then he rolled over on his back, exposing himself, and whined again.

Regina laughed. "I know that sound," she said. "Please, please," she mocked.

Calley laughed with her, and said, "He knows begging won't help. He just does it to make me laugh. He also knows why he has to return, and that he will come back here again when the time is right."

"Amanda will take him," Regina said.

Then Calley said, "Good to see you again." She collapsed into the pool, and disappeared. The wolf faded into moonlight.

Regina slowly crawled back over the tangled trees to the path, then to the horse. She turned around, walking slowly down the mountain back to the barn, letting the horse have its head.

When she arrived she found Craft waiting for her. Craft took the reins and gave her his hand, helping her dismount.

"Nice night," he said.

She smiled, looking back up at the Pine Eye. "Do you know," she said, "That we wouldn't be here without the moon?"

Craft said, "Yes. Without it, we'd all be flatter than piss on a plate."

She was taken aback by his choice of language and she laughed. As she let go of his hand she lingered, drawing her fingers along his. The charge she expected to feel was present. "Why are you here? Waiting for me?" she asked.

"Yes, waiting for you. If you hadn't returned before the middle of the night, I'd have gone looking for you," Craft said.

"In the dark?" Regina asked.

"Yes. You could have fallen, and hurt yourself badly. Finding you quickly could mean the difference between life and death," Craft answered.

"Really? Life and death?" she asked again.

"Well, no, not really," he replied. "You'd either be dead, or you could wait until morning. You wouldn't freeze." His voice became mildly sarcastic. "I would have enjoyed the ride in the moonlight."

"And do you think you could find me? In the dark?" she asked.

Craft considered his reply. He sensed the challenge in her words, and the disbelief. He decided to bait her, and see if she rose to it.

"Yes," he said without elaboration, and with more confidence than he would normally speak.

"Oh, really?" she said, thinking about her ability to sneak up on animals and people, practiced since childhood in the Highlands. "Hide and seek, then? Shall we?"

Craft grinned. She had risen to the bait. "Certainly," he said. "Tomorrow night, while it will still be bright before the leaves fill out."

"Any conditions?" she asked, slyly.

Craft thought a moment. "Yes," he said. "Once you hide, you pick a place and stay in it. I don't want to have to track your movements repeatedly. Finding you once, in the spot you pick, should prove me out."

"Aww, what fun are you?" she asked, covering her surprise that he had intuited what her plan would have been. She saw the flash of his grin.

"If you want fun, perhaps someday then, I'll chase you," Craft said, lowering his voice.

The lower register of Craft's voice vibrated in her womb. It thrilled her.

"Stop that," she said, knowing that they both knew what she was talking about. But the thrill lingered. "I'll think about it," she said, and walked away, leaving Craft holding the reins. She knew that if she stayed to help unsaddle and curry the horse, she'd probably end up 'doing him' right there in the barn, getting hay in her hair and red scratch marks from it on her ass and back.

About twenty feet from the barn door she had the sudden image of herself, on her knees in front of him, giving him her face. She turned, thinking about it. She saw him standing there in the doorway, holding the reins with one hand, the other hand's thumb hooked inside the edge of his pants, fingers pointing at what she hoped was an erection.

She saw him grin at her, then made a noise, loud enough for him to hear it, "Hmmph," as she turned her back on him.

The horse snickered.

They played the next night, as agreed. After the moon rose, Craft gave her a half hour head start, and did not look to see the path by which she entered the woods. She walked the horse up through a tall grass pasture, and entered the woods on no path at all. She stood in the shadows, holding the horse's nose, looking to watch him leave, and see where he went.

He mounted after closing the gate in the barnyard, and rode at a trot to the entrance of the path she'd taken the previous night. There was a slight breeze tonight, blowing down the mountain. He knew that when he got far enough from the barn he would be able to scent her horse from downwind.

During the day, Regina had spent the time to make four pillows out of goose down, with extra material around the edges. She had made, in effect, four big booties for her horse. When she saw Craft enter the woods she pulled them from under her bulky sweater and tied them on.

Her plan was to walk in the opposite direction from Craft, through the woods into the next vale, and walk down that until she reached the bottom. From there, she would return to the barn and wait, hiding there. She had pilfered a flask of Rachel's best scotch, and she figured that would be a good place to enjoy it. The risky part was that she had to go along the garden fence to get back to the barn. For that stretch they, she and the horse, would be exposed in the moonlight.

Craft rode up the path, searching for fresh hoof marks. Not finding any he stopped, dismounted, and examined the ground. He tied off the horse and walked for fifty yards, bent over, looking closely. He stood up, and yawned. "So, which way did she go?" he asked the woods.

He closed his eyes and extended his senses. He sensed movement off to his left and downwind. The movement stopped.

Regina, herself, had planned on a 'start and stop' manner of moving through the woods. Not on a path, she had reasoned that there were sticks buried in the leaves, and she wanted to make sure she had time to remove them from the horse's path, or walk the horse around. She had quickly discovered that there were bare spots on the floor of the woods where the wind had cleared the leaves over the winter. If she was careful, she could make it from bare ground to bare ground without making any noise.

Craft waited, but then he could not detect any motion.

Regina waited, scanning her surroundings because she could not discern the way clearly.

Craft went back to the horse and mounted. He knew a connecting path a little farther ahead that would connect him to the trail up the next ridge.

Regina could hear Craft's horse when it stumbled over a rock in the trail. She smiled. He was moving, but moving away from her. She made her way down off the side of the ridge, into the vale and down into thickets that gave way to grass along a small stream. She avoided ground that was too soft, ground that would hold a track. Now in the clear, it was faster going.

Craft found the entrance to the connecting trail, hidden, as he liked it, from a casual glance. He turned, still walking the horse, confident, though he could not detect motion while he himself was moving. The motion he had detected earlier was big. There was nothing bigger in the forest tonight than the horse.

The wolf had been watching Craft from above, and had shadowed him from before he had turned onto the connector. Since his hearing was so acute, it was not a hard thing to do, even with the rustle caused by the breeze.

When Craft arrived at the trail up the next ridge, he dismounted and knelt down to see if Regina had passed this way.

The wolf moved to a spot upwind of the horse. The horse smelled him, shied, and reared out of Craft's loose grip on its reins. It pushed past Craft out onto the main trail and bolted, dragging its reins, heading down the path toward the barn, and safety.

Craft sighed, and, since he found no sign of Regina's passing, turned, and started the near mile walk back toward the barn. Perhaps he'd find the horse grazing somewhere before he had gone all the way down.

Regina had not been back in the barn long when Craft's horse returned. She let it into its stall and gave it a bucket of grain to keep it happy.

She looked around for a place to hide. Then she decided not to bother. She went into the room they called the office—really a tack room with a desk and two chairs. She sat down, put her booted feet up on the desk, crossed her legs, and pulled the flask from an inside pocket of her quilted coat. She opened it, and took a long pull.

She shivered as it burned its way down. Slowly her eyes adjusted to the darkness.

She thought about Craft, thought about him walking now, out in the woods. She grinned broadly and took another pull from the flask.

"He's cute," she said out loud. "Perhaps, when he finds me, I'll give him a reward," and she patted herself on the lap. "If I don't pass out first," she added, taking another sip.

She thought about that, then. About what having sex with him, right there in the office, would be like. She'd been on the solo path for weeks, following Rachel's instruction. It had been so long since she'd had the real thing she told herself she couldn't even imagine any more what it would be like, what it would be like to feel it going in, warm—warm in the way her practice phalli just weren't.

It was easy to imagine him; she'd seen him naked and erect a few times. She thought about what it would be like to use some of what she'd learned on him. She wondered what would happen when she grasped him from inside, and used the strength she'd developed, the skill that allowed her, when she practiced, to stand up, still gripping the phallus inside her, and walk around with it.

She snorted with laughter. And then, while she was thinking about it, she slipped one hand down inside her pants while she took another little pull on the flask.

That was how Craft found her a half hour later; one foot still on the desk, the other on the floor, legs spread, one hand down her pants, while the other still held the flask, resting on the desk. Her head was back. Her hair hung down over the back of the chair. She was sound asleep.

She gave a little snort when she felt the draft from the open door, and came awake staring into the dark. Her eyes went to the open door. She saw Craft's outline silhouetted in it.

He said, "Olly, olly, oxen free," in a quiet voice.

She said, "Close the door, silly, you're letting all the heat out."

She sat up a little bit and shook her hair. She dropped her foot to the floor, but she kept her hand in her pants and her legs spread.

Craft took a kerosene lantern down from a peg and lit it, setting it on the desk, and looked at her. He saw her there, one hand still on the flask. While he watched, she took another swallow and set it down. She leaned forward, aggressively, and made an animal growl deep in her throat. She leaned back in the chair, slid her hips forward and began masturbating for him, her hand moved rapidly in her pants. Then she rolled her hips and moved her arm deeper under the clothing. Craft knew she'd put at least a finger inside herself.

He stood there, watching, as she masturbated—also aggressively, as she continued to growl. Soon, she tired of the constraint and undid her pants with her free hand. She alternated between looking at him and closing her eyes. After perhaps a minute he asked, "May I see?"

She stood up looking at him the whole time. She pushed her pants down toward her ankles, exposing her thighs to the lamp light. She sat down again and spread her knees. Craft moved the lamp closer and took the flask, taking a long drink.

She rolled a little to the side, so she could reach around behind herself with her other hand, inserting her middle finger in her ass. She closed her eyes, working herself with two fingers. Craft continued to watch her, not moving.

She opened her eyes, and looked at him. "Let me see it," she said. He took it out for her. His erection was as beautiful as she remembered. "Stroke it," she told him. He did as he was told.

She watched him as she continued to move her hands; watched him with slitted eyes. She gripped herself, hard, squeezing her mound from within and without. Craft could hear the juiciness. He could hear her squish. It gave him a thrill that began at the back of his head and shivered down his spine to his feet.

"Finish with me," she said in a low voice, unmistakable in its tone of command.

She crossed her ankles and picked her feet up off the ground, knees still spread. Craft went around the desk so he could see her, the faint outline of her sex wrapped around her fingers as she squeezed herself, and she squeezed faster and faster as Craft stroked himself faster and faster.

Suddenly, she came, with an "Oh!" that was as sharp as a bark. "Oh!" she said, ejaculate starting to fly around her hand. "Oh!" she said, pulling her hands away and coming in a long stream of rain, splattering to the floor. Once, twice, three times, squirting as far as Craft's legs, spattering him with her come.

It was all he could bear of beauty; and he came himself, ejaculating into her pool. She lowered her legs and watched it, breathing hard, watched his coming, shooting out. She watched his face, watched his hooded eyes watching her. One shot landed on the toe of her boot. She smiled then, dropping her feet all the way to the floor. She rubbed herself, rubbing the wetness around, making herself shiver with pleasure one last time.

She sat up and looked down at the floor, his whiteness floating around on her pool. She chuckled.

"You're it," he said.

She laughed out loud, took the flask, and a swig, and offered it to him. He put himself away and took it. She pulled up her pants and sat back down.

They said nothing, passing the flask back and forth. When the flask was empty, she stood up and walked through the pool, tracking it to the door. She turned and looked back over her shoulder. Craft, too drunk to care about the floor, turned and followed her.

They walked back up to the Mansion. When they entered the basement level they removed their boots. Before parting for their separate rooms, passing him, she paused and reached out from her side for his hand, not looking at him.

He took her hand. The friction lit little sparks in the light of the moon through the windows as she trailed her fingers away from his grasp. She disappeared into the dark.

The next morning, when Paul came down to turn the horses out into the pasture, he stepped in the still drying sticky mess and couldn't figure out what somebody must have spilled.

In the next few weeks Beverly and Paul returned to New York to begin the process of diversifying Rachel's financial holdings from arms and war materiel to more peaceful ends.

Madeleine, in particular, took on the assignment of travelling the world to look for properties that the Order could purchase as safe houses for its membership and launching places for the development of the Order. She was to focus on places where there had been wen's temples, or temples to the Goddess, historically. There were, it turned out, wen still practicing their beliefs in secret in many of these areas, even if removed by some hundreds of miles, and Madeleine could mentally connect with these groups and find them if she spent enough time in the ruins of an old temple.

She was also to look for people who could be trusted to carry out discreet assignments, as well as people—men and wen—who could serve as prospective students in the Order's curriculum.

The other wen whom Rachel had invited to serve on the first Council of the Order of the Fleur de Vie all had their own assignments, in addition to being on the lookout for prospective students and initiates. Each of these wen, persons of means themselves, was committed to returning to Stonehaven to study in the program, and would be arriving over the summer and autumn for extended stays of various lengths.

Two weeks after the midnight encounter in the tack room between Regina and Craft, Amanda received letters from Scotland that detailed the depredation of two of her groups. During the day Rachel and Madeleine had been working with her, teaching her the techniques of hypnosis: how to use her body, her voice, and her eyes, how to work in the energy fields of those around her. They had also been training her in allowing the Goddess to be within her and manifest in a controlled way; a way that could be used to extend Amanda's power in the midst of others.

After the letters came they took a final month for intensive training in these subjects. During that month Amanda dreamed of the Lama several times. In these dreams, he was always teaching her something, and she had immediately taken to journaling these experiences.

Alam returned with Amanda to Scotland as a tuft of fur secure in a pouch Amanda kept on her person at all times. There were still some tasks to be finished in the Hidden Lands and work to be done in training the children to perform their tasks. The land around Stonehaven was not safe land for a wolf, and Alam couldn't yet be in his human form for a sustained period of time. Now that She had made Her way to the New World, Calley could journey on the highest, fastest winds, returning home whenever She wanted.

It turned out that Falling Star's requirement that Calley serve Her brothers-in-law could be met in a manner far less odious than She had expected. One brother-in-law, the one in the north, was married, and quite content—His wife told Him and He listened—with what He already had. Calley had journeyed to their home once, to introduce Herself. By the end of the meeting, She found Herself on friendly terms with both of them.

One of the other brothers-in-law was the large bird form of the west that the Lama had met in the mountains. She went to offer Herself to Him and when He took Her, He was so aggressive that She quickly had to go mist on him. So self-absorbed was He that He didn't even notice for a while that She was gone. When He noticed, He raged about, making so much noise and thunder and lightning that He set His nest on fire. Calley put it out for him. Somehow, this fostered a deep affection in Him, and a deep calming, such that He would even allow Calley to pet him. His needs were minimal, even if everyone else was frightened of Him. Calley would go visit him sometimes on sunny days. They would often spend the entire time gazing out onto the world from the edge of His nest, feeling into the world, and breathing it to endurance.

The last brother-in-law was somewhat more of a problem. He was fat, and yellow-green, the shade some people turn right before they vomit. He was given to hiding sulkily for long periods of time. She found him living in a high altitude swamp in the eastern mountains, a swamp so fetid that nothing would drink there. If anything dared to approach it, he would either fart or belch, depending upon his mood. When the rising bubble burst, it would spread the stench far and wide.

He made Her sit for a long time, wheedling and begging for Him to come out. When He did emerge, dripping in slime, the stench seemed to emanate from Him.

When She explained to Him why She was there, His eyes lit up and then narrowed. He leapt for Her, slipping on the slimy water. She was ready for Him and shot vertically into the air, quickly becoming rain that poured down on Him so hard that He had to take refuge under an overhang on the bank.

When He stopped yelling at Her to stop, She stopped. He wouldn't come out however, so She lowered Herself and looked under the overhang from a distance. She saw Him crouched up against the back, drawn up into a ball, shivering and rocking. She drew closer and heard him weeping with a high keening wail.

She lay down and floated in the air a foot above the surface of the pond, Her hair floating around Her. She watched Him; simply watched Him. Little Helpers, the ones that actually ran the storms for Him, started to gather around the edges of the pond. Eventually he stopped rocking, opened an eye, and looked at Her.

"Come out," She said.

He emerged, but He had so long been trapped in melancholy that He couldn't stand on the surface of the water; He sank up to his belly. Calley sat up, crossed Her legs, and beckoned to him.

"We can't do this with you as you are," She said. "Come here."

When He got close She held out a hand to Him. He reached up and took it. Slowly He began to change. His color began to drain away, and he became translucent, clear water held together only by surface tension. His deformities melted and a true form, a beautiful masculine form, emerged. As He emerged, He rose up out of the water of the pond until He stood on the surface. As He stood there, holding Calley's hand, the clarity spread out from His feet across the pond and into its depth until it clarified completely.

Calley sniffed the air. The stench had evaporated.

"Now," She said, "Now we can get down to why I came." Together, both of Them smiling, They sank down into the water.

The little Helpers on the banks of the pond sighed in relief.

It was only a few days before the bubbles rising from the water released fecund smells. And a few bubbles contained the sounds of laughter, and sighs. The water level of the pond rose.

31

LUCKY MAN

Craft stood on the veranda of the Mansion and gave thanks for his life. Then he stood there awhile longer and studied the trees. He paid attention to the little winds that would move one treetop but not another. Then another little wind would move some other treetop. He didn't know—he was trying to determine if it was the same little wind.

Watching the wind reminded him of his time living around Native people when he was studying wildlife and the bison herd in a national park. He remembered the true grit required to live, more than required of anyone he knew, and the interminable sense of alienation—not just theirs, an alienation from the larger non-indigenous culture—but also his own sense of never, ever, being able to belong there.

He knew that this was mostly something in him, even when he was with those closest to him, those who had opened their homes, and their teachings, and their hearts to him. That was all any human could do, and he was blessed with an abundance of this—that which was all any human could do to welcome the Other, the Mystery. It was this blessing, the blessing of what was happening here at Stonehaven, for which he was giving thanks.

He continued to watch the winds. They were like people dancing in the treetops, swaying, hopping from one foot to the other. Suddenly he realized what they were. That's exactly what they were: little human shaped wind spirits dancing in the treetops.

Craft was naked, except for a light woven cotton blanket wrapped around him. He saw that the dancers had similar blankets, spreading them with their arms and causing the treetop to dance with them, like they had wings.

He asked them, "May I dance with you?" and they responded, waving their arms, and welcoming him up. When he took a step, his body fell away, and his spirit flew to the treetops.

He danced there, first in one tree, then another. He felt the other spirits laughing with joy and he started laughing with them. He felt the trees laughing under his feet.

By this time, Rachel had come out onto the veranda wrapped in a transparent summer robe trimmed in lace. She saw his body prostrate on the deck and rushed to him. She knelt and raised his eyelids, noting his eyes showed only white. As she checked his pulse she noticed he was smiling. Then she recognized the trance state.

Then the Huera came, the blonde one they had both recently seen several times out of the corners of their eyes. She was the one they had wondered might be some new Face of the Divine Feminine. The Huera danced in the trees and saw Rachel look up at Her, saw her seeing Her. Rachel saw Craft then, dancing in the trees near the Huera. The Huera smiled at her. Rachel said, "I want to dance, too." And when she reached out with her hand, her body collapsed across Craft's, and she was suddenly dancing on the treetops, too.

That was how Regina found them: Rachel collapsed over John, both of them grinning like maniacs, eyes rolled so far back only the whites were showing.

Soon Rachel found herself dancing next to the Huera. The Huera looked at her sideways. "What are you doing here?" Rachel asked. "You're not from among Them," gesturing at the little Wind Spirit Helpers.

"I asked to join them, just like you. And they accepted me."

"Who are you?" Rachel asked.

"I am not a 'who'. I am a 'What'," the Being replied.

Rachel began to lose her breath, feeling the pull of her body calling, sensing Regina touching her, calling her, seeking to follow, asked, "So, what are you?"

The Being said, "I am from Regina's mother's land." And then, "Regina brought me here."

Rachel thought, "Well, that's a problem" and immediately she was back in her body, gasping, sitting straight up, pushing Regina's hand away.

'Fuck." Rachel said. "Who are you?"

Regina, wearing a similar transparent, lace-edged belted gown, kept for guests by Rachel, said, "I am the daughter of the father of your son. This makes me your niece, at least. And you my Aunt. Perhaps it makes you my evil stepmother." And she grinned.

Rachel felt into Regina's thought, and said, "So, we teach each other? Mother teaches daughter, daughter teaches mother?"

"Yes," Regina said. "We teach each other. How else are we to know what each other knows? Between the two of us we might figure out everything he knew and turn it to our purposes, yes?"

"Yes. Turn it to our purposes. He was a patriarchal fuck" Rachel said.

"Yes," Regina said. "And he was my father. And your lover. The crossed archetypes put us at the Center, you know?"

"Yes, I do," Rachel replied. "All three of them."

"Look for four," Regina said, holding up four fingers. "When you're walking the great circle," she paused and then continued. "When you are walking the outer circle of your life there is always a fourth archetype. We must look for it."

Rachel said "I know what it is. It is the Ecstatist. Ecstasy is our birthright. It is in Ecstasy we are taken out of ourselves and into the treetops."

At this, Craft awoke. As he came awake, he moved Rachel back a little bit with one hand and sat up. Holding his head briefly he muttered, "All power is just a loan, by the way." And then, looking away from the wen into the treetops he said, "Of course the Thunder Beings have wings. Just look at their feathers, etched by clouds in the high reaches of the sky."

"Reach for that sky, John. Understand the sky." Regina said. "That one, the Huera? She is one of my Grandmothers, one of my Grandwen."

"Really?" Craft said. Not fully back yet, but realizing he had an erection he reached out and his hand closed on Regina. He pulled her toward him. She resisted, putting a hand on his chest.

Regina said, "I need a different lover."

Craft said, "Not yet."

And Rachel interjected, "Yes, you do. And perhaps I know whom."

Regina leaned forward, surrendering to Craft's pull. She leaned in close and kissed him, and when she pulled back, only a quarter of an inch, she said, "You know I need another lover."

Craft, completely back to himself, said, "Yes, I do." And he reached out and put his free hand on Rachel's thigh. He said, "I do not forget what I am, in service to you."

"Yes." Rachel said. "And do not forget to serve She whom I serve." She reached over and took hold of his erection. "It's a good thing you're useful," she smiled.

"Show me She whom I serve," Craft said.

Rachel opened her gown down the front. She spread out the blanket that had been covering John's thighs. She took his erection in one hand, swung a leg over him, and inserted him inside herself. Regina leaned forward then and kissed him again.

"Get this ready," she said when she broke the kiss. Then, opening her gown like Rachel, she faced away from her, and swung a leg over John's head and slowly lowered herself onto his face, letting him watch her descend, as she was slowly spreading and opening.

"Use your hands," she said. "I need to feel more than one."

She felt Rachel's hands upon her, too. Sighing, leaning back into Rachel's slowly rocking embrace, after taking a moment to match the rhythm, she said, "Oh, I am assuaged. I am assuaged, thank you Goddess of Mercy."

As Rachel assuaged her, Regina relaxed, and rocked herself, steadily riding. When John put a finger inside her, with Rachel guiding his hand, Regina rained for him.

All alienation fled. The dancers in the tree tops danced and watched. And then they whirl-winded, wrapping themselves around each other.

Later that night, while John Craft was cleaning up in the kitchen, Regina and Rachel sat on the veranda, watching the last of the light in the west.

"Why do you call it the 'Fleur de Vie?" Regina asked Rachel suddenly.

"The Flower of Life?" Rachel asked back.

"Yes. So many ideas are described by those words. Honestly, I don't know what any of them mean, exactly."

"Well, I mean something very specific by it. Would you like to see?"

"Yes," Regina said, nodding.

"Then go down a step," Rachel said. She leaned back against one the pillars supporting the veranda roof, pulled aside her gown and spread her legs. "Look," she commanded.

Regina bent down to see as the light faded. Rachel spread her phulva so that Regina could see the series of contractions and relaxations Rachel started. After several alternations Rachel sighed and relaxed completely.

And then Regina saw it, pink petals tightly closed, petals that opened for her gaze with one last pulse from Rachel.

Regina gasped on her indrawn breath. "Oh my," she said. "I see. The Flower of Life." She gazed at it and whispered, "How beautiful." Then, looking up at Rachel, asked, "Do I have one?"

"I don't know. Many do," Rachel said "Would you like to find out?" she grinned.

That was how Craft found them. He came and stood at the library doors and leaned on the doorframe. He watched Rachel kneeling between Regina's thighs, listened to her instructions. He knew what she was doing with one hand, holding a mirror in the other.

Craft knew, with total certainty, where he belonged: right where he was. Giving thanks for his life. Lucky man.

32

QUINN AND THE PRIEST

Quinn had followed the Priest from the Bishop's conference. He went there on assignment from Eva, hunting for child abusers, he thought, though her instructions had been ambiguous. She'd said, "There will be someone with a sexual difficulty. He will be apparent to you. Bring him here." After booking a room in a nearby hotel he'd spent time sitting in the lobby of the conference center or walking around in the parking lot.

One Priest, in particular, had been acting strangely, He had the air of someone with something to hide. He was about forty, six feet tall, of medium build, and his hair had receded only slightly and gone a little gray at the temples. When he moved, he sometimes did so stiffly, as though he were in pain. He stayed at the periphery of different groups, and left early—at least as soon as the various break-out groups finished meeting—sometimes earlier.

Quinn got close enough to read the name and parish on his nametag. When the Priest got in his car to leave, Quinn got the tag number and called a contact who was a private investigator to get the registration address. It was in different state from the parish on the name tag, so Quinn knew he hadn't updated his address.

Quinn took a train out of the city and caught a bus that took him out the interstate highway into the western part of the state. He disembarked about ten miles outside the town where the parish was and started walking overland, mostly, as was his habit, keeping off the roads as much as possible. He arrived the day after the Priest.

The parish church was small with a gated yard and a cemetery set back from the road in a narrow vale between mountains. There was a small apartment for the Priest. An office behind the church was connected by an enclosed breezeway. He kept two large dogs in the yard.

Quinn reconnoitered the small church, more of a chapel, and approached it from the side opposite the parking lot. He slipped into the church before the door closed as the Priest exited to go shopping.

He slipped the end of his staff into the door to keep it open, and when he slipped around the corner into the door he momentarily became stuck because he didn't open the door wide enough to clear the side brims of his straw hat. Recovering and cursing at himself, he entered the church.

The floorplan mirrored that of early churches with a bema, or platform, below the apse that held the altar. The bema ended in extensions to the side of the building that had been enclosed and held supplies and a small desk and chair, and, on the side closest to the apartment, an exit door and an armoire where vestments were kept.

From the desk he took a spare key to the front door of the church.

The next day Quinn was in the yard before first light. The dogs were still in the house. The Priest let the dogs out into the yard when he went over to the church to perform a morning service. There were no congregants. Quinn crouched down in an empty niche in the garden wall that gave him a view of the room with the armoire. The dogs smelled Quinn, but he had extended his field of Shadow, so they could neither see him, nor quarter his location by smell. He extended good will into the field and the dogs went around behind the church and lay down by the door to the house.

The Priest could be seen through the windows of the room off the chapel, changing into his robes. From his vantage Quinn saw him doing something very peculiar. After his robe and stole were on, comforting in the cool summer morning, the Priest removed his shoes and socks, and then his pants and underwear. He put them into the armoire that served as a closet. He turned to enter the chapel. Quinn could see that his robe was open and the Priest had a full erection, out front and proud, curving upward.

Quinn's jaw dropped, and he sucked in his breath, thinking "Now that is very strange. Let's go see what he's up to." He jumped down from the niche and landed more heavily than he thought. The dogs heard it, and barked. He reached the door before the dogs had trotted around to the front, and using the purloined key he quickly entered the church.

The Priest had entered the chapel, knelt on the steps before the altar and begun to pray, in the ancestral tongue. He felt no draft in his robe, now skirted to the floor. He did not hear Quinn as he entered and silently closed the door behind him. Quinn stood sideways behind a narrow column and watched.

The Priest stood up and climbed the stairs to the altar, lighting candles first on the left. Then he turned, erection still in the lead, and went to the other end of the table to light the candles there. He then turned back to the center, and decanted some wine into the goblet.

Quinn took this as his time to move. He ran silently up the aisle and caught the Priest with the butt end of the staff as he turned, forcing the Priest back over onto the altar, spilling the wine. Quinn pinned him there, and the Priest's robes fell open, revealing his erection, hard and falling back on his belly.

"Oh no, oh no, oh no. Please don't kill me, please," the Priest begged.

Quinn asked him, "What are you doing?"

The Priests responded, "No, no, please don't kill me."

"Maybe," said Quinn. "I asked you. What are you doing?"

"S-S-Services." he said. "Service. I say Service every morning."

"Like this? Dressed like this?" Quinn nodded in the general direction of the erection.

"Yes, yes. I have a condition. I can't help it."

"Condition. What condition?"

"I can't help it. I have a priapism."

Quinn could barely contain his smile. "And what do you do with your 'condition'?"

"Nothing! N-n-nothing! I swear!"

"You swear, do you?"

"Yes, yes, please don't kill me. You're one of them. One of the Hunters."

Quinn thought: "Hmm. Hunters, eh?" Then he said, dissembling, "Maybe."

The Priest groaned. 'No. No. I haven't done anything. I can't. I can't help it."

Quinn asked, "Nothing? What do you mean, nothing?"

"I mean nothing, I do nothing with it. I don't touch it. I don't touch anybody. I don't, I can't. I'm a priest!"

"That hasn't stopped thousands of your brothers."

"I know, I know, I'm sorry. But I'm not like that, I have a condition. That's why they put me here. Yes, yes. No more congregation here. I'm a caretaker."

Quinn grinned an evil grin, "Good to know," he said, "In case I decide to kill you."

"No, no," the Priest whimpered. "I can't help it. Whenever I pray, whenever I celebrate Service, it happens."

"And then what?"

"Nothing! I'm not allowed. I have vows. I keep them. I don't touch it. I have to wait, wait until it goes away."

"Really? You don't relieve yourself?"

"I can't, I'm not allowed!"

Quinn couldn't help himself. He laughed out loud, laughing at the situation, at the ridiculousness of the man's position, and the pitifulness of his state of being.

"That must be really hard for you," Quinn said.

The Priest, missing the pun, said, "Yes, yes, please, please, have mercy. Have mercy. Don't kill me."

Quinn backed off the staff a little, moving it down and hovering it over the Priest's still rock hard erection. "Clearly," he thought to himself, "the Priest is either a real freak, turned on by the proximity of immediate death, or he's telling the truth."

"Get up," Quinn told him. "And get on your knees." Quinn backed up to give him room. The Priest did so, leaning forward with his face in his hands.

Quinn stepped back and down three steps. "Tell me. Tell me why you get hard when you pray."

"It's love," the Priest said. "It's love. I can't separate it. It started with the Virgin."

"The Virgin? The Marinya?"

"Yes. Yes. It started when I would think of Her, think of Her as the Mother. I would get hard. I couldn't stop it and it wouldn't go away. All I had to do was think of Her. And then it started happening with the Laud. Oh, I was so ashamed. I thought I was gay. And then it started happening with the Madeleine. That's who it is now. I think about praying, and the image of Her comes. And it happens. I just get hard, She appears before me. Sometimes She comes in my sleep. Sometimes She touches me. I can't help it. I'm so ashamed. Oh, I am so ashamed."

Quinn was thinking, "This is so strange. So strange. He's in love with the Sacred. He's in love with the Divine. He loves the Divine so much it gives him an erection!" So he said again, "And you do nothing? You do nothing with it?"

"Nothing! Nothing, I swear. I used to try to do the Service. I'd strap it down, but I couldn't stand there. I'd turn red, I'd blush. I'd try to speak but I couldn't. Sometimes I would just shudder. I'd stand there and shake."

"Kriyas," Quinn said out loud.

"What?" the Priest asked.

"Never mind," Quinn said. "What happens next?"

"Nothing. Nothing happens."

"Nothing?"

"No, no, nothing. I just wait and it goes away. Three, four hours; it just goes away. I don't touch it. But I can't celebrate Service for the people."

Just then the dogs outside exploded with barking. Both Quinn and the Priest jumped. Quinn said, "Stay right there," and ran for the doors.

He threw open the doors and saw the dogs throwing themselves against the gate, snapping at a feather swirling in the air—a large feather, spotted like a young golden eagle's. In front of his eyes, a field of clear energy swirled around the feather and it popped out of existence.

He looked over the wall and across the street. He saw a winged being suddenly leap up onto the roof of a house. The being must have been in the church yard, because the gate bounced open in reaction to the dogs jumping against it, unlatched, and then they were gone, out into the street, loudly, snarling, in hot pursuit.

The being ran across the roofline and leapt off the end with its wings lifted high. Suddenly there was an explosion of light and fire as one of the wing tips crossed the electric wires running along the back yard. Quinn heard a scream of pain, and a crashing noise, as it fell into the wooden fence at the back of the yard.

Quinn took off, running hard after the dogs and in pursuit of the being. After all, it's not every day you see a winged being.

The dogs ran ahead of him. The house to the left of the one from which the being jumped had no fence in the back so the dogs went that way and into the woods behind the houses. Quinn followed, pushing through wood's edge growth of tear-thumb and wild blackberries, leaping over fallen logs, into the deeper woods. He could hear the being thrashing and tripping, while he was getting closer to it even as it ran. Suddenly he broke into a clearing, the dogs leaping just ahead of him. There the being was, face-first on the ground.

The dogs took one last leap, one going for the feet, the other for the head, and Quinn, having had enough, cried out, "Stop!" The dogs did, in mid-leap; something in them let go, some intention drained from them. When they landed they just stopped, fell to the ground, stopped in their tracks. They stood still, tongues out, wagging their tails and looking at Quinn as if he had suddenly become the master they had longed for all their lives. They sat down, panting, tongues lolling.

Quinn went over to the prostrate form. It was face down, arms over its head, waiting for the jaws to close. Quinn touched it on the heel, thinking, "Hmm, combat boots." And said, "Hey. You OK?"

The being shivered then trembled, and rolled over. At the same time they both said, "You. It's you." And then, after less than a breath, they both said, "Ah, shit."

There was a pause, and then Quinn said, "Matthews." And he dropped to one knee, put a hand on Matthews' shoulder, and said, "How the fuck did you get here?"

Matthews said, "It's you. It is you. Fuck you. What did you do to me? She told me. She always tells me where to go. Anybody. Anyone, your feet. Wherever you are. Wherever the fuck you are. Take your hand off me."

And his good wing, his left wing, beat against the ground and then faded—not absorbing into him, exactly—but a vortex formed around it and it seemed to disappear before Quinn's eyes. All fifteen feet of it. Slightly lagging behind the left wing, but in tempo with it, the right wing beat against the ground, once, twice, three times, shedding blood and feathers. Then the vortices formed around it, and the wing disappeared. Last to disappear was a feather fluff, drifting toward one of the dogs mouths. The dog snapped at it when it got close, once, twice, three times, missing it every time on its way to the ground. Right before it landed the vortices formed and it popped out of sight.

"Where do things go when they pop out like that?" Quinn asked.

Matthews replied, "Who the fuck knows."

Quinn took his hand off him and stepped back. Both dogs growled.

Quinn didn't even have to ask. Matthews looked at him, saw how his straw hat reflected the light, looking like a halo in the early morning sun.

Then Matthews told him, "You made me a child of the Earth. No, that's not right. You didn't make me anything. You didn't make me aware of anything but Her Heart. When you woke it up in me, you left me blind, lying on the floor. Fuck you. After all I did for you."

"Yeah, I read the book you wrote. I liked it," Quinn said. "I thought you did a good job, the job I was hoping you'd do."

"Yeah? Fuck you," Matthews said. He turned his head to the side, not looking at Quinn. He continued, "She gave me these." And the wings threatened to appear. "Nobody sees them. Even when they're awake. But you see them. Fuck you."

Quinn said, "I see them because they are real."

Then he said, "Get up." and extended his hand. Matthews rolled over and raised his right hand to Quinn's. They grasped hands, Matthews swung his legs under him, rolled to a sitting position and, with his feet under him, stood up in a smooth motion.

Quinn said, "So. You're new here." He turned and began walking, then trotting, back toward the church yard.

Matthews followed him, then the dogs, loping along behind, tongues lolling, drooling, happy to be in a pack. Quinn jogged between the houses, stopped to look both ways on the road—not for cars but witnesses—as they all did when they got there, including the dogs. They kept trotting, almost at a run, and Quinn pushed through the yard gate, banging it back on its hinges, ricocheting it back onto Matthews, who ricocheted it back onto the dogs as they came through. The front dog squeaked through in the bounce, the other bounded into the rebounding door, front paws forward and they all ran down the path.

Quinn burst through the church door, menagerie in tow. The Priest was on his knees on the steps leading up to the altar exactly as Quinn had told him to stay—on his knees, knees one step below his ankles and feet. The sight of it drew Quinn up short and he stopped.

He said, "Matthews, look! What is obedience, and why do you do it?"

The Priest was leaning backwards, holding his face in his hands. Quinn said, "Stop. Stop it. Let go. You are free."

The Priest let go an exhalation that echoed against the back wall of the church and rolled back forward, impelling everyone, even the dogs, out of their pause, breaking the spell of agony.

The Priest stood up, robes still open, still priapic, his erection pointing upwards along the aisle.

"See? I told you so," the Priest said.

The dogs whined and sat down.

"What do you do? What do you do?" Quinn asked, looking at the Priest. "What the fuck do you do with this?" He turned to Matthews, and caught him in the act of shrugging his shoulders.

Matthews said, "Release."

"Really?" Quinn said.

The Priest said, "Don't kill me. Please don't kill me."

Quinn turned to him and put on his fierce face. "Maybe." he said. "Shut up now. I wasn't talking to you."

The Priest went silent, and stared at Quinn instead. It was almost an empty stare, but not quite. There was surrender in that look, and a directness, too. No looking down.

The Priests' eyes suddenly resolved themselves into the direct look, quiet but steady.

Quinn said, "Do you want to know? Do you want to know what should be done here? Done with you? Done with your condition?"

The Priest nodded his head.

Quinn said, "You can't, you can't just nod. You have to say so."

The Priest said, "Yes."

And then the Priest said, "Yes. I want to know."

Quinn said, "Because you've already made vows, you have to forsake them. If you want to know, you have to break your promises. You have to break the promises you've made."

The Priest said, "That's what they tell us the Great Deceiver will say."

Quinn said, "Like nobody else could ever say the same thing. You're smarter than that."

The Priest bowed his head. Quinn said, "The Madeleine is real. I can take you to Her. Do you want to go?"

The Priest looked up, some sort of shock registering in his eyes. He said, "Really?"

Quinn said, "Idiot." He turned and walked away. He said, "Matthews, where's your car? I walked here. You didn't. And you wouldn't fly."

Matthews replied, "A couple blocks."

"Get it. You got a road trip coming," Quinn said.

Matthews asked, "Where?

Quinn said, "Where I fucking tell you. You're going to Stonehaven. And you're going to take him with you."

On the threshold he turned back to the Priest and said, "Do you forsake your vows? Right now, motherfucker. Do you forsake your vows to your misogynist fuck of a god?"

The Priest dropped back to his knees on the steps, knees below his ankles again, and raised his arms, palms up in supplication, erection bouncing, and bowed his head. "Yes. I renounce them. Take me to the Madeleine."

Quinn looked at the Priest, fiercely and directly, picking up his staff like a javelin, and said, "Lie to me. Tell me a lie so I can know when you're telling the truth. Go ahead. Lie to me or you will die."

The Priest said, "I don't want to go."

Quinn laughed out loud. "That's a pretty good gawdamned lie. You'll live. You have no idea."

Matthews asked, "What's Stonehaven?"

"The end of the world as you know it," Quinn said as he stepped out into the church yard. He looked along the walk to the gate, then into the trees across the street, and then above to the horizon and said to the world, "Now you've done it."

From inside he heard the Priest say to Matthews, "He doesn't have to cuss so much."

Matthews consoled him, "Sometimes he gets grumpy."

Twenty minutes later Matthews had the car, a four door sedan, in the small parking lot to the side of the church yard. The Priest had packed two suitcases, and was coming up the walk. Quinn motioned Matthews to roll down the passenger window, leaned on the frame with his elbow, and gave him directions. Then he asked the obvious question: "How'd you get them?" nodding towards Matthews' back.

Matthews said, "Six months after you left I hooked up with a girl who took me to an island in the Mediterranean, a Greek island named Keerkay. While I was sitting there in a chaise lounge on top of a mountain I had a vision of the tsunami wave from the explosion of the volcano Thera that washed over the island.

"Suddenly, the next day, sitting in the same place, in the same frame of mind, I had the same vision again. I'm not stupid, you know, the wings appeared. I thought of wings, I thought of flying above the destruction. Escaping. And suddenly, I felt them extend outward from my back.

"Nobody sees them. I look like I'm levitating, if they see me at all. Now, She talks to me. We talk to each other, anytime. While the girl and I were there we went to the ruins of a temple for Her; just some broken pillars and blocks lying around the edge the stone platform. We stood in the hot sun and dry grass on the large flat floor and we both had a vision—we both had the same vision. It was a vision of Priestesses doing devotional dances in the morning sun. Since then, She talks to me. And sends me images. That's how I found you.

"She is angry. She is making angels on Her own. She is making angels to defend Herself against the angels of De Murgos. They don't belong here. Not anymore. Maybe war is coming. There are others like me.

"She made me one of Her angels. I am an Earth Angel."

Quinn asked him, "Do you have any idea how fucked you are?"

Matthews thought about how to answer that. In the end he decided to say "No."

Quinn thought to himself, "Fucker just might learn something yet." Then he said, "You still see the girl?"

"No," Matthews said with a pained expression on his face. "She couldn't deal with the wings. They came out once when we were making love. She wouldn't tell me what she saw, but she became afraid and told me it was too much. I guess I kind of levitated us a little bit. Maybe she'll call me someday."

Quinn grinned at him inexplicably. Matthews was about to ask him why he was grinning when they were interrupted by the Priest, who had put his suitcases and two small bags in the trunk, and climbed into the back seat, sitting in the center. He sat there stiffly, with his stiffy, and a third small pack on his lap staring straight ahead.

"It's time," the Priest said, "It's time to be what I am." Then, leaning forward he said, "My name's Halloran. Robert Halloran. Who are you?"

Matthews replied, "I'm Matthews. That's Quinn."

Quinn told the Priest to move over. Quinn opened both the passenger side doors and whistled for the dogs. One climbed in through each door. Quinn said to Matthews. "The dogs go. Open the windows for them, will you?"

Quinn closed the doors, stepped back, and said, "Go. I will call them so they're expecting you. Just head down the driveway until you have to stop. Then make sure you do. Stop, that is. And remember, there are no Priests at Stonehaven."

Two days later Quinn got off the bus in Sally's town. He went by her house but it was closed; curtains drawn, wet flyers were scattered in the yard, steaming in their plastic bags. No car. He went by the restaurant, and sat out back on the same milk crate he'd been sitting on when he first saw her.

Eventually, Bunny came out the back door with a bag of garbage and headed for the dumpster. Quinn whistled and he stopped, turned, and then he saw Quinn sitting there, and his eyes got large.

"Where is she?" Quinn asked, wasting no words on pleasantries with an unpleasant person.

"She went back to Brazil, man. Couple of weeks after you disappeared. Said she had to talk to her brothers about something. Seems to me she could've just called them. Where'd you go man? You gonna try and pick up your last check?"

Quinn said nothing. He stood up and walked away.

33

CIRCLES OF MEN AND WEN

At the men's circle meeting the week before the Solstice, Quinn was sitting on the floor, leaving the dais to Craft, the Elder, and the High Consort. He had been invited to tell his story, and the whole of it took a couple hours. He held the men's attention. Occasionally someone would ask a question, which Quinn answered in an easy way. He had rediscovered patience here, looking into the eyes of the Feminine and seeing Her smiling back at him.

When Quinn had finished the tale, the Elder said, "He is talking about the Invader."

"Yes," Peter replied. "I think so, too. The signs are all there."

"The Invader?" Quinn asked.

"Yes," the Elder said. "A long time ago, at least three thousand years, an Outsider came into the Solar System. An Invader. As with all things eventually mortal, it had to eat. And it found us. He is the one who destroyed the ideas of the Divine Masculine for most of the world. Half the world believes he is the Divine Masculine, ruling alone without the Feminine."

Craft said, "It is because the Feminine is Antecedent that he was unable to destroy Her completely."

"We told you that the new Divine Masculine didn't exist yet, that He was emergent still. Some of the men that work with the Madeleine on becoming Seers have seen that there may be a reddish tint to His skin. That's all we know," Peter said. "That, and that there really never was a good, fully formed example of the Divine Masculine. Even those who knew the Antecedence of the Feminine pretended they didn't know and put themselves first, as if they were the true and initial creators of Life."

"All that," Quinn said. "And you know that the Divine Feminine loves you."

"True," Peter said. "Most of us are not in a hurry for that emergence to happen." He smiled, and a few men laughed.

The Elder leaned forward and said to Quinn, "She loves you, too."

Quinn smiled and lowered his face, bowing his head. "Tell me the story of the Invader," he said.

"Well," the Elder, Peter, and Craft all said at once, and everyone laughed.

"We shall each tell a part of it," Peter said.

In the wen's circle Angelica sat on a large cushion, turned three-quarters away from Diana, able to lean back on her if she needed. The wen were arranged around the room in no particular pattern except mutual interests, and were talking to each other in small groups. Many of them working on making shawls, laying out material, sometimes adding fringe, and embroidering the edges with flowers and other symbols.

Angelica clutched her shawl, holding it close, feeling the love that was present in the soul of the wen who had embroidered it with her namesake flower while she had been out of her mind in the Recovery building for a week.

She thought about that phrase, 'out of her mind', and contemplated how it was true literally. She had been ecstatic—that is, out of her mind—for almost the entire week. She could remember some of it, some of what she saw, and what she felt in her Soul and experienced in her Spirit.

She could less easily remember what she sensed in her Soma.

Her senses had been expanding, slowly at first, then stabilizing. Her vision showed her things she hadn't been able to see before. Her hearing became both acute and extended in range. That had been a part of the pain in her Soma. Her body began to feel low frequency sounds, sensing them in her solar plexus and lower belly. It seemed that her Spirit decided that she had to call it 'hearing'. Her Soul had shown her how to interpret some of the feelings the vibrations generated, and she was beginning to learn how to use both Sensing and Feeling to reduce her automatic vulnerability to the vibrations.

When she slept, she dreamed of dragons every night.

Every night in her practice, she sat on her bed and did inner exercise work. The work changed based on her instructions—all based on the division of Soma, Soul, and Spirit; sensing, feeling, and thinking. The goal, she'd been told, would be to separate these into three different forms. They might all look identical, and when she mastered it, someone looking at her would see three separate, identical, bodies.

She would do the exercises until she fell asleep, until she'd keel over. Then she'd know it was time to give it all a rest.

It still hurt, her Soma. Not all ecstasy is pleasure. It still burned when certain people, or even certain fabrics touched her skin. Some things didn't hurt: light; Diana; her shawl hanging over bare shoulders, draped over bare breasts.

She looked up and around at the wen in the meeting.

She could see the light surrounding the wen who were intentionally cultivating Love while they worked, Love that would imbue whatever they touched.

She smiled. "Good news," she said, leaning back to speak in a quiet voice to Diana. Diana responded by leaning back into her. "Good news. It would seem that it no longer hurts me to be touched by Love."

"It did for a while, I know," Diana whispered back to her. "It is good news. Are you seeing it right now?"

"Yes," Angelica whispered back.

"Try sensing it tactilely and feeling it emotionally," Diana suggested.

Angelica turned back and settled into a sit. She narrowed her eyes, first sharpening her gaze, looking for threats. She saw that Madeleine was glancing at her from under her brow. Eva was engaged in her work, and what was emanating from her felt to be a large and protective field, a field that extended to the walls of the room.

Then she saw the Moon Halter. Her face was bent toward her work, but as Angelica watched, another face appeared on the top of her head, clear as day. The face grinned at her. As she watched, Moon Halter lifted up her head and her usual face grinned at her, also. Then Moon Halter shook her head as if to say, "Unbelievable."

She turned her mind to her assignment. She let her eyes relax again so that she could see the clouds of Love surrounding some of the other wen. She picked one and projected herself in her mind's sensation of itself, across the room, reached out, and touched the cloud around the wen named Heather, a wen who had never aggravated her. Her hand sensed a vibration that resolved itself in her ears as a hum, although Heather wasn't audibly humming. Back in her Soma, she hummed the note she'd sensed. Several people, including Heather, turned and stared at her.

She returned her gaze to focus, and noticed that the top of Moon Halter's head was laughing silently at her. She stopped humming.

Diana leaned over to her and said, "Yes, that's right. That's the note. All you have to do is think it, even unconsciously, let the note hum along in the background while you're thinking about something else, dividing your attention in some way. That note will slowly operate on everyone in a room.

"Are there different notes for different feelings?" she asked.

Diana smiled at her, mysteriously, "I suppose," she said. "Now, feel it."

She used her intention to bring awareness to her second and third centers, low in her belly and in her solar plexus. They opened, in the shape of vesicas, almost touching at a point half way between them. She shifted into a receptive state, and waited.

Then she felt it. A simple love extending into the future, dedicated to whomever would use the craft work next. She saw how tendrils of love embedded themselves in the fiber, as part of the weave of the cloth, making the shawl glow from within.

The feeling wrapped itself around her, on all sides, comforting and warming her. She closed her eyes and drifted in the feeling. Her visual field shifted into an all-encompassing warm red glow.

She began to drift off in it when she heard a sharp clapping sound, twice. She opened her eyes quickly and felt a shock at the recognition of the Moon Halter standing in front of her. The Moon Halter leaned toward her and made a stroking gesture of closure around her head.

Angelica drew back, confused. When she did, she saw the Madeleine behind Moon Halter, looking over her shoulder, smiling but also confused and concerned.

"Your heads were showing," Moon Halter said, smiling.

"What?" Angelica asked.

"Your heads. Three of them. All at once," Moon Halter answered, as if that actually explained anything.

"We were concerned about what would happen if you split. We were concerned about what might emerge when your field started to turn red," Madeleine expanded.

Angelica just shook her head, both to clear her mind and to communicate that she still didn't understand. She looked around the room. Everyone was looking at her, all of them smiling at her, all smiles of sympathy or compassion.

She blushed at the attention, and leaned back into Diana again.

"It's OK," Moon Halter said.

"Yes, it's OK," Madeleine confirmed. They stepped aside and Angelica looked at Eva, who was still sitting there, smiling, holding the field.

"You were safe," Eva said. "Nothing would have happened. But everybody could see what was happening. It was very instructive."

"I am suddenly overcome with an intense longing," Angelica said. Her face twisted and she started panting, trying to control a sob. "Oh, oh," she said, succumbing to the feelings that seemed to arise from the core of her being. She bent forward, one arm around her belly, her other hand, in a fist, she brought to her face and bit down on a knuckle.

She said, "Oh!" again, sobbed once more, panted a little and then sat up straight, perfectly composed. When she opened her eyes, the people closest to her gasped.

Moon Halter immediately sat down in front of Angelica. Madeleine did also. Neither said a word. They just stared at Angelica.

Her eyes had turned green, and her pupils narrowed to vertical slits. She looked around the room, slowly moving her head from side to side, taking it all in. The air around her began to shift, and waver, and turn red.

In front of Angelica's face an odd face appeared in the red light, snouted, with long tendrils of moustache that seemed to float as if in water.

A voice issued from Angelica's throat, deeper than her own voice, and said, "Ho gved rahkhine."

Moon Halter answered, "Ho gved hamashk," and nodded.

The image returned the nod.

From the back of the room, Eva's voice spoke out, "It is said that there is one in each of us. There is a dragon in each of us, although not as strongly as it is in this one."

Many of the wen in the room nodded at this, dividing their attention along the lines of their hearing, their eyes remaining fixed intently on the apparition in front of them.

Behind Angelica, Diana, still holding her up back-to-back, suddenly felt something sliding over her thigh. She recognized it, in a general way, as having a shape like a snake. Then, in a sudden flash of real insight, she knew what it was: a dragon's tail. She permitted herself a small gasp, just the smallest inhale of breath, when she saw the form of it emerge, and could see it sliding over her thigh, edged by a darker red within the red cloud that surrounded both her and Angelica.

Eva's voice continued, "It is said that dragons are the highest aspiration and expression of our most primitive brain, our own inner reptile brain, the brain of our instincts; our instincts to fuck and feed, to fight or flee, even our instinct to freeze. If this is true—that we all have dragons within—then it would account for how globally the images of dragons are to be found."

The dragon exhaled, making a blubbery sound with its lips.

Behind Angelica, the tail had found its way up under Diana's sarong and along her thigh, the tip pressed along the length of her phulva. Diana made the same blubbery sound with her lips, sounding like a mare, impatient. She shifted her shoulders against Angelica's. The dragon, nodding, although no one in front of Angelica knew why, slipped the tip of its tail inside Diana.

The tail remained still, except at the very tip, which moved slowly in and out, making Diana tremble with the slightest tremble at her opening. She felt it as the beginning of what could happen, the beginning of a very wild ride. So she sighed, and settled down to enjoy it, enjoy the ride, whatever happened. The tip slipped a little farther in.

Eva continued, "As expressions of our instincts, they appear in our dreams, then, as well as in our art. And within us, they can be as independent as any brain, struggling to awaken and arise against the needs of our higher brains, our feeling and thinking brains, against the need of all these to function in an integrated way."

Diana could feel the tail reaching up within her, slowly, stroking her cervix. She used an exercise to draw it up, out of the way.

Eva said, "Angelica, are you in there?"

Angelica, who could sense, somehow, everything the dragon was do-ing with its tail, but seemed unable to stop it, struck by the novelty of having a tail, grinned goofily, and nodded her head.

The tail continued to the far end, far inside, of Diana, where it coiled into a ball, expanding inside her, expanding her, stretching her slowly, which the dragon then slowly withdrew, resting the knot against the inner walls, just inside her opening, lodged there like something too large to fit through a door.

Eva continued, "These three brains, then, the sensing, feeling, and thinking brains, are within us, wrapped around each other, with the reptile brain, the dragon brain, at the deepest part of ourselves. They are, in a way, what we actually are, and we are the recapitulation of the evolution of life on this planet."

The ball of tangled tail pulsed against her on the inside, and pressed against her on the outside, so prehensile that it pushed back the hood concealing the little man, and embraced it with a sucking sensation.

Diana groaned.

Angelica, paradoxically, could also feel Diana's pleasure and groaned aloud, also.

The dragon's tongue appeared in the midst of its moustaches, hanging and lolling.

Eva said, "These brains are interconnected in myriad ways, and are dependent on the rest of our nervous system for their perceptions."

The ball of tail pulsed within her, expanding and contracting. Diana uncrossed her ankles and put her feet flat on the floor with her knees spread, and her forearms resting on her knees. She dropped her head and moaned.

Angelica did the same, although no one watching could yet discern the reason why.

The dragon continued to regard Eva, the Madeleine, and then the Moon Halter. Moon Halter smiled at it.

The dragon snorted and shook itself.

Eva continued, "And, all these brains sometimes don't get along so well with each other. And so, as life is evolving, we are developing—even as we sit here—a new brain, a Fourth Brain, a brain which mediates these internal conflicts."

Diana's moan turned into a pulsing, repetitive, "Uh, uh, uh," in time to the expansion and contraction of the tangle of tail. She could feel the pressure building on her inner walls, and against her pelvic bone.

Angelica, under the intense pressure and sensory overload, echoed Diana's noise, the grunting sound of human animal sex, three times, and then fainted without falling, remaining sitting with her head dropped, although her pelvis rocked in time with Diana's.

The dragon grinned around its lolling tongue and panted, lightly.

Eva said, "This fourth brain is the seat of good judgment."

The pulsing ball drove Diana, shouting, over the edge, pounding her heels onto the wooden floor of the stage, gripping the pillow on which she'd sat.

Eva said, "It is the part of ourselves that informs us of what constitutes Good Behavior. It is the basis of Conscience."

Diana shouted then, squirting visibly up over her head. The dragon lifted her with its tail, pulling her up off the floor. She raised herself up on her hands and feet, her sarong falling back along her thighs, arching her back, ejaculating over her head, out into the room, splashing the Moon Halter and Madeleine. Moon Halter laughed out loud.

Rain fell on Angelica and the dragon as well. The top of the dragon's head started to steam.

A hissing, sizzling sound arose when Diana had finished, legs shaking, barely able to support her weight, and sat down again. Steam rose slowly from all the wetness spread around her.

Eva said, "And this new brain is connected to our heart, so that our hearts can inform us of what is good and what is not."

The dragon shrugged, and said, "Heh, heh, heh." Then the red image faded in the white cloud forming from the steam.

The wen in the room were left in a state of shock, except Moon Halter, who struggled to stop laughing. Finally quieting down, the fog wrapped itself around Angelica and Diana, leaving only the sound of faint hiss and sizzle to be heard.

Eva said, "Good behavior, indeed."

The sound faded away, and into the silence Eva said, "The Feminine is antecedent." Then she dropped her head forward, suddenly tired.

The wen responded, "The Feminine Creates, the Masculine Makes."

Diana, panting, slumping forward, head hanging, hair hanging, in the mirror image of Angelica's posture, joined in the response to the call. Unable to stay upright, Diana then fell to one side. Angelica, now unsupported, fell backwards over her.

Then Angelica's head slowly rose, returning, as if from sleep. She looked around, then sat up.

"How much do you remember?" Madeleine asked.

"Everything until I passed out. At least, what I could sense and feel. All I could see was red," she answered. "Was it...?" she asked.

"Yes, it was," Madeleine said. "Your dragon."

"Bad behavior," Eva said.

Moon Halter laughed out loud again. "Yes, badly behaved. But at least its interest in sex was laudable," and she laughed again. "Laudable. Maybe that's what we should call it. Laudable."

"Tell me, Angelica. Is it feminine or masculine?" Madeleine asked.

"I couldn't tell," Angelica said, patting her hair and looking quizzically at her hand when it came away wet. "It seemed sometimes one, then the other."

Eva said, to the other wen, "Get some blankets for these wen. Heather and Emalia, help get them moved over onto dry pillows."

The two wen helped a shaky Angelica get to her feet and move. Diana, casting her shawl aside and dropping her soaked sarong, crawled over to the new pillows and collapsed again, groaning at the effort, then she sighed with comfort. One of the wen covered her with a soft flannel blanket.

Eva came over, sat down, and put Diana's head in her lap. "Diana, can you talk yet?" Eva asked. The wen, including Angelica, gathered closer.

"Yes," she mumbled into Eva's thigh. She sat up and shook her head, trying to get the damp tangles out of her hair. Then she ran her fingers through it.

Diana looked around the room, smiling when she saw Madeleine and Moon Halter. "I heard you laughing. I see I got you; that's pretty funny," she said, and chuckled.

"Well," Eva said, leaning forward. "What was it? We could see the dragon from the front, what was happening to you?"

"The tail. It was the dragon's tail," Diana said finally. An intake of breath was heard throughout the room.

"It was unlike anything I've ever felt," Diana continued. "It started when I felt it sliding over my thigh, like a snake, but it was looking for my phulva. It was prehensile, you know what I mean? It could move around and take different shapes. Once it was inside me," and there was another gasp of breath from the circle. Diana continued "Once it was inside me, it felt like it tied itself into some kind of knot and pushed against my pelvic bone from the inside, then it bent itself around on the front and pushed against me from the outside, moving around on my little man." She paused, and looked for Angelica.

Angelica was standing in the back, deeply blushing, hiding her face in her hands. "Oh no, baby, come here," Diana said.

"My dragon did that to you? Oh, I am so sorry I did that to you," Angelica started to weep as she came over.

"Sit down here, next to me," Diana said, putting an arm around Angelica's shoulders and hugging her close.

"You didn't do that, child," Moon Halter said. "The dragon did. You don't have a tail," and she laughed out loud again.

"If you're done joking around then, Moon Halter, and if the two of you are alright," Eva said, getting nods from Angelica and Diana, "then let's get back to work and finalize the plans for the Solstice Celebration."

Moon Halter's eyes looked suddenly old as she watched Angelica. She turned to Eva, whose eyes looked similarly old, and smiled a tight smile. Eva smiled back the same way, nodding. The smile meant, 'This is a problem. We need to watch it.'

"You speak dragon?" Madeleine finally asked, incredulous.

"No," Moon Halter answered, laughing again. "I just say what appears in my mind. Maybe I understand them intuitively, I don't know. But the words just show up, and I say them."

There were no further incidents with the dragon in the days leading up to the Solstice Celebration.

Two weeks earlier Angelica had been assigned to clean up in the Formal Garden, with several others. Paths were to be cleaned and weeded and made smooth for bare feet. The fountain had to be cleaned, the flowers mulched, shrubs and flowering bushes trimmed. Grass had to be mowed.

When that was done, there was special attention to be paid to the Sunken Garden. The Sunken Garden was about 5 feet deep, with huge flagstones set for the floor, and stacked flagstones for the walls, forming a rectangular enclosure, laid out in the divine proportion, about a half-acre in size. There was a broad flagstone stair that descended into the garden from the south and was overhung with flowering bushes. Directly opposite the stairs was a spring, which filled a stone lined pool near the north wall. Close enough to reach, a clay goblet was left always in a niche. It was called simply The Well, and the spring that fed it had never gone dry.

The Sunken Garden was to be completely cleaned, the weeds and grass pulled from between the flagstones, the walls swept clean of leaves and spider webs, each floor stone washed and dried singly and immediately, to keep the spring water clean of contaminants. Then the Well water was bucketed out and the walls and bottom brushed. It was not deep, and took no more than an hour to refill. This was how Angelica came to know this was where the people would gather. But she didn't know what would happen there.

West of, and next to, the spring was a flat topped limestone boulder, called the Table Rock, or, rather formally, the Rock of the Table. It emerged from the wall and ended near the center of the enclosure.

In the northwest corner was a small beehive fireplace made of stacked stone. At strategic places holes had been drilled in the floor to erect supports for a canopy, or torches on poles. In the southeast corner was a stone bench, a long single flag of stone set in the wall like a shelf. Angelica knew the fireplace and the stairs and the bench had names but she didn't know what they were.

One evening Angelica stayed late, sitting on the bench, waiting for the fireflies to come out. As dusk deepened, the lights emerged from all around her, countless lights, so many that the tree tops were soon full. Millions of lights lingered at lower levels, filling the bushes over the stairs with so much light it illumined the steps themselves, and made the mica in the rock sparkle. The sense of magic about the place was overwhelming. She sat late, until her sense that she could breathe, and keep her head above the waters of feeling, returned.

34

THE HIDDEN LANDS

One day, She Who Is The Mind Of All Life On The Planet—that is, Mother—showed up in the Hidden Lands to visit, nominally, Her Grandchildren. She was also trying to be discreet, checking in on Alam and one of her other surviving daughters, Brighid, to see how they were all getting along, particularly in Calley's absence.

Moms can grow to be concerned about these issues and her daughters, particularly when the mate of one daughter is having sex with the other daughter. And the first daughter's children are in the picture. Many are the tragic tales of a son killing his father, even among the so-called Gods.

But their son, Balan, was pretty settled about the whole thing. His Mom loved His Dad. His Dad loved His Mom. The Sisters loved each other, and everything had been worked out and agreed to by the three of Them. This left Peace in His home, which, it turned out, was all He really wanted from his Parents. Honestly, to Him, it was simply a more matured version of the desires He had as a child: Domestic Tranquility, Peace, and Family level Bliss, even.

Then again, He was a demi-god, in the old way these things were measured. He expected it of Himself that He should take the larger view of things.

The Girls, Brighid's Nieces, were a little less easy-going. Torey, in particular, was angry that Her Grandmother had instructed Her Mother to move away. The two of Them had been accustomed to roaming and storming in the Highlands together. They would occasionally confound some shepherd together, laughing at his cursing and his prayers. Only a few times, in the hundreds of years They went storming together, were there those who remembered Them. The shepherds were rewarded, of course, but not at the level of reward that Calley had bestowed on Alam.

So, Grandmother would take the time to roam the hills with Torey. She did not have the same compunctions Calley did, so She would facilitate seductions of tourists and hikers, and the occasional farm hand out alone checking the pastures. Torey particularly rewarded the young man who tended the last shrine to Calley, moving stones into and out of the house twice a year. She had thought to reward him there, far back in the Highlands, but then thought better of it. Instead, She would meet him in the village at the pub, and pretend to be a tourist from the Lowlands out for a lark.

She knew how to seduce men, alternating between modesty and invitation in a way that he found irresistible. They would leave the pub together, arm in arm, a mystery to the other pub goers. If he found it odd that She would only have sex with him outside he never complained. She told him once that She needed the air, and he nodded as if he understood. They would make love in the alley behind the pub, or out in the park on a bench or table, or on the grass. If it was raining She might take him to a pavilion under the great trees in the center of the park. When She came, Her great drenching orgasms made him happy they were outside, and happy that he did not have to do any laundry because of it.

Grandmother approved these forays into the mortal world. She knew that, in time, Torey would find satisfaction, and even a mate if she wanted, though Torey's fierceness might be problematic. And, in time, perhaps, Torey would settle in some way, but it was always going to be Her Fate, as it had been Her Mother's, to roam the hills. Grandmother did not see Torey wanting to escape Her Fate, like Her Mother Calley did.

The extraordinariness of the way Calley had conducted Herself, the strength of Her desire to escape Her Destiny, is what lent Grandmother the insight to send Her Daughter on a Mission in the first place. She could be trusted to be what She actually was, wherever She was: The Storm.

And, She, Grandmother, had actually, out of consideration one might suppose, provided a Consort for Her Daughter's relief. Alam and the Wind from the East might meet someday. Grandmother wanted to make sure that there would be no backlash, and no stupid jealousy-based behaviors on the part of the Mortal.

Even though The Winds could be unpredictable, it was certain they would blow.

As for the Younger Daughter, Maray, Grandmother also had to spend some time with Her. The Girl disliked the taking of Life that Her Rulership of the storms over the Seas demanded. The Titanic sinking, though not quite in her sphere of Responsibility and Influence, was particularly hard on Her.

Her Grandmother reminded Her repeatedly that all things must die. It took the Girl a long time to understand the idea of Risk. There weren't many Risks for Immortals. There were many Risks for mortals.

Daring to adventure, the taking of a Risk, was often tied to the idea of Risking Death. It was in the Nature of things. It was in Grandmother's Nature, and was as inescapable as Gravity. It helped to weed out the stupid.

It only required that Grandmother reveal Her Power a little bit once. In the end She told Her Granddaughter, "You must understand. I AM You. There is no one here who is not an Invader who is Not Me. You ARE ME."

The Girl decided that She would take Her Time letting this understanding sink into Her. Nevertheless, Her Grandmother took Her out Hunting one night. She initiated Her into the taste of Blood from a man crushed by a falling mast before the boat sank. She initiated Her Granddaughter into the howling wail of the Goddess at Sea, the sustained keening of Her song. She taught Her Granddaughter how to feed upon the fear of the dying, and how to bless those who, for whatever reason, whether they Remembered Her or not, deserved to Live.

Stupidity is not a substitute for Luck.

Maray touched a very primitive part of Herself that night. She came to understand the taste of blood. She came to understand what it meant to be Merciless, and, if She so chose, to also hold within Herself Pity and Compassion at the same time. Nature's Laws, her Grandmother's Laws, were implacable, and based on a deeper and older set of Laws that comprised the Inevitable.

She came to understand that Fate was both Inevitable and Immutable. Destiny also was Inevitable but the outcome was not certain; how Destiny unfolded could be changed—it was mutable. And then there was Choice. It baffled Her how, even with the limited foresight of mortals, they would choose the stupid and foolish. Not anticipating the forces of unintended consequence, they would find themselves then trapped by Fate.

Sometimes an outcome could be changed by placation; something that floated a man in the water. But placation required extraordinary sacrifice at times, or an almost unimaginable amount of work. Sometimes Maray would be required to not only witness this application, but enforce the application of the Laws; sometimes She would even be required to cause an incident that led to the invocation of the Laws.

Mortals can't breathe water. It was in watching the Ocean take the body that She came to make the acquaintance of an distant Aunt of Hers. Since She had Her Mother's ability to go underwater, a crossing of boundaries rarely permitted to anyone who had ever lived—sky and water are separate—she followed the drowning man down to watch his suffering as he died. Her Compassion led Her to appear before him naked as his final sight. When She finished She heard a voice say, in mock seriousness, "Hey, that's my responsibility!"

And then the voice said, "I'm a distant relation. That was well done. Many are drowning tonight. Would you care to help with the work?"

Maray could not identify the source of the voice. That made Her feel suspicious, so She shook Her head negatively and ascended from the water. She realized She also felt embarrassment for some reason She couldn't explain. It took a while for Her to overcome it and cross a boundary between worlds; to venture back below the surface again.

To be fair, Grandmother took all Her Grandchildren hunting. It was how Calley had found Alam. And She, Grandmother, was disposed to help in the Work of him creating his relative immortality. She liked him.

Everything had to be paid for; the Forces of Nature, the Gods, and the People, must be kept in balance. It was the job of a Priestess of the Great Mother. Her Grandchildren knew it. It remained, eventually, only to find She to whom Balan, Her Grandson, could relate to as a Consort.

As it turned out, Balan, on his own, met the woman Himself. He was pulling a stranded cow out of a damp bog when she happened along, driving a pony wagon on her way to a high pasture to deliver lunch for the men building a stone fence. She had a shovel in the back of the cart and got out to use it alongside Balan, getting in the mud up to her knees. His attraction was immediate, as was His admiration. He was grateful He had not been in His bull form.

Grandmother warned Him of the risks of becoming entangled with mortals. He said He understood them and would develop a plan to deal with those problems, some of which would inevitably arise. In His mind He envisioned fabricating a departure, along the lines of being pressed or drafted into some army or another. In the meantime, He wanted to begin His practice of Devotion, understanding that a part of His Devotion was to behave in such a way as to avoid breaking the heart of His beloved.

Perhaps later He would ask his Grandmother for help in finding someone whose durability was more like His. She had never con-firmed the existence of such a person, but nor would She deny it, sitting there, smiling mysteriously at Him when He had asked once.

Once Grandmother had finished bringing each of Them into their Natures, the children matured to the point where each could fully take on the burdens of one part of their Mother's duties. They became comfortable in the duties, although they were somewhat more com-fortable in adopting the shapes They had inherited from their father. They also adopted some of his Gentleness and Kindness—hence

Balan's helping the cow out of the bog. He and the girl saved the cow, at least temporarily, from implacable Nature.

One day when all the young people were out in their respective territories and Alam was alone at home in the Hidden Land, he felt a chill. A darkness, a Shadow fell over his workshop while he was making a chair.

It was unusual for the weather to change so suddenly in the Hidden Land, and he thought to venture outside and take a look. At the thought, the chill went deeper and he suddenly became afraid to move, afraid that the slightest motion would reveal his presence. He could barely allow himself to breathe. The chill moved past him and he went to the window and looked.

He saw two winged beings standing in the yard talking to each other, one light, one dark. He knew them for what they were, knew them from the descriptions of Brighid and Her Mother. He knew they were Embla and Dangla, and both were creations of De Murgos. He could hear them speaking.

The Embla said, in a voice resonant enough to make Alam tremble, "Father has woken from the long dream. In it He saw the path this world is taking. He is losing interest in it, and He is thinking of leaving, letting it fester and brew, perhaps to return to feed again."

"Then why are we here?" the Dangla asked.

"Trouble. Something is working to change the mix. He thinks it will originate near here, but will manifest in the mountains of the Western Lands. He's waiting for the place to show up clearly, He has a plan and is waiting to be led to the place. The Bodhisattva He cut off has disappeared, and our trackers can't find him."

"Ah," the Dangla said. "We should just leave the poor bastard alone."

"That is His plan," the Embla said, with a hint of exasperation.

"You know what I mean. Don't play the adherent fool," the Dangla hissed.

"He wants us both to look for it together. You see differently than I do."

"And if I find it, what then? What will He do for me?"

"He will take you with us when we go, rather than leave you here, probably to starve to death."

"Not just me. He must take all of us."

"That would be the plan. So, tell me, what do you see?"

"Other than these endless hills, denuded of forest, its people gone and killed off, rubbed out, replaced by interlopers and their stupid sheep?"

"Yes," said the Embla, making a mockery of patience.

The Dangla closed his eyes. When he opened them again his face changed, his aspect grew horrid and fangs showed when he opened his mouth to breathe. He scanned the hills, turning slowly in place. He looked right over the houses and buildings of the Hidden Lands, unseeing.

"There," he said, pointing north, further into the mountains. "There is a thin column of light rising up."

"Then let's go," the Embla said. They walked a few paces, walking through the compound wall as if it wasn't there, then took a few quick steps and flew off.

Alam breathed, and then breathed deeply. "The Hidden Lands, the invisibility, held," he said aloud.

Then he said, "Agents of De Murgos standing in the yard." He sent a call of warning to his children, sending the alarm sound to each along the ground so only those of each kind could hear it. He was certain that the Embla and the Dangla would ignore the sound, even if they heard it.

Maray was posing for a painter on the coast, pretending to walk down the beach, looking out to sea. She was thinking about seducing him by allowing him to think he was seducing Her. She felt the alarm call in her horses and went still, smelling the airs for a threat.

Balan grunted and turned slowly to face home.

Torey, hiding behind a large rock outcropping near the Last Shrine, was watching the mortal move the rocks around, changing their configuration. She wasn't sure what he was doing.

That was why She saw the Embla and Dangla flying toward them. Then she felt the bleat of Her kind when afraid. She turned into her Ram immediately.

The Beings shifted phase, and became invisible except for their outlines in Torey's eyes. The mortal man saw nothing, and felt nothing when they landed next to him, continuing to move the rocks around.

"What is he doing?" the Embla asked.

"Playing some game," the Dangla answered. "He is thinking about his family."

"We saw two mortals here before we landed. Where is the other one?"

"There, behind those rocks," the Dangla said. He squinted at the rocks, trying to see the life behind them. "Not human," he said. "Sheep."

The Embla rose up into the air and looked. He saw only a large ram lying in the shade, chewing cud.

Turning around in the air the Embla said, "There's nothing but a fool playing house with stones." Then he vanished.

The Dangla, squatted down, watching the man. The Dangla could no longer see the light that had drawn them there. From the man he felt only love, which disgusted him. He, too, vanished, leaving only a sour smell that made the man stand up and sniff the air.

Torey's siblings and father had been standing frozen, feeling the terror She had been masking. They moved, and they all heard their father's voice, calling them Home. When Torey arrived Alam asked Her to summon Her Aunt Brighid.

Torey sang Brighid's wind song. She appeared, sitting in the chair that Alam was still holding. It startled Alam and made Her Laugh.

He set the chair down and said, "Agents of De Murgos were here."

The other Children arrived soon thereafter, changing form, standing still with questions and fear in their hearts.

"An Embla and a Dangla were here," Torey told her siblings.

"Here?" Balan asked, incredulous.

"Here in the yard," Alam confirmed.

"And they were at the Shrine," Torey added.

"I have called Mother. She is coming," Brighid said.

Mother emerged from the earth in the yard, a circlet of silver with a knot pattern in the middle on Her forehead. She wore the black and red cape over a deep green gown, so deep as to be almost black itself. Her arms were straight out from Her sides, dark hair suspended in the air. When the sun fell on Her dark skin, it turned a copper color.

Emerging fully from the Earth, She hung there with Her eyes closed. After a moment, Her eyes snapped open and She snorted. "Pah, the stinks of De Murgos," She said.

"They stood right there and didn't see me," Alam said.

Mother smiled. "The Hidden Lands remain hidden. I thought they would pass the test. They went to the Shrine, then, did they?"

"Yes," Torey answered, suddenly visibly shaken.

"Come here, child," Mother said. Torey went to Her Grandmother, and was enfolded in Her arms.

"I heard them talk," Alam said. "They're going to look next in the West. We have to warn Her. We have to warn Calley."

"Tell me everything you heard," Mother said.

When Calley felt Mother's call She disengaged Herself from the Wind's embrace and rose to the surface, now covered in water lilies. She rose to just above the surface, and sat, a lotus above the lilies. The East Wind emerged from the water and lay on the bank of the pond in the sun, letting it pour over His bronze colored skin. When He smiled at Calley She smiled back and dropped one foot, putting a toe in the water. She raised a hand to the sky.

Her family saw Her there, suspended over the beautiful water, pale and wearing only her long hair. She smiled hugely to see them there, and beckoned Alam to come close. She leaned toward him and kissed him on the lips. There was no concealing his delight.

Brighid stood and went to Her Sister's side, taking Her hand. Mother moved toward them and took their free hands. They formed a silent triangle, the image of them pulsing in the eyes of the rest of the family. Love pulsed with Them.

After a moment, Mother released Her Daughters' hands. The family was happy and calm again.

"Here is what We must do. We have a good shield. I will divide the Hidden Lands, and give a section to Calley. You, Alam, will go with it. Brighid will stay here with my Grandchildren," Mother said. "You all have work to do here."

Brighid and Calley nodded their assent, and, as Calley faded from sight They heard Her whisper, "I love you," smiling at them all.

"Well, then," Mother said. "Alam, pack what you wish to take. You'll leave when it's dark. And we should eat together now." To the children She said, "It will be some time before you see your father again."

They ate in the dining hall, fresh summer greens and a lamb stew. The feelings during the meal alternated between joy at the victory of remaining unseen and the sadness of imminent departure.

When they were done, they all went outside into the evening. Alam brought a bag with some favorite tools and his favorite clothes, boots, and cape. They all passed through the gate and turned and looked back at the compound. On the way, Mother told Alam what to tell Calley.

"Tell Her that the Bodhisattva is the key. The invader cut him off, and now they can't find him. For now, he is in hiding at the College. But they have trackers looking for him."

Then Mother raised Her hands and said the word, "Push." The wall with the gate in it slid back toward the house. When about two acres were free of the compound wall, She changed the position of Her hands, and said, "Lift." The free land did, hovering about two feet off the newly bare ground.

Alam hugged Brighid, kissed Her, and said something in Her ear that made Her laugh. He hugged his children, and then turned and bowed to Mother. He threw his bag up onto the land and hopped up. He looked at his smiling family. Holding his hands over his heart he bowed again. He shifted into wolf form then, and laid down, tongue lolling, still smiling.

"Go to Calley," Mother said, and the land moved slowly off, hugging the ground, crested over the mountain, and was gone.

35

INITIATION

Deep under the Mansion, the original builders had included cisterns in the design. They were accessible through wooden panels set in the basement floor. In one case, a door had been set in a wall that led down a set of steps to a store room. There was large cistern further back set in the subfloor.

Four natural rock walls, three feet thick, some ancient layering of limestone separated by twenty to thirty feet of distance, blown vertical by some volcano, ran under the Mansion and formed the basic bedrock walls that divided the space into three large compartments. The builders had dug down to find the walls, following them back from their exposure through the side of the hill, and excavated the dirt from between them.

Masons had bricked and mortared the original cisterns to slow water loss. These cisterns had been designed to be filled with run-off collected from downspouts and brick courtyards. In later years the landscape had been altered by diverting a small stream to the Mansion, running it into pipes that would carry the stream water to the cisterns. A valve in the pipe controlled the flow.

Originally, water was carried to the kitchen by bucket, hence the relatively easy access to the cisterns. Later, hand pumps were added. The cisterns were covered originally by wooden lids. These were replaced by heavy concrete lids that could be moved aside to create access for cleaning and repair. On top of these lids there were smaller hatches for bucket access.

Rachel had always been fascinated by the cisterns, even as a child. It had been a long time since they had been used to provide domestic water. Pumps, windmills, and electricity had put an end to that. The pipes leading from the streams as well as the collection channels were all blocked or had been removed.

She played in the cisterns when she could escape her parents' watchful eyes. She would climb down in, pull the access door shut and sit in the dark, waiting to see what she would see. It seemed to her that she could see lights appear in the space before her. Sometimes the lights would just move through. Other times the lights would collect and dance. Soon she noticed that she could see her own body as a pale electric blue form.

She became conscious of her heartbeat, and then of her heartbeat's echo. As the echo travelled back to her she began to hear her heartbeat in her breath. From there it was an easy thing to bring that pulsation into her mouth, and then to her lips. Eventually she could move the sensation of that heartbeat anywhere in her body. She learned to run this second heart at a different pace from her first heart.

When the wandering heartbeat found her sex, the world changed for her. The release of energies she experienced was almost overwhelming. Learning to move the energies required the development of both attention and the power of intention. Learning to control that movement was the most challenging experience of her life to that point.

She was twelve when she experienced the release of the energetic vortex at the base of the spine, under pressure from the increasing power of that second heartbeat. The experience was debilitating, but not incapacitating, for her. The barrier normally took time to harden as a child grew, crystallizing over the course of adolescence. It had not yet had time to crystallize completely in her young body. It did, however, make her ill with nausea and fevers for several days.

She had nightmares about what she called 'what goes on behind the scenes.' She developed certain powers about which, she realized, she should say nothing. She could feel what someone else was feeling. Eventually, this evolved into the power to know what someone was thinking—she had only to resonate with them. In addition, she could place an illusion in someone's mind. She could activate the second heartbeat, the one she came to call the Higher Heart, in another person by touching them, although it would fade away when she removed her hand.

She became a highly sexualized human being, learning to orgasm not just from masturbation, but simply by directing the energies to any one of her several centers of sensation and feeling. The orgasms of her spine and the top of her head became her favorites.

By the time she went away to boarding school at fourteen, she was recovered from all traces of the debility from the original vortex release. Her energetics were under control. For a couple of years, she wanted to be like the other girls and did not show her abilities to anyone. Or talk about them. She used them with the horses the school kept for riding lessons, however. She projected the image of what she wanted a horse to do into its mind. It made training a lot faster, which explained the ease with which she organized the horse circus that led to her return home.

Back home she spent considerable time in the cisterns, reflecting— far-seeing, as she called it—and honing the motion of the Higher Heart. Then, in an effort to please her parents, she went to a women's college for a year. Realizing that she already knew everything they were teaching, she became filled with the longing to learn what she didn't know. She didn't know what she was, this Resonator of the Higher Heart. She didn't know that what she was doing was called the Path of Solitary Cultivation.

She read extensively in esoteric literature looking for indications, even hints in metaphor, for anything that described what she had become. She found very little, but what she did find indicated that very little was known in the West. She made up her mind to travel, seeking out wisdom in those places whose texts contained what she believed were references. She spent a long time in Keyna, Waitan and on the Windian sub-continent studying with masters of various disciplines.

When she returned home for good, she returned to the cisterns where she was given the Vision of what to do at Stonehaven.

While laying out the plan for the Order of the Fleur de Vie, she decided that there needed to be different threshold experiences marking the transitions from one level of training, power, and authority to the next. There was to be a preliminary initiatory experience when one took the Vows of Internship. That was when someone committed to working on themselves in the ways that were indicated to them in the yogas, tantras, and alchemy. The Vows included a commitment to keep what they were doing secret from the outside world.

These vows were made in an induced trance state where the prohibition on speaking to outsiders was so deep it became almost impossible to speak about that concerning which nothing should be spoken. The Feminine Interns who took these vows were infused with the presence of the Divine Feminine, who placed a seal of silence upon them from within. The Masculine Interns were given a vision of the same energy, and the same seal was placed on them, but from the outside rather than within.

There were also to be initiatory experiences for completing the transition from Intern to Priestess or Consort, and another for transition to High Priestess and High Consort.

For the second initiation, from Intern to Priestess or Consort, she had the central cistern deconstructed and excavated from rock wall to rock wall. She had the foundations buttressed on the front and back, and covered the buttresses with dirt and rock. The space was entered through an access panel hidden in the floor of what had been the gun powder room with its iron door.

The initiate would enter the room through that heavy black iron door, where the Madeleines waited for them. They were told to remove their clothes and given a blanket in exchange. They were given a strong and bitter drink, and were handed a bucket and a gallon of water. They had to step through the panel in the floor and climb down a ladder to the dirt floor below. The ladder was removed and the panel closed and latched.

It was the last sound. There was no light.

The initiate was to remain in the grotto, as Rachel called it, for four days. The bitter drink was from a recipe that Rachel had brought back from her travels and relied heavily on psychotropic mushrooms.

The initiate was instructed that the purpose of the ceremony was for them to seek and find the face of the Goddess upon which they would focus their devotions. The ceremony was an opportunity for the initiate to work in a more concentrated way to establish the resonance of the Higher Heart and to release more of the Kundalini barrier that hindered their being.

There were also snakes.

The snakes of Snakes Knob were carefully cultivated by a select few of the High Priestesses and Consorts. Mice were bred in one of the Lab buildings, carted out to the Knob, and released in the rocks. The copperheads and rattlers were kept away, usually, by the bull snakes and the black snakes. Some black snakes were kept captive for the season, and then released, well fed, on the Knob before it was time to hibernate.

The dirt on the floor in the grotto was seeded with mouse feces and urine. The snakes were put in through little tunnels that Rachel had built into the buttressing of the foundation.

What happened when the snakes were released into the grotto was unpredictable. Some initiates were never aware that there were snakes in the room. Others discovered the snakes when they rolled over in their sleep as the snakes had drawn close for the warmth. Sometimes someone was bitten, but never fatally. The snakes weren't poisonous. Occasionally someone would tame a snake and emerge with it wrapped around an arm, or snuggled in the blanket, and rarely some terrified initiate would kill a snake, beating it against the rock walls. But there were lots of snakes.

When the Initiate emerged, they were given new robes, a white inner robe with a deep blue robe to go over it. Once fed, bathed, and any bites medicated, the new Priestess or Consort would meet with the Madeleines and be tested for conscious awareness of the resonance of the Higher Heart. They were also tested for the existence of any of the standard Siddhi Powers, such as precognition, telepathy, clairvoyance and clairaudience, clairsentience, bilocation and invisibility, materialization, telekinesis and teleportation, healing powers, and even levitation. Many showed potential in more than one power.

Not everyone showed signs of these powers, nascent or otherwise, but most showed signs of some power. The experience left them something to develop and focus on in the yogic and tantric work as they cultivated their relationships with the Divine Feminine. Almost all made progress in overcoming some aspects of the barrier and in manifesting the Higher Heart. The terror caused by the snakes was effective.

The next period of years was devoted to development and the Practices. There were three sets of duties for the Priestesses and Consorts. The first duty was the Daily Practice which consisted of five processes: Devotions, Meditations, Prayers, Illuminations, and Blessings.

The second set of duties consisted of the required work on oneself. For the Soma there was exercise, martial training, and yogas. For the Soul there was the work required to accept assignments that led to the alchemical sublimation of lower emotions and the re-emergence of that energy as higher emotions, especially with regard to the tantra of the sacred dances and the ecstasy that came from the tantra generally. For the Spirit, there was instruction in theory, the exercises in the development of the siddhi powers, and the requirement that everyone learn to play some kind of music.

The third set of duties was the requirement that everyone periodically return to life in the outer world and perform these prior sets of duties while immersed there.

Some Priestesses and Consorts were content to spend their entire lives with remaining as they were, fulfilling their duties. For others, when it was time, a sign would be given to the Madeleine and a person would become eligible for the initiation into the role of High Priestess or High Consort.

The initiations of a High Priestess and a High Consort were a different matter. Rachel and Madeleine had the storage space around the third cistern under the west end of the Mansion excavated and turned into a small throne room. The old wooden lid was replaced by a concrete slab that could be slid part way open and closed with weights and counterweights on pulleys. Inside the cistern, a set of steps was built along the circular wall leading to a sandy floor.

Rachel and Madeleine worked out the details, modeling the initiation on the legends of the descents of ancient Goddesses. They knew that the experience had to be both psychically, and psychologically, profound and productive of permanent imprint. It had to include options and inevitabilities, or at least the illusion of options and inevitabilities, so striking that the Soul would remember them forever. The commitments made would bind the Soul for life. And for Life.

Rachel applied her knowledge of shamanic and tantric chemistries to force the initiate onto the road of ecstasis, taking the initiate 'out of their mind' and into their Spirit. Their Spirit would then be taken to the world behind the world, out past the world of dreams.

They practiced together, Rachel and Madeleine, with help from Craft. Eventually, they also had help from Beverly and Paul. Careful notes were taken, and a script created that all the participants were to follow.

Rachel went first. She had to know the herbal mixture was just right. Being in the cistern was like going home to her. She had a great time. She successfully concluded negotiations with the faces of the Goddess that were appropriate to the script. Then she broke free and spent a lovely few days in meditation, both active and passive, observing the world around her as it passed by in the subterranean darkness. Alternately, she dissolved her awareness in the great Pool of Sentience.

Madeleine went next, and she also had a great time. She ended up in a hilarious conversation with the Goddess of Death. The two visited with each other like they were the best of friends.

Regina continued to work both with her solitary practices and her dual path cultivation assignments with Craft. Her own lover had not yet arrived, but it had been determined that a grandson of one of the Members of the High Council had been prepared by instruction since an early age. When told about Stonehaven he was fascinated. He was willing to take off from college to serve an Internship for a year. He would arrive the following winter after the holidays.

Regina's Initiation to the level of the functions of Priestess became necessary not long after the rituals were created. In this way, when the young man arrived, Regina would be practiced in the duties and comfortable with the appropriate power differential over him. She would be able to teach him the ways of Stonehaven, and educate him in the ways of the Consort. After a period of practice with him, she would be ready for the next level.

Given that her main siddhi power was the power to create illusion in the mind of another, there was a high degree of certainty that the young man would become entranced. The power itself was problematic, however. Regina struggled a little with self-discipline in this regard, with several illusionary tricks being played on the older adults. These were always caught and confessed to, often with laughter. But, the extent of her power, and its capacity for abuse, required Regina to develop a Conscience about when to use the power, and to practice the highest possible degree of spiritual self-effacement and humility. It was this destruction of the ego that allowed her to enter into the highest states of union with the ultimate face of the Divine Feminine.

It was thought wise, after several months of practice with her Intern, to bring Regina farther along. Rachel was expecting a cousin of the young man to arrive at the beginning of summer. Since Regina would be the primary trainer of both of these men in the ways of the Consort, it was believed that she would need the higher level of internal organization and energetic awareness afforded by the second initiation experience.

Another couple, unrelated to the young men but the adult children of another Council member would be joining as Interns at the same time. Since the extent of their ability to function sexually apart from each other and still remain true to the path was unknown, Rachel and Madeleine believed that the enhancement in authority would make it easier for Regina to control the situation. If Regina could model appropriate behavior, at least according the Order's standards, then the couple would be more likely to try to emulate it.

Since they were an already married couple, the training would have to be adaptable to their possible need to remain in a relationship exclusive of sexuality with others. They understood that as a ritual behavior this exclusivity was not the norm during their education, but they would be free to return to it, if they chose, when their training ended. The hypnagogic power of the Ecstasies was a power to compel people to return to the Well to drink again. Regina would need the young men in order to model the tantra for the couple.

In time, young wen would also come. Rachel had cultivated a network of contacts among faculty at wen's colleges. They knew of her vision, and the purpose of Stonehaven as a college to train Priestesses for the return of the Divine Feminine, and would, in time, all of them, join the work at Stonehaven. These contacts were asked to be observant, identifying the ones that were different, the loners and the disaffected, the passionate ones, and the artists. After getting to know them, discussing their openness to the idea of the Divine Feminine, some were recommended to apply for Internship. So skillful were the observations, and so engrossing the training, no one ever left or betrayed the Order.

When Regina's time came—the same vision came to both Madeleine and her on the same night—she began her meditative preparations. Her time was spent in devotional and tantric activity. She wanted to remember this world with a longing to return to it.

Two days before the ceremony she commenced a water-only fast, preparing her Soma, Soul, and Spirit for a trial she wished to face with equanimity, while also remaining empty, a vessel into which wisdom and power could be poured.

Late in the afternoon of Regina's descent, Madeleine appeared at Regina's door dressed in the finery and jewelry of an ancient age. Regina rose naked from her bed, where she and her soon-to-be Consort had been languidly practicing handwork. He rose from the bed, still naked and erect when Regina did. He bowed.

Madeleine waved away the bow and smiled. "It is time to prepare. Walter, stay. You can help."

Madeleine made a motion over her shoulder and Craft entered with a wealth of materials and cloth for draping laid over his arms. He placed everything on the bed and stepped back out in the hall returning with a suitcase which he set on the floor. He smiled at Regina and Walter. He nodded his head at them both and left the room, leaving the door open.

Madeleine clothed Regina in long drapings of transparent cloths, securing them with sashes or clasps. Walter brushed her hair from behind. The constant swish of exquisite fabrics across his phallus kept him hard. Once, when Madeleine came around behind Regina, Madeleine smiled and carefully pushed it out of the way.

When she was dressed, Regina backed up to Walter sliding his erection between her thighs. Madeleine laughed out loud, and told her to sit down. Madeleine applied makeup so stylistically as to give Regina the mien of a different wen, majestic in her sovereignty. She then did the jewelry: a girdle of delicate chain from which hung two strings of small bells that chimed high and sweetly as she moved, necklaces of fine stones, rings that hung over the ears on golden wire, from which hung tiny mirrored plates. There were rings for her hands. Finally, a headpiece: a temple dancer's crown with highly polished tiny metal plates suspended from the brow on thin strings, giving the appearance of a veil.

When she was finished, Madeleine stood back. Regina stood up and turned around. Walter gasped and went to one knee. Reaching out, he took her hands, and kissed them. Regina rewarded him with a brilliant smile. Madeleine bid her to walk out into the hall. She walked slowly, feeling every exquisite brush of the fabric against her breasts, and belly, and thighs.

Madeleine called her name and asked her to turn around. Walter, erect all this time, was standing next to her, staring down at his red phallus, his face reddening now as well. Madeleine was walking her finger tips gently and supportively back and forth along its underside. Madeleine was smiling at Regina in such a peculiar and lewd way that Regina had to laugh out loud.

Madeleine left the room, leaving Walter blushing and grinning at the same time. The wen both looked over their shoulders at him and flashed a grin back at him. Regina said, "I will see you soon."

Walter replied, "I'll be here when you return."

Madeleine took Regina's hand, leading her from her room to the stairwell on the west end of the Mansion. They descended the stairs, first through the ground floor and then down to the basement level. The stairs ended in a small platform with a door in a built-out wall. Regina had always assumed it was a closet.

"Wait here," Madeleine said. "Count to 100 slowly, then come through this door. There's a door immediately to your right. Knock on it. If I don't answer, knock on it again." Madeleine smiled, opened the narrow door, stepped through into the darkness and closed it behind her.

Regina could hear the creak of a wooden floor and the sound of another door opening, then the strike of a match. Then she heard the other door close. She strained to hear everything, taking warning from everything, because suddenly under her feeling of anticipation she felt a first ribbon of fear. She regained her sense of calm by thinking about how beautiful she must look; Walter, lovely Walter, erect all that time. How beautiful he looked.

Then she realized she'd forgotten to count. Searching her memory she tried to assign time values to her thoughts and found it hopeless. She didn't think she'd been standing there a minute, so she started with the number fifty. Remembering the fear had caused it to come to the surface again, rising from low in her belly and stopping at the level of her navel. Holding it there by an act of will required so much concentration that it made her start to sweat. At the count of eighty a bead ran down her nose from her forehead. She caught it with her tongue and swallowed, salt, memory.

It was time. She stepped through the first door, closing it softly behind her. A candle had been lit in a sconce on the wall. She turned and faced the other door. Smaller, painted with a sign that Regina recognized as an outline of the Fleur di Vie. She took a deep breath and knocked. There was no answer.

She knocked again. She heard a voice say, "Enter." She opened the door and looked down a flight of stairs, narrow at the top and widening when it descended below the level of the basement floor lit by more candles in sconces. Standing on the first wide step were two forms in black that were so disconcerting that she shook her head to clear it. The forms had no features; she realized they wore cylindrical hoods, with mesh face masks so dense she could not see through to the faces she knew must be underneath.

"Close the door," she was told by one. Then, "Descend," by the other. When she reached the wider step on which they stood she was told to "Stop." Then she recognized them as Madeleine and Craft by their voices and their forms draped in black.

They removed her headpiece and set it down on the step behind her. She was told "Step," by one, and as she stepped they both stepped with her, sideways. The other told her, "Stop." At this second step they removed her earrings.

And so it continued, stepping and stopping, with something being taken from her on each step. The third step was the necklace. On the fourth step they took her rings. On the fifth they took her girdle. On the sixth, one of them reached up and removed the clasp on her shoulder that held her clothes in place. They slid to the floor and she stepped out of them. On the last step they unpinned her hair and it fell in a twist to one shoulder.

A rough hand grabbed her at the base of her skull, twisting its fingers into her hair and forcing her to bend forward at the waist. The hand walked her, guided her, to a throne on which a goddess sat. It looked like a moving, breathing Goddess, but the face was frozen: another mask.

She was forced to her knees. Her face was held up for the Goddess and the initiate to gaze upon each other. Regina then saw a large black snake slide from under the robes of the enthroned one, and crawl across the floor. It slid behind the throne. Her belly tightened with fear. She closed her eyes and moaned, remembering her first initiation. She heard a sudden squeaking and she realized it was a panicked mouse. Suddenly the sound was gone, and all was quiet.

"Open your eyes, child," the Mask said, in a voice she knew to be Rachel's but in her ears it sounded changed. It was changed by the presence of the Goddess within: She Who Comes. Rachel had shown Her face to Regina many times.

A large wooden chalice appeared in front of her. "Drink. Drink all of this," she was commanded by the Mask. Pulled upright, still on her knees, she did. The bitterness of it almost too much. She looked around, glancing at the Goddess, the walls lit with candles and painted with the Fleur de Vie, glowing pinkly in the light. At the end of the drink the hand holding the chalice forced the last bit on her, upending the cup and spilling some down her chin and onto her breasts. The rough hand at her neck forced her head down again.

The Mask spoke, "Existence is suffering. All is suffering. You will hang on meat hooks in Hell to answer for it, and to understand it. You will forgive Life for creating the inevitability of suffering. Life feeds on Death, Death feeds on Life. I am Life, you are here to meet my sister. Death."

While the rough hand held her down she felt the skin on her back between her shoulder blade and spine being pinched out. Then she felt a quick, piercing pain that made her gasp, followed quickly by another that made her shout.

She struggled briefly when she felt the same pinch on the other side. The rough hand held her down. She shouted again, and on the second piercing briefly screamed. She felt something pull at the skin. She realized the piercings were hooks. She could feel blood run down her sides.

She was pulled upright on her knees again and looked at the Mask. It said, "You are hung on meat hooks in the Underworld. You could die on them. What will you choose?"

She was pulled to her feet and forced to turn and walk, the hooks in her back pulled on by someone she couldn't see. She felt the blood run down her back and over her buttocks. She was led to the edge of a dark hole, illumined by a single candle on the far side of the pit, with a step down into it. "Step," she was told.

Then she was given a little push, just enough to make her understand she was to continue to descend.

Then the three voices began to chant, slowly, so there was no doubt about the words.

"That which opens for me closes,
Closes around me.

"That which opens for me closes,
Closes upon me.

"That which opens for me,
Opens."

The chant continued in a round, the next repetition beginning with the second couplet, and a final round beginning with the third. At the bottom step, the hooks were pulled so that she had to back around to the edge of the circular wall. When she was in place, slack came into the line holding her, and she dropped to her knees.

"Lie down," the Goddess commanded through the High Priestess. She did, more slack playing into the line until she was prone. Then the line tugged, and stayed taut. With a deep rumble the lid to the cistern started to roll, slowly closing her in, slowly entombing her where she would meet death.

Just before the lid closed, the voice said, "Remember. You must choose."

Regina sat up and looked around. In the light of the candle on the far side of the cistern she made out the form of two buckets, one filled with water, and the other for waste. She remembered this from her first initiation. She found herself staring at the candle. The candle began to pulse in time to her heartbeat. She realized it was just her pupils dilating and closing.

She tried to sit back against the wall but the hooks were in the way. She hurt herself without thinking and she could feel fresh blood flow. She tried to cross the cistern and couldn't. She was stopped by the hooks pulling at her back. She was caught; all she could do was sit up, or lie down.

She chose to meditate. Shortly after she began, she realized she was starting to hallucinate. With the feeling in her belly and the images parading through her head, she realized meditation was impossible. She opened her eyes, and the images were still there, but she didn't focus on them. Instead she began to focus on what she could see before her.

Lines of energy moved through the cistern. Particles of light flashed, and the color in the room changed. As she looked around she saw a figure hooded in gray, seated to the right of the candle. The candle began to gutter, and terror seized her when she realized that it was going to go out. She would be left in darkness.

Then she remembered practicing seeing in darkness as a child. She remembered the state of mind she'd had at the time and returned to it.

She calmed down. The candle went out.

After a few minutes her eyes adjusted to the darkness and it seemed like the cistern was filled with a faint light, like starlight on a cloudy night. When she moved, the light moved and she realized that the light was coming from her. She closed her eyes again and saw her blue body. When she looked across the cistern with her eyes closed the figure in the gray hood had a blue body but no surrounding outline of white. This meant that the image was not a living body. At least, it wasn't humanly alive.

The body moved. Picking up its head, it let Regina see its face. It was the face of the Hag, the old wen, oily hair hanging around her. She heard it whisper, but couldn't hear what it said. Regina tried to say speak up, but her throat was dry as dust. She could only whisper, also.

The words came out like a breeze over desert sand and took, it seemed, forever to pass her lips. The skull hissed at her, and the gray form disappeared. Regina found her mind staring at lightning on an open prairie, the lightning causing grass fires.

Then she was looking at a world, some dimension where everything was connected by a vibrant green filigree. She heard her mind say, "This is my world."

She decided to practice her siddhi powers. She extended her mind, but there was no one close, no one she could find. Then she projected, looking for Walter, sweet Walter. She found him in his room on the third floor. He was sleeping and somehow still erect, with a smile on his face. She smiled. Then her mind skewed, almost violently, to having rougher sex with him than usual. In her mind, she used him, riding him, drawing power from him, him giving it to her, until she drove him out of mind and into unconsciousness.

The part of her that was suspicious of going so far beyond the gentle motions of the tantra was flooded over. A part of her that reveled in the power. The part that was fed by the power rose up in her and she smiled.

She was assailed by the images, feelings, and sensations of every lover she'd ever had. She was flooded with tactile memories of being touched by lovers whom she'd never met, all at the same time. Her voice became a tangle of groans and screams and sighs.

On her knees, she bent forward, put one hand between her legs and squeezed her breasts with the other. She worked her fingers around the little phallus, separating the lips of the phulva. Wet already, she entered herself with two fingers, stretching herself. Reaching as far into herself as she could, she curled the fingers around and squeezed herself along the inside of that wall. Palming the little man, she squeezed the gland until she started to shake. She stuck out her tongue, panting.

The stroking and caressing sensation became a moving, pulsing pressure that touched her everywhere at once. She filled from the inside with love and satisfaction and pleasure. The groans and screams and sighs became one sound. The blue-white light that filled the room began to pulse with the pressure.

She brought herself, squirting with such force that it pushed her hand out. It made her bend upright and then backwards, raining out onto that dry desert of sand. She worked the little man until she was rained dry. Slowly lying back, bending back over her ankles, she looked across the room again. In the darkness, she saw the gray hooded Hag had returned. It was now grinning toothlessly at her.

She leaned all the way back, resting on her shoulders. When the hooks touched the ground they bent, twisting inside the wound. She shouted, and rolled over on her side. She looked to the old Hag and said, "Why do you smirk at me?"

"I am happy for you," she hissed, like sharp rain falling on a still lake.

Regina got to her knees again and leaned forward until the pain from the hooks in her back made her nauseated. She threw up on the sandy floor. She passed out and fell to her side.

As she fell to her side, in her inner vision, she fell into a hole, rolling down a slope too steep for her to climb back up. A tunnel went off to the side and her choice was to stay where she was or follow the tunnel. A part of her mind knew she was in a visionary trance. Entering the tunnel she recognized the classic elements of shamanic journeying. A new hallucinogen was surging through her.

The journeying took almost two days. Time passed without Regina having any sense of it. On the journey she traversed all the continents, looking everywhere. She met many entities, some not beneficent. She found ways to use her power, the ability to create illusions in the minds of others, to narrowly escape several times. She travelled to the Bardoes again. This time her father, the Lama, was waiting for her on the open air deck. They sat and had tea and conversation under the awning. He taught her all the things about the tantra that she hadn't learned. He showed her power, and the siddhi powers, and taught her how to cultivate all of them. In the end, he blessed her, and she felt their karma end. It ended in freedom for them both.

After that, she found herself at Stonehaven, seeing it as if it were in a different dimension. She looked at Walter, sitting erect, working the internal circulation. There was a silver-white light around him. There were different lights around the other people, too. Some had only one field. Others, like Rachel and Madeleine and Craft, seemed to have different kinds of fields, each coming to the fore at different times. She saw the fields created when they had sex—great, throbbing, heart beat fields.

In one of these visions, it seemed that Rachel saw Regina and spoke to her. Rachel was riding Craft slowly. Craft was sitting up, and Rachel was sitting in his lap with her arms and legs wrapped around him. She could see lines of force, some like meridians, other swirling, in each of them. The lines crossed over into each other. The heartbeat pulsing in the field was visible. When Regina touched it, Rachel raised her head and looked directly at her.

"This is what we do, Regina. This is the field of the Higher Heart. We generate it together, and then it comes to be active in us as individuals. The life we lead then..." Rachel lost her words in ecstasy and growled.

She began again, "The Higher Heart is yours, if you want it. You must submit to the Edict of Fidelity in your own heart first. Then this will come to reside in you. The Higher Heart will be yours, but it must be in secret. It must be in service to Her, the Divine One, She Who Comes."

In the visions, Regina bowed and backed away. She turned and found herself confronted by a large man with reddish skin, wearing a dark red conical penis sheath that rose above his belly and a dark red cylindrical hood. He held a whip coiled in one hand. She felt completely overpowered by his masculinity.

He commanded her to kneel. "Do you?" he asked. "Do you submit to the Edict of Fidelity? Do you agree that if you lie and reveal us that you will die? Even the dead death? Your own heart will stop beating of its own accord."

On her knees before him, holding her face in her hands, Regina wept. She remembered the bliss of the Higher Heart, and felt its pulsing there. It travelled from her heart into her hands and then into her face. "I will save face," she said. "I submit."

The scene changed; she was swept away into some conflict she would only eventually recall.

Many days later, it seemed to her, she found herself being thrown backward down a set of stone stairs. She found that there was a tremendous pressure all round her and it was only with the utmost of her strength that she could rise to her hands and knees. A voice spoke that chilled her to her heart and she began to tremble uncontrollably.

"What, daughter?" the voice said. "Are you so weak?"

There, again, was the reddish skinned man. He picked her up by the throat, whatever warrioress garb she'd been wearing in her vision disappeared, and suddenly she felt a piercing pain in her back as the meat hooks entered her. In the vision, she passed out in pain. She thought she had died.

After a time impaled, she returned to consciousness as she was lifted off the hooks by her throat and from between her legs. She was thrown over onto the stone floor at the foot of a dark enthroned feminine form. She somehow found the strength to sit up on her heels with her head bowed.

"I am the Goddess of Death. My sister has informed you, has she not?"

"She has informed me," Regina replied, conscious enough to know that neither 'yes' nor 'no' were the correct answers.

"So you are aware of the choice before you?" the Goddess of Death asked her.

"No, I am not aware," Regina replied.

"Liar!" the Goddess roared. Regina felt a whip strike across her back. And then another, in the opposite arc, as she bowed her forehead to the floor.

"Death is merciless, child," the Goddess said. "Only Life has the capacity for mercy."

Regina groaned, feeling the blood roll down her sides.

"You must choose child. Life or Death. Or Life and Death," the Goddess said.

Regina became lost, then, in her own brilliant mind. The semantics alone were captivating. When her mind loosed itself to follow the potential consequences of the options she was now compelled to choose between, she became lost. To her, it felt like a matter of Life or Death. Then she thought that she felt something deep inside her falter; some line of her being trembled.

"Time ends for you," the Goddess said.

Regina suddenly found herself back in the cistern. The floor was damp. She heard the drip of water onto rock. She realized that the cistern was slowly filling with water. She heard a brick in the old wall give way, thudding to the floor. Water poured out.

It took a long time to fill the cistern. Lots of long, long time. Time to feel the terror. Time to feel the regret. Time to feel the sorrow. Time to acknowledge the curve of Walter's back in the afternoon sunlight. Time to feel the anger at things gone terribly wrong. Time to scream. Time to come to acknowledge that no one could hear her. It took so long it released her from her time binding…she had been bound in time. No more. Time was ending.

She was floating in the water. As the cistern filled, her nose bumped up against the ceiling and scraped; she felt blood seep into her eyes in her last breaths. She took her last breath and released it, sinking to the sandy floor. She thought, "Now I understand. I choose Life and Death."

Then she thought, "Too late."

And she died.

Blackness wrapped around her; blackness filled her, and she sank into blackness.

Her last sensation was the pulse of the Higher Heart, hovering over her own poor heart.

There was a pause then, a pause about which not much can be said because nothing can be said. It is not possible for the dead to speak, not in the way of the living. In the time of no time there is the time of eternity, the time of no time passing, the time of the moment at the end at the swing of the pendulum. Words, real words, take time. Only ideas take no time. Then ideas end. In the end of time she lay. She lay there for a long time.

When she awoke she was on dry sand. Well, not quite dry, she realized. She had died, and had shit and pissed herself in the process. She woke first to the smell of shit and piss and puke. Her dead open mouth had drooled and she had breathed sand into her mouth to replace it. She had sand in one eye and sand in her phulva.

She hurt, hurt, hurt. She moved, and the hooks in her back bled afresh. She sat up and realized that the cistern had never filled. The Goddess must have heard her choice and decided to let her live.

Her heart thudded in her chest. Suddenly she realized the Higher Heart thudded in counterpoint. She opened her one good eye and saw, in the faint blue light, the Old Hag across the cistern splashing in the water, and laughing with an evil laugh.

Regina touched her back side and felt the shit smeared there. She was revulsed. She saw the choice of roads: despairing inaction or desire driven movement. She put one foot on the ground and leaned forward. Leaning, leaning, until the flesh of her back distended. She could feel the skin ripping from the flesh, and feel the slicing as the barbs cut through her skin.

She leaned into it, felt the slicing skin part. When she believed there was not much more to go she squatted on both feet and jumped for the water. With a grunting sound and a quiet pop from her back she was free, on her hands and knees halfway across the cistern.

She looked up. The Hag was sitting there, still, smiling at her. As she watched the Hag faded into the blue light, and disappeared.

She crawled to the buckets. She poured a little water from the full bucket to the empty one and washed her hands, pouring the sandy water out. Next she washed her eye, then her mouth, following the same procedure, and using only a little water at a time. She washed her phulva and her buttocks, conserving water. At the end she washed her back as best she could, pouring water over herself. When she was finished she sat back, leaning against the wall, letting the bricks cool her.

"Wombs and tombs," she said out loud. "They are the same. In this room they are the same."

She started to chill. She leaned forward. She put up her hair in a knot, lay down with her face on her forearm, and slept.

When she woke she knew she had been future dreaming. She chose not to remember the details. She remembered only that it was a long future, a long path that went many places, and always returned to Stonehaven. She sent a mental impression of her situation to Rachel. In the vision of it, Rachel nodded at her and smiled. She contented herself with watching the light, and the energies that moved through the cistern.

When the lid to the cistern rumbled back she closed her eyes against the light. But the light was soft, only candles burning. She crawled across the sand to the stairs and crawled out. The Goddess of Life was sitting on Her throne again, Her face still veiled. Regina knelt at Her feet, and sighed. She heard a motion behind her and felt a soft blanket settle over her back.

"Tell me, child," the Goddess spoke softly. "Have you met my sister? Are you sworn? And have you chosen?"

Regina cleared her throat and replied, "I have met your sister. I am sworn. And I have chosen."

"And your choice?" the Goddess asked, as if She didn't already know.

"I have chosen Life and Death," Regina said, firmly.

Regina felt, rather than saw, the Goddess smile.

"Rise," the Goddess said. "Your choice will be recorded in the Queen's Book. You may return to the world."

Regina felt a strong hand on her arm, helping her stand. The hand guided her to the stairs and helped her slowly up, her free hand on the wall for support. At the top a veiled wen waited. The wen took both of her hands and held them for a moment. Then she turned and opened the door into the basement.

The door closed behind Regina. She looked around, returned to this time and space, and tears started to run down her cheeks. She walked that way, naked but for the blanket, weeping. She saw no one. She walked to her room.

Walter was indeed there, waiting for her. There was a basin of hot water on the side board. She could see the steam rising. He smiled. He held up a small bowl.

"They told me this will heal your back with no scars."

She nodded.

"They told me to give you this," and he held up a small talisman carved with the image of the Fleur de Vie.

She reached him and sat down, nodding again.

"I prayed for you," he said.

"I felt it. I know," she replied.

"I prayed for all wen," he said.

He washed her off, washed her back gently, wiping away the sand and dried blood. He gently smoothed the salve on the cuts.

Regina shivered, remembering the hooks. She would always remember the hooks. With a deeper tremor, she remembered the Choice and then the Vow.

36

RUNNING AWAY

Chester came home late at night after having been gone for a few weeks. He used his key to get into the trailer, quiet, sneaky. He didn't even look in Missy's room. He went straight to Lulu's, still unable to shake the image of her tattoo.

The door had been left open, as were the windows on both ends of the trailer, leaving open, also, the possibility of a breeze. He pushed it all the way open and stood there silently in the door frame, looking at her in the dark.

She had been masturbating, half asleep, moaning.

He watched, dark eyes, all pupil and no iris, no color, glittering though there was no light. His hand moved to his trousers, adjusting himself.

Lulu had recently dedicated herself to the joys of masturbation. It was safer than the boys. She was working now at the Super Burger drive-through window. Once a boy, a senior just graduated, had pulled up to the window. His pecker was out and in his hand. He showed it to her. She'd ignored it, except that when she passed him his drink she squeezed the cup a little, just enough to pop the lid off, spilling its contents over his lap and dousing his erection.

He'd come in to complain. The manager shrugged, and gave him a coupon for a free meal.

But she thought about it. It was the first one she'd seen in daylight: large, erect, pointing skyward outside his unbuttoned jeans. It became large in her imagination. She used the image of it to fuel her fantasy life.

She became aware of the presence in the doorway. She recognized the smell. She pretended that her moaning was a bad dream, and turned away. Tucking her hands under her pillow, she made sure he could see her move. She had no doubt he could see in the dark. "Creep," she thought.

Chester's mind was filled with the image of the tattoo. It blinded him. When his vision cleared, it was apparent the child was asleep. After a few moments, listening to each other breathe in the dark, he turned from the doorway and went to Missy's room at the end of the trailer. Lulu fell asleep to the sound of a bed creaking, smiling, one hand back between her legs.

She woke in the morning from a dream about Mickey. He got to her. He frightened her.

She knew enough to stay away from him. Not even polite conversation, not even an acknowledgment of his existence. She knew it was a risky strategy. But she also thought that any sign of decency she showed him would be taken as a sign of interest. And that would lead to endless cajoling and harassment. She thought she'd just go get her Momma's gun and kill him.

Not the right choice, she realized.

And the strategy of ignoring Mickey, the constant cold shoulder whenever he was at the trailer, seemed to work. At least, until the day it didn't.

Mickey had made Lulu the subject of his daily masturbation fantasies. Not all, every day, and not each time, but more than any other. One day, he became tired of his hand.

He stalked her at a distance. Learned her patterns. On a day when Lulu's car had been in the shop and the mechanic had to keep it overnight, he figured he had his chance. Lulu had gotten a ride from a co-worker part of the way home and was walking down the long road. Right before she turned into the driveway Mickey pulled up in his truck.

"Hey baby. Hey Lulu. Let me take you home."

She tried ignoring him. He persisted. Finally, because he kept nudging the truck closer to her, forcing her off the road, she stopped. Angry, she said, "Stop it. I am home."

"Not yet, you ain't."

He pulled the truck forward and turned it in front of her. There were berry bushes alongside the road, too thorny for her to escape through. He slid over and opened the passenger door. He reached out, grabbed her by the hair, pulling her into the truck. He slid back and accelerated away, holding her face down on the bench seat. The acceleration closed the passenger door for him and they disappeared down the road in a cloud of dust.

He started talking, muttering at first, almost under his breath, not loud enough for Lulu to hear. Then he told her, "Think you're so high and mighty. Think you're too good for me. But I got what you need. I got the goods. And you're gonna get it good."

He took her down to the turnaround at the end of the road where the ground was always covered in beer cans and used condoms. The dust cloud rolled up over the truck. He'd been holding her face to the seat cover so she couldn't make a sound, even when she screamed.

He kept grinding her face into the seat, imagining it was his crotch, even when he stopped the truck. He continued to mutter at her, talking about outrages to his ego, the various disrespects women had shown him over the years.

Keeping her face down, he climbed over her and opened the passenger door again. He climbed over her and out, bending her so he could keep her head down. He pulled her legs out. He grabbed her Super Burger uniform pants at the waist, hooked her panties and pulled them down to her ankles.

She continued to struggle, trying to rise, trying to kick, but it was helpless. She couldn't see it, but she heard it. She heard the zipper come down, and his grunting noises while he took it out of his pants. She heard him unbuckle his belt.

But what she felt when it touched her was small. It took her a moment to realize it was a finger. He was looking for it, looking for her opening with his finger. He found her asshole first, probed it, getting a finger in to one knuckle. She bucked her hips, fighting, twisting, and raising them up so he found the place he was looking for.

She felt it. She felt him seeking, probing, here and there, slipping up between her legs. He realized he couldn't get in. The truck was too high. He flipped her over, to her horror. He put his hand over her mouth in such a way that she couldn't scream, squeezing her jaw and lips shut at the same time. She tried to bite his hand but she couldn't open her mouth at all.

She beat at him, and he laughed. He caught her hands, one, then another, with his free hand and held them tight together, like her hands were bound, his fingers like cordage.

Then he let her hands go in order to reach under her legs and, with his shoulder, he flipped her legs up, so that they were vertical, and pulled her to him, holding the back of her legs against his chest.

He caught up her hands again. She struggled, trying to resist, but her pants bound her ankles just as surely as his hand bound her wrists.

He told her, quietly, "Scream, and I'll hurt you." He took his hand away from her mouth and twisted her breast hard to let her know he meant it.

She froze, stopped fighting. Then he took his free hand and went searching for her opening again.

He found it and she resumed her struggle. She kicked her legs against his chest. He let her hands go, so he could hold her legs against him with one hand while he felt for her with his other. She tried to beat on him with her hands, sobbing, but when she'd try to sit up to reach him, he'd bat her hands away.

He slapped her. It hurt. She closed her eyes and stopped fighting for a second.

"Look at me," he said. She looked and saw him with his fist pulled back, ready to hit her like she'd never been hit. She saw the madness in his eyes; she was afraid for her face, afraid for her broken face, afraid for her life, and went still.

He found her opening with that hand. He stuck his middle finger in, only one knuckle, she was so tight. He started to push, and she resisted. She couldn't stand it. Couldn't stand the thought of his dirty finger inside her, with its long grease caked fingernail. She felt the nail cut the inside of her and she started to struggle again, bucking her hips, kicking her feet, bound by her pants.

He punched at her, but she saw it coming. At the last moment, she shifted her head and turned her face away, and it became a glancing blow off her ear. He did it again. A second time he went to hit her and she turned the other way, still kicking. Had she not turned, the blows would have rendered her senseless and completely open to his depredations.

Her right shoe came off. He held her upraised kicking legs as close to his chest as he could, intent on pushing the finger in to the second knuckle.

Her foot came free of her pants, and he didn't see it, so engrossed was he, looking at how his finger disappeared, in and out.

When she drew her now free leg back he looked up at her suddenly. The coils of her tattoo compressed like they were a spring. With her heel, she kicked him in the nose and broke it.

The pain was blinding. The blood spurted from his nose instantaneously. He staggered back holding his hands to his face, screaming at first, then moaning, then cursing her. He staggered back to the truck again but she was gone, out the driver side door, running down the road, one leg bare and barefoot, the other clothed in held up pants.

She looked for exits, deer paths into the woods. When she found one she took it, hoping she'd cut off onto the trail before he'd seen her.

She had. Mickey was still holding his hands to his ruined nose, still cursing, and weeping so uncontrollably he couldn't see. He danced around in the turn around, holding his bleeding face with one hand, unconscious now of his deflated erection swinging in counter motion to his helpless turning from one side to the other. He blindly shook his fist in the direction he thought she'd gone.

She made it home through the woods. Chester was out, she knew. Missy was there.

"I got to go, Momma," she sobbed as she came through the door. "I got to go. Mickey, Mickey..." she sobbed and went to her knees, still holding her pants up on one leg.

"He put his hand in me," she said. "Dirty fucking hand." And she retched on the floor of the trailer.

Missy rushed to her. "Oh my gawd, yes, you do, baby. Look at your face. You got to go. Come with me and change your clothes, right now." Missy pulled her to her feet and half dragged her down the hall.

"We don't have much time, hurry," she said.

Missy tore off her uniform. "I'm not that," she said, and spat on it.

"Fuck that, child," Missy said, shocking her daughter. "Do what I tell you," Missy said. "Pack a bag. Jammies, shoes, underwear, two changes of clothes. A nice dress. Another pair of shoes. No, not those, these," she said and threw a pair of flats on the bed. "Go get your stuff," she said, in frustration, pointing to the bathroom with her head. "Get some tampons. I'll pack this."

When Lulu had changed, Missy took her into the bathroom and washed her face. The punches had done only minor damage. Missy gave her a plastic bag with some ice in it to hold on the side of her head.

She had a suitcase and a shoulder bag with her ID. Her mother drove her to a bus station in a town a hundred miles away.

"I have a second cousin in New York," Missy said, as she put her daughter on the bus. "I'll tell her you're coming. Do you understand? I won't ask her. I'll tell her. You're coming."

Lulu could only nod her head, speechless. Missy hugged her, pressed two hundred dollars into her hand, and put her on the bus. It was only at the last moment Lulu remembered to look out the window and she saw an expression on her Mother's face. It was an expression she'd never seen before.

She didn't know what it meant.

Later, when Chester called and Mickey came to pick him up, he saw the bloody cotton in his nose and the bruise forming in Mickey's eyes, Chester asked him what the fuck happened.

Mickey was evasive, saying only that Lulu had done it. All he'd done was offer her a ride.

Chester was angry when he got back to Missy's trailer. He slammed open the door, charging in to stand just inside it. Missy didn't rise. She sat at the table, with a cup of tea with whiskey in it, holding a note she'd had Lulu scribble in the car on the way to the bus station. She didn't even look up. Chester's bravado and bluster meant nothing to her now.

Chester paused, taken aback. This was not the cowering reaction he'd expected.

"Where is she?" he demanded.

"I don't know," Missy said, which was true enough.

"What do you mean, you don't know," the timbre of his voice rising.

"I mean, I don't know. She's just gone. She packed a bag and went," Missy said. "Where you been?" she asked, finally raising her eyes to him.

"Laud's work," he answered. He answered as if Missy didn't know what that meant. So close were Missy's words to the truth he couldn't tell she was covering her daughter's trail; couldn't tell she was lying. Of course, he believed he could always tell when a woman was lying. He straightened up and settled down. "You know she hurt Mickey?"

"If she did, he deserved it," she responded, still looking down into her cup.

Her tone of voice made Chester laugh. He came over and grabbed her by the hair. "Come on," he said, pulling her to her feet. He dragged her, bent over, down the hallway. "We got some worship to do."

37

ANGELICA'S DREAM

Angelica had kitchen duty the evening of the Solstice. She was not allowed to attend the rituals in the Formal Gardens. Indeed, she was not allowed to be outside on the grounds at all nor to sit on the porches. The Ceremony was for the initiated and people participated in the accompanying rituals only in so far as they had qualified to participate. She wanted so much to be here, among these people in the best way, that she accepted this restriction. She knew she was not yet ready to know, but she would be ready someday. When that day came both her Mentors and she would know it was time.

She had been told there was a vision that came; sometimes in meditation, sometimes in a dream, and sometimes during ceremony. She would bring it to her Mentors and they would have already seen the same vision. The visions might be different in specific content, but the themes of this vision were always similar.

She knew there would be guardians at the gates to the Garden so she dismissed the thought of even trying to sneak out and peek over the wall; or worse, sneak into the Gardener's shed and look through the window. Additionally, she had been assured that forces moved about on the grounds on this night and that she did not want to be caught up in their ebb and flow.

She had sent Phillip home early because the path to the barracks by the barn was unlit and the moon wasn't up yet. She wanted to be sure he was home by curfew. She liked Phillip. Two years younger than she, he was attentive. When she showed him how to do something he got it right the first time almost every time. He would try to anticipate what she wanted him to do. Sometimes she would tease him by deliberately assigning him to something he wasn't expecting. She imagined he had a crush on her.

Angelica finished up in the kitchen a little after 10, having made the advance preparations for the breakfast crew and made sure all the dishes, utensils, pots and pans were washed, dried, and in their places. All the surfaces were scrubbed. This included a complete mopping, a second mopping, and a clean water rinsing of the entire floor. She turned off the air conditioners and fans. Tonight the entire mansion was to be silent and all lights out by eleven.

She dipped her fingers in a bowl of spring water on the altar to the Spirit of the Hearth and dripped the water on the devotional candle. She replaced it with a new candle that would burn all night and lit that.

She made her way quietly up the back stairs, what used to be called the Servant Stairs, and stepped out onto the third floor. Then she remembered that she had given up her summer room in the Mansion for a guest couple who had pushed the two single beds together. She had been reassigned to a dormer room on the fourth floor, where she had slept when she first arrived, the Servant floor, along with the three other young wen who had been given permission to stay the summer.

As she was closing the third floor door, she glanced down the hall and saw a flash of white in the darkness. A head turned toward her. In the light from the 'Exit' sign she recognized the face of her friend and instructor, Diana. Her brow was set with a crown from which small golden plates were hung in strings like a veil. Her hair was tied up on top and flowing down her back like a horse's tail. She thought she saw a flash of smiling teeth as the white gown with its golden girdle disappeared behind the eastern servant stairs door.

Angelica closed her door to the third floor and made her way up the now narrowed flight of stairs, coming out on the fourth floor, illuminated in a low light from night lights along the walls. She moved quietly down the hall to her room to get her towels, summer robe and toiletries, mindful of the other wen. She could see lamp light under the door to Gina's room and another light under Janice's as she passed by to her room. Hers was Room Six in the middle of the corridor. It was on the north side where it was cooler and the night breezes would blow through.

Retrieving her things, she swept silently down the stairs at the east end of the corridor instead of going back the way she had come. With no one in the mansion tonight she could use the private shower, instead of the group shower next to it. She undid her hair and stepped up to the curtain, adjusting the water until it was just right. She loved the kind of heat that felt like a sustained hot stone massage. She let the water beat on her a moment, searching out the sore spots. She washed. The sweaty, oily grime from the kitchen swirled away down the drain. She shampooed her hair. While the conditioner soaked in, she shaved in the prescribed way, removing all hair but that on her arms and head, which she was required to grow as long as possible. She had never grown completely accustomed to the sensitivity of her skin from this activity. Every brush with every cloth, every touch, felt softer and more sharp at the same time, somehow.

She stepped out of the shower when the pipes started banging, as they always did. She dried off, wrapping her hair in a towel, and applied the essential oils prescribed for her type, even between her toes. She inspected her fingernails, and decided they needed a little more brushing to get them clean. When she was done, she brushed her teeth; two minutes, please.

Then she realized that what she had thought was the pipes banging was actually drums. Short, high pitched bursts of four, followed by a long pause, the summoning drum used to call people's attention. She heard several synchronized drums. She thought she could pick out five of them, but it was hard to be sure because of the echoes from the garden walls.

She removed the towel from her hair. Bending over, she brushed it out before wrapping it up in a top knot. She knew it would take longer to dry that way, but it would dry curly. She just couldn't stand to have wet hair hanging down on her shoulders and back in the humidity of the summer night.

She went back upstairs to her room. Checking the watch hanging from the hook on the back of her door for the time, she removed it and set it on the desk next to her phone. She hung her towels there to dry instead. Before she closed the door she stuck her head back out in the corridor. Seeing no lights coming from other rooms, she quietly closed her door and went to her cot.

Her window was opened at both the top and the bottom, as were all the windows today. She hung up her robe and laid down, the dampness of her hair transferring to the pillow and making her feel stuck. She quickly broke out in a sweat, the wisps of hair sticking to her neck.

She couldn't turn on the ceiling fan tonight. It was to be as if it were still the old days, the old ways, with no electrical humming. There was to be only the humming of the people, and the spirits of the land.

Then the drums began again. This time, it was deep drums, a single 'thoom' followed by another long pause. Then it repeated seven times; the signal to close the gates. Her pulse jumped at each beat, slowing down only to have the next beat make her jump. She felt the pulse of the drum as a push against her skin, even this far from the Garden.

She knew where the people would gather. Coming together, each dressed in a single piece of white cloth, draped or worn according to preference, often belted. Sometimes a shawl or short cloak of the same material was worn over it. She had folded them during the hours when the Interns were assigned Laundry duty.

The people would then gather on the walls above the Sunken Garden.

She sat up and moved to her chair by the window, sighing at the slightest breeze that moved. Her chin rested on her arms, which were resting on the sill. She wondered at the beauty of millions of fireflies, rising out of the grass into the trees.

It had been a cicada summer, the thirteen year cycle of the red-eyed cicada coming to life, erupting through the ground and into the trees. All day, and most of the night, the cicadas sang, calling out with their raspy leg horns rubbing back and forth, "Come find me! Come find me!"

From the top of the trees came the hum, the higher whir of the mating sound reminding her of the woo-woo-woo-woo of the flying saucer sound effect in old movies. There they were, little red-eyed alien bugs, singing their alien mating song in the tree tops, illuminated by the fire-flies.

But no, these weren't aliens, were they? They were her kin. Distant kin, but kin nevertheless. Children of one mother. The sound they made was among the sounds she made: love making, singing, singing in the arms of a lover, long sounds, rhythmic sounds, pleasure sounds.

She closed her eyes and listened as the drums grew steady. Then the chanting started. She drifted off. Sometime later she awoke to hear singing. Opening her eyes she saw forms, like clouds of mist or thin fogs moving over the grounds toward the garden, lit by the light of fireflies. She closed her eyes again, sighing at the breeze now moving through the room.

She opened her eyes again when the energy shifted. In the tree outside her window the fire-flies were pulsing in syncopated rhythms. In the garden there was both chanting and singing. There were drums and rattles and flutes, and deep horns. She heard the thumping of feet pounding on the earth and stones in unison. She felt the pounding on her whole body, on her skin, in her heart, and in her womb, as a wave in the air, bouncing up and down, almost like she was rising and falling in deep water. The fire-flies pulsed with her.

Then she fell deeply asleep and dreamed.

She dreamt she was in an enclosure. She was inside a walled stock-ade, made of tall logs set vertically in the ground with gates in each direction, closed and barred. There were guards at the gates dressed in leather armor and kilts armored with bull hide strips. They had short swords at their sides. Somehow she knew there were guards on the other side of the gate, as well. There were torches on poles. A breeze was blowing, and in the wildly flickering light she saw the people dancing, feet pounding in unison, loosely dressed in white, pinned at the shoulder, and belted at the waist. Some of the robes had become un-pinned and fallen to the waist. Others were open in front, inner thighs flashing in the light. The people were chanting and singing, each in chorus. Some wore their hair wild and loose, others pinned or braided.

All wore a necklace with a pendant inscribed in the same way but she couldn't make out the details in the subdued light of fires and torches.

She felt her own dancing, and heard her own voice. She was singing words that felt familiar but she didn't know their meaning. She looked down. Her own robe was open down the middle all the way through the belt. As she looked, the knot on one shoulder came loose, and slipped down, caught by the belt, but exposing her breast. She smiled and kept dancing. She looked at her pendant. Smiling at the symbol she recognized, a simple line drawing etched in baked clay, but she couldn't quite place where she knew it from.

Stamping her feet and tossing her hair, she looked toward the center of the enclosure and saw a platform that rose above the level of the heads of the dancers. The stage was wrapped in a dark curtain. From a trap door in the center of the platform four Priestesses emerged carrying torches on poles. Each went to a corner and planted their torch. Then they stepped to the right and began dancing, matching the rhythm of the drums and the people. They chanted at first, in unison. Then each began singing her own song, different in words and yet blending by tone into harmony with each other.

The Priestesses were dressed in long white robes, open completely up the front and slit up the back as high as the belts at their waists. Each wore a shawl over their shoulders and up over their heads, sewn with little polished metal discs that flashed in the light. As they danced their split skirts whirled. Their legs flashed.

Then, four figures emerged through the trapdoor and stood behind each Priestess. Each figure was bigger than the Priestess, so she could see their outlines when they stepped up behind the Priestesses. Their faces were hidden by cowls.

Soon, each Priestess stopped whirling and stood in place, stomping their feet and writhing sinuously. The hooded figures stepped up behind them, belly to back. The Priestesses leaned back into them.

In the light of the torches she could see the head of a large phallus emerge from between the thighs of each writhing Priestess. It emerged right at the top so the wen could ride the long rail, back and forth, side to side. The figures stood still, supporting the Priestesses as they rode.

As their excitement rose, their hands went to their pubes, stroking and separating, toying and rubbing themselves. Their eyes closed and their heads lolled back in ecstasy.

The people continued to dance and chant and sing. The drums beat the deep pulsing rhythm. Suddenly one of the Priestesses came, ejaculating out over the dancers, screaming and thrashing in her pleasure. In a moment each Priestess was coming, raining out over the crowd. The people shouted and surged forward to be blessed, washing in the sacred rain, catching it in their mouths if they could.

The people laughed and danced. The Priestesses continued to stroke themselves and rain, and rain again, knees shaking and hips bucking. Then some of the wen in the crowd, quivering in their own ecstasy, began to rain also. Both men and wen fell to their knees before them to be washed, and to drink.

Angelica knew what this was. She knew what was happening, although it had never happened to her. As she danced she could feel the pressure build. Her hands went to herself, and she came also, a great squirt of rain, and then another. She felt her knees begin to buckle and she began to fall.

She glanced up quickly at the platform one last time and saw one of the Priestesses had collapsed with her support leaning over her protectively. Another was collapsing, being let down on the floor slowly by her support.

She woke up before she hit the ground in her dream to find that she was coming, for real, sitting in her chair. There was a pool in the seat around her bottom, and rain on the floor and wall in front of her. She sat back, in shock and ecstasy, and came one more time. The rain reached up and splashed on the window sill where only seconds before she had lain her head.

She shuddered, each shudder a spasm of ecstasy. She put her head back, catching her breath as the shuddering faded. Somehow, her hair had come undone.

As she returned from an ancient Then to an exquisite Now, she heard the drums and chanting still sounding from the formal garden. Her awareness returned to her body and she felt again the wave, pulsing up and down. She could feel it extend over all the land around her, blessing the land and all that dwelt there. Blessing it with the pulse of the heartbeat of ecstasy.

She rolled off the chair and onto her cot. She lay on her back and breathed, feeling the pulse from the Garden all around her and through her. Half turning on her side, she put one hand between her thighs and smiling, slept.

When Angelica woke in the morning it was a slow return to the light. Then she remembered where she was and what her duties were in the morning. She started, a little panicked that she was late. But when she looked at the her phone, she realized it was still before the set alarm time of six AM.

Breakfast was scheduled two hours later than usual because of the Ceremony, but her daily discipline usually had her up and sitting before then. She had awakened only a little later than usual.

She remembered her dream and the familiarity of the symbol carved on the necklace she'd been wearing. She remembered raining. Her panic came up again and she looked at the chair and the wall. There was only a small damp circle on the chair, and not even a dried stain on the wall and sill. She was amazed. She remembered clearly how much she'd expressed in her orgasm.

She sat up, put her feet on the floor, and leaned over to the chair seat to look closely. She leaned down and sniffed it. She leaned closer and smelled more slowly, trying to identify the elements, unraveling the mystery of it, one odor at a time.

There was a richness, a depth that reminded her of the smell of the pool in the Sunken Garden, a richness that promised satisfaction. She touched her finger to the damp, and tasted a small drop of the wetness. She tasted a salt and a slickness that reminded her of an alkaline spring where she had once gone swimming. She felt a power in it and it made a shiver run down her spine.

Where the wall had been wet there was now no trace, nor on the sill. It had evaporated without stain. She could see the chair also soon would be dry.

She closed her eyes. She could feel the pulse over the land, still thrumming even though the drums had long since stopped. In her own heart, and belly, she felt it, too. She synchronized her heart and breathing with it.

Awake now, she swung her feet around and onto the floor. She glanced at the alarm clock, and panicked again. Then she remembered that it was the first day of summer and she was not on the early shift for breakfast. Not many would be needed then, for not many would have risen. She was on duty for brunch, one of the only eight times of the year when brunch happened.

She slipped on her summer robe and sandals and went down the stairs to the basement kitchen. The crew was there: Martin, Elizabeth and Marion. The wen she now knew as a High Priestess, Diana, was there, too. She was dressed in a deep blue, silk, summer robe, loosely belted. Her hair was down. She was leaning against a counter with her arms crossed over her chest and legs crossed at the ankles. She had been talking to the others when Angelica came in. Diana looked up at her and smiled.

Angelica could hear people moving upstairs in the dining room, and asked after David, the last member of the scheduled crew. Diana told her he was upstairs finishing up with the early risers meal.

Angelica squinted her eyes in an attempt to discern Diana's mood and availability. Diana smiled at her and uncrossed her arms so Angelica asked her, "Do you have a minute? I'd like to talk to you about a dream I had last night."

Diana said, "Sure," and nodded her head toward the shade garden, dappled in the rising morning light that shined there during these few short weeks of the year. They got cups of coffee from the urn and went outside. They sat in chairs at a garden table.

Putting her feet up on an adjacent empty chair, Diana said, "So, tell me."

Angelica hesitated. She drew a breath and blew it out, "Do you feel it? Do you feel the pulse that's all over the land?"

Diana smiled, "Yes, in fact, I do. Do you know where it comes from?"

"Yes," Angelica said. "It comes from the Sunken Garden. It started last night during the Ceremony and radiated out from there. How'd it happen? You were there, right? What did you all do?"

Diana smiled even more broadly. "Yes, it started there, and yes, also, I was there. As for what happened there and as for you, you'll have to wait to see. Now, you said you had a dream?"

"Yes," Angelica said, "I dreamed I was at an ancient version of the Ceremony, and this is what I saw." Angelica proceeded to tell her the dream in all the detail she could recall, including the orgasm and ejaculation at the end.

Diana listened closely, smiling at some parts, shaking her head slightly at times. She watched Angelica's face intently, looking for Angelica's reactions to her dream. When Angelica had finished her tale, including waking up this morning, Diana asked her, "Do you know what that was?"

"Yes, it is one of the eight orgasms a wen can have."

"That's the anatomical answer. Do you know the ritual answer?"

"Something to do with the blessing of the rain?"

"Yes, but do you know what that means?"

"No, not really," Angelica said.

Diana said, "Well, one thing that it means is that you are going to start your studies of Tantra and Alchemy. I'll notify the Curriculum Committee and make sure that arrangements are made."

"That means an assignment, right?" Angelica asked.

"Yes, usually. But your case is different. If you're not ready for it, let me know," Diana said

Angelica was thoughtful for a moment, then she said, "Alright. I look forward to it." Then, after a pause she said, "Do you think it would be OK for me to walk down to the Garden now?"

Diana said, "Alone or in company?"

Angelica said, "I think, alone."

Diana said, "Yes, you may."

Angelica took a last sip of her coffee, and stood up, looking to the northeast. She walked to the drive entrance and turned the corner. When she was out of sight Diana stood up and slowly walked in the same direction, following her.

Angelica walked around the east wing, passing the eastern court yard and continued south to the wrought iron gate and steps leading into the Formal Garden. She walked to the central circle with its fountain and brick walkway. Turning northeast again. She walked along the dirt path that lead to the Sunken Garden. She stopped to remove her sandals. This path, walked barefoot during certain rituals for certain people, was worn down and hard packed. The dust was still held down by the previous night's dew.

The path wound through bushes, some thorny, some flowering, some both. She paused to smell each kind, noticing that some closest to the path had been cut. She emerged through the hedge surrounding the grassy clearing around the Sunken Garden and stopped. Slowly scanning the grounds, she took in everything she could see and smell.

The grass of the clearing was flattened down. As she walked clockwise around the garden, she could smell the scent of it mixed with the sharp burnt odor of torch wicks. Her feet encountered wet spots in the grass, wetter than the trace of dew. Some were up to a yard across, and there were also smaller, thicker, slicker wetnesses.

At the north side, she walked up to the edge of the wall where the Table Rock emerged. Suddenly, she could feel the pulse coming up from her feet. She looked left and right along the flagstones that composed the top of the wall. Seeing the spots of wetness on the edge here and there she looked down to see the flagstone floor covered in flower petals, colorful and bruised. She inhaled the cloud of their emanations.

It made her a little dizzy, and the pulse made her knees weak. When she stepped back she slipped and fell backwards, one hand landing in something gooey. She wiped it on cleaner grass.

She got up, and continued walking around the wall. She alternated watching her step and glancing down into the pit. She came all the way around and went to the edge of the broad stairs leading down.

She stopped on the top step, raised her arms and face to the sky, and said, "May you always be full." She noticed that the belt cinching her robe was restrictive, so she untied it and let her robe fall open.

She stepped down again and stopped, raising her arms and face again, and said, "May you always be slaked." On the third step she said, "May you always be loved." On the fourth step she stopped because she suddenly heard the thrumming of the pulse. She heard it as a sound in her ears, and she could only hum with it. She stopped on the fifth step to let her heart fill with it, wishing, pushing the pulse upward and outward, she sung the pulse in a low voice.

Looking down again, she took the last step onto the floor. Suddenly, the very air around her seemed to pulse, from dark to bright. She went down on her hands and knees so she wouldn't fall.

Her ears thrummed, her voice hummed. Her nose filled with the smell of the crushed flowers, and a deeper, richer smell; the smell of sex. She crawled forward until she could touch the tip of the Table Rock, for here was the source of the pulsing. She touched it with one hand and wept. She wept at the beauty of it, at the beauty of the pulsing energy that filled her.

She got up on her knees at the end of the rock. From her knees, she draped her body as far along its axis as she could, pressing her breasts and belly and pubic bone against it. She turned her face to the right, laid her cheek on it. Her tears slid down onto the rock, and mixed with the wetness there.

She opened her eyes and looked over the side of the Rock and down into the Well. The water seemed to glow and pulse. She leaned down and reached three fingers into the Well. She became aware of someone behind her. Raising her arm she turned slightly and looked back over her shoulder to see Diana sitting on the bottom step, legs crossed under her and robe open.

Diana looked at her fiercely. "Drink," she said.

Angelica moved her fingers toward her mouth and Diana said, "Use your hand, drink."

So she leaned farther over, cupped water from the Well and drank. She shivered like she had earlier that morning, down her spine. Then the shivering spread, extending to her limbs. She lay stretched along the rock and quivered. She shook deeply, spasming along the whole length of her body, weeping and crying out in ecstasy. The pulse echoed, sounding in her voice and driving her rhythm.

At length, the shaking subsided. She felt Diana's hand on her back, quiet, steady and pulsing strongly.

Diana said, "Come. You have felt and seen and tasted. Time to go."

Angelica leaned back and stood. With Diana's arm around her waist, she turned and walked back to and up the stairs. At the top, they turned and looked back. Diana made a sign with her hand then they turned forward and walked to the hedge.

As they walked, Diana asked, "Do you know what that was?"

"Yes," Angelica said. "It was another one of the eight orgasms."

Diana laughed and said, "Yes, yes it was, among other things."

They arrived back at the fountain circle. Diana walked to the edge of the pool, kicking off her sandals and dropping her robe as she went. Over her shoulder she said, "There's a bucket by the column over there to the east. Bring it over."

Angelica turned, got the bucket, and brought it back. Diana, standing there nude, said, "Dip me a bucket, will you?"

Angelica dipped the bucket and Diana said, "Hold it up for me."

Diana dipped her hands in the bucket. She splashed and washed her face, then her arms and chest, splashing it on her belly and down her legs. Gathering up her hair in one hand, she turned around and said, "Slowly pour the rest of it on me, down my back." She washed her buttocks, then bent over and placed her other hand between her legs. Reaching back to pull water in between her thighs, she washed herself there, too, front to back. She continued on, wiping the water down the backs of her legs.

When the bucket was empty Diana stood up and turned around, saying, "Your turn next. Look down your front."

Angelica did and noticed she had been sweating. Little bits of rock, dirt and lichen clung to her belly and breasts. Diana said, "Your face, too."

Angelica smiled as an image of her face came to her mind. She gave the bucket to Diana and took off her robe. She tossed it out on the bricks, out of range of any splashing.

Diana dipped out a bucket and held it up for her. She washed herself as she had watched Diana wash. When she was done with her back she stood up, shook herself like a dog, and laughed. "Thank you," she said to Diana and smiled.

The older wen smiled back and set the bucket down. She sat down on the edge of pool facing east to dry in the sun. She motioned for Angelica to sit down beside her.

Diana stretched her legs and shook out her hair. Tilting her head to the side, she spoke, "Angelica, what do you think is going on here?"

Angelica had spread her legs and leaned forward. She was shaking out her hair.

"I don't know," she said. "Not really. The first thing I feel is that it is some kind of refuge for Nature." She heard a small creature rustle in the bushes behind her.

Angelica continued, "I feel that there is a spirit to the land here, and that there are spirits, nature spirits, that live here under its aegis."

"Yes," Diana said. "What else?"

"Well, there's what you do. What you and the others do that's going on behind the scenes. It's not just a yoga school, or a professional hospitality service for seminars. Something else is going on here that I'm aware of, and I'm aware that I'm part of it. And I want to be part of it, but I want to because of how it makes me feel, not because of what I think about it. I feel I don't know enough yet to know what I think."

"Well, what do you feel then, about what we're doing?"

"It feels powerful. I feel powerful, but the power I feel is definitely feminized. It's not an aggressive power, or a positional power, but a yielding power, and at the same time, a proceptive power; one that leads to a greater ecstasy and a greater fullness in life. If I push on it, it yields but it isn't diminished in any way. But if I stand in it, and allow it to envelope me I begin to feel myself merge with it. I become one with it, and I am extended to its boundaries, rather than just the boundary of my own skin."

After a pause, Angelica continued: "Sometimes, in morning meditation, when I'm established in the field, I can hear, or at least I think I can hear, other people's thoughts, and feel their feelings, particularly their discomfort and pain. Also, I can sense when they lapse into dreaming, and can sometimes track their dreams. Although, that's hard for me to do because I feel like I'm being sucked down into their identifications, rather than remaining still at the center of the field.

"And I feel a difference, a difference in quality, between those of us who are Interns and those who are simply students. I feel mysterious compared to them. They feel coarse to me somehow. But something constrains that mysteriousness. When I put myself in the place of my Witness, I can see a third force, something wrapped around us—the Interns—something that keeps our appearance to the students looking the same to them as they do to each other. Sometimes, I see that third force as emanating from the Meditation Leader, as something you all do on purpose, to keep us hidden, and safe, and contained."

She looked at Diana for confirmation and Diana nodded for her to continue. "Then there's the secrecy. There was a time when I wouldn't have believed in it, wouldn't have believed in the necessity of anything but transparency. But here, what's happening here, this power and this field, needs to be protected, and held close. Held secret and sacred. In the world out there it hardly exists. When it becomes apparent out there it frightens people, and they attack it. I think it has been attacked so much in the past that it has been in danger of dying."

Smiling, Diana said, "Finally, a thought. You are transitioning from feeling to thinking now."

"Yes, I am. And I think I need to know more. Like the Rules. When I'm told about a Rule, especially a new Rule, I can usually feel the rightness of it. But then I see other Interns not obeying the same Rule, and I wonder why. Especially the stuff around sex. I get that quick emotional bump of unfairness. I know it rises from my ego, so I suspend it, and wait for the chance to ask why."

Diana said, "So, you're asking?"

Angelica nodded her head.

Diana said "Different rules are in place for different people at different times. It's just like the work assignments. The rules are based on what it is happening, what is needed by the group, and what is needed by the individual based on where they are in their Inner Work. The Faculty is trained to discern these things.

"You have to remember we have all been Interns, and we have gone through what you're going through. Also what you're going to go through, one way or another. Sometimes you'll be operating under one rule, and at another time under another rule. Sometimes a rule will be reinstated for you, it depends. Sometimes there will be many rules, sometimes it will seem there are no rules.

But you will still feel constrained, most of all by the need for secrecy."

Angelica asked, worried now, "But what if I violate the secrecy? What will happen to me?"

Diana smiled. "Well, that's a secret, too."

Angelica paused, a serious expression on her face. "Well, what about the sex then? I know you and the others, most of you, and the Interns, are having sex. You let me have sex with Jake before the blowout of the Buffer. I'm not a virgin, but one of my rules right now is 'No sex' with other people. And honestly, I'm just not that interested in sex with myself."

Diana, smiling broadly now, asked, "How do you know some of us are having sex? Have you seen any?"

Angelica scowled. "No, no I haven't 'seen' any. But I can feel it. Sometimes, I think I can hear it. And I can smell it, too. I can smell where it's been had, and sometimes I can smell it on those who've had it. It doesn't matter what herbs or incense is used to purify everything. I smell it on Thomas when I'm working at the barn all the time. And you wouldn't believe what you smell like right now."

Diana threw back her head and laughed. "You can smell me? Good or bad?"

Angelica said, "Oh, you smell great. I want to smell like that."

Diana retorted, "What are you complaining about? You've just had two new kinds of orgasm in the last twelve hours."

Angelica replied, frowning, "You know it's not the same."

Diana, still chuckling, said, "I know. I know it's not the same. For now, just remember that you're going to be assigned to study Tantra and Alchemy."

Then the ten o'clock bell rang. Angelica jumped up. "Oh, there's the bell. I'm late, damn it." She grabbed her robe and sandals. Hopping on one foot, she trying to put them on with one hand while she ran, struggling into the robe with her other.

She hopped twice for one foot, twice for the other, almost got her other arm in the sleeve and went running west along the path, robe flapping and hair bouncing.

Diana called after her, "Soon! Remember!" and she heard the garden gate clang.

Over the gateway Diana had a view of Angelica dancing across the Mansion yard, naked, robe trailing and waving from one extended arm. Both arms were straight out from her shoulders, bouncing with each step. The steps were the steps of the circle dance the people had been doing together the night before. It was the dance which fed the pulse. Diana was certain that Angelica hadn't spied; Angelica learned the steps by being in the garden and sensing the movements from the traces the movements had left behind.

After her duties in the kitchen were met for the day, Angelica sat on the veranda steps beside the old dog Homer watching the sun begin to sink. The new dogs that came with the former Priest were sitting on the top step with them scanning the land.

Their introduction to Homer and Stonehaven had gone very well. The Consorts and Priestesses had worked with them, raising their levels of intuition and behavior. They loved going on patrols. They particularly loved the monthly howl that the community did. All three dogs howled along. Homer was observed more than once teaching them how to say his four words in English; "Wah-ah" for water, "Ooo" for food, "Ow" for out, and "Ehh-ohh" for hello.

Craft came and sat down next to Angelica. "He has dust in his ears," he said, gesturing toward Homer.

"Dust?" Angelica asked, lifting an ear and peering in.

"It's something to say. He's been lying here all day. He hasn't moved, he hasn't even shaken his head to clear the dust out of his ears."

"Oh, poor baby," Angelica said, lightly stroking Homer's ears. He thumped his tail once.

"He's tired," Craft continued. "Madeleine said he's going to go soon. Maybe tonight."

Angelica rested her hand on Homer's back, so when the transition began she felt it. Homer rolled over on his side, extending his legs toward Craft. Angelica's hand slid over to his side. He panted, not for long, perhaps three seconds. His legs twitched like he was dreaming of running, and then he was gone. Angelica began sobbing helplessly. She had felt the force of Homer's life leaving his body. He was the first dying being she had held. She kept her hand on the still form. She wept.

The other dogs sat up and howled, and continued howling. Craft howled. The people in the Mansion howled. Madeleine and Eva came out on the veranda and howled. Soon the veranda was full of howling people.

All the visitors for the Solstice came out onto the lawn and howled. The howling went on until the people down at the barn heard the howling and joined in. Angelica couldn't stand to sob anymore and joined, howling through the tears still streaming down her face.

Down at the archery range Quinn, Halloran, and Matthews were practicing with the crossbows. They stopped what they were doing, and howled.

The howling went on, sustained until it filled the draws and little valleys, echoing back, building. The people in the guest houses up on the county road heard and howled. Some said later they heard coyotes howling. Someone said it was a wolf.

The echo built and the pulse of the land was fed, powerfully beating in everyone. Everyone's pulse, the beat of the Higher Heart, resonated with the pulse of the land. When everyone was elevated in their feeling, and could find happiness, the howling stopped.

Almost everyone went back to what they were doing. Madeleine and Eva sat down on the top step next to Angelica, who kept her hand on Homer's cooling side. Peter and the Elder came and sat with them, down a step from the top.

The sun went down and still they sat. In the evening light a horizontal line appeared ten feet off the ground in the air in front of them. Then another line formed in the air about four feet above that line. The air between the lines changed and a picture of a beautiful country in daylight formed.

Everyone's hair began to stand up. The dogs sat up. Their ruffs went up but they didn't growl.

In the picture, the form of a wen appeared, walking toward them, dressed in white. The whole height of Her was visible only for a second, then all they could see was Her from the waist down. She came to the edge of the picture, no more than six feet from the people on the veranda, and She whistled.

They all saw an image of Homer bound up out of his body and run to Her, nosing Her hand and dancing around Her with the spirit of a young dog. The image turned and walked away, back into the beautiful country. Homer was bounding and dancing around Her.

The lines collapsed together and disappeared.

Everyone sighed for Beauty, and wept.

38

THE MOVING OF
THE HIDDEN LANDS

The journey seemed to take days, and it seemed to take no time at all. The earth turned under the land and the Hidden Land looked like the sea when it was crossing the ocean. The Land arrived in the valley of Stonehaven. Alam was still in his wolf form, tongue lolling, a dog on an airfoil. The moon was full and he howled his arrival.

Craft was sitting on the veranda with Quinn, Halloran, and Matthews, watching the fireflies. They heard it, the single howl, and felt a weight pass over them. They shivered and looked at each other.

Eva and Madeleine woke up. They felt it when the wards were breached. Rolling her eyes back in her head Madeleine saw what looked like a clear sheet, a huge clear sheet, flying over the land and settling into the Pine Eye. She got up to look out the window, as did Eva, but the image had disappeared.

Angelica moaned in her sleep and turned over.

The land settled down over Calley's thunder nest; the tangle of old toppled trees covered in moss, circling the spring in the middle. She was waiting for him. Reclining on a log, One knee raised, naked in the warmth of the summer night, pale in the moonlight, hair hanging long, smiling.

Alam returned to human form, gasping at the beauty of the sight before him: a naked Goddess surrounded by blinking lights, some swirling in a vortex above her head, filling the bower with light. He stepped carefully toward her and bowed. Then he went to one knee and laid his head on her heart.

She rose into the air, carrying him with Her to a small clearing, where the ground was covered with moss, and laid him down.

She lay on top of him, resting on Her knees. She kissed him, pouring all the love She felt for him like water into his mouth and he drank it down. His phallus rose erect between Her legs. It rose up, and as it rose it entered within Her directly, growing, connecting, joining, the fat knife of love seeking its sheath.

When he was fully erect inside Her, She levitated again. They moved together, their motion slowly bouncing them in the air, making little downdrafts and updrafts that flowed around them. The air flowed out around them like ripples from a stone thrown in a pond.

Electricity began to spark around them, flashing like the fireflies. Their bodies began to arch in opposite directions; Her's up, his down. When, in the counterpoint they would come together, the electricity and air flowed out in a disk. The disk made wind. The sparks became small bolts of lightning.

As the power built, the trees around the bower rocked slowly in the wind.

She broke the kiss, and whispered, "Truly, truly" in his ear.

She sat up then, still upon him, and rocked on him. The rocking motion created a different kind of wave, thinner and more piercing. She raised Her arms and face to the sky. She started to spin the two of them slowly.

The spinning became faster. Her hair swayed in the wake. Her body rocked side to side with it. A crystalline light formed in the center of Her, just above Her womb. Lightning flashed from Her hands and feet, igniting lightning from his outstretched arms and legs.

Out of the spherical crystal rose a vortex, passing out between the vortex of her arms and into the air above Her. The trees all swirled around them. The fireflies were drawn into the great vortex turning and turning, making light in the air above the couple.

Faster they turned, until the lights all left trails: images smeared across time and space. The air boomed, and they disappeared, leaving only the traces of light, an after-image of the vortex of Her resting on the hyperbole of him.

The morning light revealed them still coupled on the moss of the forest floor, covered with Her thick hair, blanketing them. He awoke laughing and hungry. His laughter brought laughter in Her, and it brought Her, laughing.

Then they rose to their knees, laughing and kissing. He said, "No, really. I'm hungry."

She took him by the hand, and led him to another clearing where a bowl rested on a fallen tree. "Here," She said. "Here we eat this. The spirits of the land bring it. It has all you need."

He took up the bowl and drank, hesitantly at first, then joyfully. Smiling around the edge of the bowl, he poured some slowly in. He set down the bowl, and laughed again. "Good! Good!" he said.

"Come," She said, taking him by the hand. "You must do this, what I am about to show you, every day. It will let the spirits of the land see you, and keep the age away."

She led him by the hand to the edge of her pond in the center of the Pine Eye. They waded in until they were knee deep. Calley tied up Her hair and bent over, searching on the bottom with Her hands. She brought up two handfuls of mud and put them on the bank. "Here, you do this," She said to Alam.

He bent over, and found the mud She'd retrieved. He brought two more handfuls, then two more, putting it all on her pile on the bank.

She reached over and picked up a small handful and smeared it on his chest, rubbing it in. "You must do this every day, all over, like so."

She proceeded to cover him with the mud, reaching down and bringing up more. She rubbed it into his face and his scalp. She rubbed it in everywhere, especially between his legs. She grinned at him, and said, "Wouldn't want to miss this, now, would I?"

They climbed out of the pond and covered his lower legs. He stood there, arms out to his side, grinning foolishly, looking like a mud monster from the bottom deeps.

"Turn around, let me get your back," She said.

He did as he was told, saying, "How will I do this myself?"

"Stretch," She told him. "Figure something out."

She took a final swipe on his buttocks and said, "Now stand there. Just stand still."

"Truly? I have to stand here? How long must I stand here?" Alam asked, both curious and mildly annoyed.

"Until it dries," She said. "When it dries, you can gather up the pieces and take them back into the pond with you. Then you can rinse off. Make sure you rinse it all off, including your hair."

Calley walked in a circle around him, eyeing him critically. Finally, She nodded, making a grunting noise of affirmation. The sound of it made Alam snort.

Calley looked at him and smiled. "I have something to tend to," She said. Then She backed away from him and stood in the air over the pond. Her face turned serious as She looked away in the last moment before She went mist and disappeared.

He stood there, in the morning sun, waiting for the mud to dry, He felt a prickling on his skin and scalp, sometimes as strong as a pricking. A couple of times the drying mud even pinched him. Since nobody was looking he voiced his discontent by saying "Oww!" and "Ouch!" out loud.

Eventually the mud dried and came off in chunks, little flat plates that he peeled off. He gathered them together and waded into the pond. Rinsing, he noticed that some of the color wouldn't come off no matter how hard he rubbed. Rinsing his scalp, he was surprised to see hair mixed in with the mud.

Over the next days, his appearance changed greatly. The mud removed all the hair from his body, except some on his head; leaving the sides and a widow's peak intact, but shortening and curling it all, darkening it overall but adding streaks of white. At the same time this made him look older, his muscles firmed up, giving him back the body he had when he was in his late twenties, only a little more heavily muscled.

His skin took on the color of mud mixed with the red clay of the Pine Eye.

Calley loved him.

39

RACHEL'S RIDE

Craft, Craft the sixth, rolled over in bed, suddenly cold as the wind picked up. He reached out for Rachel and found her side of the bed empty. She often got up in the night these days to wander around the Mansion, "Checking on things," she said.

He'd often gotten up and gone looking for her. She was always moving or in the study working on the Queen's Book. He'd come up to her. She'd see him coming and smile. Sometimes he would hang out with her. Other times he'd go back to bed, assured that everything was OK.

Lately, he'd taken to waiting awhile awake to see if she'd return before he went looking for her. It was a balance he'd had to find; giving her the space and privacy she needed, and not making it too obvious that he was caretaking her. Those had been his instructions from the High Council when they'd assigned him to Stonehaven.

They'd been sleeping together, mostly for company. Rachel said she liked a man in her bed, although there wasn't a lot of sex. She'd told him she liked the warmth and feel and smell of a man, and always had. What sex he needed came through assignments to various Priestesses.

Often, when he woke up in the morning, she would be sitting next to the bed, smiling at him in the first light, wearing one of her monogrammed robes, and brushing out her long silver hair.

They'd moved their joint bedroom to the room behind the second floor veranda. Rachel liked watching the sunset from there, at tree top level. Tonight the tall double doors creaked open and shut in the rising wind, cooling in the night. He could hear creaking doors from different parts of the Mansion. The wind was rising.

He stepped out on the second floor veranda wondering about the other Crafts, how many had stood here, and what they had seen. He thought about the first Craft, dead more than twenty years now. He had been standing in this spot, the spot where the current Craft now stood, when he'd had a heart attack and fallen over the railing, breaking his neck when he landed.

The physicians in the Order believed that he was dead before he hit the ground. He was buried in what was called the family cemetery high up in one of the coves coming down from the Pine Eye. He was buried next to Rachel's son David who had died on a combat mission in Laos during the Viet Nam War.

Leaning against the stiffening wind, he opened his eyes when he saw a flash of light. He realized that the lights in the barn had suddenly been turned on, including the outside flood lights. The riding corral was illumined. He could see the gate to the uphill pasture was open, no doubt left that way by one of the Interns.

He heard a rumble of thunder on the far side of Pine Eye. He saw the flash of light illuminating the mountain from behind, big and dark in silhouette. He saw movement at the barn and went back into the room to get a pair of binoculars. Returning, he saw a rider dressed in white leading a horse out into the corral. When he focused in he realized it was Rachel, wearing a white summer robe over a white gown. She was barefoot, leading the big bay horse named Roger. He was the last of her trained trick horses. He looked closely and realized she wasn't actually leading him. There were no reins or halter. The old horse was following her by habit.

When she stopped walking, the horse stopped. She turned, held his jaw and lovingly patted his forehead. She walked along his side, patting his neck. Then, pausing to gather her forces, she took hold of his withers and leapt up onto his back from a standstill.

Craft lowered both his jaw and the binoculars. He had known she was in good shape, but she was also in her eighties. The leap to horseback was spectacular. It seemed almost in slow motion to him, as if part of her lift was levitation.

She settled on the bare back of the horse, reached up and began unbraiding her hair. She shook it out in the stiffening breeze. She geed the horse to a walk, letting her hips rock, squeezing him with her knees, hair falling free. A quarter way around the corral she kneed him to a trot, still hands free. Halfway around she sped him up to a slow canter, no hands, just rocking her hips to the motion. He could see her laugh out loud with joy, shaking her head and hair as the horse shook his.

The storm clouds boiled up behind the mountain, rising higher and higher, folding back on themselves. Lightning flashed, illuminating the clouds from within.

Cantering into the wind, the robe opened and started blowing out behind her. Coming around the end of the coral the following wind wrapped the robe around her, flapping. It bothered her, so she took off the robe and held it out to wind.

A sharp gust took it aloft, and away. Craft dropped the binoculars to watch it, kiting in the wind, turning spirals as it flapped out over the forest, bright white against the darkened sky. Clouds raced along the ridge top. He turned back to watch Rachel again.

Still at a canter, she had taken hold of the mane and was on her feet. Riding in a squat, she let her feet get a grip. She let go of the mane, then spread her arms out, staying in a crouch. She started to stand, and then thought better of it. She sat back down and slowed the horse to a walk, then to a stop.

She practiced standing up on the horse's back while it was still. Grabbing the mane, coming to a crouch, letting go, then slowly standing, arms out to the side. She did it several times, correcting her wobbles. After several tries she found the nightgown restrictive and took it off over her head. She practiced, naked and barefoot, until she could stand up in one smooth motion.

She used her knees to press the horse into a trot. She leaned back, putting her face to the sky, shaking out her hair, letting the tips of it brush the horse's back behind her. She leaned forward, grabbing the mane at the withers. Urging the horse to a canter, she leapt into the crouch.

She rode that way once around the corral, flexing her knees with the horse's rhythm. Then, on a turn into the wind, she let go and stood up. Craft saw her then as she must have once been. Young, hair streaming, breasts rocking with the stride, arms out, face raised in ecstasy. Around she went, once, twice, and then she sat down again, slowing the horse to a walk. She leaned forward, patting its neck.

The clouds rolled down over the shoulders of the mountain, carrying rain in sheets. It rolled on, and over her. Craft could see her head drop. In a moment, she picked it up again. She returned to the canter, crouching then standing again, once around the corral.

The lightning flashed around her. Striking the transformer at the barn, the lights went out.

Craft kept watching her lit by the lightning. She dropped to a crouch again and then he saw something that inspired him with fear and awe. She pulled her legs and butt above her head and slowly extended into a handstand.

In a dark pause, the horse must have slipped in the sudden mud. When the next flashes came the horse was limping toward the open gate. Rachel was down on its back, leaning forward heavily, seeming to barely hang on.

She kicked the horse to a gallop, up the slope. In one flash she was sitting and lying hurt. In the next she was sitting up, arms extended, head back.

A sudden burst of wind, a column of whirlwind, came from the Pine Eye. It crashed along the forest top, breaking off the tops of trees, chewing and spitting its way to the pasture.

It caught up with Rachel and tore her from the horse's back. Up, into its body, the whirlwind took her, tumbling her, and spinning her round til she was prone and on her back.

Then it dropped her, perhaps twenty feet to the ground onto her back. She laid splayed out in the grass.

The horse came up to her, nudging her with its nose. Lightning struck. Craft saw it strike the horse's withers. He saw a blue fire travel through its neck to discharge into Rachel. The force of the strike lifted her off the ground and fanned her long hair around her.

Rachel settled and did not move.

She had not moved ten minutes later when Craft got to her. The horse was down, collapsed upon legs that must have crumpled under him. His nose was in the dirt by Rachel's shoulder, not breathing, her outstretched arm was under his neck.

Craft got to her and fell to his knees on her other side. She was smiling. He touched her hand. He felt the tremor of life fading away.

The rain came down, pelting them all, living and dead, lovers and friends.

The rain ran from her face like tears, but the smile stayed. It was a smile Craft knew; the smile she used in the presence of Beauty.

40

ON THE HUNT

Chester finished with Missy as hard as he could. Missy, on her belly, taking it from behind, allowed herself to become indifferent to the pounding. The pounding she could take, animal as it was, and use it to her own ends. The duplicity was different. It was exhausting pretending to be as stupid as she knew she had to be in order to keep Chester at bay and protect Lulu. It was hard to lie to a telepath. Hard to lie to someone with Chester's gift. Her only recourse was to pretend to be stupid and shield herself with the affect of fake grief at the imaginary loss of her daughter.

She'd had enough practice grieving in her life that it wasn't hard to weep. So she was weeping when the pounding stopped. Chester found it unappealing. He couldn't bring himself to finish. He just withdrew. Missy promptly fell asleep.

There was another reason Chester withdrew. He couldn't see what he was doing. He was still blinded by the tattoo of the little heart riding the whirlwind. He had recently allowed himself to fantasize about reaping that whirlwind, and imposing himself on that heart. After all, it wouldn't be incest, would it? Not to a patriarch. It would be a prize—his prize, his conquest—taken from some vanquished father. The mother and daughter were both his, by right, as well as possession. He would ride that whirlwind with its wayward heart until it was ground down under the weight of his sanctity and power. The girl would do as he told her, much as her mother did.

In the bathroom, wiping off his aching erection, he flashed on the image of it once again. The image of it made him ache even more. Angrily, he swore about the "fucking bitches." She would pay. In his whispered dialogue, she would pay for tempting him, for blinding him, for making him go find her.

Walking out to the table, zipping up his pants and tightening his belt, he formulated his plan. He had the money to pay for the journey, he knew. He recounted to himself how much and where he'd hidden it all. He decided that he'd have to take it all with him.

He'd have to pay Mickey his daily rate, of course. He'd have to pay for the truck as well, pay for meals, and whatever cheap motel they might stay in. But when he found Lulu—that would be expensive. He would need to put her up and keep her in until he could break her to his will. He thought of restraining her, of keeping her on a leash, keeping her tied in somewhere. His erection came back at the fantasy.

Cursing at his belt and zipper, he pulled his erection and masturbated furiously until he came on the kitchen floor under the table. When he was finished, he put the expended member away. He stepped on the ejaculate with his shoe, spreading it around until it looked like another black smear on the floor. As his vision of the present moment returned, he grunted at the look of it. He vowed to make Missy do a better job of cleaning. This time she'd be on her hands and knees.

He spread his hands and looked up, praying. "I'll need your help, Laud. You see how it is with me, how much a sinner I am. Help me, redeem me, let me find this sinner, this little girl, the one who stole my mind from you. Lead me to her, that I might return her to your ways, that I might redeem myself."

He checked in with the mental space that allowed him to see in a direction. Casting about for direction, he had a clear sense that Lulu had gone north. Good enough to get started.

He might not even come back, he thought. Once he found her, he might just settle in somewhere with her and start over. He'd have to dump Mickey somehow, of course. He'd have to break Lulu's rebellious spirit to his will, and to the Laud's will. That would make her do and say whatever was needed whenever anybody asked about it. He'd marry her, like he'd married all the others, and that would keep her under his thumb. And so, checking his powers, he concocted the his plan.

He packed two small suitcases, each with a false bottom to hold cash. He set them by the door next to his best brown Wellingtons; his preaching boots he called them. He hadn't converted all the small denominations to hundreds yet, but he wasn't about to leave any behind. This meant they'd have to sidetrack to get the rest. He'd pick it up from where he'd buried it. He realized it was a risk, what with Mickey finding out and all. "But I can handle him," he thought to himself.

Mickey came around early the next day to pick him up. He told Chester he'd had to quit a job, and needed to be paid. They'd settled on thirty dollars a day, plus ten more for the truck, and gas. This meant two hundred a week to Mickey, because he didn't count the weekend. They'd be travelling every day. Chester agreed to two hundred a week, smirking to himself about how stupid Mickey was. For Mickey it was more than he was making painting or splitting firewood for sale.

Mickey's eyes were still black from Lulu kicking him in the nose. Chester had told him he was lucky he wasn't dead. He told him his nose could have been kicked into his brain. He told Mickey that he should have talked to him about it, and he'd have set it up. Of course, Chester was lying.

Before they could head out Chester had one more piece of business to conduct in town. He had promised Missy a conversation with her boss David Harris, County Clerk. He'd been watching Harris when he was in town; waiting to see where he went at night when he didn't go directly home. He knew what nights Harris worked a little bit late, so he could honestly claim to his wife he was working late. On those nights, he would go somewhere other than home when he left work.

"A sinner," Chester thought. Especially when he had Mickey follow Harris, with Chester riding shotgun, and they saw a woman wearing a teddy meet Harris at her door. "Gonna pay for his sins," Chester said, out loud with conviction. He said it out loud for the Laud, in his own indefatigable naiveté, trying to convince Mickey's porcine mind to rise out of its feed trough.

"Unbelievable," Chester had said, as if there were anything he wouldn't believe.

Mickey agreed. "A sinner," he'd said. "Unbelievable."

In that moment Chester knew that Mickey would do anything he told him to do. Mickey never used words with five syllables.

They went and found Harris. The problem was where they found him. Chester was in a hurry so they went by the office. They hadn't known about the security camera that had been installed that week. Cheap and grainy, but focused on the parking lot; a gift from Homeland Security.

But luck was with them that night. Mickey drove past the camera and parked his truck on the far side of the lot, out of range of the camera. There was a back exit from the parking lot that was also out of range.

Chester had chosen to arrive long before dark, wanting to be sure he didn't miss Harris. Who knew? He may have decided to leave work early and Chester wanted to be sure he had the conversation he'd promised.

They waited a long time. Mickey was drinking beer and had gotten out of the truck twice to piss. Chester snorted as if he could actually smell it. Mickey piss was pretty rank but the wind was blowing in the opposite direction. Chester was never above lying to Mickey and Mickey knew it.

By the time Harris left work it was evening, just light enough to make out his form, and the parking lot was empty of cars. Chester and Mickey got out of the truck and raised the hood. While Mickey pretended to be looking at the engine Chester called out to Harris, asking if he had a flashlight, and would he give them a jump?

Harris said no, he was busy, and he didn't have any cables anyway. He got in his car and was gone before Chester could say they had cables.

"Prick," Chester said.

"Fuckhead," Mickey agreed.

They knew Harris's routes out of town, depending on the night of the week and who he was going to visit. One way took Harris past a park on the edge of town. They caught up with him there and forced him off the road, nudging his bumper with a fender in the process.

Harris, angry, got out of his car and went up to the driver's side of the truck to confront Mickey. Chester ducked out the passenger door and went around the front of Harris's car. Chester came up behind Harris just as Mickey finished rolling down his window. Mickey punched Harris in the face. Chester hit Harris in the face again from the side. Harris went down. Mickey opened his door and stepped out over Harris. He bent down and dragged him, moaning, into the park.

Chester sat Harris up against a tree and proceeded to preach at him. He preached about Harris's sins, his girlfriends, and cheating on his wife. He preached at him about harassing women at the office, and how it had to stop. Chester let him know, in no uncertain terms, that if it didn't stop Chester would make sure Harris's wife found out. That would be the end of his sweet county job.

While Chester was preaching, Mickey had returned to the truck and taken the baseball bat from behind the seat. He was standing behind Chester brandishing the bat when Chester finished the harangue and turned away.

Mickey waited until Chester was at the truck. Bouncing the bat in his palm, he stared wickedly into Harris's terrified eyes. Harris started to whimper. Mickey leaned forward and put his dirty forefinger to his lips to shush Harris. Then Mickey stood back up and said to Harris, "Fuckhead. Fuck with this," and swung at Harris's head. Chester was closing the door on the truck when the blow landed so he didn't hear the pop.

"Let's go!" Chester hollered, not even bothering to look back.

Mickey came and wiped the bat on an old rag he kept for checking the oil.

"You didn't need that. Hope you didn't hit him too hard. Unless you broke a leg," Chester said, knowing that if Mickey had broken a leg the man would be screaming. But there was only silence.

Mickey drawled, "He's all right," and started the truck.

They drove all night to Mason's Mountain. Chester had gone there once to see the monument to dead veterans with its famous carved relief of soldiers ascending into the heavens from the battlefields.

They arrived in the parking lot before dawn. Chester took a shovel and went off into the woods. Mickey got out and looked at the monument. Someone had spray painted the carving, "Is is is love." He couldn't figure out why they had used the word 'is' three times. He decided he'd ask Chester.

When he looked up, he saw that Chester had returned to the truck and was waving at him to return. When he got in he noticed the corner of a suitcase in the back sticking out from a heavy duty trash bag covered with dirt..

"What's that?" he asked, realizing he probably knew what it was. It was Chester's stash.

"Mine," Chester said, pinching the bridge of his nose and squinting like he had a headache. "Mine," he repeated, shaking his head of the vision of the tattoo that had suddenly filled his mind. "T'sall you need to know."

"All right," Mickey drawled again. "Which way?

"Back west, into the mountains. We get to high ground, the rod will find her."

Sunset found them winding up a two lane road in the foothills. Chester insisted that his divining rod worked better when there were fewer cars and travelling at a slower speed. The reality was that Chester worked better. As the last few days had progressed, he was finding himself blinded more often by the image of the tattoo. He was developing headaches, vision splitting migraines that sometimes would take his breath away with their rapid onset.

They pulled over for the night in a campground that offered showers. They spent a miserable night in the truck because of mosquitoes.

The next morning, with Chester at least cleaned up, they took a detour to a small town off the interstate highway. Chester felt sure it would have cheap tents and camping supplies. These towns acted as supply bases not just for tourists in the summer, but for hunters in the autumn.

Chester paid, Mickey noticed, with hundred dollar bills. Chester got Mickey his own tent and sleeping bag. At a pharmacy he bought a tooth brush and paste. When they stopped at a gas station for a fill up, Chester went inside to get a cup of coffee. While waiting in line he scanned the headlines on the newspapers. He flipped over the folded front page and saw a headline "County Clerk found dead." He scanned the article, about David Harris, found beaten to death in a park. Chester went cold.

Chester knew he didn't do anything that would have killed Harris, which meant it was Mickey and that damned bat. He was certain that he couldn't be tied to the crime, except by his association with Mickey. When the time was right, he'd get rid of Mickey, Chester knew, but for now he needed him. Scanning further down the article, he saw no mention of suspects or persons of interest. This meant he could probably still use Mickey to finish his mission; his mission to find the woman with her heart in a tornado, and ride her to the end. He was standing there, blinded, when someone bumped him in the shoulder, trying to get past him in line.

Suddenly overcome with panic, he had to go outside. The clerk behind the counter checked the security cameras because it looked like he might be trying to leave without paying. The clerk saw Chester holding out money to Mickey and telling him to go back in and pay for the gas and coffee. Chester gave him a hundred and told him to get what he wanted. When the clerk looked up again, she found Chester staring hard at the security camera. It made her shiver.

Mickey came back with an armload of junk food, a microwave burrito, and two extra large bottles of soda. Chester didn't ask for change and Mickey didn't offer. They spent another night in a campground. Planning to turn north the next morning, they would keep to county roads.

On the south slope of Tall Boy Mountain, near the edge of the native people's land, they pulled off to the side of the road so Mickey could urinate. Chester needed a break from the smell of microwaved burrito flatulence and decided to walk down to a little creek that ran alongside the road. Ever since he'd been a little boy he'd liked to put his bare feet into streams like this one, coming down from the mountains. He sat on a rock and took off his boots and socks. Standing up on the little sandy bank by the stream, he felt it immediately.

He felt a pulse in the sand, and when he stepped out into the water he felt it there, too. A heart beat pulse, a living pulse, running through the land in its water. At first, the sensation was pleasant. Then, tracking the path of the sensation up his legs, when it got to his scrotum the sensation became exquisite. He closed his eyes and saw the tattoo. He was hit with a bolt of ecstasy like lightning. It staggered him, and he almost sat down in the stream.

"This is magic," he whispered aloud. "Powerful magic. Nature magic. Sinner's magic," he concluded and hotfooted it out of the stream, shaking the water from his feet one leg at a time.

To Mickey, done urinating and waiting, leaning on the back of the truck, watching, it looked like Chester was dancing. Mickey laughed at the old fool.

Chester got his socks and boots and picked his way through the weeds back to the truck, still shaking. He couldn't stop shivering. He pulled a towel from his camp pack and bent over to dry his feet. He was struck suddenly by the image of the tattoo again. This time it brought blinding pain, and he fell over onto the road. He laid there, twitching.

Mickey, alarmed now, stepped back. Recognizing the seizure as the kind he saw at Chester's churches and tent meetings all the time, he stepped back to give Chester room. He fully expected Chester to burst into tongues. But Chester just laid there, shaking in a fetal position and grinding his teeth. Mickey looked around to make sure there was no one coming. It occurred to him that this might be as good a time as any to get rid of Chester; take the money and drive off. While he was getting the bat he heard Chester call his name. He closed the door and went back behind the truck to find Chester sitting up on the bumper and staring at him.

"You know, son," Chester said, "The Laud works in mysterious ways."

"I know it," Mickey said. "I been driving you around for years, and I see all the mysterious ways he gave you. I know you got powers. But let's go find this girl. Let's go find Lulu before it's too late, and we can't find her no more." Mickey clenched his fists in quiet anger.

Chester, thinking this was the longest sentence he'd ever heard Mickey utter, saw this, saw the fists, and thought of what Mickey might be likely to do to Lulu. He shivered. He knew right then that it wasn't gonna happen, and began thinking about ways that he could get a gun while they were travelling. How he could hide it. Chester knew Mickey was a killer now, even if Mickey didn't know that he knew. And Chester knew he could control Mickey, but only up to a point.

But he needed Mickey to find Lulu. When he thought of her, the image of the heart-born tornado banged in his skull. He raised his eyes to the heavens. He thought to himself, "Find Lulu. Then deal with Mickey."

Chester got in the truck as Mickey started it up. "I got a sign back there, back there at the stream. There's a poison in the land, a magic poison. I found this before, and I had to go up to the reservation to deal with it. Lot of those folks don't believe in the Laud, and do things in the dark. Mysterious things, things that would change us and lead us astray if we let their dark ways into us. I had to go up there and fight with them once, power to power. Let's head up there," he said. He held up his copper rod, letting it swing until it stopped. "Besides, the dowsing says Lulu is up that way anyhow."

"She with them?" Mickey asked, incredulous.

"No," Chester said, closing his eyes and checking in. "She ain't. She's gone further north."

Up top, Amos Sampson was sitting under his grand-daddy's chestnut tree enjoying the pulse in the earth, when he felt Chester's energy cross the boundary around the reservation. He knew the pulse drove this person crazy, like thumping on the ground will drive the worms out. He'd felt this person before.

Amos realized that this time the crazy man was looking for something. He assumed it was the pulse. He was tracking the pulse again. But the crazy man kept going, right out the other side of the reservation. In his mind's eye, Amos travelled to the hole left in the boundary magic. He got an image of a heart in a tornado in his mind.

Amos knew where the pulse came from. He'd been there. They'd given him chestnut seedlings to take away with him. They'd treated him really well. He remembered the young woman that had come to him in the night and it made him smile.

He opened his eyes and called Chestnut, the spirit of his grandfather's tree. He half-closed his eyes again and went still. In a moment he felt a soft touch at his elbow. "Go. Go to the Grandmothers House in the north and warn them. Warn their trees. Someone is coming, seeking the source of the pulse. Someone bad, bad crazy."

When the touch was gone, Amos opened his eyes and turned, watching the reddish brown bark-like back disappear into the woods.

Chester and Mickey traveled slowly north, staying on backroads. They sought out high ground whenever they could to get readings from the rod. They stopped along streams and in meadows. Chester would get out, take off his boots, and stand in the water or the grass, reading the pulse, noting where it was stronger, tracking a flow underneath the local flow, a flow that originated to the north.

Seven days into the trip, at a stop sign, the rod suddenly took a hard turn to the left. Mickey, watching it, gasped when it moved, then jumped when Chester shouted, "The sign! The sign! She's that way!" Two more days they rode.

41

BLOOD ON THE GROUND

Angelica was tired of waiting for Douglas to finish his work in the Mansion kitchen and decided to walk up to the Gate House alone.

She liked Douglas, newly assigned to her now that she had been given permission to begin her studies. To be honest, all the attention was new to her and it made her uncomfortable. She was having training sex every day now. Some part of her feelings wanted more distance than that. But it was a regimen. It was part of what she was supposed to learn and she felt the truth of that expectation deeper within than she felt her discomfort.

Still, she felt anxious. She pressed her low belly, pressed into the anxiety. She thought about the henna tattoo she'd painted there three days ago. The wen were all in the circle, experimenting with water based paints and differently colored hennas that someone had developed in the lab. The wen were practicing painting the symbol for attaining the enlightenment through sex. It looked like smoke rising in a spiral from a smoldering fire.

The painting was a part of the preparation for the next Maithuna. The symbols were a part of the costuming. The men would be painting themselves also. The High Priestess and the High Consort for the Ceremony would be required to paint most of their bodies, even their faces. It was important that there be no mistakes.

The wen talked about how the symbol, the sign of smoke rising, made them feel. For many it lit a fire deep in their bellies. At least that was how they described it. Angelica took a small vial of the dark gray henna with her at the end of the meeting and practiced in the mirror on a tilt frame on top of her dresser.

She had dropped her meeting sarong on the floor. She looked down and applied the coloring to a fingertip. Slowly she drew the spiraling line, starting at her pubic bone and ending halfway to her navel. When she looked up in the mirror, she realized that she'd drawn the symbol upside down. The narrower part was on the bottom and the wide part on the top. It looked like a tornado.

When she lifted her belly to look at it directly again, she made a small smudge right at the top of it. As soon as she did that she felt a jolt of electricity shoot through her. That was when the anxiety had started. It had actually started as a jolt of fear that rumbled the dragon within her. As she had learned, she had to be calm in order to keep the dragon from showing up unexpectedly, and, perhaps, behaving badly.

Now, walking toward the Gate House, she felt the anxiety again. She noted that whenever she paid direct attention to it, it increased in strength. She pressed her belly with both hands, willing herself to find distance, to cultivate inner distance from her fear. Then she breathed it out of her, and decided to think about something else. She remembered the seductive energy and probable sex that had been going on at the Gate House when she'd first arrived, months ago. She thought she could probably cajole Douglas into a little extracurricular sex when he caught up to her, and that stirred something else low in her belly, lower and behind the fear.

Their assignment for the day was to clean the Gate House and make sure everything was working before the guests began to arrive for the workshop beginning that weekend.

"How long could it take?" she wondered. And then she answered herself, thinking now of sex, and smiling, "As long as I want it to."

But as she walked the feeling of danger increased. She buzzed with it. At the same time she felt her heart pounding. It pounded even in her feet when she touched the ground. She knew what that pulse was—the heartbeat of the land.

She arrived at the Gate House, unlocked the door, and picked up one of the radios stored in a solar powered charger. She keyed it in. "Base, this is the Gate House, come in."

Someone in one of the houses up on the rental road was on duty twenty-four/seven. A wen's voice came back almost immediately, "Gate House, this is Base, we copy. Everything OK up there?"

"Standby, base. I'm still checking it out," Angelica replied.

Down alongside the South County Road, Craft and Quinn had been walking since shortly after sunrise. Quinn had finally agreed to show Craft what he knew about wards and their strengths and weaknesses. He had been doing a boundary walk with Craft, circumscribing the entire property, doing maintenance and repositioning. This work was usually done by the Madeleines. They had four of the younger ones and a packhorse along for the hike and the education.

They had been at a shelter about three-quarters of a mile off the Road to camp and had heard a truck go by, bouncing on the ruts, about the time they'd started walking. After listening for a moment, they'd gone back to breaking camp. Coming back to the Road, they'd made slow progress for awhile. The Road ran alongside Stonehaven Creek and the land where the boundary ran alongside it was steep. After a couple hours Craft and Quinn had forded the creek and sent the others back upstream to ford with the horse at a safer place to cross. They continued to walk up the Road.

Ms. A and her enforcers had been all over the mountains following

Quinn. They'd followed him all the way to the north where he'd gone to retrieve Halloran and back through the town where Quinn had lived with Sally. They had returned to where they'd been, at a motel in the little town down in the valley to the west, at the end of the North County Road where Stonehaven had some few small businesses.

Their path had been a zigzag, crossing back and forth, looking for the trail when they'd lose it. The longer it took them to pick it up, the harder it became to find it again. They'd spent long days driving too far down some country road, then doubling back when she was sure they'd gone past him, and then they'd look in another direction. A. knew they were probably close, but she was tired now. She had deliberately delayed two days, complaining to the knucklehead enforcers that she was waiting for money to be wired in from her Foundation accounts, but it was really just to rest. They didn't mind. Down time was still on the clock time, and, except for when they had to have sex with A., they'd either have sex with each other, or watch movies on the motel room TV.

The money would be gone soon. She'd have to go home and give up the search anyway. And this, finally, would be OK with her. She'd never really thought she'd catch him, but it had been fun to try these last few years. She was tired now and just wanted to go home and plant flowers.

This morning they'd head up into the mountains again. She'd noticed some vacation rental units up on top the last time they'd come through. She suspected she'd find him holed up in one of them.

Chester and Mickey arrived at the Stonehaven driveway entrance a few hours after sunrise. They pulled over when the divining rod began moving in circles. "She's here," Chester said intensely. "Pull over. I'll go explore and you stay here with the truck." Mickey had no idea of Chester's new found fantasy and lust for Lulu. He was never good for much walking, and had acquiesced. Chester walked down the driveway, keeping to the side. He came upon the empty Gate House.

He was standing in the woods thinking about going further down, when Angelica walked past him. Her head down and thinking, she went inside. Lulu. It had to be. She had the same hair, same long thin legs. He couldn't see her face, with her damn hair hanging down. But it had to be her.

Angelica stepped outside the Gate House and thought she heard a truck door slam out around the bend in the driveway by the County Road. Being cautious, since it was too early for guests to be arriving, she walked light-footedly along the inside bend in the driveway until she could see. She saw a scruffy looking man in his twenties with his back to her. He was working at something on the down tailgate.

She had her radio in her hand when she turned back, keying it and whispering "Security, security, security. Man at the G—". With a smacking sound, she ran into Chester's fist. The blow was so hard it turned her completely around, knocking the radio out of her hand and into the brush.

Chester picked up the unconscious girl by the collar and started to drag her toward the truck. He was blinded by the image of the tattoo. The headache caused his jaws to grind so hard he didn't hear the radio when Base issued the alert: "Base to all Stations. Security, security, security! We have an intruder at the Gate House."

Eva, sitting in her office with Diana, was never far from her radio the day before a training started. She heard the call and keyed in. "Base, this is Eva. Who's on duty up there?"

The Base operator, who had the duty rosters, said, "Checking. Checking. Angelica and Douglas. It didn't sound good up there."

Eva and Diana looked at each other and the color drained from their faces. For days Madeleine had been warning of big trouble coming, and more intruders. Even a Tree Spirit had warned them. They jumped up and ran for the four-wheeler parked outside in the lot.

Halloran and Matthews were in the Mechanics quonset hut working on a mower deck when they heard the squawk from the radio. They ran for the Barn where a flatbed truck was parked. They stopped in the weapons room and grabbed the first arms they could find; crossbows and bandoliers filled with bolts. They jumped in the truck. They drove, picking up people on the way, including Madeleine and Moon Halter who had run out into the drive looking for a ride.

Craft and Quinn had been in a radio reception shadow when the first call went out. Walking further up the Road they'd heard the chatter from Base asking all stations to check in and reissuing the security alert. They were almost a quarter of a mile from the Gate House and downhill. They started to run, Craft pulling ahead.

Chester dragged Angelica around the bend and up the drive halfway to the truck before he became tired. He dropped her on her face in the middle of the road. Almost blinded by the image of tattoo, he said, "Looky here. Look at what I got."

Mickey looked at the girl on the road about twenty yards away. He muttered to himself, "Could be her. Don't think so. Shit. Chester's blind."

Chester read something, some doubt, in Mickey's face and posture. He'd thought Mickey would be just as excited as he was. He rolled Angelica over. As her hair fell away from her face he saw clearly enough that it wasn't Lulu. Feelings of despair, then dread, formed in him and dropped into his bowels.

"No! No! It can't be. It has to be her," he spoke to the unconscious girl. Sensing that his mind was coming apart, he tried to undo her belt and the top of her pants. He fumbled at it, unable to make his mind work in reverse. He drew a folding knife from its leather case on his belt, and opened it. Hooking it under the belt, he sliced it through. Rather than try to open her pants he chose to slice that also. Grabbing under the top line from above he cut into the fabric. When it gave suddenly he lost balance a little and rocked forward, slicing into Angelica's abdomen.

Blood swelled in the cut and ran down over Angelica's side.

Chester put his knife on the ground, reached up and pulled the top of her pants down below her hips. He grabbed her underwear and pulled it down below her pubic bone.

He saw the tattoo on Angelica's belly, the sign of Enlightenment through Sex reversed. And at the same time he saw the outline of Lulu's tattoo in his brain, the silhouetting of the symbol of the Tornado Ridden by the Heart, and his brain lit up like its center was filled with fireworks.

When the light cleared he looked down and opened his eyes slowly. Before he could bring them into focus he realized that he had an enormous erection. It was so bound within his pants, and so sensitive, he thought he would explode.

Then he saw clearly. It was not her.

He reached forward, hesitant, almost afraid and almost eager. He brushed away the hair covering the rest of Angelica's face, first with his left hand, then with the right, the hand that had been pressed into the bloody ground. He looked at the face, then the tattoo. He said, "It's not her."

Then he thought, "I can have her."

He came up on his knees, undid his pants, and slid them and his underwear halfway down his thighs.

Mickey saw this and started walking toward Chester.

Chester reached out and pulled Angelica's pants down to her ankles, roughly, jerking her. Angelica moaned.

Chester said, "Come here, Mickey. Hold her down."

Suddenly, into the bubble created by the descent of madness, the four-wheeler carrying Eva and Diana roared in and braked, skidding in the gravel.

They jumped off and ran toward the figures on the ground. Eva fired a ball of energy, life force energy, toward Mickey. When it hit him he felt the push of it and gave way, backing up to the truck. Diana did the same to Chester, pushing him back on his heels and away from Angelica.

In his attempt to scramble backwards with his pants around his thighs, he fell over on his side away from the girl and out of reach of his knife. Diana held him pinned there with one hand.

The wen arrived at Angelica's prone form. Diana knelt beside her. Holding Chester back with her right hand, she leaned over Angelica to staunch the wound with the other. Eva ran to Angelica's head, knelt and lifted her head onto her lap with her back to Mickey.

Neither wen saw Mickey slide the axe out from under the spare tire in the bed of the truck where it had been stored for months.

Mickey walked quickly up behind Eva, raised the axe over his head and swung down.

The blade severed her spine, slicing all the way to her heart. She fell forward over Angelica, spouting blood, her life pouring out of her, covering Angelica.

Mickey raised the axe to strike again. At that moment, Craft came around into the entrance, crossbow raised, and put a bolt through Mickey's throat. He fell back, collapsing and gurgling. His free hand swung up to his throat, dropping the axe on the way down. Craft ran over him, reloading as he went, kicking the axe away when he stood over Mickey.

Diana screamed in grief and rage. She pulsed her hand. The life force coalesced and focused, reaching for Chester's heart.

Quinn came running around the corner of the entrance to the driveway, old limbs straining with the effort. He took in the situation in a glance and ran over to Chester. With a force unlikely for one so old, he lifted Chester into the air by the front of his shirt.

Chester, pants now around his knees, still fat-dicked but erection failing, screamed in terror.

In the next moment several things happened at nearly the same time.

The flatbed truck arrived. People jumped off the back and ran over, incredulous. Some sobbed immediately, falling to their knees. Moon Halter was helped off the back of the truck and ran to Eva. She stopped to put her hand on Diana's back, adding her force to Diana's paralyzing hold. Halloran, Madeleine, and Matthews got out of the cab. Halloran went and stood over Mickey. Madeleine ran to Eva and fell to her knees, sobbing, realizing there was nothing she could do.

Quinn used his other hand to begin crushing Chester's trachea, cutting off his scream.

From the air descended three mandorlas, one white, one red, one gold. Hovering above the ground the opaque surface cleared and forms became visible inside them.

Chester, hanging in the air and clawing at Quinn's arms, managed to croak out the word, "Laud" and pointed behind Quinn.

Quinn turned his head and looked.

Halloran looked down at the still gurgling Mickey. His grip was slipping in his own blood, unable to hold the wound closed. Halloran pointed a loaded crossbow at Mickey's eye and said, "Hey."

Mickey opened his eyes to look up at Halloran and Halloran shot him through the eye. The bolt tore through Mickey's brain and exited the skull at the back, pinning his head to the ground. In a flash of pain searing through his mind, Mickey's suffering ended. The gurgling ceased. Halloran looked over at the mandorlas and grinned.

Quinn set Chester down. Maintaining his hold and recognizing the being as the one who had bade him wait and then never returned, he asked the golden one, "Are you Laud?"

It replied, "No, but I made him."

Madeleine whispered, "De Murgos."

Diana whispered back, "Embla, Dangla," and withdrew her power to refocus it on the 'Divine Beings'.

Quinn, shaking Chester in the direction of the Beings, asked, "This is yours?"

"Yes, I made him," the golden one replied, in a voice with such a timbre that it induced terror in everyone.

Quinn turned back to Chester.

"You don't have to kill him," Craft said.

"Perhaps not," Quinn said. "But he has to die."

Quinn raised an auric cylinder around himself and Chester. It was about ten feet tall, black, with ragged flames and lightning bolts cutting across it slowly in diagonals while the cylinder turned. The last thing anyone saw was Quinn lifting Chester again, both hands around his throat.

Matthews was standing beside the fallen Eva, fists clenched, when his wings suddenly appeared and he started to levitate.

With a scream, Angelica's dragon burst from her abdomen. Angelica sat up and screamed, too, before falling back, still, unconscious. Eva fell slowly to her side in the convulsion. The dragon reared up, extending farther than ever, its long neck arching over the top of the cylinder swirling around Quinn and Chester.

Then it loosed the fire. A clear fire, blue around the edges, blew from the dragon. It filled the space with flames that licked back up and over the edges. Chester screamed again. It seemed like the flaming went on a long time.

When the dragon stopped and wound its way back inside Angelica, the cylindrical auric field came down. What was left standing there seemed to be Quinn, except that he was naked and hairless, completely covered in a layer of black that adhered to him so closely it seemed like a skin. He was holding, in one hand covered with black stuff like it was a mitten, a bundle of what looked like silver strands of rope. They had been the spirals and coils of Chester's siddhi powers. Now they hung like a handful of dead snakes.

While the dragon had been loose, Matthews had slowly levitated until he was about twenty feet off the ground. He leaned toward the mandorlas.

To them, he said, "She wants you off the rock."

Moon Halter also turned toward them. She moved forward with slow, deliberate steps. She leaned in, fists clenched at her sides.

A little tearing sound came from Quinn as the black skin parted over his mouth. He inhaled a sharp, long breath. The next thing to open were his eyes. Suddenly the skin started to morph, shaping itself around his ears and nose, seeming to be drawn into his orifices and coating the inside. When it got to his anus he made a little "EEP" sound.

The crawling skin differentiated his fingers and toes and even his prodigious genitalia like it was shrink-wrapping him.

Matthews flapped his giant wings and yelled at the mandorlas. "She wants you off the rock!"

The white and red mandorlas went opaque again and took off into the sky, disappearing from view into invisibility at no great height.

Quinn looked at the bundle in his hand and then at the gold mandorla. "These are yours then. Here." He threw the dead snakes of power at the mandorla. They spun like bolos. When they hit the mandorla they spanged and sparked. The mandorla and the silver snakes disappeared with the sound of a small explosion.

Matthews came back to the ground.

Quinn turned to the wen, now a man living in a soot suit.

The King of Salamanders emerged from the north side of the driveway and spoke the word "Food." It felt like a pressure in everyone's brain. He crawled up and took Mickey's torso into his mouth. He bit into it, tearing it loose from the head pinned to the ground, and dragged the body off into the woods.

Up in the Pine Eye, Calley had seen Ms. A. and her knuckleheads driving down the North County Road, almost to the rental properties. Calley told Alam to fly with the Hidden Lands to the intersection where the South County Road ended at the North County Road in a T. He was to lay it across the South Road so that the people in the car wouldn't see the South Road at all. Alam went wolf and hopped on, guiding it with his intention.

The car slowed as it passed the houses. Ms. A. looked deeply at them, looking for the sense that Quinn might be in one. When they got to where the South Road should have been the car stopped. A. said, "There should be a Road here. The map says there should be a Road here."

"There's no Road here, Ms. A. You can see for yourself," the knucklehead driving said. "There's no Road."

She felt out along where the road should be, searching for Quinn's energy. She had thought, looking at the map earlier, she would find him down that Road if she didn't find him in one of the rentals. Now there was no Road. And no sense of Quinn's presence.

That was the moment the thunder boomed on the North County Road. Lightning hit the ground a few feet behind the car. Looking back they could see a hail storm heading toward them. They drove off. Driving a little faster than was safe, they stayed just ahead of the storm.

They almost skidded off the Road when what looked like a big black wolf leaped over the Road in front of them.

"Shit!" all three of them said in unison.

They drove as fast as they could down out of the mountains to the small town east of Stonehaven. They stopped in a convenience store parking lot for coffee. A. was tired and able to think only of home. When the knuckleheads got back in the car, one handing A. her coffee, she said, "Let's go to the airport. Time to go home and regroup. Sleep in our own beds." She almost said, "Plant some flowers," but she thought better of it. Everything these men needed to know about her they already knew.

The thunder and hail storm up on the North County Road was only a gentle rain falling on the people gathered at the driveway entrance. Everyone had stared as the giant beast tore the body from its head and drug it into the woods. Now they turned to regard the bodies left on the ground. The rain started to mix with the blood and wash it into the dirt. A white summer robe, elaborately embroidered with the initials R.A. in light blue thread, settled down from nowhere on Eva's body, covering it.

Two golden lights appeared around Eva's body, blending. Moon Halter, watching at a little distance from Diana, recognized the Goddess and Rachel within the golden lights. The beseechment, the calling, which emanated from the lights could be felt by all. A third golden light emerged from Eva's body and blended with the other two.

Everyone but Quinn wept.

Halloran used the bolt to pluck Mickey's head from the ground. He turned to face Quinn.

Diana laid her hand on Angelica's forehead and said, "Good dragon."

42

ASSIGNMENTS

Several hours later, when people arrived for the Seminar, all signs of the conflict had been removed. The blood on the ground had been dug out and replaced with fresh dirt, tamped down and finally driven over repeatedly with the truck to make it blend in.

The guests found themselves attending a funeral. The body was laid out in the Chapel by the Family Cemetery. A Memorial was held Saturday night attended by a grandson and his wife who lived within driving distance. Interment followed on Sunday morning. The coffin was a plain pine box, lined with pillows and tapestries. Eva looked like she was asleep. She was buried alongside Rachel.

The Hidden Lands had returned to the Pine Eye.

Angelica's wound was superficial. It did not puncture the abdominal wall and required only stitches to close. There was a deeper wound, however. Something in her Soul tore from the dragon's rage. She became subject to rages that emerged from deep in her belly that would lead to wracking sobs. She had nightmares about blood. She burned with fevers that reduced her to a sweating trembling heap.

Her assignment, Douglas, had missed the entire fight at the Gate House. He encountered the flatbed, carrying Eva's body and the still unconscious Angelica, while walking up the drive to catch up with her. He was by her side when she woke up, sobbing, the next day. She would not allow herself to be touched, not even to have her hand held. The most contact she could stand was to be fanned; the air cooled her fevers.

She knew that recovery would take a while. Too much of her life was driven by internal processes of which she had little knowledge and less control. It was only when she began to dream of the Great Goddess, She Who Comes, that she found relief. She learned to take that connection into waking life. She took up a meditation practice of active contemplation that put her in direct contact with Her. She engaged in dialogue with Her whenever she could. The dialogue was instructional and led her into a place where her Spirit came to be in charge of her Soul and supervise its healing. The Goddess would reach into her and mend that which had torn. She would soothe the dragon and show Angelica how to do the same. She helped Angelica learn to talk to the dragon with her feelings and thoughts.

The dragon remained reluctant, however, and unhappy. Sometimes the best that could be done was to soothe it to sleep and will it to remain that way. As Angelica's mind grew, the Goddess began to teach her about how she would become an agent in the effort to restore the Antecedence of the Feminine.

After Eva's death Calley made it a point to appear in the dreams of each of the members of the High Council. In this way she received the blessing of each of them to become the next High Priestess of Stonehaven.

One week after that, Calley arrived. Everyone was at the windows watching. Several went outside to greet her on the steps.

A limousine, long and black with tinted windows, pulled up to the old coach stone at the end of the drive and the bottom of the portico steps. Alam liked driving, and his new assignment as Calley's chauffeur was intriguing. Learning to drive, shopping with Calley and interacting with modern mortals had all been novel and eye opening experiences.

He stepped out of the car, his white shirt contrasting with the black car. He reached back in the car and took out a black jacket and shrugged it on. At thirty-five hundred years old he was in the best shape of his life. He turned to look up at the late morning sun and his skin responded with a reddish glow.

"He will have reddish skin," Peter whispered to Craft. "Look!"

Craft nodded.

Alam walked around the car and opened the passenger side rear door.

Once straw blond, long, straight hair, going silver, white, and gray—all colors mixed with each other—She leaned out to look around. She was wearing a gray jacket, white blouse, lace bra, black back-zipped skirt, black hose with garters, lace panties. She put on black three-inch heels as Alam held the door for her.

"At last, alas, I am made flesh. It is so interesting, how different it is, and how it feels. Even my thighs brushing against each other is a new sensation."

Alam smiled. "Would that I were that sensation," he said. She rewarded him with a smile.

She stood up and glided, it seemed, over the uneven brick work, like she was walking on a cloud.

She stood at the bottom of the steps and said in a mild Scottish accent, "I am Calley Berry, new High Priestess of Stonehaven. This is Alam, my consort."

"Welcome," Madeleine said. Diana echoed it. Then everyone who had come out on the porch said, "Welcome."

Calley walked up the stairs, not touching anyone and looking everyone in the eye. Those who could see, saw in her eyes a sky filled with racing clouds.

Diana and Madeleine followed Calley up the steps. Once in the entrance hall, Diana stepped out to the left and said to Calley, "Please, this way," indicating the dining hall to the left. "We have prepared a reception."

The tables and chairs were arranged semi-concentrically in such a way that they all faced a center table. The tables were covered in white tablecloths, set with glasses, pitchers of water and low vases of short flowers.

Calley was ushered to a large wooden chair upholstered on the arms, seat, and back and set by the fireplace. She sat down and Alam came and stood behind her. Once she was seated, Moon Halter, Madeleine, and Diana sat opposite her at the same table.

The wen came in first and sat. In the back there was a row of chairs for the senior men to sit. Quinn sat down among them. The rest of the men stood behind them.

Quinn was still black, although it seemed to be fading. He looked fuzzy now that his hair was regrowing. On close examination it was determined that the black soot skin was sinking through his normal skin, pore by pore, forming a new layer within him. Patches of him looked gray.

Calley let the silence settle. She paused a long time, scanning the faces of everyone in the room. Then she crossed her legs, drawing one thigh over the other, the hose making a whispering sound that everyone in the room could hear. Alam smiled.

Calley said, "I am here now. The Mothers of the High Council and The Mother, She Who is the Mind of All Life, She who Comes, all these, have blessed this." She radiated a feeling of calm and acceptance into the room. Several people sighed.

She turned to the Elder Moon Halter and said, "Hello Regina MacGregor. Good to see you again. You have aged well. You have gone far."

There were gasps around the tables, for none but Eva and Madeleine had known her name. No one else had known she was Amanda's daughter, the first scribe of Rachel Adams' Queens Book.

"Good to see you also," Regina Moon Halter said. She hesitated, looking to see, listening to hear, if Calley wanted her to acknowledge her as a Goddess in front of the others. Regina felt the distinct impression of 'No' in her head, so she completed the sentiment with "Calley."

Then she continued, "You, too, have travelled far, and you are more beautiful than ever."

Calley laughed, a peal bursting out brightly in the room and making everyone smile. None but Regina knew quite why she laughed, how far she'd travelled through both space and time.

"And you, Alam," Regina said. "You're looking well."

"Aye, and you also, lassie. You've lived well."

Regina heard in her mind, in Calley's voice, 'Ever the seductress. You'll not trap me.' And more laughter.

Aloud, everyone in the room heard, "And how are your children? The Prophet of Conscience?"

"He is curating at the Museum of Anthropomorphic Coral on Slender Bay across the strait from Wallid. Just the other day he discovered a Pieta."

"And your daughter, the Librarian of Shambhala?"

"She's busy, Calley, thank you for asking. The conversion to digital is taking more work than imagined."

"I imagine," Calley replied, not knowing what Regina was talking about.

The room filled with silence and a cloud of incomprehensibility. These names were mostly stories to them. Few knew of their actual existence.

Calley turned to the room and said, "Regina and I have known each other for a long time."

Regina snorted. "Since I was a child," she said, which was also incomprehensible to the group, given that Regina was clearly much older. "And how is Maray?"

"She's fine, as are they all," Calley said, with a finality that closed the subject.

Calley smiled, and Regina parried the words Calley tried to plant in her mind: that there were to be no more questions. Then Regina smiled. Time soon enough for the people to know that a Goddess sat in the chair of the High Priestess of Stonehaven.

Calley turned to Madeleine, and said, "You are Madeleine here. I am in need of your support; yours and your people's." She waited until Madeleine nodded her assent.

Then Calley turned to Diana. "I must confess," She said, "I am not trained in your lineage. I will need your help. Can you stay by me?"

Diana pushed her chair back, allowing enough room for a short bow.

Calley gave her a winning smile.

Something visibly relaxed in Madeleine. She'd been trying to read Calley, probe her, for the new High Priestess seemed somehow not quite human. Calley turned back to her. "And what do you understand about me now?" Calley asked.

"Very little. But enough," Madeleine replied, smiling. "It is apparent She is with you. And She in me agrees."

"Will you both help me with Assignments?" Calley asked.

"Yes," Madeleine replied.

"Jasmine and Wade have departed for Wallid?" Calley asked.

"You—well, of course you know," Madeleine said. 'Yes. And Thompson Craft, the High Consort from Seldom Farms will be joining them in a month."

"You," Calley said, turning back to Regina Moon Halter. "You will be going back to your old home on Wallid. You will take him," she said, nodding in Quinn's direction.

"And you," she said, speaking to him. "Bodhisattva, you will go with her. Perhaps you will take the Dragon Girl with you. I am told by Madeleine."

Madeleine blushed at Calley reading her mind so clearly, having just thought those words.

Quinn squinted at Calley, trying to see into this wen who spoke so imperiously. "And what will you have me do there?" he asked.

Calley replied, "First, I would have you consider your loyalty to the Order. This is a life or death decision for you. And then, if you agree, and if you are found worthy, you will be given an assignment in the upcoming struggle. You will perform it well, or not. The odds will be against you."

Quinn, his face a mask, said, "We shall see."

Calley nodded at him, and said, "Indeed."

Calley continued speaking to the room, but looking at Madeleine, "I am told that the Dragon needs lessons in good manners. There are many Dragons on Wallid." Turning to Angelica, Calley asked, "Will you go?"

Angelica asked, "May I have some time to think about it?"

"Of course. You need not arrive for a few months, in any event." Calley replied.

Calley turned back to Regina. "You speak Dragon?"

Regina shrugged. "Apparently," she said. She looked sideways at Madeleine, who was clearly locked into some kind of telepathic download with Calley. Regina scowled, resenting that information might be shared that she would rather have kept secret.

"Beware," Calley said, in a voice that chilled everyone in the room except Regina, who grinned.

"I am so old that I can always use a little heat," Regina said. "I had been thinking that we could send Angelica to Waitan for training with the affiliate Order there."

"Perhaps. She will be needed in the battle to come on Wallid," Calley said. There was an intake of breath among the audience at the mention of the word 'battle'.

Regina leaned forward, drawing Calley's attention. It was clear to everyone in the room that Regina was communicating with Calley telepathically.

Soon, by Madeleine's face it was clear that she was actively included, whereas before she had lapsed into composed silence, eyes closed, while Calley was scrolling through her mind.

Regina touched Diana, bringing her into it, as well.

What Regina said to Calley, mind to mind, was, 'There's a problem with the Secret.'

Calley's response was, 'Tell me about it.'

So, Regina did. Madeleine had known there was a Secret, but not about the problem. Diana had not known at all. Now that she knew, her heart cried out in terror, grief, and joy all at once.

The others in the room, including all the men, observed this silent exchange. They were not curious but attentive, their minds still and at ease. With Diana's outburst they were all returned to normal mind. They looked at her, concerned.

When they saw Diana's face, openly weeping for joy, they knew what they needed to know—that all was well with their world, again.

Then, the conversation done, Calley stood and said, "Changes are coming. Everyone should prepare themselves." Turning to Diana, "Show us," indicating Alam, "to our rooms."

Passing Quinn on his way out of the room, Alam laid a hand on his shoulder, leaned down, and said, "I have an ointment for that skin condition."

Everyone filed out except Regina and Quinn.

"Are you the Regina? Regina MacGregor?"

"Yes."

"I've read much of the Queen's Book. With no particular assignments, there hasn't been much to do around here."

"Yes."

43

A PRIME NUMBER

That winter, as Lulu was riding the bus to the restaurant in the Bronx where she had gotten waitressing work with her mother's cousin Madge, she glanced out the steamed up window at a burned out pickup truck under the overpass. It reminded her of Mickey's truck. She scowled.

She got off the bus and walked a half block to the restaurant. She went in through the front door, noticing on the way that someone had posted a flyer advertising yoga classes and another advertising a tantra workshop. She felt her interest pique. And her tattoo trembled.

EXCERPT FROM
BOOK 3 OF THE
SIDDHI WARS SERIES,
WALLID ISLAND

Beth Elmyra sat on the park bench next to the falls watching the solstice sunset over the cathedral of the invader. Beth Elmyra: at least that's what the name on her passport said. She smiled.

If there was any justice in the world her passport would simply record her title: High Priestess of Bath.

As she sat, she connected telepathically with her designee, who was engaged in the Solstice Hierogamy ritual with the High Consort's designee. Both surrounded by the chanting, drumming circles of the local members of the Order de la Fleur de Vie.

She smiled again. During the positions and movements leading up to the finish, her designee had been struggling with the duality of letting the Goddess come to the forefront of her experience while she remained just in the background, yet still in control. The face of the Goddess was struggling to come to the fore and the designee was struggling with letting Her. It was important that she learn how to let Her come forward especially in high pressure situations. The Goddess would need access to her at other times if she was ever to serve in Beth's role.

Beth grinned again, and shook her gray hair back behind her shoulders. Finally the designee let go. When she did the Goddess came forward and took over. The young wen's hips bucked against the Consort, rocking. She raised her arms. The Goddess actually raised Her arms and extended ecstasy out into the world. That ecstasy contained the secret of the joy that makes life worth living.

When the ecstatic seizure ended she rose up a little creating space for her consort, Her consort, to finish. Nine times he drove the piston in and out. On the ninth stroke he finished, pumping into her nine times more. When it was finished She sat down on him. Leaning forward, she smiled and kissed him thoroughly.

Then she stood up, dripping down her thigh and along his belly. She made her way over his head and sat down on his face, letting him kiss her there thoroughly in return. She stood up shortly, made the mudras of disentanglement, stepped off the dais and was surrounded immediately by two Priestesses who hung her robes upon her and straightened her crown.

He returned the mudras of disentanglement and rolled over on his belly, his chin resting on his fist, grinning as he watched her ass bounce as she walked away from him, not looking back. He wondered if she'd grant him the boon of her favor. Finally, at the last moment before she was escorted from the room, she turned and looked over her shoulder and smiled at him. His heart opened and received the smile. He smiled back, and stood up into the robe that was waiting for him.

Beth smiled, knowing that it was done, and done well. In a few hours she would meet her designee in the Council at the Number Seven restaurant with the rest of the local Council. The men would be meeting and eating, no doubt drinking and telling men's stories two floors below them. When the time was right the wen would come downstairs and join them.

She wondered briefly where the High Consort was then decided it didn't matter. He'd been present enough in his designee, like she'd been with her's. His power was that he couldn't be found unless he wanted to be. All she could see in his direction was shadows.

She hoped he was prepared with some useful ideas about how to integrate the influx of refugees from Stonehaven.

If nothing else, she'd keep them working in the laundry over at the spa. She could probably cajole internship visas for the spa industry. Conjure up, she thought to herself, more likely. The Rules would have to be made more clear, however. There had already been an incident of a couple having sex on the dirty laundry pile. She found it remarkable that she had to specify they were to have sex on clean laundry and then wash it.

"Uggh," she said aloud and shivered at the grossness of it. Then she realized she would have to get on top of the extra-assignment sex that was sure to happen. Remote cousins getting to know each other better, she thought to herself and bark-laughed out loud. She would notify the Madeleine and her crows to begin seeing into what assignments would best serve the Goddess. She immediately heard the Madeleine's voice in her head, "Already on it."

"Of course you are, dear," she replied.

"Foresight," Madeleine said, "begins with the anticipation of need. It is as simple as that. Any further word from the High Council of the Order?"

"So, were you just waiting around so you could tell me that you were already on it?"

"No. I put it out there when I thought of it, hours ago. Kind of like voice mail, or call waiting. When you thought of me, it pinged me back and let me know you'd picked up the message. And then I tuned in to you. What time is the dinner tonight?"

"Can't you read my mind?" Beth asked sarcastically.

"Maybe. Wouldn't try. Just trying to save having to look it up."

"22:00. Third floor. Take the lift up. I'll share what I have from the High Council then. The men will be on the ground floor. Stick your head in and say hello, if you wish. "

"Thanks, dear. I will. See you then."

Beth's mind fell into silence, no sound but the water rushing over the three levels of falls. The news from the High Council was not great, but the plan felt good. She would have to work with her Craft to upgrade security. She closed her eyes and laid her head back in the last rays of the sun setting through the crenellations of the abbey. She opened her mind to the Goddess, sharing her sensation, and waited to listen to Her sense of what consequences the news entailed.

ACKNOWLEDGMENTS

I would like to acknowledge my editors, first of all. You were gracious and diligent—always a hard combination to achieve. AH, thank you for your skills and patience with some of the non-standard style elements. Thanks to Otter Bay Books for production assistance.

MH: thank you for the rendering of the icon. It is always really nice working with you. You took the vision and made it real.

Special thanks to FKV Publishing.

Author photo by RS Photography.

CPSIA information can be obtained
at www.ICGtesting.com
Printed in the USA
LVHW031651170719
624401LV00017B/1113/P